LOGIC:
THE PRINCIPLES
OF
HIGHER KNOWLEDGE

Painted by Mr Ellinger.   Engrav'd by F. John

Carl von Eckartshausen.

About the Author

Karl von Eckartshausen (1752-1803) was born on June 28, 1752 in Haimhausen, a town near Munich, as the illegitimate child of the Count of Haimhausen, and Maria Anna Eckart, daughter of the administrator of his castle. At the age of seven, he experienced dreams of a prophetic and mystical nature, as well as having "visions". His unappeasable yearning for the higher truth at first lead him to the Order of the Illuminati, which was established by Adam Weishaupt in 1776 (Goethe and Karl August, Duke of Weimar, belonged to this Order for a short while). Disappointed, Eckartshausen left this Order after one year, when he noticed that the leader of the Order, under the disguise of it being a school of initiation, in reality, pursued only political goals.

Later on he cultivated relationships with numerous mystic societies and orders, such as the Free Masons (many symbols in "Kosti's Voyage" point to Free Masonry), the Gold- and Rosicrucians, and those "Hermetic Societies" which dealt with Alchemy and the Inspired. He also corresponded with a number of metaphysicians and philosophers, among them Franz von Bader, Sailer, Conrad Schmid, Herder, Jung-Stilling. It is not known whether he joined another esoteric society after leaving the Order of the Illuminati.

He found his "Memphis", however, his "School of Initiation", in the "Inner Church", through the Society of the "Enlightened". He reports on their activities as the Invisible Brotherhood in the "Cloud upon the Sanctuary". They are not subject to time and space, but in order to be effective in the spacio-temporal world over organizations or individual Human Beings, the inner societies, more or less, remain hidden.

Eckartshausen must have found such a Human Being, who lead him to [his] "Memphis". So, in the year 1792, he writes: "The lesson which I received from a man full of wisdom and goodness, who was raised to the level of vividness ...". And in 1795, he wrote: "Whatever you understand under initiation, I do not know. If you believe that I came into close proximity to the higher truths through human lessons, you are in error. I always fled human societies because I found a faithful friend in solitude".

Eckartshausen is one of the few who, through the help of others and through the fulfilment of corresponding conditions, found their way to a new and higher consciousness, and with this derived first-hand wisdom of a higher life, which he communicated to others.

Eckartshausen was a noted naturalist and mystic, who also held positions with the Bavarian Prince Elector, Karl Theodor (1777-1793) and from 1799 with the Prince Elector, Maximilian Joseph IV. His activities included law, the natural sciences and philosophy, being a member of the Bavarian Academy of the Sciences (until 1800), as well as his writing endeavours. All of these positions served him as platforms and instruments to distribute his metaphysical, theosophical and religious knowledge. He authored well over 100 writings; among them plays and papers on the "Moral Teachings for the Bavarian Citizen", "Concerning the Source of Crimes and the Possibility of Prevention", and "Music of the Eyes or the Harmony of Colors".

This wisdom is contained in his works, such as Kosti's Voyage (1795), and also his main writings, Magic: Principles of Higher Knowledge (Aufschlüsse zur Magie) (1788), God is the Purest Love (1790), Mystic Nights (1791), The Most Important Hieroglyphs for the Human Heart (1796), and the Cloud upon the Sanctuary (1802).

REVIEWS

"... a full examination of *Magic*, or the Higher Principles, is a very unorthodox study, filled with a grave, very serious array of wonderful teachings."

"A no-nonsense approach for the serious seeker who reads this book as a matter of life and death."

— The Book Reader

"*Magic* was originally published in Brünn in 1788. Two hundred and four years later, it appears in Scarborough, Canada. Not too many books have that kind of staying power."

This German work has been rendered into a most easily readable English - and good reading it is too. At first, I was turned off by the title *"MAGIC"*, as I am not at all certain of what the contemporary "practitioners" of magic are doing. Upon closer examination, I highly recommend this book.

One of the reasons this book is important is for the wonderful look at symbols as they have been understood by the heart and not the head. The translation is fantastic because the translators have resisted what must have been a strong pull, the using of colloquial terms and jargon.

Numbers are one of the symbol-forms bearing the truths of metaphysics - not math-numbers. Pages 254 - 288 are a gift to understanding numbers, old testament symbols, and the chakras. This small section alone is worth the price of the book.

American students of metaphysics often suffer from a lack of historical background, just as many contemporary students do as regards politics and history. This is as potentially damaging in spirituality as in any other arena of the world. *Magic* contains a concept of history as well as spiritual insight. It is important to see that what you and I grapple with spiritually is not new at all - to humans - and is at best, only tinted by the socio/political climate.

Throughout, *Magic's* clear explanations are presented and a very honest critique of man is also presented. Of great interest is this critique of man, which is no less applicable two hundred years later. Let me give you a taste of the writing in this book:

"We do not understand the magic of the people of old, because we take matters much too physically and sensually." (This is great reading because this statement, especially the part about, "the people of old", which is true immediately - was expressed to a readership of

over two hundred years ago! "People of old" - don't forget we refer to ourselves as the new, and is this not the new age? Nothing changes, but things are relative - the reviewer).

To get a sense of the past thinking which goes under the present umbrella - term new age - and to reach such material without the jargon, is an eye-opening experience. It will change your impressions about the spiritual path we are all currently sharing. On top of that there is real insight to be gained from reading *Magic*. I suggest you find a copy and give it a slow but thorough going-over."

- Joseph Terrano
Friend's Review

"Although this book was first written in 1788 by a Bavarian Privy Councillor, its teachings are timeless. The book was written to convince the naturalists of von Eckartshausen's time that miracles do, indeed, occur. To the author, magic provides a way to bring the essence of Nature back to the Creator.

In a simple and inviting style (thanks to the excellent translation by Gerhard Hanswille and Deborah Brumlich), pearl after pearl of wisdom is revealed. The author's clarity makes the confusing issues of our complex world melt away. Reminding us that, "Great Secrets will reveal themselves to you.... All we Human Beings have to do is ask!", von Eckartshausen challenges the reader to find personal and divine meaning among the myriad of meaningless symbols cluttering their lives.

An excellent treatise on Western Magic, these writings speak refreshingly of the nature of material reality. Von Eckartshausen states that imagination is indeed reality, but it is a reality that needs more attention to be manifested. He warns to beware of charlatans, of evil, and of misusing any elite knowledge gained through one's explorations. More importantly, he points the way to the path of a greater understanding of Nature and gives viable insights into miracles, energy, and universal laws."

- Michael Peter Langevin
Magical Blend

Karl von Eckartshausen

Magic:
The Principles of Higher Knowledge

Translated into Englished and Edited By

Gerhard Hanswille
&
Deborah Brumlich

Merkur Publishing Company Limited
Wisdom of the Occident
Canada

ISBN 0-9693820-1-4

Cover Graphic by Amedeo Babbo

Revised Second Edition, 1993
By Franca Gallo

Printed in the United States of America

TABLE OF CONTENTS

BOOK ONE

TABLE OF CONTENTS

TABLE OF CONTENTS

TABLE OF CONTENTS

TABLE OF CONTENTS

TABLE OF CONTENTS

The Principles Of Higher Knowledge

Book One

PROLOGUE

We very seldom judge according to the matter itself,
instead, we judge according to the concept we have about the matter.
Within this lie our limitations and errors.
Let us not draw concepts out of concepts;
instead, we should get closer to the matter itself,
and then we shall find the truth.

To the Reader
The Purpose of My Writings:

This book was written with the intention of drawing the attention of the Naturalist to several things, and to prove, as much as possible, that we should not believe everything, nor should we dismiss everything.

In this book, I have shown, here and there, partly through theoretical and partly through practical endeavours, the probability of many existing, miraculous things, and at the same time, I am warning the inexperienced of the fraud and deception of the wicked, who misuse such knowledge. That is why I have explained some of these deceptions, and presented them in a clear manner. I am of the opinion that it is worthwhile to subject everything which is miraculous and incomprehensible to a cold-blooded examination, to prove that only the one who examines without passion will find the truth of things. But, the essence of this whole book is directed towards one thing - to bring the Human Being back to Nature and back to the Creator, from which Human Beings were removed through pride and depravity. In addition, I am trying to point out to the Human Being that we can find Wisdom and Truth only in God, and this can only be accomplished by walking on the True Path of Approximation. By walking on the wrong path of errors, you will distance yourself from God.

I will prove that God becomes more and more worthy of worship, and religion will become holier and holier, the more the Naturalist investigates the origin of things which are all in accordance to the Creator's generosity, proclaiming the great destiny of the Human Being.

Should my sincere effort find acceptance with honest and good Human Beings, then I will in due time, explain many secrets more

17

clearly. However, at the present time I find it necessary to keep these things shrouded due to the present circumstances, and due to the manner by which Human Beings think.

If everybody could bear the look of Truth, and if the numbers of good people would be greater, then you would not have to be concerned about the desecration of the Secrets of Nature. But as long as the majority of people are the way they are, the Naturalist is only entitled to point out the path to the Truth and the descriptiveness of things. To those Human Beings, who have an honest heart and who search, a hint is enough. They will go there and they will find what they are looking for.

I am asking the Reader to never judge single sentences unless he has also read the sentences which follow. The Reader should never forget what follows, and what preceded, when he reads. The Reader should also not consider repetition as being superfluous or unnecessary. I find at times that repetition is absolutely necessary, since I was concerned about the fact that whatever was previously read, was forgotten again.

This whole work should not be read lightly. Instead, it should be studied, and the Reader should not form any contrary concepts, but should seek to compare them with the matter or the issue itself, and he will see how much closer it will lead him to the Truth. I am making the presumption that these writings are not written for the totally ignorant Human Being, but instead they are written for Human Beings who have made healthy and reasonable concepts their own, and who seek the Truth with a good heart.

As far as the unravelling of various secrets is concerned, a certain amount of physiological and physical knowledge is of absolute necessity. The Reader must be in possession of this knowledge if he endeavours to understand higher things. Should one or another Reader have problems understanding one or another statement in these writings, do not dismiss them, but instead put this book aside and study the sciences which you require to understand; then read this book again, and the matter will become clear.

This book is not written for dull minds or for the indolent, who do not want to make any effort on their part to investigate or spend any time contemplating. This book is also not written for universal geniuses, who know everything with one look, but this book is meant for those Human Beings who seek the Truth with a good and honest heart. Contemplate on what the author Herder had to say about this: "It is almost impossible for the viewer to lead somebody else onto the path, where he himself obtained the secrets; he must leave it up to the other person and his genius, and it does not matter to what extent he is capable of partaking in these concepts."

When I speak of primary substances, do not confuse primary substances with primary beginnings. I recognize only two primary beginnings, but several primary substances. Primary substances distinguish themselves in accordance to the condition of their modification. There are some who consider the prime substance of the prime substances to be prime beginnings, and in regards to this consideration, I presume there to be several prime beginnings. Even if they are considered to be the prime substances of the prime substances, and thusly they are being depicted as prime beginnings, because of this consideration, I presume there to be several prime beginnings, even though they are only considered to be the prime substances of the prime substances.

I make the determination when I say: As the mathematical point is in accordance to the beginning of a line, that is how the prime beginning is in accordance to the prime substance. Therefore, there are two things in Nature, and they are the prime beginnings of things. Their unification is the cause of all prime substances, all the ability, which the prime beginnings obtain for the formation of the prime substances in the physical world.

There are simple things in Nature, which when they unite, bring forth a third thing, that in accordance to its nature is totally different from the first one. In regard to these things, Chemistry will enlighten you.

INTRODUCTION

Words are means by which Human Beings communicate, and we call it a language. In order to communicate, you have to have an understanding of the words you use and that is where the problem arises. The meanings of most of the words we use were learned in context with other words, and from this, we assume that we know the meaning of the word. When you do this, and your understanding of a word is the same as its real meaning, no problem arises. However, when what you assume the meaning of a word to be does not agree with the true meaning of the word, then misunderstanding is the result. It is most rewarding to understand the words; by understanding, the true meaning of the word is meant. The best sources for obtaining this information are dictionaries, encyclopedias and dictionaries in other languages.

As an example, the word "Principle" is often used. Have you ever looked it up in a dictionary to find out if your understanding of this word is the same as what it really means? Many times, of course, your understanding is correct, but be certain to avoid misunderstanding. When you read this book, your understanding of all the words are of the utmost importance.

The meaning or meanings of the word "Principle":

1. Chief
2. Beginning
3. The Ultimate Source
4. Origin
5. The Law of Nature by which a thing operates
6. An Essential Element

The example of the word "Principle" and its meaning may shed some light on the importance of understanding of the word. This book is for those who are searching for understanding. One of the keys to understanding lies in the understanding of the word, the other lies in opening your mind. If you keep your mind closed, all the secrets Nature has to offer stay hidden or secret.

Many times the word occult is used, but very rarely is it understood. Most people think of it as something sinister. This is the case, of course, if and when it is applied in the wrong sense. It actually means something which is hidden.

The Laws governing the explanations in this book are not based on man's laws or scientific opinions, but solely on Nature's Laws.

20

One ability Human Beings have that can never be deceived is their instinct. It can be fooled only temporarily. It has been the wish of Human Beings since the beginning of time "to be free".

Many people in the old days, even up to the present, believe in spirits, demons, angels and so on. Some believe this, and others do not. Primitive civilizations believed that thunder, storms and rain were caused by the gods. One question, however, always remains unanswered. Even in a laboratory experiment, the ingredients have to be put together in order to achieve certain results. In a laboratory, Human Beings do this. Who does it in Nature?

Gerhard Hanswille
1989

1. First Principle.

Only when you have a good heart, do you deserve and have access to the Secret Sciences. Any Human Being who has this quality, will use this knowledge for the benefit of mankind and not for personal, material gain.

Wisdom is like the sun - it warms every mortal and illuminates men's crown. The physical body is necessary to feel the warmth of its bliss, which commensurate with the degree of its warmth.

Evil Human Beings are not worthy of this knowledge or to know the path which leads to the "Art of Happiness". What would be a blessing for mankind through Nature, would become a curse, a plague, for mankind in the hands of an evil person.

The scent of fragrant flowers would be for nought, if you do not possess the ability to smell. To quote an old proverb: "Do not throw pearls in front of swine."

A principle of Nature teaches us that even the most wholesome herb can, through lack of knowledge of its power, turn into a dangerous poison. It is also the nature of the moth to fly into the flame because it lacks the knowledge of what effect the flame has.

These principles are very important. Think about them and remember them always. You do not obtain the understanding of this knowledge by only reading it. When you are looking for gems in a muddy area, you search slowly and thoroughly, otherwise you will not succeed.

Do not believe everything and do not reject everything, but, it is the endeavour of a wise person to examine everything. Such a person cannot be deceived by looks or appearances; his life is dedicated to searching for the truth.

2. The Hidden Secrets Of Nature
And How You Can Find Them.

The Secrets of Nature cannot be taught. This knowledge can never be taught in its totality by one person to another.

Nature is its own Priestess (Teacher), and initiates and shows her inner sanctum only to those who search and deserve it.

Those, who are in possession of some of Nature's Secrets, can point the way for those who want to know Nature's Secrets, but they cannot walk the path for them; that has to be done by the apprentice himself.

It is not the fault of the Teacher if the apprentice is bowlegged or cross-eyed, if he walks with a limp, or if he only has one eye, or when he looks up to the sky, he overlooks things and misses all the beauty which is right next to him. Nor is it the fault of the teacher when the student stumbles, even though he has been warned to walk slowly.

Never rush anything! Nature's greatest secrets are always closest to us. It is never Pride which finds them - it is always Innocence.

Not every Human Being deserves the honour of visiting the Temple of Nature. Divine Providence has ordained everything in such a way, that no evil can deceive Nature.

Birds fly in the air, fish swim in the water, Human Beings live on Earth; therefore every element requires a certain organization of the being or creature which lives on it or in it. According to that principle, the requirements of the Temple of Secrets are of a certain order and organization, and the Wise, the Sages, and the Adepts also have to be compatible with the sphere they wish to live in.

If you want to find the Secrets of Nature, you have to study the Book of Nature. The Book of Nature is written in the Alphabet of Nature. Blessed are those who know the letters of the Alphabet of Nature. Even more blessed are those who can spell the word; but, those who can read in the Book of Nature, are blessed the most.

Read this Book of Nature. Read with the Eyes of your Soul. The astral eyes are the eyes of observation.

The Eyes of the Soul have to be cheerful. This cheerfulness is attained through inner peace and by the elimination of your passions.

Only in the cleanest and calmest water do you see the reflection of the Sun. Blurred is the light of the sun in roaring mountain streams and in murky or muddy waters. This also applies when it comes to wisdom.

Wax melts in fire; dry wood burns. Whatever does not melt and does not burn has to be something more than wax and wood.

One of the most important principles is to think for yourself. If you re-think what others have thought, then you are not really thinking. Think for yourself and you are above those who do not think for themselves. Do not waste your time with things that others have done - search and think for yourself!

Reading is a good start, but thinking for yourself is better. When you read, read with a certain amount of indifference and cold-bloodedness. This cleanses the Soul of the prejudices of authority. Be calm and do not despise anything. Always be aware of Pride. Be on guard.

Pride is the greatest atrocity in the eyes of Wisdom. It was Pride which removed mankind from the Path to the Truth, thereby obstructing the access to the Temple of Nature. Pride is the reason why so many so-called learned people or scholars are always with their heads in the clouds, therefore, they can have no knowledge of the treasures which lie beneath their feet. Pride despises everything and laughs at anything it does not understand. Pride will not bend or lower itself, and this makes it totally impossible to find Nature's Secrets, which Nature will disclose only to the simplest of Human Beings. By simple, we do not mean without intelligence. Pride over-elaborates all things and everything, and natural occurrences are over-exaggerated and then become totally misconstrued.

The Proud totally forget that the key to the greatest miracles in Nature is Simplicity, not man-made education or rules.

Pride is always searching for great things, miraculous things, the sublime, yet, the true source of everything is found in the simplicity of Nature, and this escapes their observation.

Human Beings are created to receive infinite, supreme bliss or happiness. We are bestowed with the necessary drive or impulse, and the highest might of our Soul to accomplish this.

Human Beings do not recognize this might, which is at their disposal. This might is seldom or never used. They weaken themselves and search for Wisdom and Knowledge where they do not exist.

Scholars throw away the seed and write volumes on the peel. The pride of the scholars, their quarrels in our educational institutions, removes them from the path to the truth.

Truth is not for owners of Pride, but for those who seek knowledge with a sincere heart, to unselfishly help mankind.

For those of you, whose Soul is susceptible to higher things, those Human Beings and those brothers will understand these words! But, those of you whose Soul does not possess this susceptibility, will not understand these words.

Those of you, whose heart carries the Seed of Goodness will understand this language very clearly, and the more familiar you become with these writings, the more secrets will be revealed to you.

There are many things in Nature which remain secret to the majority of Human Beings, and to them, they will always be secret. The majority of Human Beings are mischievous and evil and they would only misuse God's Gifts.

3. The Obsession Of Human Beings For The Supernatural.

The immediate working energy of Divine Providence in our physical world is Nature itself.

Whoever would want to remove the Godliness from Nature, would remove the Soul from the body.

Where God has an immediate Effect, this power is the Consequence of this Effect and is Nature itself.

The weak intellect of Human Beings cannot always find a reason or an explanation for certain things in Nature and, therefore, call them Supernatural.

The Supernatural things in the physical world are nothing more than a lack of knowledge, rather than the essence of the subject.

There are Energies, Effects and Consequences. Everything which exists consists of these ingredients.

Energies and Effects are not bound by an absolute necessity, but the necessity is only relative necessity. The Consequences thereof are absolutely necessary because Consequences are children of Effects, whereas the Effect is the daughter of the Energy.

Prudence of the Eternal and the freedom of mankind is contained in this sentence.

Any Power or Energy contains infinite Effects and every Effect has infinite Consequences.

The Power, the Energy, lies in the Whole. Every Effect is in the Energy, every Consequence in the Effect. All together, this is a chain.

Without God, Nature is a dead creature. Nature is the eternal harbinger, the organ which proclaims the Creator, and also connects the physical world with God.

In Nature lies the working force and the power of God for the benefit of the physical world.

The working force of God for the benefit of the Spiritual World is much more than Nature. It contains the power, the force of becoming alike. Within this lies the reason of continuance, to immortality.

Every exception in the normal order of things is founded in Nature. Nature itself does not change, only the manner of dissimilarity in its Effect is the reason for the dissimilarity of its consequences.

Different consequences could have, as a source, the same force, but the source of their origin does not have the same effect.

Whenever Human Beings with inertia, or who are lazy by nature notice a new phenomenon, they are usually satisfied with an

25

explanation which is the closest or the easiest to obtain, and which does not cause much of an effort.

That is why people in the past attributed anything they did not understand or were too lazy to think about to sorcery.

Today, anything which is not understood is denied or dismissed. As was the fault in past centuries to believe everything, today we are faced with laughing at and belittling everything which is not understood.

Present-day Wisdom is based on what others have thought, or on what others have written or said. This has become the total extent of today's Wisdom.

There could be no greater difference between thinking for yourself and what others have thought, between what others have said, and your own thinking and your own words.

The Scholars and Teachers of this century have forgotten that Theory has to thank the Practice for its existence, and that Nature existed before Human Beings made the rules.

4. The Obstacles On The Path Which
Lead To Nature's Secrets.

Only a wise man is searching for the Secrets in Nature. In order to accomplish this, he walks his own path; he carefully examines everything, especially that which is given to him by others.

Nature is like a good friend - she harbors no Secrets for those who are worthy of her friendship.

Pertness (Vorwitz), Pride (Stolz), Self-Conceit (Eigendünkel), Blind Belief in Authority, and a Fanatic Passion for Learning are not to be confused with erudication (Gelehrsamkeit). They are the will-o-the-wisp (Irrlicht), the ignis fatuus on the path which leads to the Secrets of Nature.

Many times we believe that we are very close to these secrets, but whenever we think this, we are the furthest away.

Why do Human Beings have their own eyes, their own ears, and their own hands? In order to see for themselves, hear for themselves, and feel for themselves.

Why then do you want to see through the eyes of others, hear through the ears of others, feel with the hands of others? Why?! Those of you who understand the above sentences will be able to explain many such things in Nature. Our physical knowledge, compared to what lies hidden, is nothing but dallying around.

Nature reveals its secrets to Human Beings very infrequently. When Nature does this, however, it does it with the intent of enticing mankind into becoming more acquainted with Nature. Nature can be compared to a beautiful woman who is very reluctant to show her charms, and who very carefully covers up all her others.

There were many great Priests (Teachers) in the Temple of Nature, and when they spoke, mankind did not understand them, and their writings became the laughter of fools. This is the case now more than ever before in the history of mankind; the writings of wise men are ridiculed by so-called learned people. At the present, mankind is at its lowest spiritual level in the history of the world, but the opposite is also true, otherwise there would be no balance. To clarify this: Never in the history of the world are so many people at the lowest of levels, and at the same time, so many at the highest of levels, on the scale of human development.

Whenever you translate one language into another, you should always be competent in both languages.

Human Beings can seldom say: "this or that is impossible", because as human understanding is, it is very limited. To make such a statement requires total knowledge and understanding of all the Universal Laws.

Many things are impossible according to the knowledge we possess, but it is not impossible for Nature.

Nature is like a desirable, beautiful, knowledgeable, and noble Lady, who has many suitors, yet she will only choose the one who is worthy of her. When Human Beings have reached this lofty level in their development, they will also choose their right mate. Before this, they will make error upon error. There is, however, one consolation: their Soul will drive them on until they have reached this goal!

Nature's servants are Simplicity and Innocence. She lets the proud scholar stand in front of closed doors at the Temple of Nature, and she will not honour him with her presence. In the meantime, Nature reveals her secrets to those who honour her, and she will make them aware of the value of her treasures.

Those who are worthy of these treasures have to have the following Virtues: To think for themselves; belief in God; have feelings; examine things very carefully; have a good memory; and be willing to search.

5. A Small, Little Light For Those Who Try
To Find Nature's Secrets On A Path
Which Is In Total Darkness.

In our huge, so-called impressive, man-made buildings, where our educational institutions honour man's knowledge, man plays. They play, and it is nothing but playing - playing philosophical games. It is also the place where educated children dally around. Mother Nature can do nothing else but smile at this Puppet Show.

The Sage, the Wise Man, seeks the truth in the Temple of the Day, and in the Sanctuary of the Night.

He learns from the Sun, the Art of Separation. He learns from the Air, the Laws of Movement. He learns from the animals, the use of herbs, and from the different kinds of Air, he learns how to heal.

The morning and the evening show him the many different effects of the herbs.

The Earth shows him the power and the energy of Stones and Gems and the splendour of Metals.

The rising of the sun, noon, evening and the setting of the sun, are very important periods and cycles in Nature and, therefore, reveal many secrets.

When the dew descends from heaven, when the thunder makes the Earth tremble, when on a cool evening you see the brilliance of lightning, when you see the moon's lustre on a beautiful night, that is when Nature is ready to teach, that is when Nature gives lessons and it is then that she explains her secrets.

All we Human Beings have to do is ask! Why don't you? Examine the hurricane, examine what the hurricane is, and what kind of power or energy lies in the air. Analyze separately the components of snow and examine the tremendous energy of ice. Start doing this, and by doing so you will have taken a giant step closer to the Secrets of Nature.

Learn to distinguish Fire from Light. Dismiss the notion, the idea, the tremendous prejudice, that the sun burns. Nothing is farther from the truth. The sun is not capable of burning. Examine what the Elements are. Examine the senses of Human Beings. Great Secrets will reveal themselves to you.

First, learn everything there is to know about the physical world before you start to learn about the Spirit World. Once you have learned everything there is to know about the physical world, begin to learn about the Spirit World, and many things which are inexplicable to you now, will then be understood.

28

You have eyes, ears, a nose, and a physical body, therefore, it is within your power to see with your eyes, what others cannot see. You can hear with your ears, what others cannot hear, and with your physical body, you can feel what others cannot feel. Think about these statements very deeply and carefully. The ability lies in every Human Being, to a more or lesser degree.

Once you possess this knowledge, you will begin to understand this. You will also understand visions and premonitions; they will become definable. They are then no longer founded in you imagination, but in Nature itself, in reality.

Do not neglect to study the anatomy of Human Beings, but let Nature be your teacher. Do not study man's study of man; the horrible results which are being accomplished through even more horrible means. The most horrible of all human atrocities is invading the human body by force, under the disguise of being of benefit to humanity (1 Corinthians, 6:15). Once you have the knowledge and the understanding, you will understand the significance of this sentence in the Holy Scriptures: For whosoever hath, to him shall be given, and he shall have more abundance; but whosoever hath not, from him shall be taken away even that he hath.

Ask yourself these Questions:

What is Blood?
What are Nerve Fluids?
What effect does Electricity have on our Body?
What effect does Magnetism have on our Body?
What is Sleep?
What are Dreams?

Examine the following sentences: Everything in the physical world is movement; even the most silent of silence is movement. Ask yourself: How does movement modify itself in Nature, the movement which my coarse physical senses are incapable of detecting? The next question would be: If this finest of movement exists, how can I perceive it through the art of my senses?

An infinite amount of knowledge and wisdom is contained in this question, or better, in the answer to this question.

What is Life? What is Death? What does it mean to live? What does it mean to die? Are life and death opposites? Is there death in Nature, or is everything life?

What is the Whole? What are the parts? What is the World? What is the Universe? What are Relationships? What is Identity?

What does it mean, to be a Being? Is there a hierarchy among living beings? Are there degrees by which living beings live? What is this hierarchy, these degrees? Is there an order? What is this order? Is a plant alive? Is metal alive? Is a stone alive? How do their Life-Energies differentiate?

6. This Chapter Is Necessary To Answer All Previous Questions.

"Becoming One" is the greatest Secret of Nature. "Becoming One" is the Destiny of all things. The closer a Being is to "Becoming One", the closer this Being is to Perfection. One question, one sentence, which all Human Beings do not understand. Everything that lives in Nature feels this inner power. Everything is caught up in the wheel of time, only some sooner and others later.

The greatest, the most important law which determines this, is the Virtue which possesses the greatest of all power, and that is genuine Love, meaning unconditional Love.

Love is the active force, the means to Assimilation, the most important Link in the chain of "Becoming One".

Love is the Law of the Divinity, the Commandment which God placed into every Human Being's Heart. That is the matrix, the chain, which unites all Beings. The driving force to "Becoming One" originates with her and "Becoming Alike" is her nourishment.

The wise man has to thank her for the might of the Spirit upon the Spirit, the hidden power of the Soul, the magnetic power.

Eternal Divine God!

What tremendous power lies already hidden within our mortal shell. It proclaims that we are Your Children, God's Children.

7. Contributions To Solve One Of The Great Puzzles In Nature.

Infinite is the effect of the Light, it reaches the Intellect and the Reason.

When you know what the Intellect is, when you understand what Reason is, then you have some concept of your Soul.

The Intellect is the organ of Reason. Reason is the organ of the Spirit.

Spirit, in this sense, is the mind, but the Intellect is part of the mind. There is no Intellect without the mind. Intellect, Reason and Spirit together are the Soul, and her determination in the physical world is the Will.

Intellect is a power of the Soul, through which anything possible presents itself. The understanding of the connection with the circumstances is called the Reason. A being that possesses Intellect and Free Will is Spirit.

A thing which is conscious of others besides himself, is the Soul.

The Light is effective through the Intellect, as through an organ, because only through these means can the Soul of a Human Being receive the Light. This Light is true cognition, the emanation of the Divinity.

This Light travels from the Spirit to the Intellect, from the Intellect to the Reason. This is the path of its radiance.

Nothing equals the power of the Human Spirit. Unlimited is its effect, similar to the great power from which he emanates (Divine Providence - God).

Even though our Spirit is imprisoned in our sensuous organs, chained in flesh and bones, he never ceases to be a "Child of God".

The Spirit will always possess the splendour of the power of the Divinity. The Spirit will always have the ability to rid himself of his shackles, his chains, to rise to the greatness for which he was created.

Grand and admirable are the births of the powers of the Human Spirit. As these powers seem to be grand and admirable, they are weak deeds of the active powers, compared to the inherent powers of the Soul. This is only on the earthly plane. Even the best-organized physical body is always the prison for the Spirit, provided he is bound by sensuality.

The more a Human Being frees himself of these chains, the freer his Spirit will be. The more effective the power of the Spirit becomes, the closer the Human Being comes to the Light, the closer to perfection, the more he becomes like God.

The release of sensuous obstacles results in being closer to God. The recognition which will lead you there is the Grace. Her consequence is continuous advancement leading to perfection, and perfection to blissfulness.

There is a language of the Soul through which only similar Souls can make themselves understood. There are things in Nature, for which Human Beings have not yet found words.

Some Human Beings may laugh when I say, that it lies within the power of the Human Spirit to know and understand the thoughts of another Human Being.

It lies within the power of the Human Spirit to look through the curtain of the future and see things which are a puzzle to most other Human Beings.

It lies within the Human Soul, because the Soul is the child of the Divinity, and from her we obtain this power, through the endeavour to become like her. That is also called sanctification. Here, Nature gives us a hint and shows us those hidden powers, through somnambulism.

The more a Human Being is subject to or influenced by his carnal desires, physical cravings or coarse, physical sensuality and impressions of the physical world, the further is his Spirit removed from the Secrets of Nature.

The more worldly passions a Human Being has, the less he is able to see. All his spiritual powers are gathered in one spot, like the sun's rays in a magnifying glass, and out of the beautiful, health-producing warmth, comes a destructive fire. Everything is in the centre, and all the other beautiful things which surround this go unnoticed.

The more the Spirit accumulates the energies of the Spirit, the more his sensuality diminishes.

Nature can only speak with those who have fine organs. They can hear her voice. Only those who know how to hone their eyes to see things which ordinary Human Beings cannot see, can see Nature's Secrets.

Refinement of the senses is getting closer to the Secrets of Nature; a step closer on the ladder to the Spirit World.

8. We Have No Conception Of Anything Which Lies Outside Our Circle Of Perception.

Every Human Being's conception is limited by his surroundings. Should he then pretend that he understands the meaning of the words which are outside of his circle of perception, then you have reason to doubt that he understands or has insight into the things which are outside of his ability to comprehend.

Whenever I talk about things, especially about matters which very few people take time to think about and which most people have no concept of, I have reason to doubt that they understand what is being said.

The fountain of deceit and error would be considerably less productive if we would have no illusions and look at the face value of objects and see things for what they really are.

Most of man's illusions are the children of the ear and hearsay. That creates the tension in the Power of the Imagination and the error in your fantasy.

Most people come by knowledge through tradition. They are taught by teachers and books.

That is why most of the Sciences and so-called knowledge of Human Beings is nothing else but daughters of the imagination which entered into the Soul, not through the eye, but through the ear, which is the most timid and bashful of all the senses which Human Beings possess.

Man's fantasy is, up to now, the most inexplicable puzzle. It keeps the whole body busy, including the brain and the nerves. It is the connection and the basis of all of the delicate powers of the Soul, and also the matrix between body and Soul.

Inconceivable is the power of our fantasy; inconceivable is the power of our Soul, which is present in every mortal. Only the effect could be stronger here and weaker there; here she could be asleep and there she slumbers.

The effectiveness depends upon the form of the transitions of this energy from a dormant state to a working state.

Falsehood, lies, fraud and deceit are the deeds of our senses in the physical world.

Knowledge and truth are part of the Spirit World. Space, Time, the Future and the Past are attributes of the physical world.

The Spirit World or the Mental World has neither Time nor Space, Past or Future; there is only one condition - a continuous present.

As far as the Soul is concerned - which is independent of the physical body - the future is the present, as well as the past is the present, in this world. This is due to the Soul's conception in the Spirit World, because the Soul does not perceive through the senses; the Soul perceives directly through the true circumstances of the matter.

In the physical world, our knowledge progresses step-by-step, through our senses. In the Spirit World, there is one single overview, because everything consists of things or objects, effects, courses of action and consequences, and the Spirit World or the Mental World oversees all of this. A Human Being who knows the secret of how to separate himself from his carnal desires as much as it is possible according to his Nature, will see things considerably clearer and more pronounced, because he will see through the sight of his Soul, which

33

is independent of the coarser organization or the physical world. Human Beings have their understanding through their senses. The senses are limited. That makes us subject to deception, because our conception is limited also.

Very seldom do we judge according to the circumstances themselves, but we judge according to the conception we have of the circumstances. Our limitation therefore, lies within this concept, which through this becomes our error.

Our Soul, however, which is independent of our physical body, has an overview of all of the circumstances without any limitation, and therefore has knowledge of the effect and its consequences.

The overview the Soul has does not follow a succession, instead, it is simultaneous because the object, effect and consequence are a whole.

The physical or the coarser organs are necessary to manifest or express the Vital Energy or Life-Energy of everything in creation, but they are not necessary for its existence.

Therefore, whatever produces this Vital Force or Life-Energy is totally self-sufficient and independent of the coarser organization of the physical world.

The Vital Energy of Human Beings, among all living beings, contains the greatest and most powerful of all treasures in its effects and consequences. This of course is by degrees, from the lowest to the highest, from the most stupid to the most intelligent.

The difference is due to the amount of Vital Energy, and that causes the levels of intelligence by degrees. The more active these Vital Forces are, the closer to perfection a Human Being becomes.

The Cause of this Vital Energy we call Spirit - Soul.

The Spirit is a created Being - simple, immortal, and within the Human Being.

The Soul of a Human Being is a Child of God. To "Become Alike" (to be like God) is its destination.

The Occupation of God is perpetual creation. To "Become Alike" is the destination of every Human Being.

God created Human Beings in His Image, therefore, to become like God is the reason for being and the ultimate goal of every Human Being; this will happen to every Human Being, sooner or later. The sooner or later determines the level in the hierarchy.

9. To Search For Yourself Or To Be Lead Are Two Totally Different Things.

There are many things which are very close to us and yet they seem totally strange to many Human Beings, because they do not know how to make use of the organs or senses they possess, which would make it possible to recognize and get to know these things. This is partially due to the present condition that they cannot find this organ any more, even if they would have knowledge thereof.

Everything has a certain necessary relationship, and through this necessary relationship, the circumstances are what they are. As soon as there are changes in the relationship, it ceases to be what it was, and it becomes a different relationship.

Take a flint and strike it with a piece of steel until you have ignited it - then you have a fire. Nothing could be simpler as far as Nature is concerned, but for those who do not know this, a flint and a piece of steel are useless for that purpose.

What could be simpler than electricity or a magnet or the different kinds of Air? And what could be more natural? Yet the educational institutions, our scholars, and many of those dreadful volumes of books know nothing about these very simple things.

There are even simpler things in Nature, of which these scholars know nothing; but these things are as important as they are simple.

Every Human Being can find these things in Nature, but there is one law. In order to find them, he has to look for them himself.

This is not a small task, to look for yourself. Most Human Beings do not search themselves, they only believe that they do, yet most of the time they are being lead.

The guidance of these Human Beings is conducted by the usual guides. These guides carry names such as prejudice, partiality to authority, and self-conceit.

Books usually contain more hidden knowledge than what is written. If you do not possess this ability, this intuitive ability within your Spirit, then you do not understand many books, even if you understand what is written.

Words remain words, substance remains substance. Only the object or the substance clearly presents the knowledge, the understanding, not the words describing the object or substance. Words are only expressions of a concept of what other people understand that particular object to represent. This concept could be totally wrong. Even if they were right or true, they can become wrong, since your concept is not the same as someone else's concept of the same object.

Therefore, an object, even when described with the right words could, when conceived by another person, create an entirely different concept.
To understand what someone else understands is like making a copy of a copy. The questions then arises: "How close is that copy to the original?"

10. A Language Without Words.

There is a language without words. It is superior to any other language.

Thoughts originate through the impressions of our senses.

To be receptive to these impressions you have to have an idea, a concept of them. Then in order to remember these ideas, these concepts, you have to think. To verbally describe those concepts, those characteristics, which are in the Soul, is called to speak; in the larger sense, it is called a language.

When a Human Being wants to explain to another Human Being what his conception of an object is, language becomes a necessity.

We endeavour to express the picture our eye perceives, and all the feelings and sensations which are attached to this picture which our senses are capable of converting into sound, and to express this through sound, thereby speech was created. This is a copy, in sound, of our thoughts and feelings.

Every living creature has its language, but the language is in accordance with that being's perfection.

Animals speak, because they can make sounds. They modulate the sounds in accordance with what affects them and in accordance with their needs. The expression of joy, suffering, love, anger, and fear are, in each of these characteristics, done in a different manner. The expressions of animals are only directed towards passions and do not include trains of thought, nor do they include ideas. The language animals are capable of speaking is limited only to their passions. Only Human Beings are entitled to this privilege of expressing in words the characteristics which are lodged in the Soul.

No language can express objects or things - they can only be given names.

The difference in the impressions brings out the difference in the movement of the Soul. This difference was the first origin of the difference in the symbol, in other words, two people can look at the same object, yet get a different impression of the same object.

A certain picture is created in my Soul by looking at a tree, another picture by looking at a rose. That is how Human Beings differentiated their symbols or signs, because the language of symbols or signs leads to the language of sound.

If Human Beings would not be obstructed by the coarser organization of their physical bodies, we would recognize the impact the finest of the finest of impressions have on other people. Then a language, as we know it, would not be necessary, since a language is nothing but an explanation of the expressions.

There is a closer connection between the human Spirit and the Heart. Vividness is its language.

There are two languages, the Language of the Heart and the Language of the Intellect. The Language of the Heart is less subject to deceit than the Language of the Intellect.

The Language of the Heart receives its pictures out of Feelings. The Language of the Intellect receives its words from Feelings. The Language of the Heart has few words but says a lot. The Language of the Intellect has many words but says very little.

The more words a language has, the less perfect it is, and the more errors the language is subject to.

The hieroglyphs of old were a very graphical language and actually, the language of the eye.

The ear is the most deceiving and at the same time the weakest sense Human Beings possess, and through this sense, the weakest of all our senses, we learn all of our sciences. No wonder Human Beings are subject to so many errors.

That is why Nature has only one language, the Language of Graphics, of Light or Pictures, which of course is nothing but the Language of the Soul.

The Language of Passion has its point of view, in the eye of Human Beings. Those, who are familiar with this, are capable of looking into the mirror of the Soul and can see more with one look than what a thousand words could describe to him, and even then, it would be nothing but words.

Souls which are developed to the same degree and are in harmony, suffer and enjoy to the same degree and are subject to the same impressions.

There are occasions where you think the thought of another person. Spirits do not speak to other Spirits, their thought is their language.

Graphic Conception is their share. Graphic Conception is recognizing the object-truth, which removes you more and more from

37

error. The result: Language of the Soul.

There are Human Beings who know this language, but they are few. There must be only a few; if this language were more common, it would be to the detriment of our earthly sphere, our physical activities. It is a Universal Law that you cannot reach perfection unless it is done step-by-step.

Bound to letters, our mind crawls in drudgery. Our best thoughts turn into silence by our dead writings.

When all of mankind is capable of thinking in pictures or in objects, and not in symbols or signs, and we can speak in the nature of the thing and not in arbitrary signs, then we have given up our erring ways and our opinions. Then we have reached the Kingdom of Truth.

The Human Being who has reached this goal cannot lead another Human Being onto this path, where unbelievable treasures are available. You always have to leave other Human Beings their free will to choose. You cannot force anybody to do what you want him to do. This is left to the genius of the individual Human Being, to do or not to do the same. He can, if he chooses, follow or not follow the path to freedom.

11. Obscure Feelings:
The Reality And The Imagination.

Everything is a reality, even imagination is a reality, but a reality to a lesser degree.

Human Beings obtain their knowledge in the physical world through their senses, which are the organs.

Every sense is capable of an impression. On account of this impression, we communicate the pictures of the objects to our Soul.

The expression is kept, to a more or lesser degree, in accordance with the condition of the organ or the impression.

Human Beings have feelings, even before they can determine that they are feelings; before they are conscious of these feelings, they have these feelings.

These feelings are obscure feelings. Out of these feelings, many inexplicable things can be explained.

Premonitions, peculiar visions, sympathetic effects are founded on the theory of studies of obscure feelings.

Nothing, but nothing, no matter how small it is, is without cause. It is only Human Beings who are not always aware of the causes.

This is a story, which will explain this better: Mr. Fitzburgh was on his way to the post office to mail some very important letters. When he arrived, he realized that he had lost the pouch which contained the letters. Needless to say, he was very upset over the loss of these important letters.

That night, however, he had a dream. In this dream he saw a man in a grey suit pick up the pouch of letters. The spot where he saw the man pick up the letters was very familiar to him. He also knew that the man lived in a hotel. The next morning, Mr. Fitzburgh went to the hotel. He found the man and also his lost letters.

This phenomena is very easily explained. As Mr. Fitzburgh was rushing to the post office, he was pre-occupied with other matters and when he lost the letters, he consciously paid no attention to this. His subconscious mind, however, saw everything that happened - where he had lost the letters and also who had picked them up. At night, when his conscious mind went to sleep, his subconscious mind unfolded the events of the day.

These are obscure feelings, which our mind registers through our senses. The events were taken in, but they were not acted upon at that particular moment. At night, when the pre-occupation disappeared, it came back in the form of a dream.

This can very easily be proven with a little experiment. Take a deck of cards in the company of several people. Draw their attention to the cards by playing with them, but keep the cards face down. Then take only one card and show it face up for just a few seconds. While doing this, take a fast look around you and remember those people who looked at that card. Then, place the card face down back into the deck. Play with the deck for a few more moments, wait a little while, and then ask those people who looked at the card to think of a card. You will find that those who looked at the card will choose the exact card you showed face up earlier. Many card tricks are based on that phenomena.

The reason or the cause is very clear. The last obscure feeling becomes clear when you reflect. The first thing which comes to mind is the last obscure feeling you had about that particular matter, in other words, the obscure feelings come to the surface immediately, the minute you begin reflecting. This was triggered by the statement: "think of a card"; so you think of the last card you saw, but not consciously. Yet, when asked, it enters your consciousness.

The reason lies in the nature of our being, but remember one thing when you do this experiment, do not show more than one card, because the last impression removes the previous impressions.

Any impression of an object or matter, through our senses, makes a real impression on our Soul, and it also makes an imprint in our fibres. There are many such unilluminated impressions stored in our Soul, while our Soul is occupied with other impressions.

The ability to illuminate these obscure objects in our Soul lies within the power of our imagination.

Through the impression of our senses, our nerves and fibres are stimulated and through this, they are in a certain state of suffering.

It is within the ability of our Soul to re-create this condition without having the necessary object at hand, which was, of course, necessary the first time in order to awaken this condition. Now all that is necessary is the imagination. This imagination now becomes a relative reality. All that has to be done is to bring your nerves and fibres into the condition of perception through the imagination, in the same way as when you first saw the object, only this time you are dealing only with your imagination, without the object being present.

This ability should be developed because many things can be accomplished with it. It is very necessary if you want to recall anything from the past. You always require the services of your imagination to do this.

Through our memory we can recall the face of a Human Being, the scent of flowers, even the sound of an instrument.

A Human Being is, therefore, capable of thinking with his imagination, of music, of smelling flowers, and of hearing a bird sing, of suffering pain, and of experiencing pleasure.

Those who have knowledge of the Power of the Imagination are capable of doing extraordinary things.

Every Human Being possesses this power, to a more or lesser degree, since one person is different from another.

The difference depends on the temperament of the individual.

In phlegmatic Human Beings, the Power of the Imagination is slower in its effect. In choleric Human Beings, it is faster. In sanguine Human Beings, it is clearer. In melancholic Human Beings, it is enduring.

There are certain rules which reveal a great deal to those who think.

Here are some of those rules:

The more intense the first impression of an object is on the Soul of a Human Being, the easier it is to recall this impression through the imagination.

The weaker the impression is on the Soul, the harder it is to recall this impression through the imagination.

Similar events make you recall similar things. Something alike recalls something alike. Obscure conceptions become distinct, distinct becomes clear.

Think about these sentences. If you know how to apply them with intelligence, you will accomplish great things.

12. The Hierarchy Of Beings And Their Connection And Relationship To The Spirit World.

All creatures, from the lowest to the highest, belong to a hierarchy - from a worm to a Human Being, from a Human Being to an Angel, from an Angel to a Cherub.

God is the most perfect, absolute and purest Love.

To resemble or to be analog to this Love means nothing but total bliss. The path which leads to this are the deeds of Love.

The degree of this bliss is discernable by the manner of Love or type of Love. The highest degree of God's Love is heavenly bliss, bliss of the highest of heavens.

The more a Human Being removes himself from this Love, the more he distances himself from God, who is Love. The closer he comes to this Love, the closer he is to God.

No Being can approach God or be in the vicinity of God unless this Being becomes analogous with God. Since God is Love, you can only be like God through Love. Remove yourself from Love, and you remove yourself from God.

Those who know Love, get closer to the Light. Those who despise Love, are in darkness. Where there is darkness, there is no Love, therefore there are Spirits of the Light and there are Spirits of the Darkness.

The result or effect of Light is Good. The result or effect of darkness is Evil.

The consequence of Good is harmony. The consequence of Darkness is disharmony and destruction.

The activity of Love is infinite. Love is always active, always at work. The attribute or quality of Love is a constant endeavour to create something which is alike or similar. Within this lies the reason for creation, the occupation of all beings, our destiny.

Only the Light leads to Love. The Light only means recognition of Love; darkness is not recognition. Those who obtain this recognition through the Light, have the wish of getting closer to the Love. This wish is the effect of the intellect; the intellect is guided by the Light.

Those Beings who really get close to the Light, follow the effect of the Light on the Will, and within this lies the Morality of Human Beings.

Obstacles on the Path of Light to Love are human weaknesses. The results, when you distance yourself from the Path of Light to Love, are crimes which lead you along the wrong path, eventually to total aberration, indulging in all kinds of vice, passions and debauchery.

The natural inclination to be good and do good leads and guides Human Beings onto the Path of Light to Love. The recognition of Love makes this development much easier. In order to complete this task, you have to put what you have learned into practice.

There is no virtue without Love. Love is the foundation of all virtues.

There can be no wickedness or depravity unless you remove yourself more and more from Love; that is the only cause for the existence or formation of such characteristics.

The more a Virtue has its foundation in Love, the more God-like this Virtue is. The more removed depravity is from Love, the more abominable depravity becomes.

The highest of Love, the highest of perfection, is God. Approximation towards this perfection is beatific. The active, continued endeavour of Human Beings is virtue.

Highest of Love, highest perfection, exists in the highest unison, in the highest harmony. This harmony is similar to the sounds of music, which exist in infinite gradation, where every note, from the smallest to the highest, is in proportion part of the whole. The characteristic of perfection and harmony excludes all imperfections and disharmony. It lies, therefore, in the characteristic of the Highest of Beings to strive for perfection, to strive for harmony to the highest of Love - that is the only Path which leads to God.

According to the dissimilarity of the steps on which you approach God, the good luck of the Spirits differ.

The closer a Human Being is to God, the greater is his bliss. Even the lowest level of bliss, in relationship to the Being on that level, is considered total bliss. This is similar to the thousandfold nuances of the color spectrum which, in its thousandfold sequences, the lowest of colors in accordance to the whole, possess in purposeful perfection, the same perfection as the highest of colors.

A Being, who is in possession of the highest of enjoyment of all of the infinite bliss, is God.

This highest of levels of enjoyment of all possible bliss exists by being active with infinite power or might, and then to trigger it in other beings, so that they may attain the same level, that they experience the same enjoyment and heavenly bliss.

This highest of the active powers of God is His essential quality which, of course, is Love.

That is why there are millions of worlds in the infinite space of creation. That is the reason for the incomprehensible number of created beings, who are like steps on a ladder, progressing towards blissfulness, according to their destiny.

The incessantly working force of Divine Love turns into infinite Grace. When the highest of Wisdom unites with Grace, that is called infinite justice.

In relationship to the whole, everything is good. Everything in nature is a chain. One condition is striving for another, and one prepares for the other.

If the Human Being is the last link on the chain of the Earth Organization, then he is on the higher chain of Beings, the lowest link.

The most perfect animal being in the physical world must be, as long as it lives in the physical world, the most imperfect mental or Spirit Being in the Spirit World, in comparison to the other beings in the Spirit World.

Gold, which has not been separated from the gold-ore, is the most imperfect gold compared to the gold which has been purified or is free of all impurities.

Similar to gold, Human Beings also have this seed of purity within them, but it is surrounded by impurities, which have to be removed.

In other words, the electric current has an affect on insulated bodies or objects, the mental on Souls, which then will discharge their passions.

The Human Being, which is the most intelligent and advanced being in the Earth Organization, is the most rudimentary and underdeveloped being in his new environment, as a future inhabitant of the Spirit World.

The position of a Human Being is the last position for this, Planet Earth, and the first position for his next and future existence.

The purer a Human Being becomes, the closer he is to the next, future step in succession and the closer he gets to the Spirit World.

The more impure a Human Being is, the closer he is to the animal stage, the closer he is to the physical world, the more physical he himself is.

Having this knowledge, you can determine another Human Being's level of development in the order of things. Never let a physical Human Being dominate a mental Human Being. The result, if this happens, is that the mental Human Being would meet with disaster after disaster, loneliness beyond loneliness.

The inner drive, the effort a Human Being makes to attain blissfulness, his Spirit wanting to rise up from its weak physical existence of the animal body, is the first sign or inclination towards assimilation. It is the first hint of wanting eternity and wanting to progress.

Everything in Nature is a chain, everything is a succession, a step-by-step connection; also a connection to the Spirit World with the Brothers of a higher succession.

The more perfect a being comes, the more he resembles God; the more he resembles God, the more his Love increases, because God is pure Love.

Our Brothers, who are higher in succession than we are, are more perfect and closer to God and resemble God more than we do. They are also closer to pure Love, but they are connected to us. They invisibly participate in our well-being and in our daily affairs - they are Brothers.

A good Human Being also loves animals, cares for them, helps them where he can, and treats them as a fellow being.

Why then should a Mental Being not be a friend of a Being in the animal stage? (A physical Human Being expressed properly as being in the animal stage.) Since nothing exists without reason, nothing is without cause. That creates an effect, and the effect creates a consequence. Love is the Law of Eternity (or the only ingredient for achieving Eternity).

Human Beings cling to Human Beings; Spirits cling to Spirits; same to same, alike to alike.

This should give you a clue as to which Human Being is over the threshold and which one is not. Who do you cling to - the higher or the lower?

Everything has its order, everything has its organ (executive body) and everything in Nature has its order, its association. The sensitive Human Being searches in the physical world for another Human Being who is sensitive; a virtuous Human Being searches for a virtuous Human Being. The Spiritual Being is searching for a physical Human Being, who comes closest in ability to the Spiritual Human Being.

Same attracts same for the purpose of assimilation, and by a virtue every Human Being has by Nature.

The association with Beings on a higher level is, therefore, part of our human nature, and is not a child of our fantasy, but reality.

Since there is a succession or a level of development among Spirit Human Beings, as is the case with Earthlings or Earth Human Beings, it links up with the Spirit Human Being through the similarity of both Beings.

The inconceivability of the physical world lies within the Power of Assimilation.

This power is unknown to most Human Beings. A magnet has an effect only on something which is similar, and its outflow is wonderful.

The Magnetic Force penetrates the most inconceivable spaces, and has an effect on a similar object in the remotest areas. The mentioning of this power is just a hint.

There are hidden powers - powers of the Soul. This manner of attraction is even more wonderful than the attraction and power of the magnet.

Same ability, same frame of mind, same sound, same movement, same forms. How much inconceivability, how many wonders lie hidden in this?

Any energy, any power, works constantly to become stronger, and any energy which does not become stronger, assimilates, only one more and the other less.

There are only two ways or possibilities to assimilation - one way is positive and the other way is negative - or plus and minus assimilation. This Sentence contains many great Secrets.

The higher or the lesser power of a being lies within higher or lesser assimilation.

The power or energy recreates these Beings and it is the origin of thousands and thousands of different forms. Their growth is development; their destruction is transition.

Every being has its sphere of activity, and its purpose to serve the whole.

The existence of a Human Being is similar to the Sun. The awakening is the morning. The Moon is the physical, earthly, daily life. The evening is his death.

The Sun leaves the horizon and the bright light of the Sun changes into what our eye perceives as dusk. But for those who are on higher ground, the Sun still shines on many huts or homes, and many

Human Beings still enjoy the Sun's light.

The same as the Sun disappears, so do Human Beings when they die. His life was the moon for us, his death the dusk. He is on the other side, even though he is still effective in retrograde, even if his effectiveness is less than it was before. It can be seen by some, but not by the inhabitants of the valleys, only by those who live in the higher regions.

These inhabitants of the higher regions enjoy the Sun's light much longer than those in the valleys, even when the Sun is long lost for those in the valleys.

There are many things which cannot be seen with the normal human eye, but they do exist. Would it not be an audacity to say that they do not exist because you cannot see them, or what I cannot see, nobody else can see. Or, because I am blind, everybody else is blind, or, because I cannot paint, nobody else can paint.

Yet thousands of creatures are unnoticed in front of us, and no human eye saw them until the microscope was developed. A new world opened up. Why did he not see the world before? What was the reason? His senses were limited. Man did not possess the organ to see this world.

That is why many things are hidden by Nature and in Nature, because Human Beings do not know their organ. But do not assume that because the organ is hidden from most Human Beings, that it is hidden from all Human Beings.

Your weak eyes, mortal! Strengthened with binoculars, your eyes will discover many things you could not see before. What will the eyes or your Soul discover when they have learned the art to strengthen them.

But think!!! Only same attracts same, only like attracts like. A cube stands, a ball rolls; everything requires its formation.

13. *The Power Of The Imagination.*

The knowledge, the recognition of objects being present is a feeling, a perception; it creates a feeling. There is also another ability within us to bring forth this knowledge in the absence of the object.

The power of the imagination is twofold: One is the voluntary and the other is the involuntary imagination.

The voluntary power of the imagination is totally independent from the mechanism of the organs and their vibrations, which originates from the circulation of the liquids.

The involuntary power of the imagination has its origin when the organs have all the power of tension and sensitivity through the natural flow of the blood, and in the absence of the objects, bring their picture to life in the same manner as if the objects were present.

This leads to the conclusion that the involuntary power of the imagination can be stimulated in every Human Being.

The involuntary power of the imagination exists through the blood in the lively motion of the fibres.

When the blood is set into motion, the involuntary imagination is set into motion. We have an example when people fantasize in the case of an ailment.

A quiet and gentle flow of blood brings about quiet and peaceful pictures. A fast and stormy flow of blood brings about horrible pictures. A fierce and ebullient flow of blood brings about fright, shock, terror, anger, and rage. An inhibited flow of blood results in fear, timidness, anxiety and anguish.

The severity or weakness as a result of the above conditions depends upon the temperament of the Human Being.

The violent ebullition of the blood in a sanguine person brings forth frivolity and foolhardiness. In a choleric person, rage and frenzy.

The inhibited flow of blood has the most devastating results in Human Beings who have a phlegmatic or melancholic temperament.

The circulation of our blood and of our liquids depends upon our nourishment, the air we breathe, and the power of tension in our parts.

Therefore, these conditions arise due to the nature of things, which bring into motion the power of the imagination.

The power of the imagination can be triggered through the eye, the ear, the smell, the taste and through feelings.

Sounds, scents or odours, nourishment, friction and feelings set into motion the involuntary power of the imagination.

These are the reasons which are the foundation serving the natural magic to achieve miraculous appearances or apparitions.

You can manufacture a mirror whereby you can show different people a person they would like to see, even if the person they want to see is not present. The nature or characteristic of this mirror is based on the theory of the involuntary power of the imagination.

The mirror is based on the following basic laws: Memory and reminiscence are sisters as far as the power of the imagination is concerned.

The power of the imagination is a container of pictures, therefore similar pictures evoke other similar pictures.

All of our conceptions, may they be depending on our will or not, are either simple or complex, made from one ingredient or many.

Conceptions, where the ingredients are more than one, come from the same origin as the conceptions which have only one ingredient, because they are the combined result of different sensuous perceptions.

The sensuous conceptions are usually the right ones. The thought-out conceptions are probable. The mixed conceptions are uncertain.

Passion shows the objects as we wish them to be, and not as they really are.

The last sentence is the most important when it comes to what we see in our fantasy or appearances or apparitions in our fantasy.

1. Perceptions are impressions which our body receives from the objects which are present or from their resemblance.

2. Inner feelings are the impressions which are triggered in the Soul through the perceptions.

3. The Magician has to observe the object, which has a direct or indirect effect on the physical body, the means by which this movement is accomplished or by which means this is communicated, and also the manner of the impression.

4. The reflecting perceptions have their origin in the Human Being through a movement which is equal to and being brought forth through the presence of the objects. The power of sound can be increased to such a degree that the organ of the senses can be stirred through the power of the imagination, as if the objects were actually present.

5. Dreams exist, or have their origin, through inner movement. The feelings you have when you dream, the perceptions which develop, are just as strong and vivid as those which are caused in their presence.

6. Very seldom do Human Beings conceive things as they really are. Usually you add the impressions you receive to the reality.

7. Ask yourself: Is it right to spend more time on the past and the future than you do on the present?

8. Through the power of the imagination we do not only contain and recall our conceptions, but we join and combine them with many other conceptions.

14. The Soul.

The being, the substance in us which gives us feeling, makes us think, gives us the Will and makes us act, is the Soul.

The physical body cannot feel or perceive anything. The physical body cannot act voluntarily, but the entity, the substance, the being within the physical body which is different, has the feeling, can act and has the Will.

No created mind pervades the inner Nature of the Soul. Blessed are those who are shown its outer shell or Nature. In other words, those who are aware of its existence.

The Soul is not assembled, the Soul is not physical, the Soul cannot be separated or divided. The Soul has the ability to feel, to think and to act, but she does not feel, think and act all the time, even though she has the ability to do so all the time. The Soul and the body are joined exactly. Here is the question? How can two substances which are fundamentally so different be joined so exactly? The Soul is directly joined with the body. The direct connection has its origin partly in the simplicity of the Soul, and partly in the material composition of the physical body.

Air and Fire form the ethereal body and this etheric body is what was called in the old days the Body of the Soul, and what is now called the SCHEMA PERCEPTIONIS.

Through this ethereal, fiery envelope, the elementary Soul is functioning and informs the finer nervous system of the subtile organization of the effects it received, and from there it is relayed to the more coarse and visible nervous system.

The effect the Soul has on the body is similar to the highest rising sound, which increases in volume and then travels downwards to the deepest depth.

The effect the body has on the Soul is similar to the lowest of sounds which climb higher and higher until the sound becomes so faint that it disappears.

Our perception is also step-by-step, by degrees.

As the last nuance of the darkest of colors is in proportion to the highest nuance of the lightest colors, so are the proportions in their effect of the physical objects as far as the perception of these are concerned on the Soul.

As the highest nuance of the lightest color compares to the last nuance of the darkest color, so is the effect in proportion, what the Soul has on the physical body.

The path of radiance from the Soul to the physical body is from the light to dusk. The path of radiance from the physical body to the Soul is from dusk to the light.

Nature, through its art or skill, gives us a hint, a sign to this truth, in the same way as Nature presents objects to the eye and how the eye sees the object through its skill.

From the eye to the object, the line increases physically. What started out to be a point becomes a line, and the line graduates into an object.

From the physical object towards the eye, the line diminishes to a point.

Wherever you look you will find God's greatness, if you just take the time to look and not waste your time on idle gossip. The Sign of Immortality - the Call for Worship.

15. Immortality.

Everything in Nature is alive - nothing is dead. What is considered to be death is a transition to life.

A dead being is something impossible in Nature, an absurdity in the most ridiculous way.

Any form of destruction is a transition to a higher form of life. The wisest of our Fathers made this transition at an early stage, as quickly, as manifold, and as frequently as possible, and as the preservation of the human generation would allow.

50

Every being has its life; the difference lies in the vitality of the individual. That depends upon the particular ingredients of the particular being and the manner of its composition.

The inner power or energy of all beings is Vitality or Life-Energy. Life is the manner or fashion in which the inner power manifests itself outwardly through the coarser, physical organs or demeanour.

Everything strives for perfection, everything towards its destination, only one being earlier and others later.

There are and there will be no exceptions, only obstacles in the subject matter. Everything in this world has a specified path. Everything has its own sphere of activity.

Within this world itself, there are thousands of other worlds, only less perfect.

Even in those worlds there is life, development and transition, and there is also assimilation.

Inspect and examine the world of stones and metals, the world of plants, the world of animals.

Study the pearl on the shores of the oceans, the oyster in the shell. Marvel at the first order of the animal, and worship the Eternal, the Everlasting.

Everything in Nature is entwined through an infinite bond, everything in Nature follows a sequence and everything is linked.

Creation is a Whole, built after a master-plan. Everything has symmetry, proportion, numbers, weight and measures. Nothing can exist unless it is part of God's plan.

There are vast successions of creatures, but each of them belong to a specific branch in Nature as to area, lifespan, destination or destiny, perfection, energy or vitality, and it also has its limits.

Everything reassures Human Beings of immortality. You are being called to immortality and continuance.

Only Human Beings themselves are hesitant to accept immortality so they regress by adopting such an attitude. They also judge perfection by imperfection. How limited is such a thought, such behaviour. What judgement, what total misconception.

16. The Relationship Of Human Beings
With The World Of Spirits.

Since Human Beings are the Highest Beings in the Earth Organization, they are therefore the lowest link in the chain of Higher

Beings. It is, therefore, safe to assume that the world of Human Beings is irrevocably linked to the World of Spirits.

Every link of a chain affects backwards the next link in succession and forward the next link preceding.

A Human Being has three bodies: The physical, the astral (Soul), and the mental (Spirit-Mind).

That is why the body clings to the physical world and the Spirit to the Spirit World. That is the reason for the two-sided inclination, or the Law of the Flesh, which struggles against the Law of the Spirit. In Latin: SENTIO LEGEM CARNIS REPUGNATINIS LEGI MENTIS MAE.

This is the inconceivable mystery of the nature of Human Beings, at times sublime, magnificent as an Angel, and then reduced to the level of a worm.

The closer a Human Being is to his future destination, the closer he is to perfection.

Progressing by degrees means taking steps which bring you closer to perfection.

Being further and further away from your destination with every step you take means you are going backwards. It also means you become less and less perfect, and achieving with every step you take in that direction, more and more imperfection.

God is Love - the Creation of Infinite Love - Positive Activity.

Human Beings are the first Beings created in God's Image; created for Love and to Love.

The first Law, the Law for Human Beings, is Love, because Love is the assimilation with God, becoming alike, resemblance, progressing to higher perfection.

Blissfulness of the Spirit will multiply in accordance with Love's activity. The more perfect the Spirit, the more perfect is the Love.

The more perfect Love is, the greater is Love's endeavour to increase its sphere of activity. The Brothers of the Higher Order link up with Human Beings through Love.

The more perfection a Human Being achieves in active Love, the more he is capable of assimilation with Higher Beings.

Alike clings to alike, but in order to make that connection you require a tool, an organ, through which a Spirit Being can influence a Physical Being.

The Spirit Being cannot directly influence a Physical Being, it requires an organ to accomplish this.

Spirits can directly affect Spirits and the physical can directly affect the physical.

The physical acts upon the Spirit indirectly, and the Spirit acts upon the physical indirectly.

When two Beings are in the position where they act upon each other, the condition which causes this reciprocity is called a union.

Beings of a Higher Order can therefore communicate with Beings of a lower order, and Beings of a lower order can communicate with Beings of a higher order.

When Human Beings make a connection with Beings which are next in order of the higher order of succession, they are then in the company of the World of Spirits.

Relationships of this nature, between Human Beings and the Spirit World, do exist and are, therefore, not an impossibility, even though they are seldom.

Since these relationships seldom exist, it does not live in the inability of our nature to relate to the Higher Beings, but rather in our incompleteness to assimilate. These imperfections prevent us from this kind of relationship.

It is not the fault of the Soul. That is not the reason why the sounds of Harmony do not reach the Soul. The cause is the organ, a disharmony of this organ, which is the ear.

If you accept the possibility rather than contradict, that Higher Beings can communicate with Lower Beings, then the question arises: How is this done? Which organ do you employ to achieve this communication? How does one Being have an effect on the other?

Again, like to alike or the like affect alike, Spirit affect Spirit, mind affects mind.

The influence of Higher Beings makes itself known and relays messages directly through the power of our Soul, and therein lies the connection.

It is, therefore, impossible that the Higher Beings affect Human Beings through a hidden manner or through the power of the imagination.

It is not necessary that all communications of our Soul have to be transmitted through the outer physical organs before they can be perceived.

Can the influence of Higher Beings not be perceived directly through the finer organization without notifying the physical organization first?

The Spirit affects the Spirit, as the reflection of light upon objects.

Human Beings communicate their thoughts to other Human Beings through sound. A specific modulation of the sound creates the word. Words are expressions of our ideas or concepts - that is why we have speech. That is how we communicate our ideas and our feelings to other Human Beings.

In the physical world, the most perfect language is the spoken word; the language of signs, the most imperfect. Infallible is the language of the Soul in the eyes of Human Beings.

Objects evoke ideas through impressions which they make on our nerves. The power of the Soul to renew this impression lies within the ability of the imagination. When the imagination is triggered by certain sounds, which cause the other person to connect with other objects, this then translates and is expressed through a feeling which the Soul experiences - the spoken word, our language.

When you want to speak to another Human Being, he has to understand what you say. You have to be capable of making sounds and using words he or she understands, before the idea can be conceived, otherwise understanding is impossible.

Should I endeavour to make a person understand things he has never seen or heard of, things of which he has no conception, it is still possible to communicate on hand of similar objects, or by other examples, through things of which he already has knowledge.

We can hear in our dreams, we can see in our dreams. What does that tell us? Human Beings are capable of seeing things they saw only once, without using the rays of their physical eyes, and to hear sounds they only heard once before, without using the physical ear.

In our dreams we are capable of actually seeing and hearing. That is accomplished by bringing into motion the finer nerves which gives us the feeling of seeing. This is done in the same manner as when they were brought into motion through an object when our physical eyes were open.

The same applies when the finer organization of hearing is brought into motion. In the same manner, you are under the impression that the sounds are actually generated at that moment, therefore, you can hear and see in your dreams.

This knowledge gives you the certainty and solves the puzzle of somnambulism and magnetic sleep, but only if you understand what was said.

The Power of the Imagination, which is made up of nothing else but the power of the Soul, will give certain vibrations to the nerves, which they receive from an impression of an object. This can progress to a certain degree of intensity, which in itself is reality. This explanation may be a puzzle for thousands of Human Beings, but not for all.

In other words, you can hear and see through direct motion or movement of the finer organization, without direct or indirect motion or movement of the physical or coarser organization.

For those who have the ability to contemplate, enough has been said.

In purity, the thought of a Higher Being is superior to the thought of a Human Being. The thought of a Higher Being is much lighter in its intensity when it flows to the Soul through the finer organization of the thinker.

The thoughts of Higher Beings become the thoughts of Human Beings, but as pure as the rays of the sun, which radiate the mountain tops on a bright noon.

When Human Beings speak, the tone generates the sound and forms the word which enters the ear, and is received by the expecting Soul.

Higher Beings do not communicate with Human Beings as Human Beings communicate with Human Beings.

The tone of their voice directly touches our finer nerves and through this movement of understandable pictures, it enters into our Soul, which is prepared and receptive at this point.

Higher Beings only give information to those, in an understandable fashion, whose world is quiet and at peace, and not to those whose organs are moved by storms and passions, because it is an impossibility to hear harmonious music which is played in a raging hurricane.

What kind of effect can the fine sound of a flute have during the hammer blows on an anvil of the cyclops?

Many people are of the opinion that Higher Beings only speak to Human Beings while they are asleep.

Can a violinist play his violin when the strings do not have the proper tension? But how beautifully can he play when they are in tune and have the proper tension. This rule can be applied to all things, when properly understood.

Love, Truth and Purity are the sounds of the World of Spirits. They do not reverberate on the instrument of our Soul when the strings are not harmoniously tuned.

17. Indispensable Hypothesis
In Magic Regarding Ideas.

Every concept must be, out of necessity, accompanied by a harmonious movement, motion or nerve.

Whenever you want to recollect an idea which is stored in your memory, you have to be able to recreate the same movement of the nerves which initially accompanied the idea after you received the first impression of the object.

This occurs in three different ways:

1. The movements to which our ideas are connected maintain themselves through their own power in our memory after they have been stimulated once through the objects. Then to repeat and renew those ideas requires nothing else but the attention our Soul pays to such movements, or

2. To recall ideas is a modification of the moving force of the Soul which acts upon the fibres or the vitality, thereby causing similar movements as those which the object caused, or

3. The movements are renewed through the connection with the nerves, so if one nerve is in motion, it can cause others with which it is connected to be brought into motion as well.

We can feel this activity of our Soul if we want to remember something on purpose.

Whenever we want to retain the originality of an idea for which we are seeking or searching, we force our organs to do so.

If it is an idea which has to do with sight, we do this or accomplish this with our eyes. If it is an idea which has to do with hearing, we accomplish this with our ears, and so on.

Should we not be able to immediately connect to an idea or recollect an idea for which we are looking or yearn for, then our Soul starts to wander. This stimulates many of our nerves. Eventually the right nerve is found, which leads to the idea which we were yearning for.

Therefore, the eye can lead us to an idea which originally entered our Soul through the ear. The ear can lead us to an idea which originally entered our Soul through the eye. For example: We see a piano and it reminds us of the person playing it, or we hear a voice and that can remind us of a person.

The stronger the impression of an idea is, the more often this idea represents itself and the easier it is to recall this idea.

Those who take the time and study and understand these sentences will be able to do unbelievable things.

18. *Visions and Premonitions.*

Premonitions are preceding feelings of changes to come.

They are founded in Nature and belong to the changes themselves.

Not everybody feels a major change or notices preceding feelings because preceding feelings make a finer susceptibility a prerequisite.

The rise and fall of the mercury in the barometer is a premonition of the future weather.

When a cork is attracted, that is a premonition that an electric cloud is drawing nearer.

It is, therefore, absolutely necessary to possess a very particular organization to be capable of having premonitions, taking into consideration the receptivity of the finer effect of the impression.

In other words, Human Beings who possess a finer organization are the only ones who are capable of having premonitions.

Human Beings who possess a finer nervous system have the capability of knowing what kind of weather we will have.

Our physical body in comparison to our Spirit, no matter how fine our nerves really are, is still a coarse substance, but the nerves are beginning, at this level, to be capable of premonitions. How much more capable than are those of our internal, finer organization? How much more must our Soul's capability be?

Friendship, Love and Similarity are the objects of the feelings of our Soul, and forthcoming changes in these objects bring about these premonitions of the Soul.

Love, Friendship, and Similarity are Assimilations and, accordingly, by degrees of the same, assimilation increases by degrees, the same feeling.

Strings which have the same tension sound in harmony. Bringing one into motion sets another, which has the same tension, into the same motion.

Upon these Laws rests the Theory of Premonitions.

There are premonitions where the weaker nervous system is the origin. There are premonitions where the origin is the finer physical organization, and there are premonitions where the origin is founded in the same mood or feeling between two beings or two Souls.

There are Human Beings whose feelings far exceed those of normally accepted feelings.

There is enough evidence of people who have been born blind, and have the ability to distinguish colors, letters, etc. by touch.

There are also Human Beings who can smell what most Human Beings are incapable of smelling.

There are Human Beings who have more finely developed senses than others. Most of the time this is due to their lifestyle. Some Human Beings, who live totally contrary to the Laws of Nature, have their senses dulled to the point that they become senseless. All outside relationships are totally terminated, and those Human Beings can only rely on their memory. They have, therefore, left everything which is human.

There are also Human Beings who have developed their senses and can smell the nature of an ailment by what people have eaten.

This, of course, is a totally natural ability. It has its origin in the finer organization of the senses.

If we develop this more and more, we can see things we could not see before, and we can hear something we could not hear before. Things we thought were impossible become possible. As it is possible to see things through the microscope which cannot be seen through our normal eyes, our finer organization is capable of developing microscopic eyes.

There are Human Beings who can smell blood, even if it was cleaned, on a butcher, a hunter or a murderer. They can also distinguish human blood from animal blood. This is, of course, not only limited to blood.

This will not seem so unbelievable if you think of a dog which can find a Human Being by their footprints, even if that Human Being walked by hours ago.

Even though not every Human Being is in possession of these capabilities, there are Human Beings like this. Since there are very few Human Beings who can do this, we call them phenomenons.

Visions are based on the finer organization of our feelings.

Attuned bodies affect those who are in tune with them.

Weight, space, time, distance, past and future are attributes of the physical world. The Spirit is not limited to space, time and distance. The Spirit has no obstacles. The power of the Spirit is the Will - there are no boundaries. Human Beings can act through this in an unlimited way.

The Soul has the ability to transpose itself over the greatest distance and it can go where the physical body cannot go, because the body is limited to time and space.

Therefore, the effect of the body on the body has its limits.

The effect of the Spirit on the Spirit is not subject to the laws of the physical world.

Free from all that is, of course, the Soul. The Soul has unlimited freedom, unless you put your Soul into bondage.

That is why Human Beings who are attuned to another Human Being's Soul, such as friends, parents, spouses, or lovers, can see their loved ones immediately upon their death, without having prior knowledge. This is also not unusual for Human Beings of a finer organization.

The Soul which has left the body - in other words, the deceased person's Soul - can now, since it is free of the physical body, be seen by another Soul which is still in physical bondage, through being in harmony, and through the power of similarity and assimilation.

This has happened many times and to many people - being aware of another person's feelings. It may even be when they are ill or feel depressed, if they are in close proximity or even at greater distances.

Soul connections cannot be severed by distance or space. Souls which are the same, Souls which are in tune with each other cannot be kept apart by physical death. They find each other in death because these are the immutable Laws of Assimilation.

The Universe is a whole. No changes can take place unless there are changes in the whole. In this lies the reason for the feeling of approximation.

Approximation is a quality, a feeling the Soul has - a feeling of the finer organization. The Soul is capable of feeling the presence of such an event, whereas the physical body is still far removed from this, because for the physical body, this event is still part of the future.

Animals possess this ability; they have the feeling of impending disaster such as an earthquake, or in the case of a dog, hey feel the proximity of their master.

The finer organization of a Human Being is capable of feeling things earlier than the physical, and the Human Being who pays attention to the feelings of his Soul can take advantage of these premonitions of his Soul.

The Creator made certain when He created living beings that every being, in order to maintain itself, had in its possession the propensity of like and dislike, or sympathy and antipathy.

Animals distinguish by smell, the wholesome herbs from the poisonous herbs.

Human Beings have the same ability, however, those Human Beings who have purposely dulled their senses need a book to distinguish the wholesome herbs from the poisonous herbs, or for that matter, anything wholesome from that which is poisonous. This includes modern food and medicines. Anyone whose senses are not dulled would not take modern medicine or eat modern food.

Our organs learn many things from Nature, but Human Beings themselves have corrupted them and brought about their demise. Should we want to regain the knowledge of what Nature taught us long ago through our natural instinct, we have to study, which takes a great deal of time and dedication.

The Creator made certain that every animal had the means at their disposal for their destruction as well as for their maintenance.

When you understand the household of the animals, you can see the prudence of this blessing.

Among the means of self-preservation, you can count the feelings the Soul has in regards to Approximation.

A spider spends much of its time in the centre of its cobweb and will notice the slightest approach of any thing because it is immediately transmitted through the spider threads, which originate in the centre of the cobweb.

Very fine is the spider's web, but coarse, very coarse, when compared to the finer, inner organs of Human Beings.

Feelings of the Soul such as Love, Friendship and Devotion lead to Assimilation, because same affects same, like to alike.

In reality, the Soul only has one feeling and that feeling is Love. Friendship and Devotion are only modifications of Love.

Animosity, Hate, Dislike, Antipathy are the opposite of Love or negations.

Feelings of the Soul assimilate. It is this inclination which is the urge of "Becoming One". This is the reason, the inclination of two beings who love each other in this physical world, to unite, to communicate.

Human Beings, whose Love is pure and unselfish, do not only express their Love by physical communion with another Human Being or through embracing or kissing. The importance is directed towards the Soul of Becoming One and not towards a physical union, since the physical body is more of an obstacle rather than a tool or an organ of "Becoming One".

In all Human Beings, Love expresses itself in accordance with the Eternal Laws by degrees.

In the animals, this love is not pure. In the Human Being it is a little purer, yet in the Spirit, it is present in the purest form.

Love is in accordance with the Laws of the Destiny of the Beings. Its effect on animals is to serve the purpose of maintaining and propagating their species, in their sphere of activity.

In the case of a Human Being, where the body is animal and the Soul is in accordance with the Spirit, its effectiveness is closer to perfection. Love creates in the body the urge for procreation, but in the Soul, the propensity for communion and assimilation.

The more physical a Human Being is, the more sensual is his love. The more spiritual a Human Being is, the more exalted is his Love.

The result of physical love is only temporary delight. The result of spiritual Love is a constant endeavour of "Becoming One" - Assimilation.

This Love is not known among Human Beings, even though this Love is the only true Love - the Love of the Spirit World, which will lead us to a resemblance with God, to supreme ecstasy and blissfulness. Getting closer to God is the reason for our creation, in becoming like God, through the only possible means, Love, because God is Love. Within this lies the supreme secret of our association with the Spirit World. Through this, the puzzle is solved: Ordained Souls cannot be separated by time, distance, or through death, any kind of death.

19. Visions Caused Through
The Deception Of Our Senses.

We have discussed visions which were caused or originated through the feelings of our Soul and the finer organization. We will now discuss visions which are caused or originate through the deception of our senses, which means that our senses can be deceived.

To these deceptions belong apparitions, which are caused and can be explained due to optical and catoptrical reasons (reflections of light or mirror images).

Among those are peculiar apparitions of human-like and animal-like figures in the dark or even a reflection of your own person, or the appearance of living people, because of optical circumstances, even though the person is not present in reality.

Smoke and fog are susceptible to the reflection of light, therefore, they are capable of creating or representing shadows or silhouettes.

During the Fall, in the evenings, a thick fog usually hovers over swamps, rivers and lakes. Should you walk towards this thick fog, providing the sun is setting behind you and, of course, that includes any other person walking in the same direction, your image and also the other person's image can reflect on the heavy fog. This has the appearance, when you look at it, as if this shadow was actually walking towards you. In this case, it may be you or another person which happened to be in your vicinity. This image has the appearance of a person dressed totally in black and is either your reflection or that of the other person.

Water vapours can also form mirror-like surfaces, especially if this is enhanced by a dark background. This becomes a mirror in which you can see yourself.

This happens quite often in clothes closets located in old houses or in moist areas where it is possible for these water vapours to accumulate. Many stories and legends are based on this phenomenon and this is the simple explanation.

I have personal knowledge of such an incident, whereby a particular person saw herself when she opened the clothes closet. Needless to say, she fainted, but the whole incident was based on this principle.

Anyone who has this knowledge can create this type of phenomenon quite easily. All you require is, of course, optical and catoptrical knowledge; that means you know how rays reflect. Thousands of tricks are based on this knowledge. Mirrors can be placed in such a way that the person who looks at them is totally unaware of the fact that they are looking into a mirror.

It is also possible to project with mirrors. You can, through reflection with mirrors, make a Human Being visible in another room, even though physically that person is not in that particular room.

If you can do this with one person, it is also possible to do the same with a large party of people. You could, for instance, have a large party of people appear in an large empty room at a moment's notice, eating and drinking, and any person who entered this room would see this. You could also make them disappear at a moment's notice.

It is also possible to change, at a moment's notice, the scenery in that same room. You can change it into a garden or into night so that the onlookers can see the sky with stars.

On a large scale, this would be a very expensive proposition, but what is said here can be proven with scale models.

Anyone who is interested will find a way of accomplishing this. If everything were disclosed, it would lose its value and attraction. Enough has been disclosed if you know that this possibility does exist, and the physical reasons for this phenomenon have been explained.

Through a concave mirror you can make any object appear in

mid-air. There are, of course, many other possibilities and this is only one of them.

Here are a few more examples:

1. You can make an animal appear by preparing a tray of red hot coals and adding certain ingredients to the coals which creates a dense smoke, and the animal will appear in the smoke.

2. This experiment is accomplished with a hidden, concave mirror by employing the laws which govern the refraction of rays.

3. You can also use a vase of pure, white glass, fill it with water and let a flower grow out of it. This is also accomplished through the laws discussed.

4. Take any kind of box and let a picture of a loved one appear on top of it.

All these experiments are delusion, deception, illusions or mirages accomplished by concave mirrors. These experiments, of course, require skill and knowledge.

20. Foresight Or Forecast; Prophecy Or Prediction.

Foresight means to have knowledge of future events before they come into being, to know of their existence and their coming into being.

Human Beings measure time in accordance to the impressions objects have on their senses. That is the origin of the past, the present, and the future.

Our senses are limited, and the perception of things which enter our Soul by means of the finer organization is accomplished by degrees.

We feel that we cannot grasp many different concepts at the same time, but only one idea after the other, not many simultaneously.

If we therefore think of a being as a whole, but where the whole is composed of many different parts, we reduce this to a single thing, an Individuum. This enables us to simplify our concept and therefore we can imagine it better.

For example: A Being who has a physical body, a Soul and Spirit and whose Spirit is immortal, and is also blessed with five senses as a whole, but you can also conceive the five senses separately. This Being as a whole is a Human Being.

Time and space are attributes of the physical world. The Spirit World is not subject to these variations.

In the Spirit World, any possibility is always in the present.

Eternity does not have space or time, a beginning, or an end.

The Eternal can see all things, past and future, in accordance with his nature, because with him, everything is in the present.

The narrow-mindedness of our senses robs us of our understanding of the future. Our feelings are based on the impressions our organs perceive, which can only be stimulated degree by degree, therefore they are limited.

Only by comparing the past with the present can a Human Being draw certain conclusions as to the future. This is limited again and is in accordance with his daily experiences and what they may grant him as far as the knowledge of the future is concerned.

From experience, Human Beings know that we have day and night, and a Sun and a Moon, and Winter and Summer, and one follows the other.

Out of the manner of Human Beings themselves, future occurrences can be obtained. They are not general in substance but are from a higher synopsis which is, of course, knowledge of the future.

The higher the understanding of a Human Being, the more he knows of the future.

A natural physician determines the present and future condition of his patient with the knowledge he has about herbs, and the experience he has acquired in regards to healing. He also applies the same knowledge to determine the convalescence or the death of his patient.

Considering the prospect of the future as far as Human Beings are concerned, the following example should clarify this: Let us imagine that in front of us is a sky-high mountain. Surrounding the sky-high mountain is a range of smaller mountains, still high enough however, that if you are standing at the foot of these small mountains you cannot see what lies behind them.

Let us assume the sky-high mountain has thousands of steps, one higher than the other, leading to the summit. On the steps of the sky-high mountain thousands of Human Beings are standing, one higher than the other, right to the summit.

The people who are standing on the lower steps can only see a few hundred meters because their view is blocked by the hills surrounding the sky-high mountain.

The people who are standing on the higher steps can see a few thousand meters. Their view is blocked, not by the hills, but by the mountain range surrounding the sky-high mountain.

The people who are standing on the summit can see the hills, the mountain range and beyond. They have a total view and not a partial view.

Let us further assume that in these mountains many people are hiking. To those who are still at the foot of the mountain, the path of the future is not known to them, but for those who are on the top of the mountain, they have a deeper insight into the future than those people at the foot of the mountain. What to the brothers of the lower levels is the past and the future is to the Beings of the higher levels bright shining presence.

This is also the situation with every Human Being on Planet Earth.

The Deity is standing on the highest step of the highest mountain.

Below the Deity are the Cherubs.

Below the Cherubs are the Angels.

Below the Angels are the Spirits.

Below the Spirits are the blessed Human Beings.

Everything is according to its station in life, everything is by degrees.

Everybody has the ability to view the future, but this always depends on where he stands. It is according to his degree of development, his degree of assimilation, the heights he has attained through his diligence, and the work he has given to his development.

The more a Human Being attains perfection, the closer he comes to being a Deity. The more he ascends to be a Deity, the farther he can see into the future.

By comparing the past with the conditions of the present, a Human Being can conclude many future occurrences or events, since the future is nothing else but consequences of the present.

When you have deep insight into the characteristics of Human Beings, the temperaments, the Natural Laws, and all necessary circumstances pertaining to this and their relationships, all this makes it possible to predict many things as far as the future is concerned.

When you know the characteristics of a Human Being well, his actions then become very predictable. If you know the history of larger groups or even nations, on the basis of this knowledge you can predict their future.

The same as two times two is four, two times three is six, if you write the result down now, later, or never, it does not matter, the result remains as a consequence. Certain actions have certain reactions - some of them you know in advance.

If you pour aqua fortis (nitric acid) over limestone, it will fizz, whether you do this today or whether you do this tomorrow.

Out of these few examples you can gather that you do know many things about the future. Should you want to know more about the future, you have to increase your knowledge so that you may advance to higher levels so that you can see, hear and feel more.

Many things are right in front of everybody's eyes to see, however they remain hidden to the every-day person. Yet, when you have reached a higher level, these things can very easily be seen.

Human Beings of a finer organization can predict future happenings out of personal, preceding knowledge or predict future events out of previous knowledge on account of other ingredients.

There are Human Beings who possess this knowledge and who have the ability of predicting the death of a Human Being by looking into their eyes. It is not that person's imagination which gives him this answer, but a highly developed quality of the Spirit.

Animals have this instinctive ability; dogs react hours before an earthquake through a pitiful whining.

Swallows can indicate a change in the weather if you observe their flying pattern. Due to the clean or unclean air caused by the watery vapour, they fly high or low according to these conditions. If you have this knowledge and can interpret the meaning of this, you can predict the future.

The question now arises: Are there Human Beings who have these capabilities? Are there Human Beings who have the ability to predict the future?

Are there Human Beings who are capable of doing things which even the most sophisticated scientific equipment is not capable of doing, or even the most qualified scientist?

The answer is: Yes!!!

Remember the example of the sky-high mountain. Man's science does not fall into this category unless the scientist follows Nature's Laws.

This should not be practised for the benefit of the ungodly, but for the purpose of assimilation only and especially not for material gain, entertainment, or to prove this ability to disbelievers.

It lies within the nature of every Human Being to have the inclination to "become alike", to reach perfection. Assimilation is our Destiny. The more a Human Being assimilates with his Deity, the greater is his knowledge, the higher and deeper is his insight. He leaves the sphere of common man and enjoys purer waters. He is closer to the fountain of Wisdom.

It is also true when a Human Being of a lower degree makes contact with a Human Being of a higher degree, provided the lower Being makes the mental and physical effort, that it is considered to be a superhuman effort.

Those Human Beings who do not understand this sentence would be wise to meditate on it.

The Bible says it best. The Bible, in many instances, uses the word Fear, which is a bad translation in one way and good translation in another. In the sense that what we do not understand, we fear, the translation is correct, however, in the real sense it means respect.

The Bible says: The Fear of the Lord is the beginning of Wisdom.

In different words replace fear with respect.

Respect the Lord, as this is the beginning of Wisdom. What does this mean? Respect God's Laws and the result is Wisdom. How much lies in these words. If you understand them, you have Wisdom. All Universal Laws are based on this principle.

There is an old poem, the author is not known. It was originally in another language, therefore only the meaning is given here:

Secret, YOU! You will be the reward for those who are able to draw the right conclusions, and not those who pretend to know everything, to know all the Secrets. A man who thinks, and then draws the right conclusions, knows how to lead himself. Whosoever is ready to think will not err on the path. To the Searchers of Truth, the best of good fortune and the best of health, and I say very quietly to the indolent: God will reveal all the Secrets to those who work hard and diligently.

21. Sleep and Slumber -
The Condition Of The Sleepwalker And The Hysteric.

Our concept of the physical world depends upon our senses. The senses are the means by which we transmit the concept of an object to our Soul.

A Human Being has the continuous ability, if the senses are not dulled, to see, to hear, to feel, to smell and to taste.

It happens sometimes that a Human Being is capable of seeing, hearing, smelling, tasting and feeling at the same time, however, the simultaneous effect on all the senses results in a very unclear, very indistinct feeling.

The more attention your Soul pays to one subject or to one object, the more effective is the organ of that particular sense, therefore the perception of the particular object is much more intense. For example: If we listen to a very important story, then we place all our emphasis on the faculty of hearing and we do not see what is happening around us. Our Soul is totally dedicated to our sense of hearing. This can, of course, be done with our other senses.

Should all our senses become engaged simultaneously, this condition is very similar to anaesthesia.

If the shock which is simultaneously caused by the objects is of such magnitude that it affects all the senses, then the Soul is in a state of total confusion.

In this lies hidden the unspeakable something that at times fills our Soul. This puts us into a slumber of great delight which cannot be explained.

This condition is the condition which is an equilibrium of all our senses, a relaxation of all our organs and senses, whereby we maintain and strengthen our organs and their functions.

Any condition which brings all our senses into a gentle state of mind is the condition where our senses are being tempered, in other words, they become as strong as steel.

Divine Providence provided a harmonious condition. This is usually accomplished through sleeping.

Nature accomplishes this by softly conducting moisturizing vapours around the area of the head. By moisturizing the tense fibres, they loosen the tenseness and the result is sleep.

The type of sleep a Human Being enjoys is in accordance with the type of moisture the particular human body contains.

Thick, tenacious, or viscous moisture causes in our body a deep, coma-like sleep, whereas pure liquids result in a pleasant sleep.

Hot drinks, therefore, prevent a good rest, because they dry out the nerves and fibres. The nerves and fibres are robbed of their soft moisture with which they should be sprinkled during sleep.

As the dew falls from heaven during the evening hours and moistens the flowers, it relaxes their fibres so that they have the ability the next morning when they wake up to tense up again, so that they can open up their petals. In the same manner this is accomplished in Human Beings, through God's Grace, by conducting the serous (pure, clean and watery) liquids to the brain, thereby sprinkling the dew on the fine fibres and nerves, which relaxes them and at the same time, they recuperate.

What the dew does for the plants, sleep does for Human Beings in the economy of the physical world.

Slumber differentiates from sleep by the degree of tenseness of the nerves.

When you are in a slumber, every object of our senses has an effect on our finer organs. Since our Soul is at rest, it does not especially employ any of the senses. They are, therefore, left to their own impressions which in this state only cause a floating motion. Such as a soft wind touches the flower, like a small boat moves softly on a wind-still lake. You therefore have an almost lustful feeling when you are in a slumber.

How pleasant it is when you slumber in a garden, a soft breeze caressing you, gently soothing your sense of feeling, the sound of a water fountain in your ears, the scent of the flowers touching your sense of smell.

I remember such a feeling, falling into a slumber surrounded by Nature:

It was evening. A soft breeze was blowing gently from the west. I was lying in the grass, my mood was melancholy, surrounded by rose bushes. I was contemplating life and death and eternity. A nightingale was singing a song, the harmonious sound was touching my Soul. Feelings entered my Soul which I had never before experienced. My heart was full of very delightful feelings. It was a state between being awake and asleep. I was awake and yet I was not. The soft breeze was carrying the scent of the roses; the nightingale was singing. I could hear, feel and smell and yet I was not awake nor was I asleep. It was a state of pleasant unconsciousness. Every nerve was pleasantly irritated; it was a heavenly slumber.

When none of the sensuous organs are occupied with a particular perception of an object, the result is rest, a condition where all the organs can recuperate.

The sleep of a sleepwalker or a hysteric is not regular sleep, because the condition of the Soul of such a person is in a different condition than the Soul of a person who is enjoying a regular sleep.

Human Beings have only one sense. This sense is the sense of feeling. To better define this, you can call it the inside and the outside feeling, or the feeling which belongs to the finer organization, and the feeling which belongs to the coarser organization.

Hearing, smell and sight are only modifications of feelings. Since our body is made up of different parts, I cannot see, hear or smell, when through these parts of my body the nerves of the organ of my eyes, my ears and my feelings are not brought into motion. That means: When I do not feel, I cannot perceive.

To feel with your ear is hearing. To feel with your nose is smelling. To feel with your tongue is tasting.

Any change in any part of the body also means a change as far as the head is concerned. It will, therefore, change the hearing, the sight, the smell, and the taste accordingly.

Parts of our body, which are not in harmony with our organization, cause the rest of our body unpleasantness. Those parts of our body, which are in harmony with our organization, give our senses pleasant impressions.

Our Soul is constantly, unbelievably busy, since it cannot express itself through any other means than our sensuous organs. It therefore makes its intentions known with all its might, through these means.

There are many examples where Human Beings and other Beings have lost one sense or the other. The Soul will immediately search to replace the lost sense by focusing in on the other senses and use all its power to improve and refine them.

How much more will this active power of the Soul, which manifests itself so visibly in our physical organization, manifest itself in our finer organization, which is considerably closer to the simplicity of the Soul.

It is important to know that this finer organization, or the inner sense, is as much in need of the rest and tranquillity as is everything else.

Yet, there are people whose finer organs are not as capable of having this rest as others are. This is really an ailment because through this the laws which govern the healthy body are disturbed through this.

The inner sense is too weak when such a person is awake to show its power through the coarser organization which contains them. When such a person is asleep and the coarser organization is contained, it then becomes effective and it shows its full force. This explains the peculiar stories of the sleepwalkers and the remarkable rarities of the hysterics. The reason for this is the deafening of the external physical feeling and therefore the finer, inner feelings can manifest with all their might.

In the purity and harmony of our sensuous organs lie, to a more or lesser degree, the truth of our feelings.

The finer organs are capable of having purer and finer impressions of the objects. The conceptions are becoming more spiritual or mental; they become more genuine, and are getting closer to the simplicity of the Soul.

This condition is not to be confused with sleep because it is not sleep. It is a waking activity of the inner sense.

When a Human Being seems to sleep, he does not sleep in reality. His Spirit received the power to function through the finer senses, because the feelings of the physical senses are in a form of bondage - they have lost the ability to feel.

The question then should arise: Are our physical senses necessary, since the inner senses of Human Beings are superior?

The answer, of course, is that everything which is created, is created in accordance with the sphere in which it lives. Every organ is in accordance to its condition with the whole.

Human Beings are composed of a physical body, a Soul and a Spirit. The relationship between them would cease to exist if it would be any different. It is, therefore, similar to a filter system, from coarse to finer, to finer. From the physical to the Soul to the Spirit.

Since Human Beings are the Highest Beings in the order of the Earth Organization, and the lowest in the order of the Spirit World, the simple conclusion should be that incomprehensible capabilities must already be present in the Soul and in the Spirit, and that our present life is nothing else but a preparation for our future life.

The more we develop our Soul and our Spirit, the more unbelievable their manifestations must be, because most Human Beings judge by the nature of the physical body rather than by the nature of the Soul and by the nature of the Spirit.

22. Preconditions Which Are Essential To Explain Somnambulism.

There is a fluid in Nature which maintains everything, the prime matter of things. It is also called MATERIA PRIMA or UNIVERSAL FLUID.

All bodies, everything physical, is maintained by the Universal

Fluid. The modification of this fluid is limitless. It is the cause of all forms, the reason for all changes. Within this fluid, all the genetic forces are contained. This Universal Fluid is Magnetism, Electricity, Light, Heat, etc.

The Elements are the first emanations of the Universal Fluid. "SHE" is the Organ of Creation, the seed of all things which God called upon to create the worlds.

The first modification of the finest of all matters was the creation of the Elements. The nature of the Universal Fluid is purity and simplicity to the highest degree in physical things.

"SHE" contains and modifies everything. This includes all physical bodies. "SHE" is the cause of the growth of all the metals, the vegetation of plants and the maintenance of animals. "SHE" follows the Laws of Nature step-by-step.

The degrees in the physical world are as follows:

Light
Magnetic Fluid
Electricity
Heat
Fire
Air
Water
Earth

First Degree - Light.

The nature of this Prime Matter is made up of thousands and thousands of emanations in fulfilment of all bodies.

The Qualities are: effectiveness, outflow and back-flow.

Enveloped in the finest of all bodies it is called the Light.

The effect of the Prime Matter in the first instance upon the finer bodies is: activity, motion, circulation and life.

The Prime Matter affects its outflows and the outflows affect the matter and, through this, motion comes into being; also the activity, the circulation of things, the vegetation, and life itself.

The effectiveness this matter has on the outflows and the outflow on the matter is in accordance with that particular body, and that condition differs from body to body, which contains this outflow.

In the finest bodies, the fastest movements of these outflows are like Light.

Second Degree - Magnetic Fluid.

The second degree of Light is the Magnetic Fluid.

Enveloped in less refined particles than degree one, these outflows are set into motion accordingly and to a lesser degree. Therefore, they float around in creation, similar to the waters of the ocean.

Third Degree - The Substance of Heat.

The third degree is the substance of Heat.

The substance of Heat is composed of the concentration of many, with the outflow of Light-loaded particles, which multiply through the inner effect of this outflow. Since the outflow, in accordance with the Universal Laws, endeavours to return to its point of origin, this endeavour causes friction of these particles, meaning particle against particle, which results in the destruction of these particles and this is the creation of Heat.

Fourth Degree - The Electricity.

The fourth degree is Electricity.

The outflow of this Prime Matter is created in such a way that it continuously flows back to where it came from, according to the nature of things.

The retroactive effect is in accordance with the type of body in which the outflows are enclosed, and also in accordance with the resistance of these particular body particles.

Should the resistance of the body particles not be even towards the outflow, as it is with the Light, then the Prime Matter becomes as effective as the Light with its entire power.

Should the resistance and the energy be equal, then the body particles do not outweigh the power of the influence, nor the power or the energy of the body particles. Then, on account of this equal relationship, a Fluid Being comes into being, that we identify as a Magnetic Being.

This is similar to a scale which is in total equilibrium. This is changed with the slightest modification.

It is the endeavour of the battling, enclosed forces of the outflows, inclusive of the enclosed body particles proportionately to a lesser degree, through the effort of the influences, to return to their Prime Matter. Due to the body particles which want to contain them, ensues a never-ending battle.

Little by little, more and more outflow is the result. What a battle! This is the origin of Heat, the Origin of Creation, or the nascent state of the substance of Heat.

To clarify this further: In Nature there is no Fire; there is nothing but Light.

Whenever Light is enclosed in a body, according to the nature of the Light, it will always endeavour to return to its Prime Matter, back to its origin, back to where it came from.

It is the endeavour of the Light to break through these fine body particles. This breaking- through will result in heat, even if it is in the minutest of degrees.

Suns are not burning bodies; they are bodies of Light. These are Worlds at a very exalted level.

They set into motion their Air particles, through very fast orbits or rotations, and thereby create through this motion, Heat, Electricity and Fire.

Heat comes into being or is composed of nothing other than through the endeavour of the outflows wanting to return to their origin, their Prime Matter, by breaking through the body particles which enclose these outflows which, for a while, are being carried by the stream of Light and can then be felt. This feeling we call Heat.

It is, however, of necessity to provoke this Heat, for the substance to be brought into motion and the proper parts are being fermented. This is accomplished in Nature through the rapidity of the Light, which in turn is the cause of the circulation of the Magnetic and Electric Fluids.

As long as this endeavour of loosening or disengaging the outflows from the bodies occurs only partially, or to a lesser degree, then we only have Heat.

Should this turn into a big stream, by breaking through the body particles, then we have Fire.

This type of outflow takes with it a great deal of body particles, those which have been broken through, and those which became too weak to be retained by the substance of the body, but which were still, to a small degree, retaining parts of these influences until they were totally disposed of.

These body particles are in accordance with the particular body and so is their size. Therefore, if they are of a higher degree, that is how a flame comes into being.

A flame consists of many body particles, which are trying to dispose the outflows.

It is the constant endeavour of this enclosed matter to return to the Prime Matter and to retain these body particles which, according to their gravity, are being pressed towards the centre of the earth.

These are the reasons for the cone-shaped appearance of the flame particles and the burnings. This is the cause of the destructive forces of the fire. It is an easy task for this force to destroy or dissolve the matrix which connects all body particles.

Some light particles then discharge and rush back to the matter. This discharge disturbs the equilibrium of the electric matter and wherever there is friction, electric matter will rush towards it.

The fine outflow of electricity, or beams of Light, is nothing but the fine destruction of the finest of body particles, out of which the light breaks and rushes back to the Prime Matter. When this breaking-through occurs successively, then it is an electric outflow. Should this happen through force and the combined particles are released at once, then we have an electric shock.

The shock which the body experiences is nothing but the enclosed light particles and the already-released light particles, setting all the other particles into motion, which according to their nature, rush back to the matter, but were too weak to break through the body particles they were enclosed in. The inner effort to accomplish this caused the electric shock.

Magnetism is based on similar principles. It differs from electricity only in this respect: the light fluid is enclosed in much finer body particles, which gives this fluid much less resistance. Therefore, it does not break through, but tears it, or drags it with it. Because of its simplicity, it is much less subject to friction.

The magnetic force does not break through the bodies like the electric force, but pulls the bodies with it, therefore, Magnetism attracts.

Every body is loaded with electric and magnetic fluids, only one more than the other.

It is the characteristic of the electricity to carry away the outflows, which are closely packed in the body particles.

The quality of the Magnetism is not to break through. Because of its simplicity, it does not ferment, therefore, it does not break through, instead, it attracts. It pulls the body with it, if the weight with its power is proportionate. Any experiment will show this.

Any body has its own atmosphere. There are bodies where their atmosphere consists of electric particles; there are others, where the atmosphere consists of magnetic particles; and there are again others where their sphere of vapours consists of mixed particles.

In the case of metals such as tin and silver, the electric particles are dominant. In the case of iron, the magnetic particles are dominant.

The spheres of vapours of the bodies can be naturally or artificially increased or decreased; the same as animal perspiration.

Electric vapours increase by friction. Magnetic vapours increase through impact (strike).

The magnetic fluid maintains the equilibrium in the physical world. According to its nature, it is not subject to fermentation. In its purity, it is superior to everything else. It therefore has the quality or the ability to penetrate anything.

The magnetic fluid is the only fluid which has the ability to establish order where there is disorder; to unite those particles which were previously separated or in disorder, and to restore the equilibrium. This is a very important Natural Law.

The direction of the electric flow is from ascent to descent. The direction of the magnetic flow is from midnight to noon.

Bodies consist of Air, Water, Fire and Earth. Water, Fire, Air and Earth are nothing but modifications of the Light.

Light and Earth are Element or Prime Matter. Water, Air and Fire originate out of the dissimilarity of the mixture of Earth and light particles, and the manner and form in which these light particles are enclosed. Concentrated Air is Water.

This can be proven with a simple experiment. Mix saltpeter-air with burnable air, then introduce an electric spark. Before you introduced the spark, everything was air. When the phlogistic particles are burned and released, the air becomes condensed and turns into water.

Air is expansive water. Water is condensed Air. It should also not be overlooked that there is not only one type of Air; there is ordinary Air, right up to ethereal Air.

The expansion the Air has is maintained through the phlogiston. The more the phlogiston simplifies itself and transforms itself into light particles, the purer the Air. The result of simplification is purity.

For example: If you melt an iron wire in phlogistic-free air, this will reveal the following: not only will you see a flame which is pure and similar to daylight, but also the iron wire will melt quickly due to the fastest possible movement. Through this, the light particles of the dephlogistic air and the iron-body brought into motion the confined fire particles. As a result, the intensity grows to such a degree that the wire melts instantaneously.

This is a prerequisite for all bodies. We can see that the characteristic of a body consists of essential proportions of the mixture and primitive (prime) body particles.

76

We can also see that the measure, the proportion, and the manner of its composition are essential, inevitable laws of the body. Without these laws, all bodies would cease to exist. A rose has its necessary, essential proportions and its prime particles. Without them a rose would not be a rose.

Every one of these prime particles have their activity; they are the modifications of the outflow of the Light; they are the origin of all growth and the vegetation.

If the activity of these particles is interfered with, from the outside, the result is disorder, destruction, physical death.

Nature, therefore, establishes the equilibrium between the particles of any body which exists and it overflows all of creation with its fluid-being. This is the cause of the equilibrium in all things. This penetrates into even the smallest of gaps, prevents mixtures and fermentation, and thereby prevents a new chaos.

The purest of fluids, which can be called the Soul of the World, is the magnetic current, the Organ of Godliness for the preservation of the World.

Nature is the manifestation of God. Nature is, therefore, quite a different being, not the God the Materialist believes. Nature is a active brush. Matter can be compared to inert and dead colors. The painter is the fine working force; the artist is the Deity which brought the picture into being, the Creator.

It would be foolish to say that the brush painted the picture without the painter, or the power or energy was by itself, without the man.

The more Human Beings contemplate about Nature, the more they are in awe of God's creations.

23. The Origin Of Ailments.

In the economics of Nature, the Creator made certain that nothing is without purpose and that nothing is unnecessary.

Even the breathing of animals and plants serve a process in Nature, by which animals and plants dispose of all their unnecessary phlogiston, which would otherwise destroy them in a very short time. The Air absorbs the exhaled phlogiston, as it does the electric matter. As a result of this procedure, the phlogiston was and becomes the new source of animal warmth.

Nature impregnates the Air with various types of particles. Artistically, it shapes them into thousandfold forms. Benevolent

Nature pours, through the nursing process of the plants, balsam into the flowers and applies to the surface of the leaves, healing powers.

By paying attention to Nature, Human Beings seek help from the lowly herbs. The uncorrupted instinct taught mankind the true enjoyment and benefit, and obtained strength and convalescence.

In the equilibrium of our circulating liquids originates the health of the body. Plus or minus is the source of all our ailments.

Thousands of ailments came into being when we became careless with our health and left Nature's Path. All ailments are nothing else, but modifications of the plus or minus.

The thousands and thousands of ailments are thousandfold consequences of a very few effects.

Therefore, the remedies lost their value and will continue to do so, because Human Beings are trying to heal the consequences of ailments where they do not know the cause.

At one time, the majority favoured natural physicians, Human Beings who were knowledgeable in Nature's Laws, but mankind soon forgot all of Nature's Laws. They tried to invent their own laws, and stupidity and pride soon filled all professions as well as the healing profession, and our present-day institutions are filled with them. The more pride you possess, the more titles are bestowed upon you.

The healing powers of Nature were placed into bondage by today's man-made remedies, and the ailing person has become the victim of blind prejudice.

The exalted Spirit awoke in the Heart of the thinker. He became aware of the fact that not remedies, but only Nature could heal. He searched for the cause of ailments and he found them in the physical secretions. They either decreased or were suppressed, because of the abuse of all things - in the air we breathe, and in the passions of the Soul.

Remedies do not heal - only Nature heals - and the natural physician makes use of the means and the Art of Nature to support a weakened nature (the nature of Human Beings) when he heals. Therefore, he heals directly through Nature.

The first among all secretions is the invisible secretion, which is subject to many coincidences when it is inhibited and suppressed.

The liquids, which are usually eliminated through perspiration, thicken, the pores and lymphs become clogged. This also thickens the bile in the gallbladder, and since all liquids in the body are connected, they all thicken. The results are as follows: The circulation of the gallbladder is inhibited by the liver, and the intestines then follow by becoming constipated. The stomach starts to compost the food and digestion becomes a problem. The life-giving liquids thicken. The circulation of the blood loses its equilibrium and therefore causes a great disorder in the physical body.

Nature will do its utmost to overcome this evil. The endeavour to accomplish this is called a fever. How misunderstood this simple occurrence is.

The blood vessels swell; the result is expansion and inflammation. Many times the bile is forced into the stomach or indigestible food starts to ferment in the stomach and then decays or putrefies. This decayed food then enters into the intestines and an almost violent bowel evacuation takes place. That is also usually the beginning of inflammatory diseases.

The cause of all ailments lies in the specific proportions of the secretions. Human Beings are healthy as long as they are in an equilibrium.

Nature has guided Human Beings to higher knowledge, and gave them the means to regain this equilibrium.

The plus and the Minus-Electricity is the natural consequence of the breakdown of the physical body.

When you have an attack of fever and you feel cold, that is Minus-Electricity. When you have an attack of fever and you feel hot, that is Plus-Electricity. When a person has a fever and feels cold, all that has to be done is positive-electrify them and they start to feel warm. When a person has a fever and feels hot, all that has to be done is negative-electrify them, and the heat in their body will disappear. The reason for this is that the equilibrium has been regained.

Overeating, overdrinking and too much physical exercise are the causes of many ailments. Some have a thickening effect on the blood and body liquids and others thin them too much. The type of food we eat and what we drink disturbs the equilibrium of our fluids and causes, as a consequence, great disorder and ailments.

The Air we breathe is the source of our health and our ailments. The Air could be compared by diversity with the water. Small rivers, which flow fairly fast, are pure, and have gravel on the bottom, have the healthiest water for drinking purposes. Those waters which come from the mountains and contain sulphur, vitriol or sulfuric acid and copper, cause great damage to our health. Even more unhealthy are those waters which flow slowly, through moss-covered, swampy terrain.

The cause of all so-called contagious diseases lies within the nature of the Air. The susceptibility to infections is more or less in accordance with the nature of that particular Human Being, the condition of his liquids, and the susceptibility of his organization.

The smoke of burning wood is a type of gas which can be compared to any perspiration which rises from any physical body into the air. It carries phlogiston and therefore becomes a conductor for electric matter. Candle smoke is even more harmful. The smoke from lamps which burn rancid oil are even more harmful than candle smoke. The evaporation of coal smoke, decaying vegetation and animals are also harmful.

This leads to the following conclusion: Air which contains the most phlogiston is the most harmful for Human Beings, and air which contains the least phlogiston or dephlogistic air, is the healthiest for Human Beings.

The epidermis of Human Beings is covered with so-called little warts. These absorb the finest matter and carry this to the nerve fluids and into the bloodstream.

If you want to try a little experiment to better understand what has been said and what external effect burnable air has on the human body, all you have to do is this:

Take sulfuric acid, mix it with double the amount of water. Bend an iron rod so that it makes a right angle. Put one end of the iron rod into the liquid and point the other end of the iron rod towards your solar-plexus.

Do not touch your skin with the iron rod. Soon you will experience a soothing, penetrating heat which, in a matter of fifteen minutes, covers the whole body. The diaphragm, which next to the heart is the most refined driving force in the human body, is being set into motion. This causes a very sensitive form of tickling in the abdominal area, especially in the intestinal area.

In this way the iron rod becomes a very special conductor for the inflammable gases. They developed from the sulfuric acid and the iron, and were flowing with noticeable warmth into the skin, since it is considerably lighter than air.

This leads to the conclusion that any matter which is absorbed by our skin through the air, has to be finer in substance than the air.

The effect can be enhanced by wearing woollen clothing, because animal wool, in accordance with its nature, contains more phlogiston and therefore increases the fine outflow. However, when you are dressed in silk, the outflow is without effect, therefore you are insulated.

All particles which enter our body through absorption have to be, by necessity, finer than air.

From experience, we know that all harmful vapours which enter our bloodstream through absorption are phlogistic.

Anything which ferments and putrefies contains a considerable amount of phlogiston and can easily enter, through absorption, the animal or physical body.

The seed of many ailments lies in the absorption and inhaling, by which the infection can enter by means of inhaling air into the lungs, or by inhaling through the nose, and the air enters from there into the brain.

There are many different ways to disturb the equilibrium of the liquids in our body and also the plus or the Minus-Electricity. The plus or the minus phlegma (phlegm) is the origin of the thousand different types of ailments.

Nothing is more capable of correcting this disorder of the equilibrium of the liquids better than electricity and Magnetism. In these two lie the power to heal all physical ailments.

24. Basic Knowledge Of
Magnetism And Electricity.

Electricity is twofold: Air Electricity and Earth Electricity.

At noon, when there is no wind and there are no clouds in the sky, the Air Electricity is positive, whereas, in the morning and in the evening, the Air Electricity is negative.

Water vapour shunts the electricity. Dew and fog are the conductors for the Air Electricity to the earth.

The Air Electricity has a considerable influence on all bodies, especially on all organic bodies.

Organic Beings are the best Electrometer (an electrometer is a tool which measures differences of potential by the effect of electrostatic forces).

A Human Being who stands in the sun will become positive electric. A Human Being who stands in the shade will become negative electric.

When you positive electrify, your pulse or your heartbeat increases by one-sixth and you will breathe more often.

Electrification tightens all fibres and strengthens all solid parts; it dilutes all liquids and disperses the glutinous lymphs.

The purest, dephlogistic air is the best air for the electricity.

Only those bodies which contain Plus-Electricity can affect those which have Minus-Electricity.

Only those bodies which contain Plus-Magnetism can affect those which have Minus-Magnetism.

Bodies which contain the same amount of electricity and Magnetism cannot affect each other.

Should you want to find out what effect positive electricity has on a body which contains minus-electricity, conduct the following experiment:

1. You require clothing made of pure silk, from head to toe, including silk stockings, which have to be worn during the experiment.

2. Before you dress yourself in silk, wash yourself in clean water and fumigate yourself with white frankincense.

3. Stand up straight. Lift both your arms upwards and point your ten fingers towards heaven. In this position, you absorb the most amount of electric matter.

Since you are dressed in silk, you are insulated, therefore, you will be loading yourself with positive-electricity thereby having an effect on anybody who has a minus-electricity.

After you have loaded yourself or charged yourself, you load water with electricity. This water becomes very useful. When you wash yourself or moisten your hands with this water and rub your hands together, you can set small objects into motion, such as needles on a string, with your fingertips without touching them, or even by just staring at them.

This is the first step of Animal Magnetism.

By looking at another Human Being, you can electrify them even at a considerable distance. The effect is considerably stronger when you are in the sun and your subject is in the shade.

This can be improved upon when you are in harmony with your subject. Try this: have your subject touch some coins in your absence, which you have placed on a table. Those which were touched by the subject will, when you look at them, give you a certain feeling in your eyes. This then will tell you which coins were touched.

Once you are capable of producing the same circulation of the electric and magnetic currents in other bodies, you then will be able to do many unbelievable things.

When you are in harmony with another person, the effect you have on the other person is beyond all expectations. You have to be in harmony with yourself, then it is also possible to create the same harmony in another person. You can then feel what he feels and think what he thinks.

25. Experiments With The Electric, Harmonious Condition.

You can arrange the following experiments: Prepare yourself in the manner described, by washing yourself accordingly and dressing yourself in silk. This is an absolute necessity.

You must first establish harmony with the particular person, preferably male and female. This must be agreed upon in advance, then it can be accomplished with one look. By doing this, you electrify her. Then place your hand into her hand and look into each others eyes. Agree between the two of you on a thought or certain words. These words or thoughts should be repeated at this point, in her thoughts, very slowly, again and again. You then will be able to read even her most secretive thoughts.

When you have accomplished this, have the same person write you a letter in a room next to yours. The prerequisite here is that the harmony must first be established. You will then know the content of the letter. Later on, this person can even be in another house, and you will be able to do the same.

Another experiment can be done based on the same principles in the following manner:

When you are in harmony with the other person and this person is touched by a third person, even if you are not in the same room with that person, you will feel where they have been touched. This of course also applies when someone touches you, that the other person will feel it.

All this is based on the following principles:

1. When two bodies are charged with the same amount of electricity, they cannot affect each other. They can only affect each other if one has plus-electricity and the other minus-electricity.

2. Plus- and Minus-Electricity can be created if you have knowledge of this art, firstly through positive electrification, and secondly through negative electrification.

3. Positive and negative bodies stand against each other in complete electric effectiveness, when the proportions of the bodies are also correct.

4. Two bodies which are standing against each other in complete electric effectiveness, with total regard to their electric proportions, then become one body made up of two.

5. When two bodies, which are in complete electric effectiveness, are brought against each other, no change can take place in one unless it also has an effect on the other.

6. Since any change in one body has an effect on the other, the same applies to feelings, because feelings are nothing but a change in circumstances.

Should a Human Being, through frequent practice of these principles, be able to distinguish these electric feelings, this then becomes a very discreet type of language or an interpretation through symbols.

Strings that have the same pitch, have the same tone, or if two people are in harmony and are like-minded, the product is unity.

Since all the parts of the body are in harmony with the whole, that explains the origin of physical feelings.

If a thousand Human Beings were affected by the same electric stroke, they would then be connected by this electric stroke. They would be by comparison, at that moment, one individual, as far as their feelings are concerned, by virtue of the electric stroke.

Through the finer, electric power in a state of the finest of harmony, comes into being an even finer change and also finer feelings.

This is illustrated much more distinctly through the Power of Assimilation, which is part of everything in Nature.

Harmony is the daughter of Assimilation. Assimilation is Similarity. Assimilated Similarity - Oneness - Unity - Harmony - all together they are a Whole.

I and You. What dissimilarity!!!

Two things they proclaim are change and separation, but thank God, Nature possesses a great Secret. You stop being You when You become I. When I feel what You do not feel, as long as You are You. When You become I, then I feel what You feel, and You feel what I feel, because then we are One.

Oh! Secret of being One, how venerable are You!!! Your Laws are the Laws of supreme Blissfulness!!!

Every day God becomes more and more the reason to be worshipped - the more we become acquainted with Nature.

It is however, sad, very sad, that so few understand Nature's Language, and that what is written here cannot be better explained to those who never spent any time contemplating about these matters.

26. Animal Magnetism.

The Fluid Beings or the so-called Animal Magnetism, is nothing else but second degree Light, as it is proportionately in relationship to the physical world, and as has been explained in previous chapters.

It is an infinite, fine substance of a certain elasticity and is capable of penetrating any body.

Since it is the lightest of all of the Fluid Beings or fluid substances, it therefore has the capability of bringing everything into equilibrium and prevents the mixture of all created things, otherwise chaos would be called into being again.

In an equilibrium, chaos cannot exist. Cosmos = "in order"; chaos = "without order". In an equilibrium, all adulteration is impossible.

As a child of the Light, the quality of this fluid is motion, and it is also the cause of the motion or movement in all things.

This fluid reigns in the infinite space of all creation. It has the ability to modify itself, according to the differences of the different bodies which it penetrates and surrounds. Unique by origin or source, infinite in its modifications, it becomes the chain of things.

In this fluid, which is the child of the Light, lies the reason for the motion of all things or of all beings.

Through this fluid, all the nerve fluids in the physical or animal body circulate.

Magnet fluidum minerale, phlogiston and everything else are the result of its existence. Through the Light it receives its motion and flows continuously from the highest etheric regions against the worldly bodies or the physical worlds. Its influence upon the worldly bodies is pure and the manner of its flow is true Magnetism.

When this fluid flows back from the worldly bodies towards the regions of Light, it becomes impure and more physical. Enveloped in this shell of impurity, out of Magnetism becomes electricity, until it disposes all of the accumulated particles; then it returns purified to its source of origin, from where the outflow started.

Electricity is the first modification of the magnetic fluid, or the second modification of the Light. The Soul of the electric being or the electric substance is the magnetic fluid; that which produces the electricity is only the coarser outer shell.

We have evidence of this outflow of magnetic power or magnetic force. This energy can penetrate glass, which the electric fluid is not capable of doing.

The purer the air, the more cleansed of phlogiston it is, the more it can assimilate with the magnetic flow. The more the air is saturated with phlogiston, the more burnable it becomes, the more it assimilates with the electricity.

This Fluid Being or fluid substance is the cause, the reason for the body, and everything compounded, composed, and everything which is put together.

Also, everything which is compounded or put together races back to its own destruction, according to the wheel of time.

Bodies dissolve, destruct, but they are not annihilated; they only change their form.

Growth, development and motion are the result, the consequence of the circulation of this flow in the finest of vessels of the bodies; only the circulation differs in accordance to the condition of the bodies, and their ability and manner of filtration.

When this fluid, in similar bodies is similarly modified, then these bodies are in harmony.

The nerves are conductors of the magnetic current; they receive and modify them.

Even though we cannot assimilate to perfection in the physical world, do not despair. The ability to assimilate is within us - we have the Power of Assimilation.

Like affects alike: Similarity brings uniformity, and being alike brings harmony. When the nerves of two people are tuned in harmony, then their impressions are the same, their feelings are the same. This condition is harmony.

The measure of degree of tension is the source, the cause of musical harmony. This also applies to the animal or the physical world.

There are perfect chordas or chords - harmony and dissonance on the instrument of our nerves.

Human Beings absorb through their pores the magnetic current. This magnetic current circulates from the head towards the outer parts of the body, and follows the structure of the nerves, which are conductors.

A tree receives this current through the roots, the bark and the leaves.

The circulation of the magnetic current from one body to the other body is called Animal Magnetism.

The method which teaches us how to transfer this magnetic current from one body to the other is called magnetizing, and the person who does this is called a Magnetopath.

Magnetizing:

Any Human Being who wishes to magnetize another Human Being has to have the power to produce or increase the magnetic current and the power of circulation to transport the magnetic current without upsetting the equilibrium of the liquids in his own body.

Any healthy Human Being who is capable of saturating himself with this magnetic fluid, has the ability to affect any weaker Human Being.

The method of magnetizing is very well-known to most people who have an interest in the healing arts. Here is a brief description of this method:

The Magnetopath faces the person to be magnetized, provided they are both right-handed or both left-handed.

To establish harmony, the Magnetopath places his hands on the shoulders of the person to be magnetized and then slowly moves his hands down the arms to the fingertips. He then holds onto both thumbs for a few seconds. This should be repeated two or three times. After this, these strokes are repeated, only this time, start from the head and move down to the feet.

By doing this, an experienced Magnetopath can establish the seat of the ailment. If he cannot do this, then the person who has the ailment should be asked.

Usually the seat of the ailment is exactly opposite to where the pain is, especially in the case of rheumatism, paralysis, etc.

Then magnetize the seat of the ailment until the pain becomes critical. You thereby support the endeavour of Nature to do something against the cause of the ailment. Do not stop until you achieve this crisis, because this is the only remedy which will eliminate the cause of the ailment.

27. *I And You.*

Nature harbors so many great things, so many inconceivable things as far as Human Beings are concerned, and yet the solution to all of these puzzles is much closer than we believe them to be.

I and You are very important words. They give us the key, the explanation to many secrets which are hidden.

What does You and I represent? What am I without You? An insulated, monotonous Being. Nature does not create separate Beings. Nature's Law is unification and communion.

All of God's creations exist on the principle that everything is linked together. How unhappy, how ungodly must the link be which separates from this chain.

In Nature, one depends upon another - these relationships are absolutely necessary. These are the laws which preserve and maintain our physical world. If this is not done by one or the other Being, the result is chaos.

However, every Being is given its limits as far as their activities are concerned, but without connecting to another Being, he cannot progress or reach perfection, nor can he increase his activities. Activities increase, knowledge increases, by connecting to a Higher Being. Activities decrease, knowledge decreases when you connect to a lower Human Being. The decrease in activities is not to be confused with being busy, but you will experience that you will be busy with nothing.

As the plants depend on the soil which feeds them, Heaven gently pours the dew into the soil's lap, and the soil in turn gives this heavenly gift freely to the plants and the trees and everything else which requires the soil to live.

Everything is in order as long as this interchange is taking place. The minute this endeavour or activity stops, disorder is the result.

If Heaven would be greedy and withhold its dew, if the Earth would lock up in its centre all the treasures it received from the Air, and there would be no more interchange, no activity, then all Life would cease to exist, resulting in death.

To be charitable to each other is the endeavour of the smallest sand kernel to the stone, from the plants to the animals, from the animals to the Human Beings, from the Human Beings to the Angels.

Step-by-step, degree-by-degree, this endeavour becomes more and more magnanimous and the powers-to-be, more and more magnificent.

The needs, the requirements, were the first teachers Human

Beings had, and from this mankind learned that Human Beings are not separate entities. He therefore joined human society, became part of humanity, and thousands became "One".

The welfare of a State depends upon the harmony of the people who live there. If every citizen would treat another citizen as he treats himself, everything would be in order. When everything is I, then happiness rules, but everything starts to deteriorate when there is a difference between You and I.

The Laws of Nature are the Laws of Love. It is the endeavour of Love to "Become One".

All of God's Laws support this sentence. Love your neighbor as you love yourself. Do not think of him as another person, but as yourself. Think of another person as your second I.

The closer Human Beings come to this law and fulfil this law, the more perfect they become because this assimilates him more with his Deity, since God is perfect Love.

You are immediately standing on a higher level. You can see further into the future. A lighter, more radiant sun enlightens your intellect, and you can see further into the Secrets of Eternity.

Same is linked to same. The influence of Higher Beings bring such a person to perfection more quickly.

The purer, the more genuine Love is, the more perfect a Human Being becomes. The less somebody close to you becomes You, he becomes I, completely.

Human Beings experience a taste of this Blissfulness when they experience true friendship and gentle love. Of course, there is a difference with this holy law when it is cleansed of all impurities and of all passions.

Assimilation or "Becoming One" are words which most of our Philosophers do not comprehend, and yet they lie deeply imbedded in Nature and are without fail. They are the source, the origin of the harmony in our Soul.

There is a certain power, a certain force within Human Beings, which bring this Fluid Being, this fluid substance into motion, and it flows from Human Being to Human Being.

It has an effect from me to you and flows back to you. This condition is the condition of harmony, if the flow is harmonious. In this harmonious condition, You and I become one person. I see and hear through you, then nothing is left to me except my instinct and my moral virtues. That is the only thing your Will has left me with.

When you think, a Fluid Being, a fluid substance, circulates from you to me and has the effect on my brain, as if I would think myself.

When you read, it seems to me as if I would read, because my fibres vibrate and so do my nerves, to those conceptions you find necessary to connect to those words which you read.

When you asked me a question, I see you in the Spirit, that means: I see you in Truth, in reality, not in the flesh; that means not in error, not mistakenly, not in a lie or with prejudice.

My fibres swell through an inner power. The nerves I see with are expanding. It seems that a heavy covering, a heavy shell is being removed from every body I look at. Things which were not visible before are visible now. Even the darkest night has lit up because even the darkest night is only dark in relationship to our organization. All things becomes very clear now in my Soul. My conceptions are true conceptions because now they are themselves; they are the thing itself.

There are two currents in the air. According to their Nature they are both wonderful, yet they are as different as water and oil, which would never mix. One of these currents surpasses crystal in purity and it is light like the sunlight at high noon. The second is pale and its color has a hue of blue.

Even though those two currents resemble each other, their manner of motivation is different.

The pure current seems to originate from the sun and flows magnificently in the Spring and in the Summer. Its effect is most significant and intense one hour before noon and three hours afterwards.

The second current flows back from the Earth and the water vapours are its conductor.

The invisible Vital Energies have their origin from midnight - from an invisible mixture, as the visible Vital Energies have it out of chaos.

Their innermost is moveable. The pure powers always unite and those who quarrel are overcome and therefore purity is preserved in a perpetual cycle, the end being the beginning of a new cycle.

Basic Principles for Magnetopaths.

There is an interacting influence between the heavenly bodies, the Earth and all bodies with a Soul.

The cause of this influence is the Universal Fluid Being or the Universal Fluid Substance, which modifies in different ways. At one time it is electricity and at another it is Magnetism.

The principium of this Being is the Mother of Everything, the only archetype of fluids, or the Universal-Driving-Wheel or World Mechanics.

That is how Magnetopaths explain all the nebulous areas in physics, in accordance with the laws of physics such as: Attraction, Electricity, Ebb and Tide, Fire, Light, etc.

When this fluid flows through the bodies with its equilibrium containing quality, it establishes the harmony which we call health. Any deviation from this equilibrium is an ailment.

There is only one Health, only one Ailment, and one primary source of animal or physical life.

Since the Animal Magnetism, due to its skilful direction, is capable of re-establishing the unstable equilibrium of the fluids, it is therefore the only true remedy.

Not all bodies with a Soul are equally receptive to magnetic forces. There are even some which have opposite characteristics.

Some parts of the human body are more receptive than other parts, to assimilate the Great Agens = The Great Force (in German - DAS WIRKENDE = The Working Force). These are the polarities, the tension and the anatomical distribution of the nerves.

The Human Being is a magnetic body whose poles are not like a magnet which go from one world pole to another, but in a Human Being they originate from the Earth and proceed to the Zenith.

The equator, in terms of the human body is the solar plexus; the stomach, the junction of all influences, is the point where the inflows to the stomach take place, the liver, the mesentery (abdominal wall, small intestines, etc.), the spine is the axis, the feet are the south pole.

When you magnetize with your right hand, you touch the left side of the ailing person, and with your left hand, the right side of the ailing person. This is called magnetizing with the opposite polarity.

This is the Theory of Magnetism, which enjoyed great popularity in the 18th and 19th centuries. The discovery of Magnetism, as is the destiny of all knowledge which rises above the common spheres, had its followers, persecutors, zealots and charlatans.

Some were for and others were against. Pride, envy, stupidity and fraud entered and disposed of Magnetism for the wrong reasons. Sound judgement as to its merits became an impossibility.

One of the main reasons why it does not enjoy its proper place is because it requires a sound mind and a healthy body.

Many authors of old books will confirm what is written here.

28. Soul - Physiognomy.

There are circumstances among Human Beings, where everything wrong is considered right. Evil things are looked upon as good things; the truth is considered false, and falsehood considered the truth.

The countenance of the Spirit of a Human Being is quite different from the countenance of the physical body.

The countenance of the physical has its origin with the parents of that particular Human Being. The countenance of the Spirit has its origin from the passions and inclination, whose image it is.

The human eye can be deceived by the countenance of a beautiful physical body, but the spiritual eye cannot be deceived by the countenance of the Spirit.

The picture the mind has receives its shape, its appearance, in accordance with its inclination.

The closer the Spirit is to pure Love, the more beautiful his countenance becomes, because the attributes of Love's Wisdom are Beauty and Truth.

The condition of every Human Being is twofold: First, to love God; and second, to love your neighbor. These are the Friends of Heaven.

The love which originates evil and falsehood is self-love and worldly love. This is the fountain of evil, the source of Hell.

There are two things, two ingredients, which make up the Life of the Spirit - Love and Belief.

Love makes the Life of the Will. Belief makes the Life of the Intellect.

Blessed are those who live eternally in Love. Blessed are those who do not deface the purest of imprints of divine beauty in their Soul.

29. The Theory Of Wisdom And
The Science Of All Things.

The fondness for Truth and Goodness leads Human Beings to Wisdom. The inclination for falsehood and evil removes Human Beings from their nature.

Fraud, underhandedness, prejudice, pride and stubbornness are attributes of falsehood.

Clearness, enlightenment, tolerance, humility, and compliance towards others are attributes of Truth. Truth belongs to the Spiritual

Life - it is what you should believe. Goodness is what you should do - it belongs to an active Life.

Belief originates in the nature of a Human Being. All knowledge of spiritual things does not originate from Human Beings themselves because Human Beings do not comprehend; they conceive only what enters into their senses. He can only see what affects the sense of sight and what exists in the world he lives in. Whatever is outside of this, his world, he does not see. Since it is the condition of a Human Being to be the next link to the Spirit World, he can perceive things by no other means than through Revelation and Belief.

Love leads to Belief. Belief leads to Wisdom, because this leads to the recognition of the Light and, therefore, reaches the proximity of the Spirit of God, which is the Light.

Those Human Beings are, therefore, in the Light, who stand in Belief and in Love. Those Human Beings who do not stand in Love and Belief, stand in darkness. That also means that those who are in the Light stand in knowledge. Those who are in darkness stand in ignorance.

Human Beings are twofold: The external and the internal Human Being or the Animal Human Being and the Spiritual Human Being.

The more the Spiritual Human Being has dominance over the Animal Human Being, the closer the Human Being is to perfection. The more the Animal Human Being has dominance over the Spiritual Human Being, the more imperfect the Human Being.

Perfection and Imperfection, Good and Evil, are therefore dependent upon the dominance of either the Spiritual Human Being or the Animal Human Being. The Animal Human Being lives in falsehood and in Self-Love - that means in Evil.

The Spiritual Human Being lives in Truth and in Goodness; that is Love for God and Love for your fellowman. Love thy neighbor.

The relationship of the Spiritual Human Being towards God is approximation. The relationship the Animal Human Being has towards God is remote; it is distance. Approximation is the path to blissfulness. Remoteness is the path to destruction.

Blissfulness is the progression to higher perfection, to becoming alike, to be in the proximity of God, approximate to your Deity.

Destruction is the remoteness from the path of perfection, retrogression to the darkness.

The more a Human Being assimilates with his Deity, the more he reaches perfection. He comes closer to Truth and Love and, therefore, closer to Wisdom. The recognition of Truth is the Theory of Wisdom, and Love is the practice.

One has the Will, the other the Intelligence for the transformation of the object.

The closer Human Beings come to Truth and Love, the more they surpass other Human Beings which are below them in the chain of perfection, in knowledge. Those Human Beings are closer to the sun, therefore they are more illuminated by the sun. They stand on a higher level of progression, therefore they can see further and can see things others cannot.

Active Love or the energy required to practice depends upon the degree of knowledge. The actions of Human Beings is practice. As a result of this, the action of such Human Beings which are closer to perfection, must surpass those which have not reached their level of development. They are a reflection of the splendour of their Deity.

The path to Wisdom has its existence in respect to God, and the examination of the Sage is founded in the examination of his Belief and his Love.

Wisdom contains the Spirit of the Intellect, which is holy, united, manifold, subtle, well-spoken, agile, immaculate, sweet, loves goodness, is quick of mind, good of heart, friendly, kind, constant, certain, who has all the capabilities, understands everything, also comprehends all the Spirits, and is pure. Wisdom is the vapour of the power of God, a pure outflow of the clearness of the Almighty God. Therefore, nothing which is impure can reach Wisdom. Wisdom is the brilliance of the Eternal Light, the immaculate mirror of God's majesty, an effigy of His Goodness. Wisdom has all capabilities because she is united in harmony, she is one, renews all things and among the nations, enters into the Souls of the holy and makes friends for God and Prophets.

She is the Mother of all things and our infinite treasure for Human Beings. Those who seek, shall find her. She cultivates virtues - she teaches moderation, discretion, caution, justice and strength. These are the virtues which are most useful to Human Beings in their life. She knows and can assess everything which is past and future. She understands cunning conversation and finds solutions for the most difficult problems. She recognizes miracles and symbols before they happen, and what will happen in the future.

God bestows through Wisdom, benevolence, not to speak ill of others and to be deserving of His gifts, which He has given to Human Beings; because He is the Path to Wisdom and it is He who reforms the "Sage".

God gave the Sage the true knowledge of the created things so that he knows the nature of the circumference of the Earth, what power the elements have; also the beginning, the end and the middle of time, inclusive of the diversity and the changes of time, the cycle of time, the order of the stars, the nature of the animals, the anger of the beasts, the force of the wind, the thoughts of Human Beings, the difference of the plants, and the power of the roots. Yes, everything which is hidden and unknown teaches He, the Master of all things - the Wisdom of the Lord.

30. The Art Of Restoring Youth.

Should the movement in any part of the body stop, then that particular part dies off or becomes necrotic, and is then unable to do the work it was intended to do.

When the whole body is affected and the movement stops in the whole body, then there is sometimes no possibility of restoring the movement. This then is called the physical death.

Our physical life depends upon the success of the moving fluids and all the vessels which belong to it.

The forces which move these liquids are of considerable strength, so much so, that they would eventually totally destroy these vessels, if what is removed through this friction were not replaced.

The life of an animal is the tool itself, through which it is lead closer to death.

To assure that the animal does not die before its time, Nature replaces through nourishment whatever is lost.

The chyle (chilus) or the nutritive, milky fluid is what renews the substance of our liquids. This renewal takes place through the conversion of the vessels in the physical or animal body, which turn the food particles into animal or physical substances through body heat.

In order to accomplish this chemical work of the vessels, an uninhibited flow of the liquids is required; a proportional movement of the same with its solid particles; a certain inflection and elasticity in the vessels, and this equilibrium of the liquids and the relationship to the parts of the physical body result in the Health of a Human Being!

Should this relationship cease to exist, then the result is an ailment. If it is totally destroyed in the physical body, then the result is physical death.

From experience we know that air which does not contain anything burnable, the physical body will exist seven times longer than it would in ordinary air.

This leads to the following conclusion: air is purer if it has less burnable substances, and is therefore better suited for physical respiration.

Therefore, the main cause of the aging or the wearing-down of the vessels and the destruction of the equilibrium of our fluids or liquids, lies within the fuel which is in the air we breathe, because the physical body lives longer in air which lacks fuel or burnable substances, therefore the air we breathe is one of the first causes of our ailments, our aging and our untimely death.

We know from anatomy that age ossifies the vessels and that the limbs become lime-like, therefore, this ossification is the effect of the burnable substances. All hot liquids which contain a lot of burnable substances cause arteriosclerosis or calcination.

The only remedy which prevents this from happening and keeps the flow of the fluids or liquids in an equilibrium, and resists the phlogiston's destruction and prevents the ossification of the vessels, is air which does not contain any burnable substances.

It is therefore a remedy in Nature which prolongs life; a remedy which restores youth.

Anything which resists the ossification of the vessels, resists aging. Anything which dissolves ossification, restores youth.

The blood of young people is light red; the blood of old people and animals is dark red. In air which has no burnable substances, the blood becomes light red; in air which contains phlogiston, the blood becomes dark red. Therefore old blood contains phlogiston.

If you want to turn old into young, you have to have young blood, therefore, change dark red blood into light red blood. This is done by eating the right food, drinking the proper liquids, breathing pure air, putting your passions to rest, protection against phlogiston from entering your body, daily elimination of burnable substances which accumulate in the water and negative-electrify in the invented manner, and yet another remedy, which God kept hidden. In this lies the power of the Sages, which also brought back the youth to Jason's father.

Even if Human Beings are not allowed to be at the fruit of the Tree of Life, they are allowed by God to drink the juice of the leaves. A branch of this tree is so close to us, but only a few Human Beings recognize it.

31. *The Divining Rod.*

There is written evidence about the invention of the Divining Rod centuries ago. Since that time, in order to discover Gold and Silver mines, those who were knowledgeable (prospectors) as to the different minerals and metals that were contained in the element of Earth made use of the Hazel Divining Rod. The Divining Rod was also used to find water wells; besides that, it is not known if it was used for anything else.

However, there is reliable evidence that a farmer from Delphinat in 1692 made use of the Divining Rod to locate fugitives and murderers. Further on in this chapter, you will find in detail a report of what occurred. Although this story may seem extraordinary and puzzling, its validity should not be rejected. I will not allow myself to enter into any further demonstrations and learned quarrels, or get involved with Human Beings who do not have any insight as to the Law of Cause and Effect and who, on account of being in authority, reserve the right to belittle everything and call what they do not understand a fable.

However, may it be said that I admit that many such stories are subject to some doubt until the facts are scrutinized. But, it is just as reprehensible to reject everything due to one's own haughtiness, self-will and ignorance, and it is just as foolish to believe everything because of simple-mindedness.

The point in time that the Divining Rod was first used cannot be determined. Before the 15th century, no author can be found who mentioned the Divining Rod, except in the writings of Basilii Valentini, a Benedictine Monk. In the year 1490, he wrote: "It is true that not everybody has been given the gift whereby the Divining Rod will indicate the location of water, metal, stolen property, or where a culprit can be found. It happens also quite often that this gift loses its power. There is no less truth in the statement that the effectiveness of the Divining Rod should be accredited to the person who is carrying it, and not to the Divining Rod itself. Otherwise, if the Divining Rod would be suspended in an angle-iron, or if it would be suspended like a compass over water or metal, it should strike out, but it does not do that. Therefore, the reaction does not merely come from the inherent power of the Divining Rod itself!"

The Divining Rod never deceives because it reacts to water as well as to dead bodies and hollow crevices in the earth's crust, and to everything that has evaporation or perspiration, and to whatever has an odour.

Now, let the story be told about the farmer who, by making use of the Divining Rod, followed a murderer for more than 45 miles on land, and 30 miles over water.

In Lyon, France, at 10 o'clock in the evening on the 5th of July, 1692, a wine merchant and his wife were beaten to death in the vault of their basement, for money which was kept in a dresser in a room which also served as a bedroom. This was done with such expertise and without any commotion that, for quite a while, no one was aware of the fact that they had been murdered. That is why the murderers had the opportunity of escaping without being noticed. A neighbour of the wine merchant, who was deeply hurt by this deed, remembered a very well-to-do farmer by the name of Jakob Aymar, who was in possession of the Art of finding robbers and murderers. The farmer was asked to come to Lyon, and there he was introduced to the Crown Prosecutor. The farmer promised the Royal Prosecutor that he could find the guilty on foot, wherever they may be, provided that he would be shown the location of the murder, in order to get a proper impression.

He admitted that he would require a Divining Rod for this purpose. The type of wood used for the Divining Rod was of no consequence, nor was it important what time the wood was cut, nor were any rituals require. The judges sent him into the vault where the deed was committed. Here, they witnessed a most peculiar phenomenon. The farmer was totally beside himself; his pulse began to beat like someone who has a severe high fever. The Divining Rod he was holding began to strike out with such might in the two places where the Soul-less bodies of the wine merchant and his wife were found. No sooner had the farmer familiarized himself with the impressions, that he then followed his Divining Rod through all the narrow streets, through which the murderers had taken flight. He walked into the courtyard of the Archbishop; he also approached the Gate of the River Rhone, which was locked at that time, because it was night.

The next morning, following his Divining Rod, he crossed the bridge leading over the River Rhone, which guided him to the right along the length up the river. The three people who accompanied him attested to the fact that he, at times, was aware of the trail of three accomplices, and at times, that he was only aware of two. During this uncertainty, his Divining Rod lead him to the house of a gardener, where he was assured that there were three men. Here, he maintained that the three sat around the table, and that one bottle of the three bottles which were in the room was touched by them, because the Divining Rod indicated that. It took, however, quite a while until the two children who were there, ages 9 and 10 years respectively, admitted that this was true. Because they were afraid that they would be punished by their parents, since they left the front door open against their parents' warnings, and these three men had sneaked into their house and drank wine out of the bottle which the farmer had indicated.

The childrens' statement was confirmed by footprints which were found farther down the banks of the River Rhone. This lead to the conclusion that the culprits had continued their flight on water. The farmer, therefore, also continued on water as well, and his Divining Rod functioned as well on water as it did on land. With a boat, he followed their trail, but it lead him under an arch of a bridge where, otherwise, no one would steer his boat. That lead to the conclusion that the fugitives were on their own and did not hire someone with a boat, because this was not the normal path a boat would take.

The farmer made a stop at every place where the murderers had stopped; that is how he trailed them everywhere they went and, thusly, found out where they had stayed overnight, and he knew, to the surprise of the Innkeepers and bystanders, the beds they slept in, the tables the had their supper, and the mugs and glasses they had touched.

Finally, he came upon a camp of soldiers near Sablon, where he felt very strong emotions which he interpreted that the murderers must be among the soldiers. However, he was not allowed to use his Divining Rod in the camp, otherwise, he could have suffered great harm at the hands of the soldiers, because of the belief in those days regarding Divining Rods. That is why he returned to Lyon. He was then sent back to Sablon with a letter of recommendation. When he returned, the murderers were no longer there. He continued on their trail until he reached à la foire de Beaucaire in Languedok. While on this route, he pointed out again every bed the fugitives had slept in, the tables and chairs they had sat on, etc.

While he walked through the narrow streets of Beaucaire, his Divining Rod lead him to the gates of the local prison, where he maintained without reservation, that one of the three fugitives was imprisoned there. He was shown fourteen to fifteen prisoners; he passed by them one-by-one with his Divining Rod, but the Divining Rod only struck out at one of the prisoners by the name of Bossû. This man had been taken into custody just one hour before because of a small theft. The farmer said that he was certain that this man was one of the three murderers. He then continued with his search for the other two; this took him onto a small footpath which lead to Nismes.

At this time, the farmer was asked to travel no further. The authorities were satisfied with the capture of Bossû, whereupon they transferred him to Lyon. However, Bossû maintained and swore that he did not know anything about the murders, and that he had never been in Lyon before. Meanwhile, the same route was taken back to Lyon, which the murderers had travelled on their flight. In Bagnols, en route to Lyon, Bossû was recognized by one of the Innkeepers. Bossû admitted he had been there, as he was travelling down the River Rhone with two other men from the Provence. He also said that he was forced to do whatever they asked of him, and that he received no more than 6½ thalers from the robbery, but that he himself was not present at the time the murders were committed.

It should be mentioned that something very peculiar happened to the farmer surrounding these circumstances. On the entire way back to Lyon, he could not walk behind Bossû; he had to walk in front of him, otherwise, he was constantly plagued with nausea and palpitations of the heart. This was also the reason why the farmer could not remain in the place where the murders were committed without experiencing severe heart palpitations and feverish trembling. It was not as severe, however, as it was when he was following them on the water.

As soon as this case came before the court in Lyon, a thousand different opinions were voiced - for and against. The opinions were according to the concepts which the people had of them; they were so slanted, so one-sided and so erroneous as it happens all the time when it comes to such extraordinary circumstances. Even after so much evidence, the farmer was not believed, and that is why he was tested anew.

The farmer was lead again, in the presence of several people, to the basement where the murders were committed. And, because they were so suspicious of the farmer, suspecting him of being a cunning cheat and that he might move the Divining Rod arbitrarily, they bandaged his eyes. In spite of all these precautions and interventions, the result was the same as before.

32. Opinion On The Divining Rod
Or Rhabdomancy.

When the Divining Rod and its extraordinary uses became known, everybody immediately wanted to know the cause, the reason why you could do things with a Divining Rod, you could not otherwise do. As a result of this, the opinion as to the cause and the effect differed. Some were of the opinion that the effect of the Divining Rod was to be found in its magnetic force. Others were of the opinion that it was due to sympathy and antipathy. Those who were believers in Aristotle's theories found in this another reason for their beliefs.

Nature has only one mechanism for all its effects; only one manner to bring about the miracles of its inexhaustible resources. Nature always chooses the simplest path, the easiest and the most minimal means. Nothing is done without intention, nothing is done in vain. Everything has its cause and its ultimate object.

If Human Beings never lost sight of this principle when they examine Nature, then mankind would not remove itself so far from the truth and would not fall victim to so many errors, which cause so much shame to the human Spirit and to the human heart.

There is no effect without a cause. For the same reason, nothing can affect an object unless it comes in touch with it. However, the manner in which it is touched makes the difference. In this lies the incomprehensible, the indissoluble of so many of Nature's Wonders.

Many times our mind is too lazy to observe and examine. Our senses are too slow and too dull to distinguish the degree of fineness, the speed, and the thousandfold manner in which the bodies touch each other and what effect they have.

Then human pride laughs at what it cannot understand, and stupidity and prejudice, which are part of the same characteristic, call this the Devil's work.

Vanity is another one of the most prolific, evil human emotions which make you weak instead of strong, cringe to prejudice when bravery is met, and sows the seed of injustice which has the flower of intolerance and the ripe fruit of inequity.

The prejudice many Human Beings have, that Nature would do things differently in secrecy than it would do openly, has lead many down the wrong path.

Nature always works in the same manner, and the miraculous things and effects Nature has on Human Beings are caused by the methods, the tools and means Nature employs, which are not accepted and perceived by the senses of most Human Beings as they are accepted when Human Beings deal with ordinary things, where you can see with one look, cause, effect and consequence.

You would not view it as a miracle if you see wood catch fire and burn, since here Nature does not work in secrecy, and the whole

101

procedure from beginning to end is within the capability of our senses' understanding.

If, however, chemical factories or coal mines emit warm, dry fumes, and burn and dry out the plants and trees which surround them, we think this is miraculous, because our senses cannot grasp or perceive the fine, pungent fumes. The mechanism is, of course, the same in both examples.

These basic principles deserve a great deal of contemplation which would reveal many of Nature's Secrets. You will find the explanation here as to the reason why, and how the Divining Rod functions.

The manner in which or by which certain bodies touch is through the means of vapours which ascend from these bodies, and also the atmosphere of vapours which surround every body. Within this lies the secret of the Divining Rod.

These ascending vapours are a part of the entity from which they originate, as it is with Vitriol, which separates from the sympathetic powder and disperses in the air.

Many times there is a third entity which directs its energy from the active parts to the suffering parts.

Sometimes it is the air, which is close to the active body, and serves also as a guide, to get the effect to the suffering parts. For example, the sound of a bell reaches the tympanum of the ear.

If you, however, accept the principle of the vapours of the bodies, all the puzzles of sympathy and antipathy are explained, which are usually explained as a miracle of Nature. Whatever was understood was explained through the principle of sympathy and antipathy. Whatever was not understood was also given the names of sympathy and antipathy because these were the only means available, and gave something they did not understand a name.

Solely through the theory of the vapours you come considerably closer to the cause. How can you explain when you see a person and immediately you feel drawn towards that person; your heart makes a few extra beats - what is that immediate attraction? You would call it sympathy but what is the reason for this feeling? Here sympathy keeps its silence.

However, if you accept the fact that everybody is surrounded by vapours, an outflow of the finest body particles, which at the same time make a pleasant impression through their homogeneity on the object, then the cause of the effect is obvious.

In the case of antipathy, they are adverse impressions which are caused by heterogeneous vapours. This principle, when understood, will give you the possibility of making things which hate each other, like each other and to unite them. This is possible if you are able to change the vapours which surround them. These vapours, which ascend into the air, even though they are not visible to our physical eye, will keep the nature of the body from where they originate, because they possess the ability to re-unite at a moment's notice.

We can observe this in humid weather, when the watery particles which have ascended into the air accumulate on marble or on a window or on a wall, due to the coldness of the objects, or they descend as dew or rain and become water again.

The same can be said about quicksilver. In its many transformations, it will separate from any mixture. This can be accomplished with a very moderate fire. It separates from the finest of pores and returns to its original form.

The air is a fluid body which absorbs the vapours that float around in it, and since the liquidity of the air is much thinner than that of water and other fluid entities, it is then also easily understood that the vapours of the bodies are kept as long as the air can move, feel and carry them.

The vapours among themselves are of a different nature than the bodies from which they originate. I also assume that they differ in their colors.

We know that with spiritu nitri rectificati, even when cooled off, some vapours will rise and their color is red, when you shake the glass which contains the liquid.

These vapours have the same effects as the substance of the body itself from where they separated. Many times they can accomplish the same as the body itself, provided they are present and used for that purpose.

If we are dealing with toxic substances, the vapours of the toxic solid substance or body can be just as toxic as the solid substance.

In the old days, when Apothecaries made their own remedies, there were many incidence where the person who was distilling the narcotic substances such as opium, fell asleep from the vapours which entered into the human body through breathing.

The apple of Mandragora, kept in a room, will cause sleepiness. The breath of a person who is rabid can affect a sensitive person. When painters were using ochre oil, and it was kept for a long time in an unopened container, when this container was opened and the fumes inhaled, the result was severe dizziness. You could lose consciousness, the face could swell and it could cause death if nothing would be done.

Having mentioned many different examples, you can draw the conclusion that water-springs, ore mines, hidden treasure, the traces of people also have vapours, which affect the Divining Rod.

The feelings, the strongest of our senses, must often replace the weakness of our mind, and we feel through it the presence of body particles which escape our eye.

This explains how, when the weather changes, some animals can give you the indication. Some Human Beings also have this ability, especially those who have had an injury on a part of their body.

The branches of trees which are close to water incline towards the water. The cause is certainly because the watery vapours are drawn in and therefore they become heavier and the ascending vapours from the water put the branches in line with the water below. They grow parallel to the water as a result of this.

As the vapours have an affect on the plants and trees, they can certainly influence a Divining Rod.

The Divining Rod is attracted by the vapours toward the earth. The effect is very similar to the magnetic needle of the compass.

The Divining Rod reacts in accordance with the ascending vapours. If these vapours rise in a vertical manner, then in accordance with the magnet, the Divining Rod reacts in a perpendicular manner, to be in line with the vapours, which are parallel.

These lines of vapours are like chains which pull down the Divining Rod.

Every body, every treasure, metals, water springs, have and emit vapours which are the cause to which the Divining Rod reacts.

Many things have been written about the Divining Rod; many things for the Divining Rod and many things against. Many good people have been taken by con-artists and charlatans and this has brought the Divining Rod into disrepute.

There are books available on this subject which will describe the different techniques which go beyond the scope of this book.

This is the description of just one Divining Rod: A Divining Rod made from the pith of the Elderberry Bush. Out of the pith, form a little ball. Take several containers for this experiment and put into one or two a piece of metal. Place the containers in the sun so that they heat up a little, then use the little ball and move it over the container. It will point out which of the containers contains the metal. The cause is natural; it is the effect electricity has on the pith.

Nothing exists where there is no truth and no falsehood, therefore, a prudent Human Being dismisses nothing but examines everything.

33. The Language Of Animals.

Language is the expression of our feelings. Animals feel and express themselves, therefore, animals do speak.

The perfection of our language is measured in accordance with how effectively we can express our feelings according to the characteristic to which our Soul defines our feelings. Only the language has made Human Beings human, by containing the immense flow of its emotion and through words it preserves reasonable monuments.

Since Human Beings are the most perfect Beings in the Earth Organization, their language is therefore, according to their essence the most perfect.

The language of animals is imperfect, according to its needs and intended purpose. It is however a language.

Animals express their feelings through sound. They modulate those sounds in accordance with their passions and feelings. When they experience joy, the modulation of their voice is different than when they experience pain; different again when they express or feel love. Therefore, the sound of their voice differs with every feeling. Those who observe this will understand.

Honour, arrogance, pride, splendour - those qualities would never be the subject of their conversation. They only express desires which are simple and not complex.

A dog will not complain because his dog house does not have central heating or is not painted in a certain color. He will not ask to have his food on golden dishes and he will not ask that you, his master, make him the leader of all the dogs.

All he requires from you is his nourishment. Should you be upset with him, he will try to appease you. If you leave him alone he is sad; when you come back he is happy. He protects you from your enemies; he pursues the game or the deer and informs you where it is.

Those are the limits of his language as far as Human Beings are concerned.

Among animals, not all have an articulate language. Many animals can only express themselves through movement.

Even a dog resorts to mimicry to improve the expression of his feelings, to make himself more easily understood in his relationship with Human Beings. He expresses through this his joy, his grief, his worries, his alertness.

The most talkative of all animals are birds. The theory to understand them is as follows:

Animals do not have their own words; they do not have a

specific word for every object, with a certain specific modulation.

Their expressions usually consist of more than one sound. That means, what Human Beings usually express in a sentence, in the case of an animal, is mostly the same as one word.

The language of animals is the expression of their true feelings, therefore, it is very simply according to their needs, which are few.

The language of animals only contains the truth because it is the expression of their true feelings, therefore, it does not contain any falsehood. For example: one bird would not say to another bird, I am in love, if he is not in love, or I am happy when he is not happy.

The language of an animal repeats itself for the duration of the feeling.

This can be observed when a dog is hurt. He will express his feelings as long as the pain lasts.

The language of animals consists of continuous repetitions. The Human Being who wants to understand the language of animals, has to study the modulation of the sounds the animals make through their emotions, and he will understand the language of animals.

For instance, when a dog barks, he will continue to repeat the sound and he is saying: someone is coming - he is still in the vicinity - be careful - and he will continue to do so until his feelings and his concerns have been put at ease.

Birds react in a similar fashion. Observe them and you will notice that one and two syllable sounds are the expressions of caution, attentiveness or concern. Dogs, who are concerned about their young; cats, birds, chickens, and especially ducks, when the young ducklings are in the water, the mother duck usually expresses her concern with two syllable sounds. Birds which notice a predatory bird in the vicinity, express themselves in a similar fashion.

Sounds which follow quickly, one after the other, harmonious sounds, are expressions of contentment, of pleasure, like the lark in the morning.

Fast, indistinguishable sounds, are good messages, for instance: if a sparrow finds something to eat, he informs others and they again others.

There is a story about Appollonius of Tyana. One day when standing in front of his palace, he observed a sparrow. When asked what he had observed, he answered: a sack of grain had fallen onto the street in the neighbourhood, and this sparrow was giving the news to all the other sparrows in the vicinity. The people checked out the story, found it was true, and they were surprised.

Sounds of love differ distinctly from the sounds of joy, in the case of birds. Sounds of love are more gentle, more harmonious. Listen to the birds when they breed in the Spring. Sounds of anger are sharp, penetrating and rapid. They are not harmonious or of long duration and reveal jealousy. Sounds of sadness and melancholy are of one syllable and wailing.

Those of you who remember these sentences and practice them in Nature will understand the language of animals.

34. The Effectiveness Of Herbs
On The Different Ailments
And Their Relationship To The Planets.

1. Under the Planet Saturn

Cocles (Agrostemma githago): It has the effect of making hair grow.

Hart's Tongue (Scolopendrium Vulgare; Asplenium scolopendrium - Lingua Cervina): An excellent remedy for ailments of the spleen.

Male Fern (Dryopteris Felix - mas): An excellent remedy against haemorrhage.

Philopthetella: For a four-day fever.

Polypody (Polypodium vulgare): A remedy against consumption - emaciation.

Savine (Sabina cacumina): An emmenagogue.

Saxifrage: A haemostatic remedy (stops bleeding).

Shepherd's Purse (Capsella bursa pastoris): A remedy for diarrhoea and steeped in vinegar for exsanguination (bleeding to death).

2. Under the Planet Jupiter.

Balsam-apple (Balsamina): Serves the healing of internal and external wounds.

Barberry and Red Currant Berries (Berberis vulgaris and ribes): A specific remedy for ailments of the chest. Cools a hot liver and decreases the heat of the stomach.

Betony (Stachys Betonica): Used for constipation and blood-cleansing.

Centaury (Centaurium erythraea): Used against clogging of the gallbladder and marasmus or emaciation.

Linseed (Linum usitatissimum): A remedy to soften hardened ulcers or tumours, against consumption.

Mullein (Verbascum thaspus): This herb is used for the healing of wounds. It consolidates, but is mainly used against vomiting blood. When it comes to women, it is steeped in wine, and it will stop profuse menstrual bleeding. When you pick this herb at the full Moon in the month of August when the Sun is in the sign of Virgo, it is a remedy against all blood-flows. The herb has only to be held in the hand.

Waterpepper (Persicaria): Used against rheumatism. Heals all wounds, even gangrene.

Woody Nightshade (Solanum Dulcamara): Used against the four-day fever and similar fevers, emaciation and marasmus, and it cleanses the blood through perspiration.

3. Under the Planet Mars.

Leafy Spurge (Euphorbia esula - petite esule): Consumes and softens calluses or corns. The spirit of this herb heals hydropsy.

Nettle (Urtica dioica): The leaves soften and dry swellings and relieve Human Beings from it. They dissolve the tartarus which is the cause of arthritis and rheumatism. Nettle seeds mixed with boiled and foaming honey is a good remedy against tightness of the chest and pleurisy.

Rest Harrow (Ononis): Relieves the liver, heals anorexia, eliminates kidney stones and is helpful against pleurisy.

Thistle (Carduus): The root with the seeds of any type of thistle is a remedy against pleurisy and all stabbing pains. It also serves against emaciation.

4. Under the Planet of the Sun.

Ash Tree (Fraxinus exelsior): Used to strengthen the heart. The sugar thereof heals wounds caused by poisonous animals.

Balm (Melissa Officinalis): Heals putrefaction of the liver and lungs. The spirit and decoction strengthens older people and maintains the liveliness of youth.

Elecampane Root (Inula Helenium): The oil clears the eyes. When wine is added to the oil, it strengthens and maintains the eyesight. When this wine is taken in the morning and in the evening, it is a good remedy against tightening of the chest.

Laurel Tree (Laurus): Resists poison and heals all poisonous bites. The leaves improve polluted water.

Lemons: Strengthen the heart, stimulate and increase life-spirits. When the seeds are taken in wine, it relieves fever or pestilence.

Marigold (Calendula Officinalis): Strengthens the eyes and takes away inflammation if the eyes are washed with the decoction.

Rosmarin (Rosmarinus Officinalis): Increases the life-spirits; strengthens the heart and brain, and drives cold moisture and fluxes from the body. Also serves epilepsy and strokes.

Saffron (Crocus sativus): Its oil and color strengthen the life-spirit, and eliminates melancholy. A decoction thereof relieves stress.

St. Johnswort (Hypericum perforatum): This herb cleans wounds in an excellent manner and consolidates them, including internal wounds. When distilled, it closes broken blood vessels. It is a sudoforic and eliminates all types of worms.

The Vine Stock - Grape Vine (Vitis): The grapes produce energy and increase the life-spirits. The broth thereof extracted without fire or heat is a good strengthening remedy or restorative for all ailments caused through weakness.

5. Under the Planet Venus.

Lilies (Liliaceae): The water distilled therefrom serves women during labour by easing pain. The oil heals swollen breasts, improves facial skin and eliminates freckles.

Lily of the Valley (Lilia vallis): Lily of the Valley is a good remedy for strengthening the brain of those who are moon-struck. Serves those who have epilepsy. Can also be used by pregnant women.

Nenuphar (A certain Water Lily): Heals dizziness and cramps.

Rose: The salt of the rose wood serves in the obstruction of the uterus and is strengthening.

All fragrant herbs belong under the Planet Venus.

6. Under the Planet Mercury.

Beans (Faba): Beans are very unhealthy, but when roasted, ground like coffee and cooked in water, and taken three times daily, they are a good remedy against gravel and sand. They also dissolve stones very rapidly.

Chamomile (Matricaria Chamomilla): This herb should be picked when the Moon is in Mars with Mercury. It heals colic, opens the exits of the lungs to eliminate waste, and serves when it comes to inner clogging of the other parts of the human body.

Clover (Lotus Hortensis - Sweet Trifoil): The fragrant clover strengthens and heals epilepsy and urinary urgency. The spirit has to be extracted.

Cubebs (Piper cubeba): Strengthens memory and reason.

Dragon Root (Draccontium - Serpentaria): Used for shortness of breath.

Elder (Sambucus): The decoction mixed with the flowers serves haemorrhoids.

Hazel Tree: The spirit taken from the tree, when the Moon is in conjunction with Mercury, serves against eye pain and strengthens the eye sight.

Juniper (Junipers communis): The spirit of the wood, the leaves and the fruit heal hydropsy, colic and shortness of breath.

Marjoram: Good against lethargy and strokes when the distilled oil thereof is taken. Taken internally or externally, it is good for ailments of the nerves.

Nictimeron: Heals all internal inflammation, high fevers and erysipelas. It should be picked when the Moon is in Mars with Mercury.

Pearls (Margaritae): Used to purge the gallbladder. They dissolve stones with the salt of their tartarus when taken with water. They heal blisters of the tongue and mouth and swellings of the throat.

All herbs which have been mentioned, wherein the method of how to use them is especially mentioned, have to be prepared as a decoction.

7. Under the Moon.

Cabbage Green: The water of cabbage cleanses the gallbladder and all moisture in the body which is burned.

Garlic, Leeks and Onions: Mixed together and the spirit extracted, they fertilize the brain and bring it back to normal.

Linden or Lime Tree (Tilia): Water should be distilled from the Linden Flowers when the Moon is in the sign of Gemini. It promotes the menstrual cycle of women, heals epilepsy and ailments of the abdomen.

Mandrake (Mandagora): Works against melancholy and erysipelas.

Melons and Cucumbers: The distilled water thereof heals severe fevers and inflammation of the stomach.

Mushrooms (Champignon): When used as nourishment, mushrooms will cause a pale complexion and robs you of your natural color. They produce a water moisture and are dangerous for those who are inclined to hydropsy.

Paeony (Paeonia Officinalis): Picked when the Moon is in conjunction with the sign of Cancer, it promotes the menstrual cycle of women. The seeds have the same effect and also heal epilepsy.

Poppy (Papaver double): The double poppy is very good for the brain, if it is first cleansed with the oil of Juniper.

Poppy (Papaver simple): The simple poppy which grows wild without having been planted by Human Beings serves against heat of the liver and blood. It is very good against high fevers and erysipelas, where the origin is the inflammation of the blood.

I am adding the following to the already-mentioned herbs which were successful in my experience.

Acacia: The leaves cooked like a tea have the effect of being a blood cleanser and also used against constipation of the bowels.

Agrimony (Agrimonia Eupatoria): Agrimony belongs to the Rosaceae family. It has spiral-shaped calyces, coarsely-haired stems and pinnate leaves. The plant grows along roadsides and near houses, and blooms almost the whole summer. The leaves prepared as a tea stimulate the digestive organs and eliminates chest, liver and kidney ailments.

Aloe: One-half of an Aloe leaf cooked together with one teaspoon Juniper berries and one teaspoon fennel serves for blockages of the abdominal area, blood flushes to the head, heals white vaginal discharge and promotes the menstrual cycle.

Angelica Root (Angelica Archangelica): Angelica is an umbellate plant which almost reaches the height of a man. The root is ringed, ramose, and has many thick fibres; on the outside light brown, inside white. Cooked Angelica Root is an excellent remedy for diarrhoea,

112

chronic eczema, bowel cramps, bloating, nervous weakness, leucorrhea, chronic rheumatism and intermittent fever.

Apple: If you eat a raw apple, it is blood-cleansing. Tea made from the peel is excellent for inflammations and fever, and for sleeping. An apple eaten with sweet almonds strengthens the mind and the nerves. The last remedy is especially recommended for those who do a lot of mental work.

Balm or Lemon Balm (Melissa officinalis): Balm belongs to the family of Labiate. It grows in gardens, has ovate-toothed leaves, and a fragrant lemon aroma. Flowers and leaves taken as a tea are effective against bloating, hysteria and cramps, and used externally as a compress for the purpose of dispersion.

Barley (Hordeum distichon): Barley is mostly cooked and prepared like porridge and is used as Barley Water for diarrhoea, dysentery, severe coughs and many, many ailments. Poultices and enemas made with barley are also very effective.

Birch Leaves (Betula Alba): The leaves of the birch tree are effective as a diuretic and are especially effective against rheumatism, gout (podagra), bladder and kidney ailments and sciatica. They invigorate the mucous membranes of the stomach and intestines, and promote digestion.

Black or Bramble Berry (Rubus fructicosus): The stems, leaves and flowers boiled or a decoction thereof is an excellent remedy against asthma, urinary problems and haemorrhages.

Blessed Thistle (Cnicus Benedictus): Blessed Thistle is 30 to 40 cm high. The stem is hairy and multi-branched, because of the weight of its flowers and leaves. It very seldom remains upright. It belongs to the family of Asteraceae and grows in shady places, hedges and old ruins and has long, narrow leaves with irregular teeth and yellow flowers. When prepared as a tea, it strengthens the stomach, the digestive and abdominal organs, and acts as a sudoforic.

Blueberry (Vaccinium myrtillus): Used against diarrhoea, dried Blueberries help immediately. The leaves, taken as a tea, are an excellent remedy against diabetes.

Bogbean (Menyanthes Trifoliata): The bogbean grows near ponds, rivers, swamps and meadows. The stalks are 20 to 30 cm tall, and the leaves are long and three-partite. The flowers are rose-colored on the outside and white on the inside with reddish stamens. The bogbean is being used for abdominal and stomach ailments.

Burdock Root (Arctium lappa): Burdock can be found in forests; it has an upright stem and branched, round heart-shaped and often large leaves. Burdock is blood-cleansing and is also a diuretic. It is a good remedy for rheumatic ailments and stones.

Calamus - Sweet Flag (Acorus Calamus): Calamus has a strong, branched and jointed root-stock with many blue fibres. The bi-partite leaves are sword-shaped and pointed. Between the leaves is a double-edged, compressed stalk. The root of calamus serves digestive weaknesses obstruction caused by phlegm, and sluggishness of the intestinal tract, hydropsy and green-sickness (chlorosis). The root can be given to teething children to chew on. Externally, it can be used for bathing, and rinsing or cleansing of ulcers, atony of the gums, and all ailments which cause weakness (Asthenia).

Caraway (Carum carvi): Caraway seeds are antispasmodic, and have a calming effect, and remove the feeling of being bloated.

Carrot (Daucus carota): Carrots eaten raw serve as remedy to purify the blood. The juice pressed out or cooked is effective when applied to ulcers, sores or cankers.

Centaury (Erythraea centaurium): Centaury is also called Feverwort. The leaves are fork-shaped and oblong; the red flowers are in umbels. It grows in meadows and along the paths of fields. The dried leaves, prepared as a tea, are an excellent expectorant. It is also used for overdue menstruation due to emotional upsets, colds, and is also employed as a blood cleanser.

Coltsfoot (Tussilago farfara): Coltsfoot has heart-shaped, coarsely dentated, grey-felted leaves. It can be found on argillaceous earth, in trenches and near creeks. It is effective against catarrh and phlegm, consumption (pulmonary phthisis) and consumption of the trachea.

Comfrey (Symphytum Officinalis): Comfrey has a thick, fleshy root, dark green leaves covered with rough hair, and bell-shaped white and violet flowers. The boiled roots are a very good remedy against tracheitis, catarrh of the bowels, ailments of the lungs, diarrhoea, dysentery and internal ulcers.

Common Daisy (Bellis perennis): The leaves, flowers and roots taken as an infusion serves children as a mild laxative. It is also an old folk-remedy against ailments of the chest and obstruction of the menstrual cycle.

Cornflower (Centaurea Cyanus): The tea is effective against jaundice. A poultice or compress is effective against inflammation of the eyes.

Couch Grass (Agropyrum repens): Couch Grass belongs to the family of the grasses. It is also called Quick Grass, Dog Grass, Twitch Grass. It is a weed which grows up to a height of 50 cm - 1 m, and has spikelets of 0.9 - 2.2 cm long. This plant grows everywhere; the root and culm (stem) are effective against ailments of the kidneys and the bladder.

Cowberry - Red Whortleberry (Vaccinium vitis-idaea): Cowberries serve against ailments of the bladder and infirmities of the monthly menstrual cycle.

Cowslip (Primula veris): There are many different species of Cowslip. This particular specie grows in moist areas. The tea has the effect of producing perspiration (sudoforic), and is excellent for headaches and a swollen face.

Cranesbill (Geranium sanguineum): There are several different types of Cranesbill. This particular plant grows in forests and thickets. It has a coarse, hairy stem, upright flower stalks, red flowers and palmate leaves. It is effective for urinary ailments, haemorrhages, diarrhoea, external wounds, ulcers, and ailments of the eyes and ears. In all of these instances, the leaves should be boiled in water.

Crosswort (Galium cruciata): Crosswort has a long-branched stem, with thick, strong, oblong, downy leaves, and yellow flowers in short clusters. As a tea, it is an excellent remedy against worms (vermifuge) and it promotes menstruation. It is also effective for softening and dispersing rashes and it promotes the expelling of pus.

Cucumber (Cucumis sativa): Eaten raw, cucumber is an excellent remedy against weakness of the kidneys and swelling of the liver. The juice of a cucumber, when applied to the skin, keeps it soft and maintains its beauty.

Dandelion (Taraxacum officinale): Dandelion is an excellent remedy against ailments of the liver, the spleen, the kidneys, the gallbladder and the intestines. Also used when afflicted with diabetes, jaundice and cancer (in the old sense. Ed.). Dandelion also cleanses the intestines and acts as a diuretic.

Dwarf Thistle (in old English Mylkehtistel) (Carlina acaulis): The stems of the flowers are short. The leaves are spiny and the flowers are blueish; the plant grows where there is lime in the ground. The Dwarf Thistle strengthens the stomach and the nerves, eliminates maw worms, and has an effect on the bowels and the internal organs. It is highly recommended against impurities of the blood and skin.

Elder (Sambucus racemosa): The leaves and flowers prepared as a tea are an excellent remedy against ailments of the throat and colds, and are also perspiration-producing.

Elder Flowers (Sambucus nigra): A tea made from Elder Flowers is a sweat-producing (sudoforic) remedy, which should be employed during colds.

Eucalyptus (Eucalyptus globulus): The leaves are an excellent expectorant. Eucalyptus oil is excellent for bad mouth odour (halitosis).

Eyebright (Euphrasia): Eyebright belongs to the family of white scrophulariaceae. The stem is slender and wiry, branched pyramidal, soft-haired, with egg-shaped leaves. Eyebright, prepared as a tea, is effective against hoarseness, earaches and ailments of the head. A cloth soaked in an infusion of Eyebright and placed upon the eyes is a remedy against inflammation.

Female Fern - Bracken (Pteris Aquilina): This herb is excellent as an embrocation against rheumatism and gout. The leaves are steeped for not less than one month in a high percentage alcohol. The fresh roots of this fern are boiled and the liquid is then added to the bath for the above-mentioned ailments.

Fennel (Foeniculum dulce): Taken as an infusion, it removes bloating, stomach and intestinal cramps, intestinal gout, prevents excessive putrefaction processes in the digestive system, and increases breast milk in pregnant women.

Flax - Linseed (Linum usitatissimum): Linseeds boiled in water until they become a mucous or slimy substance, are effective against diarrhoea, ailments of the intestines, and inflammation of the respiratory tracts. As a poultice, linseeds are used for ulcers and swellings.

Garlic (Allium sativa): Garlic is, of course, a very good preventative remedy against all kinds of ailments. It eliminates disorders of the digestive system, ailments of the bowels, prevents accumulation of uric acid, arteriosclerosis, decreases high blood pressure, and especially cleanses the blood and the intestines. Garlic cleanses the intestines and removes parasites.

Gentian Root (Gentiana lutea): Gentian Root, mixed with Arnica Flowers, is very good against gout (podagra), and eliminates uric acid.

German Chamomile (Matricaria chamomilla): It should be mentioned that there are several kinds of Chamomile, each and every one having different virtues. Chamomile, prepared as a tea, is being used against bloating, stomach cramps and colic. Externally a poultice or compress can be applied against gout, toothaches etc.. Also for douching, bathing and enemas.

Ginger (Gingebere): Taken as a tea, Ginger provides relief from abdominal cramps.

Golden Saxifrage (Chrysoplenium aurea): This plant has high, hairy stems, hairy ovate leaves, yellow-whitish flowers, and grows on meagre land. Prepared as a tea, it brings relief to ailments of the lungs, mucous tuberculosis, and aids in ailments of the spleen.

Gooseberry (Ribes Grossularia): Well-ripened Gooseberries are effective against ailments of the liver.

Grapes-Vine (Vitis vinifera): Grapes, eaten in ample quantities, are favourably effective against such ailments as rheumatism, gout and diseases of the intestines or bowels. Yellowish grapes are effective against ailments of the liver, stomach pain, digestive disorders. Blue grapes eliminate skin rashes. Grapes improve the activity of the nerves. The leaves, prepared as a tea, are effective as a blood cleanser, and are also a diuretic and produce perspiration (sudoforic).

Ground Ivy (Glechoma Hederacea): The stems are long, hairy, trailing and unbranched square. The leaves are heart-shaped with rounded indentations. The flowers are two-lipped and pale blue in color.

Heather (Calluna vulgaris): A good remedy against eczema and redness of the skin. It is an excellent remedy as a blood cleansing tea, mixed with Stinging Nettle.

Horehound (Marrubium Vulgare): Horehound grows on the side of pathways and hedges. Its blooms are white and it has a balsamic fragrance. The plant has quadrangle, hairy stems and egg-shaped leaves which are covered with a white wool. Horehound proves itself when it comes to choking attacks, tracheitis and ailments of the lungs, tuberculosis, amenorrhea if caused by anaemia and jaundice.

Horseradish (Amoracia rusticana): Horseradish is an excellent remedy against impurities of the blood. It removes uric acid from the blood, also used for rheumatism, gout, ailments of the stomach and intestines, promotes the digestion and stimulates gastric mucous membranes. Horseradish can also be recommended against such ailments as diabetes, loss of appetite, sniffles and catarrhs.

Horsetail (Equisetum arvense): Horsetail, under another name, is also called Pewterwort and grows on sandy soil. Prepared as a tea and taken as such, it is effective as a diuretic in the instance of catarrh of the bladder, gout and rheumatism. Horsetail is also very effective against any prolonged types of bleeding.

Hot Sand Baths: Following a hot sand bath, a rubdown with boiled vinegar will eliminate, if repeated often enough, ailments of the lungs, catarrhs and bronchitis. Protect yourself while taking a hot sand bath from the sun with a sunshade or an umbrella.

118

House Leek (Sempervivum tectorum): The root is fibrous and the plant is a perennial, with many short stems which carry at the tip a rosette of fleshy, succulent, elongated leaves. The flowers are of a rose-red color. The leaves taken as a tea are used because of their cooling attributes against inflammation, fever and ailments of the bladder. Externally, it is being used against severe or malignant wounds, ulcers, removal of freckles, warts and corns.

Island Moss (Cetaria islandica): When prepared as a tea the taste is bitter and bilious, but it is an effective strengthening remedy when afflicted with ailments of the chest and pulmonary phthisis.

Juniper Berries (Juniperus communis): Juniper belongs to the cypress family. It grows as a small shrub or a low tree which bears dark blue berries. The branches are unwieldy, with needle-shaped leaves. It grows in dry forests. Juniper Berries, prepared as a tea, increases urination and cleanses the blood. It is also effective against urinary ailments, venereal disease, gout and hydropsy. Herbal baths prepared with Juniper Berries are an old home remedy against rheumatism, and kidney and bladder ailments.

Knotgrass (Polyganum aviculare): Knotgrass grows on the roadside and on arable land. It is a very effective tea for ailments of the chest.

Lavender (N.O. Labiatae): Lavender has rhombic leaves and greyish-blue fragrant flowers. Lavender, as a tea, is effective against congestion of blood to the head, as a compress in instances of injuries and bruises, and bloodshot eyes.

Lemon (Citrum limonum): Lemon, eaten raw, is a good remedy against weakness of the heart. Red skin turns white and becomes pliant when lemon juice is applied. It is very good for hair care, as lemon makes the hair loose, fragrant and gives it a beautiful sheen.

Lesser Burnet (Pimpinella saxifraga): Lesser Burnet grows in moist meadows and blooms white. The roots boiled in water finds its best use in respiratory problems, ailments of the throat (goitre), coughs and hoarseness, and paralysis of the tongue. It is also effective as an expectorant and a mouthwash.

Linden Flowers - Lime Tree (Tilia Europea): The tea is effective in alleviating cramps (antispasmodic), bringing forth perspiration (sudoforic) and strengthening the stomach. It is also effective against ailments of the throat and lungs, as it is for gargling, rinsing and for baths.

Lovage (Levisticum officinale): Lovage has a fleshy, thick root, and large, dark green radical leaves and one-metre high stems, and umbels of yellow flowers. Roots, stems, leaves and flowers produce a tea which is an excellent remedy against arteriosclerosis. Furthermore, it is very effective on the lower abdominal organs and the skin. It can also be recommended for compresses.

Lungwort (Sticta pulmonaria): Lungwort grows in forests and thickets. It has an oblique rootstock, and a hairy stem, first producing a light red flower which turns to bluish-violet. The roots and the mucous-tasting leaves give a healing tea for ailments of the lungs, and inflammation of the throat and chest, and also coughing-up of blood (hemoptysis).

Mallow or Marshmallow (Althea Officinalis): Mallow grows on the roadside and in meadows. Some species have white silky flower petals, and a fruit mostly containing ten parts fruit. It has a fibrous root, long stems, and finger-thick branches. The leaves are dull green, heart-shaped and crenated. Between the leaves grow the flowers which are reddish on the edges. The flower, as well as the leaves, secrete a mucous substance. A tea made from this herb is beneficial against ailments and abscesses of the throat. For ailments of the ear the tea is heated to such a degree that it turns into steam and then the steam should be directed toward the area of the ear which is affected. Caution is advised when making use of this method. The boiled root is an excellent remedy against catarrhs, chest and bladder ailments, ulcerative colitis, and diarrhoea. The infusion is excellent as a mouth wash, for eye baths and general cleansing. The well-boiled root is an excellent remedy against coughs and hoarseness and loosens excretions of the mucous membranes.

Marjoram (Origanum majorana): The leaves are ovate and dull and the plant has round white flower-spikes. Leaves and flowers, boiled as a tea, have proven to be effective in the instance of stomach cramps, bloating, uterine weakness, lymph swelling, and amenorrhea.

Marsh Marigold (Caltha palustris): Marsh Marigold has brilliant golden yellow flowers. The herb and flowers taken together as a tea are an excellent remedy against jaundice.

Melilot (Melilotus officinalis): Melilot can be found by the roadside and in moist meadows. Externally, the leaves and flowers are used as compresses against inflammation of the lymphs or glands, hardening (induration), rheumatic swelling of the joints.

Mugwort (Artemisia Vulgaris): Mugwort grows in trenches and similar places. It has grey leaves and the flowers are globular. Mugwort is closely related to the common wormwood. Prepared as a tea, or infusion, it is effective against spasmodic ailments, maw worms, jaundice and rheumatism.

Oak Bark (Quercus): An infusion prepared from the bark is excellent against bleeding of the stomach, intestinal bleeding, and metabolic diseases.

Onions (Allium cepa): Onions are being especially used against digestive disorders, intestinal catarrh (gastroenteritis), loss of appetite, nerve pain, difficulty in breathing (dyspnoea), and throat pain. Onions have significant healing potential and have a particular effectiveness. Onions increase the specific temperature in the body. They can also be successfully employed when applied to frozen limbs. Onion juice, applied to the scalp, prevents hair loss.

Paradise Apple/St. John's Apple (Pirus malus paradisiaca/Mala praecacia rubra): Eaten raw, it is an excellent remedy against disturbances of the digestive system.

Parsley (Carum petroselinum): Parsley, boiled in water, can be recommended as an external remedy for eye inflammation. The root is an excellent remedy against hydropsy, and Parsley is also an excellent diuretic.

Pine (Picea abies): Boiling two young pine cones of this particular specie and taken as a tea is an excellent remedy against consumption (pulmonary phthisis), chest and spinal cord ailments, skin diseases, ailments of the nerves, useful as a diuretic and as a blood cleanser. When the young pine cones are boiled and the fluid is then added to a bath, this provides energy to the human body.

121

Plantain - Ribwort (Plantago lanceolata): This plant is a blood-building remedy for those who are afflicted with green-sickness (chlorosis), and is effective for weaknesses of the lungs, narrow-chestedness (shortness of breath), ailments of the gallbladder, and skin impurities.

Radish (Raphanus sativus): Radish is an expectorant and promotes digestion. Radish heals and is also an excellent remedy against stones of the kidneys, bladder and gallbladder. It also aids ailments of the liver, hydropsy, and consumption (phthisis, tuberculosis).

Raspberry (Rubus idaeus): Boiling the leaves is an excellent remedy against a profuse menstrual cycle and against diarrhoea. Raw berries made into a mulch and applied to chilblains or frostbite will heal them in short order.

Red Currants (Ribes rubrum): Eaten fresh and raw, they are an excellent remedy against fever, measles and palpitation of the heart. A poultice made from ripe, crushed berries is an excellent remedy against inflammation of the brain.

Rest Harrow (Ononis arvensis): Rest Harrow blooms reddish and white. The creeping root is finger-thick, sticky and dark brown on the outside, and whitish on the inside, and has a bitter taste. It is an excellent tea against rheumatism, bladder ailments and hydropsy. The root boiled in water is a diuretic remedy, and can be recommended against urinary gravel and nocturnal emissions.

Rosehip - Wild Rose (Rosa Canina): The leaves taken as an infusion heals consumption (pulmonary phthisis) and spitting of blood (hemoptysis). A tea made from dried berries prevents formation of stones.

Rosemary (Rosmarinus officinalis): Rosemary belongs to the family of the Labiate. It has pale blue flower calyces and grows as a high bush in gardens. Rosemary, prepared as a tea, eliminates digestive problems, attacks of dizziness (vertigo), blood congestion of the head, inflammation of the kidneys and the bladder. Prepared as a herbal pillow, it can be applied externally to bruises, congestion of blood and bodily liquids, and swelling of the glands.

Sage (Salvia officinalis): Sage is a shrub with ovate, softly-haired, greyish-white leaves. The flowers are in whorls and are violet in color, and also bloom in white and blue. The flowers stand together six-fold. The tea is being used against arteriosclerosis, bloating, gout and rheumatism, because of its high content of tannic acid. It can also be highly recommended as a mouthwash (gargling agent) for ailments of the throat.

Sanicle (Sanicula Europea): Sanicle belongs to the Umbelliferae family. The flower is in umbels and is pinkish-white. The radical, palmate leaves are on long stalks. The plant grows in mountainous, shady forests. The roots and leaves, prepared as a tea, are effective against internal ulcers, vomiting of blood, ailments of the stomach and the intestines.

Scurvy Grass (Cochlearia officinalis): Scurvy Grass grows near salt-works. It is an annual or biennial plant, with spindle-shaped roots and heart-shaped root leaves, a short-stem, ovate leaves, and white flowers. Scurvy Grass should only be used when fresh as an infusion against rheumatism, hydropsy and chronic festering. It is very pleasant as gargling water or mouthwash in the instance of throat and tooth abscess.

Shepherd's Purse (Capsella bursa - pastoris): Shepherd's Purse grows in meadows and at the edges of fields. It has small greyish-white flowers and is used for abdominal pain, nosebleeds, urinary ailments. When due to the menstrual cycle, severe loss of blood is experienced, Shepherd's Purse immediately eliminates any further bleeding.

Spearmint (Mentha viridis): There are different kinds of mints; make certain you have the right mint, as every mint has its own virtues. As a tea, Spearmint stimulates the digestive organs, especially against stomach cramps, bloating and diarrhoea.

Speedwell (Veronica officinalis): The flowers are in dense, many-flowered racemes. It is a herb of a prostate habit with ascending branches. The leaves are opposite each other and oval in shape, with pale biue to rose-colored flowers, and it grows in dry areas of a forrest. It is an excellent home remedy against breathing difficulties, chest and lung ailments, phlegm in the organs of the chest, aids against old or chronic catarrhs accompanied by expectoration of phlegm. It also finds application in chronic urinary and bladder ailments.

Stinging Nettle (Urtica urens): Stinging Nettle, prepared as a tea, cleanses the blood and the whole organism and favourably affects ailments of the liver and spleen, ailments of the lungs and ulcers in the intestines. Stinging Nettle is a diuretic; it stimulates the stomach and pancreas, strengthens all organs, and is an excellent remedy for bleeding of the lungs.

Strawberries (Fragaria vesca): Useful against stone ailments, bladder and kidney ailments, lower abdominal congestion, jaundice, throat ailments.

St. Johnswort (Hypericum perforatum): St. Johnswort is recognizable by its erect double-edged and upward-branched stems. The leaves are ovate, but oblong, pellucid dots or oil glands, which can be seen when holding the leaf against the light. And it has corymb yellow flowers. When prepared as a tea it is effective against haemorrhages, diarrhoea and gout. The dried herb placed under the head is an excellent deflection against spiritual and unpleasant perceptions.

Thyme (Thymus vulgaris): The stems are long, hard, round and branched. The flowers are pale purple and the leaves are ovate. An infusion of thyme is used against coughs, mucous or phlegm (expectorant), and anaemia. Applied externally, it is useful against injuries, paresis by using poultices, and for aches and pains of the limbs, and weak nerves (neurasthenia). A bath prepared with thyme is very soothing.

Tomato (Solanum lycopersicum): Tomatoes should only be eaten raw, if they are expected to be effective for healing purposes. They are an excellent remedy for all disorders of the circulatory system, kidney stones, gall stones and febrile diseases. Also useful for festering inflammations of the stomach and weakness of the nerves.

Valerian (Valeriana): Valerian grows on hill sides, in trenches, in marshy meadows and in forests. The roots merge into a short rootstock; it has horizontal and slender branches and a blossom stem with reddish flowers. The leaves have different shapes. The root boiled in water is being used for chronic ailments of the nerves, insomnia, nervous states of anxiety, dizziness, chronic fevers of the nerves, nervous one-sided headaches, stomach cramps and colic.

Violet, Sweet (Viola odorata): Violet leaves, dried and prepared as a tea, are being used against children's chronic skin rashes. The flowers cooked with bee honey are an old home remedy against whooping cough (pertussis).

Walnut Leaves (Juglans nigra): The leaves and husks prepared as a tea are a blood cleanser and eliminate skin rashes.

Watercress (Nasturtium officinale): Watercress has ovate leaves, white blossoms and yellow dust sacs. An excellent remedy against swelling of the lymphs, blennorrhea (discharge of mucus) of the lungs and intestinal tract, chronic eczema and ailments of the bladder. In the instance of ailments of the lungs, it is recommenced to eat Watercress raw. A tea prepared from the dried leaves promotes conception.

White Dead Nettle (Lamium album): The calyx of the Dead Nettle is shaped like a bell, with six teeth and a flower corolla. Dead Nettle grows in undeveloped areas. The dried white flowers harvested and picked out of the calyces prepared as a tea cleanses the blood and has a calming effect on the heart. The dried leaves prepared as a poultice and applied to hardened swellings or tumors and old ailments is a good remedy.

Wild Celery (Apium graveolens): Celery is an excellent remedy against rheumatism, ailments of the bladder and the nerves. It is an effective diuretic and therefore disposes of all bad substances from the body.

Wild Pansy - Heartease (Viola Tricolor): The leaves and flowers, prepared as tea, are blood-cleansing, and are also effective as a diuretic and sudoforic, for ailments of the lymphs, and eczema.

Wild Thyme (Thymus serpyllum): Wild Thyme grows on hills, at the edge of forests and in dry fields. The woody roots are fibrous. The numerous stems are procumbent, the punctured leaves are on short foot stalks. The flowers are purple-red. The tea is effective against spasmodic pain during menstrual cleansing, and for disturbances of the digestive process, and for abdominal cramps.

Woodruff, Sweet (Asperula odorata): Woodruff has a slender, creeping root-stock. The stems are smooth, and there are approximately eight leaves in star-like whorls; the flowers are white. Woodruff grows in shady deciduous woods. It is effective as a blood cleanser, against urinary and bladder pain, jaundice and water retention (hydropsy).

Wormwood (Artemisia Absinthium): Wormwood, prepared as a tea, has a healing effect on the stomach. It strengthens the stomach and stimulates the appetite. It also very effectively strengthens, invigorates and heals in instances of heartburn, cholera and gastroenteritis, weakness of the bowels, anaemia, stomach catarrh, ailments of the gallbladder and liver.

Yarrow (Achillea millefolium): Yarrow leaves are effective for strengthening the stomach and have an extraordinary effect against fevers, spasmodic pain, catarrh of the lungs, and ailments of the intestines. The leaves are also very favourable towards arteriosclerosis and ailments of the heart.

35. About Words, Herbs And Stones.

The Language of Old is well-known. It is said, among other things: In Verbis, Herbis and Lapidibus are many hidden powers.

Some laughed at this statement; others took it too literally and the consequence was wishful thinking. It sometimes even took the form of fanaticism.

On the whole, the people of old were right; only we the people who followed them did not understand them and changed and misinterpreted the meanings of their sayings and writings. This has been done for centuries.

Superstition and the wishful thinking of centuries lead many Human Beings on the wrong path and this is still true today. Many false, adventurous inventions are developed due to lack of basic understanding and knowledge of Nature's Laws. These inventions make Human Beings believe they have progressed. All these inventions which are not based in accordance with and upon the understanding of the Natural Laws, lead to the destruction or to the demise of those who believe in them and those people commit themselves to a fool's paradise.

There will always be an extraordinary force in the knowledge of the Words, Herbs and Stones.

The Wisdom of the Good Lord teaches those who respect Him these powers.

Words have an extraordinary power over the heart of Human Beings, if they are words of the Soul. Every word is an ingredient of our feelings and it is mighty and effective, if the power of the Soul flows into it. There are words of expressions, words of the feelings of the Soul, and words of power.

When someone speaks with great enthusiasm, Human Beings gather around such a person in great awe and amazement. His feelings become the feelings of others, his perceptions become their perceptions.

Tears dry up and tears flow through words. In other words, they can be the cause of tears and they can stop tears. Lost courage can be regained; the anger of a person can be appeased by those who have the knowledge of the power of the word.

There is, however, one word, and this word is the word of all words. It is holy to the Angels and to Human Beings. Everything is within this word, everything what is, what was and what will be.

Every body has its necessary proportions. That means every body has its laws, in accordance that it is what it is.

Through changes of the proportions, the body changes.

Every body has its components and every component is a body in his own manner.

The body particles are divided into those which are closer and those which are more distant.

The close ones are the components of the body; the more distance ones are the components of the components. For example: the components of cinnabar are sulfur and mercury. The more distant components are sulfur.

A change in the distant components changes the closer components of the body all the time, but a change in the closer components does not always change the distant components.

A body can be destroyed if the order of the components is interfered with, and the distant components do not have to suffer on account of it. However, the distant components can never change, unless the main body changes also.

127

The different qualities of the body have their foundation in the measure of their compositions.

Every body has its own powers or energies and those which are incidental.

The energies the body has on its own mostly consist of the condition of the distant components and the incidental energies out of the condition of the form.

In other words, with the change of the distant components, their own energies change; with the change of form, the incidental energies change.

The effect of the attraction of an artificial magnet is an incidental energy. It originates out of the direction of its components, which are pure form and cannot be counted as part of the body.

Therefore, the incidental energies can be changed by Human Beings without affecting a change in the inner energies with regards to the nature of the body. Gold stays gold - it does not matter if it is shaped into a ball or a cube.

The stronger pulls the weaker, the heavier the lighter.

Strength and weakness, lightness and heaviness, consists partly in the components of the body and partly in its form.

Every body has one true strength and one incidental strength, a true weakness and an incidental weakness.

A ball of lead is incidentally weaker than a cube of lead because a ball of lead can be moved more easily than a cube, therefore, a cube of lead is incidentally stronger.

Those who study the components of the bodies, their measures, their energies and their forms will also be able to change their effects.

When you know the reason why fire burns and why certain bodies are burnable, then you can make burnable bodies non-burnable.

The effect of every body is partially dependent upon its own body, and partially upon the object upon which it acts.

There is no action without a reaction; and in each case you have parts which suffer and parts which act.

When the measure of the suffering parts in a body becomes predominant over the active parts, then a body in which the active parts are predominant over the suffering parts, can have an effect on the other body.

The measure of the effectiveness conducts itself in accordance with the receptiveness of the suffering parts.

Any effectiveness one body has on another is a form of advice given to the other body of its own power. When the powers are of equal strength, there is no communication, however, if they are not of equal force, then there are effects.

The effectiveness is always in accordance with the components.

Something is effective as long as the equilibrium of the powers of the bodies which are acting against each other are disturbed.

The equilibrium endeavours to re-establish itself, and as a result of this, we have fermentation, movement.

Similar seeks similar, like seeks alike. The power of assimilation, which is contained in every body, will work with the heterogeneous parts until they are assimilated, or until they are pushed away, and thereby change the body, or it bears an entirely different body.

When an assimilation is not possible, the duration of the conflict prevails between the fighting forces until the body particles dissolve, and those which cannot assimilate are eliminated.

These basic principles give the possibility to those who understand, of explaining how things are accomplished in mechanics, chemistry, etc. If you understand how to combine properly, you can also invent many things.

36. The Numbers.

In Magic, one of the most important subjects is the teaching of Numbers. When you understand numbers, you can obtain reliable conditions and relationships. This makes it possible to measure size, expansion, and size or proportions of all bodies.

This consists of: *Addition, Subtraction, Multiplication, Division, Sum,* which again is divided into: *Arithmetic, and Geometry.*

It is absolutely necessary that we form a concept of the equality of the amount, proportion, solidarity and transposition. The teachings of the Numbers are teachings of the proportion of the majority of things. The combination of numbers seems to extend into infinity, but they are not infinite.

A Human Being can, by means of a number which he knows in the present, discover another future number, which he presently has no knowledge of, and he can also discover a number from the past.

The power lies in the calculation of a number which is not present now with a number which is present; to find this number either in the past or in the future and make these numbers part of the present. This is done through relationship or the proportion thereof.

Numbers are nothing but repetitions of One. The number One is unchangeable. It is without parts or components; it can be multiplied only by itself and the product of the multiplication is One again.

One is the beginning and the end of all numbers, but by itself has no beginning and no end. It is the symbol of itself, the symbol of unity - it is unison.

Number 2 is the first number because it is the first majority, the measure of unity, out of which this number came into being. Number 2 is the symbol of production and of creation. It is the number of knowledge, the number of love, and the number of union.

Number 3 is the first number which stands by itself. It is also the number which is called the holy number. This number is the number of perfection. It is the first cubic number.

Number 4 is the number of the bodies. It is the number of solidity. The things of the physical world are measured by this number.

Number 5 is the child of the first uneven number, united with the first even number. It is the symbol of justness and of union.

Number 6 is the Seal of the World. It is the symbol of perfection and sufficiency. It is also the number of Human Beings, and the number of work and servitude.

Number 7 is the number of human life. It is the number of generation, of formation and existence. It is the symbol of understanding, repentance, forgiveness and of time.

Number 8 is the number of fulfilment and justness, the symbol of annihilation of timely things, the number of blissfulness and delight.

Number 9 is the number of Wisdom and Knowledge, the symbol of Human Knowledge.

Number 10 is the number of the Universe, the number of the whole of human life, the number of the Laws.

Number 11 is the number which has no meaning.

Number 12 is the number of perfection and of grace.

These are some interpretations of the old Quabbalists. Great wisdom lies in this classification of numbers. The Quabbalah is the Science of the Word.[1]

The Secret of the Numbers contains our destiny and many other secrets. Since we did not understand this, we dismissed it.

Numbers are the means by which you distinguish the majority of certain objects.

---

[1]   This is described much more explicitly in Franz Bardon's book, "The Key to the True Quabbalah". (Ed.)

We count if we want to determine the majority of certain objects. Without numbers, Human Beings cannot determine which one of the objects is in the majority.

The words of the numbers are founded on arbitrary sounds, the same as all other words. The numbers themselves are, of course, in the Nature of Things and do not lie in the Will of Human Beings.

The sequence or the product of several compounded numbers is necessary, and is based on the essence or nature of the numbers themselves before they are compounded.

Numbers multiply by unification; they produce others and lose nothing of their nature. They multiply by themselves without experiencing any losses within themselves. Even single existing numbers become parts of other numbers, and yet they are substances by themselves which consist of other parts.

Five is a number-substance, and three and two, in retrospect, are five parts of this number-substance, because five dissolves into three and two. Only three and two or four and one can be considered accepted parts of the number five. The true parts of this number are the units, because five means nothing but a number which consists of five units. Therefore, a reduction of any number of the dissolution of its components results again in a unit.

The parts of five can be two and three. Two and three are compounded parts. Two contains two units, three contains three units, therefore five has five units.

Therefore, a unit always stays a unit in its nature, but proportionately it changes its nature compared to others, and the relationship of the first unit to another is called two. The relationship of one unit to two units is called three, or two units to one unit is called three. Two to two is four.

The numbers have necessary laws. When a unit is added to a number, the number increases by necessity, and when a number loses a unit, the number decreases by necessity.

The Art of Mathematics, therefore, has necessary relationships. Necessary relationships are relationships of the matter itself. The Art of Mathematics teaches us the necessary relationships and leads us to the true knowledge of this matter.

The question now arises: What can you calculate? Answer: Everything which consists of a majority of parts; everything which has time, space and weight; anything which can be divided; everything which has an object of numbers and has arithmetic proportions and relationships.

37. Necessary Pre-Requisites
For Magic Calculation.

Objects of a calculation are size, extension and measure. There are two basic rules as far as size is concerned: addition and subtraction.

The addition is arithmetic work. This is accomplished by adding different sizes of the same kind.

Subtraction teaches us to distinguish the difference between two sizes, or how much of one, or how much is left of two sizes, whereof one part has been taken away.

The rule of multiplication is based on a product of one size of a certain matter being multiplied in a very specific way. It is a shortcut to addition.

Through division you discover how many times a certain product of one size is contained in another. It is a shortcut to subtraction.

When you add two things you have as a result, the sum or product. They are either arithmetical or geometrical by nature. The arithmetic sum is the difference between two sizes, which are compared with each other through subtraction. The equality of the sum is what is called proportion. The arithmetical proportion receives its equality due to increases. The geometric proportion is based on the equivalence of the quotient.

When a proportion has more than three numbers, then it is called a progression.

A group of the same and combinations are all different ways to divide certain sizes by taking these parts into consideration.

Transpositions differ from groups of the same, besides all changes which are in this order and those which you will be able to find, because they are contained therein.

These are some general rules in mathematics. There are many more but they are not for everybody.

The Quabbalah was the secret and symbolic Theology of the Hebrews. They had the following subjects:

Ghemetriam
Notariacam
Themuram
Mercavam
Bereschith

This is accepted by their scholars as the science of the Symbolic Knowledge of the Numbers.

The main secret of the Philosophy of Numbers is based on the Quabbalists bringing all objects of the Number three to one unit, and it was thusly condensed. Out of it derived all the differences and progressions, modifications in the relationship of Harmony.

The Relationship of Harmony is this:

System of Creation

Creator: Creature, The Connection Between Them, Love.
Nature: Existence, Co-Existence, Approximation - 3.
Similar - Dissimilar - Becoming Alike - 3.
Weakness - Energy - Equation - 3.
Resistance - Purification - Perfection - 3, etc.

The Art of being quabbalistic is the Art of finding the relationship of things according to the rules of Harmony and Disharmony.

Should you want to have a thorough knowledge of this, start with books written on this subject. However, be forewarned, there are only a few which deal with the true Quabbalah.

Those of you who have no knowledge of the Quabbalah - do not dismiss it! Investigate, examine, contemplate, think. Everything is related. Relationships are the laws of things. Those who know the means to study these relationships will experience inconceivable things.

Our language is made up of words. There is a language, however, which is founded in the matter itself and the present, the future and the past are the objects.

38. The Temple Of Health
And The Bed Of Blissfulness
Of Dr. Graham.

Human Beings enjoy through their senses, the Bliss of Life. They bring happiness as well as suffering into their Soul.

The nerves and fibres of Human Beings are, in accordance with their nature, in a state of indifference and are receptive to external and internal movement.

There are movements in the body which are necessary to maintain the physical or animal life, and these movements are called physical or animal Vital Forces or Vital Energies. When these movements can express or manifest themselves in the human body without hindrance, then the fibres, nerves, arteries and veins, the blood and the fluids are in such a condition, that everything is in its proper order, so that one does not hinder the other in constant movement. Then the Human Being enjoys true health. If this is not the case, then he is ill.

When the blood and the fluids are either too thin or too thick, the fibres and nerves are too weak or too tense, or there are variations or differences in the circulation of the physical or animal fluids. These are the first causes of ailments and pains.

Human Beings are not capable of feeling pain or happiness without considerable changes in their present condition. All feelings are changes of conditions. Their origin is external. Only when a Human Being is placed in several of such conditions through external means, will he be able to recall the same through the power of his imagination, or be able to place himself into the same state of feeling, without an external object triggering this condition.

Therefore, feelings originally depend upon impressions and behave in accordance to the condition of our organization.

Yet feelings or perceptions are different, and behave in accordance with the structure of our nerves, and their more or lesser irritability, however, mainly in accordance with the liveliness of our imagination.

Feelings can be separated into feelings and perceptions. Perceptions are impressions that the body receives from objects which are present, or from their similarity. The inner feeling is the impression which is triggered in the Soul through the perception. The feelings or perceptions can be straight or sincere, reflective or mixed.

The physical body is similar to a machine, in which all parts have to be in harmony so that they can function properly. One part is dependent upon the other. One part is capable, if it does not move, of stopping all the others.

Human Beings have two modifications in their feelings or perceptions: pain and happiness. Happiness maintains our being. It is a straight feeling, whereas pain endeavours to destroy.

Happiness tickles our senses and creates a movement in accordance to its tension. Pain gives the senses a severe shock and tears and stretches them.

Anything which destroys the equilibrium in the engine brings about an unpleasant and painful feeling.

Every sense has its own pain and its own happiness. Pain and happiness are in accordance with the force of the touch and the condition of the part which was touched.

Human Beings feel best externally with their fingertips, their lips, the back of their neck and the spine.

Through the differences in the organization, the feelings become different too. There is only a minute difference between pain and pleasure. The highest degree of physical pleasure is the first degree of pain.

Reflective perception originates through movement which is equal to the one being brought forth by the presence of the original object, and the consequences and effects are often the same.

Human Beings are usually more unhappy through reflective perceptions of pain, than through straight or sincere perceptions.

However, the more a Human Being experiences pleasant, reflective perceptions, the happier a Human Being becomes.

The sincere or straight perceptions are of short duration, whereas the reflective perceptions are of a longer duration.

Every passion is a destructive perception, which starts from the highest degree of mistaken happiness and, by necessity, turns into pain.

All intense passions disturb the free flow of our fluids, drive the blood upwards tempestuously, and exert pressure on the bowels.

Every passionate Human Being is therefore in an unnatural position, in an actual condition of an ailment.

Passions can, therefore, be the cause of ailments, and ailments the cause of passions.

There are people who are inclined towards anger; the more they are mistreated, the greater the anger becomes. This is also true for children; they become angrier when they are spanked.

I once knew an honourable lady who had such a boy, who became angrier the more he was spanked. I told her that this anger was the result of an ailment he had, caused by a pungent residue in his bowels. I advised her to give the boy enemas and proper food, and in no time the anger disappeared.

The whole nervous system is affected by every feeling and perception a Human Being has.

For example: The scent of a flower affects the olfactory nerve (smell), like an elastic string that is touched and thereby vibrates. The vibration starts at one end and eventually over the whole string provided that:

1. The nerve has enough elasticity
2. The brain is coherent and not damaged
3. The tension is proper and not above or below the limits
4. The substance has the proper consistency

This shows that the whole sensitive life exists through consistent shockwaves to our nervous system which, through necessity, must wear off little by little.

If you truly want to relax and strengthen the senses, there is nothing better than to bring all the senses simultaneously into a gentle tension.

When a Human Being attains this condition, it gives him a feeling which cannot be described. It is the highest bliss of sensuous feelings, a slumber of total bliss. This happens only when the nerves of sight, smell, hearing, taste and feeling are simultaneously brought into motion in the most pleasant way.

Dr. Graham built a bed which met all these requirements and he called it the heavenly bed. Since I myself did not see Dr. Graham's invention in London, I therefore cannot form any judgement, other than what I have been told. The idea intrigued me and I acted upon this accordingly.

The result of my experiments were: if a human body lies lightly dressed in a horizontal position on a bed with resilient pillows which rest upon elastic springs, and if this bed is in a constant gentle motion, it creates a very pleasant feeling. This feeling can be heightened through a pleasant scent, enjoying a pleasant beverage, and through the reflection of a beautiful color. This will strengthen the nerves in an extraordinary manner.

Then I came upon the idea of concentrating sounds of music to make them more noticeable and effective upon the nerves of a human being. In order to achieve this, I had a machine built which resembled a sounding-board and was large enough for a human being to comfortably lie on horizontally. In the next room the music was played under a hat-shaped funnel from which two pipes protruded which lead into the large sounding-board whereupon the human being was resting. The sounds of the music concentrated through the hat-shaped funnel and then travelled through the pipes to the large sounding-board.

The feelings which the person experienced who was lying on the large sounding-board were undescribable. The more harmonious the music was, the gentler, the more pleasant the feeling, which spread throughout the body. The more disharmonious the music became, the more unpleasant the feelings. And the feelings became unbearable when the instruments were put out of tune.

The feeling mostly expressed itself by a pleasant tickle in the abdominal area and in the diaphragm.

We know from anatomical experiences, that in a human being these parts suffer the most, when consumed by strong passions.

It would be within reason to assume that if the physicist would come to the conclusion that very intense passions can come into being, if there is a disorder in these parts.

When a human being becomes angry, you will experience that the blood moves upwards and the intestines and the viscera contract. Through this contraction, the gallbladder becomes depressed.

This condition can only be caused by a straight or reflective feeling or perception.

Should anyone become angry through an insult, this condition can only be triggered through a reflective perception. Should it happen through a defect or a condition of the physical body or organs, then this is caused by a straight activity or movement. Therefore, anger can be the consequence of an ailment.

It is always advisable to very carefully observe the condition of the physical body if you want to achieve an improvement when it comes to very passionate Human Beings.

It is a known fact that music can sometimes calm the most angry person. The reason for this must lie in the subtle vibration of the nerves. Through this vibration, the effect of the anger is eliminated. The compressed vessels in the abdominal area again attain their normal tension; they become elastic again, they become soft, and they lose their rigidity. The liver and gallbladder can resume their functions, the blood begins to circulate freely again and the anger disappears.

I hold out great hope, that the improvement of this machine will change the passions of a human being into gentler feelings.

When the moral Human Being is improving, the physical Human Being should not be neglected, especially when it comes to habitual passions. It is just as necessary to heal the ailing physical body as it is to heal the ailing Soul.

I observed that in regards to this point, many mistakes are being made when it comes to the rearing of our youth. There are children who are extremely angry or hot-tempered, even to the point that they roll on the floor like an animal. I observed that this is not always wickedness or malice, but it is mostly a hidden ailment. It would be wrong to mistreat such children or to spank them, since the blood in such a Human Being becomes even more heated-up, and this can then change from anger to shock, and the consequences could be very serious. It would be advisable to treat such a Human Being with the methods described here. The reason for their anger lies mostly in the harmful germ of pungency, which has its seat in the bowels. The best remedy is to administer beverages which improve the pungent bile.

All senses have an influence on the condition of health of every Human Being.

The finer the percipient sense is, the finer is that sense's effectiveness.

For a long time I occupied myself with determining the harmony of all sensuous impressions and making them descriptive and perceptible.

For this purpose I improved the Music of the Eye, invented by Father Castell.

I built this machine in its total perfection, so that it could bring forth whole chords of colors, as well, as tones (sounds). Below you will find a description of this instrument.

I had cylindrical glasses made of equal size with diameter of 1/2 inch and I filled them colored water. I placed these glasses in the order of the strings on a piano, and I divided the nuances of the colors, as well as the sounds in accordance to the scale. Then I had some brass-covers made for the glasses, so that when these glasses were covered, none of the colors could be seen. I fastened a wire to each of the brass-covers, and connected the wire to the corresponding key of the keyboard on the piano, so whenever you would touch a key on the piano, the corresponding brass-cover would lift and the color would become visible. As the sound would fade, when the finger was removed from the keyboard, so would the color, because the brass-cover would immediately cover the glass by its own gravity. It should also be mentioned, that the proper effect cannot be achieved, unless candles are placed behind the glasses.The beauty of the colors are indescribable - they surpass the most beautiful gems. It is also impossible to describe the visual feeling you perceive through the different color-accords.

Initially, the one who first had the idea of designing a machine for eye-music, was laughed at, with the statement, that it would be impossible to design a machine, whereby the sound and color would fade simultaneously. But I did not lose my courage and through mechanics I achieved the goal and demonstrated that you can express everything through colors as well as through sound.

39. Theory Of Visionary Music
Or Music Of The Eye.

As the Sounds of Music must harmonize, as the expressions of a Poet in a melodrama, colors also have to harmonize with the expression.

This little poem may clarify this:

1. **Expression of Words:**
   She walks, melancholy, the most beautiful of all females...

2. **Expression of Sounds:**
   Sound of a flute, gently-sighing.

3. **Expression of Colors:**
   The color of olive, playful with white and red like roses.

1. **Expression of Words:**
   ... in the meadow covered with flowers.

2. **Expression of Sounds:**
   Rising, happy sounds.

3. **Expression of Colors:**
   Changing green with violet-blue and the yellow of primrose.

1. **Expression of Words:**
   Joyful as a lark, she is singing a song.

2. **Expression of Sounds:**
   Gentle, but the sounds are in fast succession, one after the other, ascending and then gently descending.

3. **Expression of Colors:**
   Dark-blue changing to light-red, yellow-green.

1. ***Expression of Words:***
   ...and it can be heard in the Temple of Creation by the Divinity.

2. ***Expression of Sounds:***
   Majestic - Magnificent.

3. ***Expression of Colors:***
   A mixture of the most magnificent colors, blue-red-green, glorified through aurora yellow and purple colors, and lost in soft green and pale yellow.

1. ***Expression of Words:***
   The Sun is shining in great brilliance over the mountain tops.

2. ***Expression of Sounds:***
   Glorious depths and softly ascending softer and softer, gentler and gentler.

3. ***Expression of Colors:***
   Intensely yellow colors mixed with aurora yellow, getting lost in green and whitish yellow.

1. ***Expression of Words:***
   ... and shines upon the violets in the valley, etc., etc.

2. ***Expression of Sounds:***
   Thereby descending pleasantly into depths.

3. ***Expression of Colors:***
   Violet-blue, changing intermittently with different greens.

By reading and understanding this little poem and the significance of the words, sounds and colors, the fact that colors can express what the Soul feels can be demonstrated. Colors do possess this ability.

It follows that this can be extended to the sense of smell. By employing aromatic oils, they can be placed in the proper sequence in accordance to the musical scale.

The following aromatic oils are in sequence in accordance to the musical scale.

1. Orange
2. Rosemary
3. Lilies
4. Cloves
5. Bergamot
6. Jasmine
7. Roses

These scents can have different nuances. The reason why these oils have different smells is due to the sulfur they contain. The manner in which they mix is the reason why there are differences in their scent.

When all colors are mixed, the end result is the color white.

When you mix many different scents, you will always get the smell of ambra or ambergris. This leads to the conclusion that since this contains all scents, it should be possible to produce all kinds of different scents from this substance.

In order to do this, first mix this ambergris substance with substances which do not emit a smell or scent. Little by little you will be able to produce different nuances as far as scent is concerned.

This can lead to many other experiments, but the scent of each individual or combined substance is founded in the parts of sulfur it contains.

When you observe a continuous electrical spark, you see the bluish color of the electrical currents and you smell sulfur. If you bring substances which do not emit any scent or odour in contact with an electrical spark or shock, they produce certain scents, some of which are unknown, others which are pleasant. This proves that a mixture of particles and the variety of their position, through which the sulfur particles are repulsed, is the origin of the odour or scent.

Knowing this could eventually allow you to determine the ingredients of all scents.

Any ingredient out of which the odour or scent of any body or substance consists, is eliminated by that particular body, therefore, every odour or scent is the perspiration of a body.

The smell or odour is determined and according to the ingredients which perspire, and in the manner in which it is filtered or eliminated.

141

Round particles have a different effect on our sense of smell than pointed particles, and out of the diversity of feelings originates a variety of scents.

Smell, in reality, does not really lie within Nature but is coincidental. Smell originates through the diversity of the effect of body perspiration and what effect this has on our sense of smell. This feeling, which we experience, we call smell, as we call the feeling our tongue experiences, taste.

Therefore, taste does not really lie within Nature either, but is also coincidental. It is in accordance with the receptivity of our organization, and the effect the body particles have on our taste buds. The taste depends upon what substance touches the taste buds. The feeling our tongue experiences is called taste. Sight and hearing are also a feeling. The difference, however, is that this can be achieved from a distance without direct touch, whereas smell, taste and touch have to be with substance or body directly.

In the case of hearing or seeing, the nerves immediately receive the right vibration through distant objects.

No Human Being is, therefore, capable of determining the feelings, smell, hearing or taste of another Human Being, because this depends upon the organization of the individual. Therefore, what pleases one person does not please another, or what one person loves to eat, another person dislikes.

40. Sight.

When you make a serious study of sight or eyesight, you will make many wonderful discoveries.

By using the Theory of Refraction and applying this in optics, it is possible to prepare lenses or eyeglasses which, when you wear them, do not differ in appearance from normal eyeglasses, but, when you look through them and place an object at a certain spot in front of you, it disappears; even a person can disappear in front of your eyes. People can also appear without a head or they can appear with animal heads. All this can be achieved with refraction.

Many things can be achieved with reflection. If you think long enough, many modifications will create different effects.

For example, you can place an object on a table and get closer to this object, as if you want to swallow it. At this point, you change the angle of reflection and it seems to an onlooker that you have swallowed the object. At this point, the onlooker is not aware of the fact that what he sees is an illusion, and you are making the illusion disappear with the mirrors or lenses.

41. Smell.

You can conduct many experiments with the sense of smell if you understand the following sentences.

1. A stronger smell or odour overpowers a weaker smell and changes in the weaker body the particles or smell in accordance with the form of the particles of smell.

2. The particles of smell are true particles of the body and very seldom do they lose the characteristics of their body, because they are outflows therefrom.

3. Since a more intense smell of a body changes a weaker smell of another, the characteristic of another body can be changed through the means of these organs.

4. Two bodies, whose particles of smell are of equal strength do not mix and do not change.

5. When particles of smell flow out of two bodies which are of unequal force, a fight then ensues. Even if one cannot overpower the other, a third or different smell will emerge, which does not resemble the two original smells.

6. The body will lose its smell when all the sulphur particles are driven out of the body.

7. Oil contains a smell or scent for the longest time, because in oil the sulphur particles cannot evaporate as quickly as in other substances.

8. Any scent, odour or smell which is contained in spirit of wine, leaves or evaporates the fastest.

9. Heat and fire eliminate smell or odour very quickly, because the sulphur evaporates.

10. When you have water with a scent, such as rose-water, and you add sulphur proportionately, it will retain the scent much longer.

11. Scented waters which contain spirits are harmful to all Human Beings.

12. Wholesome scents are those which contain vinegar.

13. Nitrum or Nitro can also retain scent because it also contains the cleanest of air, air which does not contain any burnable substances. This air, therefore, retains much more phlogiston, and that is the reason why the sulfur particles separate more slowly from bodies of this type.

42. The Theory Of Feelings.

The nerves all over our entire body are like thousands of little branches, and all these little branches end up in what could be described as little warts. These warts are the actual tool of our feelings.

Feelings are the effect an object or another body has on these warts of feelings. Feelings are in accordance to the condition of these warts.

It is a pre-requisite that the warts are moist and are a little higher than the skin. If they do not protrude and are not moist, they have very little or no feeling at all.

These warts of feelings differentiate by numbers or amounts and by their form or shape.

Where the feelings are strong and full of life, the warts are larger in size, as they are on the tongue and the tips of the fingers. They would even be visible to the eye, if the epidermis were removed.

Under the nails, the warts of feeling are elongated and pointed; on the jaw, cheeks and upper lips they are tufted or shaggy; on the tongue they resemble upside down cones. Most of them, however, are not cone-like.

Feeling is caused by putting pressure on the nerves and this happens in different ways or manners - by tearing, pulling, pushing or shock.

The perception of feeling is in accordance to the manner, to the object or body which is causing the effect, and also according to the condition of its receptivity.

First they consist of the following: solidity or firmness, hardness and softness, form and expansion, cold and warmth, roughness and smoothness, movement and rest, tickle and itching, burning, pricking, piercing, pressing, swelling and tearing. All of this also depends upon the impression of the moisture and dryness upon the warts of feeling, and the nearness and distance thereof.

In the case of hardness, it is the resistance, smoothness or softness, how much it yields, and by the roughness and unevenness of the touching parts. When something is smooth, the warts of feeling are being touched evenly and all over.

Tickling is a soft and gentle, more sustained touch of the more sensitive open warts which are not toughened up. Itching is an unpleasant, changing irritation.

When something pierces and presses, it causes an injury to the nerves, either to a more or lesser degree.

Out of what has been said, you can draw the following conclusions:

1. Any feeling depends upon how the warts of feeling are being touched.

2. Every sense consists of the feeling you experience, may it be a feeling you have with your eyes, the nose, the ears, the tongue or the hand - it is always a feeling.

3. This feeling differentiates due to the variety of the warts of feeling you have.

4. The variety or diversity of the warts of feeling cause dissimilarity of perceptions.

5. Out of this originates, that in accordance with the dissimilarity of the organization, the perceptions differ, therefore, one person likes what the other dislikes.

6. The same type of warts of feeling bring about the same feelings and perceptions.

7. Through changes in the warts of feeling, the feelings and perceptions change.

8. Changes in the warts of feeling are essential or coincidental.

9. It is essential in accordance with the condition of the structure of the parts, coincidental in accordance with the change.

10. This change can be external or internal.

11. External, when the warts of feeling change through external influences or objects. Internal, when they change through the liquids in the body and the blood, the warts of feeling are given a different direction, for example, ailments.

12. This different direction which the feeling is taking, can be obtained by parts which perceive either naturally or artificially.

13. Pain and tickling can be accomplished through natural means or objects.

14. If pain can be triggered naturally, it can be artificially silenced through proper treatment. Even in an indifferent person, feelings of bliss can be aroused.

The following is necessary to accomplish this:

1. Knowledge of the parts of the body which are most susceptible.

2. The manner of their receptivity towards perceptions and feelings.

3. Knowledge in regards to the condition of their structure and their connection to the rest of the nerves and fibres.

4. The measure of shock they can endure. Knowledge of the relationship in proportion to the effective force of perception in proportion to the suffering parts.

Nature has hidden many great secrets in its workshop. The person who explores Nature opens the workshop of Nature, and Nature rewards such a person with exalted feelings. The pain subsides, joy becomes more joyful, bliss becomes more blissful. Through the

146

rapture (Taumel) of the highest of feelings, Nature knows how to place him into the gentlest of vibrations, to tune the highest tone of perception even higher. In other words, Nature places him into a new world of feelings. He drinks out of Nature's hand the cup of nectar of elysium to the last drop.

This is enough of an explanation!

These morsels or delicacies of Philosophy are only for its favourite sons. For the rest of the human race they are strictly secrets. It would be a crime to desecrate them by explanation. For those who can perceive what is being said, this will more than suffice.

The Theory of Feelings will explain the origin of peculiar desires and impulses.

They are mostly based in the manner of our perceptions and the structure of our tools or organs of our perception.

Divinity has placed into the Nature of every Human Being an abhorrence for pain and an inclination for pleasure.

This was absolutely necessary for the physical self-preservation.

Human Beings, according to their body, are animal, and according to their immortal Spirit, are Spirit. They therefore have the double ability to feel and to perceive, namely the ability of perception of animal pleasures and pains, and the ability of feelings of the happiness and pain of the Soul. The last one is called feelings, in order that it can be distinguished from the physical perceptions.

Feelings is the state in which the Soul is placed to experience pain and happiness of the Soul.

Perception is the state in which the physical body is placed to experience physical pleasure and physical pain. Perceptions and feelings can unite in the Human Being and very often physical perception can change over to feelings of the Soul. Examples of this are soft and gentle moods such as friendship and love.

Feelings of the Soul can very often change into physical perceptions. Examples of this are melancholy and people who are in love. In such a state, the feelings of the Soul can be the cause of painful physical perceptions.

Physical perception can outweigh, in the case of a weak Soul, the feelings of the Soul, and in the case of a very strong Soul, the feelings of the Soul can outweigh the physical perception.

The Virtuous One is strong when misfortune strikes, patient when he is in pain, and steadfast in death.

Every Human Being searches for happiness, but with one difference - one seeks true happiness and the other false happiness.

True happiness consists of true feelings of the Soul; false

happiness consists of mere sensuous perceptions.

The Animal Human Being searches only for sensuous perceptions; the Spiritual Human Being searches for the exalted feelings of the Soul.

Intelligence leads us to the feelings of the Soul and to understanding. As long as we do not have this ability, we adhere to the carnal sensuousness, one more, the other less.

To maintain the physical body, a certain degree of consumption of sensuous pleasures is required, but the amount of these pleasures should follow the guideline of reason and be within God's Laws.

You will mostly find that carnal sensuousness usually has the upper hand as far as Human Beings are concerned. The reason for this is that most Human Beings do not know what real and true happiness is, therefore, they look for it where they think that they can find it in their physical perceptions.

The origin for this lies within their natural depravity, in their inclination for evil, which mankind has by birth. This is partly due to external causes such as a bad upbringing, absence of education, and bad examples.

Every Human Being also has an inclination caused by his own temperament. The structure of his nervous system is such that he is subject to certain passions, before he is intentionally looking for them.

The basic cause of such inclination of the temperament lies mostly with our parents, in others words in the blood; a form of inheritance as far as weaknesses are concerned, sometimes also due to circumstances, the disposition of the body fluids and the blood of our parents at the time of our inception, or the condition the mother was in at the beginning of the pregnancy.

It should be impressed upon every mortal that procreation of Human Beings is one of the most important endeavours of mankind, and it should not be viewed as a mere animal tickle, but should lead to one of the most exalted feelings.

Parents do have certain duties as far as children are concerned, but it is necessary to provide for them before they are born, for their welfare, because of tradition.

The holiest of all religions united Human Beings for this end purpose through the sacrament of marriage. The commandment is moderation, reasonable abstinence and clean morals.

The curse of mankind is upon those who produce children in a senseless rage, when the blood is infested with greed or revenge, when love is experienced only when intoxicated, or those who only embrace their spouse when his stomach is full of food and drink.

It is within the nature of Human Beings, in their body-build and in the manner in which they were procreated, that sick Human Beings produce sick children, and as it is with the physical ailments, so is it with the ailments of the Soul.

That is the reason for the diversity among children, even if the parents are the same.

It can happen that good parents have evil children. That does not mean that the seed of evil passions was there from birth. It is also possible that this can be done through upbringing and education and they can be lead astray through examples. It is certain that even the best Human Being has his passionate hours, and after an hour of this, when a Human Being is in such a state, he should refrain from embracing his spouse in such an unholy hour, for mankind's sake.

However, when your heart is full of noble feelings, when you have done something great for mankind, when your inner consciousness of the greatness of your Soul fills your heart, only then should the Genius of Mankind lead you into the embrace of your gentle spouse and then heaven will reward you with children which are worthy of you.

As the basic cause depends upon the vibration of our nerves to lead to passionate perceptions at the moment of conception, they can even more so be caused by the coincidental circumstances the mother finds herself in, especially in the beginning of the pregnancy.

We know that before the embryo forms, the substance the future Human Being is made of is a form of tissue of finer nerves. These fine tissues which, little by little, develop into a Human Being, are capable of all impressions of perceptions of the mother. It is therefore her duty that she cares for the present and future moral condition as well as her physical well-being.

43. To The Seekers.

The present change in the world situation also has an effect on the minutest part, even to the last link. The more you take an active part in the fate of many Human Beings, the greater is the effect. Before any changes become noticeable, a total standstill has to be achieved, only then can a different direction be taken.

God's Laws cannot be cancelled because of some inconveniences; they also cannot be moved aside for a moment, otherwise all order in Nature would cease to exist. Then there would be nothing but chaos. To establish order, chaos has to be eliminated and not the order. Cleansing means elimination. The goal is clearness, not pollution and disorder.

The reward for God's Servant of Health is the health of the patient, not personal gain. Two people cannot harvest and eat the same apple. They could share the apple, but that would be something half and not something whole. Being partly healthy is of course not totally healthy. God is Perfection, and God's Laws serve perfection.

God's Love is perfection and it does not contain any other characteristics. The understanding of this leads Human Beings to perfection. When a Human Being is not willing to walk this path, then his characteristics remain imperfect and not pure. That then becomes the reason for all his ailments on all three planes.

Love cannot be harvested where no Love has been sown. Human Beings are the only beings who have been given the possibility to plant on Earth and to harvest in Heaven, because divine fruit does not ripen on Earth, but only in Heaven.

Earthly rewards are transitory; divine rewards are everlasting.

Anguish of the Soul is an earthly ailment - decisions on the side of earthly wants, earthly passions and cravings. Earthly power is at heavenly expense. Heaven's harvest is the price which has to be paid - an exchange of Gold for Iron.

The choice of how he chooses to spend his harvest is left to the individual. He can leave it in heaven for eternity, or he can spend it on Earth for just a passing moment. Human Beings can use this harvest for blessings or for the destruction of their own being or that of others. God's gift to Human Beings was a consciousness, a conscientiousness, and a choice. The choice gives Human Beings the possibility to sow something good or something bad - the harvest will be accordingly.

The consciousness tells Human Beings what is good and what is bad, and the conscientiousness must live with the harvest. Should a Human Being's conscience become accustomed to evil, then we are dealing with an evil Human Being, because little by little this Human Being accepts evil as good, when evil takes the upper hand. The greatest conflict appears when he is in the middle between good and evil. That is the point where it is impossible to differentiate good from evil. When someone is in this situation, only Belief in God can point this Human Being in the right direction.

44. About Passions And The Necessity Of The Study Of The Knowledge Of Human Nature For Those Who Want To Progress In The Discovery Of Philosophy.

The more intense inclinations and eruptions of the Soul which flow out of the temperament are emotions, and when they become effective, they are called passions.

Emotions and passions differ only by a degree. Passions are nothing but one or more emotions put into practice.

Passions are the result of sensuous desires or sensuous abhorrence brought to a noticeable degree.

The effect of passions on Human Beings is manifold. It is absolutely necessary for the explorer of Nature to study these effects.

They affect Human Beings in the following manner: they can be pleasant, unpleasant or mixed.

The most effective ones are: sadness, anger, fear, shock, fearlessness, courage, longing, love, repentance, modesty, melancholy, boredom, an empty heart, envy, misanthropy, ill will, hope, despair, and hopelessness.

Every effect has its hierarchy. For example: Compassion or a misfortune are the causes for sadness. Somnolence and destruction of the Spirit are the inner consequences. Fatigue and ailments of the physical body are the external coincidences.

The Progression is as Follows:
Unrest, fatigue, repentance, down-heartedness, displeasure, to succumb (defeat), disgust, and total loss of all energy.

If You Suffer Because Other People Suffer:
Sensitive to other people's pain, loss of composure, intense participation, agony, self-suffering, fear, pain, despair.

The effect follows step after step; every passion has its degree. The hostile ones are as follows:

Distance	Abhorrence
Dislike	Threat
Disdain	Insult
Disregard	Explosive Temper
Contempt	Anger
Ridicule	Revenge
Antipathy	Rage
	Hate

Great secrets are hidden in the knowledge of the passionate condition of Human Beings. Those who know these secrets have a preponderate power over other Human Beings.

The knowledge of this condition, the change-over from one emotion to another and the consequences thereof is a necessity.

Only a thorough Philosophy, a carefully thought-out association with Human Beings, and a meticulous observation as to the motives for their actions will lead to this knowledge.

This knowledge has many great benefits. Within this sometimes lies the fate or the future destiny of an individual and sometimes that of a whole nation.

It is the Art of decoding human intentions, the unravelling of the most secretive of undertakings.

You begin this Study with a thorough, unbiased examination of your own heart. You judge yourself; you examine the basis of your own good and evil actions; you study all the passions of your temperaments, such as your favourite virtues, the errors of your upbringing, the influence of the climate, and all the natural relationships.

Differentiate what is your own from what you have learned, whether through upbringing, through education, or through circumstance.

Once we understand our own feelings and from where they originate, then we can begin to understand others and why they act the way they do. However, a serene Soul is required, one that is distant from all hostile passions, otherwise we will draw the wrong conclusions.

In order to study or to understand a Human Being, observe him in his environment when he is subjected to different passions; observe his train of thought, his ideas. Examine the cause and effect all of this has on his composure, and how it affects his emotions.

Also observe how the climate, the air, the nourishment, the temperament, his station in life, and how his profession affects that particular person.

Observe such a Human Being when his passions consume him and when he is calm. Then analyze his actions into the minutest parts.

You then add the reason for his behaviour and subtract the necessary and coincidental consequences. In this manner you will eventually be able to understand Human Beings.

This Study is very important for your own good. It is, however, sad when you are sensitive, when you get to know the noblest of all creatures, Human Beings. When you observe all the glorious abilities,

152

and then you also observe how his passions deform him.

Only through this knowledge will the pride of Human Beings disappear. You become aware of the misconceived dallying of the world; you recognize fraud, deceit and trickery; you realize what is true happiness and what is false happiness. Eventually you will find that nothing is really of any value unless it is that which assimilates you with the Divinity and brings you closer to your eternal destiny.

The result of this is that you become separated from the rest of mankind, however, you are not a misanthropist. You feel sad for the great majority of Human Beings who know so little about the value of their destiny, but you never judge or hate such a person. You respect every Human Being as a Child of God. You regard every Human Being as an equal, even if he stands on the lowest step on the ladder of bliss.

You make allowances for the shortcomings of others - to be more precise, your own shortcomings. In other words, this knowledge is one of the most exalted. It reveals all the Secrets of the Real Truth.

The Bible expresses it in these words:

"Judge not, lest thou be judged."

"The Sins thou dost condemn in thy fellow creatures, were once thine, and, if thou shalt condemn the doer, they may become thine again."

"That thou judgest, thou art not past danger of committing."

"Pity them, deplore their error, but if thou condemn them, thou will not follow Him, who said 'neither do I condemn thee; go and sin no more'."

45. Psychological Secrets Or The Science Of The Sibyllisus.

The following belong to the secrets of Psychology:

1.   To predict a future course of action of a particular Human Being or Human Beings.

2.   To have knowledge of all their secret projects.

3.   To unravel their pretences.

4.   To have knowledge of their train of thought.

5.   The Art, under some circumstances, of knowing the most secret or concealed thoughts.

6.   To know the results of their actions and consequences.

7.   The equation of the combating and unified moral forces.

8.   The result of all the effects in the future.

This is called the psychological secrets, or the Science of the Sibyllines.

As there is a relationship between a unit and the first number, there is also a relationship between the condition of a Human Being and the impressions of passions. If he is indifferent, the condition becomes that which is added.

Three and four are self-sufficient substances, where three has three units and four has four units. Added up however, they make a third substance, which is seven.

Therefore, Affect (influence) and the Soul are separate substances, but if they are compounded out of necessity, they become a third different substance which, psychologically calculated, is called a passion.

As the result of an arithmetic addition relates to the nature of the numbers which are employed, therefore, the relationship in a psychological calculation is the sum of the passions in accordance to the quantum of the effects and the units.

Since it is necessary with every arithmetic progression to know the nature of the numbers and the units, and also their relationship to others, it is therefore necessary for psychological calculations to have knowledge of Human Beings and their organization: the relationship of the Affects.

For example: If I show a child something sparkling, how will the child react?

Calculation:

The Child's Soul	1
Senses	2
Object	3
2 + 3 make	5

Senses and Object produce Desire. If I add five and one, the third number is six. When you add Desire to the Soul of the Child, you have a third Product, namely the expression of want.

If I now indicate the expression of want, which here is the number six, and divide this into three equal parts, out of which the number six was made, I then get the product two, which indicates the senses.

If I now add up everything:

$$\begin{array}{r} 1 \\ 2 \\ 3 \\ \underline{6} \end{array}$$

Sum   12

This then is the result of this calculation.

The expression of the desire for the sparkling object through the senses, therefore, results as twelve, as the child is reaching for the sparkling object.

That is how a psychological theme is formed or founded, through addition, and rectified through subtraction.

Everything is founded through relationships, however, the results depend upon the Art, the ability, to place these relationships into the proper sequence.

Nothing is more conspicuous than maintaining that you know the most inner secret thoughts of Human Beings, yet, this science lies within Nature. It is based on theory of knowing pretence.

Study the temperament of a Human Being and his favourite passions. Consider his education, his upbringing, the strength of his moral character, and his weakness. Study the expressions of his most intense passions and the reaction of these in his face.

Observe Human Beings when they do the most unimportant things or when they pretend to deceive others. When you have a conversation, observe if his demeanour, his facial expression, and the tone of his voice are in harmony with the words he speaks.

Of course, all of this cannot be accomplished in one day.

The great Science of Secrets is based on psychological relationships, and it hides the future to the common man.

It was the Science of the Sibyllines, and based on or in relationships, which is not applicable for things at random, but they lie in the nature of things themselves and have truth as their foundation.

The fate or destiny of a Nation depends upon this.

The Soul is not capable of deceit. Deceit and lies are the undertakings of the external senses. Those, who make an effort to study the Soul of Man, will find the truth.

There are natural relationships; the consequences thereof are of necessity.

To know these relationships, to put them together, and to find the product of this combination is the mystic calculation, or the Soul-Calculation.

Everything which happens, happens because of proportions.

The numbers of the psychological calculations are ascending or descending. They are at a distance from the unit or in proximity.

In accordance with this calculation there are: Emanations, Approximations, Assimilations, Equations and Unifications.

The Basic Rules are:

Reduce anything multiplied to a unit. Reduce every part of the whole to a unit. Examine distance and approximation, the corresponding, and those which do not correspond.

Prepare the multitudes and observe the similarity.

Subtract the assimilation.

Unite the assimilation and measure the force of the assimilation through the equation.

Ratify the measure of the force through unification or through the unit.

Calculate the distance or nearness of the approximation. Subtract what is dissimilar and prepare the product.

46. Special Feelings And Perceptions.

Feelings and Perceptions, as explained in previous chapters, depend mostly upon the organization of the body.

Nobody is capable of determining perceptions which are alien if he does not know the nervous system of a Human Being, the circulation of the fluids, and the fast and slow impression of things on his fibres.

There are perceptions and feelings which considerably exceed the ordinary ones.

There are Human Beings who have an extraordinary irritability in their nerves, and there are also Human Beings who possess the power of imagination to such a degree that it creates amazement.

There are Human Beings who can feel with such intensity that the whole world disappears in front of their eyes, and no object can make an impression on them, only what presently occupies them.

There is a story of a young man whose feelings were so intense that, after a long separation, he saw the woman he loved again, he could not stop looking at her. His Soul seemed to be her Soul. As he was sitting down, he placed his hands behind him, and a child poured burning wax over his hands. He did not even feel or notice it.

There are Human Beings who possess these very intense feelings of the Soul, but they are more unhappy than they are happy. This extreme tension can turn from hope to despair.

Whosoever feels Love with such intensity - how intense will such a person feel unfaithfulness?

When you are a true friend, how painful it is when you are deceived?

Certainly Nature, in its benevolence, will sometimes bless such a person with happiness, of which an ordinary mortal would have no conception. But do not usually the unpleasant perceptions outweigh the pleasant ones? The reason for this is not because Nature is full of pain and misery, but Human Beings themselves are destroying the paradise on Planet Earth, and they planted thorns where there were once beautiful flowers.

It is the endeavour of every Human Being to obtain pleasant feelings and perceptions.

Every Human Being wishes to repeatedly renew a state of blissfulness, yet, due to lack of knowledge, he attempts to renew pleasures, where he often finds pain; and in place of his Soul feeling joy, it feels sorrow and accusations.

In this manner, Human Beings descend deeper into misery - out of erroneous knowledge of true goodness. He drinks out of the cup of lust and even empties it, without having the knowledge that he was drinking poison.

God granted Human Beings the moderate enjoyment of sensuous perceptions, if this enjoyment is within the limits of prudence and religion.

Sensuous enjoyment in moderation gives us pleasant perceptions and the consciousness of the Noble.

47. *The Theory Of Pleasant Perceptions.*

Study the anatomy of your body, your temperament, the measure or extent of your feelings, the impressions of things upon your nerves, and the search for permanent pleasures.

Any enjoyment which turns into misery, is not an enjoyment; any pleasant perception, which repays you with regrets or repentance, is not a pleasant, true perception. It is only a titillating agony, a deadly poison under an attractive cover.

A true sensuous enjoyment which turns into a pleasant feeling in the Soul, and repays us with bliss, even when it is not present, is a true enjoyment.

Never let gratification be the end of sensuous perception. Unite the gratification of the senses with the gratification of the Soul. The enjoyment depends upon you and not you upon the enjoyment itself.

Those Human Beings who seem to enjoy happiness do not really enjoy it. For most Human Beings, the anticipated enjoyment is the termination of the actual enjoyment.

It is not the ravenously hungry who gorge the perceptions, who enjoy, but those who know how to savour.

Feelings of bliss have to be sipped slowly and not gulped down.

When the enjoyment of sensuous happiness creates a sensuous discontentment, then you did not enjoy it in accordance to reason and religion, because those two guard over your preservation, due to their laws of Love and Self-preservation.

Build your Soul on the proper foundation and first learn the most blissful of all feelings: to feel delight when others are happy; to enjoy delight when others enjoy it. Then the sphere of your activity of your perceptions increases; then your feelings reach the proximity of the feelings Angels have, whose blissfulness is nothing but true Love.

Make use of your reason, do not neglect the Study of Nature.

There is a Science, that your nerves are capable of a gentler shock; a Science, to transform temporary blissfulness into a permanent one; a Science which removes physical misery and takes away the power of the anguish of your Soul.

Study the causes and the consequences, the connection between the smallest part with the largest.

The link which connects creatures with creatures, Worlds with Worlds, Angels with Angels, and everything in its entirety, and its connection to the Divinity.

If you worry about the past and the future, that is the reason why you cannot and do not enjoy the present, nor do you get a taste of it in its total purity.

Souls which are in an exalted state have no such thing as past and future - everything is present. They feel today as they felt yesterday, and they feel tomorrow as they feel today. Their Souls are unchangeable; they are true, in the Image of God, towards which these Souls strive.

48. Music And The Power Harmony Exerts Upon The Soul.

The sound of music continues on through the organ of hearing, to the Soul of the Human Being, by means of very subtle vibrations and therefore brings the finest of fibres into a gentle motion.

We know that any passion, through a certain tension of the fibres and nerves, expresses an effect, and the Soul of a Human Being remains in this passionate state until the state of the nerves is changed through another shock.

This leads to the conclusion that music is the most effective remedy to bring about these changes.

The following rules have to be applied:

1. The Music has to be appropriate in accordance with the condition of the passionate state of the particular Human Being.

2. The changing, continuous sounds of harmony, bring about a change to the nerves, which are brought into disharmony through passion.

3. This change has to be slow. Anger has to be appeased slowly, and the changeover from despair to courage has to occur step-by-step in relationship and in accordance by degrees with the sounds of harmony.

You have to acquire this knowledge to reach a level of perfection in this Art.

	SANGUINEUS	PHLEGMATICUS	CHOLERICUS	MELANCHOLICUS
TEMPERAMENT				
ELEMENTS	AIR	WATER	FIRE	EARTH
COLORS	Bright and Illuminating	White	Color of Fire	Color of Lead
PASSIONS	Thoughtlessness and Friskiness	Indifference and Indolence	Quick-Tempered and Wrath	Sadness and Depression
NERVES	Easily Moved	Hard to Move	Rigid and Dry	Weak
FLUIDS	Pure	Watery	Phlogistic	Thick, Tenacious
BLOOD	Light Red	Watery and Whitish	Dark Red	Black
CIRCULATION	Fast	Slow	Uneven and Intense	Stagnant
IMPRESSIONS	Transitory	Dull	Fast and Rapid	Slow and Continuous
SOUNDS	Dorius	Mixolydius	Aeolicus	Lydius
INSTRUMENTS	Violin, Haubois, Piano Flute, Harp, Mandora, Clarinet	Organ, Fagotto, Viola, Bass, Lyre	Trumpet, Bass-Drum, Drum, Cymbals, Cenele	Trombone, Trumpet with Mute, Violin with Mute
EXPRESSION OF SOUNDS	Allegretto, Grazioso, Amoroso	Majestoso, Andantino, Andante	Allegro, Praestissimo, Furioso	Adagio, Largo

From the preceding chart, you can ascertain reliable relationships. When you study the passions of Human Beings, the temperaments, the tension of the nerves and how it affects Human Beings, and the sounds, which are subject to any effect. Study! - it is not difficult to give the nerves a different tension through sounds and this thereby results in different effects. However, you have to have the ability of sound judgement and knowledge of the changeover from one passion to another.

For example: When someone is melancholy, you cannot heal his ailment with choleric instruments. The intense impression would bring forth a very unpleasant feeling in his weak nerves. It is, of necessity, in this instance, to bring his nerves into harmony. Any mood can be changed, but this can only be accomplished step-by-step. In this instance, you employ the instruments under sanguine and blend them with the sounds of the instruments of the melancholic, and then, little by little, change over to the sanguine instruments only.

49. The Angel Of Light - The Angel Of Darkness.

Those who would like to dedicate themselves to the secret, philosophical sciences should search, as mentioned many times before with their own mind, and safeguard themselves against their own gullibility.

It is not a science when you walk the wrong path, and sooner or later you turn to superstition and idolization.

A Human Being who has no knowledge of physics, is very easily fooled by charlatans because he is unaware of cause, effect and consequence. Nowadays, since our pseudo-scientific community is not aware of it either, they belittle the Law of Cause, Effect, and Consequence. They might entertain the fact that one or two of these have merit, but never three, even though our world is three-dimensional.

When you find a Human Being whose knowledge seems to surpass that of the average Human Being, study his lifestyle and how he applies his knowledge. Is he a Child of the Light or a Child of Darkness?

The Angel of Light differs from the Angel of Darkness through Love. He unites the clearest and purest of Intellect with the purest Love.

161

The Angel of Darkness is intellect without Love. Intellect without Love is the characteristic of an evil being.

The Angel of Light leads to God. The Angel of Darkness distances us from God.

The Angel of Light teaches Truth, Understanding, Knowledge, Perception.

The Angel of Darkness teaches lies, falsehood, deceit; he does not teach any knowledge.

Therefore, seek the Truth in Humility and Wisdom through the purification of your morals, because it is the dress with which virtue surrounds us, if we want to appear before Him, Who is the Source of all Sciences and Knowledge, and Who is Wisdom Himself.

50. Prestidigitators And Illusionists, Swindlers, Tricksters, Impostors And Evil Human Beings.

There are Human Beings who possess strange, odd, peculiar, natural and wonderful knowledge. They can, therefore, achieve wondrous things, because the majority of people do not know the source or cause of their miraculous powers.

As long as this type of Art or skill is shown to the World as entertainment, or to create a surprise, and the effect of such skills are based on the speed of the performance, mechanical means, optical illusions, and secrets of physics, then if presented in this manner, this knowledge presents no harm to mankind. As a matter of fact, the opposite is the case. It sharpens the mind and leads to more and higher discoveries.

As long as those who practice this Art stay within those limits, many of them are excellent physicists, mechanical geniuses, and natural slight of hand artists. There are quite a few of these artists.

However, when these individuals overstep the limits of their knowledge and give whatever they do a mysterious appearance, combine religious rituals with their experiments, create misconceptions and convince individuals or small or large audiences of this with the intention of extorting money, then they become swindlers. Our airwaves are presently saturated with individuals who employ this principle.

It is true, that when I come into the possession of a Secret or Law in Physics, I am not guilty of discovering this Secret. I can even keep it to myself; I do not have to make it public, however, I cannot mislead people with a false explanation, thereby leading them astray, especially when it affects the moral state of an individual. Among these type of swindlers are some Order of Adepts - I repeat, some, not all. They are only Orders of Adepts by name, not in reality. There are many different types of mystic orders, whose ultimate object is nothing else but to have followers and enthusiasts who are blind, who they can use to execute plans to the detriment of mankind and nations. These Orders have been in existence since the beginning of time, and there are thousands of examples of such undertakings in the history books of the World.

There are, of course, also organizations who work for the welfare of mankind, who disseminate good morals, true growth and development of Human Beings, and whose reason is Love and whose goal is a blissful state of mankind.

Secret Orders consist of deceivers and people who are being deceived. Sometimes they are one and the same person. Let this serve as a warning to those hopefuls who expect to obtain these secrets by joining such an Order. There is a great difference between "secret" and "hidden". Anything which carries the name "secret" should be suspect to those who seek the Truth.

People with the best of intentions, when they congregate for the purpose of doing good, seem to very easily take the wrong direction with their reason and their imagination runs away with them. When that happens, it is detrimental to mankind. It could turn into fanaticism and idolization, or it could be philosophical or religious by nature.

Through this, you can very easily become excessively self-important. This fosters the belief that you are better than other Human Beings; you start to despise other Human Beings and eventually persecute them.

Philosophical Orders or organizations now persecute, as religious orders once did and still do.

The Monk Passier argued that those Brothers who wore round monkshoods were the right ones, and was against those in his Order who wore pointed hoods. He, therefore, killed those who wore pointed hoods and actually believed he did a wonderful thing by saving mankind from the pointed hoods.

Any organization that withdraws from the scrutiny of the State or has more power than the State, demands blind obedience, draws enthusiasts and day-dreamers, and chains people into meaningless oaths and rituals, persecute and suppress, yet give special privileges

163

to its members over other Human Beings and trigger, from the wrong side, self-love and selfishness. Such an organization cannot be good or become good.

Plans, new laws, legislation or moral codes do not make Human Beings happier. The happiness of mankind can only be achieved through pursuing Truth and Good, not only by having mere knowledge of it, but by practice.

It is regrettable that most philosophical organizations only endeavour to teach Human Beings the Knowledge of Good, and remiss to practice the Knowledge of Good.

The Christian Religion has the most beautiful basic rules of the purest morality and the most exalted philosophy. This makes it totally unnecessary to devise new plans for the perfection and betterment of mankind. Our only pursuit or occupation should be what Christ taught us, not through books, but through His own deeds, and to bring this into practice. Nothing more magnificent or marvellous can be said about this, nor can anything more magnificent be invented.

The great lesson of Human Blissfulness He taught in the open Temple of Nature. Everybody was welcome; nobody was given special privileges. His example was active Love, gentleness was His conduct in life, goodness and generosity were His course of action. He was not interest in or envious of vain or empty honours. He taught moderation, quiet contentment and humility. He knew how to save those who had stumbled, to forgive the enemy, and to guide those who had erred.

His disciples distinguished themselves by helping others, not through expensive possessions or symbolic signs. They did not wear unintelligible signs, jewellery or paraphernalia. The degree of human love reveals the degree or height the student has attained, and how closely he is in proximity of his Master.

The disciples of the true Master-Teacher of Human Blissfulness can be found everywhere. Active love makes them recognize each other. The work is founded in love towards God and towards your fellow Human Beings.

The transformation of their heart is their activity. To make it more beautiful, to make it a Temple of God, is their occupation.

The highest honour of mankind, the noblest of all missions, is the mission of a Christian. Where is the Philosopher who can give anyone a nobler mission!

51. Magic.

True Magic means the highest of perfection of Wisdom in all natural things and of all living creatures, and the highest science of the relationship of natural things.

The person who possesses this highest of perfection of the natural sciences, dedicates this to the good of mankind, and applies and practices this, is called a real Magus.

This science was known to the Persians, Chaldeans, Hebrews and Greeks. In India and Ethiopia, they were called Brahmans and Symnosophists. The Gallic had Druids.

In Persia the Kings were taught the sciences. In Platons Alcibiades it says: Those who understand to apply the Laws of the Land, there are four: One of the wisest; one of the most righteous; one of the most moderate; and one of the most courageous men.

The first is the one who teaches the King, Magic, the Law, and the Order.

That is the reason why the oriental Kings were called Magis.

Vid. Cicero in libr. de divinatione, et Coelis Rhodiginus.

Through man, even Magic degenerated. When Human Beings have a great deal of knowledge, but do not possess a good heart, they sooner or later use this knowledge for evil purposes. That is what happened to Magic, and magia venesica, necromantia, and black magic came into being.

Even before the great flood, Human Beings caused great harm and disasters with black magic.

After the flood, Noah's son, Cham, apparently had knowledge of these hidden secrets and taught Human Beings and gave them this knowledge again according to Philostratus, Plinius, Suidas and Birosus' writings.

Cham was the Bactrian King Zoroaster. On account of his knowledge, he was given this name by the Greeks which means "living constellation."

The Secret Sciences of King Zoroaster were written in the Hebrew and Chaldean languages after the flood, in the form of books, under the following title: Ezra-Zoroastres and Mellessars - The Secrets of Wise Men.

Picus Mirandulanos maintains that he read those books. So much for history.

It seems that after the flood, Persia and Chaldea were probably the origin of our present-day Magic, but only because they were known before Egypt for this knowledge. Even though the Greeks had

165

an influence on Egypt, it was at a later date. It could also be that the Egyptians deemed this information to be sacred, so they did not divulge it to anyone who was not worthy of this knowledge, whereas the Chaldeans and Persians spread it more freely.

However, do not attempt or expect to accomplish anything in true Magic, unless you are willing to work hard on a daily basis and become totally familiar with the theory; but, theory without practice is like an ocean without water.

52. A Guide To A Better Understanding Of The Authors Of Old On The Subject Of Magic.

Many people read many books. Some read very little and others do not read at all, however, it is most important that you understand what you read. It is too often assumed that you understand what you read. Many people even fool themselves into believing it is not necessary to gather knowledge at all, and that their intelligence is sufficient.

This is especially true in regards to the subject of Magic, which is the highest of all forms of perfection. Knowledge is what everything is based upon, and there is no other form of writing which is more obscure than the subject of Magic. Nothing keeps the mantle of secrecy more than this holy, secret science. To those who have the ability to read these writings, the reason is obvious. The reason for this is that those Human Beings who possess the true Secrets of Nature use the mantle of secrecy, so that only those Human Beings who are worthy of the true secrets will be able to understand them.

They copy Nature, which conceals the diamond in a cover, and leave it up to the artist to find it and bring out the sparkle. That is why the authors of such books purposely blended fable, superstition and philosophy with their writings. It was their thinking that those who are worthy of this knowledge, would distinguish the truth from the lies and the superstition from the philosophy. If the reader is not capable of this, then he is not worthy of these secrets.

It is also worthy to note that many Human Beings, who did not possess the slightest abilities, had the audacity to approach these divine sciences, and as a result, a great deal of nonsense has been written on this subject.

Many swindlers and charlatans have written books and given lectures on the subject, using Magic and mystical terminology, and have even approached such divine and holy subjects as Alchemy.

They even tried to explain the Philosopher's Stone. Anyone who possesses reason, which is cleansed of any prejudice, can easily distinguish truth from falsehood. You have no fear when you fear God. Hypocrisy is fearing anyone but God. Hypocrisy is pride's tribute to virtue.

The Study of the following subjects would be of great help in the study of higher knowledge.

1. *Natural Science.*

This is divided into knowledge of the Body and having knowledge of the Spirit.

The science of the body or Somatology, is that which determines the attributes of the matter and the order of matter.

Pyrology	-	Science of Fire
Hydrology	-	Science of Water
Aerology	-	Science of Air
Geology	-	Science of Earth-Elements
Lithology	-	Science of Stones
Botany	-	Science of Plants-Herbs
Anthropology	-	Science of Human Beings
Quadrupedology	-	Science of Four-Footed Animals
Ornithology	-	Science of Birds
Insectology	-	Science of Insects
Ichthyology	-	Science of Fish
Conchology	-	Science of Shells, Mollusks
Anatomy	-	Science of Detailed Analysis of Organisms or Bodies
Osteology	-	Science of Bones
Sarcology	-	Science of the Flesh (branch of anatomy dealing with the soft tissue of the body)
Splanchnology	-	Science of Viscera (bowels)
Myology	-	Science of Muscles
Angiology	-	Science of Blood and Lymph Vessels
Neurology	-	Science of Nervous System
Ophthalmology	-	Science of the Eyes
Physiology	-	Science of the Condition of the Human Body in a Healthy State
Pathology	-	Science of the Nature of Disease
Therapeutic	-	Science of Healing
Chemistry	-	Science of the Composition of Substances

The Sciences mentioned are no more than mere preparatory work. They cannot become part of you, but they can help you to distinguish Truth from falsehood, and help you to better understand the Secrets of Nature:

This also includes the following:

Arithmetic	Geometry
Phoronomy	Mechanics
Hydraulics	Optics
Catoptrics	Dioptrics
Perspective	

This should be absolutely necessary and finally, Metaphysics, which is subject to the study of the following:

2. *Teachings of the Temperaments.*

Teachings of the Effects of the Imagination. Teachings of the Effects of Passions upon the Soul.

Physiognomy.

Teachings of the Effects of Speed and Delusion.

Teachings of Feelings.

Teachings of the Senses.

Teachings of the Power of the Soul and the Imagination.

Teachings of the Interdependency (links) and Similarity or Sympathy.

Teachings of Visions and Premonitions.

Teachings of the Science of Things to come in the Future.

Teachings of knowing what thoughts other Human Beings think.

Teachings of the Relationship of other beings in the Hierarchy of their development.

The Teachings of the Temperaments are the higher Sciences or true Magic. The first degree of this knowledge would be a Philosopher of Magic. The second degree would be a Pansophist, who is a person with universal knowledge. The third degree would be a Magus or Magician, who has knowledge in accordance with God's Laws and applies this knowledge for the betterment of mankind.

Very few Human Beings reach this last degree, because it requires the greatest of knowledge of a person's weaknesses, and the understanding that nothing can be accomplished through weaknesses - everything is accomplished through God only.

When Human Beings lose sight of this thought, then the light in their Soul disappears and they return to the Children of Darkness.

Their concepts become confused; they forget all holy or divine secrets which they are not worthy of, since they are only reserved for those who seek wisdom with the deepest humility and a pure heart, which wisdom comes only from God.

There are many good books written. It should not be difficult to distinguish books which contain this information and those which do not, by using the knowledge gained in these writings, if they are understood.

Never forget, however, that Human Beings should be like a bee in this respect, which gathers only the honey from the flowers.

* End of Book One *

The Principles of Higher Knowledge

Book Two

Information To The Reader
On The Contents Of This Book.

Here begins the second part of this book: Magic - the Principles of Higher Knowledge. This information is intended for those who have read and ruminated the first part of this book. This book was not written for the impertinent, the doubter or the sceptic, but for those who seek the truth and who have the ability and the knowledge to do so.

When you want to calculate with numbers, you have to have knowledge of the numbers. The next step would be counting, then combinations of adding and subtracting, and from there you progress further. When you want to read, you first have to learn the letters, but, experience has taught me that most Human Beings want to calculate without having any knowledge of the numbers, and they want to read, without having any knowledge of the letters.

I am asking the reader not to blame me, when you do not understand me. The reason for your problem does not originate with me, but with you. I am not an inventory. I copy the oldest documents which are stored in the archives of Nature. Those who want to understand me, must learn how to read, because the inner content of the letters of my words are unrecognizable for many Human Beings. The key to decoding these words lies within the Soul of very few Human Beings.

In the Land of the Blind, one with eyesight spoke of the sun and was laughed at. In the Land of the Deaf, one with hearing spoke of the harmony of sound and was mocked. In the Land of the Odourless, one who spoke of the scent of a rose was treated with contempt.

There have been no changes in this respect, even in our present century in the Land of the Scholars. Human Beings insist on seeing without their eyes and hearing without their ears. Remove the scales from your eyes, and remove the waste from your ears which makes you deaf. When that is done, you will be able to hear and see.

Every Human Being should remember that a physician who is in possession of his reason, will first cleanse an ailing human body before he will prescribe strengthening remedies.

The strengthening remedy behaves in the body in accordance with the cleansing. Why do you belittle the healing power of the fever-barks (Peruvian Bark)? It is a wonderful remedy, but it will turn to poison for those whose body is not cleansed. Therefore, always cleanse the body first, before taking any healing and strengthening remedies.

It is an absolute prerequisite to have this knowledge: Before you can give a healing or a strengthening remedy, the body must be cleansed. Most Human Beings want the remedy, without cleansing the body. The healing power is only given to the remedy when the body has been cleansed. Cleansing is always first, then follows the stillness of the passion.

There are also many who want to see, but they have weak eyes and do not want to make use of eyeglasses.

Others drank vinegar and then tried to taste cherries and experienced an aversion. The cherries were not to blame. They did not think that they had ruined their sense of taste.

If you want to progress, the rules have to be followed conscientiously because everything has its laws. Laws are necessary relationships, since without them, the thing will cease to be what it is.

Nothing in the teaching of higher things is arbitrary; everything is in accordance with the eternal rules, the eternal laws. There is really no better example at this point than the following:

1 2 3 4 5 6 7 8 9
9 8 7 6 5 4 3 2 1

When you add any two of the vertical numbers, the result will always be ten. There are, however, Human Beings who want to change the order of things, and in spite of being contrary to all laws and their relationships, expect to have the right results. I do not know what those people should be called - fools or insane. When you want to play a flute, you have to learn the finger positions the way the music teacher teaches them; when you want to sing a song in harmony, then you have to modulate your voice either higher or lower, according to the way the song was written. You have to follow these same rules if you wish to play the Piano of Nature. Should you not follow these rules, then you will be an incompetent bungler, and the Sage will close his ears when he hears anything which is not in harmony.

I can say with certainty, that the Spirit (Mind) of very few Human Beings is ready or receptive to higher things. I was surprised to find that the number of enlightened Human Beings are so few, until these Human Beings themselves convinced me that it was so.

A letter I received from a man who read this book explains it best: How few Human Beings will be able to foresee, to feel, and to know how to make use out of the true sense of your work, and what the ultimate object really is? How many complaints will your Publisher receive from silly, impertinent Human Beings who, by reading this book, will not achieve the expected results because they expect to be Magicians by the time they finish reading it, only to deceive others and appear to be superior.

1. Nourishment For The Spirit
And Light For The Soul.

Nourishment for the Spirit is Recognition (Knowledge), because Light is the nourishment for the Soul.

Whosoever wants to nourish his Spirit must be hungry in the Spirit, and must know how to choose the nourishment for the Spirit. He also must be able to digest the nourishment.

What applies to the nourishment of the Spirit, also applies to the nourishment of the body. Sometimes even the best of food cannot be digested by many stomachs, since the stomach has to be strong to digest strong nourishment.

No food can be turned into nourishment for the body if it cannot be digested, and the finer substances do not enter into the fluids. Food for the Spirit does not become nourishment for the Spirit if the Spirit does not know how to digest it, so that it can become the Spirit's property. In the stomach, where the acid is, milk will curdle.

That is how food for the Spirit will change, in accordance with the condition of the Spirit who consumes it.

Even the Spirit is, of necessity, subject to dietary rules in regards to its nourishment. There are spiritual gluttons, where the food of the Spirit lies undigested on their Soul. Those who eat everything or mix many different foods, and digest nothing, will do great harm to their body.

Those who read many different writings and do not digest anything, do great harm to their Spirit.

The body does not live so it can eat, but instead, he eats so that it can live.

The Spirit does not nourish itself only to have knowledge, but he has knowledge so that he can live spiritually.

If you want to have light, you must know wherein you can find the light.

The Sage takes a flint and steel. The fool and a child would take cardboard and a red beet.

It is not enough to strike a spark; you have to have tinder which catches the spark. If you strike a spark and let water catch it, you will never ignite a lamp.

You will also not ignite your lamp when you use rotten wood, even though rotten wood lights in the dark. Everything requires the knowledge of the inner attributes.

2. The Glow Worm -
A Necessary Tale For The Seeker.

A lonely glow-worm was shining in the grass and its light caught the attention of passers-by.

One of the passers-by said: Look, there lies a diamond in the grass, I will take it and have a ring made.

The other said: Look, there is a light with which to light to my pipe.

When they tried to take what they thought it to be and discovered they were deceived by their own suppositions, they became very angry and tried to kill the glow-worm.

"How cruel can a Human Being be?!", said the Sage, "Can you blame the glow-worm because you are fools? Look at things the way they really are."

"This creature is a glow-worm. It emits as much light as the nature of its being allows. I will take it in my hand and study the greatness of its creation."

3. Seekers And Finders;
Fishers And Tempters.

Human Beings, who possess reason, seek to earn the secret, but the fool wants to tear it out of the heart of the Sage.

There are seekers and finders, fishers and tempters. The seekers search for the truth for the sake of the truth, and they find it. The fisher, catches the fish for his own sake, and that is how the tempters tempt.

The seekers do not employ an instrument to catch the truth. They search with an inquiring eye and a sincere heart. That is why they find the truth.

The fisher, however, makes use of a net and a fishing rod, and fishes in the waters of the
truth, so he can carry something to market and sell it as a rarity. The tempter is similar to the fisher. He imagines the truth to be a big park, containing the rarest of birds. This big park, however, is surrounded by mountains. The tempter is too lazy to climb the mountains to reach the big park, therefore, he places his nets outside of it and begins to imitate the birds, hoping to catch some of them. Once in a while, he is successful in catching a rare bird, and he immediately shows the bird and sells it with the remark: "Look at this rare bird, it comes

from the big park and the owner of the park gave it to me". He neglects to mention that he really stole the bird. As a result of this, people who hear this story become very curious about the big park, and begin to question him about all the other animals in the park. Since he never set foot inside the park, his imagination gets the better of him and he begins to describe animals which do not exist. At this point, even before he is aware of it, one of the birds he caught escapes and flies back to the Park of Truth, informing all the other, even rarer birds in the park, that there is a tempter who is trying to catch them; and for this reason, the tempter will not be able to catch another bird so easily.

4. The Braggarts.

The Path to the Truth is a straight path, and anyone who tells you that he rode on it on a horse, is a liar. The path is so steep, that neither pride or arrogance should make a Human Being dizzy.

Even the one who is dressed in golden robes and claims that the truth made him a gift of the golden robes is a braggart, because the truth loves simplicity and not pomp.

The door through which Human Beings enter into the Temple of Wisdom is very straight. Those who are bloated with arrogance will not be able to pass through this narrow door.

Also, those who will not bend and bow their heads, will not be able to enter because this door is made for humbleness and innocence.

Should you want to have a better understanding of the straight gate, the narrow path, which leads to the truth, the blissful life, the eternal life, the Kingdom of God - study the following.

5. The Path To
The Temple Of Secrets.

The Temple of Secrets is located on a high mountain, and there are thorns everywhere covering the path leading to the Temple of Secrets.

The inconceivable, mysterious height of the mountain is the reason why many people doubt the existence of the Temple of Secrets. Some think of it as a fairy tale, some consider it an old myth, and others believe it to be the Truth.

Pertness and curiosity urge many Human Beings to see this

Temple, but soon, very soon, they become disillusioned by the height of the mountain and they retreat, disappointed and dismayed by the thorns on the path up the mountain.

At the entrance of the narrow path stands IGNORANCE, with her sisters STUPIDITY and LAZINESS. They tell awful tales to the travellers of horrible adventures the travellers will encounter if they set foot onto this path. That is how lazy and fearful Human Beings can easily be persuaded to turn back.

Not all Human Beings can be so convinced. There are a few Human Beings on which ignorance attempts her deceptions in vain. They climb up to the first part of the thorny, steep path, and when they are about half way up the mountain, they reach a plateau on which they find the Temple of Self-Love. Next to this Temple stands Self-Conceit, Pride and Know-it-All, and they offer the traveller a cup, out of which he drinks his own Self in great gulps, thereby becoming intoxicated with himself, with his own "I".

These travellers then become so intoxicated with themselves that they imagine that their Temple, the Temple of Self-Love, is the Temple of Secrets and there is nothing, but nothing, above them. The inscription on this temple, the Temple of Self-Love, reads as follows:

The Sanctuary of the Wisdom of the World

Desires, passions and wantonness are the servants of these priests, however, those whose heart searches for the truth, will not find any satisfaction with this, and they will keep on searching.

A few thousand steps from this Temple you will find a very secluded little hut, inhabited by a hermit, with the following inscription above the door:

The Residence of Humility

The man who lives here guides the strangers to the residence of humility which, in turn, leads them to Self-Recognition. This Divine Beauty becomes the traveller's companion, and with her, he conquers the inaccessible mountain. Whosoever tries to reach the Temple of Secrets without this Divine Beauty, can very easily be misled by his Self-Love, and as a result, will follow the wrong path. His greed for knowledge will lead him to the Temple of Curiosity. The inhabitants of this Temple are: fraud, seduction and deception, the founders of most of the secret societies, and those Human Beings who search for the Truth and for the Temple of Secrets will, if they join these secret societies, be robbed of the ability to see with their Soul. They are then lead to the top of the mountain, where they fall into the abyss, or into the labyrinth or maze, in which they will walk in circles for eternity, without finding the Truth.

Humility alone is the best guide. This alone will lead the seeker to the Master of Teachers of all Secrets. This Master Teacher is the Pure Will.

This Pure Will becomes the friend of the highest of knowledge, and together they enter into a bond of eternal union.

The Seekers of Truth are invited to these marriage festivities, and the same union is awaiting them with the Sisters of Truth to strengthen their bliss.

Then Wisdom emerges, the most beautiful of all graces. Lovingly she waves at you and leads you into the Temple of Secrets, which she gives as a dowry to the Pure, who are her suitors.

6. True Magic.

The knowledge of the effects of the Eternal Light of Godliness in all created beings is True Magic in Theory.

The conception of this Light, or the transition from the intellect to the will, is True Magic in Practice.

A true Magus is a wise man, a Sage, who has the power to convey his God-given Light to others, and through the Laws of Assimilation, to influence others and to assimilate them also.

All Wisdom and Knowledge comes from above as the result of all Good and Truth.

The Souls of Human Beings have been created to receive the Divine Light, however, the manner in which this Light can be received depends upon the natural condition of the organization, and as far as the moral condition is concerned, depends upon the purity of the Will.

A well-organized body can, in accordance with its nature, come into various knowledge. This knowledge is an outflow of Light, but it does not become part of such a Human Being unless the Intelligence and the Will are united in Good and in Truth.

When the outflow of the Light of Godliness is without any reaction in a well-organized body, then it is called natural Wisdom. In other words, even though the natural understanding of a Human Being receives Light through his Intelligence, the Will still remains in the shadow and is without Light.

Since Human Beings, in accordance with their nature, are capable of reason, it is the attribute of this ability to be receptive to the Divine Light. This receptivity is in accordance with the nature of the Human Being, the same as the receptivity of the rays of the sun react in accordance with the body, which the sun illuminates.

Therefore, natural Wisdom is nothing but a borrowed Light, which will never become a Human Being's property unless he assimilates the purity of his Soul with the Divinity from where he receives the Light.

When the natural Wisdom remains to be an object of Reason and does not pass over into the Will, then it is similar to the top of a mountain, which is illuminated by the rising sun (Aurora) and glistens, but there is no warmth, and when the Light disappears, nothing but the bare stones are left.

When the Divine Light of intelligence (reason) does not enter into the Will with the greatest of purity, then it changes its warming and productive character and becomes a consuming fire. It can be compared to the gentle sun rays, which invigorate in the flora in the meadows in the spring, whereas, in sandy areas, the sun's rays consume, every flower withers and all the plants die.

False magic distinguishes itself from True Magic by the true Magician's Intelligence and Will, since they are illuminated by the same Light, whereas, the false Magician's Intelligence has only the Light, and his Will is in the shadow or even in total darkness.

The Intelligence is receptive to the Light, and the Will is receptive to warmth, because when the Light changes over from the Intelligence into the Will, it becomes very beneficial warmth; the same as the Good, when practised, turns into Truth, and when the Good and the Truth unite, they become Wisdom and Love.

It is the natural sequence of the Light, after it has been received by the Intelligence, that it is transferred to the Will.

When the Will is pure, then the Light changes into Divine Warmth. When the Will is impure, then the Human Being stands in darkness with his Will, therefore, the transition is a consuming fire, which ravages and destroys.

The pure Will joins the Good with the Truth. The impure will joins evil with falsehood; that is the origin of false magic and the abuse of knowledge, by turning Love into hate.

The purity of the Will is in accordance to the measure of Love.

Pure cognition united with pure Love, is becoming angelic.

Knowledge without Love is becoming satanic. Convergence vs distance.

7. Secrets Of True Magic.

There has been no century which has been as peculiar as the present one.

Many Human Beings occupy themselves or are interested in the secret or occult sciences. The inclination towards the unusual is extraordinary.

Everybody is searching for Enlightenment and Wisdom, however, the majority are searching for it on the path of unrighteousness.

There is only "One Path" to true wisdom and only the true Sage travels this path; he lives like a monk on Mount Lebanon or Mount Hermon.

This path is the Path of Spiritual Love, separated from the love of the world and self-love. The love of the world and self-love lowers the Spirit to the level of sensuousness. The Love for God and the love for your neighbour lifts the Spirit upwards and thereby closer to the vicinity of the Divinity.

The same as crystal glistens when the sun comes closer, and it becomes warm as it absorbs the sun's rays, that is how the Spirit of Human Beings becomes brighter, and his love becomes more active through the Divine Proximity.

The whole secret of True Magic lies within the laws of the divine proximity. The more a Human Being becomes assimilated with the Divinity, the more effective his power becomes, but the more incomprehensible his existence.

The proximity consists of the union of the Will with Knowledge or the warmth with the Light; Love with Truth. Wherever this union does not take place, true wisdom has no place to stay. Human Beings can have the ability to recognize - they can have the Light - but when the Light does not change into warmth, and knowledge-recognition does not change into Will, then the Light will extinguish as quickly as an oil lamp without fuel.

They are like trees who blossom, but bear no fruit, because the gardener transplanted them from the spring meadows into stony ground, where there is eternal snow.

8. God.

Incomprehensible is God for us in His Omnipresence. He becomes comprehensible through Nature, which is His organ. His

Being is Love. Nature is the interpreter of His Being, the herald of His existence. Christ said: The only ones who know the Father and the Son are those to whom the Father and Son make themselves known.

But, thank you, Lord of Heaven and Earth! That You have hidden the great treasures of Your knowledge from the Sages of the Earth and that You reveal them to those who worship You in the purity of their Soul, and in the Innocence of their Spirit.

Indeed, you cannot point out God with your finger. Certainly, there are no words to describe God, but there is a concept of feelings for those who are given the Secrets of the Kingdom of God; however, the Children of the World do not understand this concept.

God is Love. To be God means to be Love; His Being, His Nature, His Character is Love; His existence is Wisdom.

Between being and existence, there is of course, a difference, but in God, through their union, they are One, because Love is contained in Wisdom, and Wisdom is contained in Love. Love is the Wisdom of God and Wisdom is God's existence. Every flower proclaims His Wisdom and Wisdom proclaims His Love.

God is the Life and Source of all Life, because He is Love and Love is the Life. It is the warmth, just as Wisdom is Light.

The Divinity reveals herself through her infinite powers and in infinite ways.

Everywhere these powers proclaim her existence, everywhere she makes her influence known through the organs, which proclaim her existence.

God is the Primordial Power of all powers; the Soul of all Souls. Without Him, no Soul can come into being; without Him no Soul can function.

The whole of God's world becomes a kingdom of material powers, where there is not one thing which is not connected to another, because only through this connection and its reciprocal effect, all appearances and changes come into being in this world.

God is the Primordial Source of all thoughts - the source of origin of the power to think - whose Intelligence and Will are One.

In accordance to the eternal laws of His Being, God works and thinks to perfection on all things in ways only conceivable to Him.

His thoughts are not wise, they are Wisdom; His works are not good, they are Goodness.

Not through coercion, not through arbitrariness, but out of His eternal and His essential nature, He is the original, absolute Goodness and Truth.

Everything functions in accordance to a Principal Power, in

accordance to eternal rules of Wisdom, Goodness and Beauty.

This Principal Power, Omnipotence, is the Divinity. All powers and energies of Nature function through Him organically. Every organization is nothing but a system of living energies, who serve in accordance to the eternal rules of the Omnipotence. It is the characteristic of the Light, to illuminate; it is the characteristic of the warmth, to heat.

It lies within the nature of the Light, to bring forth; and in the nature of the warmth, to produce. The source of all Light is the Divinity, as it is the source of all warmth. Knowledge and Will are united in Her, as is Light and Warmth, Power and Activity.

The sequence of this unification is Love; her existence is Wisdom; her product is Creation - Life. Wisdom is what the Light of the Spirit is; Love is the Warmth of the Spirit. The attribute of the Light is to illuminate; the attribute of the Warmth is to bring forth. Illumination and warming-up are necessary sequences, orders of the Light and the Warmth; they are the necessary sequence, consequences of love and wisdom, creation and bringing forth (production).

The first work of Love, is therefore, Life; maintenance is the object of Wisdom which unites the Good with the Truth, or Recognition and Will, Divine Omnipotence and being active everywhere. Within the Wisdom, as within the Light, lies the Good; within Love, as in the Warmth, lies Truth.

There are laws under which some of us rule and others serve. The internal make-up of every being is unification with the same kind (homogeneity). Whatever is in opposition-separation; but eventually becoming analogous with one's self and then the imprint of your Being upon another Being.

These are the effects and consequences through which the Divinity reveals herself and not through anything else. Nothing higher is thinkable or possible.

Within the purest of recognition lies the purest of goodness. It is absolutely necessary to recognize the highest, the greatest good (possession = Christ) in God united with volition, which is the character of the Law of the Divinity, and this union is in God the Truth, and the product of this union is Love; therefore, Wisdom, Truth and Goodness, are the powers of the Divine Trinity.

The Father is, therefore, the most perfect Wisdom; the Son, the most perfect Goodness; the Holy Spirit, the most perfect Love, therefore the Trinity which fulfils everything, but in God it is still only One.

Every creation behaves according to this Divine Being because creation is the activity of love, type of divinity and life, therefore, God is in everything and everything is in God.

The Being, whose necessary conditions were never subject to any changes - nor can this Being ever be subjected to any changes - is Eternal. The attributes of Eternity are constant; they are unchangeable, everlasting existence; therefore, only God is eternal.

God is the Being who is in possession of the highest Recognition of all which is Good, and He connects His eternal Will with this Good, which is the Truth, and this consciousness enjoys that which makes up His highest of Blissfulness.

Power and Might are an eternal part of Him, as a Law of His Being. That means, the power to recognize every possible Good, and the Might to exercise every possible Good.

The power cannot exist in Him without the union of the Might - in God, they are One. It cannot be, to recognize the most perfect good, without wanting the most perfect good.

This unification of the recognition of the most perfect Good with volition is Divine Love. The source of creation and the determination of creation exists to bring forth Beings similar to God, and to lead them to similar blissfulness.

This "Bringing Forth" is what is called Creation. Wherein, from the largest to the smallest part, Omnipotence expresses Herself in accordance to the wisest and the best Laws of Necessity, in which any power in the Kingdom of Change is always new and maintained, and is always functioning through attraction and repulsion, through friendship and animosity, and continuously changes her organic garment, until it rises to the level of the most possible resemblance with the One Who is the Creator. Therefore, there is no death, no rest in creation; everything is continuous transformation, everything is an eternal endeavour towards the Laws of Necessity, which lie in Nature, which make out of chaos, order, and out of abilities which are asleep or dormant, active powers.

Any fear disappears when a Human Being, with joyful optimism, becomes aware of creation, where even in the minutest part, the whole God is present with His Wisdom and Goodness.

The Kingdom of God is different from the Kingdom of Time, in that everything which is possible is present. Whereas in the Kingdom of Time, everything which is possible has come into being, therefore, the "opposite" also belongs to the highest of goodness, because one aids the other and advances it to perfection, and through unification to similarity.

Unchangeableness is in the Being of Divinity. A succession of perfections is for the Divinity, an impossibility, since all possible perfections are already present.

God does not have a mere ability or a waning energy; everything is power and activity. A God, without a Being outside of Him, is as unthinkable as the sun without light. In the Being of Divinity lies being the "Creator", because creation is His Existence, His Life.

Everything which is possible is created by God, and everything was created all at once. The Kingdom of God is not subject to time. Everything is there, but everything tosses and turns through perpetual refinement, and changes towards God's Image, to become similar to God. Everything exists - the present through His Existence, the future in its source, the past in its activities.

On the whole, evil does not exist, only what we call evil, relative evil. On the whole, goodness and perfection for God and all Beings is outside of Him.

God is unique and eternal; the Being, whose necessary condition or circumstances were never subject to change, nor can they be now, or in the future. Therefore, this Being is Eternal. God is the most perfect Being, Who is infinitely true and infinitely kind; therefore, the Eternal Will wanted Him to bring forth similar Beings and they are destined to receive similar blissfulness.

Therefore, a simultaneous perfection, according to the Laws of Being was not possible for any creature, because it would cease being a creature and it would become God.

The Being can only have a resemblance, changeableness and a goodness in accordance with that. That means: A Being can only have a successive perfection, and within this, consists the Work of Creation.

All things outside of God are things which can reach perfection or levels of perfection. They reach this goal of perfection by becoming similar to God, in His Image, step-by-step.

The reality, which is outside of God, is called Nature. Through Him, Nature is alive, and therefore, Nature is His organ, and it is called the working force of the Divinity in the material sense.

The Great All of everything which is "Brought Forth", is the world, the Universe.

The World does not only mean our Earth alone, the seemingly present form of Earth; not only the visible solar system, but the world is the whole, the actual outside of God.

The millions of stars, and stars which belong to the nexus of the Whole.

9. The Human Being.

It is not the body, nor is it our shape or form which makes us Human Beings. The orangutan, the ape, the snowman - all of them have a shape or form. Even though they resemble Human Beings, they are not.

Intelligence and Will make out of the animalistic humans, Human Beings, because without Intelligence (Reason) and Will, Human Beings would be nothing but animals. That could be more or less according to the receptivity of his Will and the direction of his Intelligence.

Therefore, there are animalistic Human Beings and Spiritual Human Beings. Animalistic Human Beings are those who are lead through their Will, without Reason. Spiritual Human Beings are those who lead their Reason (Intelligence) through the Will.

Human Beings are in regards of the bodily (physical) organization, like the physical world.

The Spiritual Human Beings are in regards to their Reason (Intelligence) and their Will, like the Spirit World.

The animalistic human is a microcosm in the physical world; the Spiritual Human Being is a microcosm in the Spirit World. As the animalistic human is in contact with the physical world, so is the Spiritual Human Being in contact with the Spirit World. As the physical affects the animalistic human, so does the spiritual have an affect on the Spiritual Human Being.

The ability of the animalistic human to rise to the level of a Spiritual Human Being is a move which is within the capability of his character, and it is this which distinguishes the Human Being from the animal, and the existence of this ability, which is within us, is the form or imprint of the Image of God. The ability of the animalistic human to elevate himself to the level of a Spiritual Human Being is an ascending power, and this ascending power is called "Human Designation" or Approximation.

The necessary conditions, which arise out of the Nature of this designation, are the Laws of the Beings (essence), or necessary conditions. Without them, a Human Being would not be a Human Being, but only an animal, because a Human Being distinguishes himself from an animal by the ability which lies within him, namely, to act in accordance to his knowledge. Through this he becomes a spiritual animal; without this he would only be a simple animal.

The Soul and the Spirit of Human Beings have three levels to which they can elevate themselves. Through their Reason and Will, those who reach the third level of Approximation are the first Human Beings who are the closest to the Angels. The ability to reach all three levels of Approximation lies within the spiritual essence of the Human Being, in the attributes of the Will and the Reason.

Reason and Will have the one ability: To feel the effect of Divine Approximation. This Soul-Feeling is Enlightenment, or the ability of the Soul to receive the Light of the Spirit World.

The Will elevates, the Intelligence (Reason) enlightens; this is not done through your own power, but through the conception of the Light of the Omni-Bonitas (the All-Goodness).

This Light illuminates the Soul and makes her inwardly visible, but remains concealed to those Human Beings who have not reached this level of Approximation.

Through this Enlightenment, Wisdom comes into the Soul of Human Beings; everything physical and moral is revealed in its full truth; he sees the connection between things - the basic urges, the source, the effects and the consequences. With one word, everything comes into view.

That is why Wisdom comes from God. Even the simplest of Human Beings, who elevates the pure Will of his Soul to a higher level of Approximation, receives this Holy Enlightenment.

There is not much difference between natural Human Beings and animals (I Corinthians 2:14). The difference lies only in the ability to recognize the Good and to exercise the Truth. When this ability, to a more or lesser degree, changes to reality, then the natural Being becomes, more or less, a Human Being. Should this ability be neglected, then he descends in the order of levels and returns to being an animal.

This knowledge gives you the ability to measure all the infinite degrees from the most imperfect to the most perfect Human Being.

The perfection of a Human Being depends upon the progress. This progression takes place through the recognition of the Good, and exercising the Truth. This is the Path to Assimilation.

The recognition of the Good comes to pass through the Reason (Intelligence); exercising the Truth takes place through the Will, or the identification of the Good with the Truth produces the perfection of a Human Being. That is what connects Human Beings with the Angels, and the Angels with God.

It lies within the ability of Human Beings to connect the Good with the Truth. The organ which accomplishes this is the Reason and the Will. The actual connection of the Good with the Truth is called Approximation or Assimilation.

Assimilation is in accordance with the manner of the recognition and the Will. The purer the purity of the Will, the more distinct the recognition.

The reflection of the Light is in accordance with the degree of Assimilation. The degree of Assimilation stipulates the knowledge of a Human Being and therefore, he has the knowledge another Human Being does not have - but only Angels have, who are with the Human Being on the same degree of assimilation.

When a Human Being is standing with his Soul in the Light, he then comes in contact with those who are on the same degree of enlightenment as he is. This alliance comes into being through the Eternal Law: similar to similar, same to same. That is the reason why this possibility for a Human Being exists, to make a connection with the Angels.

Every assimilation works towards "Becoming One"; within this lie the eternal Laws of Assimilation. The effect of "Becoming One" is the organ through which a Human Being can be in contact with the Spirit World, while he is still in physical form on Planet Earth.

The natural has no effect on the spiritual, but the spiritual has an effect on the natural, because the stronger affects the weaker, not the weaker the stronger.

When a Human Being is standing in the same Light as an Angel, then his thinking is the same as that of an Angel. Similar to similar, same to same. This is the reason for the relationship between Human Beings and Angels.

The thoughts of Angels become the thoughts of Human Beings. This is what the Language of the Spirit (Spirit-Language) consists of.

As soon as the Will in a Human Being rises in purity, then what follows is the Knowledge (Recognition), in an analogous degree of purity, and the effect is the same among all of those on this level, because everything in creation is based on Harmony, because it is Harmony.

10. Light And Warmth.

When the Light changes over into Will, then the Light becomes Warmth. The attribute of Light is to illuminate; to bring forth the attribute of Warmth.

As the world-light illuminates physical objects, so that they become visible to the eye of the Human Beings, that is how the Spiritual Light illuminates spiritual objects, so that they become visible to the eye of the Soul - that is, Recognition.

Since a world-light and a world-warmth exists, there also exists a Spiritual Light and a Spiritual Warmth. The world-light is the cause or source of all physical sight, or the perception of the physical eye. The Spiritual Light is the cause or source of all spiritual sight or the perception of Reason or Intelligence. The physical warmth is the cause or source of vegetation and bringing-forth; the Spiritual Warmth is the cause or source of spiritual or mental bringing-forth.

As the Art with physical warmth in the desolate winter, while Nature is asleep, brings forth wonderful flowers in greenhouses, that is how Spiritual Warmth produces Human Beings with miracle powers.

As the warmth in the physical world promotes growth and gives life to physical bodies, that is how the Warmth in the Spirit World promotes the growth of the Spirit and the Soul-Life.

Through the world-light, objects take form in the physical eye, as the theory of sight proves; that is how spiritual objects take form in the eye of the Soul through the Light in the Spirit World and become visible to the Soul.

How clearly the physical eye can distinguish objects depends upon the condition and the organization of the physical eye, partly in accordance with the refraction of light. The clearness to distinguish in regards to spiritual sight also depends upon the condition of the organization of the Soul, and in accordance with the refraction of Spiritual Light.

11. Reality And Imagination.

Whatever appears to most Human Beings to be uniform, constant and generally common, is accepted as reality.

This reality is totally dependent upon our organs, in accordance with our organs and is, therefore, within itself not an absolute reality, but a mere appearance. With other senses, we would have other realities.

Everything which is contrary to generally-accepted appearances are called illusions, imagination, and optical illusions, and we do not think about them. We do not realize that everything we perceive, every sensory feeling, is an illusion, and not at all the reality of the matter, but the consequence of an impression upon our organization. Whenever our feelings do not generally agree with what we accept to be the common consensus, or what we accept to be the general imaginative faculties, is usually considered to be an illusion or an

190

imagination and within this lies great error and great misunderstanding. This belief is one of the greatest obstacles, as it prevents Human Beings from making progress in regards to Higher Knowledge.

There are, of course, feelings which are more subtle and infrequent or rare. They are separate appearances; they cannot be compared with the common appearances, but within themselves, they are realities, just as well as what we accept and understand as the common realities, because, in itself, everything is an appearance.

In accordance with this, the feelings of all Human Beings are measured, and there is never a thought given to deceit or fraud, which human feelings are subject to. Every feeling has its limits; the common human feelings are in accordance with the condition of their preservation.

We look upon this world as it appears to us through our senses, but the world is not as it appears to be. That which we call reality, is only relative to our senses - it is not absolute. This applies to sound, scent, taste, feelings, lust and pain, bitter and sweet tastes, pleasant and unpleasant sounds. This does not only apply to things, but also to the impressions of things, and their effect on our organization.

From this knowledge the following rules can be established:

1. When the senses change, then our presumed realities change.

2. The coarser the senses are, the more capable they are of accepting coarser appearances, and they lock out the finer ones or are not capable of receiving them.

3. The finer the senses are, the more capable they are of receiving the finer appearances.

4. The appearances of the refined senses consist and exist of necessity in a totally different world of finer realities.

When it comes to the development of the power of the Soul and to the perception of the finer senses, the same applies, as it did with the perception of the coarser senses. For instance: What would a Human Being know or experience, if he would have only the sense of sight? He would be deaf, have no smell or taste. What would such a Human Being know about the scent of a rose, the harmony of a flute, or the song of a nightingale? If there would be such a world with Human Beings such as that, then they would follow a system based on the following rules: A rose has no smell, a bird does not sing, the apricot has no taste. When a Human Being who possessed more than one sense, which included hearing and smell, would enter into such a world, then all the other Human Beings would not understand him. They would call him a dreamer, or even worse, because they are of the opinion that they have the only reality of things.

In reality, we live in such a world, because we judge everything according to our senses, and insist on explaining or dismissing all appearances, depending on our perception of it. Should we not instead at least endeavour to think about these things, and consider that the possibility exists, that we cannot feel with our coarser senses, but that they are a reality of our finer organization.

Ordinarily, we judge things in accordance with the perception of our senses. We see a rose, we judge the rose as such, in accordance to the impression it leaves on our eyes, and on our sense of smell. However, if there would be a human eye which, by looking at a rose, would discover a thousand different things contained therein - which we were unable to discover - what would our world say when they encountered a Human Being with these capabilities?

What would they say and what would they do? It would be handled in the same manner as all such things are handled, especially in our times, the times of the so-called scientific achievements: First, they would try to explain it in accordance with accepted rules such as: doubting, erring, bickering, disagreement, rejection, overruling, dismissing, and repudiating. The Rules of the Ignorant would be applied as they have been practised by Human Beings since their existence, but never more so than now, because Human Beings have never been as ignorant as they are today.

12. A Treatise Regarding
The Human Body - Somatology.

Nothing consumes: The parts one body loses, another body assumes. This surrender or release of the bodies and the acceptance of other bodies makes the life of things. Everything is, therefore, only change, nothing is dead. With every change, there has to be a body present which accepts the release of parts of another body.

The recipient is usually the air. The air accepts the parts of most bodies in accordance with the form or shape of the circumstances, and then in turn, imparts it to the other bodies.

There are, of course, other bodies which do accept and those which do not, and through this acceptance and non-acceptance, the attractive and the repulsive powers come into being.

Everything in Nature has its measure and its equilibrium. Whenever this measure, this equilibrium, is destroyed, then everybody seeks to unload its excess or seeks to replace its departure. The ones, who have too little, attract those who have too much, reject, and do not accept any more.

When there is no body available which accepts parts that are given up by another body, then no changes can take place in the body which is giving.

13. Exaltation And Enhancement
Of The Spirit.

Any Vital Force, may it be on a lower or higher degree, is capable of exaltation, and every exaltation is Assimilation towards the Spirit, and has a higher power.

Any exaltation, or raising of the Vital Power changes fundamentally the internal body, and its consequence is refinement, and its effect on similar refinements.

We find proof of this in electricity. Through the friction of bodies, the internal power of the bodies become exalted and the body, which is electric, has an effect on others and sets the internal powers of other bodies into motion.

This can also be observed when it comes to the coarser organizations. For example, in the instance of melting metals, which is nothing else but a work of exaltation of the finer internal spirits which lie hidden under the coarser shell. Since the warmth is assimilated by the inner spirits to a great degree, the inner spirits exalt, expand, and without breaking through the body particles in which they are confined, they assimilate in this manner and become soft.

As long as the exaltation lasts, that is, the duration, or how long the change of the condition of the body lasts, the body will return to its previous condition. But that depends upon the degree of release in accordance with the cause of the exaltation; in this instance, it was the warmth.

The relationship of the exaltation of the inner powers progresses step-by-step through infinite modifications from the coarsest to the finest of bodies. This also applies to sound, which behaves in the same manner, after a string is heightened or exalted.

Lesser or higher tensions, which are not in accordance with the nature of the string, result in dissonance, but should they be in the proper ratio to the whole, then the result is harmony.

All works of the Spirit (Mind) such as: writing, poetry, eloquence, powers of persuasion, the ability to touch the emotions of others, are consequences of the exaltation of the inner Vital Forces. This is why the following sentence states a universal truth: If you want me to cry, you cry first.

That also includes the tremendous force of passions; the effect of gentle feelings which, through the inner, exalted life-forces, assimilate others, and through this, are being set into motion.

The greatest Secrets of Magic are contained in the Truth of these sentences; within this lies the Theory of Effect and Consequence.

The every-day Human Being experiences the exaltation of his inner power through external determinations, through which his Will is being determined. He sees, wants and demands.

The Will is, therefore, Soul-Electricity. The more the inner power receives through recognition, the stronger the effect becomes.

The expansion in the inner life-forces is incomprehensible to our senses; it is exalted life, exalted Life-Energy, refinement, Assimilation to the finest.

Recognition lightens; the Will exalts; Recognition (Knowledge) brings Light; the Will brings forth Warmth.

Knowledge changes through the Light; the Will changes through the Warmth.

In the Will alone lies the Power of Assimilation; the purer the Will is, the mightier its power becomes, because it changes into something more sublime.

The exaltation of the Will has its own gradation, its germination, its progression, its growth.

The more a Human Being cultivates his Will, the more alive a Human Being is. Cultivating your Will means to raise it to the most possible purity of knowledge or rather, to practice the knowledge which has reached the level of purity. Through this, Human Beings assimilate with the Divinity. Since this becomes power and activity, the Human Being becomes Knowledge and Will.

Within this lies what is commonly called the Rebirth of Human Beings, Spiritual Life, Soul (Vital Force).

Our future condition in the sequence of succession of progression behaves in accordance with the manner of this Vital Force.

This gives our Soul the organization to more or less live in higher spheres; within this lies our determination after our death.

14. Death.

Death is the transformation of the continuation of my "I", my Ego. Dying means to discontinue to see or to recognize here, and to continue to see, to recognize there. It means to receive a different organization, to change your receptivity, to see objects in an entirely different manner, to discard the external shell, and to penetrate deeper, in order to get closer into the inner of the powers. Dying means to be born, and to be born means to die; ceasing to be active in one form, in order to appear and be active in a new form.

Death is the transition from seeing objects in one manner, and starting to see them in another manner. That is the step-by-step progression into the Inner Being; a matter of a higher transition, a gradation in the sequence of succession.

15. Existence And Reunion.

As far as our "departed" are concerned, we still exist for them and they exist for us. They exist for us through our memory, and we for them, through something which is more than memory, and for which no special word has been coined.

Their "I" remains to be presently a part of the universe, even though it is beyond us. Everything is connected through the great chain of things and operated invisibly in respect to our normal senses, but it operates essentially.

Every creature is not just a spectator of the world he is dependent upon; the power lies within him to work his way up to higher spheres and the joy to look into the interdependency of many things or parts.

The departed exist for us through our memory, and we exist for them through "something", which is more than memory. It would be wonderful if there were a word to describe this, however, there is no word in the human language which can express this.

Memory is Soul-Reality; not a mere ideal thing, which is only a figment of our imagination.

Nothing is really imagination; everything is reality, but everything is not a physical reality. You must differentiate between the reality of the condition of the Soul and the reality of the condition of the physical.

When I think about a rose in the winter, then the rose is not present in physical form, but the memory of the rose gives me her real existence in my Soul. Therefore, remember what was previously mentioned in this regard, that even what we consider to be physical realities are only appearances of the senses, and these appearances, these realities, represent to our Soul that which they have always been.

When you think about a friend who is not present, then you are with him in your Spirit. Should the disposition of his Spirit be finely tuned, then his Spirit will feel your presence; only the outer shell of his body will prevent the physical unification.

We speak with and to physical Beings. With Beings who are finer than physical bodies, there our thoughts become our language.

These beings not only exist, they are with us, but our shell is not capable of feeling their existence. Only our Soul has the capability of feeling their existence and refinement. Homogeneity makes it possible for them to become visible to us.

Even when it comes to physical appearances, it is absolutely necessary that the object has an effect on us, and we also must be able to feel its effect in order to physically see the object. This is, of course, much more of a necessity when it comes to finer beings.

Every appearance, and that applies to physical objects as well, can only occur when the object has the ability to have an effect on us, and we notice the effect of whatever the object or the finer being might be. Therefore, to notice any appearance, the appearance has to have an effect on us, and we must notice or perceive the appearance. Who has the audacity to deny that things or objects which are outside of us, and are connected to the chain of the whole have no effect on us - that we cannot perceive their effect, and that everything belongs to the whole, the universe, and everything has an effect on each other? Certainly everything has an effect on us, and we can feel these effects. Perceiving in the physical body through our Soul is called to foresee. Perceiving through the eye is called to see.

Whenever a departed friend has an effect, and the effects are perceived by the living friend, for such a person, the "departed" has at times, visible existence.

16. Existence And The Shape Of Things.

The world as we know it, and its composition in our retrospect, is nothing but a mere organic appearance. The world, therefore, appears to be for us, in this or that form, with this effect or with that effect, because our organization comprehends its existence in such and such a manner. If we would have different types of organs, then the world would change for us and it would be a totally different world.

A Being without eyes would feel the warmth of the Sun, but it would not enjoy the light. A Being, who would have more than eyes, would see what we call the Sun as something that we could not speak of, because we do not posses the senses necessary for this type of perception.

With this or that type of inner receptivity comes into being for us the existence of this or that type of object, because the receptivity exists in the feelings of our senses. Whatever our senses do not feel, does not exist for us. Existence for us is only what our senses feel. Whatever is not perceived or is not sensible to us means that it is non-existent.

Out of all this we can learn that the finer our senses become, the more things exist for us. Also, our receptivity grows after this refinement, and we are able to see things which other Human Beings cannot see.

A new world comes into being for us, which essentially already exists, but it appears to us in accordance to our organization. That means, in accordance to our perceptibility.

Whosoever has keener eyesight can see objects clearer at a distance, which shortsighted Human Beings cannot see.

The same applies to the inner sight. Through the natural refinement of our senses or through artificial means, we will come in contact with a world which is totally unknown to us.

17. The Refinement Of The Senses.

The smallest separation of the Spiritual Human Being from the coarse physical Human Being causes, at all times, extraordinary and unusual sensations and effects.

In order to allow a clearer insight, Nature has means at its disposal which totally dissolve the close contact between the Soul and the nerves, fibres and the anatomy of the physical body.

Such an artificial condition in our life is of very short duration; the means to accomplish this cannot be found in the ordinary school philosophy.

Any exaltation of the Spirit enhances the refinement of the senses, because everything spiritual assimilates everything refined.

Everything refined comes closer to simplicity; all simplicity comes closer to the Truth, whose recognition exists on account of greater insight; the physical truth is the object itself.

We can see the power of refinement in the works of the Spirit, in the spiritual exaltation of the poets, in those who are seekers of truth.

Any exaltation is a multiplying Vital Force, and any knowledge is in accordance to the more or lesser Vital Force. Therefore, there is greater insight, and more truth in an exalted state.

Some people might get the idea that even fools sometimes enter into an exalted state, therefore, they also have greater insight. It becomes a necessity to answer this question so you have a clear concept of spirit-exaltation and the refinement of the senses.

Without exaltation, there is no refinement of the senses. The exaltation is therefore absolutely necessary to refine the senses.

Everything in Nature has its time and takes its time; everything progresses step-by-step - first germ, then flower and eventually fruit.

The exaltation of the Spirit has to be in accordance with the refinement of the Spirit.

The greater the refinement of the senses, the more they can tolerate a greater exaltation of the Spirit.

A sudden exaltation of the Spirit, without the step-by-step refinement of the senses, does not lead to insight but to folly.

This matter is easily understood. The exalted state requires the finest of organization, so that there is no difficult obstacle to overcome.

Should the exalted Spirit find any opposition in the sensory organs, then out of necessity, the Spirit will destroy everything in its path.

The most fragile glass will be able to tolerate, undamaged, the greatest heat, when the heat is increased little by little, so that the receptivity can be organically determined.

The sun rays are reflected from the hard rocks to torture the tired traveller, whereas the clear, pure spring accepts them contentedly. Here the sun appears in an entirely different manner, strengthening the weary traveller with gentle refreshing coolness.

The condition of the fool is exaltation without sense-organization. Therefore, the monotony of their ideas, the unalterability of a once-conceived idea, the cause of all this is the lack of fibre-elasticity and the lack of the refinements of the senses.

The scholar who studies much, exalts his Spirit many times, and he leads a lifestyle which gives him the momentum to be more easily receptive to impressions, but if he deprives his fibres, such a person is on the edge of insanity.

In order to have fine feelings, it is necessary to have a fine organization, therefore, proper dietary rules are an absolute necessity. This does not only apply to the outer, coarser organization, but it also has an effect on the inner, finer organization.

You never tune the string of a violin by tightening it suddenly in order to get the right pitch. This is accomplished by the tightening of the string little by little. There are also other external means used to strengthen the expansibility of the string, and you will achieve a height of harmonic sounds, which can only be applied for music belonging to the higher spheres.

Inner peace and silence of passions is of absolute necessity to achieve outer and inner Soul-Refinement, because any passion makes your senses coarser. There is a great difference between feelings and passions. Feelings are restorative, invigorating vibrations, whereas passions are destructive vibrations, which wear out the organization and through this, the organization becomes totally useless as far as refinement is concerned, because the inner senses become coarse and unreceptive.

Out of this you can gather and see the truth in the teachings of the people of old - the Truth of Morality, the Truth of Religion, their unfailing accuracy, and their greatness.

Passions are storms; curable is their shock. They heighten our feelings when we are at war. However, should they become more to us than just a passing storm, when they become one with us, and we make them our own, then our Soul can be compared to an ocean, where a continuous storm keeps the ocean in constant unrest.

Yet how much purer is the area of the heaven, how much nobler are the meadows and the forests there; the purer the Soul is, the more heavenly are her feelings.

The scent of a flower is much more aromatic in the mountains because the thunder clouds pass by below her. None of the vapours of earthly puddles can rise up to the flower. She receives the purest of dew and the first rays of the sun.

That is how a Human Being can be, if he rids himself of his passions little by little. Then he is close to Divinity. He enjoys the dew of his Spirit, and a holy fire enlightens his Soul and strengthens the Soul to incomprehensible effects for those children who live next to the swamp in the valley below.

18. The Inner Sense.

The centre of all senses, or the inner power of Human Beings, through which a Human Being is capable of feeling the impressions of the effects on the entire senses, is called the Inner Sense.

This Inner Sense is the pictorial power of Human Beings through which the different impressions, which come into being through the senses, are then identified and simplified and after that, they pass over to the Soul.

The Inner Sense is the interpreter of our Soul. Whatever the bodies speak through the impressions they make upon the senses, the Inner Sense interprets to the Soul in the language of the Spirit, or rather, the Inner Sense makes out of physical feelings, spirit-feelings, and out of temporary impressions, independent and self-reliant impressions.

19. The Life Of The Soul.

The Life of the Soul is made by the Will; or the Soul, which is in the Soul, is the Will.

This ability lies dormant within the Soul, since she comes into the world imprisoned in a physical shell and develops through the Inner Sense.

This Inner Sense gives the Soul its step-by-step formation (development). The Soul learns through the outer senses, everything physical first, and then through the inner senses spiritual volition.

Therefore, the Soul is immortal, because the Will is its life, and this Will becomes its property, which is inseparable from its being. She, therefore, lives spiritually, eternally.

She lives more or less in accordance to the condition of her Will, and her future condition depends upon this condition.

Knowledge (Recognition) and Volition are the first abilities of the Spirit. This is unified in God, but in a Human Being, the sequence is step-by-step.

Therefore, Human Beings have the power within them to recognize and to will, and this is the power which is expressed in the sentence: To be created in the Image of God.

God has the highest of knowledge-recognition, and as a consequence of having the highest of all Knowledge, that is the highest Good.

His Volition makes it possible to carry out this highest Good, and this, His Knowledge and His Volition, is the law as to the identity of His Character, His Omnipotence, His Omni-Activity, His Love.

The ability to execute or to carry out the highest good is the highest truth. That is why we call God: Truth, Love and Goodness.

The consciousness of this Omnipotence and Omni-Activity is the highest blissfulness of the Divinity.

To recognize and to want the highest good therefore requires creating Beings similar to God, and determining them to similar blissfulness, otherwise, the knowledge and volition would not have been unified in God, therefore, God would not have been Omnipotent and Omni-Active.

Out of the Divine Law of Being came into being the Law of Being of all Creation, which is also eternal and unchangeable.

The Law of Being exists so we can become like God, because in the assimilation lies determination (intended purpose) of Human Beings, the blissfulness of Human Beings.

In order for Human Beings to elevate to this blissfulness, it became absolutely necessary for God to give Human Beings this power. However, He could only give Human Beings the power which was within Him and that is, to recognize and to will.

This was the creation of the Soul; the union of Knowledge (Recognition) and the Will is freedom. To possess this power was absolutely necessary for Human Beings because of what benefit would knowledge be?

It is, therefore, possible for a Human Being to have knowledge and not to have the Will to want because of limited knowledge. God could not bestow upon Human Beings the highest knowledge because if that would be, then all Human Beings would be God.

Within the limits of our knowledge lies the lack or deficiency of our volition; within the deficiency of our volition lies the evil, the withdrawal (remoteness-distance), blissfulness and not being blissful, and the life and death of our Soul.

20. Punishment And Reward.

Essentially, as an eternal relationship, punishment and reward lie within the Laws of Being and the Soul-Organ which communicates this to us is our consciousness.

The reward for Approximation is clearer recognition with a better volition. When it comes to the opposite, then the reward is punishment for any distance or remoteness.

It is the determination (mission) of the Soul to become like the Divinity. Becoming alike is her element, which is her own, and her unification is her blissfulness.

All hindrances which stand in the way of this unification places the Soul into bondage and because of this, the Spirit suffers because he is being detained from reaching his destination, from his determination.

21. Being Blissful And Suffering.

The first Law of Being of all things is the inclination towards unification. This Law is an absolute necessity because within it lies the energy of Assimilation.

Without this energy there can be no life, no aspiration, no becoming alike.

Every hindrance towards this unification brings forth an aspiration to dispose of these hindrances. In physical things or matters we call these aspirations suffering.

That is how a dying Human Being suffers and moans for loosening, because his ailing body is still retaining his Soul, which is struggling to reach the Spirit World.

That is how the animalistic body suffers, when hindrances of the unification of the parts destined for separation takes place, and then this struggle in Nature occurs to remove these hindrances. This effort the physicians call fever or...

This also applies when it comes to the magnetic needle uniting with what attracts. This is visible and invisible suffering.

The magnetic needle suffers, even if it lies on a flat board; but its suffering is not visible to our senses, however, if it rests on one point, then it can express its suffering endeavour.

In Nature, suffering is coincidental, as hindrances are coincidental. Only where there are hindrances is there suffering. Wherever there are no hindrances, there is the enjoyment of blissfulness.

Therefore, only in God alone there is no suffering.

The more hindrances there are in a body, the less the body can pursue its natural purpose or destination in accordance with the Law of Being, therefore the more this body suffers. The less hindrances, the less the body suffers.

On account of these reasons, we have the proof that there is actually no absolute suffering, but all suffering is only relative (because all destructive forces are relative; truth and blissfulness are absolute), and belongs to the refinement of our condition.

As long as we experience hindrances, that is how long we will suffer. As soon as the hindrances or obstacles have been removed, then the suffering ceases to exist and we come into an existence of peace, of unification. That also leads to the conclusion that even finer bodies are subject to suffering. That is why the Soul can suffer, because the Soul can have hindrances when it comes to her unification.

The Law of Being, as far as the Soul is concerned, is her yearning for the Light; that means to say: to pure Knowledge.

Everything which is impure cannot unite with what is pure, because unification takes place only in Assimilation. That is why oil does not unite with water, or the water with the oil, because of the dissimilarity of their parts.

The destination of the Soul is the unification with the Divinity. To this unification belongs the unification of the Knowledge with the Will.

As long as that condition does not exist, a unification is not possible.

Any distance the Soul takes is Soul-Suffering, but it has to be from the higher Path to Approximation. Through this, the concept of the condition of purity and what is considered to be Soul-Pain becomes understandable and honourable, and you can see that religion does not teach a dream or a vision, but reality, which becomes more and more venerable, the more we become enlightened through the knowledge of natural things.

22. Revelation.

The news that the sun is a reality, is a revelation to the blind Human Being. Revelation is knowledge of certain conceivable truths, which are possible only when under a different type of organization.

Therefore, there are also truths in revelation, which we are able to conceive and they become clear to us, when there is a change in our organs.

It is necessary and good to make Human Beings suspicious of their present and previous knowledge in order to arouse their exploring Spirit, to unite what has been revealed with the reality of what has been recognized already, so that in some instances, the impossibility of the unification can be realized and through these examples, truths of a different and higher order can be surmised and suspected, so that the connection can be established between this new future world and the present world, and the start can be made while in the present world, to live for the future organization.

Living for the present organization is an animalistic life or a worldly life. To live for the future life means a Spirit Life or a Spiritual Life.

23. Physical Life And Spirit Life.

Human Beings have three lives: The physical or animalistic life for the present organization; the Spiritual Life for the future organization; and a median life, which is between the World and the Spirit Life - this life we call the moral life.

Within this moral life lie the Laws of Being of the future organization, or the Laws of Sequence, the Approximation. Whosoever cannot live morally cannot live spiritually.

Within every Being lie dormant, the necessary conditions, which prepare the Being for his future circumstances. The development of these dormant conditions are the abilities. The being of the whole tree is already present in the seed; but, the conditions lie dormant - they slumber - until the whole tree develops. This explains the parable of the mustard seed.

Everything that has a transition, must have a medium. Everything must have an organ, everything must have a connection, a sequence, a chain. That is how the Spirit unites the body with the Soul.

Out of necessity, every body must have a Law of Being, because it belongs to the maintenance of the body.

Out of this Law of Being originates the cohesive force of the bodies. In animals, it is the instinct, the driving force for self-preservation or self-love.

Self-love belongs to the animalistic organization, and it is in an animal that which we call instinct. This also applies to Human Beings who are more animalistic than they are spiritual. They act only in accordance to their instinct or self-love.

Human Beings which have reached a level higher than the animalistic Human Beings, or those who are at the gradation of a

Spirit Human Being, also have a higher level of guidance, and this guidance is Knowledge or Spirit Instinct.

The more self-love a Human Being has, the more animalistic he is; the more he rises above self-love, the closer he comes to being a Spirit Human Being.

The more a body has the power of expansion, the more effective it becomes. The more effective it is, the more it loves, the higher its Vital Force, the higher the Assimilation.

The reciprocal effect of the development to perfection is Love, or the force-to-be towards Assimilation.

The one body has an effect on the other, the more this body loves.

Even though this word is essentially the spirit attribute of the finer organization, it is also present in coarser bodies, but in a different form with different effects.

In every body lies an incomprehensible force of expansion, which acts in accordance with its refinement.

One should observe the force of expansion of the bodies in smoke, the force of expansion of gold.

The greater the expansion, the greater the effect; the more spiritual, the more wonderful.

The more noble a body is, the greater the force of expansion, because the sphere of activity is increasing.

Only in the expansion of the body lies inner life, vegetation and bringing-forth.

More refined bodies have more life, therefore, greater growth of the Vital Forces, from the coarsest to the finest, from a Human Being to an Angel.

This life is in accordance to the Vital Force, and the Vital Force is in accordance to the effects.

Therefore, everything has the ability to Assimilate. Out of the development of this ability originates the unification, the inclination and the aspiration for perfection or love, attraction to alike, and repulsion to dissimilarities.

In the Kingdom of the Spirit, this attraction also exists. Her medium is Knowledge and her organ is the Will.

The purer the Knowledge, the purer the Will, the greater the Spirit Life, the greater the Spirit Attraction. The lesser the Knowledge, the lesser the Will; the greater the Spirit repulsion, the greater the inactivity, lower life.

The Spirit, therefore, lives through Knowledge and Volition.

They are her Laws of Being and are inseparable. That is why the Spirit lives eternally.

Even in an animalistic Human Being, the Spirit has Knowledge and Volition, because his gradation is the transition to the Spirit Human Being.

Therefore, Human Beings have, even in that organization, the ability to live spiritually; but since the Spirit is imprisoned in the body, the Human Being receives his Spiritual Life only through morality, which is Soul Formation.

24. Soul Formation.

The first Vital Forces of the Soul first start to develop in the body, because the Soul begins to gather Knowledge and Volition on Planet Earth.

Sensory knowledge and sensory volition are physical life, Spiritual Knowledge and Spiritual Volition are Spirit Life.

When the physical body decays, it no longer has sensory knowledge and sensory volition, but its Knowledge and its Will are Spiritual. The Spirit World, therefore, becomes a totally different world for us.

To expose and develop your Soul on Planet Earth to Spiritual Knowledge and Spiritual Volition, is Soul Organization for future conditions, which the Soul expects, in the sequence of succession.

In accordance with the condition of this organization, this is how we will enter into the Spirit Life after our physical death, as our present life relates in accordance with our past physical organization.

A Human Being with two senses feels differently than one with five senses; the one with three senses is different from the one with two.

Therefore, the feelings are different where there are only:
Feelings and Taste. Feelings and Smell. Feelings and Hearing. Feelings and Sight.

And different again where there are only:
Feelings, Smell, Taste. Feelings, Smell, Hearing. Feelings, Smell, Sight. Feelings, Taste, Sight. Feelings, Hearing, Sight.

And different again where there are:
Feelings, Smell, Taste, Hearing. Feelings, Smell, Taste, Sight. Feelings, Taste, Sight, Hearing.

206

And finally, where you find all five senses together, you will find that the greater or lesser effect is dependent upon the condition of the exaltation.

Having this knowledge makes it possible to understand that by the changing of the worlds, the organization must change, and by changing the organization, the world must change also.

On top of the highest mountains, where the air is the finest, Human Beings with a human organization cannot live, whereas, in areas where the air is fine but still adaptable to breathing, it is possible for Human Beings to live, but they will suffer under such conditions, because their organization is not in accordance with the sphere in which they are trying to live.

This also applies to the Spirit World. Wherever there is more or less Spirit Organization, there is more or less Spirit Sense, or more or less Spirit Feeling, and depending upon these feelings, suffering and joy are experienced in the Spirit World.

When, in the physical world, only sensuality enters the Will, and the Spirit is not given the opportunity to Spiritual Volition but only the sensuous, then the condition will be one of suffering, where there is no physical world, because what exists is a perpetual volition without any satisfaction, and that is Soul-Pain.

The condition of Spirit-Suffering in worlds where there is a finer organization, depends upon the sensuous volition.

However, the progressive Spirit suffers of necessity, until clearer Knowledge changes the Volition, whereby he becomes more organized with the Spirit World.

25. Appearances.

Whatever a finer organization has, has no effect on the coarser organs, but, it has an effect on the finer organs, because the coarser organization has no perception of the effects of the finer organization.

In order to feel the effects of the finer Beings, a finer organization is required - a spirit armature, reinforcement and exaltation.

The spirit armament towards a finer perception is twofold: the internal and the external.

The internal is the spirit purity, because the spirit purity is spirit refinement or the refinement of perceptibility of the inner senses.

The inner senses in their exalted state, or when the external senses are separated to a degree from the inner senses, then the inner senses can see, hear and feel things which the external senses, because of their coarser organization, cannot. Therefore, the inner senses can see objects which the eye allows to pass through, but it will only reflect in the eye of the Soul.

That is how a sun ray flows through a glass unnoticed, but becomes visible in a mirror, which was made for the purpose of reflection.

Between the external senses and the internal senses exists an effect (action) and a counter-effect (reaction). The external senses filter the impressions of the objects until they pass over through the internal senses to the Soul, because every sensory feeling is an impression of the objects and true contact.

The objects, which come in contact with the internal senses without being perceived by the external senses can, however, through their effects on the inner senses upon the external senses, become visible to the external senses. Through the connection the inner senses have with external senses, comes into being the aspiration to communicate. This aspiration is the Power of the Imagination. The more active this is, the more effective they become, and project pictures to the outside, which become visible to the external senses, but they are still the pictures of the finest organization.

The whole Theory of the Imagination is based upon this, which is still reality and consists of finer or refined sight.

Through this, the Realities of Appearances can be explained, which come into being through the inner sight, and are brought forth from the inner senses, to the perception of the eye.

The principle is similar to that of a concave mirror. The object, which is not visible to the eye, is caught by the concave mirror; the concave mirror concentrates the simple impression of the pictures through its cavity and, therefore, forms or projects a body outside, which becomes visible to our organization.

This is how the inner senses function. They take a picture which is not visible to us, and reflect it through the concentration of the impressions upon the external senses.

But what do we see? Objects which are outside of us; realities, like the impression of a rose outside of the concave mirror is a reality, an impression, a true or real appearance, just as any reality is only an organic appearance.

Many who will read this explanation might come to the conclusion: If the picture is a reality, how come it does not remain when the picture, whose imprint is being formed, no longer exists?

The answer is very simple. When you place your hand on an elastic body, then the pressure your hand exerts is reality; when you remove your hand, there is not a sign of your impression left to see. The same applies when it comes to picture reflections. Study optics, do not indulge in prejudice, and then you are dealing with the purest teachings of the Soul.

26. The Power Of The Imagination - Picture Creation And True Appearances.

The effect of the inner senses upon the external senses is creating pictures or it is Picture Creation.

These Picture Creations are for the external senses, the power to think or Thinking Power. When the pictures are temporary, for the inner senses they become permanent. That is why the Soul possesses the ability to form, to produce images of external objects of the senses, which are not present; however, they are present for the inner Soul.

The Picture Creation is in accordance to the manner of our aspirations, the communication or the Power of the Imagination which, in an exalted state, produces real pictures externally.

All of us can remember circumstances whereby you think of a friend in retrospect and you can see this friend as clearly in front of your eyes as if he were present.

That is how our palate craves certain foods which are not present, and our tongue has an aversion to the taste of man-made medicine, when this enters into our imagination.

These examples give total proof of the reality of Picture Creation and the Power of the Imagination.

Therefore, there are false and true appearances. False appearances occur when the impressions of objects which are already present in our Soul, become visible through the power of our imagination.

True or actual appearances occur when, through the actual perception of the finer senses, finer objects (which only the finer senses can perceive because the coarser are not capable) become externally visible to our physical eyes through the Power of the Imagination and the Picture Creation by the inner senses. Within this lies the secret of true appearances.

27. The Appearances Of Spirits.

There has been no other century as peculiar as our present one, where there is so much written and spoken in regards to superstition and no belief, atheism and agnosticism, philosophy and nonsense, truth and falsehood, where the seeker is sighing for the truth in a maze of misunderstandings and errors.

The question is: Are there such things as Spirit Appearances? Is this possible, do they exist in the essence of Nature?

One person says "No", the other says "Yes", and the third person repudiates it totally. Then a fourth person comes along and reports a totally credible incident and makes out of all the others, doubters again.

The unequivocal statement can be made: Spirits do appear, and their foundation lies within the essence of Nature.

Whosoever wishes to understand the possibility of such appearances must study the nexus of these things, make all the essential requirements his own, and he will find the truth of the matter.

There are three different types of Spirit Appearances.

1. The artificial or contrived appearance, which is based on optical fraud.

2. Those pictures which are produced through the Power of the Imagination, because the imagination has the capability of producing external pictures.

3. The third one is, of course, the true, actual appearance of Spirits, which is only visible to the inner sense. Through this inner sense, it can be turned into a picture for the external sense, and then becomes a true appearance.

28. Appearances Which Are Being Produced Through The Pictures Of The Powers Of The Imagination Because The Imagination Has The Ability To Produce A Picture Externally.

The exalted Power of the Imagination produces pictures externally and the Theory of Appearances through the Power of the Imagination is based on this.

The question is: How can the Power of the Imagination become so exalted that a picture which now lies in its Soul, can be transferred to the external senses and become organic for the eyes?

In order to answer this question in its totality, it would be a prerequisite to make certain assumptions in regards to the different explanations as to the effects of the Spirit and Soul, and especially, we should reflect in regards to the might of retrospect.

The knowledge of the theory of the manner in which the senses operate is a must. This will be discussed in the next chapter. The examples are borrowed from daily human life and are taken from a collection of peculiar appearances, which serve this purpose well.

29. The Sphere Of Operation Of The Senses.

1.

When external objects produce an adequate movement in the nerves, and through this have an effect on the brain, then the Soul receives an impression accordingly. A blow upon the hand provokes a certain feeling of pain. The impression is that much greater, not only because of the greater preceding movement of the brain which produces the impression, but it is also based on the superiority of the present receptivity of the Soul. To a person who is totally occupied with his thoughts, the pain he feels from such a blow would be minimal, whereas it would be more painful to a person who is not lost in his thoughts. The statement cannot be made that the receptivity of the Soul is always the same, and what causes the difference depends only on the body, because for many other reasons a Soul could, through the perceiving of one idea, be prevented from perceiving other ideas. In other words, perceiving many ideas all at one time, which means to be infinite.

2.

As soon as the Soul has received the impression, then she does what every familiar substance does upon which an influence has been exerted by another substance. She acts in return upon the object of influence. When a sound penetrates the ear and is heard, then the muscles which tighten the eardrum are animated in such a manner, that their tension is in accordance with the sounds they receive. When light penetrates the eyes, then the muscle-fibre of the star of the eye changes. In the eye of a blind person, the light will do as little as it does in the eye of a dead person. At this point, the question might come to mind: Is it really true that in all these examples, the Soul

211

really produces the retroaction, and is it not really the body? In the first place, there is no denying that the retroaction could presently take place only through the body without the help of the Soul, but certainly, the retroaction is also in the Soul itself. In accordance with the previously established principles, the Soul receives, through the uniform movements of the brain, impressions in different degrees, depending whether she possessed at that time more or less receptivity, and if she at that point contained other impressions or not. The noise which Archimedes would not hear because of his preoccupation with his compass, would trigger the attention or make a strong impression upon an idle person. Would the retroaction be solely dependent upon the preceding movements of the brain, then strong, preceding movements of the brain on account of the Soul being presently distracted would have very little, unnoticeable Soul-Expressions. If that were the circumstance, then each and every time, if the impression would be weak, the retroaction would have to be extraordinarily strong and conversely, when it comes to very strong impressions, the retroaction would hardly be noticeable.

All this is, of course, totally contrary to all experience. The movements of the body, which arise through the Soul, are always in proportion to the size of the imagination, and that includes the disposition of the body towards movement.

This is even more noticeable when it comes to the Power of the Imagination. Through this, retroaction occur, as they do through the senses. The little taste-buds on the tongue do not only rise when you eat, but they do the same when you crave food, and when you imagine that you eat certain foods. If this retroaction originates only in the brain, and not out of the Soul, then the same must occasionally occur (namely, if the impression to an adequate degree of the preceding physical movement is being interfered with, and should the Soul be distracted or through other circumstances be interfered with), without all the desire or imagination of the object.

On the other hand, through the strongest of desires and imagination, nothing will occur, because when there is very little movement in the brain, the great receptivity of the Soul produces a strong impression. Many other observations can be made; for example, it quite often happens that epileptics who, through retroaction-produced movements, receive only at the moment when the perception comes into being, and it is often necessary to produce a passion, fear, hope, etc. They are not only increased or decreased through the imagination of the Soul, but are also revealed in some instances and, subsequently, through the perception, the movement of the body is stronger than the ones which provoked the impression in the Soul. All the preceding writings are being confirmed with these conclusions, however, it takes time to read them all and understand them.

3.

It is of great importance to look for the secrets which are within these laws, because the Soul executes these impressions in accordance with these laws. "No retroaction occurs through sensory impressions without the preceding movement of the brain, because no such sensory impression can be produced without such a movement."

The effects of the sensory impression are only noticed in certain parts of the brain; not all, but only certain parts are equipped to provide us, through movement with the pictures of the eye and with the feelings of sounds. Therefore, we do not experience the impression of sight in every part of the body, not in the throat or the foot, but only where the muscle-fibres of the star of the eye are located. We hear where the eardrum is located, wherever that certain movement takes place.

This part is without doubt the one which gave the Soul the impression.[2] This is a logical conclusion based on the nature of retroaction, which is always directed towards the foreign object which causes the influence.

This observation makes it very clear and teaches us, that the impression of wantonness arouses movement in that place, wherever the stimulus was produced; painful contractions in the heart trigger convulsive movements of the heart. If another part of the brain other than the part that caused the influence would be struck in a spot which is void of nerves or contains nerves of an entirely different origin, then there is either no reaction, or through the reaction, a different part of the body is being set into motion. Should the thought be entertained, that a different part would feel this effect, yet the nerve would lead into the same area, there would be no objection to this assumption and it is not contrary to these laws.

The imagination is a repetition of past sensory impressions and brain movements. Both work retroactively towards one area. For

---

[2]   It is, at this point, of no consequence if it takes a few parts which take the impressions to the Soul, or if there are others who, through a movement which was produced by the bodies, carry it out. The Soul, in this instance, will react in one of two ways: either not at all, because no nerves are struck, or if there is a reaction, then a certain part of the body will be set into motion. The part being set into motion is where the sensory impression originates.

example, this particular area, in the case of a wantonness imagination, provided it is stimulated, will produce the sensory impression of wantonness.

The retroaction produces a movement in one point of the brain, but this movement is not limited to the brain only, instead it continues, should the impression and the retroaction be very strong. It continues through the whole course of the nerves and the source of origin is the one point in the brain and also extends to the parts and machines to which the nerve is connected, for example the muscles, and the retroaction then takes the opposite path of the first movement.

This law is confirmed by all the experiences discussed, and this conclusion can be drawn out of the relationship the nerves have in connection with their source of origin in the brain, and on the other hand, with the other parts of the body and the muscles.

The above examples should enlighten us enough, that the magnitude of the preceding movement and the Soul-Impression are the ones that together determine the magnitude of the effect. Since both are the originators, but sometimes, both express it more and sometimes less, therefore, it must be measured by the degree of the effectiveness of both.

A conclusion of great value can be drawn from these experiences.

A sensory impression has an effect on that part of the brain which produced it, and through the same upon the nerves, which have their origin there, and on all the parts which are connected, and that is returned more or less in accordance with the magnitude of the mobility of the brain and the magnitude of the impression. OR: A movement, which comes out of one part of the body through the nerves and the brain, and penetrates the Soul and makes an impression there, always has another movement as a result of this. The following then takes place - that this movement comes from the Soul at precisely the point of the brain and through the particular nerves to the parts they affect, and in exactly the opposite direction, towards the same part of the body.

A multitude of experiences can be quoted to substantiate these experiences. There will be a few more examples in addition to those already given.

When you eat, the little taste-buds on the tongue rise. Should the skin suffer a strong external sensation such as cold, then the skin contracts, and perspiration lessens. Should a very tasty liquid be tasted by the back of the tongue, then the throat is lured into swallowing.

4.

There is one comment which has to be made in regards to the consequences of this retroaction, and the relationship which exists in regards to the consequences of the external or internal objects existing in the body which produce the impression, or generally, with the physical condition. Many times the retroaction is increased or substituted by the effect of the external and internal sources of origin and through the physical condition, which is produced by this effect. This may occur through the unification of the retroactive movement with the effects of the external and internal objects and the physical condition, or through such an emotion of the body, through which the body becomes capable of producing such effects. Through contagious vapours or through internal causes, through this fire of the Soul, the heating-up of the blood is produced. This fire by itself increases the heat of the blood. The bite of a rabid dog could be another cause for being enraged; but anger by itself has the ability to bring about the change of the liquids in the same manner, as if it were rabidness in the true sense. A Human Being, who was bitten by a fighting cock, experienced something very similar, as if he would have been bitten by a rabid dog. A young man who bit himself when he was in a rage, also experienced something very similar. (Reference: v. Gaubii Sermones II. de regimine mentis, quod medicorum est p. 97).

What has been discussed so far should enlighten the reader, and he should therefore come to the following conclusion by himself: the physical condition which produced the impression through which the capability cannot only be enhanced, but also has the capability of being totally changed, and therefore, becomes subject to a new revolution.

30. The Mode Of Action Of
The Powers Of The Imagination.

We should now have the knowledge to determine the sphere of operation, or the mode of action of the Powers of the Imagination.

1.

Frequent repetitions of physical movements produce as a consequence, a proficiency.

The external physical body makes the proficiency obtained by these means visible. The trained foot works, dances and jumps more skilfully, whereas the untrained foot is slower and awkward and that applies to the movements of all the external parts. However, as soon as these movements are executed more often, the movements are executed with more ease, much more quickly, and with greater success. Nothing makes the accuracy of this observation clearer than the fact that all this is done by organic association. (You could attempt to explain that all this is accomplished through the abilities, which are obtained through the inner brain and through ideas, but that would be in error). Insects still mate after they have been decapitated, provided they have done so before. Some decapitated Human Beings moved their arms and hands, as to remove the shackles and free their hands. There are many reported incidents such as those mentioned here.

This can be seen much more clearly when it comes to the proficiency which we obtain through daily exercises in our brain, and especially in those parts where the movement is absolutely necessary to serve the imagination. The result of these exercises are a better and more lively memory and an increased Power of the Imagination. A greater liveliness of the memory and the Power of the Imagination cannot take place unless there is a greater mobility in the brain. Lesser mobility can be caused through a fall, or too much water in the brain which causes stupidity, etc. Is it, therefore, not a fact that through exercise, the mobility of the brain and its proficiency to mobility can be increased?

Perhaps the possibility exists that the brain and its mobility can only grow through exercise, but not some parts, which communicate an impression through a certain movement of the Soul and thereby receive a greater proficiency in regards to this certain movement. This statement requires a more detailed explanation.

If we think because of a sensory movement, that does not mean that any movement of any part shows any arbitrary idea, nor does any single idea require the movement of all the parts of the brain, but, it requires certain movements of certain parts to show or produce certain impressions. The movement which gives you the impression of sweetness does not give you the concept of "black". It is also a fact that this impression does not require the movement of all the parts. If now, frequent movement causes greater proficiency of the same, it can, therefore, expand to other parts because not all parts were set into motion; only those which produced the impression of sweetness or those which produced the concept of "black".

These examples should give the reader enough proof and, at the same time, enough to think about (any additional examples would become repetitious). However, the knowledge which the following sentence contains should be taken to heart: In accordance to certain impressions, the corresponding parts of the brain, through repetition of their movements and also of the impression, take on the proficiency to produce them again.

It is also not necessary at this point to give a detailed explanation in regards to the above two instances other than that the same, or even contrasting ideas, correspond always to those movements of those parts which follow the particular sequence which triggered it in the first instance.

2.

When you think about these matters long enough, you will come to the conclusion that this must leave some after-effects, or consequences, in the Soul. This observation should not be overlooked unless you find a reason, a priori, and you realize its impossibility; or, you will find through experience, that the growth and the decline of the Effectiveness of the Soul corresponds totally to the growth of the body. These are two statements which are very hard to prove. It seems, however, that general ontological concepts, and especially the experiences of the Soul, will add to this.

One substance will be entirely modified through one impression, at least as long as this impression lasts. Should the Soul, when the impression leaves, return to its original condition, to the point as if the impression never existed, then there would have occurred something of great importance - a cause without a consequence - a certain, very effective condition upon a Being without any reaction upon the same. There would also never be a permanent, internal change; instead, there would be only external changes in accordance with the situation at hand and, among other things, if this would occur quite often, there would be a disproportion among several connected substances. For example: The Soul and the body to the Soul. However, it would never happen only to the body in accordance to the external condition. In addition, the relationship the body has with the Soul would also have to change. Another condition would also have to occur; whatever was compatible in the beginning would no longer be compatible.

Experience favours these conclusions:

It has been mentioned previously that it is the Soul itself, due to its restricted nature, can only grasp a certain amount of objects, even if the body would give the Soul all the support the Soul would need. This is one instance, and there are many more, where the Soul is not governed, or at least not totally, through the laws of the body, but what she does is being governed through her own peculiar laws.

Continuous practice improves our skills to grasp several objects all at once, compared to what we were capable of before we practised, even when present ideas become considerably more difficult when compared to the previous ones, because we have come into the possession of a greater proficiency. That includes our actions, which we execute in accordance to the peculiar Laws of the Soul. Should all of this not lead us to the conclusion that practice is not only a physical function or a physical motion, but, when we practice, that this strengthens also the operation of the Soul itself? Also, that often-repeated sensory impressions make the Soul more receptive to these impressions?

Certainly objections could be raised in regards to these conclusions. For example, what seems to be a strengthening of the brain could be interpreted as an improvement of the brain, but these arguments cannot be dealt with at this time, and it would be a deviation from the actual goal. In addition, it would be inexcusable, since proving this point would have little or no effect upon this theory.

If we accept the conclusions which were made so far, what happens in these instances in the Soul is without doubt a proficiency which makes all previous concepts we had easier, faster and with greater liveliness, especially when they are expressed in a certain sequence. This is a proficiency which has a relationship with the newly-attained and previously described proficiency of the corresponding brain particles in regards to particular movements and united with her, reaches the great purpose of Nature.

3.

There was already a connection, from the first sensory impression between the Soul and those physical particles that carried the motion to the Soul and which, through the retroaction of the latter, received another. From the place of contact, the physical particles delivered immediately the impressions to the place where the Soul could receive them and, conversely, from those who directly received the movement from the retroaction to those where this was being transmitted to. They are connected in a most precise manner, because without this connection how could such consequences occur? This connection can be improved upon through practice, partly because the particles become more receptive, and partly because they accept the movement from the objects much more easily, especially when they have received them frequently. Therefore, through external object contacts, provided all circumstances are equal, sensory impressions are much more easily produced if they have happened before, or if they have occurred many times before. That applies conversely to the Soul as well who, through the retroaction, produces movements much more easily if they have occurred many times before. The hands' ability to feel something more easily and to distinguish finer objects, is much greater if the hands have done this many times before. The same applies to dancing, jumping and walking - if you have practised, you become much more proficient.

4.

The greater the ability towards movement or the imagination, the easier the movement and the imagination occurs. However, in order to bring the movable particle into actual motion and the ability of the imagination to the actual manifestation of the imagination, requires a new awakening cause. Where can this cause be found? There is no external object available, as there is when it comes to the sensory impression; therefore, either the Soul awakens out of itself the slumbering imagination in accordance to the peculiar laws, and through this awakens the corresponding movements of the body, or the particles of the brain are the ones who awaken first, while the dominating motion of a point communicates to the other interdependent points and through this also awakens the changes in the Soul; or either this happens and then that happens.

On one side to make a decision on this question is very difficult, complicated and extensive, and as far as this theory is concerned, not decisive. It should, therefore, suffice that instead of all the observations and conclusions, we will concern ourselves only with the results. They are both great difficulties, yet they explain all the reciprocal communication of the movements of the brain amongst each other. For the present, they are subjected to an even greater extent than the ones which are in opposition. (How else would it be possible that previously perceived but now absent objects reappear in our Soul?) Out of necessity, one of these two means are being called forth through previous conceptions.

5.

The Soul awakens again, with or without the help of the brain, the previous impression.

In the instance of the actual sensory perception - it was the impression of the Soul which caused the retroaction through all parts of our body. This impression is now available again, and the Soul must express, in the instance of the same cause, the same effect. That means the Soul must, as in the past, in accordance with these same laws, in these same areas, with these same successes, work retroactively even more so, because the body is more disposed to the same movements. That also applies when it comes to the reception of the same movements, when they come out of the Soul and also out of those particular parts of the brain. Therefore, take notice: Should the idea however be weak, then the success as far as the external body particles are concerned is only visible to a small degree. If the idea is as lively as the sensory impression itself was, then these same consequences must prevail throughout the whole body to the same degree.

Out of this knowledge great results can be derived:

A concept of fantasy can bring forth the same effects in the body as the sensory impression from which it originated, as soon as it reaches the same level of intensity or strength.

Many examples could be given to substantiate and illustrate the conclusions made. Here are just a few:

When certain Human Beings are tickled on the soles of their feet or on the side of their body, this can result in convulsive movements of almost all the muscles in the body; some people even suffer through mere fear of it, in the same manner. It is also not impossible when you dream that you have fallen, you received a blow, a bruise, etc., that real blue bruises develop. The placebo effect is also not unknown. There is a report by a physician by the name of Bonet, who had a patient who insisted that the physician should supply him with a strong purging remedy, but instead the physician gave him silver-covered breadcrumbs. The patient took them in the belief that they were the strong purgative he had asked for and, as a result, he vomited once and had five bowel movements. The same physician had another patient, a girl who was supposed to have taken rhubarb in the evening but, because of the bad taste, did not take it. That same night, however, she dreamt that she had taken the rhubarb, and when she awoke in the morning, believing that she had taken it the previous evening, purged in the same manner as if she would have taken it in reality.

A physician by the name of Pechlin reports of a patient who took 20 grains of Houndstongue tablet, and since he believed them to be a purgative, he purged, whereas in reality they are an opiate and therefore constipate. Another patient took 15 grains of white vitriol in the belief that it would induce perspiration and he did perspire, even though this remedy should induce vomiting.

These assumptions in regards to the Theory of the Power of the

Imagination require the establishment of rules so that a clearer concept emerges in regards to the pictures of the fantasy.

1. The Soul awakens again, with or without the help of the brain, the former impressions.

2. In the instance of the actual sensory perception, it was the impression of the Soul which caused the retroaction throughout all the parts of our whole body. This impression now exists again or is available again. The Soul must, in the instance of the same cause, express the same effects as mentioned in previous chapters. The Soul must react in the same manner as she did previously in accordance with these same laws and the same areas with the same success. When the idea is weak, then the success on the external body parts is hardly visible; should the idea, however, be as lively as the sensory impression was by itself, then these same effects must prevail throughout the whole body to the same degree.

It should, therefore, be repeated: A concept of fantasy can bring forth the same effects in the body as the sensory impression out of which it originated, as soon as it reaches the same level of intensity or strength.

By many examples we have proven that through the fantasy we can feel, see, hear, taste and smell because all these abilities are based on the same theory. The question now is: How can we give the fantasy the same strength which was given to the sensory impression?

The answer to this question represents the most important part of Magic. The fantasy can be brought to this level of exaltation partly by coincidence and partly artificially.

In any case, it is always necessary that the inner sense has a greater effect on the external sense than the external has on the internal sense.

Since the Picture of Fantasy is a creation of the internal, it is absolutely necessary to have the following abilities:

1. Ease of Fibre-Motion.
2. Spirit Exaltation.

Both of these abilities can be brought forth by coincidence and artificially. Our object is the artificial bringing-forth, whereas, the coincidental bringing-forth is strictly an object of pathology.

In the instance of the artificial bringing-forth of Pictures of the Fantasy, the first question must be: What has an effect on the fantasy? The answer: Everything which has an effect on the Spirit.

The theories taught in the first part of this book should not be forgotten: The Theory of Similarity and Dissimilarity, Spirit Exaltation, Assimilation, etc.; Similarities effect similarities; Spirit effects Spirit; same to same, like to like.

Since the fantasy is a power which produces the picture from the internal, the motion of the fantasy must occur on the inside.

What are the means necessary to accomplish this?

Nature beckons all of us from the Theory of the Body to the Theory of the Spirit. Observe how we treat people who are unconscious; what do we do to awaken their Spirit?

We employ means or remedies which are homogeneous with vitality (Life-Spirit) and the same applies to the fantasy as well.

What has the greatest effect upon the fantasy?

This question can very easily be answered due to the knowledge of the Life-Spirits (Vitality) and the theory, which must be the prerequisite in this particular regard. All of this will be explained.

Spiritual things, narcotic incenses and other agents which act upon the finer, inner organization, are the most useful. In order for us to obtain a clearer concept and understanding of the use of such things and agents, the following prerequisites are absolutely necessary:

1. Anything which has an effect on a certain matter, has the most effect on those parts of the human body where such matter is present.

2. Spiritual, subtle things, act again upon spiritual, subtle things; therefore, they have the most effect upon the parts of the human body where spiritual and subtle things are present.

3. The fine Life-Spirits in Human Beings can be diluted, extended and condensed. The dilution, extension and condensation always brings forth different effects in the human body and, therefore, requires different means or agents to develop.

4. The Life-Spirits can also be heated up, tempered, and cooled off. The heating up, the temperateness and cooling - each of these have a different media.

5. There are powers of the Spirit which produce, and there are powers of the Spirit which rob.

6. Every producing-power can turn into a robbing-power, and every robbing-power can turn into a producing-power.

7. The robbing-power dries; the producing-power softens.

8. The producing-power causes inner assimilation; the robbing-power external.

9. The abilities to coagulate (thicken) and to expand lie within the Spirit.

10. The finer the Life-Spirits become, the greater expansion they are capable of.

11. The finer the body is, the greater coagulation it is capable of.

12. The more compact a body is, the greater the ability of expansion; for example: Gold, smoke, etc.

13. The nobility of a body is in accordance to its subtile, inner spiritual parts.

14. The body, which has the ability of the greatest of expansion, also has the ability of the greatest of coagulation.

All powers of the body, the growth, the vegetation, consist of the expansion and the coagulation of the inner spiritual parts of any body.

The greater the expansion, the greater the sphere of activity. The greater the power of assimilation, the greater the attraction of similarities.

All passions in the human body have, as their source of origin, the different motions of the Life-Spirits and are, therefore, the source of origin of the different passions.

The Life-Spirits differ by some having a greater similarity with Air; the others with Fire.

The attributes of the Life-Spirits consist of the inclination to multiply, to leave the coarser, and to join the finer.

Every confined Life-Spirit dilutes if he cannot join with what is similar. The more the Life-Spirits multiply, the more they coagulate (thicken). The more the Life-Spirits disperse, the more they dilute.

When you are in possession of this understanding, then the different effects of the passions in the human body can be explained.

All passions can be classified under extension, dilution, condensation, heating, temperateness, and cooling of the finer Life-Spirits. Passions can, therefore, cause ailments and ailments can cause passions.

An ailment of the gallbladder can cause the fervent, passionate condition of indignation, impatience and anger; and out of the fervent, passionate condition of indignation, impatience and anger, the ailment of the gallbladder, can develop.

A passion, which extends the Life-Spirits, can be caused through the extension of the Life-Spirits and destroyed through the opposite; and this is how it is with the dilution, condensation, heating, temperateness and cooling.

Whatever dilutes, extends, condenses, heats up, tempers and cools, can bring forth or produce passionate conditions and, in accordance to the shape and condition of the passion, the opposite can be achieved.

The dilution, extension, condensation, heating, temperateness and cooling can be triggered either through internal or through external causes.

These causes are through nourishment, which brings forth dilution, extension, condensation, heating, temperateness and cooling; or, through incense, which can cause dilution, extension, condensation, heating, temperateness and cooling; or, through retrospect, which can cause through the fantasy, the condition of extension, dilution, condensation, heating, temperateness and cooling, and the same condition of dilution, extension, condensation, heating, temperateness and cooling can be produced again, through the powers of the imagination.

The Life-Spirits require, for their subsistence in the human body, three essential substances:

1.   An unconstrained motion.
2.   Temperature.
3.   Conforming nourishment.

When one of these requirements is disturbed, then the Life-Spirits suffer.

The unconstrained motion is disturbed either through dilution or

224

condensation. Everything which impedes the circulation of the Life-Spirits, coagulates. All opiates and narcotics belong to this category.

Under the category of passions belong fear and sorrow. Fear and sorrow therefore cause the coagulation of the Life-Spirits, and any coagulation of the Life-Spirits can cause fear and sorrow.

The extension of the Life-Spirits is caused through sulfuric vapours.

Passions which cause these extensions are very passionate joys.

All of this, and the following, will show the order of things - the system.

Coagulation
All narcotics and opiates coagulate the Life-Spirits, such as:

Opium	Poppy seeds
Henbane	Mandrake
Hemlock	Nightshades

These are the simple opiates. The compounded opiates are as follows:

Methridates and Theriacs
Trifera
Laudanum Paracelsi
Diascordium
Philonium
Pilulae de Cynoglossa

Coagulation can occur when such opiates and narcotics are consumed. However, the coagulation can also be caused through incense and ointments made out of ingredients such as opiates and narcotics.

Consequences of the Coagulation
of the Life-Spirits.
A slow circulation of all body fluids.

A higher level of the Power of the Imagination which, at times, can be brought to the highest level of liveliness, because the fibres are tensed and thereby lose their elasticity.

Heavy dreams, nightmares and peculiar fantasies; transposition into a dream world can occur.

Observation

When the coagulation is caused through artificial agents, then the natural condition of the body is impeded. The artificial coagulation can cause, in accordance with the condition of the organization, more or less harm, or even evil. The consequences can be apoplexy, insanity or rage. For this reason, preliminary preparations are necessary to prepare the body for the conception of a harmless coagulation of the Life-Spirits.

Be aware of how risky such experiments are when narcotic incense is employed, especially when they are used by Human Beings who possess no knowledge of the Natural Sciences.

The appearances of Spirits, which were described in the first part of this book, belong to this category, and are nothing but the effects of the Power of the Imagination. They are produced through a particular incense. It is absolutely impertinent when tricksters, under the disguise of performing sorcery, endanger the health of other Human Beings to the extent that these people become insane, or, for long periods of time, through a corrupt imagination, disturb the natural condition of health.

The author has personal knowledge of people who, through lack of knowledge of this type of incense, had very bad experiences due to the fact that the experiments were done without the proper care. Do not experiment, especially without proper knowledge.

People who have done these experiments without proper knowledge and care will, in retrospect, relive the hour and the uneasy feelings which were connected with this, especially in the dark.

It is an atrocity when certain so-called health professionals play games with mankind in this manner and thereby expose many Human Beings to great danger, even to the point that they may lose their health, reason, or even their life.

Of great concern is, that in spite of everything which has been said, there still may be some of you who would misuse this knowledge. Therefore, in order to prevent any improper use, no clear description of ingredients or preparation of incense will be given.

Not being aware of danger is more dangerous than being aware of it, however, all that can be done through these writings is to warn you not to be present where magical manifestations are being produced through the burning of incense, unless you have full knowledge and are fully convinced of the abilities and good character of the artist, otherwise, your health will be in constant danger. Should you come into the possession of such incense, never burn it, especially when the content of the ingredients and amounts are not properly given. By doing so, you are inviting self-poisoning, which could not only cause you to lose your mind, but also your life. The author also has personal knowledge of people whose power of imagination became so corrupt through the burning of such incense, that they believed spirits were always around them, and were not healed of this until the day they died.

Be forewarned and do not walk into an open trap. It may not always be the burning of incense; other methods can also be employed. All these things are well planned and are not coincidences. There is an army of charlatans of ghost-seers travelling the world, and they are also in institutions of evil. Their single-most purpose in life is to gain political power over the People of the Nations and they expect recognition. The result is that these charlatans and their teachers, through their atrocious teachings, now have half the population of the world committed to hospitals and insane-asylums.

In this book, I will refrain from giving detailed instructions as to the preparation of these incenses which have an effect on the imagination, but, as a warning to the noble and to expose the charlatans, I will give the ingredients of such magical incenses and ointments, but not in any order and following no system. Every physician can judge for himself how much devastation these ingredients can cause among Human Beings.

Ingredients which are used for such experiments are:

Hemlock	Mandrake
Henbane	Nightshades
Saffron	Black Poppy Seeds
Aloe	Succus Apii
Opium	Ferula

By preparing the above ingredients as ointments or incense, in the proper proportions, either by themselves, or the fluids or seeds thereof, can result in a total poisoning of the imagination.

For those who have no knowledge of this subject, and those who will try anything without proper consideration, I will try to give an understanding of how dangerous these ingredients can be. The consequences of using these ingredients can be devastating.

Hemlock: The herb and root can cause cardiac arrest, severe heart problems, severe gallbladder ailments, rage, induce sleep, a light dark swelling of the whole body and of course, death.

Henbane: Causes unreasonable behaviour, severe burning in the abdominal area, unbearable thirst, loss of sight and rage.

Mandrake: Causes senselessness, sleep, severe tiredness and total lack of understanding.

Saffron: This is one of the strongest narcotics. There have been reports of people dying by just sleeping on a pillow of saffron.

Aloe: It is irritating and analgesic.

Nightshades: Poisonous and analgesic; the same as black poppy seeds.

This should suffice to give the reader an idea as to the effects of the main ingredients.

Anybody who is in possession of the knowledge in Nature's Kingdom knows that all burning of incense irritates, especially those made from burnt herbs. I once gave a very knowledgeable physician the recipe for such an incense. The physician examined the ingredients very carefully and his reply was as follows:

These ingredients, which are used as incense, are narcotics. They have an effect on the imagination and should only be used with the greatest of care, otherwise, they will cause apoplexy, madness and by increased use, insanity. This incense, and other forms thereof, are employed by charlatans and their victims to produce appearances of Spirits. Should you be invited to witness such a spirit-appearance, or you are aware that you will be subjected to such a fraudulent presentation, then soak little sponges or cotton in good wine vinegar and place them in your ears and hold a cloth soaked in good wine vinegar over your mouth and nose. The effect can also be thwarted by throwing a few grains of sulphur into the burning incense. Should a Human Being, however, be so unlucky and be totally deceived by such a charlatan, and his imagination be totally poisoned, then the only solution to the problem would be to use the remedies which are used by those who have been poisoned by narcotics. The best antidotes are frequent, very small blood-lettings, enemas, and the use of good wine vinegar and acidic beverages. The peculiarity of such incense is that it affects the imagination so vehemently, that a Human Being is virtually transposed into a dream state and, even after a long, long time, the smallest reminiscence can produce the same condition as it did when it was actually done.

Another knowledgeable physician said the following, after he had examined the burning of such incense:

The burning of such incenses transposes those who are subjected to it into a dream world. When I exposed myself to the smoke of the Hemlock herb, I became totally anaesthetized and after that, fell into a sleep and dreamt very peculiar things. For a long time afterwards, I did not feel very well.

These examples should suffice to show how much care must be taken when such incense is being burned. At the time, enquiries should be made as to the temperament of each person who will be present when such incense is being burned, so that no harm can come to their health.

If this is done only to seek the truth in Nature, and if the proper precautions to gain these experiences are taken, then no reasonable Human Being will have any objections, but if this is done for the wrong reasons and in order to deceive people, then it is inhuman, especially when it goes too far.

However, should such Human Beings whose belief and confidence can be enhanced, be chosen for these endeavours, then such an experiment is safe. There is also considerably less need for the burning of incense because through belief and confidence, their fantasy is already exalted, and the appearances always have the same consequences, no matter in which manner they occur.

I am, however, certain of one thing: If I would have revealed the recipes of such incenses, they would have been misused. The reason for saying this was substantiated by letters which I have received. Only a small percentage of people who wrote to me had a healthy mind with a healthy reason, and even a smaller percentage had a human heart. Here are some excerpts of the letters I received:

1. I would be very much obliged to you, if you would send me your incense so that I could make the Devil appear. I have tried many different such experiments and conjurations but so far, without any result. If, through the burning of incense, the Devil can be invoked faster, then these methods of accomplishing this are faster and better. I am a man of honour and I will not misuse them.

ANSWER:

Dear Sir,

Your concept of Spirit-Appearances through the burning of incense is incorrect. It is the fantasy which is being stimulated through the narcotic herbs, and they produce the picture you see. They are not reality.

2. What Fantasy! There is no such thing as fantasy. These devils are real. In this respect, you can be sincere with me. You do not have to worry, I am not afraid of the Devil. As long as the scoundrel gives me money, he then can be on his way again, but, I want to burn incense, even if I require 2 pounds of incense every day. Send it immediately....

This was the general content of most of the letters which I received. How can you answer people who write such letters, and who will not accept any other concepts?

The best thing you can do is not to answer any of these letters. It is, however, a pity that I could not properly answer the letters of those people who have a much nobler character, and it has to be said, that I received a great number of letters from them. Unfortunately, time, and other obligations, made it impossible to satisfy all of them. I hope your goodness will pardon me, and that these writings will give your curiosity the proper satisfaction.

31. True Appearances.

I said that true appearances exist, and I repeat it. These appearances originate essentially in Nature.

I can imagine what some nit-wits might say when they read this, but, it is not the one who is negative on everything who enlightens human intelligence, but the one who examines, can explain things and knows how they are put together.

Unbelievable!, some people might say. He maintains that Spirits exist; Spirit-Appearances! For God's sake! There you can see how even he contradicts himself. He himself wrote about superstitions. But, Ladies and Gentlemen, you must understand me correctly. I do not know the concept you have of spirits and ghosts, or what your understanding of this subject is. I only said there are true appearances.

Even though there may be a thousand false ones, thousands which are produced through optical illusions and, again, thousands through the fantasy. All this does not exclude the contention that true appearances do exist.

Now the question arises: What are true appearances, and what do I understand under true appearances?

A true appearance is an appearance, when a body or being which actually exists in Nature, but which was not perceptible to my conventional previous organization, becomes perceptible through the changes of my senses or through a Medium. I do not think that anybody can deny this.

These appearances have their gradation from the finer to the finest bodies to even finer and even finer yet, as the finest of bodies are.

For example, there are thousands of objects in the air, but they are invisible to our organization. Through a magnifying glass, however, we become aware of a new physical world. We see beings we did not see before. Seeing these things depends upon a stronger organization. There are also things and beings in existence which no ordinary microscope has yet discovered. All of this is appearance. As it is with our sense of sight, that is how it is with all our other senses.

We can see things which could ordinarily not be seen; hear things which we ordinarily could not hear; feel things which we ordinarily could not feel; and we could taste and smell things which we ordinarily could not taste or smell.

Some bodies are invisible to us because of their minute size, and others, because of their diluted expansion. Every sensory feeling exists because of a contact which is being made. Whatever is too small or too expanded for us, does not make contact with our senses and therefore, it cannot be felt.

There are things which our senses allow to pass. That means to say, just as a sieve cannot hold water, fine objects cannot be held by our organization, but they are allowed to pass, as a ray of light comes through a glass window.

Now there can be a media, which either makes refined objects more physical or they make our organization finer. In either instance, the appearance is the consequence.

When bodies, which are so diluted that they are invisible to our eye, coagulate to the degree that they become visible to our eye, then the result is also an appearance.

When all these prerequisites are met, this proves the possibility that all objects which our senses do not feel, can become perceptible through a change in our organs or through a change of the objects, and through this, the possibility of the appearance is proven. Also with refined senses or with magnified or condensed objects, things you do not feel must become perceptible. That is the second proof through which the certainty of the appearances can be proven. This proof leads to the following understanding:

Things which are not visible to our eyes become visible either through their artificial or natural magnification, or through their artificial or natural condensation.

Things which, because of their minuteness, cannot be perceived or felt by our eyes must, out of necessity, become visible through artificial or natural magnification, appropriate to our eyes.

Things which are not visible to our eyes because of their expansion must, by necessity, become visible through condensation, appropriate to our eyes.

Things which we could not feel with our previous organization must become perceivable to our changed organization, if the organization becomes so refined that the now non-perceivable things become perceivable to the changed organization.

Within this, the whole theory of true appearances are contained.

Now the question arises: Can Spirits appear? That prompts another question: What do you understand under Spirits?

Not everything is already Spirit, what we believe to be Spirit. There are bodies in the finest of form, but they are still bodies.

For example: As long as Human Beings have perspiration from the parts of the physical body, that is how long they have man-like forms. They can be condensed artificially or naturally, and this results in appearances which represent misshapen human figures and, therefore, are not ghosts nor are they Spirits, but a collection of impressions of humans through the Art.

That is why it is possible that above the graves of dead Human Beings, artificially or naturally, human figures can become visible. They are the parts which essentially still belong to the physical body and, therefore, represent a number of similar forms which are not ghosts nor are they Spirits. That is what the people of old called "Umbrae", and they became visible on battlefields or in cemeteries. There are burning incenses which are the medium to concentrate such parts and to produce or form such a figure. All of this belongs under the physical appearances and not under the appearances of the higher gender.

Under the appearances of the higher gender, I understand appearances of beings, which become visible through the inner sense of our eyes. Among these types of appearances belong the beings who are on a higher level in the hierarchy, of which you can find many examples in the Scriptures.

As little as our Soul is created for the perceptibility of physical objects, that is how little our physical body is created for the perceptibility of spiritual things; everything must have its proper organ.

We have assumed that the organ by which means the physical body communicates its perception to the Soul, and the Soul communicates her perception to the physical body is the inner sense. We are trying here to reiterate the remarks which were previously made in regards to the inner sense.

The Soul starts to see spiritually when she opens her eyes. That means, through the Power of the Assimilation.

She sees objects of her future condition, beings in their future dwellings, and comes into contact with what we call the Spirit World. However, to be able to have inner sight, total purity of the Soul and the physical body is required, so that the communication of the inner sense with the external organization can take place.

This condition of purity made the connection of the Saints with the Spirit World possible. Their visions and appearances were not mere figments of a heated-up fantasy or of a corrupt, irritated body, but totally natural and necessary consequences of their Soul Assimilation.

Since the condition of the Soul is not limited to time and space (this statement is only true from the physical world point of view, since only the Akasha is not limited to time and space), therefore, the Soul possesses an all encompassing concept of clearness, which our organization of the senses does not allow. It is, therefore, easily understandable, that the smallest glimmer of Light, which shines from this Soul Transfiguration through the dark physical body must be, for the ordinary Human Being, a wonderful apparition. For those Human Beings who think more about these matters, it proclaims to a greater degree the greatness of God and the holiness of religion.

I do not know if this book was written one century too early, since I am making claims in regards to the truth of which, of course, the most simple Human Beings have a better concept of than the most fashionable Philosopher, where the rapture of Paul triggers his fantasy, whereas the appearances of John trigger his frenzy. The most beautiful physical truths lie hidden in things which the so-called Philosopher repudiates without having examined these truths with absolute purity.

All is harmony in the whole, but the sound cannot be heard by every ear. They cannot be heard due to the noise of the world and the racket of the scientists and philosophers. In peaceful solitude and in many hours of the night, when our Soul raises up to God, resounds the sound of wisdom out of the harmonious All of the Divinity. You do not hear the sounds under the confusion of Human Beings and the storms of passion.

The corpulent, complacent ignorance which does not examine anything, considers every uncommon appearance to be the Devil's work, and the pride of some of our present-day philosophers makes everything they cannot explain or do not understand, a figment of the imagination. No greater error could be committed in both instances.

These errors will not cease to exist as long as the great ego of the scholars stretches out the sceptre of their despotism in the kingdom of science. Only where the sincerity of love reigns, the truth approaches the Sage, who seeks the Light in his innermost.

32. The Higher State Of The Soul.

Life, and the Primary Source of all Life, is God. Without God, there would be no Life, because He alone is the Prime Origin, the Prime Origin of all the beginning of Life.

GOD LIVES and His Life is composed of Love and Wisdom. Love and Wisdom are Spirit-Life, and they are for the Spirit, what light and warmth are for the body.

The physical world receives its light and warmth from the sun; the Spirit World receives Love and Wisdom from God.

All things in the physical world receive light and warmth from the sun; all Beings in the Spirit World receive Love and Wisdom from God.

The more active the Vital Forces are, the nobler is the physical being; the nobler the Spiritual Force, the nobler is the Spiritual Being.

The Spiritual Light is Wisdom; the Spiritual Warmth is Love; and Wisdom unified with Love is Spiritual Life.

Without light and warmth, there is no physical life; without Wisdom and Love, there is no Spiritual Life.

Human Beings possess Reason and Will as Spirit-Abilities, and those abilities are Soul-Organs, spiritual-reception tools of Wisdom and Love.

The physical body cannot live without air, and the Soul cannot live without Light. Our Will behaves in accordance with Love; our Reason in accordance with Knowledge.

The perception of Truth is the consequence of the pure Will.

The viability of the Soul is in the Knowledge; the activity of the Soul is in the Will.

It is the endeavour of the Activity and the Will to unify because those are the Laws of Love.

The organ of Wisdom is the Reason; the organ of Love is the Will, through which the Divinity acts upon the Life of the Soul. The Reason receives from the Will the power to ascend. The purer the Will the purer the Reason.

Light can only be found where there is purity. Purity of the Spirit creates the ability of conception of the Divine.

The ability of conception is inner Soul-Exaltation, Energy-Approximation to divine feelings, a higher state of the Soul.

33. Advancement Of The Soul.

Recognition begins with the Ego. The closer you are to your Ego, the closer or better you know yourself; the deeper you penetrate within yourself, the more you get to know yourself. That means: the purer the understanding of our own nature is; and if we act upon this knowledge accordingly, the purer becomes our knowledge of external things and their source of origin.

All Recognition (Understanding) must be controlled by the Will. All knowledge must be warmed-up through being, otherwise, everything remains idle talk.

Wherever this warmth is not present, there is no true recognition, no true understanding.

First, the Will must be guided, prepared and disposed towards goodness.

All this cannot be accomplished through words alone, nor through cold teachings and sentences which do not strike the heart.

In deed and Life, in Spirit and development, exists the power of our Soul, the spark of Divinity which lies within us. If we follow this, then we come closer to her Nature.

Do not speak, search, or declaim with the pupil in regards to the Divinity. Whenever it is your intention to impose a concept which is too high for the intelligence of your pupil, and if you do not realize that all teachings have to have their origin in the Will, then the wrong conclusions will be drawn by your pupil's concepts and your method will be proven incorrect.

Through habit and by example, the heart is guided to the Temple of Virtue and is taught to exercise the duties of mankind, and to love thy neighbour. Develop the pupil in such a manner, that it becomes a sweet, refreshing habit.

Also, develop the pupil into a pure Human Being. Then you have laid into his heart the source to understand God. This is a fountain which never runs dry.

Once he feels this spark, and he begins to become a moral Being, when this Will, this heart, this conscience, becomes active in him and he becomes aware of his feelings in regards to his relationship towards God, then it is time to direct his sight out of the innermost to the objects in Nature and to read in the Book of Creation, and in these works, learn to recognize the Almighty hand of the constructive Creator.

A heart which has been prepared in these feelings and touched by the beauty of creation will never misunderstand the voice of Nature which keeps calling: There is only one God!

Then he is receptive for the revelation of Nature. He feels the contradiction of all things which are without order, and to think of this order without a primary source, he understands that there must be Beings who existed, before he himself existed.

Speak about this Being with deep emotion; about the necessity of His Existence; about the solace of the Belief in Him. These solemn words will be forever engraved in his mind.

Inform him of what it means to recognize God though His Works, and Nature will become a mirror of His Omnipotence; but, once and for all purify his inner sense.

Experience teaches the Wise in order that he constantly comes closer to God, the more audible the voice of conscience becomes in him and warns him to do goodness.

The Wise understand that this sense, as all the others, is born with him, and he has to thank this sense for everything.

Neither words, systems, nor dogmatic regulations teach the Wise who God is. His sense, his heart, feels the great need. This heart, this inner sense, drew him to God, and the more he followed this Genius, the happier and the more like God he became. Not through words, but through action, life and deeds.

Even though every Human Being must, sooner or later, reach an understanding of God, it depends greatly upon the circumstances under which he lives; what inner condition his inner constitution has; if his spiritual sight is pure and free, or if a fermenting mixture of harmful passions stops him from penetrating the nebula of sensuousness earlier.

Never can the Blissful thank Divine Providence enough, who were placed by her into such circumstances, which were favourable for the growth of their spiritual life, like fruitful soil and the mild springtime air of the sprouting flowers.

You! Whoever you might be, who have a heart which is soft and benevolent, give thanks to the Infinite, when the germ of harmful and destructive inclination was removed from your heart at an early age.

Blessed is the one who, at the time of his early youth, lived among good and noble Human Beings who, in the morning of his life, guided his first steps and placed the seed of goodness into his heart.

Blessed is the one who grows up to be a Human Being whose quiet, cheerful and wise life is already an example of virtue and who does not brood on the subject of the Divinity, but who gives, through true practical Christianity, teachings of understanding, and convinces more by examples than through words.

In a blessed circle of good Human Beings, where friendship, love and domestic bliss reigns, there the thousandfold active forces of good, well-organized Souls develop. The sight of noble deeds triggers the endeavour to Assimilation! Activity becomes a need; benevolence becomes your life's duty.

As the sense of a young painter develops through continuous viewing of great masterpieces of art, that is how the advantage of tactfulness for everything morally good and beautiful is honed, and this keenness is the advancement of the Soul or Soul-Development.

34. The Forces Of Assimilation.

Within every Human Being lies the ability of Assimilation. The forces of Assimilation slumber within him and develop in accordance with the purity of his Soul.

Every Human Being has his own relationship towards or with God, which only he can feel. Accordingly, they determine the measure of his inner forces and his Soul-force, and then they become again, accordingly the measure of his value, his perfection and his blissfulness.

This yearning for the primary source, this anticipation of God, this inner religion, can only be felt. Words cannot express this, however, it is certain that no earthly bliss can surpass these moments where, through the sight of such a moral beauty, the Sage becomes enchanted, like through a Seraph, out of the sensory illusion into the intellectual world. Then the Soul feels the highest virtually within herself so close, and begins to sink into deep worship.

What is like the bliss of the feelings when a good deed has been done, which unseen by Human Beings, the willing heart out of love to God accomplishes, and in silence sacrifices?

The good Human Being feels these heavenly moments; they disappeared like an apparition, therefore, the feeling of goodness is more than a mere mortal tongue can describe.

Silence is the greatest of all feelings of the Soul, inspired by the knowledge, the anticipation of the Omnipresence of the Eternal. That is how the butterfly feels the flame of the fire; if he flies too close, his wings become singed and unconscious he falls into the dust.

35. The World.

The reality which is outside of God has been brought forth through Him - this All is the World.

The concept of the World is not this Planet Earth alone; this seemingly present shape or form of Planet Earth, and not this solar system which is visible to us, but that which we call the universe, and not only the present state of this universe, but also the past and future state, because all of this belongs to one whole. The concept of "the World" is not this planet alone, nor the seemingly present shape or form of the Earth, nor our visible solar system alone, but the whole universe; not just the present state of the universe, but also the past and future state because all of this belongs to one whole.

The world is not infinite because it consists of expansion and space, and infinity of the space and of the expansion does not exist.

Space and expansion are appearances, illusions, therefore, not infinite space, not infinite expansion.

The concept of infinity arises from our inability to think of limits. Only so much can be said with certainty: this world consists of as many parts as it is possible and she is as good as she is capable of being.

The world is not eternal because the eternity of the world would be infinite time; time is an appearance, an illusion. Eternal time would be an inability to think of a beginning without an end.

Everything has a connection; all is a whole. Nothing exterminates itself; everything exists through changes in conditions. Everything has its cause and consequences; everything has its effects and its life. In every cause and in every change, all consequences are already contained. The forces or powers of the beings are determined through the development and the effect to bring forth the immediate ensuing forces, because everything is the development of a preceding condition.

Every effect is founded on a preceding one; one occupance is the result of another. Not only is the change of one world-particle connected among each other, but they are also connected with all the other particles and changes in the world.

Nothing can become a reality, that which contradicts another change to become a reality. All changes are in harmony and establish themselves reciprocally.

The ability to bring about your own changes means to act or to be active, and the ability to bring forth other changes which are appropriate to this world means to be suffering.

Nothing changes in this particular manner, which is dissimilar in its ability to change; and when something changes, then corresponding changes develop.

We have the ability to comprehend things (objects) which are in this world, but of only a few do we have a clear concept. Having a clear concept and a clear understanding are essentially different matters.

Understandable is a matter of which I have a concept or an idea, and the understanding can be measured in accordance to the manner of these ideas.

Conception consists of the total understanding and includes at the same time, the whole present, past and future condition.

Everything is, at the moment of its existence, that which it must be. More or less reality would be, as far as this object or being is concerned, imperfection.

At times, however, what may seem to be an imperfection of a thing at a certain moment of its existence, is not an imperfection or deficiency, but is the greatest perfection which it is capable of at that moment, only we do not see it.

Human Beings do not possess the ability to realize the inner, essential relationship of everything for the common purpose. They judge in accordance with the goodness and perfection of a thing by employing the restricted and narrow relationship they have, and the circumstances they are aware of; again, in accordance with the influence it had under the circumstances at that time, and the result is relative evil.

The perfection of the world and all its parts are successive by nature and, therefore, the change lies essentially in the world.

Successive perfection is perfectibility, and this is the great law and the determination, according to which the world changes as a whole, and as well changes in all parts occur.

This perfectibility of things is the reason why Human Beings divide world changes into good ones and evil ones, because through comparisons arise relative imperfections and evils.

In as far as looking back upon a perfect thing as to what it was - it could have been better and it could have been worse in respect to what it will be. This imperfection is only by comparison, because it lies within the nature of things to climb from the lower to the higher, therefore, every change of condition is in respect to the whole, in regards to the thing's total perfection.

The evil which we see in the world and all the imperfections which we believe to have discovered, apply and relate to the limits of our understanding.

The narrower our point of view is, from which we look upon, view or observe things, the more evil and the more imperfections are the result. The more, however, this point of view broadens, the more these evils disappear due to the superb framework of the infinite prime source.

In the World of Ability, the condition of the Spirit to be in a state of blissfulness is greater, and the evil is less and also less visible, therefore, our blissfulness depends upon the enlightenment of our intellect, since we are leaving our narrow-minded circumstances so that we can increase the feeling of our blissfulness by broadening our mind's outlook.

Through true enlightenment and by broadening our mental outlook, we increase our true blissfulness; we penetrate deeper into the essence of the matter and we clear the path through higher understanding and insight to the most blissful feelings.

Through this far-sightedness, the falsehoods disappear and we come closer to the truth, due to a greater clearness.

False air, false greatness, false sensuality, and false passions disappear; the storms in our Soul calm down; our heart becomes more peaceful; the hour of the holy contemplations and amazement approaches and cradles us in the feeling of eternity.

Human Beings! Should you want to be happy and enjoy, and want to have permanent happiness and enjoyment, enlighten your understanding and learn to be above the narrow-minded circumstances. Pray to God, Who created everything so magnificently. This world was not only created for the blissfulness of Human Beings, but also every being in God's creation is entitled to be as blissful as the present association and well-being of the other fellow beings allows.

God feeds the raven, nourishes the worm in the ground, and maintains the lambs in the meadows.

36. *Truth And The Illusion Of The Senses.*

Everything we feel and recognize very seldom leads us into the centre of the matter itself; it is only the result of the influence of things which are outside of us. This applies to those who are in this organization and not in another. Therefore, there must be two truths: one truth which is the matter itself, and the other which indicates what the matter is.

The first is Absolute Truth, and the other is Relative Truth.

Absolute Truth is only in God. Relative Truth is in Human Beings and is more or less by degrees in accordance to the approximation to God.

Relative truth does not lead into the centre of the matter or into the inner of things, even though it is brought forth through it; it only determines how things appear and how they must appear with this receptivity, may it be under these circumstances or under those. We then call this truth and reality.

Sensuous truth, or what we call reality, is dependent upon our organs and we call this physical truth. In most Human Beings this represents itself to the senses in this or that manner, as perception. Therefore, the stone is hard, the snow is white, the rose has a scent, aloe is bitter, and the sound of the flute is in harmony.

From all of this, we can gather that most physical truths conduct themselves only organically towards us, and these sensuous truths will change, and must change, when our organs change.

There are also abstract truths or realities which are not always made perceptible through physical objects and the senses of the power of our perception. They are either perceived through concepts which we connect to or associate with physical objects, or through observation of effects which are not perceptible through the coarser senses, but which reach the perception of the Soul in this manner.

These abstract truths are considerably more subject to the danger of deception than the sensuous truths, because the abstract truths are brought to our perception through words, and these words would represent our concepts, and these concepts should represent the impression. How much accuracy and harmony of all the circumstances

241

is required for this? It is, therefore, necessary for the speaker to connect the concepts he has with the proper words. Should we, however, connect entirely different concepts with the words, then that particular abstract truth is not being conveyed - it is only believed to have been conveyed. Due to this lack of perception, errors upon errors are accumulated; that is why there are so many disputations and quarrels amongst the scholars.

In the instance of abstract truths, we experience the same problems as with sensuous truths; every Human Being judges in accordance to the perception of his senses. Therefore, he cannot comprehend things which Human Beings with other senses perceive differently.

We judge, when it comes to abstract truths, the type of thought in accordance to the concept we connect to the words, and not in accordance to the concepts the speaker connects to his words.

We require logical knowledge and a clear terminology to more clearly and accurately understand abstract truths. But how many Human Beings are in possession of logical knowledge? There exists, however, a terminology in the public domain, and it should therefore be of no surprise that there are so many disputes and misunderstandings, because there is so much lack of understanding as to the real meaning of words. It should not be a surprise when Human Beings read books regarding abstract truths, and judge the content of these books in the same manner as a blind man would judge colors. It should also not be a surprise that many Human Beings do not even understand half the book, and most do not understand the whole book.

Since the beginning of time, this has always been the fate of books which dealt with the subject of abstract objects, and the fate of this book will be the same.

Abstract matters are for thinkers and not for those who do not want to think. There is a proverb which states: There are books which bring salvation in the hands of the thinker, and destruction in the hands of the fool.

Since Sensuous Truth exists, so exists Spiritual Truth, and that is the clearness of the matter itself - that is the true, Absolute Truth. But this Absolute Truth has its boundaries in accordance with the ability of our understanding.

The primary source of Absolute Truth comes from God, Who is Goodness and Truth. Goodness is in this consideration the Mother of Creation; Truth is the Daughter of Goodness and the Mother of Existence.

Truth is the matter itself, therefore, there is only one truth.

Sensuous Truth or Relative Truth are only approximations of Absolute Truth. They are more or less truth in accordance to the degree of their relationship with Absolute Truth.

Error or untruth is organic. They originate within the limits of the senses and in the erroneous perceptions.

God is not subject to error! He cannot be subject to anyone because He does not perceive through the senses. His perception is based on total clearness, simultaneous overview, not successive perceptibility.

Understanding (Recognition) in Human Beings is the successive power to obtain clearness, and its organ is the Will. With the Will, the understanding increases and attains the ability to accept the influences of the Divinity, and through God, through the Truth, to recognize.

There are degrees of understanding or recognition. The one who receives his understanding through the senses, understands the least. The one who understands through the Spirit, understands more. However, the one, who understands through God, possesses the highest understanding. That is why God is called the Truth, the Path and the Life.

Human Beings only possess successive abilities to progress towards perfection. We must possess within us the power to ascend, progress, and of necessity, this Law of our Being and this power of ascent, is the Will. Through the Will alone we become an active creature, otherwise we would be passive (suffering). The Will is, therefore, the staircase to understanding.

Every improvement of your Will is one step closer to the Divinity. There we receive a brighter light and remove ourselves from error, which lies in the sensuality.

37. The Will.

The Will is the consequence of Recognition (Understanding).

Sensuous Recognition (Understanding) brings forth sensuous Will and Spiritual Recognition (Understanding) brings forth Spiritual Will.

The sensuous Will has as the cause of his being, self-love and world-love. The Spiritual Will has God's Love and Love for thy neighbour.

Seeking to recognize (understand-realize) God is, therefore, the most necessary endeavour for Human Beings in order to change their volition, because only the change of the Will from the sensuous to the spiritual is Approximation.

Since God as a Spirit would be incomprehensible to our organs, this is communicated to us through Nature. He makes use of this organ to proclaim His existence and through His benevolence, He attracts our curiosity, so that we get to know the Originator of all the beautiful things which He created. He also made certain that the Will becomes the first consequence of recognition (understanding).

Human Beings have the ability of sensuous recognition (understanding) and sensuous volition, spiritual recognition and spiritual volition.

Human Beings have within them a double, twofold power, and a double, twofold ability, because Human Beings are animal beings and Spiritual Beings.

The ability of sensuous recognition and sensuous volition belongs to the animal; spiritual recognition and spiritual volition belongs to a Human Being because the spiritual recognition and the spiritual volition unite when the state of a Human Being has been reached, and it prepares a Human Being for his future existence.

Upon this development, his future existence is dependent; the greater his spiritual recognition, his spiritual volition, the more he prepares himself for his future level on the staircase of development.

Sensuous recognition and sensuous volition require the maintenance of the animal body and belongs to the necessity of the animal existence and the physical life. Spiritual recognition and spiritual volition require the maintenance and existence of the Soul, and belong to the Soul-Life.

Sensuous recognition and sensuous volition are attributes of the Animal Human Being. Spiritual recognition and spiritual volition are attributes of the Spirit Human Being.

God does not have sensuous volition because He is Spirit and He does not possess senses; therefore, only the spiritual volition of the Divinity can assimilate, which is Spirit; sensuous volition cannot assimilate.

Since no effect is without consequence, recognition must have also a consequence, and this consequence, as was mentioned before, is the Will.

The sensuous Will is being determined through self-love and world-love, or the link which unites the sensuous recognition with the sensuous Will, that is world-love and self-love. The link which unites the spiritual recognition with spiritual Will is God's Love and Love for thy neighbour (charity).

In this union of the spiritual recognition with the spiritual Will lies the foundation of all morality, since morality is based on the necessary relationship to unite the spiritual Will with the spiritual recognition and to transform into Beings of a higher continuance.

If the Spiritual Will is the consequence of Spiritual Recognition, then, out of necessity, an impetus emerges within us to want the Recognition; this impetus is Approximation, Advancement, Soul-Development.

Spiritual advancement depends upon the purity of our Will, and the purity of our volition depends upon the assimilation of our Will with the Will of the Divinity.

Nothing is without action and reaction; the recognition (realization) has an effect on the Will, the Will effects the recognition and, depending upon the state of the reaction of the Will, the future gradation of recognition will conduct itself accordingly.

If the volition would not have a retroactive effect on the first degree of the Spiritual Recognition, then the recognition would have no advancement. Through the effect of the retroaction upon the Will, the future recognition increases and, on the other hand, the future volition through the future recognition also increases.

Some of you might think there are contradictions in these statements, but if you properly examine these sentences, you will find no contradictions. Even though the Will is the only consequence of the recognition (realization), it is, however, only the volition which leads to the realization (understanding). We must not forget that Human Beings first want sensuous and then want spiritual. And we must not forget that there are will powers and a driving force of the Will.

Human Beings always want the good; they only seize the evil as a pretext. Their volition of sensuous goodness leads them to contemplate spiritual goodness and therefore becomes the first reason towards spiritual recognition (realization).

When a Human Being begins to recognize spiritually, then his sensuous Will changes into spiritual Will, since the first step of spiritual recognition consists of the greatest purity of the sensuous volition, because this purity gives you the ability to have spiritual recognition (understanding).

The question now arises: Is sensuous volition not also the consequence of sensuous recognition? And when a Human Being recognizes only in a coarse sensuous manner, then his volition can only be coarse sensuous?

This question can be answered as follows: You must differentiate the volition or the Will from the determination of the Will; or the volition in its development from the volition in its existence (being).

245

The volition in its development lies within us before the recognition and it is the driving force of the Will. The volition in its existence is determined first through the recognition (realization) and it is the determination of the Will, a consequence of the recognition (realization).

Everything in Nature is a chain; the recognition is in accordance to the volition in its development; the volition in its existence is in accordance to the recognition.

The recognition is the determination of the Will, therefore, the Will in its existence is the consequence of the recognition. The Will in its development alone must be of this determination and that is the willpower, because in the order of things is Cause, Effect and Consequence - willpower, recognition (understanding-realization) and the driving force of the Will.

But how, in a Human Being, does the volition originate in its development and its existence?

The volition in its development originates in a Human Being first through self-love; this leads him to sensuous recognition (understanding), sensuous goodness, and this sensuous recognition leads him to sensuous volition.

This self-love leads him also to objects outside of himself and teaches him the want for others; that is also the gradation from self-love to love for other Human Beings.

Human Beings receive a twofold power of their volition, thereby increasing the circle of their recognition and it is then determined by the love for others.

Human Beings are in possession of powers (forces), abilities and driving forces. Freedom is the ability to unite the volition with the recognition. If Human Beings would not possess this ability, then Human Beings would not be capable of volition. The Will, in its development, is a consequence of freedom, as the Will in its existence is a consequence of the recognition.

There is the driving force of recognition (understanding) and the driving force of the Will; recognition-power and willpower.

The recognition-forces ennoble the willpower, and the ennobled willpower produces new recognition-forces through which comes into being ennobled willpower which, in turn, effects retroactively the recognition and increases the recognition-power and perfects the willpower, which is being brought forth through this increased recognition-power.

God is goodness and truth. His recognition is goodness, His volition is truth. His highest purity is governed by this volition.

The union of the spiritual Will with the spiritual recognition is the union of the recognition of goodness with the practice of the truth, and this is the Path of "Becoming One".

38. The Miracle Powers Of Nature.

There are wonderful appearances in Nature which are incomprehensible for Beings like us, in the way we are organized. Incomprehensible, since we have no concept of these things - no idea. Ideas are impressions, organic appearances. This incomprehensibility is mostly dependent upon our organization. That means we are not organized in a manner in which we can accept this or that matter.

This does not leave us with the consequence that everything which, up to now, was incomprehensible, has to remain incomprehensible.

With the change in our organs or with the change of the objects, things which are now incomprehensible, can become comprehensible.

Many abilities slumber in Human Beings, which are necessary for our future state of development, and with the development of these abilities, our organs change and the abilities to comprehend matters which were incomprehensible to our organization before this change increase.

Nature beckons us with high anticipations. Within the seed of the fruit lies the future tree, even though it appears to our eye only as a seed. It then starts to develop, becomes a sprout, a young tree, which bears blossoms and fruit, and everything becomes visible to us, but when it was still a seed, we had no organs to see this.

The incomprehensibility of many wonderful things lies mostly therein, because we judge them in accordance to the perceptibility of our organs, sometimes also in accordance to the abstract concepts which we have of the visible impression of things, before we have made certain ontological truths our own, without considering that a change in the senses changes the perceptibility, and that through Soul-Exaltation, the inner state changes.

Because of this misconception, this error, the effects and the magic appearances are, to most Human Beings, incomprehensible, because they are measured in accordance with their own knowledge and judged in accordance with their own concepts.

If you want to measure something, then the object should determine the measure, and you cannot, unless you have measured the object, judge its dimensions; but, this is how it is most often done.

The Physicist says: "This is an illusion, that is tomfoolery, this has no foundation in Nature, they are charlatans!" It is easy to belittle and despise things. Instead of criticizing, they should examine things more thoroughly because it is not a foregone conclusion when you have a measuring tape of one thousand meters, that there are no things for which this measure is too short.

Very few Human Beings think about the innermost of things. Contemplate on the following sentences as they will answer many great questions:

1. There is an All (Universe), and this All makes a Whole.

2. Everything which is in this All, belongs out of necessity, and it is connected to the Whole.

3. Everything is One. Things seem to differentiate by form and shape, and through this they differ.

4. Human Beings are in one respect different from all other things.

5. Human Beings do not have to remain indefinitely the way they are - they can change.

6. There are things which are outside Human Beings that are a reality.

7. These things which are outside of Human Beings, can have an effect on Human Beings.

8. These things are the ones, and Human Beings are the ones who bring forth these changes.

9. I am also different when they bring forth different effects out of me.

10. These certain things appear different to me, when I myself or my organs have changed.

11. Those things are not really what they seem to be because they appear to be different when the organs change.

248

12. These certain things must, with changed organs, out of necessity, appear differently.

13. But they are something, because everything is something; there is nothing which is nothing, even an idea is something, an imprint, a picture.

14. There are things which cannot really exist, but they are, in and through others, a reality.

15. Expansion, composition, body and figure cannot be listed under this, the last category.

16. Among the composition of matter, there must be finer things hidden.

17. These refined, hidden things are the reason for all effectiveness, the phenomenons, the matter, and the compositions.

18. There are hidden forces which produce, in us all, organic appearances.

19. Whenever the form, figure or shape, and composition of a thing changes, then a change also takes place in the inner forces.

20. We are capable of bringing forth this inner change of the forces, if we determine these circumstances under which these changes of shape or form have taken place.

21. All causes which are similar bring forth similar effects, and similar effects produce similar causes.

22. I am something permanent, that is constantly being modified.

23. My body is a composition and it cannot be permanent.

24. My "I" is essentially different from my body.

39. There Is One All And
This All Is Whole.

Everything the Creator created, belongs to the Whole. It exists out of necessity and belongs to the harmony of the universe.

Therefore, the smallest matter is important because everything is in contact with the Whole. That is why the Creator counted every grain of sand on the shores of the ocean and all the dust particles in the air, which can be seen in the rays of the sun. They all belong to the All - without them, the Whole would not be.

It is a Law of Being that nothing is destroyed, it is only changed. Every change belongs to the Great All and takes place in accordance to the Laws of Harmony.

Human Beings!, in the smallest of changes study the changes of the greatest. Every change has a very small beginning and grows into the greatest possible change. Study the connection of the parts; study that everything great is composed of many small particles. and often the smallest change can bring forth an infinite amount of other changes, therefore, many effects of Magic will not be unknown.

40. Everything Which Is In This All
Belongs Out Of Necessity
And It Is In Contact With The Whole.

Every effect is already a change and every change has an effect. Whosoever acts, changes, and whosoever changes, acts.

Since the smallest is in contact with the greatest, every change which takes place in the smallest has an effect on the greatest, but the effect upon our organization is in an incomprehensible manner.

Since "I" belongs to the Whole, every change has an effect on me, and when I act and change, then there is an effect in me and a change occurs because I am a part of the Whole.

Therefore, there is an infinite gradation of changes, from the noticeable to the unnoticeable.

Everything - whatever will be - is already present. The past through the causes, and the present through the effects, and the future through the consequences.

Future and past are only for Human Beings in relationship to their organization; in the All of Creation there is eternal present.

41. Everything Is One:
Things Only Differ In Their Manner,
And Through This They Vary From Each Other.

Everything is One. This is one of the greatest statements of the wonderful appearances.

The thousandfold modifications of this One are the cause of the diversity of things. The manner of the perceptibility of this One is the Origin of Being of the differences. Everything which exists is a part of the Whole, of this One.

They become parts relative to our perception, which does not embrace the Whole.

The number one is the cause of origin of all numbers, and all numbers reduce to the number one again. The thousandfold changes or variations, millions, trillions are nothing else, but repeated units. The many different modifications of the number one are the cause of the thousandfold changes of the numbers, out of which so many wonderful things come into being.

42. Human Beings Act;
They Were Not Always The Way They Are -
They Can Be Changed.

The effect is the consequence of the power. Action of effect can also mean when the power sets into motion other abilities.

To work, or to be active, is one of the most marvellous attributes of Human Beings. The ability to accomplish this lies within the innermost, because Human Beings have abilities, powers and effects.

The ability is a slumbering power. The power is the developed ability. The effect is the consequence of the power, and everything together is One.

Within the ability already lies the power and the effect. The power is in accordance to the ability, and the effect is in accordance to the power.

Life is nothing else but a declaration of developed, effective powers.

The more the power, the more life, the more effectiveness. The more you work, the more you live. Whosoever lives a lot, works a lot. Activity is a declaration of life.

Nothing is without power; only sometimes the powers are in a slumber and are waiting to be developed.

Powers have an effect on abilities; that means, active powers have an effect on slumbering powers, or powers have an effect on abilities, which make out of slumbering powers, through development, active powers.

In order that this effect can be obtained, equality is a necessary ingredient, because only the same powers have an effect on the same slumbering abilities which, however, very often in the course of their development, become stronger than the active powers.

One body has an effect on another body through motion, because motion is developed ability and becomes physical or body power.

The power is in accordance to the manner of the motion; strong motion, strong power; weak motion, weak power.

All life is motion; everything which has life-ability (viability), has energy (power).

Bringing forth motion means to develop life-forces, to produce energy (power) out of slumbering abilities, of which the consequences are effects.

Therefore, we can see that Human Beings who want to have an effect on objects outside of themselves must recognize the innermost of things.

The same forces do not have an effect against each other; one must always be stronger than the other. Such is the Law of Things in the coarse, physical world, and it is also so in the subtle, and in the Spiritual World.

That which we call Spirit has more life than the physical body, because the physical body receives its life only through the Power of the Spirit. Therefore, the Spirit has a higher sphere of activity, a higher life.

In the Spirit, the life-energies are constantly being developed. This constant development is the Life-Law of the Spirit.

This constant development brings forth the life in the animalistic bodies, and that is what we call animation.

To receive more and more life means to become more and more spiritual, and to become spiritual is the Path to Assimilation which, through infinite gradations - as we can see in all creatures - progresses from the lowest developed life-force to the highest.

Within Human Beings lie abilities which are essentially different from the abilities of the bodies. That is why Human Beings exist in a manner which is different from the manner in accordance to which the mere physical bodies exist.

Since there are many different abilities within Human Beings, therefore, different powers develop within Human Beings. These powers bring forth special effects, which the mere physical body is not capable of bringing forth, through which the Human Being proclaims his exalted powers and his Soul-Continuance.

Nature shows us that the inner powers and abilities are entirely different from those which we call the external or outer abilities, and everything "wonderful" in the physical world consists of the developed inner abilities, because they are concealed to our senses.

That is why the power of the magnet, the effects of electricity, give rise to general admiration, because they were developed inner abilities, inner powers.

The more inner abilities a thing contains, the more are the slumbering powers and the more exceptional are the effects such a thing can produce.

Within Human Beings lie the greatest abilities, the greatest slumbering powers, in infinite gradations. Within Human Beings alone lies the power to do the most wonderful things, through their developed powers, for their fellow Human Beings.

The greatest mistake which is made in finding the solution to the puzzle of peculiar appearances is judging things in accordance to their outside or external powers, because we have not taken the time to study the inner powers.

43. There Are Things Which Are Reality
Besides Human Beings.

A thing, an object, which I perceive through my organs, is outside of myself.

The more organs there are, the more things there are outside of us; the clearer the organs are, the clearer the things outside of us are. The duller the organs are, the more blurred are the things which are outside of us.

The more ill the organs are, the more incapable they are of receiving impressions, therefore, the less things are outside of us. The organs, therefore, make things which are outside of us, appearances to us.

Appearance is a manner, which is in accordance to the Power of Perception of our senses.

Since there are things outside of us, and everything has abilities, powers and effects, such things which are outside of us can affect us necessarily, through their developed powers; only these effects are always organic. There can, however, also be things which are within us, and these things which are within, must be different from the things which are outside of us.

Things which are within us cannot be physical things; they must be different from the physical things, because they cannot be perceived through the physical senses.

Since there is nothing without an organ, there is nothing without connections. There is however, an organ of the inner perception, and this organ is the inner sense of which we spoke earlier.

In the inner sense also lie abilities, powers and effects. They are abilities which are different from the physical abilities of the body; powers, which are different from the physical powers of the body; and effects, which are different from the physical effects of the body.

Why then is the world surprised about these inner, developing powers, about these inner effects? Because very few have a sense for the perception of these things!!!

44. Things, Objects, Which Are
Outside Of Human Beings
Can Have An Effect On Human Beings.

The fact that things which are outside of Human Beings can affect Human Beings organically, is not subject to contradiction, but we should be aware and think about the fact that these effects are only organic. You have the knowledge that every effect has infinite gradations. Through these gradations come into being the differences of sounds, from the coarsest to the most refined; and the nuances of colors, from the darkest to the lightest.

All this is of the utmost necessity - necessary for the thousand-foldness of the perceptible organs.

A question which is on a higher level is: Can things, which are within Human Beings, have an effect on things which are outside of Human Beings?

The answer is: Yes - certainly! And the effect is twofold. Either the inner affects the external by means of the senses upon the objects through the inner power of the senses, or the inner of the Human Being immediately affects the Inner of Things and develops in the same, slumbering, spiritual powers and brings forth wonderful, physical effects, wherein lies a great part of the Secrets of Magic.

45. Things Which Are Outside Of Myself
Are The Ones, And I Am The
One, Whereby Changes Are Brought Forth.

Since the effects of the external things behave towards Human Beings organically, and since there are infinite gradations from the most imperfect to the most perfect organs, it is, therefore, essentially necessary that the power of perceptibility modifies just as manyfold.

Any weakening, any strengthening, of the organs therefore brings other appearances forth. What kind of substance for infinite Works of Magic?

46. I Am Different When Things Bring
Forth Different Effects In Me.

In the difference of the effects of things lies the difference of things. It is not always necessary to change the things themselves, but only the organs, which perceive the things, and works of wonder come into being.

All sorcerous deceptions are based on this theory. This is done by changing the perceptibility of the organs. No sooner is this accomplished, and the Human Being is placed into an entirely different world.

Therefore the following statements can be made: Certain things appear to me to be different, when I myself or when my organs are changed. These things are in themselves not what they appear to be, because they appear to be different to me, in accordance to my changed organs, and they can be measured in accordance to this basic rule.

47. Things Which Are Outside Of Myself,
Even Though They Affect Me Only Organically,
Are Something, Because Everything Is Something.
Nothing Exists Which Is Not Something, Even An Idea
Is Something - An Impression, A Picture.

Everything is, therefore, something, really something; everything is an impression, everything is a picture.

My picture in the mirror is an impression. The picture of a rose in the eyes of thousands is a thousandfold impression, therefore, a thousand pictures of a rose in the eyes of millions, millions of roses. Yet, it is still only one rose with millions of different impressions, of which each impression behaves organically. What an immeasurable field for contemplation!!!

Every vapour of the finest evaporation of the rose is again, totally a rose, in accordance to the perceptibility of the organs of her appearance.

Take the smallest of snails and pulverize them. Then, through a microscope observe every particle and you will find in the tiniest part, as you do in the largest part, the sketches of Nature.

Pulverize, for that matter, any being to such a degree that you only have the finest of dust left. You will find that every particle of dust has the picture of this being. It is nothing but an external change. The same as gold will always be gold, even if you reduce it from a large quantity to the tiniest particle; you can change the form, but you cannot change the inner quality of the matter.

Only when the Inner of the thing is changed, the pictures cease to be organic for us, and they become different forms.

Add to the pulverized snails a drop of nitre and all at once, all forms are changed.

There are things which, in a way, cannot exist, but they become in and through others, a reality.

Expansion, composition, body and figure cannot be added to the category of the latter things. Among the matter of composition must be concealed other refined things.

These refined concealed things are the reason for all effectiveness, the phenomenons, the matter, and the compositions.

48. Powers And Forms.

There are powers in natural things, which have their source of origin in a mixture of the elements; such is the power of heating-up, to cool-off, to dry and to moisten. These powers modify again in accordance to infinite gradations.

There are also other powers within the matter itself. That means that there are objects whose ingredients consist of different mixtures of their Primary Matter, of which each part is again a whole in Nature, but to our organization, all of these parts appear to us totally as a whole.

To be ready, to digest, to dissolve, to soften, and to harden - those are her powers. They are called drying, consuming, burning, condensing, opening, evaporating, strengthening, sweetening, attracting and collective things.

It lies within Nature, that the unequal distribution of Primary Matter must bring forth different effects.

How infinite must the number of modifications be, when you contemplate on the following:

Fire - Air - Water - Earth, when mixed in equal proportions, bring forth different conditions, than when Fire - Air - Water are mixed in equal parts and the Earth has less or more proportionately in respect to the other three elements. The following chart will illustrate this better:

Fire	-	Air	-	Water	-	Earth
Predominates						

Fire	-	Air	-	Water	-	Earth
		Predominates				

Fire	-	Air	-	Water	-	Earth
				Predominates		

Fire	-	Air	-	Water	-	Earth
						Predominates

If you would calculate all the transmutations and combinations of all the predominations you will be able to see all the possibilities of the transpositions.

When you calculate the transpositions with the number ninety, then there will be a total of a million transpositions.

In accordance with the multiplicity of the transpositions, the following basic rules can be established.

Any Primary Matter must, in accordance to its mixture with others, bring forth different effects which are more or less appropriate to its inherent powers.

These effects were called by the people of old, qualitates secundas, because they do not follow the effects of the Primary

257

Matter, they follow the effects of the mixture; or, because they are not the consequences of the effects of the Primary Matter, they are consequences of the mixtures.

Therefore, there are progressive consequences, and to the effects of heat, belongs softening.

Progressive consequences of cold are hardening and freezing. Then there are effects which the people of old called qualitates tertias, which express themselves in certain specified objects.

These qualitates tertias are the consequences of the qualitatum secundarum, as the qualitates secondariae are the consequences of the first qualities; so that every consequence becomes an effect and thereby brings forth another effect.

All things consist of these three attributes and within these three attributes (qualities) lies the Great Mysterium, to which the people of old gave the number three. They coined a name for this number and called it "The Mighty Number".

The three attributes (qualities), qualitates tertiae, are determined through the homogeneity of the parts which are present in the suffering bodies and upon which the active parts act.

Upon the knowledge of these conditions of the inner qualities, which the bodies have towards one another, the works of wonder are founded, which seem to contradict things in Nature. For instance: The invention of fire burning in water; the invention of oils which extinguish fire; the invention of lamps which always burn; artificial lights which do not consume themselves; and flames which do not burn.

The first effects of things are founded in their Primary Matter.

These effects behave in accordance to the mixture of their Primary Matter, and the diversity of the mixtures of the Primary Matter brings forth again a diversity of effects.

The first reason for every internal change lies within the change of the mixtures of the Primary Matter.

In order to bring about the opposite effect, I must have knowledge of the inside of the matter, and then weaken the inner powers or, I must have the capability of changing their effects.

There are also powers (forces) which do not have the internal as their source of origin, but are a consequence of the external, and that is the form.

The form is the external of things, and this external comes into being through the mixture of the internal. That means to say, this or that mixture of Primary Matter, or of the internal, brings forth this or that form.

As mentioned before, different effects behave in accordance to the diversity of the transpositions of the inner forces and therefore bring forth coagulations, compositions, expansions, hardening, etc., through which things acquire their external form which, out of consideration to us, conduct themselves organically.

Every thing has its concealed attributes or qualities! They are called concealed attributes because our organs do not notice them and they lie hidden in the Inner of Things.

The figure or the contour are essentially different from the form, because the figure or the contour are external parts of the form.

Those who shape or sculpture contours, change only the external parts of the forms, never the inner of things.

Since everything which exists belongs to the Great All, the powers of the forms or the things cannot be calculated separately or individually for us in accordance to their being; instead, they contain within them higher powers and these forms we cannot perceive.

Since everything is One and everything is a Whole, no change can take place in the Whole unless this change effects to more or lesser degree, all parts of the Whole. This effect has infinite gradations, but within itself, it always remains to be an effect. This explains what the people of old called "Influence".

49. Influence.

Influence or effect, participation, has no other meaning than the consequences of a change which occur in some of the parts of the Whole, and then affect the remaining parts of the Whole.

It was mentioned earlier that everything is a Whole and the difference of the things emerges only in the manner of their being. This clearly proves that body upon body, and thing upon thing, or matter upon matter must necessarily be effective in accordance to their manner of being.

The effectiveness or the consequences are in accordance to their powers, the powers in accordance to the abilities, the abilities in accordance to the manner of the being of the thing. Through this chain comes into being direct and indirect effects from the first member to the last member. That is how the number one affects every possible number, and its power is in accordance to the action of the numbers, which in itself are only progressions of the number one or they are repetitions.

So, everything is in proportion to each other. Our world-body has

259

proportions, viewed as a part of the Whole, to all the other possible world-bodies in the Universe, even to the remotest, and these effects have infinite gradations.

Every stronger body has an affect on a weaker body, or plus-power upon minus-power. Through this law, all effects and activities come into being. That is how the Sun makes its effects known, through its approximation or through its distance.

Every approximation and distance is a change; every change an effect.

Our new generation holds the belief that the planets have no effect upon our world-body, and thereby dismiss the whole system of influence. This belief contains the highest and the greatest of errors. We cannot view our world separately or singly - our world is part of the whole universe. Our world belongs to the Whole, and in the Whole, one part has an effect on the other. These reciprocal effects make the chain of the worlds; they are responsible for all life in the whole universe.

50. Unravelling The Puzzle Of Some Magic Secrets.

We do not understand the Magic of the people of old, because we take matters much to physically and sensually.

Within the symbols of the people of old lie wisdom and greatness; in order to reach an understanding, you must penetrate into the inner of their secrets and not be satisfied with the surface of the matter.

The knowledge of the numbers are the rudiments of Magic; they are what the people of old called the Quabbalah. The concepts which most Human Beings have of the Quabbalah, are to the highest degree sensuous, contradictory and absurd.

Those who do not have the ability to think into the inner of Magic, are the originators of all this ridiculousness.

People without understanding want the secrets of the Quabbalah, which lie in the inner of the matter, to be on the exterior, and they do not think that the exterior is coincidental and changeable, whereas only the inner is Truth alone.

Numbers are arbitrary determinations, as are the letters of the alphabet, if we accept them as we do the letters of the alphabet. In order to find the Truth, you must connect the spiritual with them.

The numbers lie essentially in Nature; that means, not the signs from 1, 2, 3, but the unit with its progressions.

The system of the Universe consists of three triplicities, therefore, the threefold triangle, according to which the people of old signified as God.

The following belong to the First Triplicity (Qualitates Primarias):

Prime Prime Ability	-	in German = Ururfähigkeit
Prime Prime Power	-	in German = Ururkraft
Prime Prime Effectiveness	-	in German = Ururwirkung

The Second Triplicity (Qualitates Secundariae):
Prime Ability
Prime Power
Prime Effectiveness

and, finally, the Third Triplicity (Qualitates Tertiaea):
Ability of Matter
Power of Matter
Power of Effectiveness

We count among the First Triplicity the Prime Prime Ability, the Prime Prime Power and the Prime Prime Effectiveness. To this belong the attributes of the Deity, which the people of old expressed in the simple triangle.

The first ability of the effectiveness of all things or matter is the number one. It is the number of unity, the number of the Deity. The first ability's first effectiveness is the number two, the number of production. The first effectiveness' first consequence is the number three, the first number of perfection.

The number three, or the First Triplicity altogether are One, because ability, effectiveness and consequence are One.

In consideration to the Deity this three is: Wisdom, Love, and Creation.

Wisdom, Ability, Love, Effectiveness or Power, developed Wisdom, Creation, consequence of Love, of the developed power.

The Second Triplicity or Prime Abilities, Prime Powers, Prime Effectiveness originate out of the First Triplicity and, therefore, become the first effectiveness' first consequence, or the first ability of continued effects, number four or the number of the body.

This ability has again its effects or existence and out of this originates the number five or the number of the senses, and from this, all possible numbers of physical things or matter can be perceived and finally the consequence of the developed power of the number of perception - the number six.

The gradations are as follows:

Number 4 - is the physical body.

Number 5 - is the senses or to perceive the physical bodies.

Number 6 - is the true perception of the physical bodies, through the senses.

Finally, there is the Third Triplicity, which originates successively out of the Second and First Triplicities.

The consequence of the preceding triplicity produces the first ability of the continued effects, or the number seven.

This ability has its effects which, in its progression, is the number eight, and the consequence is the number nine.

The sequence in which this Triplicity stands is

7

8

9

therefore, the development of the physical bodies, especially the main-epochs of Human Beings subsequent to the number seven.

Through this, this question is solved: Why does a child who is born in the seventh month have a better chance of staying alive than a child born in the eighth month? The seventh month is the number of ability; the number eight is the number of development which, out of necessity, must have as a consequence the complete number, which is the number nine.

When a child comes into the world in the eighth month, a further development is taking place at this time which, through the consequence of birth, is being taken away, namely, the order to reach maturity. It, therefore, cannot continue out of its sphere - it cannot live - because this sequence, this consequence, belongs to the life. In the ninth month, however, the ability, effect and consequence are completed.

Out of these three triplicities, which consist of the Spirit and the Body Abilities, the powers and effects come into being a Fourth Triplicity, or abilities, powers and effects in a further progression, as brought-forth abilities, powers and effects of the first three triplicities, and this one is the Moral Triplicity.

The consequence of the latter triplicity gives again the ability of the first, namely the last consequence is existence and existence results again in ability.

The Fourth Triplicity, in consideration of the previous triplicities, has the number ten or the Numerum Universalem, which leads back to the unity (1), and it is, therefore, called the Numerus of the beginning and the end.

Its development takes place in the same manner as it was with the first triplicities: Its power is eleven, its consequence twelve. The whole impression of the First Triplicity, God's Image, Human Abilities, Recognition, Will, Deed.

These are the true mysteries of the numbers, the reason for the quabbalistic calculations, which do not exist because of arbitrary words and letters of the alphabet, but because of a chain of abilities, powers and effects.

Through this exists the Harmony of the Whole, and one has an effect upon the other, it assimilates, it rejects, and it makes itself similar to the unity.

Since the number ten is Numerus Universalis, and it originally emerged through progression from the number one, the people of old expressed through the repetition of the number one, the ten names of the Deity and they, therefore, placed the ten names of the Deity in accordance to the ten numbers.

The name of the Deity as far as the number seven is concerned, for example, is nothing other than the relationship of the first ability of the First Triplicity compared to the ability of the Third Triplicity. Therefore, the people of old gave every name a number, which is saying nothing but the effect of the divine ability. These effects or numerations have their gradation through the first three triplicities.

The first name is EHIEH. His numeration is Kether; the meaning of this is, the most simple Deity or the Deity in its being.

The second name is JAH. His numeration is Chokma; it means God's existence, since God's being is only the ESSE of the Deity.

The numeration Chokma means Wisdom or the consequence of God's existence.

The third name is Jehova Eloim, whose numeration is Bina, that is, effect and providence.

This completes the First Triplicity and shows the progression from one to three. That is, God's Being, Existence and Effect: Wisdom - Love - Creation.

The fourth name is Elhoa, the Almighty God's ability, and has to his numeration, Haesset - goodness, effect of the first abilities in the Second Triplicity.

The fifth name is Elhoim Gibor; his numeration is Geburah; that means, strength.

The sixth name or God in the third degree of the Second Triplicity is Elhoa, and the numeration is beauty and life.

The Third Triplicity in which the seventh name of God, or where God stands as ability in the Third Triplicity as Jehovah Tsebaoth; and the numeration is Netsah; that means, completion of strength.

The eighth name, Elhoim Tsebaoth; the numeration is Hod or order.

The ninth, Elchäi, the numeration is Jesod, or the reason of connections or unions.

This is the end of the three triplicities and the fourth comes into being - the Moral Triplicity.

In the number ten is the name of God as Adonai Melech, and his effect is Kingdom, God's Temple and the reasons for religion.

These examples should give us an idea that the Quabbalists have an entirely different meaning connected to their teachings than what the whole world thinks it to be.

The Theme of the Whole is as follows:

The First Triplicity.

The Prime Prime Ability, Number 1; Name: Ehieh; Numeration or effect: Simplicity of the Deity.

Prime Prime Power, Number 2; Name Jah; Numeration or effect: God's Existence.

Prime Prime Effect, Number 3; Name Jehovah Eloim; Numeration or effect: Divine Effect and Providence.

The Second Triplicity.

Prime Ability, Number 4; Name: Elhoa; Numeration: Goodness.

Prime Power, Number 5; Name: Elohim Gibor; Numeration: Strength.

Prime Effect, Number 6; Name: Eloah; Numeration: Beauty, Life.

The Third Triplicity.

Ability of Matter, Number 7; Name: Jehovah Tsebaoth; Numeration: Completion, Strength.

Power of Matter, Number 8; Name: Elohim Tsebaoth; Numeration: Order.

Effect of Matter, Number 9; Name: Elchäi; Numeration: The reason for all connection or unions.

The System of Creation is based on these triplicities, because abilities, powers and consequences make a Whole. This Whole is the Creation.

The reality of the exterior of God is the world, and this world exists through developed powers and consequences.

Every triplicity has, therefore, its worlds, and their gradation leads to the highest creation.

Therefore, for every world, there are organic creatures from the lowest level of creation to the highest.

These creatures of these different worlds are divided, in accordance to their triplicity.

The First Triplicity contains three Spiritual Worlds:
1.   The Beings of the first World are called Seraphims.
2.   The Beings of the second World are called Cherubims.
3.   The Beings of the third World are called Intelligences.

The Second Triplicity also contains three Spiritual Worlds:
1.   The Beings of the first World of the Second Triplicity are called Dominations.
2.   The Beings of the second World of the Second Triplicity are called Might (Authorities).
3.   The Beings of the third World of the Second Triplicity are called Powers - Forces.

The Third Triplicity has also three Worlds:
1.   The Beings of the first World are called Ordines.
2.   The Beings of the second World are called Archangels.
3.   The Beings of the third World are called Angels.

The Fourth Triplicity or the Moral Triplicity has only one Spirit World, and the Beings of this Spirit World are the Souls.

Unto this World borders the physical world and that is the first level of progression to the Spirit World.

These three triplicities, which we have just discussed, are the ones which the Quabbalists call the Hierarchies, and they are divided into the high, the medium, and the low.

Within the comparisons of these triplicities lies the origin of the true quabbalistic calculations.

51. Principles To Quabbalistic Calculation.

The Quabbalah is the science which takes into consideration the abilities, forces and consequences of matters, substances and things; and out of the Nature of a few known abilities, forces and consequences, finds other unknown abilities, forces and consequences.

The Quabbalah is, therefore, a calculation of things. Quabbalistic calculation means to compare abilities, forces and consequences amongst each other.

A quabbalistic result is a found ability, force or consequence.

All ultimate things are in accordance to a certain measure that comes into being through the multiplicity. This multiplicity is, in itself, only a repetition of a unit.

In arithmetic, these multiplicities become numbers; in the Quabbalah, they are called progressions - that means, abilities, forces and effects.

Out of the different classes of units come into being the numbers of arithmetic. Out of the progressions of the unit comes into being the abilities, forces and consequences in the Quabbalah.

Each of the nine numbers in arithmetic contains a different value as soon as it takes a different place.

Therefore, when it comes to quabbalistic calculations, every ability receives a different force, as soon as it takes a different triplicity.

To number in arithmetic means to give the product of several numbers one name.

To number quabbalistically is to designate the abilities, forces and effects of one thing.

In arithmetic, when we verbalize large numbers, they are placed into classes, therefore, the quabbalistic calculation of things are divided into the triplicities.

Quabbalistic addition means to place together abilities, forces and consequences. If you place the number one to the ability and the number one to the force, the consequence of this addition is the number two or the number of the product.

Quabbalistic subtraction means to subtract the present abilities, forces and effects from the preceding ones.

Quabbalistic multiplication means to unify the consequences with the forces and the abilities, or the abilities with the forces and the consequences, or the forces with the consequences and the abilities.

Quabbalistic division means to place the abilities, forces and consequences into their proper place.

Out of this you should be able to come to the conclusion that the true Quabbalah is not merely a figment of the imagination or a fantasy, but the Quabbalah is a true and superb science which has been practised in silence by the admirers of wisdom for thousands of years. The Quabbalah is the basis, the reason of science of all things, or the knowledge of the divine progressions in creation.

The one who bases the quabbalistic system upon the triplicities, and properly classifies the things in accordance to the forces which are indicated, will be able to bring forth in the comparisons, seemingly impossible things.

There has been enough revelation of information and we should remember at this point what a wise man once said:

I give into the hands of a labourer, metals, and I say to him: These metals contain gold; cleanse them of their waste and you will find the gold. If you do this, the apprentice does the work himself. If I give him the pure gold, then he does not require his own energy to purify the metal, instead, he would put his hands into his pockets and live in luxury from the gold, without work.

52. The Work And Deeds Of Human Beings.

All work which a Human Being brings forth is nothing but a painting of his plan, an imprint of his Inner, a drawing of his thoughts.

Human Beings endeavour to give as much resemblance to their copy as it is possible. He assimilates it as much as he can with the original, which lies in his Soul, so that he can give in the best possible manner, an impression of his thoughts.

If every Human Being could read the thoughts of another Human Being, these visible signs would not be necessary. Then the thought would be work and language, as fast and speedy as the thought itself.

But the Soul languishes in body-chains and the eye of recognition is apathetic to the perception of the Inner.

The Soul is forced to seek out sensuous tools for sensuous Human Beings and to make its Spirit-Language physical. Therefore, she gathered words, drawings, and hieroglyphics, and they are the tools of the impressions of the Inner.

The Soul makes use of these material-tools to prepare a Being for her thoughts which resemble her, since the body separates Souls from Souls. Therefore, the Soul makes use of everything at her disposal to unite herself with other Souls again, and the Soul designs in words

267

and deeds her picture and her existence, so that they may follow her inner inclination to unification and the particular union which lies in Nature; but the body excludes the Soul from this.

Within this inclination of the Soul lies the miraculousness of the Speakers and the Poets. How communicative is the Soul in all her feelings, how great her endeavour to assimilate the thoughts of others with hers, with one word, to Become One?

The inclination to unification is the Law of Being for the Soul. The general activity depends upon this law, and the incomprehensible inclination which we admire daily in the physical world, the reciprocal attraction of the bodies, their approximation, and their assimilations.

There lies a necessity in the Being, an inner compelling force, which every individuum, the Beings which surround it, are being drawn equally into their union. This is how the whole of Nature strives more and more towards unity. That which was separated, joins; that which was on the circumference, moves towards the centre; that which was hidden, comes to the Light. In this manner, harmony and order become victorious over disorder, thereby keeping all the Beings active. This great Law of Being is the impression of the incomprehensible Unity of God. He placed the same into us, and our destination is unity, to return to God, and unification.

His language lies within every creature in Nature. These are the letters, the words, through which He speaks to Human Beings: Your Destination Is Unity.

This language is the language of Love. The blissfulness, the welfare of the creatures, lies within the unification with God. If Human Beings would have never been separated from the Unity, then they would not be victims of their own error here on Planet Earth. Only in the distance, in the separation, lies the punishment, and the loving Deity placed all possible means into the Being of Things to remove this separation, which is so much in opposition to our being blissful.

53. The Word Of The Deity In Nature.

In every Being in Nature exists, for the Ones who think of God, ability and energy. Everywhere there is a hint of divine harmony of the purest of unison. Everywhere there are means of support, healing, rebirth and new creation.

Everywhere there are outflows of life, to save Beings from the clutches of death. They would wilt like a flower should they be separated from that which is life and energy.

This reunion with the primary source of life is the destination of Human Beings. We carry the imprint of unity and we proclaim this inclination towards unison in all that we do, in all of our activities.

Everything proclaims a greatness in us, which is worthy of the Creator Who created us, but how distorted has this picture become? This did not occur through God, nor through Nature, but through ourselves - we, who distanced ourselves from the Unity.

54. The Condition Of Separation
From The Unity.

Human Beings seek and God possesses; Human Beings inquire and God understands; Human Beings hope and God enjoys; Human Beings doubt and God Himself is Belief (Conviction) and Truth; we fear, and in God there is no fear, only Love.

God's greatness consists of the impression of His Image in every Being, and our greatness consists of the destruction of this impression and in the annihilation of the creatures.

The Creator of all Beings provided for all our necessities. He created the elements for our welfare and all the secret driving forces in Nature, and we employ them for destruction, to produce human misery.

We, who should be proclaiming the truth, are instead their pursuers and the followers of errors.

The whole of Nature is calling us and telling us: There is only one God, but the ones who God made Lords over Nature, we, Human Beings say, there is no God.

God, Who the whole of Nature proclaims through Love, Human Beings proclaim through atrocities and by desecrating His name. Human Beings determine, decide, judge, deceive, victimize, suppress, subjugate, strangle and murder in His Holy Name, the One Who is total Truth and the One Who is total Love.

God created all of us for the same blissfulness, and we separated ourselves from Him and rage against ourselves, against our brothers, who were created in the same image, and who have the same rights to God's Kingdom. This is the condition of being distant. Error and confusion are our punishment. Being created for a higher purpose can only occur through a union with God. Assimilation can place us closer to our bliss of unity.

55. The Voice Out Of The Clouds.

Those of you who have recognition without Will, that is power without Love. Those of you who have left the Path of Truth and seek the darkness, and remove mankind from the path of salvation - how cruel can you Human Beings be?! Why not admit the misery of your condition? You mutilate the language of Nature and your passionate clamour drowns out the voice of gentle Love which speaks in every Being. Through you, Truth should have declared its rights, instead, you built altars from lies and falsehoods and for error. How can righteousness, the Light and the Truth of the World become known, if you suffocate the pure concepts in your heart and do your utmost to extinguish every letter of Love which God wrote into every Being in Nature? How should Human Beings know that their Prime Being (in German = Urwesen) is holy and eternal when those of you who teach the ignorant are addicted to sensuality and passions?

You do not proclaim Love through hate, and you do not proclaim good deeds through blasphemy. Order and Life cannot exist where there is confusion and death. Raise up your heads and observe the degree of your remoteness on which you stand. Hear the mighty voice: Blissfulness exists only where there is assimilation with the Deity, and destruction, when Human Beings separate themselves.

56. The Alphabets To The Secrets.

There are only four letters in the Alphabet of Divine Matters. Therefore, those who judge this language according to the twenty-four letters of the alphabet, will not understand it.

The closer you are to the Deity, the less letters you require to make yourself understood.

It was a language which surpassed any other language in its simplicity, and the alphabet of this language consisted only of four letters. This language is still in existence, but the aberration of Human Beings removed Human Beings from its simplicity.

There is also another language and the alphabet of this language has twenty-two letters. The words are composed as well of the temporal, as they are of the spiritual bringing-forth of the great Prime Being.

There are also Human Beings who have in their Spirit-Language eighty-eight letters, therefore, they can never read the words of a language which contains four and twenty-two letters. Whosoever wants to learn the first two alphabets must, as much as it is possible, separate himself from the earthly, because these two alphabets belong to the Spirit-Language, and lead to clearness or a clear understanding.

57. Signs Of Nature.

The simplest observation in regards to what we call the Elementar-Light, beckons us and shows us how high Human Beings should ascend to receive the Light of the Spirit, because the Laws of the Spirit-Light have much in common with the Laws of the Elementar-Light.

It is a necessity of every Light to have its original prime beginning. Every light requires a basal surface, reaction, and a certain amount of receptive Beings.

The Forces of the Light express themselves through the number four:

1. The Prime Beginning
2. The Basal Surface
3. The Reaction
4. A Certain Amount of Receptive Beings

This is the manner in which the people of old understood this.

In the abyss of the Earth, the metals are robbed of this Light. The vegetation receives it, but without any benefit. The animals see it and enjoy it, but they do not possess the ability to observe it and to have it penetrate into their Innermost. This preference is reserved for Human Beings only.

Therefore, only within Human Beings lies the destiny of the benefit of the Light. There is, however, an essential difference in the classes of Human Beings:

1. There are Beings who separated totally from the receptivity of the Light.

2. There are Beings who did not totally separate from the Light but, in their instance, the Light has an effect only on the surface, without penetrating into the Innermost.

3. There are Beings who receive internally the ray of the Light, but who have not the faintest idea as to its effects.

271

4.   Then there are Beings who take part at the Prime Source of the Light from where it flows; they receive it, they see it, they enjoy it and they benefit. This condition is the highest enjoyment of the Light.

This benefit, this enjoyment, was once shared by Human Beings, but Human Beings wanted to transpose the fundamental principles of all Light. Yet to transpose the fundamental principles meant nothing but to lose them, and to lose them, meant to be robbed of them.

In doing so, Human Beings left the paradise of happiness which was designated by God to be their place of residence, thereby stepping down to a very low level from their first destination, to where they can hardly recognize the intellectual Light, even though it maintains itself in its brilliance, regardless of the coarse shell of the physical body.

58. Time.

Due to the deterioration of the Will, Human Beings separated from the Unity because they united with other things which were put together.

They came out of the Land of Clarity and entered into a place of residence of appearances. They left the Prime Source of the Light, the general point of lucidity, and entered into successive circumstances. These mixtures of things bring forth, through their blends, the appearances of time, and that is how out of Children of Eternity, we became Children of Time, and out of simple Beings, we became Beings composed of a mixture of things. This is the reason, the prime origin of separation, dissolution and death.

Whatever the composition is, it is subject to change; only the physical is subject to death and decomposition. The simplicity which comes from the Deity is immortal. Time causes the changes of things in the physical world and, at the same time, imprisons the eternal Soul of Human Beings in a dungeon. Similar to water, whose might it is to dissolve everything, either faster or slower, this changes the shape or form of the body. That is how Gold loses a nineteenth degree of its weight when it is poured into water, and it becomes the symbol of disparagement of our dignity.

59. *The Symbol Of Progression.*

Successive approximation towards the Prime Source of the Light, from which Human Beings are removed is the Law of Being of the Soul, and its necessity lies within the original relationships.

Imagine a mountain where, at its summit, the Prime Source of Light has its throne. Little by little, as the traveller gets closer to this Light, the area becomes more and more illuminated and he has a farther view. His sphere of vision increases in accordance to the degree and the level which he reaches. He notices other travellers before and behind him and he no longer doubts their existence, even if these travellers are not visible to his eyes, even those who are already higher up the mountain than he. Courageously he follows them; he is not upset by obstacles, and he follows the course of his destination.

The One who is imprisoned must break out of his prison, which holds him at the foot of the mountain. The One who is in shackles must break his chains, which are attached to heavy boulders at the foot of the mountain, if he wants to get closer to his Fatherland, which is located at the summit of the mountain.

The more the Prime Substances of the body change over to simplicity, the more power they receive, and when the Air is cleansed of all coarse physical substances and fills a room, even the imagination would shudder or shrink back from such a room.

60. *The Laws Of Progressions And The Laws Of The Numbers Of The Sensuous Things.*

There is an invisible Prime Fire, out of which originate all kinds of peculiar substances which form the bodies.

This Prime Fire becomes noticeable through the phlogiston, which every matter in its dissolution exhales. It is also called the substance of warmth.

This Prime Fire has three noticeable manifestations. It brings forth the material and visible fire. This visible Fire manifests itself in animals in the form of blood. The coarser Fire is threefold, because every material fire contains water and earth.

Regardless of this triplicity, it is still considered to be simple because it essentially has no special separation.

The second effect of the separation of this visible physical Fire is a watery, flowing, coarser substance.

The flowing, watery substance is twofold, because it is united with the earth and it is a product of the second action (actionis secundariae).

The third action separates the earth from the flow and brings forth the solid and the form.

The form appears to our eyes to be simple, but it becomes threefold through its measure and outflow and because this form is a compounded triplicity, that is the reason why it is the opposite of the fire, whose triplicity is simple.

Such are the Laws of the Progressions and the Numbers of Things, and the abilities of creation of the universe or the powers of production. You can observe how things become more and more physical the more they descend from the simplicity. The same as things conduct themselves in accordance to the Laws of Descent, there are also Laws of Ascent; that means from the physical Body to the first Powers of Production.

Through these ascending laws, the solid and the earthly disappear, it becomes soft and turns into water. The water becomes volatile and vanishes because it becomes volatile through the Elementar Fire. The Elementar Fire disposes of all its compositions and changes it over to its phlogiston and Prime Fire.

61. The Elements Are The Organs
Of The Upper Powers.

Fire ascends, Earth descends, and Water passes through a horizontal line and proclaims the upper powers of which the elements are the organs.

Gold proclaims to us, through its expansion, the remarkable powers of expansion of Nature, which reach the remotest being and bring forth the general harmony and conformity.

Plants lap up all the impure evaporations in the atmosphere and blend them with their own evaporations and return them to the atmosphere in pure form. They become a symbol to us that the existence of all Beings of Nature have no other ultimate reason as to maintain order and goodness.

The different effects of plants, their powers by day or by night, if they are in the sun or if they are in the shadow, are measures in accordance to the power of the reaction. Within this lie the secrets of healing.

In the animal kingdom, the quickness of the circulation of the

274

blood from the heart to the most outer parts becomes the symbol of the greatest generosity of the Creator.

Air unites the Earth and brings forth in the bodies effect and counter-effect, and it is the means of motion of the universe. It shows everywhere Omni-Might and Omni-Power - especially when you contemplate on the fact that Earth has its Air, Water has its Air, and Fire has its Air.

62. The Law Of Perfection Of Nature.

All bodies which are in Nature seek to dispose of their coarser shell in order to assimilate with the Prime Power which vitalizes them.

The inner Fire, which every body has received, contributes to this great work of purification and assimilation of the substances.

Fire has the power to vitrify the bodies, namely, to purify the bodies, so that they receive their natural simplicity and purity. What wonderful changes do not manifest if they are brought to the highest of purity?

We see it in the glass, the most beautiful symbol of purity. Through the glass we have become familiar with the remotest areas, discovered invisible new worlds and thousands of other miracles to which the unclean physical substance did not have the necessary abilities.

If the purification of the coarser substances brings forth such miracles, then how will the purification transform the Spirit and the Soul?

Everything in Nature is an analogy. Therefore, the purification of the Spirit and the Soul does not occur without an inner Fire. This inner Fire is the Will, which unites with Recognition, because Recognition in the Spirit-Life is Light, and in the Will, it is Warmth. Through the Warmth of the Spirit the Will receives his exaltation, separates from the physical volition, becomes simple and comes closer to his Prime Source. The physical shell, which holds the inner sense in chains, vanishes. The pure and vitalizing outflows of the Deity begin to have an effect upon the purified Soul; she receives them and reflects them immediately into a mirror. Through this reaction, she unites herself more and more with the Deity, and forms the link of unification and harmony, until she totally changes over to a unity. This unity produces the object and the goal of the actions of all Beings of Nature.

Through this unity with the Deity communicate all the Vital

Forces of the purified Soul, and she becomes the purest organ of the Deity. She penetrates the physical, changes the earthly, drives away darkness and evil, spreads Light and Goodness, and changes everything which surrounds her, according to the Laws of the Eternal Truth. Within this lies the condition of the sanctification, the explanation of the miracles, which essentially lie in the nature of the assimilation.

63. Reaction Or Counter-Effect.

The secrets of the highest and true Magic are based on the reaction of the Soul in regards to the influences of the Divine Light.

Without reaction, the Soul cannot ascend; there is no unification, no imparting of the divine Omni-Power and Omni-Might.

Everything previously discussed provides the complete theory of the true and the highest Science, and this Science is the true Magic, the highest Wisdom. It must not be blended and confused with the natural knowledge which Human Beings have out of their own self, which they did not seek in God.

The Tree of Science of Good and Evil divides into double branches, whereof some bear the fruit of Goodness and some bear the fruit of Evil. That is how the Sciences of Magic are divided into Good and Evil.

The true and highest Magic is the Theosophis, Knowledge of God, approximation, effectiveness through God.

The second classification is the Anthroposophia, the Science of Natural Things, the Science of Human Intelligence. You can be an Anthroposoph, but never reach the dignity of a Theosoph. However, if you are a Theosoph, then you are also in possession of the Knowledge of Anthroposophy.

The evil Magic divides itself into Cacosophia and Cacodemonia. The first is deviation from God, distance, darkness, self-love; her sister, the Cacodemonia, is the science of poison (contamination), and also the different secrets of destroying Human Beings, and human misery. Since it is the aim of the Theosoph to live in accordance to God's Will and to strive for the Light, the Cacosoph, in contrast, seeks only darkness, depravity, destruction and corruption and he is the cause of his own misfortune, which is the consequence when you remove yourself from God.

The Sciences of our World, which are usually taught in our schools, are based mainly only on mere natural knowledge. Very seldom are students lead to a higher level. They are left on their own, therefore, many degenerate and seek wisdom within their self and through this are lead into error because the self of Human Beings stands in darkness and the light of the natural reason is too weak to illuminate it. Therefore, all the true and the highest Science comes only from God, because He is Truth and Wisdom.

In order to make it more interesting to reach the level of the highest Science of the true Magic, I assumed certain main principles. Let us, therefore, examine some of these basic principles which belong to the knowledge of the secrets of the Anthroposophy, and out of the miraculousness of Nature, let us study the highest Wisdom of the Theosophist.

64. The Miraculous Works Of Nature In Hieroglyphics.

There are many natural miraculous Works which are founded in the knowledge of the forces of Nature.

The people of old concealed this knowledge in their hieroglyphics and, through this, continued to propagate the secrets of these sciences for centuries. It was also necessary to use this method of carefulness because passionate and ignorant Human Beings would misuse the knowledge of the forces of Nature to the misfortune of their fellow Human Beings.

Through the misuse of the knowledge, the misery of mankind multiplied. The sciences abandoned the centre of love and instead formed a new circle of their "Self". This therefore resulted in the increase of misfortune for mankind.

The stronger the forces of evil make their affect known, the more means they receive to express their powers, and the more mankind will suffer.

It is, therefore, a main principle to take away from the evil Will the tools with which to act. God, therefore, arranged everything in such a wise manner that evil will lead to darkness, not to knowledge, but to ignorance.

We all know the causes of the invention of gunpowder, the harm and misery it caused.

Ignorant Human Beings concentrate everything upon their self and therefore the misuse of things. In order to expand this self, these inventions are used for the downfall of mankind and this is the general fate which the higher secrets can expect when they become commonly known among Human Beings.

The majority of mankind consists of ignorant Human Beings. Other than themselves, they know nothing. Wherefore, the crime of Epimetheus, who opened Pandora's Box, through which so much evil came into the world. Therefore, the great disaster caused by Sisyphus, who told others of the secrets of his King which, for the thinker, the people of old described in the most beautiful of allegories.

Such was the depravity of the Danaides, who strangled their husbands, and if it would not have been for the virtuous Hypermenestre, then forever the hundredfold numbers of this family would have been destroyed. It was, therefore, the sentence of the Gods that they would eternally fill containers which had no bottom with water. The point this allegory is trying to make is that any effort the ungodly make to obtain any secrets out of the fountain of Nature will be in vain.

Therefore, no reasonable Human Being will criticize the carefulness the Sages employed up to the present times to conceal the great Secrets of Nature before the Children of Sensuality.

The fables point out vividly, in the allegorical pictures of the giants who wanted to conquer heaven, the misuse of knowledge, and Phaeton, who wanted to rule the Sun-Horses. This is the symbol of the misuse of knowledge in the hands of careless Human Beings.

The wisdom and the knowledge of secret things is only meant to be for good Human Beings. King Athamas received the golden twig only through his piety and through his bravery and courage. Theseus received the thread from Ariadne.

Minerva was the daughter of Jupiter and her shield protects those alone who deserve it and to those to whom she imparts the shield.

All the fable teachings are hieroglyphics for those who investigate the Secrets of Nature, and everywhere they will find greatness and veiled truth.

The times of the human race have their epochs, as have the years of a single Human Being. Their childhood, their teenage years, their maturity; every age has its certain knowledge. They can be measured in accordance to their powers.

First a child is taught the alphabet, then he is taught how to form words from the letters, and, finally, how to read.

The past centuries were the times of the hieroglyphics; the teachings of letters of the higher secrets for the greatest part of the human race. Our present centuries are the times of the apprenticeship of the art of the spelling of the secrets, and the future is the time when the human race will ascend to a higher level, and it will be the time of reading.

The times of the dark and solitary hieroglyphics have passed; the time has begun to enlighten Human Beings through compositions; to teach them how to spell in the Book of Nature.

Blessed are those who make speedy progress and who can read before the others can because he can place himself into the existence of future centuries.

I urgently beseech the reader to read this chapter many times - it will clarify or enlighten the reader about the Whole.

The sphinx protected the temple of secrets of the Egyptians and it was a symbol to show how much the Light was located under a shell of secrets and darkness. Oedipus was not forbidden admittance to the Inner of the secrets. He solved the puzzle and, through this, killed the sphinx. The puzzle itself, which he solved, is the highest proof that there is only "One Word" which holds the key to solve all secrets; and this word is the wisdom and that is God.

These were the secret teachings which were hidden under all the allegorical secrets of antiquity. These secret teachings were contained in the mythology of the Greeks and Egyptians, in Theogony, in Cosmogenesis, and in the religious teachings of the oldest civilizations. In the Shastras of the Hindus, in the Zend Avesta of the Parsis, in the Edda of the Icelanders, in the Chou-King and the Ly-King of the Chinese - with one word, in the oldest and holiest traditions of all nations on Earth. But, this was only clear to those who penetrated the most inner of the secrets.

65. The Secrets Of
Natural Magic Or Anthroposophy.

The secrets of the natural magic are being contained in the science and knowledge of natural things, which are hidden to the majority of Human Beings.

Their ultimate object is the knowledge of the causes, motions and inner Forces of Nature which are available or open to those who penetrate the inner Sanctum of the Temple of Nature, close to which the everyday Human Being is not allowed.

In this Temple of Nature, those who seek will become acquainted with the secrets of the composition of the bodies, the hardening and the cooling-off. The maintenance of the different types of bodies is the first step to which the apprentice of Nature is being lead. He will learn the secrets of what type of manure to use for the soil, and the compiling or gathering of the different substances which bring forth the fruitfulness.

Then Nature will instruct him as to how to search through the inner of the spring and the water and how to produce through the Art, what Nature produces in her workshops.

He learns the secrets of the air-appearances, the emulation of the snow, hail, rain, lightning, thunder and the coming-into-being of animals and insects, which the air hatches.

That is how the apprentice ascends to higher observations. His objects are the air; he studies the different kinds of air, the different components, their effects; he learns how to tinge, to moderate, and to make the air suitable for the health of Human Beings and for healing. He learns the secrets of curative baths, strengthening remedies for the nerves and the Life-Spirits, the manner, the know-how of having an effect on them, how to exalt them, how to coagulate, how to dilute, and how to call forth what has been extinguished.

He is lead to the Secrets of Nature and to their effects on trees, plants and fruits; he learns how to change the colors of the flowers, the taste of the fruit and the effects of the herbs.

Following this sequence, after the kingdom of vegetation, the object becomes the kingdom of the animals. He studies the characteristics of the four-footed animals, their passions, their effectiveness among each other, and their relationship towards Human Beings; the bringing-forth of insects and worms, their effectiveness in their life, their effectiveness in their death, their antipathies and sympathies, and their relationship to the Whole.

Then finally the Human Being becomes the object of his activity. He studies the effects of their characteristics, their passions, their conditions of health, as well as their conditions of ill-health, their Soul-Effectiveness, progressions, sympathy and antipathy. He studies the causes of the powers of healing of herbs and roots, their effects upon the parts of the human body, the causes of ailments, the inner healing, the effects, the circulation of the liquids, the causes of their change, and their diversity.

The higher secrets consist of the simplification of things in their assimilation. As far as the mechanic is concerned, the object of his work is the new and unknown inventions to the simplification of the things. He learns, through mechanical furnaces, to give physical fire different directions: to make the flame burn more, to make it more cutting and concentrate it more, and to increase and to distribute the warmth with more endurance; to emulate the warmth of the Sun and to examine the effects of the warmth of the manure, the animals and their temper and through this, to bring forth miraculous things.

Among the higher secrets belong also those of the light and the rays, the theory of the shadows, colors and pictures, the bringing-forth of the different ways of the refraction of rays, the inventions of new methods of magnification and condenser glasses.

The theory of incense and vapours, their effects upon the body and the Vital Spirit or Life-Spirit, the theory of the effectiveness of sound, taste, and the doubling forces in mechanics are the objects of his work. Through the compositions of all these things, their application and the knowledge of the parts and the Inner, he produces the magic wonder-works of Nature.

66. Prerequisites To The
Theory Of Sympathy.

The natural transition of the Spirits from one body to the other, or the artificial transposition of the bodily outflows into other bodies, brings forth the most exceptional effects, in which lies the greatest part of the secrets of natural magic.

The sympathy and the antipathy have their foundation in these outflows.

Everything which has an effect must have a counter-effect, otherwise it would not have an effect. In accordance with this counter-effect, the forces of the effective things and their consequences can be measured. The Spirits of the bodies will either be accepted as homogeneous or they will be rejected as being heterogeneous. But, should the repulsive forces not have enough strength to immediately repulse the closing-in Spirits, then a form of fermentation takes place which causes a quarrel and out of this come into being the most peculiar effects.

There is one main fundamental principle which has to be observed when it comes to all of these effects of the outflows or Body-Spirits; the body, towards which the effect is directed, must be prepared for acceptance and it must be weaker than the effective force.

These effects can be brought forth much more easily when it comes to ailing Human Beings, women and children, because they have a more refined nervous system.

The Poet had his reason when he said: Nescio quis teneros oculus mihi fascinat agnos?

He only speaks of the lambs, not of the sheep or the animals of the coarser organization.

As it is with Human Beings, so it is with animals, and with all the bodies on the whole. The changed force, which should bring forth the effects, must always seek weaker objects - those who are either weaker by nature or which are made weaker through the Art.

When it comes to these effects in the instance of Human Beings, the belief, the trust, the hope, are infinitely necessary for the acceptance of the effective Spirits. This lies within Nature. They are the expansive passions which transport the circulation of the blood, which open the pores to perspire and thereby make the organs become the recipients sooner.

We presupposed that every true change which takes place in the bodies, takes place all the time out of the change of the finer, inner components. This can be observed when it comes to melting and all the chemical operations; also when it comes to epidemics, illnesses and infections.

It can be said without contradiction, that the finest of outflows have an effect upon the inner of the bodies and then bring forth a real change of bodies. The Air is proof of this; the evaporations of flowers and herbs leave such traces.

All of Nature is a whole; one always affects the other, but the effect is not always noticeable or organic.

In Nature everything is in an equilibrium. The constant interference with this equilibrium and the endeavour of Nature to re-establish the equilibrium, makes the life of the things, the quarrel of the forces towards assimilation of the coarser to the finer.

As soon as the body is overloaded with electric matter, it will seek to dispose of it, and attracts the one which is less electrically loaded to take its excess electricity and to impart this electricity again to other bodies, until the equilibrium is re-established.

The effects one body has upon another is not alone dependent upon the outflows; sometimes it can also be composed of their form and gravity, which behave in accordance to the central-force. The effects are mainly in accordance to the general expansive and contractive forces of Nature, which are in accordance to the distance or approximation to the Sun.

It can be said without contradiction, that wherever there are expansive forces in Nature, through the Art, contractive forces can be brought forth; and wherever there are contractive forces in Nature, through the Art, expansive forces can be brought forth, and based upon this are many wonderful things.

The Life-Spirits are exalted through the imagination and a firm Will, therefore, they receive a higher expansive power and can bring forth effects on other bodies.

When there is Will on one side and on the other side there is Belief, then we are dealing with action and reaction, and natural effects come into being which have their foundation in somatology which were dismissed as mere figments of the imagination.

We discussed the theory of reminiscences, about the association of ideas, and it is therefore, no wonder, if in the instance of weaker Human Beings - especially if there is a firm belief present - that many ailments can be recalled and also can be made to disappear.

When passion is united with the imagination through reminiscences, all the same passions can come into being again; they actually must come into being again out of necessity, when the body is placed into the same circumstances in which he was, when he experienced the passion.

We must remember that all passions can be placed under the category of either the expansive or the contractive forces and, therefore, whatever the contractive or the expansive forces bring forth, also bring the passions forth, which belong to this classification.

We also know that the Human Body consists of different types of liquids which have their place of origin in the different parts of the body.

There are many different things in Nature, herbs and plants, which in accordance to their nature, have an effect mainly upon certain liquids and parts, and therefore have the capability of artificially bringing forth passions which otherwise would come into being through other impressions.

Everything which enters the body can bring forth effects in the body, may it be through indulging (food = taste), inspiration, smell or hearing. On this theory the first miraculous works of Nature are based, and the effects of Human Beings upon Human Beings.

Sound has as much of an effect upon the Spirits of Human Beings as does Light.

Light is the finest mobile; it sets into motion the finest of Spirits. Infinite are the gradations of her motions, therefore, the peculiar effects of colors, and the theory through which can be brought forth wonderful effects in Human Beings.

The people of old divided the main effects into seven categories. To make it easier to understand, they called this classification the Chart of the Seven Planets, not that the seven planets bring forth these effects, but to make the difference of the things clearer.

They understood through this the secret of the seventh number which is composed of the number three and the number four, or the unification of the spiritual and physical.

The main parts of the Human Being are arranged in accordance to this number as: The heart, the tongue, the liver, the lung, the spleen and the kidneys.

The main parts of the human body: The head, the chest, the hands, the feet and the reproductive organs.

The seven main passions: Arrogance, avarice, lust, envy, anger, intemperance, laziness.

The seven virtues: Wisdom, recognition, counsel, strength, science, piety and fear of God.

The mysteries of the number seven are depicted by the people of old by the seven burning lamps in the Temple of the Deity.

The secrets of these numbers lies therein; that the people of old know how to determine and classify the changes of the triplicities of Prime Matter and they employed seven classifications.

In accordance to these seven distributions of the primitive elements or Prime Matter, the bodies and everything which belongs to the physical world, were classified into seven charts - Human Beings, the areas and the regions of the Earth, animals, plants, metals, stones, abilities and energies. And through this they determined the effects and the consequences. The effort to study the charts of the planets in detail is really worthwhile because they will give the clearest of information and they illuminate the student to much of the higher knowledge.

Present-day Human Beings look upon these systems in an entirely different way and give these systems an entirely different meaning. They are dismissing it by making it look ridiculous, and instead of gaining knowledge, they lose it. What should be done is to make an effort to understand the Spirit, the mind of the people of old. These are only hints for the Seeker of Truth. Whosoever is willing to make this effort from this point of view and study the old books of magic, will find an extensive field to satisfy his searching Spirit, by making wonderful discoveries.

67. Sympathy And Antipathy.

Since ancient times, much has been said about Sympathy and Antipathy, but only a few knew the true reason for these rare phenomena.

Human Beings quarrelled constantly about the words without searching through the Inner of Things.

Multa in spiritus humanos agunt ex Sympathiae et Antipathiae viribus, is what the knowledgeable Baco said.

The teachings of Sympathy consists of the knowledge of the effects of Spirits upon Spirits.

It is very important to properly understand the expressions used, in other words, be certain as to their true meaning.

I understand in this instance under the term Spirits, the finest components of the bodies. What is meant by that are the evaporations, which are still physical enough to have an effect upon our organization.

Therefore, there are many gradations in existence among these Spirits which change over from noticeable to unnoticeable. For instance, the rose, which causes her scent upon our organization. The evaporations of every flower which cause a scent for us.

The knowledge of the noticeable leads Human Beings to the knowledge of the unnoticeable.

We observe, in the instance of the scent of flowers, different gradations which behave organically for us.

This scent is noticeable to us as long as the fine body-particles are perceptible and have an effect upon our organ of smell. The weaker the effects become, the less noticeable the scent or smell becomes. Eventually the flower is without scent for us. Even though the same outflows continue, they are no longer perceptible to our organs of smell.

We see that the finest in Nature has an effect on us. These effects are accepted through our senses - the eyes, ears, feelings and taste. Proof of this is the Air. She maintains our life and brings forth the finest electricity in our body.

Our body possesses many tools of suction, through which it receives the finest particles of other bodies. We have proof of this in the contagion (contagious diseases).

It is well known how quickly the finest particles of other bodies pass over into our body. This is also contagion, especially through different kinds of rabies or through love-epidemics, plagues or pestilence.

We also know that when you hold a needle close to an electro-static machine, almost instantly it becomes electrified; however, make certain when holding the needle that you are insulated.

All these observations lead us to a more thorough explanation of Sympathy and Antipathy.

Even the Art of Healing - if we can avail ourselves of this

terminology - consists of sympathetic and antipathetic effects because the inner of herbs brings forth effects and healing.

It is definitely not the coarse physical that we perceive in plants, but the finer, which causes the healing.

This, then, is called the finer Spirit, or the finer forces, and the good effects can be called the Power of Healing or Sympathy. You may call it one or the other - it is not a matter of words. What is important is that the principle is understood.

Under the provisions of these assumptions, it is possible to get closer to the matter and we must observe the quarrelsome forces which are in Nature and bring forth this effect.

The fine evaporations of the bodies have an effect on other bodies, if the other bodies have the capability of accepting them, and mostly they are changed substantially.

We can observe this when we place different bodies together with different scents. The stronger scent imparts it to the weaker body.

That is how the evaporations of poisonous herbs poison; and that is how pleasant, aromatic fragrances strengthen. With one word: everything which has an effect upon the Inner of the bodies can bring forth inner effects.

Everything acts in a particular manner and this effect behaves partly in accordance to the components of the active bodies and partly in accordance to the condition of the receiving or passive bodies.

Every effect expresses her forces mostly upon those parts which are the most skilful to accept her parts.

In every suffering body a change takes place, either through an expansive force or through a contractive force, and this change has her necessary consequences. All passions of Human Beings, as was mentioned previously, have been placed into two categories by the famous English Physician, William Falconer, and they are classified as the expansive and the contractive forces.

He says, from a certain point of view, all human passions can be placed into these two categories. To the expansive belong those which awaken the forces of the life-system, the ability to maintain the activity of the body; and the contractive, which weaken and suppress those abilities.

In the first instance, all of the Inner life particles are being awakened; the heart is given a new might and it vitalizes the circulation of the liquids. The unnoticeable evaporation is being promoted and increased; the chest is breathing free and easy, and all the abilities of the animalistic economy are being strengthened.

In the second instance, the might of the heart is being weakened;

the pulse becomes irregular and weak, the circulation of the blood becomes inhibited, the unnoticeable evaporation becomes disturbed.

Among the first classifications you can account for the following: Love, happiness, hope; and to the second classification: Anger, hopelessness, sorrow, shame, avarice, and jealousy. All the different remaining passions are only gradations, and every passion has from the first unnoticeable feeling up to the strongest in its progression, its consequences, which are in accordance to this progression.

If those Human Beings who have the ability to think know in what manner these passions come into being in the human body, which parts suffer the most when they are in a passionate condition, and when you study, in addition, the effect that one body has upon the other, the pathology, the effects of herbs upon the human body, then it will not be difficult to bring forth artificial effects.

Therein contained lie the wonder-works of the fascination, which also have essentially their foundation in Nature.

Incense, evaporations from the different herbs, plants and roots can bring forth the most strange effects in the human body. But luckily, mankind is safe to a degree since this knowledge is in the possession of very few Human Beings as this requires great dedication and the right contemplation. If this knowledge was common knowledge, Human Beings, without a doubt, would abuse it.

68. Epilogue To Sympathy.

It is without doubt that the forms of the finest or most refined particles are the reason for their wonderful effects, which we have given the names Sympathy and Antipathy.

It lies within the Laws of Being in Nature that same unites with same and rejects what is dissimilar.

Proof of this is when you pour different types of oils and different types of liquors into a glass, they will, little by little, separate. You can observe in this mixture the quarrel of the parts amongst each other until eventually same comes to same and produces the unification of the same.

The heaviness and the lightness of the bodies also depends upon the forms, because the forms are the reason that some bodies are more and others are less compact.

The people of old observed a certain friendship and animosity among all bodies which they called Sympathy and Antipathy.

It is also true that within the evaporation of the bodies, which also belong to the body, there are different effects which cannot be denied. Proof of this are the different fragrances - some are nauseating and disgusting, while others create the feeling of fresh air.

Of course, not all of the peculiar effects which the same and the dissimilar bodies have amongst each other have as their reason only the evaporations. There are also other reasons, and they are falsely attributed to the friendships and the animosities. Many times certain types of plants perish, if one is planted next to another. It is not that they contain heterogeneous parts, but that they require too much of the same nourishment out of the soil and, therefore, due to lack of nourishment, one destroys the other.

Certain plants bloom where there are plants other than their own species, and very often the reason for this is because the other plants do not require the same nourishment as they do.

When it comes to such instances, it is very important that this is properly examined, otherwise it could lead to great error.

The following are important fundamental rules:

1. In every body, where there are senses present within this body, there is a Spirit, protected or covered by a coarser body, and this Spirit causes the decomposition and the putrefaction.

2. This Spirit is not a force to us, but a fine, invisible body, who has his place and his space.

3. When this inner Spirit or Vital Spirit of the bodies leaves the bodies or parts of the body, then they dry out; when the Spirit remains enclosed, then the Spirit softens and brings forth life; and when he no longer communicates with the Air, he brings forth putrefaction.

4. This Vital Spirit of the body is capable of different modifications. He can be thickened, diluted, increased and lessened (coagulation, dilution, propagation and diminution), and with every change he brings forth different effects.

We previously discussed this subject in more detail, therefore, we do not want to repeat all the fundamental rules, only the consequences which apply in regards to Sympathy and Antipathy.

Also the animosities and friendships which are present within Nature can only be classified under the expansive and contractive forces and their maximum and minimum, and they can be judged in accordance to the main, fundamental rules of these forces.

We assumed that according to the observations of the most learned physicians, all passions behave in accordance to these forces and are either expansive or contractive, and that all ailments which the human body is subject to, also belong to this category.

If you think in a mature manner about these fundamental rules, then you will find in Nature the reason why so many sympathetic remedies heal, and you will have no reason to belittle and condemn them.

In all these matters you will find that the people of old had a considerably deeper insight into the inner of things than we have now. I will give a few examples of such sympathetic remedies and I will also give an explanation in regards to them.

There is a very common remedy for stopping a nosebleed. When a person has a nosebleed, ask them to let a few drops of their own blood drop on a piece of bread and then ask them to eat this piece of bread. Proof exists that this remedy has been used with good results.

The reason why this remedy is so successful is due to the revulsion the person experiences when eating the bread. This feeling of revulsion brings forth the contractive effect in the body. The greater the revulsion, the sooner the effect is experienced, and it must necessarily take place because this remedy produces the same conditions as do the common remedies which are being employed when bleeding occurs, as an astringent remedy.

Hope, fear, love, shock and expectations bring forth different passionate conditions, if they are used in accordance to the rules of the expansive and contractive forces, and in this manner, many wonderful changes can be achieved.

When someone has hiccoughs and you tell him that he stole something or embarrass him in a different manner, the hiccoughs will sometimes stop immediately. Hiccoughs belong to the contractive category, embarrassment to the expansive category, therefore, out of necessity, this effect should be the result.

Certainly the effect will be without success if the person who has the hiccoughs is made aware of these methods. The reason should be clear, that under those circumstances it cannot be achieved.

Different, unintelligible words, certain ceremonies which draw the attention of a Human Being to a totally different object, can also be employed as aids, because the expectation, the belief and hope change the inner and must, therefore, have their consequences.

We should also not forget that Human Beings are only capable of successive perceptions. They cannot feel pain and happiness at the same time, therefore, unexpected joy or a sudden shock can bring about the most peculiar effects.

There is an account of a carpenter who cured the agonizing toothache of a friend by tightening a wooden screw around his thumb. He did this until his suffering friend no longer felt the toothache, but only felt the screw on his thumb. By that time the toothache had disappeared.

The successive perception was the reason why the agonizing pain lost itself in the tooth. When the pain in the thumb became stronger than the toothache, then the nerves experienced a shock and took on a different direction.

In the same manner, shock, joy or any other passion which is triggered quickly can achieve this.

The whole theory of Sympathy and Antipathy is based on the knowledge of the Spiritual in the Human Being, because all effects in the human body can be brought forth through the finer motion of the Inner. Since the Spirit is the origin of the motions, it is, therefore, totally natural that through the Power of the Imagination, which rules these motions, the most wonderful things can be brought forth.

69. The Art Of Bringing Into Motion The Inner Spirit.

The Inner Spirit of a Human Being can be brought into motion in many different ways.

The most wonderful and the rarest is the Power of the Imagination. This is triggered through the belief and confidence a person has, in the artist and in the art. The Power of the Imagination can be stimulated and increased through memories and reminiscences, through ceremonies, and also through artificial effects such as herbs, vapours and incense.

The rules which can be applied as far as the effects of the Power of the Imagination are concerned are the following:

1. Everything which has an effect upon the senses can also have an effect upon the imagination.

2. Everything which has a pleasant effect upon the senses will bring forth pleasant fantasies.

3.   Everything which has an unpleasant effect upon the senses will bring forth unpleasant fantasies.

70. Additional Rules.

Every sensuous feeling can be re-awakened through the Art and through reminiscences.

A feeling which, through reminiscences was artificially awakened, brings forth a sequence of other feelings in accordance to the Theory of Association of Ideas. Every feeling a Human Being can have can be triggered again through any sense. For instance, the feelings of the eyes, the feelings of the ears, the feelings of taste, the feelings of smell etc., in accordance to all possible transpositions.

Smells which provoke or tempt will bring forth passions which provoke or tempt. The same applies to tempting foods, tempting bodies which respond to touch, tempting colors.

All things which have an effect upon Human Beings behave in accordance to this fundamental rule. To make the whole matter clearer and simpler, only effects, feelings and causes should be classified and placed into these charts, and the Whole is in accordance to the four Powers, as:

1.   The Power of Dilution and Coagulation or virtus rarefactionis et condensationis.

2.   The Power of Assimilation or virtus assimilativa.

3.   The Power of Unification or virtus appetitiva.

4.   The Power of Communication or virtus communicativa.

Within every body lie these powers or forces; they are only separated through media.

If this medium is changed or disposed of, then the powers are effective in their full abundance, wherein the wonders of Nature have their origin.

71. Observations Regarding Magnetism.

Nothing has been more peculiar in this century than the revival of Magnetism.

When you read the writings of the Authors of Antiquity, you will find traces of this Art of Healing; only this Art of Healing was sometimes known under entirely different names.

The disagreements which ensued in present times in regards to this age-old phenomena were based on the belief that some were of the opinion that the forces of magnetism were the property of one fluid Being located in Nature; whereas others thought of it as the effects of the imagination.

These different opinions were the cause of many writings, which were written in favour of and against magnetism. It would probably be much easier to get to the truth in any other century than in our present century, because the majority of scholars excluded cold reason and an unbiased examination, and decisions are made out of passion.

In this book, we do not wish to become part of the argument or side with one party and not with the other, but rather give our opinion in an unbiased manner, with the wish that it might serve to clarify the doubts.

Some say the moral Human Being, as the physical, is and forms himself only through two abilities; he forms himself and perfects himself through the emulation; he acts and becomes mighty through the imagination.

The emulation is the first medium of perfectibility in a Human Being; she modifies a Human Being from the beginning of his life to the death.

The imagination is a progressive ability, an outstanding acting ability, creatress of good and evil. Everything lies before her, the future as well as the present, the worlds of the Universe, as well as the point on which we stand. She magnifies everything, whatever she touches, and this magnification produces her strength.

Through this strength, she awakens moral sources, doubles the physiological powers, and Nature obeys her voice and the whole of Nature unveils herself in front of her. When the imagination speaks, the masses obey and nobody fears danger, or obstacles. One Human Being orders and thousands obey.

You also know the disorders, the confusion, which causes a fast and lively impression upon the human machine.

The imagination impedes or renews the animalistic activities; she stimulates through hope and solidifies through shock.

She has the ability to turn the hair grey in one night; in one moment she can take away your speech, and give it back in another, and destroys or develops evil and Good.

This is the imagination, with which the majority of scholars oppose magnetism and the peculiar appearances of Magnetism are attributed as their effects.

This opinion is based on too many probabilities, but as far as I am concerned, it is not satisfactory or adequate.

It is true, however, that the imagination is very active in those who are being magnetized, but the means through which the imagination is being set into activity is always through something which is essentially different from the imagination, but whereof the imagination is the consequence.

In all the observations I have made in regards to this rare force I have found no remarks which better describe this force than those of Dr. Gmelin of Heilbrunn:

Now my vista is clearer, luminous and encompassing! Now I have closer and better knowledge of the Being which penetrates and enlivens every fibre of my body and every drop of my fluids.

The excellent effect of my contact upon the nervous system teaches me that the nerves are splendid conductors of that Being, which enlivens the mechanism of my body and calls it into motion, and out of the power of the same strives towards the Laws of Affinity of mixed bodies.

When I think of my nerves as being a body, which is loaded with a matter very similar to electricity, then its effectiveness and the influence of the external things upon the nerves is much easier to comprehend.

The condition of being awake is based upon the discharge of the nerves and the condition of sleep is based upon the loading (overloading?) or by not discharging the nerves. One condition causes sleep with dreaming, and another sleep without dreaming. Now I fully understand the intimate sound connection of the animalistic warmth, the turgor vitalis with the Life-Force itself. I understand the reason for the coldness of death and the shape of death. Many previously puzzling appearances in healthy and ailing Human Beings, I see them now in the dawn.

Now I recognize the medium imparted, through which I am in contact with the Universe, and I now comprehend the reason for my attachment to this world and why I only have a sense for this life. Now I also know the reason why Human Beings have a natural fear of death! Yes, I understand how, through certain changes in this medium, love for life can degenerate into indifference, how in the nerve-fibres it can degenerate to stupor - it can even degenerate into being tired of life itself.

I am convinced that we, due to a constant, instantaneous loss of our Vital Force, will find enough of a substance as replacement in the sunlight and in the electricity of the Air. For this reason, the condition of the Air, the influence of the Sun, the four seasons, the climate, the local and regional conditions, next to the fortunate organization, the measure, the refinement, the intensity and the modifications, determine our Life-Forces and our powers of the Soul. It is a most probable conjecture that on the degree of bonding of the components of the nerve-substances and upon this relationship amongst each other, the reason for the different tenacities of the life among Human Beings and animals, and again among the different species of animals, is preferably based.

My experiments have taught me that through my contact with another nerve-ether, communication takes place, and my Will alone cannot (even if the Will is strong) effect a keenness and exaltation for the senses in the nerve-ether of another, and in that manner raise the animalistic instinct. But, that at the same time, the influence of the spiritual principle, whose main-attributes are self-consciousness and volition, diminishes and eventually, as long as the effect is continuous, totally disappears. Appearances in ailments have also taught me that the ones which are the human Soul's own organs, can come into a very strong but orderly motion, without the Will and without the self-consciousness. Under these circumstances, Human Beings can execute works of contemplation, reflection, reason, and imagination, without being conscious of it. This cannot be accomplished when the influence of the spiritual principle in the organs of the human Soul is re-established. Due to the increased effect of my nerve-ether transferred into another nerve-ether, I am allowed to conclude that the excessive overloading of my nerve-ether into another can bring forth the power of divination, delirium, a crisis can occur to the magnetizer, convulsions, and eventually even total destruction of the organs. Out of all this I have come to recognize how my animalistic, electric matter (Magnetism), my animal-being, is tied to my human Soul, and my human Soul is tied, in turn, to my Spirit, and all three are being bound into One; or as the animal in the Human Being borders on the Angel.

The degree of assimilation of the nerve-ether, its greater approximation or distance from the nature of the electric matter, the degree of the connection of the same with the whole nervous system, the amount and the proportional distribution of the same through all the particular parts of the nervous system, the direction and intensity and stability of the currents of the nerve-ether, the structure and condition of the nerves themselves, in as far as they become through these splendid conductors of the nerve-ether and become very skilful, does not only determine the nuances of the human character, the sensitiveness and indolence, the conspicuous animal-being or Human Being, the hardness and softness, the phlegma and fire, the slowness and the swiftness, the firmness and the fleetingness, the stubbornness and the yieldingness, the courageousness and cowardliness, steadfastness and hopelessness and other attributes of human characteristics, the differences in the humour and moods, but they also contain the reason for the natural effects of the nerves, as well as the nerve-ailments in the actual brain. It can, at the same time, illuminate, as well as through mere physical means or remedies transform a character, and also generate and eliminate nerve-ailments and Soul-Ailments. This concluded the Physician Gmelin's remarks.

I agree with the opinion and I am convinced that objections which are directed towards Magnetism are not merely the effects of the Power of the Imagination. When this is subjected to closer scrutiny, this idea will find no place.

It is no secret that our language is made up of slogans which are accepted by the majority of people and are thereby entered as facts, which they are not. One of these is: This or that can only be the effect of the imagination, and nobody makes the effort to examine what the imagination is, what the imagination is made of, if the imagination does not require a reason for coming into being.

Since there were so many peculiar and varied opinions on the subject of Magnetism, I decided to take a closer look into the matter and became a silent observer of magnetic experiments.

In my travels, I visited the cities of Strasburg and Karlsruhe (Germany) where I was given the opportunity to observe the most honourable gentlemen being occupied with this subject. There was no doubt in my mind that they were very serious about this, and that they would not spend their time on something nonsensical.

I made a point of reading whatever was available for or against Magnetism and then thought about it thoroughly. I examined, without prejudice and with cold-bloodedness, as a silent observer, different types of experiments and was present during several magnetic operations.

In an open forum in Strasburg, besides normal operations, there was nothing special to draw my attention, since there were also only a few people present. One somnambule, however, triggered my curiosity. She suddenly called out in her magnetic sleep that her regular Magnetizer, who had been ill for a few days, would arrive any minute. No sooner had she made this remark, than the Magnetizer entered the room.

There were gentlemen present, with a thorough background in learning, who spoke without prejudice about the peculiar effects of Magnetism; and it was their only occupation to search for the truth. The Laws of the Harmonious Society are proof of the integrity of their intentions.

Since it is my way of life not to join any Societies or Unions, I did not seek any closer connections there, but considered myself to be an impartial observer, following my own path and doing my own research.

I observed that very few Human Beings seek the truth with cold-bloodedness, and that some travellers would attend a forum just so that they could say they attended, without observing or understanding the subject matter.

Some become enthusiasts, others become cynics, and this way one agrees with this and the other disputes that, without knowing why.

It so happened that I made the acquaintance of an honourable gentleman who promised to satisfy me of some of my curiosity.

After magnetizing an ailing woman for a short period of time, she became somnambule; she spoke of peculiar things in her magnetic sleep, and when this occurred a young man who was also present in the same room placed himself into a rapport with the Magnetizer. He then took a book from the table and started to silently read a few paragraphs from the book.

The somnambule, who had her eyes totally closed and who was at least ten steps distant from the young man who was in rapport with the Magnetizer, began to read aloud the same paragraphs in the book which the young man was reading. When asked how she could read these paragraphs, since her eyes were closed and she was at a distance, she gave this as her answer: I am reading through the eyes of the person who I am in rapport with, because for the Soul, everything is unity, everything is One.

At this point it was decided to examine this matter under closer scrutiny, and somebody took a letter out of their pocket and had the young man, who was in rapport, read a few lines from it. At the same moment the young man started to read, the somnambule began to read aloud what the young man was reading in silence, and this convinced everybody of this incomprehensible effect, and that there was neither fraud or deception perpetrated.

Even more remarkable was the next experiment, which the Magnetizer performed with the ailing woman.

After the woman awoke from her magnetic sleep, the Magnetizer showed us her whole bare arm. He said: Look at this arm and notice it is a natural, healthy arm. The arm was well formed, totally pliant and had a good color. After magnetizing it twice, the arm became rigid, pale and was like the arm of a dead person, without any feeling. The Magnetizer took a needle and forced it through the ailing woman's finger without the slightest reaction, and without any pain. Next the Magnetizer moved his middle finger from her shoulder down to the wound, and the blood started to flow. He then went up with his finger and the blood stopped flowing.

Finally, he took an astringent remedy and applied it to the wound and he then magnetized the whole arm again. Except for a very small, unimportant wound which was hardly visible, the arm was as natural and healthy as it was before.

One of the gentlemen present asked to be magnetized, and reported that he did not feel anything in particular except for a heaviness in his feet. The Magnetizer said he would like to produce a certain effect, and the gentleman agreed. The Magnetizer pointed his thumbs in the direction of the gentleman and slowly proceeded to walk backwards. As he did this, the gentleman had to follow, through an irresistible force, and it was no longer within his power to remain where he was. The Magnetizer then made a few steps to the side. Now the magnetized man felt he was glued to the floor. He could not lift a foot, nor would he dare to make a step. The Magnetizer moved slowly towards the gentleman and again pointed his thumbs towards his body. When the Magnetizer pointed his thumbs and came closer to the gentleman, he had a feeling similar to parts of the body falling asleep; for example, when a foot falls asleep. The Magnetizer also produced a few other effects such as an appetite for fruit and then a disgust for fruit. After a while, the Magnetizer was asked to produce the same effect again. This time the gentleman stood on a table, but even there, the effect was no less - he followed him in whatever direction he pointed his thumbs.

This feeling was definitely not the imagination. Something entirely different must have happened in his body, which brought about this peculiar feeling, but I am of the opinion that this part of the book is not the place to give long explanations.

72. Rules.

1. An eternal and immutable Law lies within the essence of things, and this Law is the proportion and modification of all abilities, effects and consequences in accordance to the Unity of the Prime Power.

2. This Prime Power enlivens all the original beginnings of things, which come from up-above, and take on coarser and coarser coverings, to impart themselves upon the bodies.

3. The condition of the things in this physical world is such, that there is no Being without necessities and this necessity is the driving force towards unification; this is the whole endeavour of the Beings.

The Earth would be unfruitful if the vapours would not rise from her lap and unite with the higher forces. Pregnant with heavenly power, they plummet down to earth as dew and bring life and fruitfulness.

Human Beings can become as unfruitful as the Earth if they do not elevate their Inner and ascend to higher spheres, and obtain from the Source of Light, the holy anointment and life.

How great must be the Might of a Being that is the closest to the Prime Power of all things, and obtains the drink of Wisdom out of the first fountain!

There are pure invisible forces that directly originate from the purest of Prime Powers and effect the spiritual (intelligence) of Human Beings.

How the effects of the Prime Power express themselves depends upon the condition of the body. The more the body is separated from the coarser senses, the stronger are the effects.

Truth and vividness of things are the consequences of these effects. The vividness depends upon the degree of purity.

Every exaltation of the Spirit brings forth powers for the Spirit, which are in accordance to the condition of the separation of the senses.

This can be observed by Poets and Speakers. When their Spirit becomes exalted, they totally withdraw into themselves, and are totally taken up by the spiritual object. That accounts for the wonderful works in poetry and the magical powers of the art of speaking.

All great deeds came into being through the exaltation of the Spirit, which either received their exaltation through passions or external influences.

The exalted Spirit affects other Spirits, assimilates and unites.

Every Spirit exaltation proclaims the approximation to the higher, progression to the Prime Power, therefore, double the energy and wonderful retroaction.

There is only one Prime Power from where everything earthly receives its power, through which it is effective. The Prime Power modifies itself in accordance to the organs which accept this Prime Power.

All possible goodness lies within this Prime Power, because she comes directly from God, therefore, beauty, light, harmony, powers of healing, are contained therein because she is the power of perfection, the attraction towards perfection.

The manner of her influence is in accordance to the power of the Human Being and this power can turn, through this process, into a healing force, assimilates, but distant from the sensuousness, it weakens the medium which prevents the influences of the Prime Power and brings forth effects which are different from the effects of the bodies.

Therefore, Magnetism, is the healing force of Human Beings, not the imagination, not the effects through fantasy, but an entity, which lies in Nature and which has the exaltation of the Spirit to the object.

In accordance to the purity of the Human Being, in accordance to the assimilation of his Spirit to the spiritual, he receives purer and purer outflows. The more he assimilates his Spirit with the Prime Power, therein lie the wonder works of sanctification, the central-power of divine outflows, which express their effects through the purity of the Spirit and exaltation.

Therefore, the Light is in God, which illuminates the knowledge of Human Beings and becomes the Light of the reason in the Human Being's Spirit. It then changes into thoughts and flows through the Human Being's reason and has an effect upon the imagination, without changing its simple substance. If we then impart her power to the finest organization of the body, which in turn imparts it to the coarser organization, and in this manner, in accordance to the Law of Assimilation, shapes Human Beings which are similar to God, which in accordance to the steps of approximation on which they stand, must surpass the common type of Human Being by necessity.

73. A Necessary Consideration
Of The Former.

There was once a time when there was no Evil. In order to understand this sentence, you must not look upon Human Beings in their degradation of days past, as slaves of habit and prejudice, who are controlled by their habits and subject to their varied types of feelings.

Everything was good as long as the Laws of Unity were followed.

These laws are truth and goodness and they, therefore, exclude everything which is false and evil.

The Blissfulness in the regions of Eden was the descriptiveness of the Powers of Unity, and the delight and participation in the divine Prime Power. Only when Human Beings left this descriptiveness and searched for the pure products of the infinite in the finiteness, did this error become the first thought, which lead to falsehood and evil. Without this thought, there can be no evil; only this thought became the father, the producer of all calamities; before him, there could have been no Evil, as there can be no product that did not have a creative beginning before.

The Divine never had a part in falsehood and evil; the Divine never had a part in all the disorder which destroys the Creation because the Divinity is purity itself. The Divinity was in itself the law of her own Being and all of its works, and as an eternal activity, she could not be in a suffering state.

The whole of Nature is proof of this sentence. All destruction which prevails in Creation never has the primitive things as objects of its effects, only the objecta secundaria.

The greatest destructions in the physical world change only its physical production or the way it is brought forth; they never upset the pillars of the foundation of Nature, which no human hand can upset, only the Hand of the Eternal, Who created them.

Whenever Human Beings are wrongly judged in regards to this object, the reason is that they looked at the great Law of Being of all things with closed eyes, and misunderstood the essential signs of differentiation, which exist between God and the world.

The Human Being left God, the Prime Power of all things, through which everything lives and receives all the Light and thoughts, and sought in themselves what they do not have in them and what could not be in them. So they walked from the Light into darkness, and that is how the falsehood originated, because it lacked the descriptiveness, the clearness to accept the truth. That also applies to the evil, which is the consequence of falsehood. That applies to all disorders which destroy the world. The Prime Power is the origin of all harmony and the distance from this Prime Power destroys this.

Human Beings are destined to have control over everything physical because of their connection through their designation to the Deity. Everything would have been subject to them, because Human Beings' power was outflow, reception of the first Prime Power, but the Human Beings left this power and became the victims of materialism, all changes, suffering and death.

The first Human Being therefore changed his Spiritual Being, distant from the Prime Power of Life. The Life could no longer be active in him, and he became a slave of time and a child of death.

When Human Beings were still connected to their Prime Power, there must have been a means, a connection, which united him with this Prime Power.

This connection, this means, was the Will, because only the Will, as a reaction to the recognition, could have been the medium, the connection, with the Creator and the Beings.

This Will changed and took a different direction. The Will separated from the spiritual and connected the Being with materialism. The consequence as a necessity, because of this change was as punishment: misery.

But one thing the fallen Human Being was left with was the ability of recognition, a leftover of divine Omnipotence, which was once united with him.

Through this recognition alone, the loving Power of God is still active, and since the attribute of Love is an active endeavour, she was effective against those Human Beings who were separated from her and she searched for a new connection, a new medium, to re-unite with those who were separated from her.

In this, the most blissful condition in which Human Beings were, the knowledge which was given to them by the Prime Power of the Universe was abused, and the necessary punishment of this abuse was the loss of this knowledge.

The more Human Beings removed themselves from the Prime Power, the more they removed themselves from the Light.

The more distant Human Beings became from the Unity, the more materialistic, the more divisible, the more compounded became their foundation; therefore, more imperfect, more compounded; therefore, the distance from the Light; therefore, the chains, which chain a thinking Being to matter.

301

In this World we cannot totally regain the lost Light. Only through the progression to the Unity, through simplification, is it possible to ascend again to the Light and Life, to the Prime Power, to God.

Only from God, the Origin of Light, flows the Light into the knowledge; this knowledge was the purest, as long as she was next to God.

Human Beings did not enjoy this blessed delight for long. United with the corruption of his Will, he descended to the mixture of things and lost his place, which connected him to the Unity, the Paradise of Life.

Through the distance, he lost the World of Descriptiveness and entered a region of successive appearances. He, a child of eternity, became a child of time, and felt that time was a tool of human suffering, and that it is the mightiest of all obstacles, which keeps him away from the Original Source.

He, who was destined to conquer her, lies now conquered through her in the chains of the flesh, chained to compounded substances, whose perpetual separation is the cause of his suffering and his death.

The time is the interval between action and consequence, and consequently only appropriate to the physical, not to the Spirit, for which only unity exists.

The time is an obstacle for the activity of the abilities of a Being and changes the spiritual existence in the step-by-step development.

The Unity does not pass through space or time, she only passes through herself. Only the distance from the Unity has space and time and disappears for the one, who is getting closer to the Unity again.

74. The Numbers Of Nature.

Whosoever knows the Numbers of Nature knows the most secret paths; but, there is a great difference between the Numbers of Nature and the common numbers, which are used for addition and subtraction. Most Human Beings have no concept of the Numbers of Nature.

Instead of promoting these Sciences, they have been suppressed by the Scholars of the World. They dictated laws to the seeker and issued interdictions so that the people should not look for the truth anywhere else, but in their decisions.

They did not think of or know that there was a Science in existence that does not tolerate any pressure, which is like water collected in the bladder, and when pressure is applied, it ruptures and leaves in the hands of the ignorant, natural Scientist, dry remnants.

Those Human Beings who have not applied their knowledge towards the understanding of the Numbers in Nature should not seek any enlightenment from the Scholars or Scientists of this world, because they build buildings upon opinions and not upon Truth. They have dried out the sources of the sciences and, instead, produced skeletons of learning. The nourishing liquids disappeared from under their eyes, and they had no knowledge of the Art to control them.

The Numbers of Nature are invisible coverings of the Beings, whereas the bodies are visible coverings of the Numbers of Nature. Everything has its beginning and its formation, and the medium which unites the beginning and the formation is the Numbers of Nature.

The laws and attributes of the Beings, Nature sketched upon its perceptible coverings, through which they feel our senses and they are the expression and the activity of the Laws of Being and the attributes.

That is how it is with the numbers. The invisible attributes and Laws of the things are their expressions, as the perceptible coverings are the expressions of their perceptible powers. There are numbers which are there for the Primary Being of the things. There are numbers for the activity of the Beings - for their beginning, for their end, and for the different progressions and, at the same time, there are limits wherein the divine outflows remain and flow back again towards their beginning and, at the same time, throw back the picture of the Divinity into the unity, in order to obtain life, measure and weight for the physical world.

There is a mixture of numbers to express the unification of Beings, their abilities, powers and effects.

There are central and median numbers, numbers of the circle, and numbers of the circumference; and also false and corrupt numbers, and through all of these numbers, the whole of Nature can be calculated. Place the number four between the number one and zero and you will find the relationship of harmony, the relationship of Unity. Remove this number from the medium of this progression and place it in a circle by itself, and you find the prime source of destruction, the disharmony of things.

Place the number one in the centre of the number four and the disharmony will cease and the Laws of Unity will reappear.

These three lessons are the most important of the great Number Calculation of Nature, because within them lie the past, the present, and the future.

303

75. News Of The Voyage To The Truth.

In was very early in the morning as we reached, with our Guide, our destination. We had to leave our horses with a farmer because the path which lead to the hut of the hermit was narrow.

After approximately one-half hour of walking, we reached the hermit's hut. When we arrived, he was praying. The moment he noticed us, he hurried to meet us.

He said: I was aware of your coming and we receive you with happiness. He offered us breakfast which consisted of bread and milk.

After breakfast he lead us off to the side into a cave. There was a spring and he asked us to bathe and cleanse and then he gave us white, clean clothes, precious oils for anointing and precious incense. We followed his directions. After about half an hour, he came back and lead us into the depths of the mountain. There was a cavern which was very dimly lit by a lantern. He lead us into this cavern and asked us to have courage. As we ascended deeper and deeper into the mountain we saw five more hermits. They were sitting around a table and were calculating with the Numbers of Nature. They showed us the destiny of the future, and the centuries of the past. They calculated the original name of every herb, every original energy, and most every secret and most hidden thing in Nature; and they showed us the greatness and majesty of Creation.

We were in awe. A feeling of reverence overcame us and it was not necessary to convince us. We saw what seemed up until now incomprehensible, and for the common Human Being, it will remain eternally a puzzle.

We stayed with these Holy Men for five hours and as we were leaving the old hermit told us: You have, after proper preparation, seen for yourself, and satisfied yourself that it is possible for Human Beings in this lifetime to reach the level of clearness of things, which most Human Beings consider to be impossible. But, do not believe that this Science can be learned through the study of physical Nature alone.

The moral Human Being, in his Inner, has to reach the purity of an Angel, before he is capable of seeing with the eyes of his Soul; Angel purity is the receiver of the outflow of the Deity. The first knowledge of higher Philosophy and the necessary energy must be obtained from within God Himself, through which you can act and have a clear view.

Then Religion becomes holy to you, the Secrets reverend, and the wonder-works become understandable, which the Beings of a purer nature can accomplish through the outflow of the Power of God. Have a healthy life, may God's blessing be with you, and may He maintain you pious and virtuous.

These were the words of the hermit as he accompanied us to the farmer where we had left our horses. After changing into our own clothes, before we left, he gave us many blessings and good wishes and we left with such cheerfulness and contentment of the Soul, that it is impossible to find the words to express these feelings. We thanked God for the Love which lead us closer to the Light and the clearness of His Greatness and Majesty.

76. The Seekers Of Truth.

Those of you who seek Wisdom to be wise; those of you who seek Truth to act truthfully - do not let your devotion cool, do not let your endeavour become weary. Every thought is a step closer to the sanctuary, every wish of the heart an approximation to the Deity, which is being rewarded with more Light.

Separate yourself from conceited relationships with fools who seek the Wisdom within their own Ego, and attach yourself to those who, with the simplicity of their hearts, walk the Path of Truth.

Walk with a good and pure Will and you will make the acquaintance of the highest of secrets in Nature. You will have a reverend concept of the greatness of the Deity and you will marvel in His Love, His Omni-Goodness. His Spirit will lead you into the Workshop of Nature and what was incomprehensible, will become clear to you - that which has been present in Nature for centuries.

The quarrels of the world elite, as far as knowledge is concerned, will disappear for you because where there is truth, there is no error and no quarrel; there is unity, there is harmony, there is agreement. Bowed down deeply, you will pray to the Eternal and marvel at the greatness of the Deity.

Only when God begins to lead your pure heart, will you begin to revere the holy Secrets of Religion, the Secrets of Creation, the Secrets of the First Fall, the Banishment of the Human Being from the Region of Eden, his present condition, the cause of his death, the condition of the Soul in the world, his condition in the future, the punishment for evil Human Beings, the rewards for good Human Beings, the connection of the Human Being with the Spirit World, the great work of salvation, and the rebirth of Human Beings. All of this is so essential, so beautiful, so harmoniously woven into the Whole,

305

that it will deeply entrance Human Beings to worship Jehova, who has His Throne in the Halls of Eternity.

Human Beings! Make an effort to make a new Human Being out of yourself and receive out of the Hands of Wisdom the treasures of rebirth and to approach the Unity from which we were removed because of our first crime. This is our occupation, our destiny.

Therein exists the approximation of the Human Being towards the Deity, by removing the barrier which The Sin erected between the Unity and the Human Being, so that he again can receive the Light from the divine Sun, to become illuminated through her knowledge and through her Love, warm-up, from whence all Goodness and Truth flows.

Oh, how blessed will be our condition when our knowledge becomes united with the Will, when this is our practical work, and to establish the divine Harmony internally and externally of ourselves, and as God's Children to be received in God's Kingdom and to act through Him.

This great destiny lies within us; the morality and religion is our guarantee; her treasures are right under our eyes, but we are blind and cannot see them.

The freethinker scoffs, laughs, about things he does not understand. He wants to calculate in Nature, but he does not even know the first numerals, the one of all things, the Deity.

It should be no surprise that all his calculations are in error. Who can begin his calculation with zero, which has no progression?

Calculate with the numeral one and you will solve the toughest assignments, because she is the simplest of all numerals and she is not subject to any division.

Add nothing, otherwise she loses her simplicity and you will not know the first numeral in the nature of things.

Only when the compositions cease, then all progressions disappear; only the One, the Prime Source of everything is eternal and unchangeable. Therefore, identify your whole Being with the One of the Divinity and your reward will be sanctification and blissfulness.

77. Inscription At The Entrance To
The Temple Of Wisdom.

It is the destiny of us all to take part in the greatest attributes of Unity. There is a force within us to ascend to this Unity, and this power is given to us by the Being, which is the Unity itself.

Everything which is perfection is this type of Unity, everything that nears itself to perfection, nears itself to the Unity.

Distance from the Unity is the transition to the composition, and every composition is subject to separation.

Unity excludes time and space;, she is the centre of all active forces. Through her, everything is active, whatever is within her radius, stronger or weaker, in accordance to its proximity or distance.

Human Beings can be effective in the Unity, with the Unity, and through the Unity. Sometimes Human Beings are even effective without the Unity and contrary to the Unity.

Whosoever seeks Wisdom, must not seek her in second causes, but must seek her in the first, also the base-line cannot be material.

The effects which have the basis in the first powers of things must not be explained through the powers of the second manner.

Never forget that there are different paths on which Human Beings seek the truth, but there is only one path which is the true path, and this path is the path which leads to the Unity.

Who can explain the number two without the number one? Who can explain the number four without the knowledge of the progression of the first three numbers?

Learn to differentiate science from Wisdom, because this is the purpose and measure of all of science.

Human Beings only acquire Wisdom step-by-step. We must walk with humility, submissiveness, stability, devotion and attentiveness, and Wisdom must find us to be ready at any hour, to follow her.

The Wall of Rocks, which represent the barrier between Human Beings and Wisdom, can be removed much more easily with patience than with force.

Gentleness and Love lead to Wisdom. There is only one Unity, only one Blissfulness, only one Wisdom, only one Harmony.

Human Beings are created for the harmony of the universe; their activities must not be dissonant with the Unity.

The time will come where there will be no more dissonance. Those Souls, which are not in harmony, will exclude themselves from the pure concert of the Unity.

78. The Staircase For Human Beings
To Knowledge And Wisdom.

The first step, upon which Human Beings stand, is the step of the childhood of human intelligence.

His knowledge languishes in the bonds of darkness. Everywhere he enjoys the charity of the Deity, but he enjoys it like a child, without having the knowledge from where it comes, and without recognizing the hand which provides it for him. His condition is only suffering. He does not recognize the true nourishment for the Soul, which consists of the activity of Life. A large portion of Human Beings remain upon this step, and no further progress is made.

The second step is the step of the years of adolescence of the intelligence.

The Human Being suspects that there is a Being which is the beginning of Nature. He feels the inclination to recognize this Being, but error or mistakes, seduction, passion and sensuality confine his Spirit and hold him back from ascending, and other than having a very faint notion, he does not progress any further.

Upon this step, another great portion of Human Beings remain and do not progress any further.

The third step is the step of recognition of the Highest Being; the sense of a necessary relationship of this Being with the Universe; a sense of Spirit and physical laws; the reason for a Morality and Religion. But only darkness assimilates these senses with passions, and many Human Beings do not progress from here.

The fourth step is the recognition of the Highest Being and the knowledge of his relationship with the Universe, recognition of the Laws of Morality and Religion. Again, many Human Beings remain at this step, without having proven the recognition through practice.

The fifth step is the recognition of a Revelation - Belief, mixed with erroneous concepts. Here, many return to the darkness and walk in superstitions and fanaticism.

The sixth step is the right concept in regards to the Revelations; the right Belief, humility and submissiveness, but without unification of the Works with the Belief. Here, again, many Human Beings remain and do not ascend again.

The seventh step is the true recognition of the Revelation, with the unification of the Works with the Belief; transformation of the heart to the Temple of God; participating with the common harmony and the divine Unity.

This is the step to which the true Sage ascends.

Through this ascension, he enters into the proximity of the Prime Power of all things and he becomes a participant of her powers and effects. But, how few Human Beings raise themselves to this Greatness? And, how true become the Words in the Scriptures: Many are called, but only a few are chosen.

79. Principal Recollections In Regards To The Whole.

So far, everything said belongs essentially to the true Magic. Through these Laws alone can these things, which are otherwise incomprehensible to our reason or intelligence, be explained. The great Secret of the Wonder-Works (miracles), is to be working in God and with God.

It is a certainty that the greatest part of the human race will not be satisfied with these explanations, even though every possible explanation to higher things is contained in these two books.

It is the wish of most Human Beings to be able to perform miracles, or wonder-works, without making any effort to think. And when it comes to the sensuous Human Being, he is still afflicted with the punishable thought: we want to eat from the fruit of the tree and, at the same time, become equal to the gods.

The wishes of many Human Beings are equal to the wishes of unintelligible children who have no understanding of the fact that Skanderbeg's Sword serves no purpose when the arm does not have the power to wield it.

That also applies to the higher Magic. Human Beings have to be guided when it comes to the preparation of their Soul, to strengthen the powers of their Soul, to strengthen the powers of their Spirit. Then their ability develops by itself. This is the Path to Wisdom, there is no other.

The Unity is the Centre of all Things; Nature is situated on the circumference. Only in the centre, all radii of a circle are concentrated and out of the centre the power of the Unity is effective in equal measure upon the circumference.

To seek out remarkable things, wanting to do things which exceed normal concepts, or wanting to become a Magus, without preparing your Spirit and your Soul for Magic, is nothing but nonsense which leads to destruction.

This nonsense distances us from the Truth, and concentrates everything upon our Self and upon incidental powers which cannot exist without the Power of the Unity.

That is how Self-Love very soon leads us astray onto the path of error. We turn the knowledge of Nature into the servant of our passions and heap misery upon our crown because we are walking the path of falsehood and evil.

You! Whoever you are, You! who feels an inclination to approach the great Temple of the Holy Nature and to search for her

309

Secrets and to listen to the Wonder-Works of Creation, do not approach the Fire of the Deity until you are as pure as crystal, so that the Flame of Nature will not find anything in you which it can consume. However, if it is your belief that you are strong enough to be lord over your Self-Love, and be able to determine your feelings in accordance to the Feelings of the Unity, and your Heart in accordance to the common Harmony of Nature, then give me your hand so that I can lead you to the Throne of the Deity, which the Sage in his Spirit worships.

Child of Error! You search for Wisdom! You search for the Light and you are sitting in the Darkness.

Wisdom is only there where there is Truth; Light, where Goodness is united with Truth; there, where there is Life and Peace, and Life and Peace are only there where there is Harmony, and Harmony is only in God.

Look around! Where do you live? In the Valley of Misery, where one hour consumes the other, one moment destroys the other; a Slave of Time, a Child of Change.

Happiness and suffering change from hour to hour. In vain your Soul languishes for everlasting joy; your chest breathes in vain for everlasting delight. Desire triggers desire, and does not satisfy you; the Night conquers the Day, and one moment destroys the work of years.

Distance, death and separation tear out of your arms what you love. Age, illness and worries rob you of the happiness of your days. Death causes the pallor on your loved one's cheeks, and in the evening, the roses wilt, which the morning made you a gift of.

This is your residence now, chained to the shackles of the flesh, incarcerated in fragile bones, wherein your Soul is sighing for freedom - the same as someone who is a prisoner in a prison.

When the Sun rises, there is a reflection of the Sun in the tears of misery and the Moon shines upon the sleepless eye of the one who is submerged in his worries. The grove hears his sighs; the brook which flows through the meadows, his whining. Wherever you look, monsters terrify you. There, armies murder, and here, Laws and Judges; here the peaceful Poor immerse their bread in tears, and there feast the heartless wealthy who make their stomach their god. Hecatombs fall for their gluttony, with which they fatten their adventurous selves and innocence, virtue and morals are banned, and languish in chains, and die in prisons or bleed on scaffolds.

That is your place of residence. And where do you think this misery comes from? Who unfolded this Kingdom of Nature in this manner? Who turned the divine Eden into a desert? Who? Nobody but you yourself! You separated yourself from God, from the Unity, where there was only Goodness, Love, Truth and Harmony.

You - Human Being! You are the cause of your own misery; you have changed the point of view, the place which the Deity assigned for you. The first cause of your misery occurred by removing yourself from the Unity. Therefore, there are no other means, no other remedies, but to approach this Unity again, to unite yourself again with the Prime Force of Life and Light, where there can be no suffering, no death or darkness.

Learn to know this Unity, learn to know God. His Being is Goodness, His existence is Love. He is the Light, Truth and Life. Without Him there is only Evil and Falsehood. Without Him, there is only error, darkness and death.

Goodness and Truth is His Law of Being; Goodness and Truth the bond that connects us again with Him, the Bond of Love, the mood or the atmosphere to the Harmony of the Whole.

Unity is the attribute of God - Power and Deed - Volition and Activity - this is the hint towards reaction, towards Love-In-Return to the Deity, towards separation of the bonds of our Self and the World which, up to now, made up the centre of Evil and Falsehood.

Self-Love and World-Love are what separated us from the Deity. It was the distance from the Truth, the transition from the Spiritual into the material, the cause of separation, the misery, the death.

Approximation to the Unity is God-Love and Love for thy Neighbour, reaction, Assimilation, the Laws for Human Beings towards happiness and rebirth, to ascend to the Light and distance from the darkness and death. Within this lie the Laws of Morality, the Holiness of Religion, and the Miracles of the Sanctification.

There are, of course, things which are for the coarse, sensuous Human Being, incomprehensible, and they will also not become comprehensible unless he removes the scales from his eyes, which covered the Eye of his Soul with blindness.

80. Zozimus:
To His Students.

Learn to know God, my Son! The Being that is, that was, and that will be for Eternity.

This high designation explains the necessity of His Being and the fullness of His Existence.

311

No mortal can understand the infinity; the created do not understand the uncreated, only the feeling leads us to His recognition, through Nature. The Human Being is created to Love this Being, not to probe or explore this Being.

The Name of God should bring joy into your heart. Among all Beings who inhabit Planet Earth, if you are one of the Beings who is capable of recognizing his Creator, this difference shows you your greatness.

The Being, My Son, which cannot recognize God, descends to the lowest class of the sensuous Beings and lowers himself even to the level of an animal! All Beings and all creatures which surround you remind you by calling: We are, as you are, we came out of God's Hands, Who created us to serve you, to instruct you that there is a God, and that this God is total Love, to teach you and to coerce you to Love Him.

The Name of the Deity, My Son! is written in legible letters into every Being, upon the wings of the smallest insect, and also upon the wings of the eagle, who ascends to the Sun. God's Name is written everywhere, in the whole of Nature, and everything repeats to us His eternal existence.

What kind of concepts did Human Beings have from time immemorial about this Being? An oppressive fear towards an unknown might gave them false concepts of a God of necessity and blind coincidence. From this point of view they looked upon the Being of Love, and to this day, there are still many Human Beings who view God from this point of view.

To believe in God means to recognize the Highest of Beings, Who is in control of everything through His Wisdom; to love your fellow Beings, as He loves them, to keep His Laws, and to relinquish yourself to His Providence, Goodness and Righteousness. The Righteous sees his God everywhere - in Nature and in society. He sees in every created Being the active hand of his Creator, which is active within him.

Being of all Beings! Most Human Beings do not know your Name. The world laughs at those Human Beings and scorns those Human Beings who sing Your Psalms and Praises. Oh, how unfortunate are those who close their mouths to the Hymns of Nature, which ascend to the Deity.

My Son! God is Spirit, that is what the Belief tells us, but He is a Spirit which cannot be compared to any other created Spirit. To be in His manner, His perfection, transcends our common concepts and there are perfections within Him, which are far beyond the capabilities of our thoughts. God is holy and only that Being which ascends to Him, to Him, the Centre of all Reality, approaches this sacredness; without this, a created Being languishes in darkness and in misery.

When we think of the years of Eternity which the Belief proclaims, then our feeling convinces us that we Human Beings are created for the Unification with the Creator, and this Union is the work of the Religion which Christ taught.

Not the Majesty of this Truth, which is so deserving of the divine Love, places the Human Being against the imperviousness of God's resolutions into astonishment, but instead, our sensuousness clouds our Spirit with darkness and we cannot, therefore, recognize the Truths of the Eternal Light.

God is the Soul of our Soul. This Soul, our Soul, is without Life and without Light if she separates from the Soul which vitalizes everything. The Spirit of the Human Being lives only through the Spirit of the Deity. Only when Her holy Light illuminates the Spirit of the Human Being can the Human Being see, and when Her flame burns in him, then he becomes active and he performs works of Love.

Our Life is only the childhood of our existence; the eternity which follows this is only the continuance of this Life.

Wrapped in our physical body, the sensuality cannot be the destiny of our Soul, because the Soul languishes in the bonds of the flesh, yet the future beckons her towards the knowledge of the Harmony, the Order and the Beauty.

The Holy Truth, which is inhabiting the heavens, is the source of Life for all thinking Beings out of which they gather the Light, and this is the sole source.

In the lap of religion rests the magnificent pledge of divine Love, surrounded by the rays of the Deity, who illuminates those, who with a sincere heart seek instructions and wish to know what they should be and what they should become.

But only the one who in quiet and solitary hours contemplates about the Truths of Religion, will be able to make her heavenly feeling, the feelings of his own Soul. Then the gift of the Deity, the Belief, will secure his work.

Not in the great circle of the world or on the stages of passion will the ear hear the sounds of harmony of Nature. The music of the spheres can only be heard by the Sage in solitude.

The true Philosophy feels the necessity of help from Religion. On her hand, she glides with courageous steps between blind Belief and contempt; out of her, she receives the guidance of reason, which leads her from the wrong path, the path of passion, to the Temple of Truth.

The Religion is to the Soul, what Light is to the eye. Without that, Human Beings walk in darkness, but the heart, as well as the eye, can open or close itself to the Light.

God does the greatest things in Human Beings; with His help, Human Beings are capable of doing everything, but Human Beings cannot take any credit and attribute this to their own powers Human Beings can only consider themselves as a tool of the One, Who alone is Great and Almighty.

As To The Conclusion Of This Book
A Chapter That Should Be Read Three Times.

I am beseeching the reader: Should you not understand the Higher Principles of Knowledge in their totality, and if you are not totally convinced, to put this book aside and delay any judgement until later.

I am also asking those readers who admire the Secret Sciences to probe their heart very carefully in order to protect it from the impressions of daydreaming or fancies.

There is nothing more dangerous than the extraordinary inclination towards miraculous things. The Powers of the Imagination are very easily deceived, and then the Human Being is very easily seduced to daydreaming.

In this century, there are many Human Beings who indulge in daydreaming when they occupy themselves with the Secret Sciences, and according to Zimmermann's account of it, they are people who, with a burnt brain, believe to have read in mystical writings something which is not contained therein. Hopefully, through the most venerable solitude and the most exalted style and out of the most devout, sought-after union with God, those Human Beings are not lead down the wrong path, and instead of finding the true Wisdom, they become a game of the imagination and a victim of a fanatic deceit.

For those who search in Nature, who want to walk the dark paths of mysticism, it is absolutely necessary to study the symptoms of mysticism. Through our sensuality, they very often take the most peculiar turns, and we believe that it is nothing but a separation from our senses, that there is a change in our sensuality, since when we daydream, there is enough evidence to appease or satisfy us.

I repeat again: Nothing is as dangerous as occupying yourself with the mystical Sciences and then falling victim to daydreaming.

Every century has its share of people who speculate. There are also a number of sects that practice mysticism, but who totally fail to achieve their ultimate goal, and instead of finding the Truth and clearness, change over to folly and fury.

It is true, however, that the Soul of a Human Being can be set slowly into an exalted state, of which very few Human Beings have a concept.

The Soul, being separated from the tight bonds of sensuality, receives the impetus of clearness, to which only a few Human Beings ascend. Pythagoras confirmed this when he said: The Soul dissolves into the One when in the view of God, and there is a condition, when all relations between the Soul and the physical body cease, and the Human Being ascends to Enlightenment through Prayer, Solitude and Silence.

We, Human Beings, should never forget that the abilities which are present in our Soul, which belong to the future development of our condition, do not belong to the present, and we should not neglect these forces which God has given us for our present Life on Planet Earth.

Because of lack of proper understanding, mysticism leads many hundreds of people astray into daydreaming. Those people dream of nothing but solitude, silence, no physical labour, a place of peace and rest, and to remove themselves of all other duties, to which they were called upon by God.

Not holy indolence, but true activity of Love is our destiny.

The Wise enjoy the joys of Life with reason and with gratitude towards God. He develops himself on Planet Earth into a useful tool of His Goodness; he learns to be intelligent among fools and wise among clowns. He learns to conquer his passions, because they also belong to the life of a Human Being.

All these matters have to be taken into consideration and they should be remembered, because there is enough proof that many Human Beings think about the higher Sciences from an entirely wrong point of view.

Every passion is dangerous and to the detriment of the human race. Every passionate condition is an unnatural condition - the religious daydreamer, the philosophical daydreamer, the sensuous daydreamer, only the objects are different.

We should not forget that the Power of the Imagination has more control over a Human Being than reason, therefore, it can very easily get out of hand.

A person who is intoxicated by wine is no more in a natural state than the one whose Power of the Imagination is fired up in a different

315

manner. Continuous contemplation, excessive overheating of the imagination, bring forth a kind of passionate Human Being of an entirely different category.

Sensible abstinence, knowledge of Nature, a healthy Philosophy united with a noble and good will and true religion, all results in a Christian Philosophy.

We should never forget that the Human Being who lives on Planet Earth, has a physical body and a Soul, and the physical body in his present existence, in accordance to God's design, is absolutely necessary.

The Soul must be the ruler over the body; the body should serve her and not rule the Soul; this is the Law of the Philosophy of Religion. On the other hand, the Soul must treat the body as a servant and not as her slave, who she totally wants to destroy, since the Deity assigned the body to the Soul as a fellow worker on Planet Earth.

We have to remember: As long as a Human Being lives, the Soul has an effect on the body and the body has an effect on the Soul and, therefore, these effects and counter-effects have their laws and should not be violated.

To follow and obey the Laws of Reason and Religion, is in every point the measure of the behaviour of the Wise. It is his duty to keep the Power of the Imagination within its boundaries, because anything which outweighs the equilibrium, destroys the order and confuses the harmony of things.

It cannot be repeated often enough: Anybody who studies the secret Sciences should not be fascinated by the Powers of the Imagination and take chimeras for the Truth.

To explore secret things with calmness is the activity of the reasonable Human Being. To be fascinated by daydreaming is the attribute of a fool.

However, a large number of fools will always surpass a small number of Wise. Bene Vale!

THROUGH A WINDOW SMALL
By Gerhard Hanswille
An apocalyptic view of our present and future times with spiritual guidance being a focal point to deliver oneself from bondage. Detailed accounts of coming events are presented to the reader from the year 1992 through 2000. Comforting and contemplative! (194 p.)

PHILOSOPHIA MYSTICA:
THE PROPHECIES OF THE PROPHET DANIEL
By Paracelsus
Paracelsus unveils, for the attentive reader, the Mysteries of the Old and New Testament. Truth, Wisdom and Love are attributes of God and are also the basic principles of the Mysteries. Truly insightful for the serious seeker! (158 p.)

ALCHEMY UNVEILED
By Johannes Helmond
The author discusses in detail the highest perfection a human being can achieve on planet earth ("Alchemy)". It also deals with the various levels human beings have to attain in order to reach lofty spiritual heights (Philosopher's Stone). Rousing and to the point! (182 p.)

THE ADVENT OF CHRIST
By Jakob Lorber & Gottfried Mayerhofer
This 92-page treasure contains words spoken by Christ to the world and to his disciples dealing with the events surrounding His Second Coming (with special mentioning of His initial appearance in America). It also leaves no doubt as to the final victory of Christ over the Anti-Christ. A must! (92 p.)

THE GOSPEL OF JOHN
By Jakob Lorber
This monumental work reveals never-known insights regarding all questions pertaining to God, creation, the reason for living and eternity. Unprecedented and incomparable! (6 volumes = 2,113 p.)

THE CHILDHOOD OF JESUS
By Jakob Lorber
This work is the Gospel of St. James which was received again by Jakob Lorber. James recorded the whole life of Mary and Joseph starting from their birth. A comprehensive and wonderful description of the birth and childhood of Jesus of such intimate, exalted beauty and might, that not one heart can deny the origin and truth of these precious writings. We experience in the Child the first wonderful activities, and we receive with joyous astonishment, undreamed-of insights into the Holy Secrets of the person Jesus. Soul-clenching and illuminating! (402 p.)

SUNSET INTO SUNRISES
By Jakob Lorber
Among the writings about "life after death", this book ranks very high. Amazing and enlightening! (487 p.)

JESUS' WORDS
By Jakob Lorber
A collection of the Words of Jesus from the works of Jakob Lorber. Uplifting and heart-warming! (176 p.)

GEMS OF THE MASTER OF ALL MASTERS
By Jakob Lorber & Walter Floreani
A beautiful selection of the Lord's Words which will give inspiration to contemplation and reflections, with photographs by Walter Floreani. Visually and emotionally scintillating! (108 p.)

A SPIRITUAL VIEW OF LIFE
By Jakob Lorber & Gottfried Mayerhofer
This book reveals from a spiritual point-of-view, the spiritual anatomy of man, the spiritual vision of the universe, light and sound-spiritual elements and the essence of the natural order. Profound and revealing! (236 p.)

FUNDAMENTAL PRINCIPLES OF LIFE
By Walter Lutz
The content is taken from the wealth of the messages of Jakob Lorber regarding the most important questions of life. Fundamental, convincing, and precise! (3 volumes = 1,064 p.)

THE LORD'S SERMONS
By Gottfried Mayerhofer
This book contains 53 sermons for every Sunday of the traditional church year. A quote from the epilogue: "These sermons should be like steps which gradually should teach you to know Me, My Teachings and yourself better, and expand your insights." A ray of light! (326 p.)

FUTURE MERKUR TITLES

THE WORKS OF PARACELSUS
Containing his comprehensive theological, medical, philosophical, and hermetic writings.

THE GARDEN OF HEALTH
A concise treatise of herbal remedies and the application thereof.

THE HOUSEHOLD OF GOD
By Jakob Lorber
The primeval history of mankind is revealed, starting with the Secret of Creation until the Time of Noah. (3 volumes)

MW01063183

Tough Luck

ALSO BY SANDRA DALLAS

Where Coyotes Howl
Little Souls
Westering Women
The Patchwork Bride
The Last Midwife
A Quilt for Christmas
Fallen Women
True Sisters
The Bride's House
Whiter Than Snow
Prayers for Sale
Tallgrass
New Mercies
The Chili Queen
Alice's Tulips
The Diary of Mattie Spenser
The Persian Pickle Club
Buster Midnight's Cafe

Tough Luck

A NOVEL

Sandra Dallas

ST. MARTIN'S PRESS
NEW YORK

First published in the United States by St. Martin's Press, an imprint of St. Martin's Publishing Group

TOUGH LUCK. Copyright © 2025 by Sandra Dallas. All rights reserved. Printed in the United States of America. For information, address St. Martin's Publishing Group, 120 Broadway, New York, NY 10271.

www.stmartins.com

Design by Meryl Sussman Levavi

Library of Congress Cataloging-in-Publication Data

Names: Dallas, Sandra, author.
Title: Tough luck : a novel / Sandra Dallas.
Description: First edition. | New York : St. Martin's Press, 2025.
Identifiers: LCCN 2024027069 | ISBN 9781250352309
    (hardcover) | ISBN 9781250352316 (ebook)
Subjects: LCGFT: Western fiction. | Novels.
Classification: LCC PS3554.A434 T68 2025 | DDC 813/.54—dc23/
    eng/20240628
LC record available at https://lccn.loc.gov/2024027069

Our books may be purchased in bulk for promotional, educational, or business use. Please contact your local bookseller or the Macmillan Corporate and Premium Sales Department at 1-800-221-7945, extension 5442, or by email at MacmillanSpecialMarkets@macmillan.com.

First Edition: 2025

1   3   5   7   9   10   8   6   4   2

Tough Luck

Chapter One

Ma hadn't been in the ground more than an hour when my brother Cheet sold the farm. It wasn't his to sell. I told him that. "Cheet," I said, "the farm isn't yours to sell."

"If it's not mine, I don't know whose it is. It surely ain't yurn," he told me back.

"It's Pa's."

"Pa's dead, and ain't nobody going to raise him up like Lazarus."

"You don't know he's dead."

"He left in 1859 and it's now 1863, and he ain't writ more than three letters that whole time. The last was near two years ago. That means he's dead, and Ma wasted away from knowing it, and that's a fact. Her dying words were, 'Hello, Manley.'"

"That doesn't mean she saw him in heaven."

"You think she's in hell then?"

Cheet always twisted my words.

"I'm saying we don't know Pa's dead."

I can be stubborn when I want to, even if I don't do any more than repeat myself. I could have argued Pa's leaving didn't kill off Ma. She'd been poorly since long before Pa left, and to tell you the truth, I think that might have been one reason he took out.

"You already said you don't know Pa's dead. I say he is, and even if he ain't, who's going to run the farm until he decides to come home?" Cheet asked. "You think I'm going to slop the pigs and spread manure until Pa shows up with his tail between his legs and with nary a word of thanks? You know how he is."

"He'll come home proud and rich," I insisted.

I believed in Pa, although nobody else in the family did. Ma nagged him all the time, and Cheet laughed at him, so maybe that was why Pa had taken me up. He taught me to fish and to plow the field and ride astride like a boy. He said I was the best *son* he had, although he had Cheet and Boots. My older brother said I was too young to have known Pa for a failure. Maybe so, but somebody had to believe in him. And Pa believed in me. Before he'd gone off, he'd made me give him my solemn promise that if something happened to him, I would be responsible for the care of Boots. It was my sworn duty, and he'd repeated that in his letters.

There'd been only three of them, as Cheet said, and they were short because Pa couldn't write very well. I'd read them so often, I had them memorized.

Dear wif and fambly, he'd written in the first one. *I have got to Colorado and gold mines are scarce to find. Im lonesome as a skunk too. Cheet give up cards and do your part on the farm and Haidie you don't forget your promise about Boots. Afectionate your Pa Manley P. Richards.*

He didn't say anything to Ma.

Cheet and I were sitting in the kitchen now, him next to the cookstove, which was the only warm place in the house. He spent a good deal of time in that chair, even before Ma died—there or in the barn studying on cards and ways to cheat, him thinking he was going to be a riverboat gambler with a silk vest and a string tie. He made me play against him of an evening—Grandpap had taught us both—and the truth was, I was a better player than Cheet, and better at cheating, too, but I usually let him win, because he'd get mad enough to chew splinters when he lost.

After it got too cold in the barn, Cheet said he had to be near Ma in case she needed somebody to lift her up, and he was the only one strong enough. That meant me and Boots had to do the farm work.

Boots was out milking now, and I'd join him just as soon as I finished washing up the dishes folks had left. The women had brought us raisin pie—funeral pie, we called it, because that's what they always took to a laying out—and cake and baked beans and bottles of bread-and-butter pickles they'd put up, although I didn't know why anybody'd want to eat pickles after a funeral. Cheet had just cut himself a big piece of butterscotch cake, spilling crumbs across the table, which I'd have to clean up, too. I wanted to tell him that he could help with the milking now that Ma was dead and buried and didn't need lifting up anymore. But I knew better than to aggravate him when he was doing some deep thinking.

"I'll bet you a dollar Pa never comes back."

I snorted at that. "If I won, you'd pay that bet out of the money we got for the farm."

Cheet shrugged. "Well, it's done with and nothing you

can do about it now," he said. "The farm's sold. I signed the papers even before Ma was in the ground."

"How much you get?" I asked.

"Nine hundred and fifty dollars."

"It's worth fifteen hundred. You were snookered." Truer words were never spoke. Like Cheet said, this was 1863, and it looked like the war was going to go on a long time, North versus South. Our good Illinois cropland was worth even more than fifteen hundred.

"Bird in the hand."

"What are we going to do with that money?"

"*We?*" he snickered. "You mean what am *I* going to do with it? The money's been give to me. I didn't see no name of Mary Haidie Richards on it. I am nineteen, and I can dispose of it any way I want to. You are fourteen and a girl and have no rights. Tough luck."

His words took me back. I hadn't thought things through until now, not that anybody could blame me. I hadn't expected Pa to be away so long and I hadn't studied on what to do if Ma died. And I hadn't expected Cheet to sell the farm either, and now that he'd gone and done it, I had no idea what the three of us would do. I did not care to live on a riverboat while Cheet gambled away the money, but where else could me and Boots go? Besides, if I didn't keep an eye on Cheet, he'd use up the money faster than wheat grows in a good rain. "Best give me the money to keep?"

"Best give me the money to keep," Cheet repeated, teasing me. Cheet was mean to do that. "It's my money. Why'd I give it to a child like you?"

"Because a third of it's mine, and another third is Boots's, and I don't trust you not to gamble it."

"Here's you your share then." He reached into his pouch and took out two twenty-dollar gold pieces.

"Forty dollars! My share is forty dollars?"

"Both your shares, yours and Boots's. I'm being over-generous. That's more than anybody else has where you're going."

I stared at my brother. "What do you mean 'where we're going'? You mean we're not sticking together?"

"I got plans for me. I got plans for you, too."

I stared at Cheet for a long time, while I pondered what he said. Did Cheet mean me to be a hired girl? I wondered what other kind of work I could do, and then I thought about the women who worked on Red Feather Road, and shivered. Surely Cheet didn't expect me to become one of them. Cheet wasn't much, but at least he'd protect me if we were together. Without him, what would become of me and Boots?

✳ ✳ ✳

Cheet's plan, it turned out, was to put me and Boots in an orphanage. He'd already arranged for us to board at the Smoak, Illinois, Good Shepherd Home for Foundlings and Orphans.

I protested, of course. "We are not foundlings, nor are we orphans either, ma'am," I told Mrs. Jessica Tallbridge Walker, who was the matron. She said we were to call her Mrs. Walker, as if she thought I might call her Jessica. I had been taught better manners than that. "We have a father who is temporarily out West discovering a gold mine."

"Well then, when he gets back, he can pay for your care, Mary."

"It's Haidie, ma'am."

She looked down at a paper that Cheet had already filled out. "It says here that your names are Thomas Benton Richards and Mary Haidie Richards. Your name is Mary."

"I go by Haidie," I said stubbornly, refusing to look at her but instead glancing around the room, which was ugly and very plain. There was a desk, wooden chairs lined up against a wall, a cross that was five hands high, and a picture of the Virgin Mary looking woeful. If there hadn't been a sign saying "orphanage," you wouldn't have known what it was, because there was not a toy nor a picture to suggest children lived here.

"Haidie is not a proper name for a girl. You are Mary, named for the mother of our Lord, are you not?" The Good Shepherd home was Popish, although Mrs. Walker wasn't one of your nuns. After all she couldn't be a bride of Jesus and be *Mrs.* Walker at the same time, could she? The Good Shepherd was not such a bad place for an orphanage. I knew because I used to go there with Pa when he sold them potatoes. But it wasn't as good as the Jewish Home for Unfortunate Children. Pa sold potatoes to them, too, the good ones. The Good Shepherd bought the culls. If I had to be an orphan, I wished I was a Jew.

"Well," Mrs. Walker said, and I had to think back to what her question was. "Aren't you named for the Holy Mother?" she prompted.

I was not named for anybody's mother, but for my aunt,

Mary Haidie, a woman of uncommon size who believed in castor oil for croup and willow switches for children. Whenever we visited, she threatened to snatch me and Boots bald-headed for misbehaving, something with which she was mightily familiar if the wig that perched on her head like a small badger was any indication. Pa had hoped she would leave us money in return for giving her naming rights to me, but in that we were sorely disappointed, because the only thing she left us was an oil picture of herself. Her money went to the foot-washing Baptists. I did not protest that the painting was sold with the farm. In fact, it was some time before I realized it was gone, because we kept it in the barn. "Yes, ma'am, I guess I must be named for Jesus's mother," I replied, because that was what she wanted to hear, and it did me no harm to say so.

Right here, I'm going to inform you of something you ought to know about me. I lie. I do not do it to be ornery or because I am wicked. I lie because it is to my benefit, and it might be to yours, too, if you'd like to try it. And it is an easy thing. I can look a person right in the eye and lie myself silly. I see no harm in it, none at all.

"I'm trying to tell you, me and Boots, we're not orphans. Cheet has no call to put us here. He sold the farm for near a thousand dollars, and he wants to keep it for himself to spend on wickedness."

The matron turned to Cheet, who glared at me. "She's a liar," he said. "Ma whipped her and whipped her, but she couldn't whip out the lying. Haidie—Mary, that is—is lacking truth in her nature. It's a curse she was born with." He might have been afraid he'd said too much and the matron wouldn't take us, because he added, "Other than that, she's all right, a hard worker."

"Now who's the liar?" I said. "My brother's got near a thousand dollars, and he's going to spend it on riverboat gambling. If he's going to dump us here, he ought to be man enough to enlist again for the Union. The war's been on two years, and it needs men, even worthless ones." The war was not going well for us Yankees, but Cheet could not be blamed for that, because he had come home after two months, saying he'd been wounded and mustered out. Myself, I believe he had deserted.

"If you are their guardian . . ." The matron frowned.

"Yes, but I am on my way to the seminary, where I will study for the priesthood."

I stared at my brother with my mouth open so wide you could have tossed a potato down my throat without touching my tongue, thinking I had never in my life told a whopper like that. Mrs. Walker crossed herself. "A priest. Why, that is a fine thing. All of the children in the orphanage will pray for you. We are honored to take your brother and sister."

"Ask him if he knows the books of the Bible," I told her. "Ask him to quote you something from the book of George."

Cheet gave me a sad smile, and I knew I'd lost. He could charm the leg off a chair. "You have my permission to smite her on the right cheek and smite her on the left and smite her on the fanny, too, whenever you want." With his finger he drew a cross in the air.

"Now what are Mary and Thomas's ages?" Mrs. Walker asked Cheet.

"It's Boots, ma'am. You can call me Mary if you want to, but my brother's Boots. He wouldn't even know his name if you called him Thomas."

"Boots is not anybody's name."

She was wrong about that. My little brother had been Boots since the day he learned to crawl and got his head stuck in one of Pa's boots. Now he looked from Mrs. Walker to me, not sure who he was going to be. "His name is Thomas," Mrs. Walker said, glancing to see if Boots would challenge her. He did not.

"Now as to ages," the matron continued. "You said Thomas is ten, and Mary is twelve."

Once more, I started to protest. I was fourteen, almost fifteen. But I kept my mouth shut after she added, "We do not keep girls over the age of fourteen, so we prefer young children, but being as you are going to be a priest, we will accept Mary if she is twelve."

Now you might wonder why I did not protest that. It was not because I knew Cheet would argue with me if I gave my true age. It was because I wanted to keep an eye on Boots. He'd never been by himself, and he'd be afraid without me.

Besides, a plan was already forming in my mind.

"Cheet, being as you're going into the priesthood"—at that, I drew a cross on my chest with my finger—"I'd like you to give me Pa's letters that you have in that carpetbag. You know as well as I do they don't let beginner priests have things of a personal nature." Cheet didn't know but what that was true. Besides, he didn't have any use for the letters. So he reached into the bag for them. But I was too quick for him and pulled the bag to me. My fingers found the money pouch and slipped two coins into one of the envelopes. Something else you should know about me is I can be a sneak thief if I want to be. In fact, I had given some thought to being a cutpurse, but nobody in Smoak ever had money to put into a pocket.

Cheet signed some papers, and then he drew a cross over our heads. I wished him good luck. I didn't hate Cheet, although he cheated me and Boots out of our share of the money and dumped us in an orphanage. He wasn't cut out to be a father any more than he was cut out to be a farmer. He wouldn't have fared any better raising us than he would raising crops and would have run us as well as the farm into the ground. At least in the orphanage, we'd have something to eat and Boots would learn to read and write better than I could teach him. Cheet wasn't a bad person. He just wasn't a very good brother.

"Be good, you hear?" Cheet called to us.

"Bless you, Father Cheet," I said.

Boots watched the matron walk our older brother out of the room, and then he turned to me, his face solemn. "What's going to happen to us?" he asked.

"We're going to stay here and be the best damn orphans they ever had. Then in the spring, we're going to run off and find Pa."

* * *

If I did not know that me and Boots were going to run away one day, I would not have stayed in that orphanage as long as I did. Ma was dead. I'd grieved for her long before she crossed over. She was a testy woman and never strong, and after Pa left, she just withered away. When Pa's letters stopped coming and Ma convinced herself he was dead, she spent most of her time in bed, saying she didn't have a reason to live. I guess she didn't consider me and Boots reasons. She didn't want anything but to join Pa in heaven, and her dying words, as Cheet said, were "Hello, Manley," Manley being Pa's name, of course. It helped me considerably to think she was happy at the moment she crossed over, although I believe God or the angels or whoever's in charge was fooling her. Nothing in the world could convince me Pa was already dead.

Since I'd known she wasn't long for this world, I'd had my grief worked out. But Boots, he cried and cried, and I cursed Pa then. A pot of gold wasn't worth all the misery he'd brought on Boots.

✳ ✳ ✳

I thought I was done with sorrow by the time Ma passed, but I missed her like a good rain. She'd been a poor mother to me and Boots. Still, she was a gentle soul, and she loved me in her way. Every morning, she'd asked me if I'd said my prayers and washed my face. I'd come in at the end of the day and sit by her bed, holding her hand, and she'd smile at me, and on Ma's good days, which weren't many, I'd think we were like one person, her the soul and me the body, just as we'd been when I was small. We were the only females in that house. Besides Cheet and Boots, Ma'd had seven or eight other boys who'd died when they were born or shortly thereafter, none of them living long enough to get a name. She and I were the only ones who sorrowed over them. I knew how much she'd grieved, because the other thing she said when she died was

"Hello, babies." So even if Pa wasn't up there in heaven, Ma was with her lost children.

✳ ✳ ✳

I reckon you've heard the stories about how they treat orphans in an asylum, how they starve them and beat them and work them half to death. There might be some truth in it, but I have to say the nuns at the Good Shepherd weren't all bad. They ate the same porridge and black bread we did, and they tried their best to teach us to love Jesus and wash our necks. Of course, they didn't have any money, so the orphans had to work hard to earn enough for food and the coal bill.

Boots was assigned to the garden, but as it was still winter, he didn't have anything much to do, so he went to school, which was in the basement of the orphanage. He did not like it much, because he was new—fresh fish, the other boys called him, and challenged him to fight. Now Boots was a fighter. I myself have been wounded by him. But he wasn't much good against three or four boys at one time, especially when they were larger. So he had his share of bruises and bloody noses. Sometimes in the night, I heard him cry out, "Haidie," but as I was in another room and the nuns slept beside the doors, I couldn't go to him.

I was put to work in the washroom, and I will say here that it was not an easy thing for me, as I have never equated cleanliness with godliness.

Washing was hard work even on nice days, and it was purely hell in winter. We boiled the clothes in scalding water, then rinsed them in freezing water we hauled from the creek. Sometimes, we had to break the ice to get to it. If we had

had to wash only the laundry of the orphans and nuns, we wouldn't have minded so much, but the orphanage supported itself by taking in the washing of half the town of Smoak—the dirty half. For five cents each, three for a dime, a man could have a shirt covered with barnyard muck and pig fat washed clean and ironed stiff as a church pew. The price was so cheap that I myself would have spent one of my gold pieces having Boots's and my washing done—only our laundry got done for free. At the end of the day, my hands were raw and bleeding and my wrists so tired from the rubbing and twisting that I could not unbutton my shoes.

Being a washer-girl did have one advantage. Like I say, sometimes I heard Boots call for me at night. When I asked him about it, he said he was dreaming, but I saw the fresh bruises. So one day, I got him in a corner and said he'd have to let me know what was going on or I'd tell Mrs. Walker something was wrong.

He replied that he wasn't a tattletale, and besides, he'd get tromped and called a sissy if the boy who was thrashing him found out he had complained. But I said if he didn't tell me who was tormenting him, I'd leave him behind when I left to find Pa.

So Boots confessed that Dolph Bates was his enemy and egged on the other boys to beat up Boots. I'd known Dolph before he was an orphan. He was a bully, meaner than a nettle, and I wondered that I hadn't figured out myself that he picked on Boots. "Why's he got it in for you?" I asked.

"'Cause he's plain mean."

"He is that."

"What are you going to do, Haidie?"

"Just watch me," I said. "But you have to do something. Next time he picks on you, you tell him you've got something in store for him. When he asks what, you just smile."

"But he'll smack me."

"He'll smack you anyway. But it won't be for long. I have a plan."

Another thing about me is I am good at plans.

Like I said, I worked in the laundry. Once a week, the kids in the orphanage changed their clothes, as each girl orphan had two dresses and each boy two shirts and sets of overalls. I made a point of remembering what Dolph wore, and I grabbed his shirt when it came into the laundry. After I washed and ironed it, I put tiny burrs into the pocket, so that when Dolph put it on, the burrs made scratches across his chest. I told Boots what I'd done, and he said all the boys giggled when they saw Dolph rubbing his chest, although they didn't let Dolph see them. That made Boots feel good, but it didn't keep Dolph from picking on my brother.

So the next wash day, I filched some red pepper from the kitchen, and I rubbed it inside his overalls, right over where his skinned knees touched the fabric. He yelped and jumped around, and the boys laughed again, not caring so much if Dolph saw them this time.

That still wasn't enough, however. So on the following laundry day, I rubbed the red pepper over the front of his overalls, down where I figured the material came into contact with his private parts. It wasn't so bad when Dolph put on the overalls, because he was standing up and the overalls were loose. But when he sat down at breakfast he started to howl and itch, then scratch himself with both hands, until

Mrs. Walker got up from her place at the head of the table. When she saw what Dolph was doing, she smacked him on the side of the head and told him if he didn't stop, he would go blind.

She told Dolph to stay in his chair when the other children left the room, and she'd let him know his punishment. When Boots walked by, he looked Dolph in the eye and grinned. The other boys didn't know what had happened, but they knew Boots had gotten even, and that was the last of the bullying.

* * *

When our work in the laundry room was done, we had classes. We girls had to learn to read and write and work as maids, because that was the only job an orphan girl could expect to find. I already knew manners, because Ma had been a Haidie from Chicago, which in Illinois meant you were as fine as frog hair. Since Ma had taught me a fair hand, Mrs. Walker put me in charge of penmanship, and that was how I got to keep an eye on Boots.

He knew how to read and write, too, but I told him to act like he was no good at it so that he could stay in my classroom, where he sat up front. Sometimes when I pretended to correct what he was writing on a slate, I would scribble a little note, like "Keep your chin up" or "Anybody need red pepper?" Once when I was going around the room checking what the orphans were doing with their chalk, I saw that Boots had written on his slate, "Wen are we finden Pa."

"Soon as the weather turns good," I wrote back.

Some of the other girls at the orphanage taught, too,

because the nuns had too much to do. Being married to Jesus was no picnic, not like you were the wife of the mayor of Smoak, who sat around and drank tea and ate cake. Jesus expected his brides to milk the cows and slop the pigs and toil in the fields, and believe me, they were no lilies. Most of them were as ugly as buckets. I asked one of the prettier ones, Sister Teresa, who was a nun-in-training, why she would join up to be a nun? After all, she was a pretty, pigeon-eyed little thing who could turn any boy's head.

"Wasn't my idea. I'm what they call an incorrigible. It's my nature," she said.

I didn't understand the word, but I didn't want to admit it, so I asked, "What were you incorriged to do?"

"I got in the family way," she explained.

I understood *that*. She had begotten. "Is the baby an orphan?"

"No, my pappy gave it to my sister before he put me in here."

"Who's the father?"

"I ain't telling."

"You can tell me."

She considered that, running her tongue around her lips. "Why'd I do that? I never told anybody else."

"Why wouldn't you? Maybe I could help."

"How'd you do that?"

"I'm good with plans, and besides, I don't think being a nun is such a good idea at your age."

Teresa didn't reply.

"It's Billy Stover, the one that delivers the laundry, isn't it?" I'd seen the two of them making cow eyes at each other,

Billy trying to slide his hand up her dress. Sister Teresa always cried when he left.

"The same," she admitted.

"Why didn't you marry him?"

"I wanted to. Billy even has a farm. But I was too young, and now that I'm going to be a nun, I can't. They won't let me out, and who'd marry us anyway? The priest that rides through Smoak every now and then would tell my pappy if I tried to get married, and Pap would stop it. He says I'm a sinner, and he hates sin worse than God does."

"You could ask the Campbellite minister to marry you."

"And be married outside the church! Then I'd go to hell for sure. I'm stuck."

"Maybe not," I said, an idea forming in the back of my mind. "If I was to help you, would you help me back?"

"I would." She frowned.

"Would you promise on the cross?" Seeing as how we were in the washroom of a Papist orphanage, I thought that would be binding.

Sister Teresa nodded. "But what could you do?"

"Just you wait and see."

⁕ ⁕ ⁕

Much as I was mad at Cheet, I had to admit he wasn't all bad. Once a month or so, he came back to see us, telling the nuns he was a regular priest now and that the seminary had sent him out to do God's work among the heathen, meaning gamblers, I suppose. The closest he ever came to working for the Lord was using marked cards to take money off a free-will Baptist. Mrs. Walker thought he'd been chosen to help the downtrodden, however, and told me that by making the decision to be a priest at such a young age, he was just the holiest person she'd ever met.

"I could do so much more if I had not taken a vow of poverty," he told her, looking like a hound dog whose rabbit had just ducked into a hole. Mrs. Walker couldn't help him there, saying she hadn't enough money for the poor and hungry orphans in her own care. When I got him alone, I told Cheet anybody who stole money from the orphans was lower than a snake's belly, that if he did so, he'd be taking food from me and Boots.

"Why, I'd never consider such a thing," he said.

I knew better. "You would, but you do it, and I'll snatch you bald-headed as Aunt Mary Haidie," I told him.

I wasn't sure why Cheet came around to see us after the way he'd dumped us at the Good Shepherd Home. But I am judging, and that is not the province of orphans. I was glad he came, because he was family, and I guess I loved him. Maybe there was a tiny bit of decency in Cheet, or he felt guilty about the way he'd treated me and Boots, because he brought us penny candy. He gave Boots a wool cap and me a silk scarf that smelled like perfume, so I suppose he lifted it off a fancy girl, but it was the thought that counted.

☀ ☀ ☀

I waited until after the snow was gone, before I asked Cheet to do me a favor. "You owe me, and it's not going to cost you a thing," I told him.

"Aw, come on, Haidie. I ain't a real priest. I can't officiate. It won't stick," he said, after I explained what I wanted. I'd told him only part of my plan, because I knew he'd be against the second half.

"You and me's the only ones that know that."

"It would be a sin."

"So's cheating at cards, and pretending to be a priest. And since when did you care about sin anyway?"

"This'd be worse than gambling. I'd be promoting criminal connection."

"They already connected."

"But I ain't a real priest."

"You could have fooled me."

Cheet looked at me funny at that.

"Well, you fooled Mrs. Walker, and that's all that matters." Indeed, he'd fooled Mrs. Walker so much that she'd asked him to hold a church service for the orphans. Cheet said he'd not do it because that was the job of the regular priest, who wouldn't like somebody else butting in. "Don't tell him I said so, but it's about respect," he'd told Mrs. Walker.

Now, Cheet tried to figure out if there was a percentage in my proposition, but other than clean laundry, there wasn't. "Why'd you want me to do it?" he asked.

"Because she's kindly to Boots."

Once Cheet agreed, I went to Teresa. "You remember your promise, if I got you out of here, you'd do something for me?" I asked.

She nodded, watching me like a dog waiting for a bone.

"I got a way to do it."

Teresa put her hands together to form a little steeple. Then her face turned blank, and behind her, Mrs. Walker said, "Girls, there's work to be done."

Teresa said, "Mary here just asked me if I thought she could be a bride of Jesus one day." Teresa bent her head to one side and lowered her eyes. "I said she would have to repent of her sins."

I liked Teresa even better then, because I knew she was a good liar, too, just like me, and that would help me and Boots.

"Is that so, Mary?" Mrs. Walker asked.

I was getting used to that name of Mary, but I'd be glad to drop it once I was out of there. "Yes'm. But I got a pokeful of sins. I'm not so sure Jesus would want me. I might defile his house."

Mrs. Walker thought that over. "You're a little young yet."

"I'm fourteen!" Then I clamped my hand over my mouth. I'd get kicked out of the orphanage if she found out my real age.

"You're twelve. Your holy brother told me, and he also said you're a liar. Lying is a serious sin."

"Yes'm."

"So is slothfulness. There's washing to be done. You wouldn't want to go to the Lord in dirty clothes."

Teresa and I went off together and broke out laughing as soon as we reached the laundry room. "We fooled her," Teresa said, although I wasn't so sure. Mrs. Walker would bear watching.

As we were bent over the scrubboards, I brought up the subject of her leaving the orphanage.

"I can't run away. Where'd I go? They'd make an awful

stink, and they'd run me down like hound dogs take to a fox."

"What if you could marry Billy?"

"I told you, the priest wouldn't do it without Pappy's say-so, and if I got married by anybody else, I'd be living in sin and would surely perish in hellfire."

"My brother's a priest. He comes to see me sometimes."

Teresa stopped rubbing overalls on the scrubboard and turned to stare at me, as the idea took hold of her. "If there was to be a real marriage with a priest, then Pappy couldn't put it asunder. Your brother truly is a priest?"

"Truly," I said. As I had told Cheet, Teresa would never know she'd be living in sin the rest of her life, so what harm was the lie?

"He can perform marriages?"

"That's what priests do, isn't it?"

Teresa wiped soap scum off her hands and shook out the water. Her hands might have been pretty if they weren't so red and chapped. "You'd have to be married in secret, of course, but once the wedding's over, you could live right here in Smoak at that farm Billy owns, the one you told me about. And maybe you could get your baby back."

She nodded. "I surely would like that. You think your brother'd do it? Mrs. Walker would be awful mad."

"He will. But first, I'll tell you what I want in return."

✳ ✳ ✳

It wasn't long before Cheet came back and I reminded him of his promise to me.

"I guess it won't do no harm. They got any money to pay me?"

"No, and don't you go bothering them for it."

"I was just asking." He paused. "What am I supposed to say?"

"You've been to enough weddings."

It was our good fortune that Mrs. Walker and the nuns had gone to market that morning. So I took Cheet into the laundry room, and we waited with Teresa until Billy showed up with a pile of washing.

Cheet took out a Bible I'd stole from the church and asked Teresa and Billy to stand in front of the washtubs.

"Oughten we to get married in a church?" Billy asked.

Cheet shook his head. "A laundry room's a fine place, a place for washing away your sins and all that." Cheet was getting into the spirit. He cleared his throat and began, "Dearly beloved, we are gathered in this place . . ."

Billy interrupted again. "Aren't you supposed to marry us in Latin?"

"You speak Latin?" Cheet asked.

"'Course not."

Cheet nodded, and then he began talking in French, words he'd learned from a hired man once. I think he said, "I ain't going to shovel manure" and "Do you have a bottle on you?" And there were some other words that were never before spoke in a house of God, but as Teresa had been an incorrigible, she should not have been shocked, although she didn't understand French either. When Cheet was finished, he said, "Done!"

"Now get Teresa in the laundry wagon and drive like

hell before Mrs. Walker comes back," I said. "And you, too, Cheet, git!"

"Why me?"

"Because when Mrs. Walker finds out, she will have a fit of apoplexy. And the wrath of Mrs. Walker is worse than the wrath of God."

"All right," he said. "I'll come see you next month."

Tough luck, I thought. *Me and Boots won't be here.*

＊ ＊ ＊

Mrs. Walker was boiling mad when she found out Teresa had married Billy Stover, but as it turned out, she wasn't mad at Cheet, just at Teresa. And there wasn't a thing she or Teresa's pappy could do about it, because the happy couple had been married by a priest, or at least that was what they thought.

"If I'd known what she was about, I'd have warned Father Cheet. That girl's as slick as a snake on a marble floor," Mrs. Walker said. She shook her head, while I wondered where she'd picked up an expression like that. There surely were no marble floors at the orphan home. "He'll have to explain himself to the Good Shepherd board."

"Yes'm," I said. "He'll take the responsibility. Wasn't a thing to do with you."

"Well, I hope not." She was more concerned about what the directors would think than she was about losing Teresa, who wouldn't have made much of a nun anyway. If what she'd told me was true, she liked connection too much.

I was afraid Mrs. Walker would refuse to let Billy Stover come to the orphanage after that, but she needed the laundry money, so Billy still came three days a week, and he grinned at me when he said that marriage could wear out a person.

There was quite a commotion at the orphanage about Teresa getting married, because nothing much happened there. So I waited until it calmed down, until spring was almost over, and then I reminded Billy that he and Teresa owed me.

"She's waiting," he said. "You want to go out in the laundry wagon?"

"No, then they'd come looking for you. An hour after the lights go out, you wait a mile down the road. We'll find you there."

I hadn't told Boots about the plan for fear he would brag on it to the other boys. So not until that night, after supper, did I tell him we were running away that very evening. "When you go to bed, you put on all your clothes, everything you got, and I'll come get you," I said. A nun slept in the boys' room, but she was a lazy thing and usually was snoring before the boys even settled down.

I waited until she was sending up a racket with her honking. Then I put my second dress over my head and gathered up my things, which weren't much—Pa's letters, Ma's wedding ring, and the little money Cheet had given me from the sale of the farm (plus the gold pieces I'd stolen from him). Then I sneaked into the boys' room and touched Boots's arm. He didn't answer. He'd gone to sleep. I pinched him, but he only whimpered. "Boots," I whispered, and then louder, "Boots!"

"Haidie?" he yelled. That woke the nun. "You boys be quiet," she ordered, and then to my horror, she got up. I rolled under Boots's bed and listened to her footsteps as she came down the aisle between the beds, stopping next to where Boots lay. "We'll have no whispering, young men," she said.

That woke Boots for sure, and the boards under his mattress squeaked as he sat up and said, "Haidie, that you?"

I was in for it now. She took a step toward the bed, and in the moonlight, I could see her bare feet, her toes cramped up. I reached out and pinched her big toe between my fingernails, just like a tiny bite.

She flinched and yanked back her foot and said, "God damn rat!" I almost laughed at the blasphemy. But the pinch did the trick, and she marched back to her bed and wrapped herself in her blanket and went to sleep. I reached through the boards and poked the mattress three or four times so that Boots would know I was there and wouldn't doze off. We waited until everyone was asleep again, then I crawled out from under the bed, and me and Boots sneaked past the nun, out of the room, and down the stairs.

I'd forgotten about the front door. Mrs. Walker locked it every night with a big key that she wore around her neck. We tiptoed to the kitchen, but one of the nuns was setting the bread to rise for the next morning. So I took Boots down to the laundry room. It was dark on the stairs, and we could hear the rats running around.

"Maybe we ought to stay," Boots whispered, but I told him we'd never find Pa if we didn't get away now. This was our only chance. So he crept along behind me, holding on to my skirt.

Moonlight was coming through the window high up in

the laundry room, and I could see the door that Billy Stover used. It wasn't even locked. We scooted out and ran down the road, hoping Billy hadn't given up and gone home. But he was there. We climbed into the wagon, and Billy covered us up with sacks. "If anybody comes along, just pretend you're a bundle of laundry," he advised.

Billy larruped up the horse, and we rode along in the dark, Billy stopping once to talk to a man who passed in a buggy. "Are you up early with the laundry or out late?" the man asked.

"Out late," Billy said. "I just got married."

The man said some words that weren't in French, but Billy just wished him a good evening and went on.

With the rocking of the wagon and the heavy sacks to lie on, me and Boots fell asleep and didn't wake up until Billy stopped again. "Here we are."

I sat up and looked around. "Where's the river?"

"That's the thing of it. We can't get the boat until to-morrow night. You have to spend the day here, with Teresa."

"It's the first place they'll look for us. Mrs. Walker knows me and Teresa are friends and that my brother officiated at your wedding."

"He did what?"

"He married you and Teresa."

"Oh, you don't have to worry. Teresa's got a hidey-hole for you."

"Not in a privy," Boots said. "I wouldn't hide in a privy."

"Wouldn't expect you to. There's a little ole tree house back in the woods. Me and Teresa used to go there—" He broke off. "It's got a blanket and a jug of water, and Teresa put vittles in a box where the coons can't get at 'em. I'll come get you tomorrow night after dark." He left to put away the horse.

✳ ✳ ✳

That tree house was a fine hideout. With all the branches and the leftover leaves in the way, you couldn't see it if you were standing directly under it, and from high up like that, we could look out over the Mississippi. Me and Boots slept better than we ever had at the orphanage, and we ate better, too, because there was white bread and boiled eggs in the box. We just sat there in that cozy place and listened to the birds sing all day until evening was coming on.

Boots was trying to sound like a robin when I heard a noise below, and clamped my hand over his mouth. "Hush," I whispered. It was probably just Billy Stover with the laundry wagon, but I wanted to be careful, and that was a good thing, because a minute later, I heard a man's voice cry out: "Teresa Stover, there's two orphans missing from the Good Shepherd, and they better not be here."

Teresa came out of the house, mad as could be, and yelled, "They ain't here. You search the house and barn if'n you think so."

"I guess we'll just do that. And the chicken coop and the backhouse, too."

Through a crack in the boards of the tree house, I could see Teresa standing in the dooryard, her hands on her hips, glaring at two men.

They went into the house, then came out and searched the barn, then stood in the yard, one of them asking, "Where'd you hide them?"

"Why you asking me. I never had truck with boys at the orphan home."

"One of 'em's a girl."

"A girl?"

"Mary Richards."

"Well, hallelujah. That's the best thing I've heard since I left."

"You're too pert," one of the men said, but the other told him to go on, that time was wasting, and they'd better hurry up and look elsewhere if they wanted to get the reward.

"What reward?" Teresa asked.

"Ten dollars."

Teresa watched the men leave, standing at the gate and studying on them until they were far down the road, and then she climbed up into the tree house. "Did you hear that? There's a reward for you."

"Are you going to turn me in?" I asked.

"Not me, but Billy might."

"Your husband?" I asked.

She nodded. "Billy's not what I thought he was," she said. "He used to be real nice with his sweet-talking ways, but now that we're married, he expects me to wait on him, and he slaps me if I don't please him. Billy rules me. He's a fool for money, too. Why, he goes through the laundry looking through pockets to see if anybody left a coin or something he can sell. Before we were married, he was the sweetest man that ever broke bread. I guess you never can tell."

"Just because a cat's born in an oven, that doesn't make him a baker's pie," I said. "Are you sorry you married him?"

"It's better than being a nun, but not much. Mostly, I wanted to get my baby back. But the baby calls my sister Mama. It would break my sister's heart if I snatched it back. I couldn't do it." She smiled at me. "'Tain't your problem, but you got another'n all right. Once Billy finds out about that reward, he'll turn you in quicker than you can say Yankee Doodle. I guess we got to hide you somewheres else."

I'd already done some thinking. It hadn't set right with me that Billy hadn't found a boat the night before, and I'd wondered about him, whether he might be waiting for the orphanage to offer a reward, then double-cross us. "I guess me and Boots better git. You tell Billy that after those men showed up, I got scared and asked directions for the post road. Tell him I didn't want to stay around anymore, and me and Boots aren't strong enough to row across the river by ourselves."

Teresa nodded. "That's a good plan. I'd go along with you if I wasn't married to him. It's a sin to leave your husband. But I got no choice."

I jerked up my head. "You do. My brother's no more a priest than Mrs. Walker. He just pretends he is. By rights, you aren't married."

"I ain't?" Teresa looked at me, dumbfounded. "That means I could leave Billy, but where'd I go. Pappy wouldn't take me. I'd be worse off than ever."

"We're going west to find my pa. Why don't you come along?"

It didn't take Teresa half a minute to make up her mind.

She wrote Billy a letter telling him she was showing us the post road, then she'd spend the night with her sister.

"Can he read?" I asked.

Teresa blinked and cocked her head. "I don't know. I never asked."

Me and Boots got our belongings, while Teresa put a dress and a pair of boots in a sack, along with the food she had in the pantry. "You think we need blankets, too?" she asked.

"Won't Billy notice they're gone?" Boots asked.

"You think he won't notice I'm gone?" Teresa replied and went to fetch the blankets. Then she said, "In for a penny, in for a pound," and for good measure, she took the money in Billy's poke, leaving him three pennies and a two-bit piece.

"One more thing," I said, asking Teresa to get me a pair of Billy's britches and a shirt and to cut off my hair.

"Why?" she asked.

"They'll be looking for a boy and a girl. Besides, if me and Boots are to tramp west, I'll have an easier time of it as a boy. There's nobody who'll hire a girl to tend horses or drive wagons."

"It's a sin to transgress like that."

"The Bible says it's a greater sin not to take care of your brother. Haven't you read that? It's in the book of George."

"I was never partial to Bible reading." She found a pair of scissors and hacked off my hair, doing such a poor job of it that I looked not only like a boy but a poor one at that.

Just as the sky was darkening, we found a rowboat cached along the riverbank, and the three of us rowed across the Mississippi.

Chapter Two

Teresa had made the decision to run off, with no thought to what she'd do once she was away. She reckoned she'd stick with me and Boots until she figured it out, which suited us all right, at least for a little while. If the orphan catchers crossed the river, they'd be looking for a boy and a girl, not a mother and two sons. We thought the men we'd seen wouldn't go all that way just for ten dollars, but we weren't so sure about Billy Stover. So to be safe, we floated down the river for a day in a boat we'd thieved until we reached Fort Madison. Then we stowed the boat and walked into town.

I'd never been anyplace more than five miles beyond Smoak, and I'd figured the rest of the world wasn't much different. So I was surprised to find a dozen houses that were a hundred times fancier than anything at home. Teresa called them mansions, and they surely were, big houses with towers and turrets and porches and balconies. They had iron fences in front and tee-toncey little iron fences on their roofs. There was a business district with brick buildings three stories high, tall enough to make you dizzy just looking up; a bank, half a dozen stores, and a place that sold nothing but books.

I hadn't thought there were that many people in the world who could read. "I think this must be like New York City," I told Boots, who was staring at the buildings, his mouth open.

But Teresa scoffed. "It ain't even Chicago," she said with authority, for she claimed she'd been to that city. She stopped at every shop window, her eyes wide at the fancy dresses and geegaws. "I would like that," she said, pointing to a useless yellow bonnet with satin ribbons as long as a horse's tail, hanging down from a bow. The violets pinned to the hat looked almost real.

"Best save your money," I told her. "You won't need that where we're going."

"Where's that?" she asked.

"To Colorado Territory. To find our pa." I'd never let her in on my plan to find Pa. I hadn't known if she could keep a secret and was afraid she'd tell someone at the orphanage, or Billy. Of course, I was just being cautious about Billy. I hadn't known that he was a traitor.

"Colorado! That's a hundred miles, isn't it? How are we going to go all that way?" She didn't sound quite so worldly then.

"It's not so far. We'll work for our keep. I'm as good as any boy with horses, and Boots is a sight better than most his age. We'll hire on with somebody going west. I've studied on it. There's a sight of people headed for the territory."

"Why don't you take the train?"

"We don't have the money. Besides, it doesn't go all the way to Colorado."

"I'm afraid of Indians," Teresa protested.

"No need to be. There's soldiers that's been mustered out that are wanting to find their fortune in the West. Why, it'll be like market day in Smoak out there on the prairie with all those people." I lied about all that, because I didn't have the least idea about Indians.

"I don't know," Teresa said, staring at the bonnet. Her hand went to her pocket, where she kept Billy's money. "Maybe I ought to stay here."

"And do what? Do you think Billy's going to let you go? You hurt his pride, running off like you did after you'd been married only a month. What if he crosses the river and checks all the towns. A lady all by herself, folks will know you're here, and when Billy asks around, somebody's bound to tell him. Besides, what would you do? All's you know is cooking and keeping house." *And connection,* I thought, but I didn't say so. "If you go to Colorado, you'll likely find a rich man to marry."

"I would like that," Teresa said. "You sure you want me to go with you?"

I wasn't sure at all. I figured me and Boots might do better on our own. Teresa would need tending, and she'd slow us down. Me and Boots would have an easier time of it by ourselves. But Teresa was my friend. And without her, I'd be back in the orphans' home. "We'll stick together," I promised.

I may be a liar, but when I give my word, I keep it.

* * *

I was in a hurry to leave for Colorado. I was anxious to see Pa, but I was worried about Billy, too. The more I thought about him, the surer I was he'd come looking for Teresa. Having your wife run out on you is a powerful shock to the soul. Besides, he'd waited a long time to get married, and from what Teresa had told me, Billy sure did like somebody to cleave to. It would be easier for him to find his old wife than a new one.

So as soon as Teresa agreed to go west with us, we went to the stable where two covered wagons were being loaded. We let Teresa do the talking for us, since she was claiming to be our mother. She approached one man, telling him she was taking her children west to join her husband in Colorado Territory. He licked his lips while he looked her over and said he'd be happy to take her along, only he didn't want a pair of brats. Well, I couldn't blame him there, because me and Boots appeared slight, both of us tall and skinny, me with my hair looking like roof shingles. But Teresa told me later that even if she'd been by herself, she wouldn't have traveled with him. She thanked him and turned to the other man. His woman spoke up and said they already had enough kids to do the work. She was a homely sort, her mouth all stove in from where she'd lost her teeth, and after she appraised Teresa, she added that she didn't fancy another woman to get in the way. We took her meaning and figured we'd come back the next day.

Then a man who was loading a wagon with supplies said he was going to Omaha, and if we didn't mind sitting on top of the crates and barrels, he wouldn't object to the company. He wasn't going all the way to Colorado Territory, but we ought to be able to hook up with a wagon train in Omaha. If Teresa would cook and me and Boots would help with the mules, he'd consider it a fair bargain. "I'm an easy man to

please. The grub I like best is whatever I can get," he told
Teresa.

She turned to me for my opinion. I'd feel safer traveling
with a family instead of a solitary man, but he seemed nice
enough, friendly, big, chesty, arms that looked as hard as an
oak knot, and sandy hair that was a little thin on top. I wondered if he was after Teresa and would try to get rid of me
and Boots later on. I studied on that a minute, but I knew
we didn't have much time. A mule team would be faster than
oxen, and this was a swell outfit: six mules, all black, not
a lazy light-colored one among them, and no signs of sore
mouth that I could see. The wagon was well built, with a
brake, so we wouldn't have to stop and lock the wheels when
we came to a hill. So I nodded, and Teresa held out her hand
to the man and said it was a deal.

"Me and Boots will help you load, mister," I said.

"So he's Boots," the man said. "And how are you called,
boy?"

"Haidie," Boots said. It was too late to change our names,
but maybe it didn't matter. He was the only one in Fort
Madison who knew us by name. So if Billy asked for Teresa
or Haidie or Boots, nobody'd know who we were. "The last
name's Richards," I said before Teresa could tell him she was
Teresa Stover. We'd all have to have the same last name, of
course. "We're Boots and Haidie and Mrs. Richards."

The man studied us for a long time, sizing up me and
Boots, then looking over Teresa. Most likely, he was thinking
that Teresa didn't have enough wear on her to be the mother
of two boys as old as we were. But he didn't remark on it. He
touched the tip of his hat and said, "I'm pleased to make your

acquaintance, Mrs. Richards. I'm Jacob Crowfoot, but you're to call me Jake. And my dog over there"—he pointed to as ugly a mongrel as I ever saw—"that's Tige. Now you go sit in the shade, Mrs. Richards, while your boys and me finish loading the wagon. I figure we can leave at sunrise."

"I got shopping yet. My shoes are wore through." She took out Billy's money and counted it. Me and Boots had each got a fair pair of boots from the orphanage that were in better shape than Teresa's shoes, and I hoped they'd last the trip. I figured we'd need our gold coins for other things. Teresa didn't know about our money. I didn't mistrust her, but if she knew about the gold pieces, she might think a third was hers. She probably figured that like all orphans, we were flat busted, and that was okay with me.

Teresa left us then, and when she returned, she was wearing a pair of heavy shoes—and a yellow bonnet with purple violets and long ribbons hanging down to her waist. "It was just calling to me," she explained.

I didn't say anything. It was her money to spend. But Jake snorted and teased, "By golly, Mrs. Richards, it's said them Indians have a preference for yellow." "By golly" turned out to be Jake's high curse words.

He was a good packer, a freighter, he called himself. He took goods to Omaha, where shopkeepers marked them up about a thousand percent and sold them to folks going west. Then he brought back buffalo robes that were shipped from the Mississippi to tanneries in the east. "I don't usually freight people, but I ain't in so much of a hurry this time, and I can stand the company." He looked at Teresa when he said that, and I was glad she'd decided to stick with us. I don't suppose Jake would pick me and Boots for company.

"Fetch the rest of your gatherings, so we'll be ready to go soon, at dawn light," Jake told us, placing Teresa's sack of clothing in the wagon.

"We don't have anything else," I said. When Jake frowned at that, I added quickly, "Me and Boots, our carpetbag fell right off the ferry boat into the river."

"Couldn't they fish it out?"

"It sank like a millstone. Sank like the rock of ages," I added for emphasis.

"Wasn't no way to fish it out," Boots added.

"Well, you can't go west with no coat." Jake dug into his pocket and took out a gold coin. "You go find the mercantile and buy you both a coat and an extra pair of overalls. And more boots wouldn't hurt either, since after Omaha, you'll be doing plenty of walking, while your ma rides. Unless you want to go barefoot, which I don't advise. I'd have to pay wages to a packer, so I guess I won't be out none if I shell out something for you boys to wear."

Me and Boots hurried off and found a store and looked through the offerings. "We expect a better price seeing as how we're buying two of everything," I said to a man who scowled at us.

"You expect a better price, do you? Two!" He curled his lip. "Who are you, President Lincoln outfitting a hundred boys to go south to fight the Rebs?" He sounded a lot like Cheet.

"Yessir. I expect the second pair of boots we buy to be half price."

"Well, I'm not in the business of giving away the merchandise to cheeky children."

"I guess us cheeky children will go elsewhere then," I told him, and me and Boots headed for the door.

"Now you two hold on," the man called, but we kept going. "I said hold on."

I turned and repeated, "Half price for the second pair."

"I'll give you twenty-five percent off."

"Come on, brother, he is wasting our time."

"He's a sharper, that boy is," said a man who was leaning on the counter. "Best you give in to him or you'll lose the sale."

"Oh, all right," the shopkeeper said. "My good nature will be the ruin of me."

"Not so's you'd notice. You are still making a good profit," I told him. "And half off on the second pair of overalls. And the coats."

"You'll beggar me by the time you're through," the man said, sighing. But when I asked to see the overalls, he took them down. I held them up to me and Boots, and they seemed the right sizes. Still, I handed back my pair. "The stitching's come out on the side."

"Imagine a boy seeing to the stitching," the lounger said. "What did I tell you? He's a sharp one."

I checked out the second pair of overalls. Then me and Boots tried on heavy leather boots and wool coats. "I need yarn for knitting socks, and needles," I said. Then lest one of the men remark on my knowledge of needlework, I added, "Our ma will make them for us."

The man wrapped our purchases in brown paper and

tied the package with string. I gave him Jake's coin, and he handed me back change. I counted it, then counted it again and said he was three cents short. He counted the money himself and fished in the till for the three pennies, slapping them on the counter. As I picked up the money, I said, "How about two sticks of candy to seal the deal? We're off to the gold fields and won't see candy for a long time."

"And will cheat someone out of a gold mine, no doubt."

"We cheat no one," I said.

"You got three pennies in your hand. Spend them on the candy."

"I may need them in case we encounter Indians."

"I imagine your looks will scare them off."

The lounger gave a good long laugh and said, "How about it?"

The storekeeper grimaced, but he took two peppermint sticks from a glass case.

Jake approved of our purchases and seemed surprised when I gave him the change. "Your young 'uns are honest," he told Teresa.

She raised her chin a little and said, "I raised them that way."

※ ※ ※

Teresa wanted to spend the night in a hotel. She'd never slept on a feather bed before, only corn shucks, and she said she might never have the chance again. That morning, we'd passed a fine-looking hostelry in the business district, a big lamp with about a million glass drops hanging in the lobby over a wooden counter with a marble top. It looked as nice as anything I'd ever seen, and I thought a place like that would have not just feathers in the tick, but sheets on the beds. I said I'd always wanted to sleep between sheets, and Teresa agreed she had, too, and this was her chance. But I didn't want to spend the money, even if it was Teresa's, and I said we ought to get used to sleeping on the ground, because that's what we'd be doing till we reached Colorado Territory. So after Teresa fixed supper and we washed the pan and the tin plates, we bedded down under the wagon for the night. The ground wasn't any worse than the beds in the orphanage. We'd had a hard time of it the last few days and were tuckered, so we went right off to sleep. But not Jake. He told us he was going into town on business and would see us later. I figured he'd be making the rounds of the saloons, because there weren't likely to be any until we reached Omaha.

Along about three or four in the morning, I heard somebody stumbling around, and thinking it couldn't be Jake, because he was making too much noise for a man getting ready to roll up in a blanket, I raised up my head. But it *was* Jake, and he had a harness in his hands and was about to put it over one of the mules. I was afraid he had forgot we were under the wagon, and I sat up and said, "Hey, Jake."

"Hey yourself, young feller."

"Aren't you going to bed?"

"I figured we'd get an early start."

"Why's that?"

"I went into town and drank too much, and now it seems a waste of time to sleep for just an hour or two." He paused as he slid the harness over one of the mules—Big Blue his name was. "I got to jawing and lost track of the time. A man was telling me his wife run away from over across the river, and he'd come to fetch her. He said he'd make it warm for her. I asked him what he done to make her run off like that, and he near sliced me with his knife, so I figured I ought to cut out."

I felt Teresa beside me draw in her breath, and I knew she was listening. "Likely he's punk. There's men that don't know any better than to take a broom handle to their woman. We had a neighbor once that was so mad when his wife burnt up his dinner that he ran a fork through her arm. It swelled up, and she had to have it taken off," I told him.

"You don't say."

"You didn't bring that fellow with you, did you, Jake? We wouldn't care to travel with a man like that," I said, knowing that Teresa was holding her breath.

"I didn't fancy him myself. He was drunk as a pigeon when I left. I figure he won't wake up till the sun's high. You want to help me here? We can leave your ma and your brother to sleep till we're ready to light out."

I scrambled out of my blanket. Teresa got up, too. "You'll be wanting breakfast," she said.

"We'll go a piece, then stop after the sun gets high. We can let the mules rest then." He turned away to get the second mule, Old Samuel.

Teresa whispered to me, "Imagine that. He ran into Billy. It's a good thing he don't know I'm Billy's wife."

But he did know. It was clear as still water to me, and that was why we were leaving so early. Jake was a good man. He must have realized as soon as Billy started talking that the woman Billy was looking for was sleeping under his own wagon. And Jake had come right back and begun hitching the mules so that Teresa could get away. I liked him for that and vowed that he'd get his money's worth and more from me and Boots.

We put our blankets under the tarp that covered the goods in the wagon, and I checked the ropes to make sure they were good and tight. "You want me to feed those mules?" I asked.

"Done it already," Jake said.

Jake surely did know what he was about, because before you could turn around twice, we were on our way, him and Teresa sitting on the wagon seat and me and Boots stretched out on top of the tarp.

With the jogging of the wagon and sunrise a long way off, Boots went back to sleep, but not me. I lay on my back staring up at the sky, looking for stars. I'd missed seeing the stars at the orphanage and promised myself I'd be where I could see them every night for the rest of my life. But there weren't any stars just then. It was as dark as Egypt. Jake must have known where he was going, however, because he hurried along those mules. The night was nice, a little cold, and I was grateful to Jake for my new wool jacket.

Except for the clip-clop of the mules and the jangling of the harnesses, there wasn't a sound. I could smell the flowers in the yards we passed—lilacs, mostly. I knew, because we'd grown them on the farm. But there were others whose names I didn't know. I wondered if there were flowers in Colorado.

"What you thinking, Haidie?" Boots asked. I hadn't realized he was awake. We were out in the country, passing farms. Here and there a woman was up early, already at work in the kitchen. I could see her through the window. Smoke was coming from chimneys, and windows were lit up with candles and coal oil lamps. Off in the distance, a rooster crowed.

I put my hands under my head and looked up at the sky, where there were tiny streaks of gray. "I'm thinking maybe Pa has a big house with lots of servants to wait on him."

"Then why hasn't he sent for us?"

That was a good question, and I knew the answer might be that Pa hadn't found anything at all and was ashamed. But for Boots's sake, I put that thought out of my mind and replied, "I expect he wants everything just so."

"You think he'll have a pony for me to ride?"

"Naw," I said, teasing. Boots sighed. So I added quickly, "I expect it will be a real horse. You're too big for a pony."

"You reckon Pa knows how big I am? Maybe he thinks I'm still a baby."

"If he doesn't, he'll know when he sees you."

"I bet he won't recognize me. You think we'll recognize him?"

I'd wondered about that. What if Pa'd grown a beard and we passed him on the street with not a glance? But I couldn't tell Boots that. "Sure we will. You'd recognize me, wouldn't you."

"Well, I can't hardly tell you with your hair all cut off like that."

I shushed Boots, because I didn't want Jake to hear him.

In a minute, that ugly dog, Tige, started barking. He'd been running along beside the wagon. He was a strong dog, big, with hair as thick as a Persian carpet and jaws like a snapping turtle. Jake had introduced us proper, and I was glad, because I wouldn't want to run afoul of him.

"Hush," Jake told Tige, then turned around in the seat. "Likely he smells a cat."

I scoffed. "What's a big dog like that care about a cat?"

"I ain't talking a kitty cat. I mean a big cat, a cougar."

I shivered a little. "He'd let you know?"

"Yep, he tells me when there's big cats and bears and Quantrill's Raiders. He's the worse dog I know for smelling such."

"Well, I hope he don't smell them, because I am fearsome of them," Teresa said.

"Now, little lady, you be easy. We're not likely to run into Mr. Quantrill this side of the Missouri."

I figured Jake didn't want to scare Teresa, because no river ever stopped that murderous southern rebel. I'd heard all about him, even in the orphanage. Still, I didn't give much thought to Confederates or the war in the South as we rode along as nice as you please in the early morning light. We heard cows mooing off in a distance and roosters. Sometimes we heard a man shout, and two or three times we passed farm wagons going in the opposite direction. We never stopped for breakfast. After a while, Teresa reached into the vittles box and handed around cornbread from the night before, and we gnawed on that.

Jake waited until the sun was high overhead before he stopped the mules by a stream and said it was time to take a resting spell. Teresa offered to fry bacon and whip up batter cakes if he'd build a fire, but Jake said we'd wait until evening. We could eat leftover cornbread and cold beans and drink buttermilk that he'd bought early that morning on the way back to the wagon.

Me and Boots watered the mules, while Teresa got out the leftovers, and we'd just sat down under a nice tree when that dog Tige began to growl. Jake put a hand on the dog and looked off down the trail to Fort Madison. We were so busy hunting for Billy Stover coming up behind us that none of us saw the fellow slip out of the trees from the other direction.

Tige barked, but Jake told him to quiet down. The fellow was a boy, and he was dressed in the sorriest set of clothes I ever saw, even worse than an orphan. His shirt was ragged and his pants were held up with a rope. He was barefoot and carried a pair of homemade shoes over his shoulder. He seemed as surprised to see us as we were to see him.

"Hello there," Jake said, his hand on Tige. "We're about to have us some buttermilk and cornbread. You look like you could use a bite."

He stared at the cornbread and licked his lips. "I wouldn't say no."

"You from around here?" Jake asked.

"Around."

Jake studied the boy for a minute, then grinned. "I expect you're off to join the Union, running away, if I'm not mistaken."

The boy glanced at Jake, a guilty look on his face. "I'm going for a soldier, all right. You won't tell nobody, will you? Pa would whip me and fetch me back home."

"Not if you're for the Union. I might tell on you if you was to go for a Reb. I'm a Union man myself, got wounded in the leg at Shiloh and am no more use as a fighting man than a one-legged chicken. Jake Crowfoot's the name."

"Minder Evans, but don't say you met me."

"I'll make you a deal. We won't tell nobody we seen you, if you won't tell nobody you seen us. Anybody ask if you passed a woman or a couple of kids with a mule team, you say no, sir. And if anybody asks if I seen a boy with shoulders like an ox, I'll say I didn't."

"Deal," Minder Evans said.

There was a commotion near the road, and Jake glanced back over his shoulder east, while the boy looked west, but it was only a deer in the trees. After a time, the boy shouldered his pack and put a chunk of cornbread inside his shirt. Jake wished him a good day, and we watched him head off down the trail.

"I didn't know you were a soldier," Teresa told Jake.

"Mrs. Richards, there's aplenty you don't know about me, none of it of interest to a lady such as yourself. I have been around a good bit and seen a mess of sights, but the worst thing I ever saw was a battlefield with a bunch of poor boys lying dead with their heads blowed off and their guts spilling out. They was boys that had joined up as a lark and had no idea what war was. I hope I may never see such again." He looked off into the distance, but what he was seeing was inside his head. "I'd be glad if you didn't ask me about it again."

Me and Teresa did not say anything, but Boots asked, "Can I see your leg?"

"You can see both of them." He rolled up the pants on his left side, and we didn't see anything but a gnarly leg. Then he rolled up his right pants leg, and we saw a scar that went from his knee down inside his boot. The leg was half the normal width, and the knee was turned the wrong way.

I felt bad for Jake. His leg hadn't been any of our business, but he didn't seem to mind showing it. He stood, and I noticed then that he favored his right leg. I guess he had all along, but I'd never paid it any mind.

"Them mules has rested enough. If we let them stay here any longer, they'll turn lazy and refuse to pull the wagon. It's best we get going pretty soon, in fact sooner than that." He glanced back east toward the road, and I realized then that he'd picked a hidden place for our nooning.

We passed eastbound travelers, and a few men on horseback went by us, but not many. Those mules kept up a good pace. It was a lazy day for a trip. Me and Boots just lay out on that tarp as comfortable as you please. The sun shone down on us, but every time we got to thinking it was too hot, along came a breeze. We heard bird songs, and after a time, Teresa started singing. She'd never sung at the orphanage, and her voice was as sweet as honey. Jake must have thought so, too, because after a time, he joined in, and the two of them sounded better than any choir I ever heard, her singing high and him low. Teresa started out with church hymns, but Jake liked patriotic songs. He sang "Tenting on the Old Camp Ground" and "Tramp, Tramp, Tramp" and "Lorena."

Me and Boots weren't much as singers, but we were loud, and we sang, too, my favorite being "Oh! Susanna." We kept on until Jake said it was time to find a stopping place. He turned off the main road and picked a spot that was surrounded by trees, and if you were passing by, you wouldn't even see it. I figured if Billy was following behind, he'd never look for us there.

* * *

Of course, I was wrong.

Me and Jake took the mules to the stream to water them, while Teresa got out the fixings for supper. We'd skipped breakfast and hadn't had much for dinner, so we were all hungry enough to eat buzzard bait. But Teresa fixed us better. She made a batch of cornbread in a Dutch oven and fried up pork, then cooked a mess of greens we'd found along the creek and added vinegar to them. With the buttermilk Jake had bought that morning, we had a fine dinner.

While Teresa cleaned up—since I'd turned into a boy, I didn't have to help with the cooking—me and Jake and Boots just lay in the tall grass, looking up at the sky, watching the day go down. Jake took out his pipe and lighted it with a stick from the campfire and leaned back against a rock, smoking. We were so content that we didn't pay much attention to the noise in the bushes. Even that ugly dog Tige was dozing.

Then came a voice out of the dark. "Don't nobody move. I got a gun. You got no more chance than a worm in a chicken house."

Boots slid over close to me, while Jake sat up straight, not scared but not about to rush into something stupid either.

"Billy!" Teresa cried. She sank down onto the ground and squinched up as if she could make herself smaller. I felt awful for her and reached out my hand, but she was too far away to touch.

"That's right. I come to fetch you, Teresa."

Jake still didn't move. I knew he had a gun, but it was

in the wagon, which did us no good. "Now hold on there, young fellow," he said, quiet as if he was talking to me or Boots.

"Hold on yourself, old man. You taken my wife. I ought to kill you for that. Maybe I will."

"I done no such thing. This lady's going west to meet up with her husband."

"She's got a husband, and he's right here."

"Billy—" Teresa said.

"You shut your mouth. You're not worth a milk bucket under a bull, but you're mine, and I won't take none of your smartness. I showed you before how you ought to shut up, but it didn't stick."

"She isn't your wife," I said.

"You be still yourself, you. You open your mouth, I'll take you back to the orphan home." He glanced over at Jake. "She's a runaway. Her brother, too."

"She? I thought that one was a boy." Jake didn't sound all that surprised.

"And a smart one, too. You best watch out for her. She's liable to steal you blind. Took my money and my food and my wife."

"She's not your wife," I spoke up again.

"I told you hush."

Teresa clasped her hands together and rolled over onto her knees, like she was praying. Jake didn't seem all that upset, but then, nobody had threatened to take *him* back to Smoak. He knocked his pipe against a rock and put it into his pocket. Then he got up, slowly so as not to rile Billy. Standing there, his back against the fading light, standing easy, he looked twice as big as Billy, who was a good-sized chap himself but seemed to shrink next to Jake. Billy held out his gun and said, "Don't you dare to move, mister."

"Wasn't thinking of it. Now, Billy, is it?"

"Mr. Stover to you."

Boots giggled, and I clapped my hand over his mouth.

"Mr. Stover," Jake repeated. "It seems like you want to take your wife home, but she don't want to go. Why is that?"

"It ain't none of your affair. She's an ornery woman, and best she learns who's boss." He added in case Jake didn't understand, "That's me."

Jake nodded, as if he was considering Billy's words. He scratched his shin with the toe of his other foot. "By golly, I don't know any more about it than a rabbit, but it appears to me you ought'n to make a lady go where she don't want to."

"It's my right," he said.

Jake glanced at Teresa. "How come you don't want to go back?"

Teresa looked from Jake to Billy, then back to Jake again and said in a low voice, "He was so mean I didn't know what to do. He threw a pan of dishwater over my head once, and I expected to get hit 'bout all the time I lived with him," Teresa said. "He riles the animals, too. He kicked the cat against the door and put out her eye. And he whips the horses when he gets mad."

"I can't abide either one, hitting women nor animals." Jake took a step forward, but Billy raised the gun and made a motion for Jake to back up. Jake didn't, but he stopped.

"Teresa's my wife," Billy said stubbornly.

"She's not," I said.

Billy swung the gun around to me, but Jake stepped in front of me and raised a hand to tell Billy to be still. "Why do you say that, son?" he asked me.

I glanced down at Teresa, who looked like she hoped a big hole would open up and she could fall in. I guessed things between her and Billy had been even worse than I'd thought. "She's not married—"

"We was married by a priest. Haidie's own brother. She knows that," Billy interrupted.

"Is that right?" Jake asked.

"Sort of. They were married by our brother, Boots's and mine. Billy's got that part right. But Cheet isn't any kind of priest. Shoot, the only time he'd ever go into a Catholic church would be to rob the poor box. Cheet isn't any religion, and he sure isn't a priest. He just made that up so the orphan home would take me and Boots, on account of our mother died and our Pa was out West."

"Aw, don't listen to her. It ain't true," Billy said. He sounded confused.

"Yes, it is," Boots butted in. "Cheet's no more a priest than your horse."

"He married us in Latin."

"French, and you don't want to know what he said. You've been living in sin," I said, not that Billy would care.

"Teresa wouldn't have done that," he said.

"Oh, she didn't know either. I figured neither one of you would ever find out, so what difference did it make? As long as you thought you were married good and proper, Teresa wouldn't have to be a nun and she'd help us run off from the orphan home. Of course, we wouldn't have done it if we'd known you'd turn out to be a bully."

"I ain't a bully. I'm just treating her like a wife. All's she is is a woman." He paused and thought a moment. "Is that true, Teresa? What she says, is it true?"

Teresa nodded, but in the dark, Billy couldn't see her, so she whispered, "It is."

Billy seemed more confused than ever and looked down at his gun hand, while Jake inched forward. Billy caught him and motioned him back, and Jake took a step or two to the side. "I guess it don't matter none. We already lived together as man and wife. We can get married by a real priest. Shoot, Teresa, we got a kid."

"A kid that my sister's raising. You didn't want him. You never once went to see him when I was in the orphanage. Heck, Billy, you don't even know his name."

Billy frowned and seemed to consider that. Then he said, "You *say* he's mine. He could have been Hugh's."

"Billy, you know he ain't!"

"You drop your clothes like a molting hen."

"I never!"

"Fact is, I wondered at the time if Hugh—"

Teresa clenched her fists and sprang at Billy.

I guess Jake had waited for that moment, and he yelled, "Tige, attack!" Now you might wonder what that ugly dog Tige was doing all this time. He was sitting by the fire, snoozing. But with that command Tige lunged at Billy, sinking his teeth into Billy's jacket. Billy dropped the gun, and Jake picked it up. When Jake saw Tige wasn't doing any real damage but was only shaking Billy up a little, he let the dog have his fun. But after a time, he called him off. Billy lay there cursing and crying, saying his arm was bit through to the bone, although his jacket wasn't even tore. At last, Jake got tired of the whining and said, "By golly, boy, you best stop your sniveling before I let that dog have a bite out of you."

"You wouldn't do that," Billy said, sounding like he wasn't so sure.

"You were ready to shoot me. Mrs. Richards. Or these two boys."

"The gun ain't even loaded. Hell, Teresa took all my money. She didn't leave enough to buy bullets."

Jake checked the gun. "Well, don't that beat all!" He turned to Teresa, who was looking from Billy to Jake. "How come you got mixed up with such a useless fellow, ma'am?"

Teresa looked down at the ground and shrugged. "He bragged on me, and that turned me foolish. I wish I'd knowed better."

"I guess we got ourselves a dilemma," Jake said. Then he looked down at Billy lying on the ground. "You had anything to eat?"

"No." Billy was pulling at his coat sleeve in the firelight, looking to see if there was any damage.

"Would you be willing to fix him a plate of food, Mrs. Richards? I believe we can afford to be generous, seeing as how he isn't holding a gun on us anymore."

Billy jerked up his head at the name "Mrs. Richards," but he didn't say anything. Teresa dished up cornbread and left-over pork that she'd planned to serve for breakfast and held it out at arm's length to Billy, as if she was afraid he'd snatch her hand. He didn't. He was too hungry and grabbed the tin plate, using his hands to shove the food into his mouth. Me and Boots built up the fire, because we didn't want Billy slipping off in the dark. When Billy was finished eating, he leaned back against a rock. He didn't look so dangerous then, more like the laundry delivery boy he used to be.

"How come you was to find us?" Teresa asked.

"Somebody at the livery seen a man with a woman and two kids taken out early in the morning. I passed a fellow on the trail that was carrying his shoes in his hands and asked him if he seen you, but he said he'd come a long way and there was nobody like that behind him. Might be better if I'd turned back then."

Jake nodded. "Like I said, we got a dilemma."

Teresa looked at me to see what the word meant, and I told her, "A problem."

"We got that, all right," she said.

We all turned to Jake and waited for him to lay it out. "You come here with your gun and tried to captivate Mrs. Richards. She don't want to go, and being as how you ain't married, she's got that right."

I wondered if Jake would have sent Teresa with Billy if she *had* been married.

Billy stared sullenly at Teresa. "Don't make no difference."

"Does to her, and being as how I took on the responsibility to get her to Colorado Territory, I got to stand by her. If we leave you here, how do we know you won't be following behind all the way to St. Joe, causing trouble?"

"I thought we were going—" Boots started to say, but I

clamped my hand over his mouth. That Jake was smart as a skinned cat.

Billy smirked and stared at the ground. "I found you one time. I guess I could find you another."

"So maybe it's best we just shoot you and be done with it."

Billy glanced up quickly, but Jake wasn't smiling. "You wouldn't do that."

"You'd have shot us."

"I told you I didn't have no bullets."

"We didn't know that."

Billy considered that, not sure but what it made sense. "She took my money. If she'll give me my money back, I'll go on peaceable. She wasn't much of a woman anyway."

Teresa ignored the insult and said, "I don't have your money."

"Well, you took it."

"I spent it. I bought a bonnet and a pair of shoes. The money's gone."

I knew that bonnet had been a mistake.

We all sat there a minute, trying to come up with a solution. Then Jake reached into his pocket, but I knew what he was about to do, and I didn't want him paying off Billy Stover. Billy was our problem. Besides, I didn't want to be beholden to anybody. So I spoke up. "I got a ten-dollar gold piece. You can have it if you promise to God you'll go off and never come back looking for Teresa."

Billy's head jerked up, and I could see his eyes gleam. "Where'd you ever get money like that?"

"From my brother Cheet. He gave it to me after he sold

the farm." Cheet hadn't done any such thing. The ten-dollar piece was one of the coins I'd stolen from him the day he put us in the orphanage. "If you take it, you got to promise to God you won't come after us and if you go back on your word, terrible things will happen to you."

"What terrible things?"

"Pestilence."

"What?"

I didn't know what "pestilence" meant either, but it sounded bad. "You'll break out in boils. You'll grow hair on your hands, and then you'll go blind. You'll end your days in the insane asylum." The nuns had threatened the boys with those very words, although it hadn't been for breaking any promise to God. It was for practicing what the sisters called the "solitary vice," which is something the Irish do more than anybody else, they'd said. I thought that threat would scare Billy more than if I told him he was going to hell. Most folks figured they were going to hell anyway. "Isn't that true, Teresa?"

She nodded solemnly, although I thought I saw her mouth curl up a little at the ends.

We all stared at Billy, and he muttered, "Ah, hell."

I held up the ten-dollar piece and let the firelight shine on it. Billy's eyes gleamed, and he reached out his hand, but I closed my fist around the coin and put it against my chest. "You got to promise, first."

"Okay, I promise," Billy said.

"Promise what?"

"I promise I won't follow you no more."

"You got to say more than that. 'I promise to God I will

go back to Smoak and never come looking for Teresa or Boots or Haidie again. I'll never tell anybody where they are, and if I see them, I'll pretend I don't know them.'"

"That's an awful lot to promise," Billy said.

I shrugged and put the ten-dollar coin back in my pocket. Billy started to get to his feet. Jake put his hand on Tige's head, and the dog began to growl. Billy sat back down, saying, "That sure is one ugly dog."

"What?" Jake sounded offended. "He's as pretty a dog as I ever seen, ain't he?" I thought he winked at me, but it was too dark to be sure.

"He surely is," I told him and Boots nodded.

"Yes, sir," Billy mumbled.

The fire had died down, and Boots went for more wood, piling it onto the embers, which blazed up.

"What are you going to do, Billy?" Teresa asked.

"I guess I'll say that promise, but I can't recollect it," he told her.

I didn't remember it, either, so I made up new words, and Billy repeated them. Then I made him cross his heart. I gave him the coin, and Billy bit it to make sure it was real. Then he said as how he was tired and hungover, he figured he'd go to sleep. I didn't want him sleeping with us and started to say something, but Jake shook his head. "Best we let him stay with us so he don't go sneaking up on us in the night. You ought to know, Mr. Stover, that I'm a light sleeper, and I wake up every time somebody turns over. So you best not try anything. If I don't hear you, Tige here will, and you don't want to rile this pretty dog."

Billy was still sleeping when we got up the next morning.

Teresa woke him and gave him a plate of the breakfast that she fixed for us. We ate together, then me and Boots went with Jake for the mules, leaving Tige with Teresa. She and Billy must have talked things over, because when we returned, he was saddling his horse and seemed to accept that he was going back to Smoak by himself.

"You lost yourself a good man," Billy told Teresa as he swung up into the saddle.

Not so's you'd notice, I thought, but Teresa, being nicer than I am, replied, "I guess I did at that."

"I won't never see you again."

"No, it's not likely."

He started off, then stopped and turned around. "What did you name that kid, anyway?"

"I named him William, for his pa."

Chapter Three

We never did see Billy Stover again. For the next few days, Teresa looked over her shoulder every five minutes. But Jake never bothered to see if Billy was following us. I guess he knew Billy was gone for good. Most likely, Billy went back to Smoak and bragged that he'd sold his wife for a ten-dollar gold piece, the most money he'd ever had in his life. Or maybe he drank up the money in Fort Madison. He could have bought some bullets and returned, hoping to shoot us down, but if so, we'd gone too far for him to ever find us. Maybe, believing we'd gone to St. Joseph instead of Omaha, he'd headed there. Or it might be he was too afraid of that ugly dog Tige to come back at all. Whatever it was, he was out of our lives, and after a time, Teresa seemed to accept that.

"I don't miss Billy," she told me.

"I can see that," I said, looking from her to Jake. She seemed to have become right smitten with him. "What about your baby? What about William? Don't you miss him?"

"I never knew my baby, which was took away as soon as it was born. When I went to collect it at my sister's, the baby

didn't even know me. In fact, it cried for my sister when I tried
to pick it up. I love it, but it's not mine anymore, so it's best
I go far away." She paused. "And the name ain't William. It's
Sarah. Billy never asked me whether it was a boy or a girl,
and he never even went to see it. Now if he goes to my sister's
to make trouble, he'll be asking for a boy. Don't that beat
all!" She appeared proud of herself at the deception, and I
had to admit that was as big a whopper as my telling her that
Cheet was a priest. "But he won't go looking," Teresa continued. "What's a man like him want with a baby anyway?
He didn't care about her when I was in the orphan home, so
why would he care now?" She stopped walking and looked
away off into the trees, maybe a little embarrassed. "I can't
say I'm sorry I was incorrigible, because Sarah's a peach, and
my sister loves her like she was her own. So how can it be
wickedness like the nuns say when you get a precious little
baby like that?"

We'd stopped to noon beside a stream, and Teresa and I
had walked down it a ways. Now we sat on a rock and put our
feet into the water. Although I had my orphan boots and the
ones that Jake had bought me, I wanted to save them for the
walk from Omaha to Colorado Territory, so I went barefoot
most of the time. Besides, it was hot, and the boots made my
feet sweat, and that caused blisters. I'd been knitting stockings for Boots and Teresa and even Jake. But I hadn't gotten
around to making any for me.

"You miss Smoak?" I asked.

"Not one bit. I feel free and easy in Iowa. How about
yourself?"

I nodded in agreement.

"You ever been on your own before?"

"Only at the orphan home, and we weren't exactly on our own."

"We were not!" She splashed her feet in the water, kicking up a spray that landed on us. The cold water felt good. She turned away from me and stared out into the trees, where the sun caused a golden glow on the leaves. "I've been thinking I might just stay in Iowa and not go on to Colorado Territory at all."

"Omaha's in Nebraska, not Iowa." I turned to look at her. "And what would you do there?"

She shrugged. "I could find something. I'm a worker."

"In a laundry?"

"I'd do anything before I'd take in washing. Anything."

"Anything?" I hadn't known much about Red Feather Road in Smoak where women in their underwear hung out of the windows, calling to men, or even went out into the street and grabbed their hats so the gents had to go inside to fetch them back. But at the orphanage the nuns threatened us, telling us if we didn't say our prayers and mind our betters, we would end up in a Red Feather house. So I got a pretty good idea of what was going on there.

Teresa gave me a sharp look. "Well, not what you're thinking. I might be incorrigible, but I'm not a hoor."

I was teasing, I told her, although I wasn't so sure about that. Wearing fancy dresses and drinking wine in exchange for crawling into bed with some man seemed an easier way of earning your living than rubbing dirty clothes on a scrubboard. "What were you thinking of doing then?"

Teresa turned away, but not before I saw that her cheeks

were pink. "I wouldn't know. Jake said he thought I could do most anything. Honest labor, he calls it."

That set me to remembering the last few days. Now that I thought on it, I realized that Teresa sat awful close to Jake on the wagon bench. She gave him his plate first and was always ready to jump up from her own supper and pour him more coffee. And I'd seen her fix herself up. Now why would a woman in the middle of a wilderness smooth her dress and touch her hair and bite her lips to make them red, a million times a day, if not for a man? And why did Jake stare at Teresa when she sat by the campfire of an evening and ran the brush through her hair, lifting her chin so that her long black waves rippled down her back just like a waterfall? And then I remembered waking in the night and going for the water bucket, stepping on Teresa's blanket and finding it empty. I thought she'd gone to find a private place, but maybe not. It was none of my business, of course, but that didn't stop me from asking, "Have you had connection with him?"

"Why, Haidie!" she said, giving me a look that said she was greatly offended. Still, she didn't deny it.

"Well?" I asked.

"I am a lady."

"Oh, don't put on airs with me, Teresa. I know you lived as man and wife with Billy Stover and you weren't married at all."

"And whose fault was that?"

She'd gotten me there. But then I remembered that being incorrigible was the reason she'd been sent to the orphanage. I didn't remark on it, however. I just said, "I like him—Jake, that is."

"He's the best man."

"He is that. If it wasn't for Jake, me and Boots would be orphans again, and you'd be back with Billy Stover. We got boots and coats out of it, too. You could do worse than Jake Crowfoot."

"You think he's already got a wife?"

I took my feet out of the water and studied the underside of my big toe. I'd stepped on a thorn the day before, and the pricked place still smarted. There was a scab the size of a needle point where I'd pulled out the sticker. "I couldn't say."

Teresa thought it over. "I think he'd have told me."

"Would it matter?"

Teresa wiped her feet on the grass and stood up, straightening her skirt. "I don't know, Haidie. I've been stupid all my life. There's the baby and living with Billy and other things you don't know, so taking up with a married man wouldn't be the worst thing I've ever done. I guess I could stand it if he was, but I'd rather he wasn't."

"Maybe you could find someone better in Colorado."

"Maybe. But if Billy Stover's any example, I'm not so good at picking men. And to tell you the truth, I don't know if I even want to go all the way to Colorado. Jake says it's all prairie with not a tree in sight, until you reach the mountains, then it's Katy-bar-the-door, mountains so big it would take you a year to walk over them."

"Sounds like Jake's the one who doesn't want you to go to Colorado."

Teresa didn't respond. She put on her shoes and buttoned them up and told me we'd been sitting too long, that Jake would be anxious to get on the road.

✳ ✳ ✳

We were booming along. Those mules could cover twenty-five or forty miles a day, so it wouldn't take us even two weeks to get across Iowa. When I said my prayers at night, I thanked the Lord for bringing us to Jake Crowfoot. We surely were proud to meet him.

Like Teresa said, he was the best man, but he wasn't anybody's fool. He might have been soft on Teresa, but he kept me and Boots hopping. It seemed like he'd forgotten I was a girl. Sometimes we had a pretty good time and sometimes tough. Jake said he was training us up to join a wagon train to Colorado Territory and that we'd be glad later on that we knew about mules and packing freight and sleeping on the ground. And maybe he was right. He expected us to help him harness those mules every morning, and a mule is as rotten an animal as ever lived. They are sneaky, too, especially a mule like Big Blue. The minute I thought I had him ready to go, he'd slip out of his harness. He bit me on the shoulder once, and I thought Jake would take over for me, but he just said that if I couldn't think quicker than a mule, I wasn't much good. He made me start all over with Big Blue. But I didn't mind. Like Jake said, if we wanted to join a wagon train, we had to know how to work.

We'd been gone from Fort Madison for days and were not so far from Omaha, and sitting at supper one evening, when a voice in the trees called out, "Hello, the camp."

"Billy," Teresa whispered, and she slipped over next to Jake.

Jake got up slow and went to the wagon, where his gun was kept. "Show yourself," he called.

At that, a man stepped out into the firelight and came to within a few feet of where me and Boots and Teresa were sitting. It wasn't dark yet, and I had just built up the fire, so I had a good look at him. He was a clean-shaven man, with a black mustache that drooped down around his mouth at either end. He was dressed in a white shirt with a ruffled front that made him look like a pigeon, a breast pin whose diamond "headlight" sparkled in the fire, and a scarlet neckerchief that shone like silk. He had on a frock coat and Confederate Army pants tucked into patent leather boots, which were a little worse for wear. The man was a dandy, by the looks of him. When he saw Teresa, he took off his tall hat (beaver, it was) and held it in front of his chest while he bowed almost to the ground. "Madam, a pleasure," he said.

"Who would you be?" Jake asked.

Still holding the hat, the man turned to Jake and announced, "I am Cornelius Vander." He pounded the ground for emphasis with a gold-knobbed ebony walking stick.

Jake studied on him. "Not Cornelius Vanderbilt?"

The man laughed, as if Jake had said the funniest thing in the world, although me and Boots and Teresa didn't get it. "I see you are a man of the world. That would be my illustrious cousin. It is my misfortune that the family split many years ago, and I was bequeathed only a truncated name."

"What's 'truncated' mean?" Boots whispered.

"Swedish," I told him, not knowing myself.

"I see," Jake said, his hand still on the side of the wagon.

"And with the less illustrious fortune, as well. In fact, sir, I am without a farthing. I am flat broke. You bet."

Jake didn't comment on that. Instead, he asked, "What are you doing all the way out here in that fancy getup?"

"A misunderstanding."

Jake must have decided the man was harmless then, because he left the gun in the wagon and walked over to the campfire and studied Mr. Vander. Then he snorted. "A misunderstanding over cards or was it some other flimflam?"

"Sir, you have no right—"

"Answer," Jake said harshly.

"I was accused unfairly of cheating at cards. My opponents were not gentlemen but rather scoundrels. Such profane language they spoke. I had to open the window to let out the cursing. They were the roughest cut of men I have ever come across, not at all like the high-class type of traveler one encounters on a steamboat."

"Our brother's a riverboat gambler." Boots spoke up before I could stop him.

"Indeed. And may I inquire of his name?"

"Cheet. Cheet Richards."

"Ah, yes." Mr. Vander put his hat back onto his head and clapped his hands. "A delightful young man. I have encountered him in my travels, as honest a man at cards as you could wish, a worthy opponent. I myself have lost sums to his superior knowledge of the pasteboards. He would go further if not for the unfortunate first name."

Me and Boots exchanged glances. "You reckon there's two Cheet Richardses?" Boots whispered.

I knew better. "You're a liar," I said, which was like the

kettle calling the pot black, although Mr. Vander wouldn't have known that. "Cheet's not honest, and he's not worthy. You never met up with him."

Mr. Vander rose up as tall as he could, which wasn't much taller than Teresa, and puffed out his chest. "Men are dead who have called me that," he thundered. "You are fortunate you are but a boy, young sir, or I would make you rue your words. No one calls Cornelius Vander a liar."

"You're a liar and a gold-leaf braggart. Now you leave be," Jake warned. His voice was low but hard.

All the air went out of Mr. Vander, like a pig bladder that's been cut. "And would you have the boy apologize?"

Jake looked at me, but I shook my head. "I would bet a million dollars he never met Cheet in his life," I said.

Jake cocked his head as he studied Mr. Vander. "I'd like a piece of your bet."

"I was merely being polite," Mr. Vander said. "I meant no harm to your son."

Jake didn't correct him. He blew out his breath, then said to Teresa, "I expect we got a little supper left." He turned to our guest. "You eat, have you?"

"Not in some time." He glanced beyond the fire to where Teresa had stowed the leavings of our meal. "I wouldn't want to rob you."

"You won't," Jake told him. The man started around the fire, but Jake held up his hand. "I'd as leave have your gun."

Mr. Vander looked as if he might protest, but as he turned to Jake, he spied Tige. He reached into his coat pocket and took out a revolver and handed it to Jake. "I hope I will not be sorry I trusted you," he said.

"The other'n, too." Jake held out his hand.

"Sir?"

"The other gun. I never knew a gambler but what he had two guns."

Mr. Vander sighed and took off his boot, removing a one-shot pistol from an ankle holster.

"You won't mind if I check for a third?" Jake asked.

"Sir, I would as lief dress in a suit of armor as carry three guns." But he let Jake search him. Jake didn't find any more guns, but he did remove a knife, a wicked-looking thing, sharp as a cuss word.

"You would leave me naked?" Mr. Vander asked.

"Better that than you murdering us in our sleep." Jake motioned Mr. Vander across the fire, where Teresa handed him a plate. Then while our guest wolfed down Teresa's cooking, Jake made a circle around our campfire, going farther and farther back each time.

Mr. Vander didn't take notice of Jake until the man had finished his supper. By then, Jake had almost reached the trees. Our guest sighed and said, "Over there under the oak."

Jake picked up a pair of saddlebags and brought them to the campfire, opened them and dumped the contents on the ground. Besides an extra shirt and pair of drawers, there were two decks of cards; a container holding dice; a tiny metal clamp that I recognized as a holdout, an implement used for cheating at cards; a razor strop and a razor; and three sets of business cards. Jake handed them to me, and I read them out loud: "Cornelius Vander, Esq., Solicitor," "Rodney Cornelius, Insurance," and "Sir C. Vanderbilt, By Order of Her Majesty the Queen."

"An honest man," Jake scoffed.

"I prefer to think of it as enterprising."

"It's that all right." Jake went through the gatherings again. "I don't see no money."

"Alas, as I told you, I am broke. My small purse was taken by the very band of scoundrels I spoke of earlier." Mr. Vander wiped his plate with the last of his cornbread and started to put it into his mouth when he glanced at Tige. Changing his mind, he held out the gravy-soaked cornbread. I would as lief a dozen wolves ate from my hand as Tige, but Mr. Vander wasn't afraid. Tige got up and sniffed the hand, then gulped the cornbread and wagged his tail.

Jake looked dumbfounded. "Tige generally don't go to nobody but me," he said.

"He is a noble animal, a creature fit to be the boon companion of a king," Mr. Vander said. "He must be descended from a line of champions. Never have I seen such a superb animal. 'Dog' is too common a name for him."

"I never saw Tige take to anybody like that," Jake repeated and studied on Mr. Vander for a long time. "What happened to your horse?"

"He abandoned me, I am ashamed to say, and me a lover of all animals. I had unsaddled him and was watering him when the ingrate bucked, and away he went. I was left with only the saddle and the bags you have in your hand. The saddle must needs be left behind, but I have trudged along with the bags. They contain all I have in this world. The brute left me no choice but to travel by shank's mare."

"You got somebody following you? Answer true, now."

"A band of ruffians, but I believe they followed the horse,

so for that reason I am thankful for the animal's perfidy. I swear to you, sir, I did not take their money. I am an honest man."

Jake gave him a look telling Mr. Vander he doubted that, but he didn't comment on it.

"I would be grateful if you would let me accompany you wherever you're going."

"You'll let him ride with us?" Teresa asked.

"Don't be alarmed, Mrs. Richards. Tige takes to him. Tige's the best judge of character I ever met," Jake told her.

"But he's a flimflam man," I protested.

"Like your brother?"

He had me there.

"At least he didn't abandon a couple of kids in an orphanage," Jake said.

"You don't know what he did," Teresa said.

"No, but I have a feeling."

We were all quiet, thinking. Then Boots spoke up. "I reckon it's Jake's wagon."

"I won't take him if he makes you uneasy. But I believe we can't leave a man alone out here, him with no horse, no food, nothing. It seems not right."

"I hadn't thought about that," Teresa said. "Besides, you took us in and didn't know nothing about us."

"And I was right about you."

Mr. Vander stood off a little as we talked about him as if he wasn't there. I half expected him to tell us we should be honored with his company, but he'd lost his bluster.

Jake studied on him a moment, then looked at Teresa. "I expect you can join us, Mr. Vander, but you'll have to sit on top of the freight with the boys." I was glad he didn't see any need to let the man know I was a girl. "And if I find you so much as looking at our belongings, I leave you off right where we are, no matter if we're in the middle of an Indian camp. That's the way of it."

"Splendid, sir."

"And we'll expect you to do your share of work. Ain't nobody going to wait on you."

"I would not have it otherwise."

Jake went over to the man and held out his hand. "Jake Crowfoot's the name. And this here is Mrs. Richards and Haidie and Boots. Call me Jake."

"And you must call me Corny, as my friends do."

Jake gave a wry smile at the word "friends." Then he told Corny to help me water all the mules.

"I'll take Old Samuel. You take Big Blue," I told him.

✳ ✳ ✳

Corny wasn't a bad sort. He was cheerful, and he knew more about mules than I did or ever wanted to. Whenever he worked, he wore gloves. He wouldn't do anything that might hurt his hands. "In my profession, one needs to keep the hands soft and pliable. A mere hangnail could affect the turn of a card," he explained. Then he added, "For want of a nail the horse was lost."

"Huh?" I said.

"I doubt the Republic is based on the turn of a card," Jake told him. For a freighter, Jake was more learned than I'd thought, although I still didn't understand what Corny was getting at.

"He keeps his hands soft so's he can feel where he shaved the cards," Jake explained. I got it, but Boots didn't, so Jake added, "He's sanded down the edge of the high cards. You can't see it with your eye, but a good cardsharp can feel it."

"What if the fellow he's playing with can feel it, too?" Boots asked. "Ain't he in a pickle then?"

Jake's eyes twinkled. "I expect that's why Corny there run off without his horse. He must have had a pretty warm time back wherever he came from."

Corny raised his chin a little to show his displeasure at Jake's words, but he didn't deny anything. That Jake was pretty good at sizing up men—women, too, I thought, looking over at Teresa.

Although we knew Corny was a flimflam man, we were glad to have him with us. He picked green weeds along the way—herbs, he called them—and added them to whatever Teresa was cooking. They flavored the food better than salt and didn't make me as thirsty either. His singing wasn't much, but he played a good mouth harp and kept up with us on our songs. At night, after supper, he told us stories about the famous people he'd met and the games he'd won and lost. Of course, when he won, it was because of his skill, and when he lost, it was because scoundrels and blackguards had cheated him.

Some of his stories were whoppers. He claimed he won his stovepipe hat from Abraham Lincoln, and he told us his knife came from Jim Bowie hisself. He said he'd been a Bowery Boy and fought Dead Rabbits in a riot.

"Who'd fight a dead rabbit?" I scoffed.

"They were despicable young men, called Dead Rabbits because one of our noble band threw a deceased hare into their midst. I was on the side of honor. We celebrated many a victory with prodigious amounts of rum." He turned to Jake. "You would not have a bottle of that nectar of the gods, would you, sir?" he inquired of Jake.

"I would not."

"That is just as well, for I could consume the bottle as fast as you could a cup of Mrs. Richards's excellent coffee." He looked a little sad and was silent for a moment.

"You been in the army, have you?" Jake asked. It was sort of a trick question. I figured if Corny was a Confederate, he was doomed. Jake would throw him out of our camp faster than you could say, "Damn Reb."

"I was not. I tried to join numerous times, but I was rejected because of a congenital defect, that is, a bad leg." He held out both legs, and I could see that the left one was shorter than the right. I'd seen him limp, but I thought that was because he'd been walking.

"And was it the Union side you tried to join? I've heard the Rebs are not so particular."

"It was indeed. I am proud to say I am a Union man through and through and will leave at once if you do not share the sentiments."

"I am myself, but I was wondering where you got the Secesh pants."

Corny looked down and smiled. "Why, I won them in a card game, of course. There is more than one way to fleece the South."

"Where do you hail from, Corny?" I asked.

Jake looked startled at that and told me later it was a western custom never to ask a man where he'd come from.

But Corny did not seem to mind. "From Kentucky, young sir. I was raised with Abraham Lincoln and accompanied him to Illinois, where we rode the circuit together."

"Is that so?" Jake asked.

"Indeed it is."

"Then how is it you was a Bowery Boy at the same time?"

"With great dexterity, sir."

Jake laughed at that. We all knew that Corny was full of hot air, but his stories livened up the evenings.

What I liked best about Corny was that he taught us new ways to gamble. He started with the nutshell game. He took three walnut shells from his saddlebags and asked if I thought my eyes were pretty good. I said I did.

"And what would you wager on it?"

Jake put his hand on Mr. Vander's arm and squeezed. "We'll have no gambling here, Corny. I won't have you cheat the boy."

"Sir!" Corny said, looking wounded. "I am an honest man. Would you object to betting horse nails?"

Jake allowed as that was all right and went to the wagon, coming back with a handful of nails. "Winner gives them back to me," he said.

Corny took out a smooth board that we carried in the wagon and set it on the ground. Then he placed the walnut shells cut-side down on the board. He removed a tiny marble from his vest pocket and set it on the board. "The trick is to see if the hand is quicker than the eye," he told me. He moved the shells around, going as fast as lightning, sliding the marble under one shell and then another. When he had finished, he looked satisfied and said, "Now, lad, I will bet you a nail you cannot tell me which shell hides the marble."

Jake winked at me to tell me the game was a trick, but I only frowned and studied the shells. I touched one shell with my finger, then changed my mind and pointed at another.

"That one?" Corny asked. "Will you bet two horse nails on it?"

"Five," I said. Instead of turning over the shell, I grabbed Corny's hand and turned it over. The marble fell onto the ground.

"Why, boy!" Corny cried.

"Got you!" Jake said. "A cheater loses all his nails. Give over."

"It is only a trick, to test the boy's eyes."

"I already know the shell game," I said. "Cheet taught it to me. I will not get shaved by you."

Corny had to laugh. "That's a ripper. You would make an excellent capper."

"That's an accomplice," Jake explained. "When things get dull, he steps up, puts down his money, and then he finds the marble under a shell and wins the bet. He goes off shouting about how he whipped the shell game, and that causes things to liven up."

"You and I could make a team. Here, have a dollar cigar, which I purchased for the munificent sum of five cents, while you think it over," Corny said.

Jake intercepted the cigar and announced, "Haidie don't smoke, but I do."

Corny took out a second cigar for himself and a tiny gold cigar cutter, which he handed to Jake. "Pity, I could teach you the way of fine tobacco, too, Haidie, sir."

"We're going to Colorado to find our pa," I said.

Jake had lit his cigar and made a face, and I thought the cigar must taste as bad as it smelled. Corny only laughed and puffed on his. "Then I shall teach you some skills, should your paterfamilias search turn out to be for naught. You have a quick mind and hands as small and as soft as a girl's."

Boots started to giggle, but I sent him a stern look.

So at our noonings and after the evening meal, as well as the hours sitting on top of the freight in Jake's wagon, Corny took the cards and dice out of his saddlebags and taught me how to use them, taught me things even Cheet didn't know, like All Fours and Old Sage. He showed me ways to cheat, too, how to shave cards and to attach the holdout to my jacket sleeve and slip a card into it that I palmed from the deck. Corny wore a huge diamond ring—at least, he said it was a diamond. I thought it was glass. Corny showed me how, when he turned it toward his palm, it acted as a tiny mirror, so he could read the cards being dealt. He said I was a natural, that he was surprised Cheet had not taken me as his accomplice, because he figured the pair of us could have made a pretty good living with the cards. He asked me again to be his capper and rope in suckers for him, but I told him that nothing would stop me and Boots from going onto Colorado Territory. "A pity," he said, and I thought he was truly sad. It could have been an interesting life, so I was a little sad myself.

＊ ＊ ＊

We didn't make as many miles each day on the last part of our trip to Omaha. Jake said that was because we'd added Corny to the wagon, but he was a puny little guy and weighed not much more than a sack of flour. I think Jake slowed down a'purpose, so he could spend more time with Teresa.

She told me she'd asked if he had a wife, and he'd said no. "There'd be nothing lower than a man with two wives," she said.

"You believe him?"

"I do." She looked a little uncertain. "Of course, I ain't much of a judge about men. I believed everything Billy Stover ever told me. I guess there's no hope for me."

"Jake's a better man," I said. Then I asked, "Is that what you're after—marriage?"

She shrugged. "I guess I was lucky I got to try out being married to Billy, kind of a sample marriage, you could say. Lord knows what I'd be doing if I really had married him. I'd have been stuck, wouldn't I? You surely did me a favor by having your brother pretend to marry us." She paused. "Jake hasn't asked me or anything, and I don't know if he will. He hasn't even asked me to stay in Omaha, only hinted at it. I guess I'm counting my taters before I dig them, by golly." She'd picked up Jake's favorite cuss words.

Jake might not have asked Teresa to stay with him, but I figured that one way or the other, Teresa would be leaving us in Omaha, and I couldn't say I was sorry. Much as I liked her—and much as I owed her for getting us on that freight wagon with Jake—I thought me and Boots might have an easier time of it on our own. Somebody driving a covered wagon was more likely to take on two boys who could help than two boys and a woman.

✻ ✻ ✻

We were a day out of Omaha and had stopped early for our last night. Jake said the mules were tuckered, but I thought he was dragging out his time with Teresa. Maybe he intended to do a little courting. Much as I was anxious to get to Omaha, I didn't mind the extra rest. I was sore from riding on top of the freight, and of course, those mules went too fast for me to walk, the way you would beside an ox-drawn wagon. Besides, I was hoping that Jake was thinking about marriage.

Me and Boots and Jake watered the horses, then hobbled them so they could graze. Teresa got out the skillet to fix supper, and Corny collected wood for a campfire. Jake had picked a nice spot, an open area surrounded by trees, just off the road. We weren't worried about Billy Stover anymore, so we didn't have to be careful to find us a place that was hidden.

When we were finished with the mules, me and Jake dragged some logs near the fire so we'd have a place to sit while we ate supper. It was real cozy. We sat around the campfire after we'd finished the vittles, and Teresa and Jake sang "My Old Kentucky Home." Corny sniffed at the words— maybe he really was from Kentucky and had a mother or even a wife back there. He rubbed his eyes and got up and said he'd go to the stream and look for some greens that

Teresa could cook up for breakfast. Of course, it was as dark as the inside of a boot out there, with the moon not up yet. He couldn't see a thing. But none of us said a word about that. I guess we knew Corny felt the need to be alone. We'd developed a liking for him. By golly, we even trusted him. So we just sat there, not even looking up when he walked off, wearing his tall hat, as usual, and carrying the walking stick, like he always did.

Jake and Teresa sang another song, and I lay on the ground with my head on a log, listening to the night, thinking if we never found Pa, I wouldn't mind a life as a mule-skinner. Of course, we'd have to get some age yet as well as our growth, but me and Boots could work with somebody like Jake, maybe even Jake himself, and by the time we'd saved enough money, we'd be old enough to buy a team of mules. Mules weren't my favorite animal, but I'd gotten to know them. "Now there's some that try to beat sense into a mule," Jake had told us. "But a mule's like any other animal. You be nice to it, and he'll mind. Of course, they're stubborn and have a mind of their own, and it is all right to swear at them, because they don't understand it and it helps your soul. But you'll get more cooperation with kindness than meanness. I believe that's a lesson for life, with mules and with folks both."

I lay there wondering what would happen if we didn't find Pa. Or didn't hook up with a freighter. Maybe me and Boots could find a gold mine on our own, but we'd have to have somebody show us how.

I looked up at the sky, wishing the stars would come out, listening to the singing and the sound of Corny coming back through the woods, thinking he was making a lot of noise, because he was usually quiet as a mouse. Then I felt prickles in my back because I suddenly knew it wasn't Corny making that noise. Jake must have realized the same thing about the time I did, because all of a sudden, he stood up and started toward the wagon, still singing, as if he didn't want anybody to know he suspicioned a thing. The wagon was where he kept his gun. It was also where he'd tied up Tige. That ugly dog had chased a rabbit right through our campsite, knocking over Jake's supper plate, so he'd tied him to a wagon wheel. Now, Tige was barking and jumping around.

Jake was too late. "I wouldn't do that. You just stay put," a voice said. Two men stepped into the light of our campfire, guns in their hands. They were mean-ugly, with ragged beards and their hair cut worse than mine. Their eyes were cruel and glinted in the firelight.

"Well, what have we here, a family, is it?" one of them asked. He ran his tongue across his bottom lip as he looked at Teresa.

"You're welcome to supper," Jake said, as if the two men were a couple of boys who'd stumbled onto our camp.

"We ain't here for supper." The man gave a mean laugh.

I studied on their faces, making sure I'd recognize them if we ran into them again, and then I had a terrible thought. Most robbers, at least the ones I'd seen pictured in Cheet's magazines, had handkerchiefs over their faces so that no one would recognize them. If these men didn't have their faces covered, maybe they didn't care if we saw who they were. Maybe they meant to kill us.

Jake didn't seem to get it. He was as nice as pie. "You

fellows sit, and we'll fix a pot of coffee for you. It gets mighty cold in these woods at night."

"I'll do it." Teresa stood but the man kicked at her with his boot, and she fell back down.

I expected Jake to spring on that man, but he only said, "Here, now, there's no need for that." He paused and asked, "What can we do for you fellows?"

The taller of the two men stared at Teresa for a long time. "Maybe I got an appetite after all," he said, spitting tobacco juice onto the ground.

Jake hands became fists, but he didn't say anything.

The man squatted by the campfire and looked Teresa in the face. "She's a young one," he told his partner. "Kind of pretty, too. I always liked the pretty ones."

"Well, who don't?" the second man responded.

"You leave be," Jake snarled. He glanced back at the wagon, where Tige was straining at the rope, his teeth bared. But Jake had tied him up too good. He couldn't get loose.

"You'll not be telling me what to do. I'm the one's got the gun."

"Aw, leave her alone," the other man said. "We ain't that kind of men."

"Well, first, let's get that wagon hitched up." The smaller man turned to Jake and gave a hoarse laugh. "We surely do thank you for hauling these goods all this way for us. Yes, sir, we surely do. We'll get a goodly price in Omaha. Of course, we won't get full price, being as how we'll have to sell them fast. But we'll make do. Ain't that right, Dan?"

"Now why'd you go and tell them my name?" Dan asked. "I guess we'll have to take care of them."

"The mules won't go to nobody but me," Jake told them.

He started to rise, but the second man waved his gun at him and said, "Mules is too dumb to know anybody. They'll go to anyone that hits them hard enough. We'll just whack them with a log if they gives us trouble. Now, you sit still. You try something, and . . ." He paused, then added, "Maybe you ought to think about your kids."

Boots moved over toward me and tried to make himself small. I put my arm around him and hugged him to me, thinking what we could do and wondering where Corny was. Then I had an awful thought. What if Corny was one of them? What if Corny had set us up to be robbed? After all, the two men had come into our camp about the time Corny took off. He might have met them in the woods and sicced them on us.

"You go get the mules," the small man said.

"Me? You get them," Dan replied.

"And leave you to look after these folks? You remember what happened afore."

"Ah, stuff it. That weren't my fault."

"I said get the mules. Do as I tells you."

Dan sighed, but he got up then and moved off toward the woods where the mules were grazing. Then he stopped. "Maybe that big boy can help me. I don't fancy getting stomped by a mule." He pointed his gun at me.

I sent a pleading look at Jake, but there was nothing he could do.

"Get up, boy," Dan said. "You do anything funny, Lige over there'll shoot your ma."

"Now who's giving out names? Well, it don't matter." He

thought for a minute. "Here, give me your gun. You don't want the boy to jump you."

Dan shrugged and handed the gun to his partner.

As we moved off toward the mules, Lige called, "Remember, boy, you try anything, I'll shoot your mother."

"You hear that?" Dan asked me, and I told him yes, sir.

"Now you just find me those mules."

I thought it would be better if we first got the mules that had wandered the farthest from camp. That would give me time to think up a plan. Maybe I could talk Dan into forgetting he was going to rob us. Sure, and maybe I could talk the Mississippi into flowing north. "We'll get Big Blue first. If we get him hitched up, the others'll be easier."

"I never knowed a mule that was easy."

"Big Blue's a good mule," I said, wondering if I could get him to bite Dan's head off. But even if I did, Lige was sitting there at the campfire with two guns pointed at Jake and Teresa and Boots.

We went through the woods toward where we'd hobbled Big Blue and Old Samuel. It wasn't far from camp. I could still see the glow of the campfire. "There they are," I said, pointing.

Dan stared at me, and suddenly he said, "You ain't a boy, are you? I always liked young gals." I took his meaning, but before I could run, he grabbed my arm and pulled me toward him. When I struggled to get away, he ripped my shirt. He held my arm so tight that it hurt, and he grinned at me and licked his lip. "Say now," he said. Then he stopped. "You hear something?"

"Maybe a cougar."

"Ain't cougars in these woods."

"There's bear."

"Yeah." He laughed and began to pull me closer. All of a sudden, something smacked his head, and he uttered a loud "Uhhh." Then he fell and was still.

Lige must have heard the noise, because he called out, "What's going on there? Everything all right, Dan? Where's them mules?"

"Damn mule!" called a voice that sounded almost like Dan's, and I looked up to see Corny grinning at me, the walking stick in his hands. He wiped the knob with his handkerchief, wiping off blood, it looked like. "You all right?" Corny whispered.

I looked away, embarrassed that Corny knew what Dan was going to do to me. Then I whispered back, "That man is killed."

"And good riddance. I apologize that I did not strike him sooner." He studied me, then said, "I believe we shall keep details between ourselves, Haidie." Corny leaned over Dan and felt for his wrist. "He is not yet dead, but his life is ebbing away." He raised the cane again and was about to slam it into Dan's head, when I grabbed the end and said, "No, Corny. That'd be murder."

Corny reconsidered. "I can always do it later. Now, tell me what has transpired. I was returning to the camp when I saw the two desperados. I knew they were up to no good."

So I told Corny what had happened. "Problem is Lige has two guns, and we've got none."

"A problem soon corrected. Now, young sir, you rush back to camp and tell the footpad that his partner is in a precarious state. He may not believe you, but his senses will be dulled as he thinks what to do. That will allow me to position myself behind him."

Corny might have been able to smash in Dan's skull in the dark, but it wasn't likely he could creep up on Lige unawares. Still, it was worth a try. I couldn't think of a better plan. It was sure that Lige would shoot one of us, but if Corny could knock him down, Jake might get to Lige to grab one of his guns.

I gave Corny enough time to get to the far side of the campfire. Then I yelped and rushed back to camp. "That man's hurt. Big Blue kicked him, and he's laying on the ground," I gasped.

"What?" Lige stood up, and he motioned me to join the others. He wasn't anybody's fool. "What'd you do to him, boy? We should have shot you all before we went for them mules. I guess I got to do that now. You first, big man." Lige pointed his gun at Jake.

"Sir!" I couldn't see Corny, but I heard his voice loud and clear.

Lige whirled around, and at that instant, there was a gunshot.

Jake? Corny? I thought. _Which of them got hit?_

But it was Lige who fell to the ground, dropping his guns and clutching his chest. Jake swooped up the guns, just as Corny stepped into the firelight, a pepperbox in his hand.

"Why did you wait? Why'nt you just shoot him? What if you'd missed?" I asked.

"I would not have missed, sir. Have you ever known a gambler who wasn't a good shot? Our very lives depend upon it. You bet. I called him out, because a gentleman does not shoot a man in the back."

Jake leaned over Lige, his ear over Lige's mouth. "He's dead. What about the other one?"

"On his way to perdition when we left him. I recommend that we tie him up, lest there be a resurrection."

"How'd you get him?"

"With my walking stick. You see, the knob is not gold but cast iron coated in gold."

Jake shook his head at that, then asked, "That fellow left his weapon here with his partner. Where'd you get the gun?"

Corny grinned. "You said you never knew a gambler who did not have a second gun. Well, sir, I never knew one who didn't have a third. I call this revolver 'my pet.' It was in my hat, sir. In my hat."

Chapter Four

Dan was still breathing when we found him in the woods where Corny had brained him. He was used up bad, although Jake said he would live. We carried him back to camp, and by morning, he had begun to moan and move around. We were eating breakfast when he opened his eyes. He was confused at first, but then he recollected us and tried to get up and would have if Jake hadn't already tied him to a wagon wheel.

"Where's Lige?" he asked.

Jake pointed to the ground. "Gone under, although I'd say hell's too good for him."

"Why, you're lower than a snake's belly," Dan said. "You all killed him and jumped me."

"Not us," I said, "Corny." I pointed to Cornelius Vander, who was sitting on a log and looked no bigger than a boy.

"A puny fellow like that couldn't take me," Dan insisted.

"I guess you're some punier," Teresa said. "And cowarder, too."

"Well, you got the jump on me now. I guess you've took

my gun. You can leave it down the road after you go. I'll find it there."

"Like hell!" Jake said.

"You pert near killed me, but I won't tell nobody if you leave me be. Half-killing a man's a serious offense, maybe even a hanging offense."

"Not when he tried to kill us first. Maybe we should have done you the same way," Jake scoffed. "Besides, we let you go, you'll likely rob the next freighter that comes along. By golly, if we loosed you, you might even get ahead of us and hold us up again before we get to Omaha."

"I ain't even got a horse."

"You're right about that. We found him out in the woods, tied up, along with your partner's horse. I guess some of us will ride to Omaha now. Won't be you."

Dan saw he couldn't bluff his way out, so he began to whine. "I didn't do nothing to you. Me and Lige was just funning."

"The lady didn't see it that way," Jake said.

Jake glanced at Teresa, who was stirring a pot on the fire, but I was sure by the look he gave me that Dan meant me.

"I never hurt nobody," Dan said.

"You didn't come to our camp to talk. You come to kill us." Jake stirred his breakfast with his spoon—mush with some weeds Corny had picked—then dug in. "You want to give him some vittles, Haidie?" I was helping Teresa dish up breakfast.

Dan smiled at me, which was a mistake, because he had only half a mouthful of tobacco-stained teeth, and his smile made me shiver.

I handed the plate to Jake. "You can give him some, if you want to, Jake. He can starve for all I care."

Jake frowned at me, then glanced at Corny, who shook his head, and I knew Jake had figured out something had happened with me and Dan in the woods. He set the pan in front of Dan. "Here, eat up, and we'll be on our way."

"Well, how can I eat when you got me tied up like this? Let loose my hands."

I sent Jake a frightened look, and he said, "I guess you'll have to make do. Eat from the pan or not. It makes no difference to me, by golly, but I believe you'll find Mrs. Richards's offerings better than what you'll get in jail."

"Jail?" Dan stopped with his head halfway to the pan and looked up.

Corny gave a loud laugh. "Do you think we would loose your bonds so that you could practice rapine and pillage? No, sir. We intend to have you incarcerated. You bet."

Those words made Dan so mad that he pulled forward, tugging at the ropes, but Jake had tied him good. Tige got up and growled and bared his teeth, and Corny grabbed his walking stick and held it up. "Be still. Would you have another pounding, sir? It would be my pleasure to administer it." Corny sure was full of ginger that morning, but anybody who'd done what he had most certainly had the right to be.

Dan gave up then and leaned over and began to gobble from the pan, smearing cornmeal mush over his beard. He looked so funny that Boots laughed. When he was finished, Dan tried to wipe his beard on his shirt. Then he glared at Corny. "You didn't get Lige alone."

"Of course not. The boy over there implemented a diversion." He turned to me. "You are a spruce lad, young sir. I could not have shot the highwayman without you and your brave action. I believe you shall share in the reward."

I was sure then that Corny knew I was a girl, and he didn't want to give me away. "Reward?" I asked.

"Most assuredly there will be a reward."

I turned to Jake, who nodded. "I expect the sheriff will be mighty glad to find out who's been robbing freighters along the trail. Most likely, this fellow'll hang, seeing as how his partner got killed."

"But I didn't do the killing," Dan protested.

"A mere formality. Your partner was killed in the process of committing a crime. That makes you guilty," Corny assured him. "Yes, it will be prison or hanging."

"One's hell. The other's damnation," Jake said.

"You'd let me hang?" Dan asked.

"I don't give a dead rat if you do," Jake told him.

Dan's face turned white, and he whined again and begged and even swore on his mother's name that he'd turn his back on his evil ways. He kept it up all the way to the Missouri River. But he didn't fool us.

Late that day, when we arrived in Council Bluffs, across the river from Omaha, Corny riding on Dan's horse and me on Lige's, we asked directions to the sheriff's office. When we got there, Jake set Tige to watching Dan, who was tied up on top of the freight, and went inside and told the sheriff about how the two men had tried to rob us, how they would have killed us if it wasn't for Corny. He came back outside and the two unloaded Lige's body, which was wrapped in a blanket on top of the freight. The sheriff pulled Dan down off the wagon where Jake had tied him and kicked him into the jail. Dan protested, but the sheriff said, "There's some freighters here would like to get their hands on you. When they find out who you are, they'll get up a necktie party. I reckon you know what that means."

Jake told us Corny was likely to get a medal for killing Lige and capturing Dan. There was a three-hundred-dollar reward posted for the outlaws, and the sheriff would give it to Corny the next day. "By rights, it's his," Jake said.

"He deserves it. We'd be dead if it wasn't for him," Teresa said. "You're a brave man, Mr. Vander. You could have gone off, but you came back and saved us."

Corny ducked his head. It was all right for him to brag on himself, but not for us to do so. "We will divide it four ways," Corny said, then looked at Boots and corrected himself, "Five."

"Why would you do that, Corny?" I asked.

"It is only right." He looked away, as if he didn't want to talk about it.

"Why, that's more than twenty-five dollars each," Teresa said.

"Sixty to be exact," I told her.

"Sixty dollars! I never had so much money." She turned to me. "I can pay you back your gold piece."

"It was the price of the trip and well worth it," I replied.

"No, you take it. I'd only spend it on hats. I'm not much good with money. It gets away from me."

"You best find somebody to see after you," I told her.

I went over to Jake, who was tightening the rope over the

tarp, and asked him why Corny would share the reward. After all, Corny was broke and the three hundred dollars would give him a nice stake.

"You don't know much about gambling men, I see," he replied. "They might cheat you blind, but they're the most generous men I ever encountered. They'd divide their last potato. And they're not showy about helping folks either. Why, a gambler's more likely to go broke giving away his money than he is losing it at cards."

I knew he hadn't met Cheet.

* * *

The next morning, we crossed the river to Omaha, each of us with an extra sixty dollars in our pockets. Me and Corny had horses, too. After he found out neither of us owned a horse, the sheriff said he believed the animals ought to be part of the reward. So when we reached the Nebraska side of the river, Jake and Teresa rode into Omaha on the wagon, Corny on Lady Luck, and me and Boots on Outlaw. We hadn't asked Dan what the horses were called, so we named them ourselves. We looked spruce. Outlaw was black, with two white stars on his forehead. The sheriff gave me the saddle, too. It was decorated with silver stars.

Corny glanced around until he figured out where the saloons were and said he'd be on his way. "I do not like to part company with such a fine assemblage, but the pasteboards call," he told us. He removed his hat and bowed, then kissed Teresa's hand. He shook hands with Jake and said he might have perished back there in Iowa if Jake hadn't taken him in.

"I shan't forget such kindness," he said. He even shook Tige's paw and said, "You are a prince of an animal."

Finally, he came over to me and Boots, both of us sitting on Outlaw. "You are a brave boy," he told Boots. "When faced with adversity, you acted like a man. You will go far."

Boots might not have understood the words, but he squirmed with pride.

Then Corny took my hand. "You are a noble lad, young sir." He pulled at his mustache, which he had just waxed so that it shone like a black candle, and winked at me. "You, too, have acted the part of a man." Corny touched the diamond headlight on his breast. While the rest of us had set up camp the night before, Corny had found a dry goods store and bought himself a white shirt. He'd had his coat and pants brushed, his hat steamed, and his boots blackened, and he looked like a dandy again. The diamond blinked like fire against the shirt, which was as white as the moon. Corny removed the stickpin and polished the stone on his flowered vest. "I believe someday you might wear this in remembrance of me," he said. He opened my coat and secured it in the inside pocket.

Embarrassed by the gesture, Corny stepped back and coughed. "I wish you success in finding your father. If I may be of service at any time, or if you change your mind about joining forces in a business way, step into any gambling hall and ask the whereabouts of Cornelius Vander."

As he mounted Lady Luck, Corny tapped the false top inside his hat, and put the hat onto his head. Then he turned to Jake. "Remember, sir, three guns."

Then he said to me, "If Lady Luck is against me in Omaha, I might perchance see you in Colorado."

We stayed where we were while Corny rode off. He didn't turn around, but we watched him anyway, until he disappeared into a stream of freight wagons and prairie schooners.

"What's going to happen to him?" I asked.

"Oh, he'll do fine for a while, maybe even a long time. But one day, he'll get shot dead by somebody over a poker game or he'll have a streak of bad luck and end up in the gutter. Once gambling's got its hooks in you, you never give it up. It's a squirrely business."

Jake flicked the reins on the mules' backs, and me and Boots followed him to a freight depot and sat outside with Teresa while he sold his goods. "What are you going to do?" I asked her. It had occurred to me that Outlaw couldn't carry three of us all the way to Denver and that we'd have to buy another horse if Teresa came along. That would cost us much of our money.

"Jake said he wouldn't mind if I went back to the Mississippi with him."

"Married?"

"He didn't say that."

"What if you run into Billy again?"

"Oh, we wasn't thinking of going back to Fort Madison. We might go south to Keokuk or maybe even up north to Galena. Jake says freighting's an awful good business right now, what with all the gold mines in Colorado Territory. We might even run into you there someday. You think I ought to go with him, Haidie?"

"I like him."

"Oh, there's nothing about him not to like. That's not the question. I asked, should I go?"

I wanted her to, but I said only, "You got to make up your own mind about that."

Teresa nodded. "If it don't work out, I can always go on to Denver and meet up with you. I guess by then, you'll be living in a fine mansion."

"I guess."

"Are you going to stay in Denver, do you think?" she asked.

I shrugged. "We'll stay with Pa, wherever he's at."

"You think you'll find him?"

"Of course." I tried to sound sure. "He wrote us he was in Georgetown, west of Denver, but maybe he's moved on."

"What if he's dead?" Teresa asked.

Boots, who'd been drawing in the dirt with a stick, heard the question and looked up at me. If I'd studied on it, I'd have known there was a good chance Pa was in heaven, but I hadn't let myself think that. He couldn't be dead. Somebody would have written us, wouldn't they?

"You think he's dead, Haidie?" Boots whispered.

"I do not. Pa wouldn't do that to us." But we all knew that Pa might not have had a thing to say about it. "He'll be so glad to see us, he'll grab us up and say you've grown so big, he wouldn't have recognized you."

"You think so?"

"I do." But my heart was heavy to think that might be the worst lie of my life.

✳ ✳ ✳

That night, Jake took us into a restaurant and bought us a
fine dinner, with meat and potatoes and applesauce, beans
and bacon and bread, and custard and three kinds of pie for
dessert. Me and Boots had never eaten in a restaurant before,
let alone one with a tablecloth and a knife and a fork and a
spoon for each of us. I wished the orphans could have seen us
now with this high living.

Jake said he'd pay for a hotel for us, him and Teresa in
one room and me and Boots in another. Teresa was game,
but I'd got used to sleeping on the ground and said me and
Boots would go back to the wagon with Tige and keep an
eye on things. I didn't want to be any more beholden than
I already was.

Boots didn't like that. "I could sleep with Jake and Teresa,"
he said, but I told him someone had to keep me company,
just in case Dan got loose and came looking for a freight
wagon to steal.

"Don't think nothing of it if we're not there at sunrise.
I'm mighty tired," Teresa told us, as me and Boots went off
to roll up in our blankets.

She surely was right about that, because Jake and Teresa
didn't show up at the wagon next morning until the sun was
high in the sky, with Teresa looking foolish. She must have
been incorrigible all night. Her nature was getting pretty
well worn out.

The two of them didn't seem to be in any hurry to head
back to Iowa, but I was anxious to start for Colorado and asked
Jake where we could find us a ride. He took me and Boots
down near the river where folks were loading Conestogas.
There were fourteen of them, the big wagon covers as white

in the sun as Corny's shirt. Another train of wagons was just leaving, and we watched them strung out along the road like a necklace of pearl beads.

"Who's the wagon master?" Jake asked, and someone pointed to a man who was hefting a table into a wagon. Jake motioned for us to follow him, and me and Boots fell in line behind him. We'd let Jake do the talking.

"You need a hand there?" Jake asked. Before the man could answer, Jake picked up the back end of the table, and the two shoved it into the wagon. Then he helped the man load a rocking chair, a washstand, and two barrels. "Be careful of them. My wife's china's mixed in there with the flour. She wouldn't like it if her dishes got broke before we even left," he said.

"Heading for Colorado Territory?" Jake asked.

"Denver."

"I got two boys here that are awful good workers. They're going to Colorado to find their pa."

"I already got boys, three of them, in fact."

"Don't look like they're much help." Jake looked around to where the boys were playing.

"They will be when they get hungry." He nodded at two women who were washing dishes in a basin beside a wagon. "You might ask them. They're going to Colorado, too, and haven't got a man to help them."

Jake thanked him and walked up to one of the women, removing his hat. "Good morning, ma'am."

She looked up and asked, "What's good about it?"

Jake thought that over and said, "For one thing, the sun came up in the morning." She didn't reply. So Jake told her,

"I've got two boys here who'd like to work their way to Denver."

"Do we appear to need help?" she asked.

"They'll work for grub."

"Sister and I can manage by ourselves, thank you." She turned to the other old maid. "Why is it men believe we cannot make this trip without their aid? Before we reach Denver, we will have shown them we are as capable as they are."

"That is our purpose, sir," the other woman said. "We might have taken a stagecoach, but as my sister says, we are determined to prove we are every bit as capable as men."

"Perhaps better," the sister said. "It will be an adventure for us."

"Adventure!" Jake scoffed. He went from wagon to wagon then, asking if anybody would take me and Boots with them. Men studied on us, but I guess they figured we were too small. And while the women looked at us kindly, I could see they all had a passel of young 'uns to take care of and didn't want us added to their burden. Nobody seemed to think we could do a day's work.

"What about that one over there?" I asked, pointing to a single man who was hitching up a team of oxen to a wagon.

Jake sized him up, then looked at me. "You don't want to go with him."

"It looks like he could use the help."

"Maybe, but I don't trust him."

"You didn't trust Corny, and he saved our lives," Boots said.

Jake shook his head. Then he squatted down beside me and took my hand. "There's things about men you don't

know, Haidie. If he finds out you're a girl, it'll mean troublement. There might be troublement even if he doesn't."
He studied on me a moment, then said, "Well, maybe you
do know."

I was worried. What would we do if we never found a
wagon to take us? Me and Boots couldn't just go across the
prairie by ourselves. We could run into Indians or get lost or
one of us could break a leg. Then what would we do?

As I sat there puzzling, a man dressed in a leather shirt
and heavy pants with pieces of buckskin sewn on the seat,
with a long beard hanging down to his chest, came up to Jake
and asked, "You be making the trip, pilgrim?" He scanned
the wagons, with all the furniture and trunks, and boxes and
barrels of provisions lined up next to them. "We be leaving
maybe a thousand years next month if they don't hurry up."
His laugh was a happy one.

Jake laughed, too. "No, I'm not going, but these boys
want to."

"We're looking to find our pa," I added.

"I knowed plenty of folks going to Colorado but none
of them looking for their old man. They want to find gold.
Want to scoop up nuggets and tote 'em home in a wheelbar-
row." He narrowed his eyes. "How come your pa didn't come
to fetch you?"

"He doesn't know we're coming," Boots spoke up.

"Our ma died, and our brother put us in an orphan home,"
I explained. "But me and Boots left so that we could find Pa."

The man nodded.

"You know anybody who'll take them?" Jake asked.
"They come to Omaha with me and my mules, but I got

to turn back. They're right good workers and such good-hearted boys you never met. Haidie here knows a thing or two about mules."

"I never liked a mule." The man thought a minute. "Either of you pilgrims know how to cook?"

"Haidie can," Boots spoke up, and I clapped my hand over his mouth before he could burst out that I was a girl.

"Cornbread and beans, over a campfire?"

"Yes, sir," I said. "And biscuits."

The man turned to Jake. "They your kin, are they?"

"I never saw them before they asked me for a ride in Fort Madison. But I can guarantee them."

"That your horse?" the man asked me.

"It is now."

"It was give to him by the sheriff in Council Bluffs on account of he helped bring in the men that was robbing the freight wagons. They come to rob me, but he helped get shut of them. One's dead. Most likely, the other'll hang," Jake said.

"I heard about that. A hard lot they was." The man scratched his beard, while I stared at the fringe on his shirt. He caught my eye and said, "That fringe ain't there just to be pretty. It keeps the flies away."

He sized up me and Boots again. "I've been hired on as scout for this sorry company. I figured to pick up a boy from one of these wagons to help me, but if you'll drive the wagon whilst I scout for the train, you'll do."

Jake looked at me, and I nodded. "You won't be sorry. If I had boys, I'd like them to be just like these two." Jake was laying it on pretty thick, but I didn't mind.

"I guess they'll protect me if we run up against any robbers. What be your names?"

"I'm Haidie, and he's Boots," I said.

"Ben Bondurant." He held out his hand, not to Jake but to me. "I'll provide tuck for your horse, too. Is that ugly dog coming?"

Jake shook his head. "He's mine."

Mr. Bondurant didn't seem to care. "There's too many of 'em already." He told Boots, "You have permission to kick any dog that barks at us."

We'd said our good-byes to Teresa that morning and brought our bedrolls with us, our extra boots and clothing and Pa's letters wrapped inside, just in case we joined up with a train leaving that day. Jake handed them to Mr. Bondurant, who stowed them in his wagon.

"You see to them good, Mr. Bondurant, or you'll hear from me."

Mr. Bondurant nodded. "They do their part, they got nothing to worry about."

Jake shook hands with Mr. Bondurant, then with Boots. But he hugged me. "You're an awful good kid," he whispered. "Maybe we'll catch up again one day. But if I don't see you again, I'll meet you in heaven." He walked away, stopping every minute or so to wave, until we couldn't see him anymore.

✻ ✻ ✻

We left that afternoon and made just two miles. People around us complained that we hadn't gone any farther, saying we might just as well have stayed where we were and left the next morning. But Mr. Bondurant said crankily that if we'd waited until morning, folks would have unloaded their wagons that night, then spent half a day loading them up again, and we wouldn't have left until afternoon. "Best we get a start, any start, or we'll be here for three or four years."

Even in that short distance, I learned something about oxen. They're as slow as treacle. A mule can cover more ground in a day than an ox in two or three or four. You can walk faster than an ox, which is why most people walk across the plains beside the ox team instead of sitting on a hard wagon seat. Noah in the Bible would have drowned if he'd had to wait for a pair of oxen to get aboard the boat.

A mule's as smart as a human, compared to an ox, which is as dumb an animal as God ever created. A mule gets mean if you hit it and will bite you if it can, but an ox just stands there and waits for another blow. However, oxen are stronger than Samson. A mule's better company, but an ox is the best animal to pull a Conestoga wagon.

Mr. Bondurant picked a nice place for the three of us to camp, not far from a stream. The wagon master said we ought to form a circle with the wagons, the way he'd heard other plains travelers did, in case we were attacked by Indians. The pair of women who'd turned us down looked at each other and smiled. I guess Indians were part of the adventure they were looking for.

"Sir, we can see the lights of Omaha," Mr. Bondurant boomed out. "We are in greater danger of being scalped by the gamblers and hoors and ruffians of the city than we are by Indians. Best you not frighten the ladies just yet." The man started to argue, but when he saw the look Mr. Bondurant gave him, he kept his mouth shut. "I have signed up with a

wagonload of fools. I suspicioned it before, but now I know
it for a fact," Mr. Bondurant said as he watched the man walk
away. "We'll see to the animals lest one of them pilgrims
mistakes an ox for a buffalo."

He and Boots left to water the oxen and the horses, whilst
I began on the supper. I wasn't much at building campfires
yet. The man Jake had warned me about came over to help.

"Here, boy, I'll do that for you. The way you build fires,
you won't eat till morning."

I told him I'd rather do it myself, but he tried to push
me aside.

"Sir!" I said, wishing my voice wasn't so high.

He stopped and watched me. "Might be I'll bring my
vittles over and eat with you 'uns. No need for two fires when
one will do."

It wasn't my place to tell him no. For all I knew, he and
Mr. Bondurant were friends. I just grunted and said he'd
have to ask Mr. Bondurant when he came back.

"I'm called Patrick Fitzgerald." He spit a wad of tobacco
juice into the kindling.

I nodded.

"Ain't you got a name?"

"Haidie Richards."

"Never heard that name before."

I didn't reply, just arranged dried grasses over the sticks.

"I said I never heard that name before."

"No, sir."

"You're very little of a talker."

"I'm trying to make a fire."

"Well, you wouldn't have to if you'd let me help you.

Ain't that right?" When I didn't reply, he added, "No, you sure ain't much for palaver."

I wished he'd go away, but Mr. Fitzgerald sat down in the dirt and took off his hat, which was greasy and worn, like the rest of his clothing. Instead of using braces or a belt, he held up his pants with a piece of rope. One pants leg was stuffed into his boot top. The other had come out and dragged on the ground. Heavy spurs were attached to his boots, and they jingled when he walked. I took a quick glance at his face and didn't like what I saw. He was a thin man with stringy black hair that matched his mustache, both of them greasy, and he looked stingy and mean.

He fixed me with his hard black eyes and asked, "What you staring at, boy?"

"Nothing, Mr. Fitzgerald."

"You can call me Pat on account of we're going to be friends, ain't we?"

I got up and went to the wagon for a lucifer, then struck it and held it to the dried grass. The grass caught fire, but just as I thought the kindling would light, a breeze came up and blew out the flame.

"Here, boy, let me do it." Pat reached into his pocket and took out a flint. With a couple of tries, he got a spark, and the dried grasses caught fire again, then the kindling, and finally the broken branches. "I always liked a fire." His voice was hard, and his eyes glinted.

"He's got himself some nice horses, don't he?" When I didn't reply, he added, "Bondurant, that is."

"Seems like it."

"I might could take one off his hands. Reuben over there ain't been doing so good." He pointed to a horse that had been tied to the back of his wagon but now was hobbled.

"You don't know if Bondurant wants to sell a horse, do you?" He sounded casual, as if he really didn't care, and took out a showy gold watch and clicked it open. I'd have bet one of my gold pieces his name wasn't the one engraved on the lid. "I have in mind that black horse."

"That's Outlaw. He's *my* horse," I told him. "He's not for sale. Ever."

"Don't have to be your horse. How about one of Bondurant's?"

I shook my head. "I got to start supper." I hoped he'd get the hint to leave, but Pat made himself comfortable. He took a ropelike piece of tobacco and offered it to me. I almost gagged at the idea of biting off a chaw and murmured no thank you.

"Don't have the habit yet, do you, boy?"

"No, sir."

"I could learn you to chew. I learned me how to snuff when I was half your age." He leaned toward me, and I caught his scent, which was stronger than horseradish. "I hear you and your brother's going west to find your pa."

I moved a little away and measured out cornmeal and water, mixed them and put them into a skillet, then set it on the fire, which had burned down a little.

"Lots of people disappear out there in the gold camps. Die of the ague or pneumonia, fall down a mine shaft or get crushed in a mill accident. I know a man got shot sitting in his cabin reading the Bible. You ought to know what happens to men out here, in case you don't find him. It'll save you some pain."

"We know where he is."

"Yeah, well, men move around a lot. Maybe your old pap don't want you to know where he's at. You ever think about that? Maybe he run off."

"Not my pa!" I said.

"Maybe he got in a gunfight over cards or a hoor. I done it myself."

"You killed a man?"

"More than one." Fitzgerald raised his chin. "Fact is, I don't know how many. I'd have to go back and study over it."

At that moment, Ben and Boots returned, and Ben frowned when he saw Pat. "What do you want, Fitzgerald?"

"I was just being sociable. The boy don't even know how to light a fire. A muckle he made of it. If I hadn't of been here, he'd have used up all your matches."

"The boy does fine."

"Well, I thought as how we're all batching it, we might as well eat together."

"You'd expect the boy here to cook your meals for ye?"

"Don't see why not, seeing as how I'm learning him a thing or two."

"Nothing worth knowing, most likely. You do your own cooking."

Pat sniffed. "Well, I guess that's all right with me. I have an independent heart."

"Independent, but not free."

Pat Fitzgerald slowly got up, as if he was ending a sociable call. "Nice talking to you, son," he said. "You get tired of living with a squawman, you're welcome to camp with me. Your brother, too." He and Ben exchanged a glance. Pat added, "A man that has to do with an Indian is lower than a pig."

"But not lower than an Irishman," Ben retorted. Pat gave him a dark look, and Ben added, "You interfere with me and these boys, and I'll make it warm for you."

After Pat was gone, I asked, "What did you mean, independent but not free?"

Ben pondered that. "He is on his own, all right, but his heart is as much a captive of the devil as if it was in jail in his breast. He's a child of sin. Best to stay away from him, Haidie. I don't reckon he'd harm you, but he'd steal the bones out of your feet. Keep a sharp watch when he's around."

"He might like to buy a horse from you."

Ben narrowed his eyes and then gave a chuckle. "We'll see. Patches maybe, but not Stormy. I'd never sell Stormy." He winked at me.

"What's so special about Stormy?" Boots asked.

"You'll see."

✳ ✳ ✳

I burned the meat, and the cornbread was raw. The weeds I'd picked along the creek, which I thought were the same ones that Corny had gathered, gave us all sour stomachs. But Mr. Bondurant said the food suited him. "The best kind of eating there is—food cooked by somebody else," he said, "and eaten with folks you like." He glanced over at where Pat Fitzgerald had set up camp.

After the pans and tin plates and spoons were put away,

we sat at the fire and listened to the sounds of the camp—
the oxen bawling, wagons creaking, babies crying, a woman
calling to her kids to keep where she could see them lest they
be trampled by oxen. A man asked Mr. Bondurant to look at
the hoof of one of his oxen, which he thought was lame. The
two left, and when Mr. Bondurant returned, he told us the
man had been cheated by a sharper. "That ox won't make it
a hundred miles. If he hadn't brung along four pairs of ox,
I'd have told him to go back to Omaha and buy another'n."

A couple next to us started to bicker, and we heard the
man say, "I ain't hauling this picture of your old mother all
the way to Colorado. We should have left it behind with
her." Something crashed onto the ground, and the woman
wailed. Then there was a slap, and she was still.

"People! I never liked 'em much," Mr. Bondurant said.

"You like us, don't you, Mr. Bondurant?" Boots asked.

Mr. Bondurant laughed. "You aren't *people,* Boots. You
and your brother are boys. I get along with boys just fine. It's
when they get growed up and think they're smart that they
trouble me."

"Maybe you never growed up yourself, Mr. Bondurant,"
I said.

He laughed and slapped his knee and said, "Maybe you
got that right, young Haidie. The only thing I like about a
man is he can play cards."

"I can play cards," I said.

He scoffed. "Old Maid, I expect."

"I have enjoyed a time or two at it, playing Old Maid,"
I said. "But I know some other card games. Have you ever
heard of Seven Up or Old Sledge?"

Mr. Bondurant looked startled. "Now, what would a boy like you know about such things?"

"My brother is a riverboat gambler," I said.

"And Corny taught us, too," Boots added.

"Corny?" Mr. Bondurant asked.

"Cornelius Vander. He's a gambling man, too, only he's better than our brother. He came with me and Boots and Jake and Teresa. He's the one that stopped the men trying to rob us."

Mr. Bondurant nodded. "I have heard of him, although I haven't made his acquaintance. They say he's the runt of the litter, a pocket-size hellion. And he learnt you the cards?"

"Yes, sir."

"Then I'd best keep my eye on my pocketbook. I heard he'd rather cheat even when he's dealt the winning hand. Old Sledge, you say. What say we play for lucifers?"

"I haven't any," I told him.

"So I have to give you your matches, so you can win my matches."

I looked him in the eye. "Yes, sir, Mr. Bondurant."

"Well, if we are going up against each other man to man, you best call me Ben. I don't suppose you'd rather play the shell game."

"Only if you let me move around the shells," I said scornfully.

"Oh, you know it, do you?"

"I could play you three-card monte, too."

Ben laughed. "So Vander learned you how to cheat, but did he learn you how to play poker?"

"Right well."

Ben took out a worn pack of cards and shuffled them. "We'll see."

"Are they marked, the cards?" I asked.

"Whoa now. I've shot men for accusing me of less."

"Corny says that, too. Gamblers sure are a touchy bunch. It seems they'd shoot a man for saying just about anything."

"I ain't really a gambler, just a fellow who likes to take a turn or two with the cards. But I've done my share of winning."

We played for matches. I started with ten, and so did Ben, and when we gave it up for the night and unrolled our blankets under the wagon, I had eight lucifers, and Ben had twelve. I figured I'd made a poor showing, but Ben told me, "There's not many that can match up against Ben Bondurant. I've a quick eye for cheating, and I can say you played it straight. Ye didn't cheat, did you?"

"No, sir," I replied. But I did.

* * *

In the night, I heard loud voices, and although we were still only two miles from Omaha, I sat up, wondering if the Indians had attacked.

"Here, you, what are you doing there? Get away from my wagon."

"Hush up. I got a call of nature," a voice said.

"And you was going to answer it in our flour barrel?"

"It's too dark to see. I thought it was my wagon. Go to sleep. No harm done."

"What've you got in your hand? That looks like a fry pan."

There was a thud as something fell to the ground. Then

the first man called, "Who are you? Where'd you go?" He paused and added, "A darned sneakthief."

The thief must have disappeared, because the man called out again, demanding to know his name. But there was no answer. The thief went undiscovered. But I had recognized Pat Fitzgerald's voice.

✳ ✳ ✳

We were not bowling along, as we had with Jake and the mules. We were lucky to make ten or twelve miles a day. I drove the oxen, while Ben took charge of the horses or rode ahead of the train, looking for likely camping spots and watching out for Indians. Mr. Samuels, the fellow they'd elected to be the wagon master, didn't know anything about going west, and Ben said if we followed that man, we'd likely wind up in Cincinnati.

Boots spelled me on the oxen from time to time so that I could ride Outlaw, but mostly he ran off onto the prairie with the other boys, looking for rocks or flowers, picking up kindling for the cook fire. Ben told us about the animals—rattlesnakes that could kill you in a minute if they bit you in the right place; antelope, which were so curious, they would come up right to the wagon train to see what was going on. And there were coyotes that Ben said were cast-off cousins of wolves. "When He created the coyote, the Almighty had a use for them, but He kept it to himself."

Once, Pat asked Boots to help him with his oxen, promising to pay him a nickel a day, but Ben warned Boots he'd never see a penny of the money. Boots tried it for a day, but it was hard work, and Boots told me that since he had sixty dollars, he didn't have to work for five cents a day.

One evening, a woman complained to me that somebody must be stealing her flour, because it was going twice as fast as it should. She said her breast pin had disappeared, too, although she thought she might not have pinned it tight to her shawl. Maybe it had just dropped off. I told Ben about that.

He said others had complained about things disappearing. "Now that happens sometimes in a wagon train, because folks get careless and leave their pans and dishes behind by the campfire. But I believe we got a sneaksman amongst us." He glanced over at where Pat Fitzgerald was camped, and I took his meaning.

It wasn't more than a week later that Pat's horse, Reuben, gave out.

"Why didn't he bring a better horse?"

"Patrick knows his horses. Reuben might have been the best he could find."

"What'll he do?"

"Most likely try to buy a horse off me. He looks poor as a drought, but he has money on him."

"Would you sell him one?"

Ben chuckled. "Maybe I would."

"But wouldn't he treat the horse bad?"

"No, Pat cares for his horses. Reuben was just played out. I'd sell him Patches for the right price, just not Stormy."

Ben's eyes twinkled, and I knew he was up to something.

Not more than a day later, Pat came up beside me when I was driving the oxen and got sociable.

"Ben's got too many horses," he said, real casual, like he

was just making conversation. He'd put away the tobacco, and now he reached down and grabbed a blade of long prairie grass and chewed the end of it. "Too many horses like that, he's liable to lose one. It'll run off or an Indian'll grab it. Ain't no way he'll ever get it back." When I didn't respond, he said, "What do you think about that, boy?"

"I guess Mr. Bondurant knows about horses."

"You do, do you?"

I remembered Ben talking about Stormy, and I said, "Maybe he'll sell you a horse, just not Stormy."

"What's so special about Stormy?"

I shrugged. "I don't know. I just know Mr. Bondurant won't sell him. He said he might sell Patches."

"Patches, eh? That the funny-looking one, looks like a pail of paint fell on him?"

I nodded.

That night, Pat wandered over to our campfire and sat down without being invited. Me and Ben had just got out the cards, and Pat gave Ben a scornful look. "Taking candy from a baby, are you?"

"He's got to learn."

"Well, I got a proposition for you."

Ben shuffled the cards, then shuffled them again, but he didn't deal. "What's that?" he asked.

"It seems I need a horse, and you got more horses than you need. Or want, either. I seen you trying to keep 'em together."

"I do all right."

"Maybe now, but not when we get into Indian country."

"Indians don't scare me."

Pat took out his tobacco and offered it to Ben, but Ben said, "Never developed a fondness for it." He removed his pipe and lighted it with a sliver of wood that he took from the campfire. "So you want to do some horse trading, do you?"

Pat snorted. "I got nothing to trade. I want to buy a horse."

Ben thought that over. "I might could sell you Patches, but not Stormy. I'd never sell Stormy. Patches is a good horse, though."

"What's so good about Stormy?"

Ben smiled. "Don't matter none, since I won't sell him."

"I believe Stormy's the only one that'll do."

"You don't have enough money to buy him."

"How much'll it take?"

Ben shook his head. "He ain't for sale. I wouldn't sell him for pie. Take Patches for a hundred dollars."

The two of them went back and forth like that for the better part of an hour, Pat chewing and spitting into the fire and insisting he wanted to buy Stormy, Ben puffing on his pipe and saying the horse wasn't for sale. I thought they'd sit there all night, and I guess Ben did, too, because he yawned and said he was too sleepy to bargain anymore.

"I tell you what, Ben, I'll give you a hundred and ten dollars and a real nice breast pin that was my mother's. And you sell me Stormy."

"I got no use for a breast pin." Ben yawned again. He looked ready to fall asleep right there. "Oh, well, you wore me out. Take the horse."

Pat grinned, but after a time, the grin faded, and he narrowed his eyes. He sat like that for a long time. "How come you didn't want to sell that horse, but now you do? Changing your mind like that ain't like you."

"It's the breast pin," Ben said.

"Hell, you could buy one for a half-dollar."

Ben gave a sheepish smile, which he tried to hide behind his hand, but Pat saw it.

"You've been playing me. Why, it's highway robbery."

"You'd know more about that than me."

"I know your game. You tried to trick me into buying Stormy. Well, it won't work. I'll take Patches. He's the one you wanted to keep, ain't he?" He took out a buckskin bag and threw some coins on the ground. "Here's you your money. I'll get my horse in the morning."

Ben gave him a sour look and sighed. But he put the money into his pocket and turned his back on Pat.

※ ※ ※

In the morning, as the women were cooking breakfast and the men hitching up the oxen, Pat sauntered over toward our campfire, calling in a loud voice, "I come to get Patches." He had Reuben's saddle in his hands.

Ben gave him an angry look and took the saddle.

"Yes sir, you tried to trick me into taking Stormy. Think I'm a damn fool, do you? You can't get the best of Patrick Fitzgerald." Ben didn't reply, just took the saddle and disappeared. In a few moments, he returned with Patches and tied him to the end of his wagon, which was at the edge of the camp.

"I guess I just proved I'm no sap-head." Pat added in a loud voice, "This old sharper tried to smoke me into taking old Stormy off his hands." Pat turned to the men, who were listening, and raised his chin and grinned. Then he put his foot into the stirrup and threw his leg over Patches. "Don't count out Patrick—"

Patches put his feet together and arched his back and sent Patrick straight up into the air. Patrick held on with all his might as the horse came down. But as soon as his feet touched the ground, Patches rose up on his hind legs, Patrick clutching at the pommel with one hand and the horse's mane with the other. Then Patches kicked his hind feet in the air. The horse repeated that business two or three times, with Patrick hanging on for his life, his eyes as big as puff balls. The third time, Patches came down hard on all four feet, and Patrick flew off, landing not a foot from our campfire. Ben had insisted we camp a little away from the rest of the train, and now I knew why.

People had come from all over the camp to watch, some of the men grinning, the women covering their mouths with their aprons so as not to seem to be enjoying themselves. Patrick was not a favorite, and it was all the gawkers could do not to cheer when Patches bucked him off.

Two of the men went to help him up, and Pat took off in search of the horse, which had run off half a mile.

Ben stayed where he was, chuckling.

"You knew he'd choose Patches," I said. "How?"

"He's too smart for his own good. If he knew I didn't want to sell Stormy, he'd be suspicious when I gave in. I told you I mostly win at gambling."

Trying to follow that line of reasoning made my head hurt, but as it turned out well, I decided Ben knew what he was talking about.

✳ ✳ ✳

Pat Fitzgerald had given one hundred and ten dollars and a breast pin for Patches. As we were preparing to head out, Ben went to the woman who had complained that her bauble had been lost and asked if the pin was familiar.

"You've stole it!" she said. Then she called her husband. "Jeffrey, come here. This man has stole my breast pin." Her voice was so loud that others heard and came to glare at Ben. Jeffrey picked up a stout stick and advanced.

"Now, hold on there, sir," Ben told him. "Do you think I'm fool enough to take your wife's jewelry, then show it to her?"

Jeffrey stopped, frowning as he thought that over. "Then how came you to have it?"

"Pat Fitzgerald give it to him for the horse. I saw it," a woman said.

The others looked in the direction Pat had gone. Then a man said, "I'm missing a knife. I laid it out, and in the morning, it was gone." Someone else mentioned a stolen pan, and before you knew it, a dozen people were walking toward Pat's wagon. By the time Pat returned, holding Patches by the bridle, there were about ten thousand items lined beside his wagon—a penknife, a fork, a red shirt, hand-knit stockings, a girl's dress. And there was no way of knowing how much of his sugar and flour, salt and saleratus he had thieved. Pat looked at the plunder and didn't say a word.

"I believe stealing on the trail's a hanging offense, ain't that so, Bondurant," the wagon master asked Ben.

"Oh, no. Surely not," Ambrose Tappan spoke up. "Even those who believe an eye for an eye is proper revenge would not demand such retribution. A man's life is worth more than a little property." The Reverend Tappan had just graduated from seminary and liked to advise us on churchly matters, even when nobody asked. He was a seriously pompous man who liked to show himself superior to everyone in the train, including his wife. She was pretty and shy, but she was as good as bread and had helped me with my cooking.

"Besides, we haven't seen a tree in a week. How can we hang a man if there isn't a tree?" I asked Ben.

"Banishment's the usual punishment," Ben said.

"Then I believe you'll be leaving us now," Mr. Samuels told Pat. "You want us to take a vote on it?"

Pat shrugged. He knew he was done for. But then he had an idea. "Maybe I'm guilty, maybe I'm not, but you all know Ben Bondurant cheated me out of a good horse. You can't turn me out with a horse I can't ride. What if I run into Indians?"

The men looked at each other, a little uneasy. They didn't like Pat, but they didn't want to be responsible for his getting killed. Was it right to send him off on a horse he couldn't ride? they asked each other.

"How about it, Mr. Bondurant?" someone asked.

Ben scratched his head. "He bought that horse fair and square. Some of you saw it."

"Yeah, but he can't ride him."

"Never asked me if he was rideable."

"Well, make up your mind. We got to be on our way," the wagon master said.

"How about we cut cards for it?" Pat asked. He reached into his coat pocket for a deck.

"With your cards?" Ben scoffed.

"I wouldn't trust that deck of yours, Bondurant."

"Then we'll let the boy cut them—cut one for me, cut one for you."

"Sounds fair to me," the wagon master said, and Pat had no choice but to hand the cards to me. They were dirty, greasy even, I thought, as I felt along the uneven edges. I started to shuffle but dropped the deck and had to pick up the cards one by one. I set them on the wagon tongue and shuffled them a time or two, slowly, awkwardly, as if I wasn't much good at it. "Who gets the first card?" I asked.

"I do," Pat said.

I shuffled the cards again, not much better than before. Then I cut the deck and turned over the jack of hearts. Pat picked it up and grinned. "Beat that, Bondurant," he said.

My hands were sweaty and I wiped them on my pants. Then I felt along the edges and cut a second time, holding up the king of spades.

Pat scowled, but he didn't say a word. He hitched up his oxen, tied Patches to the back of his wagon, and turned it around. Then he headed back to the east, and we watched until the white top of his wagon was a speck the size of a marble. "We turned the dog out," Ben observed.

"It's a long way back to Omaha. What's going to happen to him?" I asked, as we got under way.

"Oh, he won't go to Omaha. He'll join up with the next train, claiming he'd started out on his own but figured he'd be safer with a train," Ben replied. I was driving the oxen then, and Ben walked beside me for a time. "Pat shaved the deck," he said.

"And a mighty poor job of it," I replied.

Chapter Five

While Patrick Fitzgerald might not have been fit to associate with hogs, I still didn't wish him dead.

"You think Pat'll mend his ways?" I asked Ben.

"Oh, he'll lick his wounds like a yellow dog. He's been bad hurt with humiliation. But by and by, he'll be well enough to backslide."

I was glad, too, that Pat wouldn't be traveling by himself, since we'd begun to come across Indians, and while Ben said they were friendly, he also told us it wasn't safe to be out there on the prairie all alone. He warned me and Boots to stay close to the wagon when the Indians came around, because they might kidnap young boys. I wondered what would happen if they captured me and discovered I was a young girl? Nothing good, I figured.

Sometimes, I almost forgot I *was* a girl. When we'd reached Omaha with Jake, I could have put on a dress, since nobody was looking for runaway orphans anymore. But I figured we had a better chance of finding someone to take us west if they thought we were two boys instead of a boy and a girl. Besides, being a boy was more fun. Nobody told me to mind my manners or keep to the wagons or that young ladies shouldn't run across the prairie the way I did. I could ride Outlaw astride, and it sure was more comfortable wearing pants than a long skirt and petticoats that dragged in the dirt. I wasn't in any hurry to turn back into a female.

Still, I did a girl's work. After I figured out how to cook, we ate good. I sewed up a rip in Ben's pants, telling him Ma had made me learn to sew because she didn't have any girls at home. I washed me and Boots's clothes when we camped by a stream, although not Ben's. He didn't want them washed, because he said the dirt softened the buckskin.

Ben had warned us about Indians, but I didn't see what all the fuss was. The first ones we met were a family who came into the camp just as we were unhitching the oxen. The wagon master got jumpity and asked Ben whether we ought to put the wagons in a circle. "Most likely, they're spies, checking to see what we got."

"Most likely, they're hungry and want to trade for food," Ben told him, fanning himself with his hat, because it was so hot. "If an Indian scouts, he don't come begging to a wagon train. He watches you from afar where you can't see him. Look at that horse they got. That's no war pony. It couldn't outrun a chicken. And an Indian don't take his wife and young 'uns with him when he's making war, neither." Ben shook his head.

"Should we hide ourselves?" one of the spinsters asked Ben.

He told them not to worry. "Indians ain't partial to old maids."

"Sir!" one of them said.

"Yes, ma'am?" He stared at the woman until she turned away, and then he winked at me. "Indians want a woman that behaves. Any Indian that took that one would throw her back," he said. I didn't know if the woman heard, but she straightened her shoulders and raised her nose in the air.

"She'd drown in a rainstorm," I whispered.

Ben said sternly, "I expect she'll have to forgive you for that." But the corners of his mouth turned up when he said it. He watched the woman walk away and added, "I got to say that while they're first-class suggesters when there's a thing to be decided, those two biddies pull their own weight. They're usually right about their suggestions, too. They ain't asked for quarter. There ain't many women that can yoke an ox the way they can."

The Indians came up to our wagon then. They were dressed peculiar, the man in old Union Army pants with the center part cut out and a buckskin apron called a breechcloth hanging over himself. He wore a dirty vest and a woman's blouse that had been white once but was now caked with dirt.

The man sat on the horse, while his wife, who wore a buckskin dress with a man's red shirt over it, walked beside him with two little boys, who wore nothing but moccasins.

"An uncivilized custom," one of the spinsters said.

"Ain't no different from Adam," Ben told her.

"Well, this is not the Garden of Eden," she flung back.

"No, it surely is not. More like Sheol," her companion added, wiping her forehead with her sleeve. It surely was as hot as hell.

Ben tied his horse to the back of the wagon and went over

to the Indians and made some kind of gesture. I guess it was
the Indian way of saying howdy.

"Hello. Got tobac?" the Indian asked. He grabbed Ben's
hand and shook it like you would a pump.

"No tobac," Ben told him.

"God damn. Bees-kit?" the Indian asked.

"Nope. We ain't got biscuits."

"Swap."

Instead of answering him, Ben began making gestures
with his hands. When Ben was finished, the Indian made
his own signals. "Sign language," Ben told me and Boots
over his shoulder. "That's the way Indians talk when they
don't know each other's language. He wants flour and a dab
of trinkets, and he'll trade a toy bow and two arrows for it.
You want 'em, Boots?"

"Yes, sir!" Boots's eyes shone. He'd never had any toys
except for a wooden gun I'd carved for him after Pa left.

Ben handed Boots the bow and arrows. They were first
class. Even I could see that. The bow was decorated with
feathers and beads, and the points of the arrows were as sharp
as knives.

Ben palavered with his hands a little more, then said,
"Haidie, fetch me that red neckerchief that's in the sack
hanging in the back of the wagon. The sack's where I keep
my trade goods. Might as well bring the string of blue beads,
too."

I climbed into the wagon and handed down the two
items. The Indian reached for them, but Ben wouldn't give
them up. The two bargained some more. Then the Indian
woman reached into her dress and pulled out a buckskin doll

with horsehair on its head, its mouth a cluster of beads. The eyes were beads, too—one red, one green. She held it out. Ben scoffed, as if to say we didn't want any dolls.

But I held out my hand and took the doll. I was too old for toys. Besides, I was a boy now. But like Boots, I'd never had a toy in my life, and I loved that little buckskin girl. "I got a dollar hid away," I said to Ben. "I bet I could sell this in Denver." It wouldn't do to let Ben know I wanted it for myself.

"That's too much. Besides, they ain't got a use for hard coin." He bargained some more with the man, then told me to get a scoopful of flour and put it into the woman's buckskin sack. "Break off a piece of that sugar cone, too, for the boys."

After I'd done what he'd asked, Ben handed the flour and the sugar to the woman, then gave the man the kerchief and beads. The Indian tied the scarf around his arm, but instead of giving the woman the beads, he put them over his head.

"Hey, they're for her," I said, pointing to the woman.

Ben shook his head. "She's lucky if she gets a taste of that sugar."

"But I bet she made the doll."

The Indians had nothing else to trade, but they still hung around camp. Ben talked to them in signs, and they took off, the man riding the horse, the woman and boys walking alongside.

"Indians don't look dangerous to me," I told Ben.

He sniffed. "Don't be so sure. You ain't seen a real Indian brave yet. There's no man on earth more fit than an Indian warrior. And there's no sight that sends chills up your spine like a passel of them coming toward you on their war ponies, whooping and hollering and holding up their bows and arrows. A few's got rifles now, too. I hope you never see such a sight."

Just the idea made me shiver a little. "You think the Indians will attack us?"

Ben shrugged. "Maybe not, if we're careful. We got to ride in each other's dust, not strung out like we have been. And we got to keep a sharp eye out."

"But you're the scout."

"I can't be everywhere. But don't you worry yourself, young son. Most trains get through just fine."

* * *

I liked it out on the prairie. You could see all the way to tomorrow and back to yesterday, without a house or a tree to block the view. There were jackrabbits and squirrels and those cowardly coyotes. I spotted animals I'd never seen before—sage hens, which made awful good eating, and antelope. The antelope were curious as chickens and would come running if you held up a red neckerchief on a stick. But they were skittish too, and if they got spooked, they'd take off across the prairie, disappearing before their dust settled. Sometimes Ben shot one of them, and we had antelope steaks, threaded on sticks and held over the fire, for supper.

There were birds I'd never seen either, and fish and snakes and rodents. One of the old maids found a dead mouse in her flour barrel. "I guess we will have to sift out the little fellow and his calling cards," she said, which surprised me, since spinsters were supposed to screech and jump on chairs when they saw a mouse. I'd have thought she'd go hungry before she'd eat the flour, but she used it for flapjacks that night.

The animal I really wanted to see was a buffalo. Ben said there were herds of buffalo as far as you could see, moving like waves in a big black ocean. "Worst thing I ever saw was a buffaler stampede. Why, if you got in the way, you'd get flattened ten feet in the ground," he told me.

"What's a stampede?"

"It's when the whole herd gets a notion to move, and they just go, running as fast as they can, with a sound like thunder out of hell. They make the earth shake. Sometimes they get set off by lightning. But other times, it's Indians. The Indians'll get the herd going toward a cliff, and half of the buffaler falls over. Then the Indians pick 'em off, if they're not already dead."

I kept a sharp lookout for buffalo, but I never could spot them. Then one day, Ben pointed out some specks on the horizon. "Buffaler," he said.

I squinted at them. They were no bigger than lap dogs, and I was disappointed. "By golly, they're not so much," I said.

"You just wait, young Haidie. They'll be big as a house when we get up close. You know how to shoot a gun, do you? I never asked before."

"Yes, sir."

"Well, if you think you're cut out to shoot a buffaler, I got an extra gun for you. What say we get us a shaggy? Go ask one of the Samuels boys to help Boots with the wagon. We could be gone a time."

I went off to the Samuels wagon and told Mr. Samuels me

and Ben were going after buffalo and would one of his boys
please help Boots with the oxen.

"Buffalo? Why, I'd like to shoot one my own self," Mr.
Samuels said. "You tell Bondurant I'll be along directly."

"Damn me!" Ben said after I returned to our wagon and
told him that Mr. Samuels was going with us. "You can't
never trust him. He don't have no more idea than a yellow-
legged chicken how to shoot a buffaler."

"We could give him the cold shake," I suggested. But
Ben pointed out that Mr. Samuels would come chasing after
us, so there was nothing to do about it but let him come
along.

He joined us in a minute, all lathered up and shouting
"Huzza!" Ben told him to hush, because he didn't want any
more farmers taking out with us. "That's no herd out there.
Likely it's just a few buffaler that's wandered off." He studied
the air a moment, then told us to follow him. Instead of going directly to the animals, Ben led us in a roundabout way.

"I thought we was going to shoot buffalo," Mr. Samuels
said.

"You don't want 'em to smell us, do you?" Ben gave Mr.
Samuels a scornful look.

Ben took off north of the buffalo. I fell in behind him on
Outlaw, but Mr. Samuels squeezed between us, telling me,
"Boy, you stay behind. This is men's work."

"Boy rides with me," Ben said. "Haidie, come alongside."
Mr. Samuels glared at me as I came up abreast of Ben.

I guess the buffalo didn't see us as we circled around them,
because they didn't pay any attention. Ben was right. They
were as big as a house, humpbacked with huge heads that

were covered with shaggy hair, and had spindly legs. They weren't much of a herd, Ben said, but to me they looked like all the buffalo in the world. Mr. Samuels raised his gun to shoot, but Ben grabbed it. "You ever shot a buffalo, Samuels?"

"Can't be much different from shooting a cow."

"Oh, you shoot cows, do you?"

Mr. Samuels didn't reply, but he lowered his gun.

We were near a coulee, and Ben dismounted and tied his horse to a dead tree, and we crept along until we got a hundred yards from the herd. "Now you get a bead on the one you want—" Ben began, but just then, Mr. Samuels raised his gun and fired. That gunshot set off the herd, and they stampeded, just like Ben had told me they would. I felt the earth shake as they thundered off, and in what seemed no more than a minute, they faded into the distance in a huge cloud of dust, running about a thousand miles away.

"I winged one. He won't go far," Mr. Samuels said.

"Oh, you did, did you? Well, you go chase him if you want to. Chances are if you hit one, he'll carry the bullet for the next fifty years. You're a blammity-blam fool, Samuels."

"I won't take that from you, Bondurant. I'm the wagon master."

"And not much of one at that."

I reckoned the two of them would get into a fistfight, but at that moment, we saw an old buffalo come walking up over a rise, and Ben put out his arm and said, "Hush up. You spoil this, Samuels, and I'll tell everyone in the wagon train about it."

"I expect he's deaf and didn't hear the others run off," Mr. Samuels said in a low voice.

"And didn't feel the earth a'shaking, neither," Ben replied, rolling his eyes. "Now you hold your fire till I tell you. We'll just wait patient."

We slipped down into the coulee and hid behind a dead cottonwood tree. There was a stream near us, and Ben reckoned the buffalo had come for a drink. "We'll just stay put until he reaches that water. Then when I give the word, all three of us will shoot."

Ben turned to me. "A buffaler ain't the easiest thing to kill. His hide's as tough as an oak tree, and a bullet can get lost in his beard. Now tenderfoots'll shoot him in the head, but he won't hardly feel it there. The way to kill a buffaler is to shoot him in his heart or his lungs."

"Where are they?" I asked.

"Just beneath the shoulders." Ben studied me a moment. "Just aim at the buffaler, young son. That gun you got shoots a might high, so figure that in. Think you could hit a house?"

"Yes, sir."

The buffalo was heading directly toward the water, and I could hear my heart pounding, thinking he might attack if he saw us. Up close, he seemed even bigger than a house, more like the size of a barn, and I figured he could trample all three of us without raising a sweat.

The buffalo wasn't in any hurry. He walked slowly toward the water, grunting and snorting, his legs looking like they'd break under all that weight. "On three," Ben whispered. "We all fire at the same time. Ready?" He looked at me, and I nodded. He glanced at Mr. Samuels, but the man wouldn't catch Ben's eye. Ben raised his gun and steadied it, and I did the same thing. Then Ben said slowly, "One. Two. Three."

There were three gunshots, but they sounded like one, because we'd all fired at the same instant. The buffalo stopped, but he didn't seem any more hurt than if he'd been bitten by a horsefly. He snorted and shook his big head, turning it a little as the eye on the right side of his head sought us out.

"Again," Ben said. We'd reloaded, and we all shot a second time.

The buffalo was stunned then. He rolled his eyes and seemed to hunch his shoulders, making himself even bigger. He bellowed and pawed the earth, lowering and shaking his head, blood running out of his nostrils. Then he gave an enormous bellow and fell over, kicking his feet fast, at first, then slower and slower, until at last he was still.

Mr. Samuels jumped up and raised his gun in the air, stamped his feet, and shouted, "Huzza! Huzza! I got me a buffalo!"

"*You* got him?" Ben scoffed. "That's a ripper, all right." Then he muttered to me, "Likely, his bullet got the buffaler through the tail." I looked and saw that the buffalo's tail was indeed severed from the body.

Mr. Samuels didn't pay Ben any attention, just ran to the animal, then stopped. "Now what?" he asked.

"You get out your knife, and we'll butcher him."

"I didn't bring one."

"I figured ye didn't. How 'bout something to carry the meat in?"

Mr. Samuels shook his head.

Ben nodded. He got out a wicked knife and sharpened it on a whetstone. "I'd make you cut your own meat, but you're liable to ruin the knife." He sliced open the buffalo and ripped away the hide. Then he butchered the animal, handing the liver, the hump meat, and the ribs to Mr. Samuels to put into the bags that Ben had tied onto Stormy, who he'd brought along for a packhorse. When we had as much as the horses could carry, Ben wiped his knife on his pants and stood up.

"What about the hide?" Mr. Samuels asked.

"You want it, you get it."

Mr. Samuels must not have wanted it much, because we left it there on the prairie.

When we got back to camp, Mr. Samuels took his meat to his wagon, but Ben handed out most of ours to the other travelers, including the old maids.

"Mr. Samuels tells a thrilling tale of how he cornered the buffalo," one of them told us.

"That story is highly undependable."

She narrowed her eyes at Ben, as if she was deciding whether to believe him.

"The way Samuels tells it, he shot the buffaler by himself. That tail shot was as close as he come. His other one went wide," Ben told me later on, after he had built a fire and the chunk of buffalo hump was roasting in a kettle.

"Then why don't you tell folks?" I asked.

Ben considered that as he watched me dump a handful of sage into the pan. Corny had taught me about sage. "Truth is, your shot could have been the one that got him. But if I told it about that Samuels had been outshot by a boy, he'd be mad and take it out on you. Sometimes it pays to let the other feller take the glory, even if he don't deserve it. And it don't hurt you none. There's reasons. Think on it, young Haidie."

While I was pondering that, Marianna Marble came up to us and asked for a piece of buffalo. She was crossing with her husband, and she reminded me of the women I'd seen on Red Feather Road. It wasn't just that she wore satin and velvet and a hat with an ostrich plume, while the other women in the wagon train dressed in calico, their skirts hemmed to their boot tops. It was her attitude. She skinned up to the men and looked at them with hog eyes before she asked them for favors and sometimes when she didn't even want favors. Ben said she was as hot as a billy goat in a pepper patch, which I did not fully understand until I thought about how much Teresa liked connection.

If that was what Mrs. Marble was after, it surely was not with me, because she caught me staring at her once and said, "What you looking at, boy? You see something you like?"

When I replied, "No, ma'am," she called me fresh.

"Is she a hoor?" I asked Ben.

"Maybe not one that gets hard money for it," he answered. "She will bear watching."

As far as I could see she wasn't much of a wife. She made her husband do the cooking, and I never saw her at the streams we crossed, washing Mr. Marble's shirts.

Now she gave Ben that piggy-eyed look as she asked him for the buffalo meat. "Hump, mind you. I won't eat the inferior parts."

"There's a little piece left," he said.

She told me, "Well, then. Boy, call me when it's cooked."

And such was Mrs. Marble's command of people that I did just that.

❋ ❋ ❋

We were more than halfway to Denver by now, and the farther we went, the more scared I got about Indians. I wasn't
the only one who was worried. Some of the men began carrying their guns with them when they walked beside the
wagons, which was a danger in itself, since one tripped and
shot off his dog's nose. And I overheard one of the spinsters
tell the other, "We must be prepared, dear. We are well aware
of the depredations."

I didn't know what a deprivation was, but I reckoned it
had something to do with being made to marry an Indian.
"Oh, don't worry, ma'am," I told her. "Ben Bondurant says if
they captured you, they'd throw you back."

She laughed and said, "Take consolation, sister. It appears
we are safe."

Her sister remarked, "Not all the insolents in this country are red Indians."

I had to think about that for a minute before I realized
she meant me.

Every now and then, we saw a bunch of braves riding back
and forth on the horizon or one or two kneeling or standing
beside their horses, watching us. "Them's the ones we have
to look out for," Ben said, "them and the ones you can't see.
When you don't see Indians, that's when they're the thickest."

"Have you seen them?" I asked.

"Have I seen the ones you can't see?" he asked by way
of pointing out what I'd said didn't make sense. "No, but I
think maybe there's a passel of 'em back over the hills."

"I wish we had that ugly dog Tige."

"That sure was some ugly dog, all right," Ben said. He wasn't looking at me but far off in the distance where the wind was blowing up the dust. "Haidie, go get Samuels," he said suddenly.

Something in his voice made me jump to. "Yes, sir," I said, telling Boots to mind the oxen. Mr. Samuels was at the head of the line of wagons, sitting on his horse while his boys drove the oxen. I rushed up to him on Outlaw and said, "Ben Bondurant wants to see you."

"Well, I'm right here. Can't he see?"

"He wants you to go to him."

"He does, does he? I'm the wagon master. I don't answer to him."

"Please, sir," I said. "I think it's important."

"Then he can act proper and come over here."

Mrs. Samuels leaned out of the wagon and said, "Man is unmannered. Don't let him play you finer."

"Samuels!" Ben bellowed. "Didn't the boy tell you to come over to where I was? I wasn't sure myself until a minute ago what it was. I could have used another pair of eyes. We got Indians coming."

"What do we do?"

"You get the wagons in a circle, and you do it fast. Now."

Mr. Samuels got down off his horse and began yelling at the oxen, while his wife picked up a whip and flicked it over their heads. Ben swatted Mr. Samuels on the side of the head and yelled, "Your wife and boys can do that. You got to tell the rest of the wagons to circle. Ain't you the wagon master?"

But Mr. Samuels was in such a panic that he didn't hear Ben.

Ben grabbed the lead oxen of the Samuels wagon and began to turn them. As he did, he ordered, "Haidie, you tell the others to get them wagons in a circle and do it fast. Tell them that dust means Indians. I'll be along directly, after I get these oxen turned."

"Yes, sir!" I said, kicking Outlaw. I rushed along the line of wagons, yelling, "Indians! Corral your wagons!"

There was a good deal of confusion then, although the men had been taught what to do. When we'd started out from Omaha, Ben had made everyone practice putting the wagons in a circle.

"You're scaring the women," a man had chided Ben.

"Yessir, pilgrim, that's just what I aim to do."

"Can't we outrun the Indians?" a woman had asked.

"No, ma'am. A two-legged horse could outrun an ox."

Each night for weeks, Ben had given the order to corral the wagons, the wagon tongues toward the center, the wheels of one wagon adjacent to the next, the stock safe inside the circle. So now, when I gave the order, the men fell to. So did the women, urging the oxen to turn, gathering up the children and thrusting them inside the wagons, shooing the animals inside the growing circle. As soon as the wagons were in place, Ben yelled at the men to get their guns. That was something else Ben had taught us: the men would shoot, while the women reloaded.

After I warned everybody about the Indians, I rushed to our wagon, which Boots had already turned and put into place. He had taken out the guns, too, and was searching for the bullets. "You think Ben will let me fire a gun?" he asked. Boots had been disappointed that he hadn't gone on our buffalo hunt and was itching to shoot something. "I'd sure like to get me an Indian."

"This isn't any game, Boots. Those fellows mean to kill us," I said, watching my brother's face as he suddenly understood what was happening.

"You don't think we'll get hurt, do you, Haidie?"

I shook my head, but I wasn't so sure, and I was afraid. By then, the Indians were more than a cloud of dust. I could hear them yelling, and I thought I saw splotches of paint on their bare bodies.

"Don't let nothing happen to you, Haidie. I don't want to be an orphan again." Boots looked ready to cry.

"Ben'll protect us," I said, as much to reassure me as Boots.

Ben had come upon us then, had loosed his horses. "You won't let anything happen to Haidie, will you?" Boots asked, his voice trembling. Boots was more worried about being left alone than he was about getting killed.

"Blamed if I would," Ben told him. He picked up his rifle and the shotgun. "Get under the wagon." He turned to me. "When I hand you a gun, you reload, you understand?"

"Boots can do that. Don't you want me to shoot, too?" I asked.

"You think ye could kill a savage? It ain't the same as shooting a buffaler. Killing a man's harder on the soul than killing a critter." He thought that over for a second. "Well, most times."

"I could do it if he was going to shoot Boots."

Ben didn't say anything but handed me the shotgun. "Boots can reload," he said. "Now get ready. They's a'coming."

I thought we'd have a whole tribe of Indians attacking us, but there were only ten or fifteen, their faces painted with red-and-black designs that would scare a ghost. Only one or two had rifles, but Ben had told us that an Indian with a bow and arrow was more deadly than just about any white man with a rifle, and quicker, too. A red man could fit an arrow into his bow faster than you could reload a gun.

As we crawled under the wagon, Ben yelled to the men, "Let 'em get close before you shoot. No need to waste ammunition." I doubted that anybody heard him, because some of them had already begun shooting. They hadn't hit anything but the dirt, however. I watched as Ben held his rifle steady, sighting with one eye. Then he called, "Spit fire at 'em!" and he squeezed the trigger. An Indian slumped over and fell off his horse.

"You got him," I said.

"He's still moving. See if you can do better."

I held up the shotgun, waiting until an Indian came close. Waiting beneath that wagon was the hardest thing I'd ever done, worse than when I lay under Boots's bed at the orphanage the night we ran away. I wanted to shoot just to get it over with, but I knew my chance of hitting an Indian was better if I waited until he got close. I sighted on an Indian mounted on a chestnut horse that had black circles painted around his eyes, which made him look like a devil horse. He scared me as much as the Indian did. I remembered what Ben had said when we went after buffalo, that the gun shot high, so I lowered it a little just before I fired. I lowered it too much, however, and instead of shooting the Indian, I killed his horse. The Indian jumped off just as the horse fell. I hadn't even nicked him, and he started for us. But at that moment, Ben fired, and the Indian fell. "Me and you got him," Ben said. Without looking, he handed the gun back to Boots and grabbed the shotgun from him and fired at another Indian.

That Indian went over his horse's head onto the ground and lay still. A few wagons away from us, another Indian crashed into the ground. I heard a man shout, "Huzza!" and knew Ben wasn't the only one who had gotten a savage.

Then I heard a scream, and a woman cried, "Josiah!" She gave a long, shrill wail after that, and in a moment, Mr. Samuels was at our wagon.

"Josiah Marble's got gut-shot with a arrow," he said. "He ain't going to make it." I wondered if the Indian had been aiming for the ostrich feather on Mrs. Marble's hat.

"Well, what do you want me to do?" Ben asked, not looking up.

"Give him something, make him stop screaming. Can't you hear it?"

"You want me to put down this rifle to play nursemaid? Do it yourself, man."

"Ben!" I yelled. An Indian had come up close, and I didn't have the shotgun, because Boots was loading it. But before Ben could pick off the Indian, there was a shot, and the Indian fell off his horse.

"Got him, sister," a voice called, and I glanced at the wagon next to us to see both of the old maids holding guns.

Ben chuckled and said, "Can you beat that!"

Mr. Samuels, who was still with us, shook his head and said, "Those women are unsexed."

"You'd rather the Indian shot you?" Ben scoffed. "Get away, Samuels. Give that man some whiskey to ease him."

"Where'd I find whiskey?"

"In the drawer of the bureau in your wagon," I said, remembering that Jake had helped Mr. Samuels load his belongings and had told us about the whiskey.

The fighting had tapered off. We'd beat the Indians. They were gathering up their dead and wounded and starting off.

"Huzza! Huzza!" a boy called, as the Indians rode off. Someone else yelled, "Run away, you cowards!"

I guess that riled the savages some, because one of them turned and fired his rifle into the wagons. I heard an "Oof!" sound next to me, and one of the old maids rolled onto her side. "Sister, I am shot," she cried.

Ben handed his rifle to Boots and crawled over beside her. Then he called, "Haidie, fetch me that medicine box from the wagon."

The man who'd been hit with an arrow had stopped yelling, and I figured he was dead. Men were calming the animals and checking them for injuries, while the mothers let the children loose to run around inside the circle. Three or four women were on their knees, thanking God for delivering us. Slowly they became aware that one of the old maids was injured, and several of the women hurried to the wagon, bringing water and cloths.

"Dern savage shot her," Ben said, when I handed him the medicine chest.

A woman gasped, while another said, "We are here to aid, Mr. Bondurant."

"'Bliged," Ben said, "but me and Haidie is up to it."

I blanched. I didn't know what we were up to, but I had an idea, and I didn't want to deal with any gunshot wound. I sneaked into the wagon on the other side of the old maid. She was lying on her back, her arms stretched out, perspiration running down her face, which was white. She'd begun to shake. I didn't see anything wrong with her until I looked down at where her left hand ought to be and saw it was a mess of raw meat. It had been beat all to smash. "She got her hand shot off," Ben told me.

I turned away, thinking I'd be sick, but I swallowed down the bile so as not to embarrass myself.

"The hand's got to go. Ain't no way to save it. You want me to take it off?" Ben asked the other old maid.

"Don't talk about me as if I'm not lying right here," the wounded woman muttered.

"She will have to give you permission herself." The old maid turned to her sister and said, "Lizzie, you heard what Mr. Bondurant said. Do you wish to have your hand cut off?"

I expected a simple yes or no, but wounded like she was, the woman was still proper. "I do not wish it at all, Arvilla. But there is no choice. Cut away, sir."

"Anybody got whiskey?" Ben asked the women standing around.

"I do," the other spinster said. "Haidie, will you fetch the bottle just inside the wagon. It is wrapped in a red-and-white quilt."

"Arvilla," Miss Lizzie whispered, and Miss Arvilla had to

lean down now to hear her sister. "Tell him to fetch the quilt, too. I'm as cold as Greenland."

"And bring a basin filled with flour," Ben added.

When I returned, Miss Arvilla uncorked the bottle and held it to her sister's lips. Miss Lizzie took a whale of a gulp, and then another. Miss Arvilla put the quilt over her sister as gently as if she'd been a baby. Then she clutched Miss Lizzie's good hand, while Ben examined the other and shook his head. He told me to find a stick for Lizzie to bite on when he did the cutting. I picked up a stick the size of a finger, wiped it on my pants, and put it into her mouth. Then I knelt down next to Ben, who was fixing to take off what was left of the hand with a small saw he'd removed from the medicine chest. He glanced at the sisters, and when Miss Arvilla nodded, he sawed through Miss Lizzie's wrist and handed me the amputated hand. It couldn't have taken a minute. "We'll bury it so the dogs don't get it," he said. He thrust the old maid's stump into the basin of flour for a few minutes. Then he placed some herbs from the medicine chest around it and wrapped it in a clean cloth that one of the women handed him.

"Will she be all right?" Miss Arvilla asked.

Ben shook his head. "Too soon to tell. Keep her hand dosed with whiskey. Keep *her* dosed, too. She'll need it, and when you run out, let me know. I'll find more. Haidie'll cook up some broth with the buffaler that's left. Your sister's thin as gold leaf, but broth ought to give her strength. Don't think nothing of it if she says her fingers hurt. That's the way of it." He turned to me. "Come on, Haidie, we'll make a place for her to ride in her wagon. I don't suppose Samuels will let us lay by a day. We'll have to go at first light."

The two of us climbed into the old maids' wagon and
began rearranging the trunks and crates.

"She didn't even cry out," I said.

"I never saw a woman so stout outside an Indian. She held
up better than any soldier I ever seen. Them sisters has got
iron."

We shoved two of the crates together, and Ben grunted.
"Furniture, most likely. Marble tops. Why's women got to
have so many fool things?"

I fetched a pile of quilts and put them on top of the crates
for a mattress. Then me and Ben picked up Miss Lizzie and
laid her on top of the bed we'd made. She didn't weigh any
more than a lace hanky. She was still passed out, but she was
moaning now.

"Don't you worry about supper. I'll fetch it to you. My
boy's already took care of your oxen," one of the women said,
as Miss Arvilla climbed into the wagon next to her sister.
Another whispered, "We got whiskey if you run out."

Miss Arvilla nodded her thanks, and Ben and I started
to climb down from the wagon. But Miss Arvilla took Ben's
hand in both of hers and said, "How can I thank you, Mr.
Bondurant? If my sister lives, it will be due to you." She
paused a moment and added, "And to you, too, Haidie."

＊ ＊ ＊

We stayed put the rest of the day, because we had a bury-
ing to attend to. I'd never paid much attention to Josiah
Marble, and as far as I could tell, his wife, Marianna, hadn't
either, at least not since we'd left the Missouri. I heard her
tell Mrs. Tappan that when she married Mr. Marble, "He was

worth fifteen thousand dollars. Today, he isn't worth fifteen cents."

Now that Mr. Marble was dead, however, she carried on as if he'd been her true love all along. She sobbed and screamed and would have fainted, I figured, but there wasn't anybody close enough to catch her.

Despite Mrs. Marble making a fool of herself, I couldn't help but feel sorry for her. How could she yoke her oxen and drive them all by herself? Shoot, she couldn't even build a campfire.

"Oh, don't you worry about it," Ben said. "A woman like that always makes out."

We had gathered beside a grave that the men had dug. Reverend Tappan read from the Bible, then talked about God and vengeance and repentance, and prayed so long that someone muttered, "Give us a rest."

Reverend Tappan raised his head and sent a black look over us, but he finally said, "Amen."

"It is his first burial service, and he does want the Lord to approve," Mrs. Tappan told me.

We sang "The Old One Hundred" and "O Come, All Ye Faithful." Then the men lowered Mr. Marble's body into the grave and covered it with dirt. At that, Mrs. Marble began to cry and carry on again. She said she wanted to jump into the grave with her husband, but instead, she threw herself at Reverend Tappan and said she didn't want to live.

Mrs. Tappan patted Mrs. Marble on the hand and told her that from then on, she would take her meals with the Tappans, which I thought was a Christianly thing to do, seeing as how Mrs. Tappan had lent her sewing box to Mrs.

Marble and when she went to get it back, it wasn't to be found. "My husband and I will help with your wagon," she added.

"You see," Ben said to me. "That woman'll doubtless be all right. I ain't so sure about that sin-buster."

* * *

Miss Lizzie lived just fine. In a week, she was driving the oxen, holding the whip in her good hand. Ben said he'd never seen anybody recover so fast.

"I'm real sorry, Miss Lizzie," I said, feeling responsible for her. Maybe if I'd got that first Indian, things would have turned out different.

I thought she'd be downright mean about her hand getting shot off. After all, she and Miss Arvilla hadn't been all that nice before. But instead, she said, "Now, don't you worry about me, Haidie. The Good Lord saw fit to give me a second hand, and thanks be to Him, that hand's the one I use for writing. And He gave me a sister to button my dress. She and I could have hired a driver and servants to go west, but we wanted to prove two women were every bit as good as two men. Well, I guess I have made my bed."

"No, ma'am, me and Ben made your bed. We moved those crates together so's you'd be more comfortable. They were awful heavy. What's in them anyway?"

"Why, can't you guess?"

"Furniture maybe."

Miss Lizzie shook her head.

"Whiskey?"

Miss Lizzie looked shocked, but then she smiled and said,

"You assume I am an imbiber because I was drunk as a fiddler when my hand was taken."

"That is doubtless correct." Miss Arvilla laughed.

Miss Lizzie smiled at her sister, then said to me, "The bottle was brought along for medicinal purposes. My sister knows I never got a taste of whiskey in my life until that day. Yes, it was my first taste of whiskey." She glanced at Miss Arvilla and added, "But perhaps not the last." Then she said to me, "No, dear, the crates do not contain spirits. They are filled with books."

"Books!" I'd never heard anything so foolish. From what Ben had said, half the gold-seekers couldn't even read. "Who'd want to buy a book in Denver?"

"We are not planning on doing commerce. My sister and I have a brother living in Denver, a Mr. Matchett. He is a banker and one of the town's leading citizens, not that that means much in a place that is as new as a chick. But he believes Denver one day will be a metropolis and is anxious to bring culture to the city. So he has invited my sister and me to open a school for girls. We have brought books to teach reading and ciphering and deportment. We expect to open in the fall. It will not be just for the quality but for all who wish to improve themselves."

"Oh" was all I could say. We were walking alongside the old maids' oxen, and I heard Boots holler. "I got to go," I said and started to turn away.

"Haidie," Miss Arvilla called.

I turned around. "Yes, ma'am."

"If you would care to be our first pupil, my sister and I would be pleased to accept you without charge."

I thanked her and took a couple of steps. But then I stopped and looked around at Miss Arvilla. "I thought you said it would be a *girls'* school."

Her thin lips turned up at the corners. "We would make an exception."

Chapter Six

Miss Lizzie's hand had scabbed over by the time we reached Mingo, which Ben told us was the wickedest town between Omaha and Denver.

"What's that mean?" Boots asked.

"It means cowboys and gunfighters and imbibers and ladies in short skirts," I explained.

"Or no skirts at all," Ben added slyly.

"Why'd anybody want to see that?" Boots asked.

"Son, you got some growing up to do," Ben told him. "I expect we'll refuge here for a spell. I'd like the satisfaction of a drink." He looked me over, then shook his head, and I realized I would not get that same satisfaction.

"Look at that sign up there. What do you think of that name for a saloon?" I asked, pointing to "Lucky Duck" written on a board hung from a building.

"I don't know," Ben said. "I can't read." He headed for the door.

I didn't see any of those gunfighters—or naked ladies, either—only a couple of cowboys who weren't any cleaner than we were and a drunk stumbling out of a second saloon.

But heck, I'd seen drunks before. Shoot, I'd seen Pa drunker than that man, and maybe Ma, too. So Mingo didn't surprise me. It was just a dusty, dirty town with scalped log buildings that looked ready to sink into the ground.

Still, it had been a long time since we'd seen a town, and we were mighty glad to be there. Some of the men went into the saloon, while the women crowded into the mercantile to gawk at the goods, which were mostly covered with dust and fly specks. At home, nobody would have given them a second glance, but after three months on the prairie, the women were hungry for a look at what they called civilization, not that a spool of white thread, turned gray from the dirt, could be called civilized. The thread had sat there since the beginning of time. Judging from the ragged clothes on the local folks, I guessed they didn't do much sewing.

Miss Arvilla pushed through the women crowded around the counter and asked if there was a doctor in Mingo.

"We got a barber," the shopkeeper said, laughing at his joke.

"My sister does not need her hair cut, sir. Her hand was shot off by an Indian." Miss Arvilla glared at the man, who shuffled his feet behind the counter and pulled at his beard.

"Well, then, go in the far saloon and ask for Doc. He's the best we got. Hell, he's the only we got. It being early in the day, he might be sober."

Miss Arvilla grabbed hold of my shirt and told me to come along.

After Miss Lizzie got hurt, I figured Miss Arvilla would ask Ben to make me do her cooking or lead her oxen or gather buffalo chips, those big circles of buffalo dung that we now used for fires. But she did none of that. When I offered to help, she told me, "We will not ask further of you. You are both mother and father to your brother, a faithful companion to Mr. Bondurant, and you have proved a worthy friend to my sister and me. You did not flinch or turn aside when called upon to aid in her surgery. And now you are offering to be an even greater friend to us. We shall not forget your kindness when we reach Denver, Haidie."

I followed her to the farther saloon, which did not have a name, as far as I could see, where she told me to go inside and find Doc, it not being fit for a maiden lady to go into the doors of a den of iniquity, as she put it. I did what she asked, going up to the man behind a bar where bottles were lined up. He was polishing a glass with a dirty rag, and since there wasn't any washbasin near him, I thought he didn't wash the glasses, only wiped them out. That was of no consequence, I believed, since the whiskey he served would probably kill anything left in the glass.

"I'm looking for Doc," I said, and the bartender jerked his head at a man who was sitting by himself at a table, a bottle and a glass in front of him. I went over and stood beside him until he looked up.

He studied me for a moment. "You touch that bottle, boy, and I'll wring your arm off."

"I don't want any whiskey."

"Then what are you doing inside a barroom?" He sounded sober enough. "Does a young snot like you think you can buy it by the dribble?"

"Sir, are you a doctor?"

"Well, I am and I am not. Who wants to know?"

"There's an old maid outside that needs your help."

He snorted. "There's a lavish plenty of old maids been after me."

I took his meaning. "This one doesn't want *you*. She needs a doctor."

"Tell her to come in here."

"She thinks it isn't fitting, her being a maiden lady and this being a den of iniquity."

"Oh, one of your high-toned biddies, too good for the likes of Mingo."

"No, sir, she's a right nice lady." I looked around for Ben, but he had gone to the Lucky Duck, and I didn't recognize any of the other men from our wagon train. There'd been a lot of talking when I came in, but now the men in the bar quieted down to listen to us. I put my hands into the pockets of my overalls and kept my head down.

"It is an ill-convenient time for me to leave," he said, glancing at the bottle. "If she wants to see me, she can come in here." He looked around the room to see whether the others heard and approved. Nobody said anything.

The doctor poured himself another drink. I could stay there and argue with him while he got drunk or go fetch Miss Arvilla and Miss Lizzie, which is what I did.

"You tried your best," Miss Arvilla said. "Come, sister, I believe the man's expertise must be of dubious quality, but I would feel some little assured if he examined your hand." They followed me back into the saloon, and the three of us stood beside the table.

The doctor knew we were there, but he stared at the bottle

and helped himself again. Finally, he turned his head, running his eyes up and down Miss Arvilla. When he saw the look on her face, he stood up and said, "Ladies." He made a grand gesture, taking off his hat and bowing, then indicating they were to sit down. They remained standing.

"We understand you are a doctor, although what sort of doctor keeps office hours in a saloon, I would not know," Miss Arvilla said tartly.

"The only doctor in town," he replied.

"You will have to do until we reach Denver. My sister's hand was shot off. The circumstances are of no consequence, so I will not elaborate. Mr. Benjamin Bondurant of our train amputated it. He is a man of uncommon abilities. I would have you look at it to see if it is healing properly."

The doctor thought that over and nodded. Then he said, "Well, I can't do it standing up. Sit down, ladies." Miss Lizzie sat beside the doctor, and Miss Arvilla next to her. And as I was a lady, even if I didn't look like one, I sat, too. Miss Lizzie held out her arm and removed the bandage. The doctor leaned over and peered at it. Then he picked up the arm none too gently and moved it back and forth. Miss Lizzie winced, but she kept still, pursing her lips together.

Some of the men got up from their tables and came over to look at the arm until I moved behind Miss Lizzie to block the view and Miss Arvilla stared them down. "Gentlemen, have you nothing better to do? This is not your affair," she told them.

They didn't pay her any mind, and one asked, "Shot it off, did you? Ladies shouldn't play around with guns."

That made me boiling mad, and I said, "An Indian did it. Miss Lizzie knows how to handle a gun. She shot a warrior that was going to kill us. We'd be dead without her."

"That right?" the doctor asked.

"That'll be enough, Haidie," Miss Arvilla said, without answering the doctor.

"Well, you must be a regular sharpshooter," the doctor said. "Herman, did you hear that? You ought to get up a shootin' contest, les'n it was her shootin' hand that got cut off." The doctor laughed, but none of the men did. He had gone too far.

Miss Arvilla stood. "Come along, Lizzie. We are nothing but objects of ridicule. There is no one here of consequence."

"Now hold on," the doctor said, but Miss Arvilla pushed her sister toward the door, while the doctor muttered, "Cheated out of a half-dollar."

"Ma'am." A tall man who was cleaner than the others and clean-shaven, too, came up close to Miss Arvilla so that no one else could hear him.

She stopped and eyed him.

"I've had some experience with wounds in the war, ma'am. It might be that I could take a look." He lowered his voice. "He's not really a doctor, you know. He just calls himself one. Me, I wouldn't go to him for a mosquito bite."

"You are a doctor yourself?"

"No ma'am, just a homesteader, but I was in battle, fought for the Union. The name's Tom Earley."

She looked around for a table, but Mr. Earley led us outside where the light was brighter—and there were fewer lookers.

Miss Lizzie stretched out her arm, and Mr. Earley took it, gently touching her wrist and the stump where the hand had been. It was red and puckered and scabbed. "Does it pain you?" he asked.

"Some."

I knew it was more than some, but she wouldn't admit it.

"My fingers hurt, and they're not even there," she continued. "I don't understand it."

"Phantom pain, the soldiers call it. The nerves that go to your hand don't know it's gone, that's why." He let go of Miss Lizzie's arm. "Whoever did the amputation did a mighty fine job. I've seen some wounds that turn black with gangrene, and the whole arm has to be taken off. Or maybe the soldier just dies. What's the white powder on it?"

"Flour."

"Flour! I've heard of that, but I never saw it myself." He studied the hand again then said, "From my experience, I'd say you were just fine. It wouldn't hurt to have a doctor in Denver look at it when you reach there. Put some bacon grease on the end of it. That'll soften the skin a little."

"We thank you," Miss Arvilla said. She took a little purse from her pocket and opened it, but Mr. Earley pushed it away.

"My opinion isn't worth a continental. I ought to pay you for the embarrassment inside. We're not used to ladies here. No harm was meant."

"You are a man of culture," Miss Arvilla said. She turned to me and said, "Haidie, please bring me a volume from the crate with a three written on the top."

I went to the wagon. The crates weren't nailed shut, and I

lifted off the top and took out a copy of a book titled *Shakespeare's Sonnets*. Then I carried it back to Miss Arvilla.

"A token of our appreciation," Miss Arvilla said, handing the book to Mr. Earley.

"These are favorites of mine. I am grateful to have it, but I wouldn't want to rob you," he said.

"Give it no thought. We have ten copies."

"Opening a bookstore, are you?" Mr. Earley asked.

"We are starting a school in Denver."

"Civilization is coming west then."

"At a snail's pace," Miss Lizzie said, then glanced around. "And not to this place at all, it appears."

"Give us a hundred years or so." He bowed to the two ladies, then shook my hand. "It wouldn't be a bad idea for you to know this book, too, son," he said.

"I can read," I told him.

"We have invited Haidie to be our first pupil. But he has not yet accepted."

* * *

Two of the men, the ones who had purchased mule teams instead of oxen to pull their wagons, told Ben they were leaving the train to push on to Denver by themselves. Without the oxen to slow them down, they could travel twice as fast and reach the city in two or three days, they said.

"You be fools," Ben told them. "There's Indians 'tween here and Denver City, and they're on the warpath. Ain't you had enough of them back yonder? Traveling by yourselfs, you'd likely lose your scalps."

"An Indian don't scare me," one of the men said.

"Think about your kiddies, man. And your wife."

"Now, Mr. Bondurant, there's no need for that kind of talk," Reverend Tappan said. "You'll frighten the ladies."

"I mean to. Likely you've never seen a woman that's been ravished by Indians. Indians are almost as bad as white men."

"Sir. We are civilized," the reverend said, and I guess he was, if talking through his nose and setting folks to rights was civilized.

"You're of that opinion, are you? I can't say as I agree. But I'll not argue with you. I'll just say it's a terrible risk just to beat the rest of us to Denver by a day or two, and not fair to the train, as we will have to come along and bury you."

He turned away, leaving the two men looking sheepish. "I guess the missus is scared enough now to make it hot for me if we go on," one of the men said, and the other nodded.

"Mr. Bondurant is a profane man," Reverend Tappan told Mrs. Marble, who had come to collect him for supper. "I believe any man, red or white, can be tamed if he will just hear the scriptures." He patted a little Bible he carried in his pocket.

"Need them like they need a big wind," Ben muttered.

"They do not have your breeding, Reverend Tappan," Mrs. Marble said, leading him off. She still wore the fancy hat, the white ostrich feather now brown with dust, and smiled up at the minister, tightening her grip on his arm. "You are an extraordinary man," she whispered, as she walked past me.

"What's going to happen to her?" I asked Ben.

"I dasn't dare to think."

⁎ ⁎ ⁎

We were all anxious to reach Denver City now and hurried the oxen along. But no matter how much the drivers yelled at them or hit them with their whips, the oxen only plodded, moving no faster than they had for the million miles we'd come since we'd crossed the Missouri. As we walked beside them, we strained our eyes to be the first to see the mountains.

"Four days to Denver," Ben said one evening as we unyoked the oxen. When he put it like that, I felt a flutter of excitement. Four days to Denver, then maybe another two days before me and Boots reached Georgetown—and Pa!

"Did you hear that, sister? Four days to a proper bath," Miss Lizzie said, then added, "and to Edwin, too, of course."

"Brother can wait. But a bath!" Miss Arvilla smiled. "I have enough dirt on me to grow roses."

"Well, you don't smell like them," Miss Lizzie told her.

"A bath," Ben scoffed. "Now who'd care about a bath? A bottle of Taos Lightning is more like it. Young Haidie, I think you deserve a nip yourself after all the miles we've crossed."

I grinned, but Miss Arvilla pinched her nostrils together at the idea of me having a slug of whiskey. She didn't comment, however, as the two women turned their oxen into the wagon circle. Then Miss Arvilla asked Ben, "Do you think they might graze on the open prairie tonight? Surely there is no danger of Indians this close to the city."

"I don't advise you to do it. I seen Indian signs all along."

"Then we will follow your wise counsel and keep the animals close," she said.

She started to lead the animals off but stopped when we

heard a ruckus coming from the Tappan wagon. "You must return my sugar nippers. Ambrose, speak to her," an angry voice cried.

The Tappan wagon was parked on the other side of the spinsters' wagon. Mrs. Tappan was boiling mad, and we could hear every word.

"Shame, Emily, you know the Bible bids us share," the reverend admonished his wife.

"Share? Is that what you call it? Share? The Bible says, 'Thou shalt not steal,' too."

"Oh, here, take them then." Mrs. Marble threw the nippers to Mrs. Tappan, but she threw short, and the nippers landed on a rock and broke in two.

"Oh!" Mrs. Tappan cried. "They are spoilt. And they cost too much to replace."

"You must not worship earthly goods," the Reverend Tappan told her.

"Tell that to that . . . that . . . woman," Mrs. Tappan replied. "She has already 'borrowed' my hairpins and my sewing basket, and I cannot find my good jacket."

"She is a poor widow woman."

"She is a thief and a painted harlot."

"Emily!" the reverend said sternly. "Such language from a woman, and a minister's wife at that!"

"She simpers and pouts and flirts shamelessly with you, Ambrose. I can scarce believe you don't see it." Mrs. Tappan put her hands over her face and climbed into her wagon. If I could have, I'd have climbed in there with her and told her she was a hundred times better than the Widow Marble.

Mrs. Marble shook her head in sympathy with Reverend

Tappan. "My poor dear reverend, to be saddled with such a shrew, and a plain, mousy one at that," Mrs. Marble said, rubbing her hand up and down his arm. She lowered her voice, but I had slipped to the front of the old maids' wagon, although I could still hear her. "You poor, poor man to have to put up with such an ungrateful wife. If you were my husband, you would know what it means to be satisfied."

She smiled up at him, but when she saw me, she dropped her hand, and Reverend Tappan jumped back, blushing. "Get away, you nasty boy. What do you think you're doing, spying on your betters?" she said.

"I've seen fancy women at home with better manners," I said. I hoped I'd got even with her for Mrs. Tappan.

The reverend's face was as red as a dog with a fit. He blustered and foamed, but he couldn't get out any words. Finally, he said, "We will not countenance such rudeness with a reply." He turned, and as he walked past the wagon, he called, "Emily, you should be about our supper."

Although Mrs. Tappan had been in the wagon, she had seen everything. As she slowly climbed down, I saw that she was trying to hide a smile. "You, Haidie and Boots, you come around after supper. There's a dried-apple cake." She paused. "No, come around before supper, there's only half a cake left, maybe you can eat it all up, so there's none left for . . . them as consider themselves 'betters.'"

* * *

Three men guarded the camp each night, each working a three-hour shift. The third guard was responsible for waking the camp at four in the morning. But the following day, no one banged on a washtub to get us up, and it was nearly day-light when Ben yelled, "Awake, the camp!"

The men sensed something was wrong, and they gathered around Ben, me and Boots with them. "Where's the guard?" a man asked.

"*Who's* the guard?" came from another.

"Tappan," Ben said.

"Fell asleep, did he? Probably bored himself spouting scripture," said the first man. "Where's he at?"

"He ain't *at*," Ben said. "I searched the camp. He's gone."

"Did you look inside the Widow Marble's wagon?" some-one asked slyly.

"First place," Ben replied.

The men were silent a moment. "Did an Indian get him?" I asked.

Ben shook his head. "No dead body. Besides, an Indian might sneak into camp to steal, but these Indians around here are dog soldiers. They're about killing. If one had got into camp, there'd be others, and we'd all be laying on the ground with arrows sticking out of us."

"Maybe the reverend went back to his wagon to sleep."

The men turned to the Tappan wagon, and I noticed that Mrs. Tappan was sitting on the seat, her head in her hands. Ben went over to her and asked, "Your husband here, ma'am?"

"Gone."

"Where'd he go?"

"Ran off. Took his carpetbag and all our money." Then she looked up at us. "His Bible, too."

"Where's Mrs. Marble?" I asked Ben.

Mrs. Tappan looked at me and nodded. "I expect she's gone, and taken our horses." The reverend had brought a team of mules, as well as two sorry horses.

"They'll answer to me when we find them!" Mr. Samuels promised. "I'll horsewhip a man that leaves the camp unguarded."

"Leave be. We got to hitch up the teams," Ben told him.

"Ain't we going after them?" Mr. Samuels asked.

"Why for?" Ben said. "They're grown folks. If anybody catches them, it'll be Indians, and then we'd risk our lives just to scrape them off the prairie."

"I guess they asked for it," Mr. Samuels agreed.

The men went to fetch the animals, while the women returned to their wagons to start breakfast, but Ben and I remained behind with Mrs. Tappan. "You know how to drive a mule team?" Ben asked.

She nodded. "But I can't hitch 'em up."

"I can," I said. "Jake Crowfoot taught me." I was proud I could help Mrs. Tappan. I followed her to where the animals were corralled and asked her to point out her mules. They were a poor team, brown ones, and I didn't know how they'd made it this far. As she was leaving, I said, "Ma'am, I'm awful sorry. I expect wherever Reverend Tappan goes, he'll meet up with Judas."

※ ※ ※

I didn't just hitch up the mules, I drove Mrs. Tappan's wagon for her, because she wasn't able to do a thing for herself that morning. She set out the makings for her breakfast but forgot to light a campfire. Then she sat on the wagon seat but didn't pick up the reins. So I tied Outlaw to the back of the wagon and climbed up beside her and slapped the reins on the back of the mules and yelled, "Giddup, you good-for-nothing, pie-eyed, God damn fools," the way Jake did.

Then I bit my tongue, afraid Mrs. Tappan would call me a blasphemer, her being a minister's wife. But she muttered, "God damn mules, God damn husband, God damn whore of a woman, too." I liked her even more for that.

I cleared my throat. "You all right, ma'am?" I asked.

"The Lord has put me down in the middle of this godforsaken country, and my husband has left me for a harlot, and you ask me if I'm all right?"

"Sorry." I felt as low as a toad in a hole.

We sat there silently, until I asked, "Are you going on back home?"

"I have no home. I was an orphan until the day Ambrose plucked me out of that place and said I was to be an instrument of the Lord."

"Like me and Boots. We weren't instruments. We were just orphans. We were in a Catholic home."

"I have no use for Catholics. A Catholic hit me over the head with a skillet once."

"Me and Boots aren't Catholics either. I wanted to be a Jew. Their orphans eat better. But if you ask me, an orphanage is no place for a child."

Mrs. Tappan smiled at that.

"Did you marry Reverend Tappan because you loved him or because he got you out of the orphan home?" One of the mules turned its head and bit the mule beside him. I flicked the whip at his ear and yelled, "Hey, you, God damn mule." I liked swearing, and I believed I did a fine job of it.

I thought Mrs. Tappan hadn't heard my question, because it took her a long time to answer. "I guess you know about orphanages, all right. All the future I could see there was marrying some dirt farmer or working as a maid, cleaning up somebody else's messes. Then came Ambrose Tappan and his talk of bringing God to little heathen babies and setting up a church in the wilderness where we would lead sinners to Christ. He wanted a big church, the biggest in Denver, and said we'd be as good as any banker or storekeeper in the city. I reckoned I could wear a velvet coat with brass buttons and carry a fur muff. I always wanted a muff. All's I had to do was marry him." She shook her head. "He was the mouse in the meal. But I figured he was a sight better than a hog farmer, even if he did like to wallow around at night." She thought for a moment. "Ambrose wasn't a bad man. He tried to live a Bible life, and I was a good wife to him. I was meek and wore plain clothes, because Ambrose said a woman with fancy clothes was like a crow with a feather fan." Mrs. Tappan glanced at me out of the side of her eyes.

"I have come to the conclusion that his words were highly undependable. He came into knowledge of the Widow Marble," she said.

"Did they have connection?" I asked, surprising myself that I could be so forward. But I figured "knowledge" and "connection" were the same thing, which meant she had brought up the subject. Besides, why else had he gone off with her? They weren't sitting around a campfire reading Genesis.

"What would a boy like you know about that?" Mrs. Tappan sighed. "Oh, that's right, you grew up in an orphanage."

I stared at the rumps of the hind mules.

"What choice did I have?" she continued. "As you can see, I am not a pretty woman. Ambrose told me that often enough."

"He's punk! He was a liar, Mrs. Tappan! You're a beauty." I lied myself at that, for she was only middling pretty.

Mrs. Tappan patted my hand. "You are to call me Emily. I am eighteen and not much older than you."

"Without her fancy clothes on, Mrs. Marble surely isn't as fine-looking a woman as you," I said. That didn't come out right, but Mrs. Tappan—Emily—took my meaning.

"Once we get to Denver, I'll never wear plain calico again."

The sun was high in the sky by then, and it was hot. I liked driving the mules, liked it better than walking along beside a team of poky oxen. We passed patches of wildflowers, and if I hadn't been driving, I would have picked a bouquet for Emily to make her feel better.

Every so often, she put her head in her hands and sniffed. She didn't make any noise, but I could tell she was crying. Then she'd wipe her face with her hands and stare out over the mules and sigh and ask, "Why am I sorrowing for a man that ain't worth it?"

"It's because you're a good person," I told her.

We rode along without talking for a time. Then I asked, "What'll you do when you reach Denver?"

"I've been giving it some thought. There's not much I can do."

"You can wash clothes, I bet. That's what I learned to do in the Smoak orphan home."

"How'd you learn laundry if you're a boy?"

I'd been careless, and I quickly added, "There was a shortage of girls at that place, so the boys had to help. I hated it because it was girls' work." I tried to lower my voice a little when I spoke.

"I never heard of that, boys washing clothes. I never heard of an orphanage that didn't have a preponderance of girls neither. Have you?"

"That's a good word, preponderance," I said, hoping to change the subject.

"My husband taught it to me. It means having too much sin. Now, what do you say to what I asked?"

"I couldn't say. I'm not acquainted with a preponderance of orphan homes," I said, grinning. She stared at me, waiting, until I said, "Everybody learned to wash. It's a right handy thing to know. I expect some of the bachelors on this trip were orphans. Haven't you seen them washing their clothes?"

"I have not. But I have seen them pay Mrs. Samuels's girl a nickel to wash their shirts."

"Washing's not such a bad way to earn your living."

"'Tis, and you know it." She studied me, then asked, "You're a girl, ain't you?" When I didn't reply, she added, "I never saw it before, but now I reckon I do. Well, I won't tell."

"Nobody knows but me and Boots, not even those two old maids. They're real nice."

Emily nodded. "They said I could eat with them. How come you pretend to be a boy?"

"Who'd want to hire on a girl to drive oxen?"

"I see what you mean."

"And being a boy, I don't have to ride sidesaddle."

It was hot as an angry mule now, and Emily fanned her face with her hand, then held open the front of her dress to let the air inside. "I'll tell you one thing, Haidie. I sure am glad I'm not in the family way. And it's a surprise to me with all the rutting the reverend did."

"Did you like it?" I thought she'd be as shocked as I was with the question, but instead, she thought about it.

"Not at first, but it grows on you."

"I know a girl named Teresa who was taken with it. I never tried it myself."

"I was pretty good at it, I think."

"I didn't know there was a way to be good or bad. I'd thought it just was."

"Oh, yes. There's ways."

I was about to delve into that subject so that I could enlighten myself, but Ben held up his hand and called a halt for nooning.

"You can eat with us," I said. "There's no reason to build two campfires."

"I don't feel much like eating. I got thinking to do."

✳ ✳ ✳

I unhitched the mules and fed and watered them, then turned them out. When I was finished, I walked over to where Ben and Boots had built a campfire. Boots had set out the cornbread and cold beans from last night and was pouring water into the coffeepot.

"Ben says Indians most likely got that reverend and Mrs. Marble," he told me. "Those two mares couldn't outrun an ox. I suppose they're shot full of arrows about now." He seemed to relish that thought. "Shot full of arrows with their privates cut off."

"Where'd you hear all that?"

"From Ben. That's what he told Mr. Samuels. He said they might carry off Mrs. Marble and ravish her. What's 'ravish,' Haidie?"

"I don't know," I lied. "Maybe it means paint her face, you know, the way the Indians painted themselves before they attacked us."

"I know you to be a liar, so I don't think that's what it means at all."

I ground a handful of coffee beans and threw them into the pot.

"Besides, she already wore paint. I saw her put something on her cheeks to turn them red," Boots said.

"She was an unnatural woman."

Ben came up to us then. "You drive them mules like a muleskinner," he told me. "When that fellow back in Omaha told me you could drive mules, I didn't believe him. But now I'm right proud of you."

"I said I could."

"Yeah, but you can be a liar."

That was the second time in five minutes I'd been called a liar.

"Ben," I said, after we'd dished up our dinner and were

sitting cross-legged on the dirt, eating. "What do you suppose will happen to Mrs. Tappan?"

"Well, now there's a good question, and I can't rightly say. Best thing for her is to find a man and get married again. There's one or two right here in this wagon train that might be looking for a wife."

"What if she doesn't want to get married?"

"She could take in washing. A man'll pay a half-dollar in Denver to get his shirt washed and ironed by a white woman."

"What if she doesn't want to do laundry?"

"She could take in boarders. That is, if she found a place where she could set up."

"What if she can't cook?"

Ben nodded, thinking. "You sure are full of questions. There's other things she could do."

"You mean things like Red Feather Road in Smoak?"

Ben wiped his plate with a piece of cornbread, then shoved it into his mouth. When he was finished, he brushed the crumbs off his beard. "I ain't acquainted with it, but I take your meaning. Yes, I guess there's things like that."

"It's not right. He lit out, but she's the one that's got to make do."

"It's a mean world out there, young Haidie, filled with liars and cheats and men of the worst stripe. Best you learn that."

* * *

Not more than an hour after our nooning, we spied the mountains. For the past hundred miles or two, we'd driven across prairie covered with tall brown grass, with a few red or blue or yellow wildflowers stuck in them. Some days there wasn't a tree in sight. So I'd been waiting for the mountains, but I admit when I saw them, I was not impressed. They were just a little raggedy blue line along the horizon. I had expected great humps of rocks, but these mountains didn't look any bigger than the hills along the Mississippi. I didn't know what all the fuss was about. Those men who'd bragged about how rugged the mountains were told bigger whoppers than I ever had. Ben pointed to one mountain that was higher than the others and said, "That there's Pikes Peak. It started the Gold Rush, but there ain't nary a spec of gold ever found there or ever will be."

"I can tell you I am greatly disappointed in the Rocky Mountains. It won't be a thing for me and Boots to go into them and find Pa."

"Just you wait," Ben said, grinning.

I figured we could reach Denver, which was at the foot of the mountains, by sunset, but when Ben called a halt, we seemed to be no closer than when we'd first spotted the Rockies.

"Ben says that's because the air's so thin," Boots told me.

I had never heard of thin air—or thick air, for that matter.

Just as we were having our air conversation, we heard horses. The men in the camp rushed for their guns, and someone called, "Indians!" but Ben put up his arm the way he did when he wanted the wagon train to halt and said, "Indians don't wear spurs. Can't you hear 'em jingle?"

We waited until a dozen soldiers rode up to the wagon train and dismounted. Ben and Mr. Samuels went out to meet them and talked a long time. When they returned with an officer, they looked solemn. "Friends, gather around," Mr. Samuels yelled, which was unnecessary since we were already gathered.

"Friends," he said again, "in this world we have come to expect sorrow. We must prepare ourselves for the sad duties the Lord entrusts us. Our days upon this earth are few, and we must always be prepared to meet our maker, prepare by living a righteous life."

I'd never heard such talk out of his mouth—it was as if he'd become the Reverend Tappan.

"Friends, I am the captain of this wagon train and have tried to run it justly. I have tried to maintain—"

"Soldiers found two bodies on the prairie," Ben interrupted. "They's Mrs. Marble and the reverend."

We gasped, while Mr. Samuels glared at Ben for spoiling his oration.

"There ain't no use to drag it out," Ben told him.

"The soldiers found them on the prairie, only a few miles from where we camped that night they run off. They didn't get far," Mr. Samuels said quickly, before Ben could say more.

"Serves the adulterers right," a woman said.

"The soldiers was taking them to Denver, but seeing as how we know who they are, we said we'd bury them right here."

"I want to see them." The men had started for the wagons to get shovels, but they stopped, and people hushed when Emily said again, "I want to see them."

"Ma'am?" the officer said.

"One of them is my husband. I want to see them."

The officer looked at Ben and shook his head. "Best not."

"You dasn't," Ben added.

"I have a right to see my husband."

Ben whispered to the soldier, "He taken out with another woman."

"Well, he paid a mighty price," the officer whispered back.

"Retribution," Mr. Samuels said in a loud voice.

Emily didn't pay any attention to the men. Instead, she walked past the prairie schooners, past the soldiers, who had dismounted, and went to a freight wagon where the two bodies lay. Ben followed her, and I slipped out of the circle of wagons after Ben. All three of us peered through the slats of the wagon at what had once been Mrs. Marble and the reverend. Neither one had on clothes. The reverend's hands and a few other parts had been cut off, and Mrs. Marble had been stabbed maybe a million times. Her face was so bloody I wouldn't have recognized her if I hadn't known who she was. Emily just stared, her body so rigid that she couldn't move. But I turned aside and lost my dinner. I hope never to see such a terrible sight again in my life.

Ben realized I was standing next to him and said, "You shouldn't have looked. It's not fittin' for a young lad to see—or a lady, either. Hell, it ain't fittin' for a man."

"I wished them dead, but not like this. I didn't wish for this," Emily cried. Her face was so pale that I thought she would faint. Ben picked her up and carried her back into the circle of the wagons, where she rallied. "I shouldn't like to see them buried like that. They might have come naked into

the world, but they shan't go out of it that way. Ambrose left
a formal suit behind. It's in a trunk in the wagon."

"I'll fetch it," I said.

"And best you bring a white dress that's with it. Mrs.
Marble should be covered, too."

I found the trunk and took out the clothes, then brought
them back, where Ben said he'd dress the two bodies. "By
rights, a woman ought to attend the lady. But it ain't right
to ask a lady to see what's been done."

"I'll do it," I said.

While Ben put the reverend's clothes on him, I slid the
white dress over Mrs. Marble, thinking it was a shame that
Emily's best dress was covering up a woman who'd been so
badly mutilated. Mrs. Marble being a sizable woman, the
dress didn't fit. I tugged and pulled, staining the dress red,
but the buttons in the back wouldn't match up. Well, there
was nobody that was going to look close. Indeed, as soon as
the bodies were clothed, we wrapped them in blankets for
shrouds, and when the men were finished digging the graves,
we laid them side by side.

There wasn't much of a service. The army officer read
from the Bible, something about sinners repenting and the
Lord's vengeance. Then we sang "O God, Our Help in Ages
Past."

While others went back to their wagons, Emily stayed
until the last clod of dirt was in place and the men placed
rocks on the graves to keep the wolves from getting the
bodies. I stayed beside her and held her hand, which was as
cold as the body I'd dressed. When the men were finished,

they lifted their hats to Emily and told her she'd best return to the camp. But Emily stood by the graves for a while longer, staring at them in the moonlight. Finally, she took a deep breath that seemed to come from her toes, and her face wet with tears, she turned, and we walked back to the wagons.

"That was a real nice thing you did, giving your good dress to Mrs. Marble," I said when we reached her wagon.

Emily stopped and put her hand on the wagon tongue, wiping her face with the other. Then she said, "It was my wedding dress."

Chapter Seven

All we'd seen for the last hundred miles was flat prairie. Denver was set on flat prairie, too, but two creeks crossed it, and it was right in front of a range of mountains. Ben said that was where the first argonauts had panned for gold. Argonauts—and sometimes sourdoughs—were what they called gold-seekers.

Denver was about a thousand times bigger than Smoak and growing every hour. Ben said that in the spring, a fire had burned down most of the city, ridding Denver of the trashy log cabins and flimsy board buildings that had been built after the first gold-seekers arrived in 1858. So we saw brick buildings going up along Larimer, the main street. I spotted an apothecary shop, a bank, an embalming studio, and even a bookstore, along with blacksmith shops and saloons and dance halls, fancy women standing out front. Ben told us there were almost five thousand people living here.

Piano music came from the saloons, and if it hadn't been so noisy on the street, we'd have heard roulette wheels and dice, too, I expect. There seemed to be as many saloons as houses, and I thought Cheet sure would be disappointed that he hadn't come with us if he knew the opportunities for him to get cheated out of his money in Denver.

I got to wondering about Cheet then, what he'd thought when he went to the orphan home and found me and Boots were gone. He'd know we'd lit out to find Pa, and maybe he'd followed us.

I thought on that for about a minute, before I asked myself why would Cheet want to come to Colorado? He wouldn't know any more what to do with us here than he had in Smoak. He'd just look for another orphan home for us. I loved Cheet in my way, and I felt sad that my brother didn't care about us. But Pa did. He'd be so happy, so proud that we'd come all this way on our own, that he'd dance a jig. I almost hugged myself, thinking how close we were to finding him.

The streets were packed with teamsters and freighters. They yelled at sourdoughs, who made their way through the muddy streets with their donkeys, though in Denver, Ben told us, they were called burros. Men swore at the animals and each other and at people who got in their way. We were near run down by a team of mules hitched to a big wagon that couldn't be stopped, the driver pulling on the reins and shouting at people to get out of the way. Dogs seemed to be everywhere and fought each other and chased cats. "Any cat with a tail is a tourist," Ben told us.

There were banks and mercantile stores, barbershops and hardware stores and smithies. I saw a tin shop and a place that advertised daguerreotypes and thought it would be a fine thing for me and Boots to get our picture taken. But there was nobody to give it to. Cheet wouldn't care about a picture of us, and the orphan home wasn't likely to put it into a gold frame and hang it up with a sign that said "escaped orphans." I wondered about Teresa then, where she was and whether she and Jake had gotten married or whether they were just being incorrigible together.

The merchants who stood in front of their buildings were dressed in rusty suits and starched shirts, just like the ones me and Teresa washed and ironed at the orphanage, but the men in the street were dressed in dirty canvas pants and flannel shirts, greasy hats and cracked boots. There wasn't a uniform in sight. "Is this place Yankee or Secesh?" I asked Ben.

"Yankee, but most of the men that was patriotic enough to fight already enlisted. Men here care more about gold than the war."

We finally stopped on Wazee Street at a place called the Elephant Corral, and I was mightily disappointed that there weren't any elephants there. After all, on the trail, we'd passed enough go-backs—men returning east—who told us they'd "seen the elephant," that I was looking forward to spotting one. Ben told me the Elephant Corral was just a name, because the place was so big. Well, the Elephant Corral was big as an elephant, all right—big and crowded with prairie schooners and freight wagons, animals milling around, kids running everywhere, and men shouting.

I was driving Emily's wagon with Outlaw tied behind it when Ben directed us into the Elephant Corral. As I stopped the mules, I asked Emily, "You figured out what you're going to do just now?"

"I have. I'm going to sell this team and wagon and everything in it, and if nobody wants it, then I'll just leave it here."

"Then what?"

"Never you mind." She looked around and called, "Mr. Bondurant, if you'll act as my agent in selling my wagon and goods, I will give you ten percent."

Ben didn't say anything but beckoned to a man who was sitting on a log and told him Emily wanted to sell her wagon. The man looked over the mules and said he didn't know how they'd made it across the plains, them being old and brown and grass-fed. He climbed into the wagon and poked through Emily's belongings.

"Hundred dollars, as generous an offer as you'll ever find," he said, holding up a Bible and squinting at it. He opened it, and when he realized what it was, he tossed it back into the wagon. "Hundred dollars and a penny."

Emily nodded yes to Ben, but instead of accepting the offer, Ben scoffed. "Worth three hundred." They bargained for a time, Ben saying as how the box of Bibles was worth twenty-five dollars easy, and the man saying he might sell the whole box for a dollar to somebody who wanted them for paving stones. I'd been in Emily's wagon and knew the pots and pans and the clothes weren't worth much, the sugar was gone, and there wasn't but half a bag of flour. But the altar was big and might make a nice chopping block in a butcher store.

Ben said he might find somebody who wanted to take his family back East so's he could sign up to fight in the war, but the man scoffed. "You'll find the talk here ain't the war anymore. It's mining."

Finally, the two men settled on two hundred dollars. The buyer gave Emily the money, and she handed Ben a twenty-dollar gold piece, but he shook his head. "Obliged, but it wouldn't be right taking money from a widow."

Emily tried to give it to me then, but I wouldn't take it either.

"Well, I don't understand," she said, putting the money into her purse. "Ambrose never turned down as much as a penny in his life."

"Where you going now?" Boots asked her.

She gave her answer to Ben instead of Boots. "I've heard talk, amongst the men in our train, of the Progressive Club. Do you know the place, Mr. Bondurant?" She looked fierce, as if she was waiting for Ben to object.

He studied her a moment, but he didn't protest. Instead, he nodded. "That'd be the best of the lot. I wish you had a better plan, but good luck to you all the same."

She turned to me. "Later on, if I pass you on the street, it's all right if you pretend you don't know me."

"Why?" Boots asked. But I knew. It had taken me a minute to understand that the Progressive Club was like those places on Red Feather Road and I felt heavy in my heart that Emily was going to work in one. I hoped it beat washing clothes.

"Best give me directions, Mr. Bondurant," Emily said.

He pointed down the street, and we watched Emily walk off, not taking a single thing from the wagon with her, not looking back.

As Emily disappeared, the two spinsters came up.

"We've already sent a boy to alert our brother, Edwin,

that we have arrived," Miss Lizzie said. "Haidie, you and Boots are welcome to come with us until you make arrangements to go into the mountains. You might like a bath."

"They'll just get dirty again," Ben remarked.

"We did not make the offer to you, sir, seeing as how it would be fruitless." She turned to me, and I said no, because we didn't have time for baths. "A meal then, Haidie," Miss Arvilla said.

I shook my head. "I expect we're anxious to find Pa." I wouldn't mind a supper that wasn't cooked over a campfire, but I was afraid the sisters would try to get us to stay in Denver and maybe attend their school.

"Then you must call upon us when you return." Miss Lizzie told us to ask directions to the Matchett house. "Meanwhile, we wish you Godspeed, all three of you. Mr. Bondurant, I would have died without your medical knowledge. If there is ever anything we can do for you, sir—"

Ben made a gesture, brushing aside her thanks, and said, "Oh, bother with that!"

"I understand, but we are in your debt—you, too, Haidie, for your kind assistance. If we may ever aid you, do not hesitate to call upon us."

I felt as embarrassed as Ben with all those awkward words and only muttered, "Thank you, ma'am."

Just then, a man called, "Lizzie! Arvie!" I'd expected the spinsters' brother would be as proper as they were, dressed like Corny in a white shirt and flowered vest and top hat. But instead, a big man in corduroy and rough woolens swept a hat as weather-beaten as Ben's off his head and swooped up the two women. They squealed and hugged their brother.

"Nobody believed me when I said my sisters were coming here by themselves. But I knew you were keen on adventure." He stopped when he saw Miss Lizzie's arm. He stared at it a long time. Then his gaze slowly rose to her face.

"Indians," she told him. "But there is no need to worry, Edwin, I have a perfectly good hand on the other arm and can still whip you at cards."

I stared, because I had no idea the sisters played cards.

"Poker," Miss Lizzie told me. Then she said to her brother, "Of course, I wouldn't be here if it weren't for Mr. Bondurant, our faithful guide. It was he who removed my afflicted hand and kept the rot from spreading up my arm. And it was Haidie who assisted him."

Edwin turned around and saw the rest of us for the first time. "Bondurant. Ben Bondurant, I'll wager. I've heard of you, sir. I am grateful to you for what you did for my sister, for both of them." He added affectionately, "I know better than anyone that they can be a trial." He shook Ben's hand, then introduced himself. "Edwin F. Matchett at your service."

"Eh? E. F. Matchett that owns the bank?" Ben asked.

"The same."

"I heard of you, too."

Miss Arvilla introduced me and Boots, then said we were going on to Georgetown to find our pa.

With all that greeting and introducing, I felt out of place and whispered to Ben, "Me and Boots are ready to head out if you'll point us to the road." I'd already put our belongings into a sack and tied it to Outlaw's saddle.

"You're not going to wait for a guide?" Miss Arvilla asked.

"It's only fifty mile, and the road'll be packed with men. There won't be any need," Ben told her. Then he turned to me. "I'll take you to where you start." We said good-bye to the Matchetts, and Ben told the Samuels boy to watch the wagon. Then he mounted his horse, and me and Boots got on Outlaw, and we rode down the street. A few blocks later, Ben turned west and stopped. "That'll be the way," he said, pointing to a road. "You get to Golden—that's where the mountains start—then turn you up the canyon to the diggings at Central. Once you're in Central, you ask for the road that goes over the mountains to Idaho Springs, then on to Georgetown." He reached into a pouch and handed me a gold piece, but I refused to take it, telling him our bargain had been meals.

"I won't force it, but it's waiting when you need it. I never met a man I admired as much as you," Ben said. "If'n you come back to Denver, you'll look me up and let me know how you make out, won't you?"

I swallowed and straightened my back. I'd never had such a swell compliment in my life. "Where'll you be?"

"At the Progressive Club, I expect. You can inquire inside of Emily, if that be her name then."

I felt tears come into my eyes, so I kicked Outlaw into a trot, and me and Boots took off.

✶ ✶ ✶

I'd been wrong about the mountains. From far off, they hadn't looked like much, but up close, they were the dangest things I'd ever seen—big as an elephant, rugged, ragged, with steep sides and pointed peaks reaching halfway up to heaven. There was even snow on the tops of some of the far mountains, and it was summer!

We spent the night in Golden, wrapped up in our blankets under a tree, and in the morning, I spent two bits for us to eat breakfast, because I was tired of campfire cooking. And besides, we didn't have any pots and pans. Then me and Boots mounted old Outlaw and headed up the canyon.

Well, here was another surprise. I'd already revised my thinking about the mountains. I knew now they were bigger and rougher than I'd thought, but I'd expected them to be pretty, with trees and streams, maybe some flowers. They might have been at one time, but now the stream that ran through the canyon, which went by the name of Clear Creek, although it wasn't any clearer than the Mississippi at flood, was lined with men, and I never saw such a mess of goings-on.

Some men had gold pans as big as turkey platters, and they were squatting beside the creek, dipping the pans into the water and swirling them around, picking out specks of gold the size of nits. Others dug up the creek and dumped the dirt into what they called sluice boxes, and ran water through them, which washed away the dirt and left little dinky flakes of gold, and when they found them, the men put them into their pokes. After they were finished washing the dirt, they dumped it back into the creek, so the banks of the stream were lined with piles of used-up rock and mud, where nothing grew.

The trees at the diggings had been cut down to build cabins or to burn as firewood. So there wasn't more than a spot or two of green in the whole canyon. We stopped Outlaw to let a freight wagon pass us. It was filled with rocks—ore, I told Boots, because I'd heard men on the wagon train talk about it. While we were sitting there, a man came up and offered me a job at a dollar a day shoveling dirt into his sluice boxes. He said he'd pay Boots fifty cents to do odd jobs, too.

"Let's do it, Haidie. We'd be rich as those old maids."

I was mightily tempted. Another two weeks wouldn't matter much in finding Pa, and I could tell already that our money wouldn't go far. But I shook my head. "I bet it would cost us two dollars a day for a bed and board. We got to keep on finding Pa."

"Oh, yeah. You think he'll pay me fifty cents a day to work for him?"

"Maybe more, if he's found a gold mine."

The road was poor and crowded, and we had to turn out every so often to let one of those ore wagons pass us. The road was muddy, too, and the noise was so loud that Boots put his hands over his ears. I had to yell as loud as I could just to make him hear me.

As we got higher up, we saw the mines. You could tell that's what they were by the huge piles of yellow tailings that were spread out like a skirt down the mountainside. "You expect they got gold rooms inside those mines?" Boots asked. "All's you'd have to do is take a penknife and scrape off the gold every day, just say to yourself, 'I need two dollars to buy a pig,' and you'd go in there and whittle off a little hunk, maybe a little more to buy a candy stick. I expect if you took a kerosene lamp in one of those rooms, you'd get blinded by the shine."

"Gold just comes in little bitty strings," I told him. "You have to dig out the rock, then crack it open to get to the gold. Why, they say unless you know what you're doing, you can stare at the richest gold mine in the world and not think it's anything more than a rock pile."

"I bet Pa's mine has a gold room," Boots insisted.

"Maybe you're right," I said, thinking to myself, *If he even has one.* There were just too many other argonauts.

Before we left Denver, I'd asked Mr. Edwin if he knew Pa. He said the name sounded familiar, but he wasn't sure. I took that to mean he'd never heard of him and was just being polite. I inquired of a man in Golden, who told me, "I can't say as I've heard of him."

"You think maybe Pa isn't even here?" Boots asked.

I thought that over. "These men live in Central. If Pa's found a mine, it's over the mountain in Georgetown."

"You know what's the first thing I'm going to do when we find him?"

"I do not." We had slowed down because we were behind a prospector walking a burro that was loaded down with a gold pan and pick, an iron skillet, a blanket roll, tent, and some items I didn't recognize.

"Buy a saddle for the pony Pa's going to give me, a saddle with gold stars all over it, just like the silver stars you got on Outlaw's saddle."

"You're sure about that pony?"

"If you owned a gold mine, wouldn't you buy a pony for your little boy?"

What if Pa's just like that prospector in front of us, I thought, *wading through the mud in old boots with cardboard inside the soles to keep out the wet?* But there was no need to worry Boots. "I sure would," I said.

"You know something else, Haidie?"

"What's that?"

The prospector had stopped to bite off a chaw of tobacco, and we passed him. He had a bushy beard, and his hair was gray, and I wondered how long he'd been looking for gold—and whether he'd ever find it. Maybe he'd fall off a mountain or catch the influenza or go to sleep in the snow and never wake up. I shivered to think maybe that had already happened to Pa.

"What's Pa going to buy you?"

I thought that over. There wasn't much I wanted. "Maybe I'll go to the old maids' school," I said.

Boots was disappointed, and then he asked, "Why do you think Pa didn't write to us anymore, Haidie?"

I wished I could think of a better explanation than I'd given the last time he'd asked, but that question had been worrying me, too.

"Maybe he wrote, and his letter got lost," Boots continued.

"Why, of course! You know how Postmaster Mueller's always getting the mail mixed up at home. I bet the fellow who runs the post office in Georgetown is no better. Pa's letter might be down in Mississippi. Or Texas," I said. I kicked Outlaw to hurry him up.

We rode until the sun had started its slide down on the west side of noon. Then we stopped, and I took out some bread and cheese that I'd bought in Golden, whittled the mold off the cheese, and handed a piece of it to Boots, who broke off some of the bread. We were both hungry. So was Outlaw. Ben had tied a sack of oats to the saddle, which was a good thing, because there was no place in Clear Creek Canyon that Outlaw could graze. So I fed him, too. Then me and Boots stretched out on a pile of rocks, looking up at the sun, which was brighter than I'd ever seen. We finally reached Central just as it was getting dark.

I feared someone would thieve Outlaw if we tied him to a tree or a fence post, so we found a livery stable. "You boys by yourselfs?" the man there asked, as he ran his hand over Outlaw.

"We're looking for our pa," I told him. "He's in Georgetown."

"Well, you can't get there this evening. You'll be wanting a place to spend the night. You can sleep here, if you'll shovel manure for an hour. I'll throw in feed for the horse. That's a mighty fine animal. He ain't for sale, is he?"

"We'd never sell him," I replied.

He nodded. "Can't say as I blame you."

Finding that stable was a stroke of luck. So we agreed to shovel horse droppings for a place to sleep. Me and Boots set to with a will, and we didn't stop until we'd cleared all the manure out of the stable.

When the livery man saw how hard we'd shoveled, he said, "Well, don't that beat all, two young 'uns that know how to work. I guess I could stake you to supper, too." He took a pot of beans and bacon from the top of a potbellied stove and dumped the contents onto three tin plates, then handed around the plates. He gave us bread instead of spoons to shovel the beans into our mouths. We didn't say a word,

just ate like we hadn't eaten in a week or two. When me and
Boots were finished, the man added dried beans and water to
the dirty pot and set it on the stove, saying he'd start in on
tomorrow's supper.

"Don't you want me to thrash out that pot?" I asked.

"What for? I haven't washed it since I got here. It gives
flavor," he said. He pointed to the hayloft and told us to
spread out our blankets.

✳ ✳ ✳

That straw was the best bed I'd slept in since we left the
farm, maybe even better than that, because Boots could turn
over without flopping on top of me. With nobody pounding
on a washtub and telling us it was time to gather the oxen, I
slept till sunup. Boots was still asleep when I got up, so I left
him there and went in search of breakfast. I found a woman
who was selling hot rolls, three for a nickel, so I bought five
cents' worth, and when I got back, I gave one to Boots and
another to the livery stable man.

"I'd be obliged if you'd point us to Georgetown," I said as
I rolled up our blankets.

The man had already saddled Outlaw for us and didn't reply right away. He ran a hand over Outlaw's withers and said
again, "You sure you don't want to sell him? I'd give you fifty
dollars in gold and throw in Rusty over there." He pointed
to a swayback horse. When I shook my head, he said, "How
is it two boys like you accumulated him?"

"It was give to us," Boots said. "For a reward. Haidie helped
Corny capture Dan, who was a man that was going to kill us
and steal Jake's freight wagon. I expect he's dead of hanging

by now. The sheriff said as how Dan wouldn't be needing Outlaw, Haidie could have him."

"That's mighty fine. There's a job here for you young 'uns if you ever want it. Just come back to Central and ask for Ed Simpson. That's me. Good luck to you, then." He pointed us over the mountain and said to turn right when we got to Idaho Springs. Then just before we left, he leaned in close and said, "Best you stay away from the livery in Idaho. When he gets liquored up, that man's known for whipping a horse. And he ain't going to let you sleep in his hay, neither."

The trail was steep, but it wasn't as crowded as the Clear Creek Canyon road, and we made better time, reaching Idaho Springs while it was still light. I was willing to keep on going, but Boots was tired out. Remembering what Mr. Simpson had said, we went on past the livery stable and camped out under a tree, where we ate the last of our bread and cheese.

* * *

I slept so hard that I didn't hear Outlaw run off. When I woke up in the morning, I went to get him, but he was gone. Boots searched one way, calling his name, and I went another, thinking he must have wandered to the stream for water. Outlaw couldn't have gone far, because he was hobbled. Still, I couldn't find him. Neither could Boots. I said he might have followed some other horses into the camp, and we decided we'd cache the saddle and our blankets and go in search of him. But when I went for the saddle, I discovered it was missing, too. And then I saw Outlaw's hobbles on the ground. "Outlaw's been stole!" I told Boots.

Boots's eyes grew wide. "How are we going to get to Georgetown?"

"We're going to find that horse!"

We picked up our things and went along the road, where men were already cooking their breakfasts. "You seen a horse with two stars on his forehead and silver stars on the saddle?" we asked, stopping at each campsite.

Finally, one prospector scratched his head and said, "I seen him in the middle of the night. I wouldn't have, but the danged horse almost stepped on me. I told the man riding him I'd bust his leg if he ever let that animal step on me again. He told me to shut up and said he was sorry his horse hadn't kicked me in the head."

"*His* horse?" I asked. "Outlaw's *our* horse."

"He's been thieved," Boots added.

"It's a mighty mean man that done it. He jammed his Mexican spurs into that horse and hit him with a whip."

I shivered. Even Dan hadn't treated Outlaw that way. "Did you see which way he went?"

The prospector shook his head. "But whatever way it was, he was going fast."

Me and Boots found the sheriff's office and explained that Outlaw had been stole, but the deputy said there wasn't much he could do about it.

"How'll we get to Georgetown to find Pa, Haidie?" Boots wailed.

"I guess we'll walk."

But the deputy spoke up. "No need. You can hitch a ride on a wagon." He went out into the street and stopped a freighter. "These boys got their horse stole, and they need a ride to Georgetown. You think you could give them a lift?"

The freighter agreed, and me and Boots climbed up onto the wagon seat beside him.

"I can drive the mules if you get tired, sir," I said.

"A boy like you?"

"Just try me. Jake Crowfoot taught me. He's a Missouri man."

"Crowfoot? Why, I've come across him a time or two. He's as good as bread."

"You hear that, Boots? He knows Jake." I turned to the freighter. "Did he have a woman with him, name of Teresa?"

"I can't say he did." Then he told me, "If Crowfoot taught you, I guess you must drive pretty good."

I nodded, thinking the man would hand me the reins, but he never did, and by the time I was ready to offer again, we had reached Georgetown.

✳ ✳ ✳

First off, I was disappointed in Georgetown. It wasn't any prettier than Central or Idaho and a sight smaller. But I liked the way it sat in that mountain valley.

"How are we going to find Pa?" Boots asked.

"We'll go to the post office and ask."

So we did. Me and Boots waited in line, and when it was our turn, we asked if the postmaster knew a man by the name of Manley Richards.

"Seems I do." He looked through a pile of mail and pulled out an envelope. "If you find him, tell him I got a letter for him." He held it up, and I recognized my own handwriting. I'd written Pa right after Ma died.

"You have any idea where he might be, sir?" I asked.

"Well, if he ain't got his mail, he ain't here, is he?"

Boots spoke up then. "Please, sir, he's our pa. We walked about twenty thousand miles to get here, and if we can't find him, they'll send us back to the orphan home."

"That's not a thing to be believed. Why'nt you help the boys out?" a man behind us spoke up.

The postmaster shrugged. "Seems to me I remember meeting somebody by that name. But I ain't heard it lately."

"What'd you say it was?" the second man asked.

"Manley Richards. He's from Smoak, Illinois," I said.

"Say, ain't he the fellow that discovered the Hangover?"

I had to laugh at that. If anybody discovered the hangover, it wasn't Manley Richards but his son and my brother, Cheet.

"The Hangover's a mine," the man explained. "But he doesn't own it now. Joel Thacker does."

"And a mighty poor job he does of running it," the postmaster added.

"If Pa doesn't own it now, where's he gone?" I asked.

"You could inquire at the mercantile. They might know. My guess is if he sold it, he's gone to Denver."

We thanked the men, and as we went in search of the mercantile, Boots asked, "What if he *started* on home? What if we passed him out on the prairie, him going one way and us the other?"

"Then we'll turn around and go on back to Smoak."

"But what if he finds out we went to Colorado Territory to find him, and he turns back, too?"

The idea of us crossing back and forth, passing each other twenty or thirty times like coyotes in the dark, made me laugh. "We'll go back to that livery stable in Central and get us jobs and write him a letter," I said. I was lighthearted knowing that someone in Georgetown had heard of Pa.

The Georgetown Emporium had a long counter, and behind it was more merchandise than I'd ever seen in one place—picks and shovels and gold pans, bolts of cloth, cans of peas and peaches, felt hats, pants and shoes and dresses, and hanging from a nail high up was a hoop to go under a skirt. I had time to take it all in, because the man in front of me was bargaining with the man behind the counter, grub-staking, they called it.

"You already got your pick and your pan from last time, and I gave you enough beans and coffee, fatback and flour, crackers and cheese to last you the summer. I'm not staking you to whiskey. Last time all's you did was sit under a tree and drink it and throw away the bottle."

"Now, Mr. Olson, you know that bottle hit pay dirt."

"Yeah, and you were too lazy to file the claim. You let somebody else get ahead of you on that."

"Well, I won't again."

"Lightning don't strike twice. I'm not giving you any more whiskey."

The two argued for a time, then the prospector signed an X on a piece of paper and left with his stake.

"You boys looking for a grubstake, too?" the man asked,

as me and Boots pushed against the counter. "I'm not such a soft touch. That there man is my wife's brother."

"No, sir. We're trying to find our pa, and the postmaster said you might have heard of him. His name's Manley Richards."

The man scratched his chin with his knuckles. "Sorry, boys. Men come and go in these towns. I hope you find him."

As we left the mercantile, I spotted a bank, and I suggested we check to see if Pa was a customer. Heck, with all the money Pa must have gotten for selling the mine, his picture might even be on the wall. But there weren't any pictures at all on the wall. That room was as plain as a feed sack. I went up to a man standing behind a brass grille and said, "I'd like to know if Mr. Manley Richards keeps his money here."

"Oh, you would, would you?"

"Well, does he?" Boots asked.

The man rose up on his toes and leaned over so that his nose was almost touching the grille. He stared at us through glasses clipped to his nose. "That is confidential, young gentlemen. We do not give out the names of our patrons."

"Well, he's our pa, and he's got to put his stash someplace," Boots said.

"Then why don't you ask him?"

"Please," I said, kicking Boots to shut up. "We came all the way from Smoak, Illinois, to find our father, and we don't know where he is. He used to be in Georgetown, but the postmaster says he hasn't been to collect his mail in a long time. He discovered the Hangover Mine."

"The Hangover. That was a likely prospect at one time, but it's poorly run."

"Could you tell us if he keeps his money here?"

The man thought for a moment, then he held up a finger and walked to another man, this one sitting behind a desk. They whispered for a moment, then both approached us. "I'm Mr. Wilbur Toll. I own this bank. My teller says you're looking for Manley Richards."

"He's our pa. We ran away from an orphan home where our brother put us after Ma died. Jake gave us a ride to Omaha, and we almost got murdered by two outlaws, but me and Corny stopped them, and the sheriff gave me a horse, but it was stole last night in Idaho Springs," I told him.

Mr. Toll nodded and held up his hand to stop me. "That story is too unlikely to be a fib. So I guess you must be who you say you are. We are charged with keeping the names of our patrons in confidence, but seeing as how you are the children of the depositor and you've come all this way, I reckon I will answer you." He led us back to his desk and pulled up two chairs for me and Boots, then sat down himself. "I did not know a Manley Richards, but my teller tells me he came in and closed his account a year or two ago. Took out the entire amount, a dollar and six cents. He seems to remember your father saying the mountains didn't agree with him and he was going to Denver. Of course, I can't say for sure, but that's where I'd go if I had a nice chunk of cash. You came through Denver, did you?"

I nodded.

"Well, it's a shame you didn't check around when you were there. It would have saved you a trip. What'll you youngsters do now?"

"Go back to Denver. I sure wished we had Outlaw to ride. That's our horse, which was stole," I said.

"Be that as it may, you will get there all right. I will help you find a ride, but first, I am taking you to the Prospector and buying you a beefsteak. When's the last time you ate right?"

I thought back. "Two days out from Denver."

Mr. Toll bought us our supper in a restaurant. Me and Boots thought it was the finest meal we ever had. "You just tell your pa when he finds another gold mine to come and see me."

"When we find Pa, he'll take us to supper in a restaurant, and you, too, Mr. Toll," Boots promised.

✳ ✳ ✳

Me and Boots camped out that night with a freighter who hauled goods back and forth to Central City and promised to take us as far as Central in one day. He hitched up before first light, and we were almost to Idaho Springs by the time the sun came over the mountains. It took the rest of the day to reach Central City, and the stars were out by the time we got there. Since the freighter was nice enough to take us with him and even share his dinner with us, me and Boots helped him unload his wagon. He offered to let us sleep in the empty wagon with him, but I decided we should go back to the livery and bed down on the straw.

Ed Simpson wasn't there. In fact, the livery stable was empty, except for a pair of horses way down at the end. Me and Boots would have waited for him, but we were too tired, so we just climbed the ladder to the hayloft and bedded down in the hay.

It was the middle of the night when I woke up because two men were exchanging words just below the hayloft.

"What'd you bring him here for?" I recognized that voice as Ed Simpson's.

"Where else you think I can put him up? You want him right out there on the street where somebody'll recognize him? I hid out for two days, near killed myself riding in the dark, and I ain't going to do it again tonight. I'll light out before sunup. Ain't nobody going to come looking for him."

"You get him out of here early, before somebody recognizes those two stars on his forehead. And you get rid of that saddle, too. Anybody can see those stars a mile off."

I jerked up my head, clapping my hand over my mouth to keep from crying out. But I must have moved, because hay sifted down onto the floor below.

"What's that? Somebody up there?" the man asked.

Mr. Simpson scoffed. "You getting jerky, are you? It's only rats."

I shivered at that. I hated rats. But I hated those two men more, and I was scared to think what they'd do if they found me and Boots in the hayloft.

"I never taken a horse from a pair of kids before."

Mr. Simpson said, "Yeah, it's a shame. I kind of liked those kids." I heard him sigh, then add, "Likely they stole the horse theirselves, the liars. They said they got it for catching a thief." He laughed.

"Yeah, well maybe somebody'll steal it from you before morning."

I thought that over. That's exactly what me and Boots would do. As soon as the men left, I'd wake Boots and we'd sneak out of there with Outlaw. We'd be halfway down the canyon before Mr. Simpson knew the horse was gone.

"Not likely. I'll stay right here till you come back, me and Betsy'll keep watch." He cocked a gun.

Just as the thief seemed to be leaving, I heard another voice, this one calm, sounding a little friendly-familiar. "I seen a real nice horse come in here just now. Thought I'd ask is he for sale?"

"That horse ain't none of your business," Mr. Simpson said.

"You mean he's not for sale?"

"I mean he's none of your business. Now go on out of here."

"It just might be my business at that. I believe I know that horse. The saddle, too. Where'd you get him?"

"You're mighty nosy for a stranger. Maybe we should send for the sheriff."

"You do it!"

The barn door blew shut, surprising me so that I moved, letting more hay sift through the floor. Boots moved a little, too, and I reached to put my hand over his mouth so if he woke up, he wouldn't say anything.

"Unless you're looking for trouble, you best turn around and forget you was ever here," Mr. Simpson said.

"Last I knew, two boys owned that horse. Never would I think they'd sell it to the likes of you. Swindling Simpson, isn't that what they call you? If you have laid the weight of your hand on those young fellows, I'll make you sorry for it."

The voice was familiar now, and I peered over the edge of the hayloft. In the light of a kerosene lantern hanging on a nail, I could see Mr. Simpson was just below me, his gun in his hand. Beside him was a man I didn't recognize. But confronting them was Jake Crowfoot! I was so relieved, I could have shouted. There was no sign of Tige, however, and I was greatly disappointed at that.

"Yeah?" Mr. Simpson's voice sounded almost sad. "I don't hardly see any way you can do that. Looks to me like you come into my stable to steal a horse. We tried to get you to leave, but you was too stubborn. Now I guess we don't have no choice. Bob here will tell the sheriff we caught you red-handed. Of course, you can't say nothing, because you won't be able to talk. Nobody cares much about a dead horse thief."

The other man seemed startled. "Aw, you can't do that, Ed. We could let him go if he promises to keep his mouth shut."

Ed scoffed. "I wish we could, but you can't never trust a man to do that."

From where I was perched, I could see Mr. Simpson slowly raise his gun. At that instant, I was aware that Boots was awake, crouched beside me. His eyes were wide, a look of terror on his face. I thrust my arms to the floor, and Boots, realizing what I was about to do, shoved his hands into the straw, too. I nodded one, two, three, and then, together, we shoved about a ton of hay over the edge of the loft onto Mr. Simpson and his friend.

The hay came down like leaves in a windstorm, covering Mr. Simpson and the horse thief. They raised their arms to keep the hay off their heads and out of their eyes, and as they did, me and Boots jumped out of the loft onto their shoulders. "Get the gun, Jake," I yelled, kicking Mr. Simpson in the head with my foot.

We rolled around the floor, until Jake yelled, "Stop it. I got you covered." Me and Boots scooted out of the way, then went to stand behind Jake, who held a gun in one hand and his mule whip in the other.

"What the bejesus?" Mr. Simpson muttered.

"It seems you stole the wrong horse, by golly," Jake told him, slapping the whip a time or two against his pants leg.

✳ ✳ ✳

Boots ran for the sheriff, while the two men whined and said they didn't mean any harm. "Mr. Simpson sent his friend after us when we wouldn't sell Outlaw," I explained to Jake. "You saved us."

"Oh, damn that."

When the sheriff arrived, he told us he'd suspicioned Mr. Simpson of horse theft but never had any proof. He took the two men off to jail. Then me and Boots got on Outlaw and went off with Jake to his camp.

"What are you doing here?" I asked.

Jake grinned. "Couldn't keep away, I guess. I made some little trips around Omaha. Then a fellow hired me to freight a load to Central City. Teresa said, 'Let's do it so's we can see Haidie and Boots again.'"

"Where's Tige?"

Jake shook his head. "I left him to guard Teresa. I should have taken him with me."

By then we'd reached Jake's camp, and I was just as surprised to find Teresa there as I had been to see Jake. To be truthful, I had been afraid he'd gotten tired of her and left off.

That beautiful dog Tige jumped all over me and Boots, and then Teresa, sounding not the least bit surprised to see me, said, "Hi, Haidie Richards."

"Hi, yourself, Teresa Stover."

"It's not Stover," she said.

"Well, whatever it was before that."

"It's not that either. It's Teresa Crowfoot. Me and Jake got married."

"By a real priest this time?"

She giggled. "I don't trust priests anymore. We got married by a Methodist preacher."

"That's fine, Teresa." Next to finding Pa, Teresa getting married was the thing that had worried my heart most. I loved Teresa, and I was happy enough to shout, "Huzza!"

Teresa grinned. "It's all right to be incorrigible when you're married."

She held out her hand and showed me a ring about the size of a piece of thread. I had to peer close to see it, but I told her it was the prettiest thing I'd ever seen. "You've slept between sheets?" I asked, remembering how she'd wanted to in Fort Madison. I figured Jake would have taken her to a hotel with sheets on their wedding night.

"Not yet." She paused. "There's another surprise. Guess who we brung with us?"

"Corny," I said, thinking it had turned out to be a good day after all, what with getting Outlaw back and meeting up with Jake and Teresa and maybe even Corny.

She looked disappointed. "I didn't think you'd guess."

"You wouldn't have brought Billy Stover, and it's not likely you took in Cheet. So who else could it be?"

"He caught up with us a day out of Omaha, said someone was making it hot for him. He'd won a lot of money."

"Is he in Central?"

"Naw, he stayed in Denver. He told us he was going to see a man about a horse, and that you could find him at a place called the Progressive Club. I think it's a restaurant or a boardinghouse or something."

"Or something," I said.

Chapter Eight

Me and Boots weren't about to let anybody steal Outlaw again, so we waited in Central until Jake found a load to haul to Denver, and we helped him put it into the wagon and hitch up the mules. I thought Big Blue recognized me and was glad to see me again, until he tried to bite a piece out of my hand. I was sorely tempted to forget Jake's advice to treat mules kindly.

Before dawn, Jake was up, and we were on our way down the road that me and Boots had come up just a couple of days earlier. "We wasted our time. We should have looked for Pa whilst we were in Denver. It looks like he sold his gold mine and lives there now," I told Jake.

"Yeah, in a big house," Boots added. Then he said, "We think he sent for us, but the letter got lost. Most likely, he's real sad, living there all alone with about five hundred servants. By golly, he'll be happy to see us." I was glad to hear Boots so joyful.

"He'll be surprised, too," Jake said. "I can guarantee you. Who'd think two orphans could cross the country on their own and find their father?"

"We won't be orphans anymore," Boots told him.

We made good time getting to Denver. Outlaw was tied to the freight wagon, and me and Boots sat up in front, crowded between Jake and Teresa, and watched the prospectors jump out of the way as Jake, driving like Jehu, barreled down the canyon. We left the two of them when we reached the Elephant Corral and asked directions to the E. F. Matchett house.

Everybody knew where it was because that house was a mansion. We followed the directions to Curtis Street, which seemed a long way from the Elephant Corral, with brick houses surrounded by iron fences. Trees had been planted, and there were flowers and even grass. Me and Boots never would have thought when we met those spinsters that they would live in such a place. It was the kind of house we figured Pa must live in now, made of brick with a tower and an iron fence and a cast-iron dog in the middle of the yard. We sat out front on Outlaw for a minute or two, just staring at the house, getting up our nerve to go to the door. "You figure they're as rich as Pa?" Boots asked.

"Maybe richer." We dismounted and tied Outlaw to the fence, then went up and yanked on the doorbell. It made a dull sound, like a bell scraping across a rock.

In a minute, a maid in a white apron with a tiny good-for-nothing white hat on her head answered the door. The hat was more cappy than hatty, and it looked silly on her. "Yes?" she said, looking us up and down. I could tell right away that she was not impressed.

"We came to see Miss Lizzie and Miss Arvilla," I told her.

"Oh, you did, did you? They are indisposed. Perhaps another day." She started to close the door.

I glanced over at Boots, then down at my clothes, and realized we looked like a pair of foundlings or maybe a couple of street toughs who would wipe their hands on the tablecloth or steal salt spoons off the table. Maybe the maid thought we were beggars. I felt ashamed. But then I told myself we couldn't help the way we looked. "Please, ma'am, we're acquainted with them," I said.

"And likely President Lincoln and the Pope of Rome, too. Go on with you," she said, and tried to shut the door.

Boots was too quick for her. He stuck his foot in the door and said, "We saw Miss Lizzie get her hand cut off. She's real brave. Ben said he never saw a lady as stout as she was."

The maid paused at that.

"We came on the trail with them," I added.

We still didn't make much of an impression on her, because she blocked the doorway and tried to push Boots's foot away. But then we heard a noise in the house, and Boots called out, "Miss Lizzie."

It wasn't Miss Lizzie but Miss Arvilla who stuck her head out of the door and said, "Oh my goodness."

"I tried to get rid of them, ma'am," the maid said.

"Get rid of them? Why, Martha, these are the very children who accompanied my sister and me to Denver. Without them, we might not have made it. Come in, come in. Don't just stand there. Martha, ask Miss Lizzie to come down." Miss Arvilla held out her hands to us and led us into a room she called the library. This one had about twenty-five times more books than the library at Smoak.

She told us to sit down, but me and Boots were dirty enough that we were afraid we'd soil the furniture. So we just

stood until Miss Lizzie came into the room and put an arm
around each of us. I got the arm without the hand. "Why, I
was never so glad to see two people in my life." She lowered
her voice. "Our brother's house is very nice, but we miss the
prairie." She, too, told us to sit down, so at last we did—on
the floor. And Miss Lizzie sat right down next to us, although
she was wearing a silk dress. She looked nice, in that red dress
with the black trim and a lace collar, her hair done up with
fancy combs. She looked less like an old maid, too. I glanced
up at Miss Arvilla then and saw that she was dressed up like
her sister, wearing a gown the color of the blue wildflowers
we'd seen on the prairie. A pin with a lady's face painted on
it was fastened to a ribbon tied around her neck. Her hair was
combed into a lot of little ringlets, and she didn't look like
an old maid either.

Miss Arvilla laughed at her sister as she perched on
one of the chairs that looked as hard as the board seat in
Ben's wagon. "Now, tell us at once. Have you located your
father?"

"We found out he had a mine in Georgetown, but he
doesn't own it anymore, and he isn't in Georgetown either.
We think he came to Denver, but we don't have any more
idea than a dead man when he did."

"Do you know where he might be?"

I shook my head, while Boots said, "He probably lives
around here somewheres. I expect he owns a house like this."

"You are doubtless correct," Miss Lizzie said. "In the
meantime, you will stay with us." She reached up for a little
bell on the table and shook it.

Almost before the sound died away, Martha came back.

When she saw Miss Lizzie on the floor, she cried, "Oh, ma'am, you've fallen."

"Nonsense, Martha, I have chosen to sit on the floor with our friends, the way we did on the trail. Now if you would just fix a supper of beans and side pork, I'd feel right at home."

"Ma'am?"

"A jest, Martha. You have already met our friends Haidie and Boots. They will need baths, and then you can go out and find some proper clothes for them. Theirs are almost worn through. Use your judgment on the sizes. They will be staying with us indefinitely."

Martha looked us over good, as if she thought we were covered with graybacks, and she pursed her lips together until they were a thin line.

"They are our guests," Miss Lizzie said sternly.

"Yes, ma'am." She took us upstairs to the nicest room I'd ever seen, with a brass bed that shone like a twenty-dollar gold piece. It had sheets on it, too. I could hardly wait to tell Teresa! Martha lugged a tin bathtub into the room, and in a few minutes, she brought in kettles of hot water. I told Boots he could use the water first, and he flung off his clothes and sat in the tub so long that the water turned cold. I didn't mind, because except for the few times we'd gone swimming on the trail, this was the first time since we left the orphan home that he'd had a bath. After he got out of the tub and wrapped himself up in a towel the size of a Persian rug, Martha knocked on the door and said she'd empty out the dirty water and bring hot water for me. I didn't even have to use Boots's cold water!

I sat in the tub as long as Boots had, washing the dirt
off me and even soaping my hair and ducking my head into
the water to wash it out. Then I got out and was just wiping myself off when Martha knocked at the door one more
time and said she'd brought us some new clothes. "I'll close
my eyes and bring them in," she said, opening the door and
stumbling toward the bed. That wasn't necessary, because
by then, both me and Boots had towels wrapped around us.
That was a good thing, because she opened her eyes after all
and looked us over. "You clean up pretty good," she said.
"Does your pa really own a gold mine?"

"Not anymore. He sold it," Boots said. "He's richer than
Miss Arvilla and Miss Lizzie. If you're nice to us, he'll give
you a gold ring."

"Go on," Martha said, but she smiled at us for the first
time.

I went to the bed and handed Boots his pants and shirt.
There were even drawers, and I had to explain to Boots what
they were, because he'd never worn them before. Then I
found more boys' clothes for me.

Mr. Edwin was waiting in the dining room, but we didn't
see him at first, because we were looking at all the silver and
china that gleamed like the sun on water in the light of about
two thousand candles. The wallpaper looked like somebody
had painted bright blue curtains on it, and it matched the
velvet drapes at the windows, which were held back with
gold cords. Underneath them were long panels of white lace.
I knew that people on the street could peer through them to
see us inside, because me and Boots had walked by the big
houses in Smoak and looked through the windows at people

eating their supper. Back then, I wouldn't have bet five cents on a sure thing that me and Boots would ever be eating our supper in one of those houses.

The two of us sat down on one side of the table, with Miss Lizzie across from us. Mr. Edwin and Miss Arvilla sat at the ends. A maid brought in little cups of soup, which disappointed me. I thought such a fine place would have bigger bowls. Boots grabbed his bowl to drink the soup, but Miss Lizzie cleared her throat, and we watched as she picked up a spoon and dipped it into the liquid. We each had three spoons in front of us, and I didn't know which one to use. "Always start with the fork or spoon on the outside," she whispered. I nodded, but first I picked up my napkin. At least I knew enough to tie it around my neck.

After we had finished the soup and the maid was taking away the bowls, Mr. Edwin said, "My sisters tell me you believe your father is in Denver."

"Yes, sir. Do you know him?" Boots asked.

"Perhaps I do. What is his name? It has slipped my mind."

"Manley Richards. They told us in Georgetown he owned the Hangover—" I stopped suddenly. It might not sound right if Pa named the mine for a hangover. They might think he was a drunk. "He owned a mine, but he sold it, I guess."

"I don't know a Manley Richards, but I will inquire. My sisters are anxious that you find your father, but they are not anxious to have you leave. Arvilla has even told me her hopes of connecting you with her school, that is if she stays unattached long enough to start it."

"Edwin!" Miss Arvilla said, blushing.

Miss Lizzie leaned across the table. "My sister is already

being courted. A banker friend of our brother's has called on her three times. He seems quite smitten."

"With the Matchett money, you mean," Miss Arvilla muttered.

"Does that mean you won't be an old maid anymore?" Boots asked.

"You hush up," I told him, but the other three only laughed.

"If twenty-seven makes me an old maid, what are you at twenty-nine?" Miss Arvilla asked her sister.

"Smart enough not to reveal my age," she shot back.

That soup wasn't the only thing we had for supper. Martha brought in the best food I'd ever had in my life—roast beef, potatoes, and green beans, lettuce and tomatoes. Then for dessert, there was custard with syrup poured over it. The Matchetts finished with what they called cordials, but they weren't much because they came in glasses the size of thimbles. They didn't offer any to us, but it didn't matter because by then, me and Boots were so tired we were about to fall off our chairs. So Miss Lizzie told Martha to take us up to bed, and we'd see about finding Pa in the morning.

As we started out of the room, I stopped and said, "Outlaw. I forgot all about Outlaw." I rushed to the window and looked outside, but my horse was gone. "Somebody's stole him again."

"Never fear," Miss Arvilla said. "He's in the stable. The groom took care of him."

"Miss Arvilla, me and Boots never had anybody be so nice to us in our life," I told her.

"Boots and I," she said.

"Boots and you what?"

"Never mind." She took our hands and led us to the stairs. "Tomorrow, we will start the search for your father." She exchanged a glance with Miss Lizzie that I think I wasn't supposed to see.

* * *

In the morning, me and Boots went down to the Elephant Corral and asked about Pa, but nobody'd ever heard of him. We inquired in the saloons, too, and even went to the Progressive Club, where we saw Emily, although we barely recognized her. She had her hair pinned up, and her cheeks and lips were painted, and she wore a dress that was cut so low you could see her bosoms. Nobody would have taken her for a preacher's wife, but then, I don't suppose anybody went into the Progressive Club looking for salvation. She was the spit of a Red Feather Road girl.

She saw us and jumped up and asked if we'd found Pa, but we said no and asked her to keep an eye out for a man named Manley Richards.

"I asked in here, but nobody remembered him," Emily said.

I thanked her, then asked how she was getting along.

She thought that over for a long time before she answered. "I guess everybody at home would be shocked how I turned out, but it's not so bad. I was pure as snow when I married Ambrose, but he told me all the time I was a sinner. Now, I'm a sinner, but . . ." She shook her head. "I know it's wrong what I do, but the Lord didn't give me any other choice. Maybe this is what He meant me to be.

For now anyway." She smiled. "You know what, Haidie? I think I'm going to meet a nice man here, and he'll marry me, and we'll have a house and a baby, and he won't care how we met. He won't spend his time Bible reading in the evenings either."

"Why, I bet you're right," I lied. Maybe Emily really believed that, but I'd heard stories about girls on Red Feather Road who drank too much and took dope, and I'd seen them sitting in the dirt, asking people for money.

⁂ ⁂ ⁂

We didn't find a soul who knew Pa, and I was plenty discouraged by the time we returned to the Matchett house later that day. But Miss Arvilla met us at the door and said, "Our brother has something to tell you."

"You found Pa?" I asked when we went into the library, where Mr. Edwin was sitting in a chair the size of a Conestoga wagon.

"No, not exactly. But I have an address. I'll call on him in the morning and find out if he is indeed your father."

"No, sir. That's up to me and Boots. We came all this way to find him, so we want to see him for ourself." Then I added quickly, because I didn't want to be rude, "But we thank you all the same. Nobody's ever been so good to us, even our own family." I thought about Cheet and said, "Especially our own family."

"Haidie, we don't want you to be disappointed," Miss Arvilla said.

"We won't be, not if we find Pa."

Miss Arvilla started to say more, but Miss Lizzie raised

her arm, the arm with the hand on it, and said, "It's not our place, sister."

I wanted to go out that night, that very minute even, but Mr. Edwin said it was too dark, and there were dangerous ruffians on the street. The sisters and their brother were acting strangely, and I couldn't figure out why. Maybe they didn't want us to leave so soon.

The next morning, Miss Lizzie said she and her sister would drive us in their carriage to Pa's house, but I turned her down. She sighed, and in a few minutes, the groom brought Outlaw, who had been curried until he shone like a racehorse. The saddle had been rubbed with oil and the stars shined until they looked like, well, stars.

Mr. Matchett handed me a piece of paper with Pa's address and instructions on how to get there. Then me and Boots were off.

We rode past the Elephant Corral and the Progressive Club to a street with a bunch of shabby houses—houses worse than the one we'd lived in on the farm—and Boots said, "Pa wouldn't live in any of these."

"Likely, he's waiting for us to get here so's we can help him plan the mansion."

"You think so, Haidie?" For the first time, there was worry in Boots's voice.

We'd find out for ourselves in a minute, so I didn't lie to him. "We'll see." I stopped Outlaw in front of a house.

I was as excited as I'd ever been, but I was afraid too. Why would Pa live in such a poor shack, with only a door and one window? The boards were unpainted, and the front yard was dirt.

We sat on Outlaw and stared at the house, just the way we had at the Matchett mansion, until I said, "Ready, Boots?"

"By golly!" Boots said, sounding like Jake. "By golly, Haidie!" And he jumped off Outlaw.

Boots ran up to the door as fast as he could. I was slower. I was afraid to knock and find out who was behind it. But I didn't have to, because Boots was already pounding on it.

A long time passed. I knew somebody was inside, because smoke was coming from the chimney, and I thought I saw the curtain in the window move. At last, the door opened, and Boots cried, "Pa!"

But it wasn't Pa. Instead, a woman stood there. She was pretty, although her hair hung down over her face, and she wore an old dress. And I could see she was going to have a baby any minute.

"I ain't nobody's pa. That's for sure. But I'm about ready to be somebody's ma, in maybe twenty minutes." She rubbed her back, sticking her stomach out, and smiled a little at us. "Oh, don't worry. It'll be a while yet. What do you want?"

"I think we got the wrong house," I told her, relieved. I put my hand on Boots's shoulder and said, "We're looking for Mr. Manley Richards. Do you know where he lives now?"

"Why, he lives right here. Manley," she called over her shoulder, "somebody's here to see you."

"Who is it?"

"I couldn't tell you, but they're not bill collectors. You come on to the door."

And in a moment, there was Pa. He was older, his hair gray on the sides and his face thinner than it had been in Smoak. He stooped a little, too. "Pa!" Boots cried, and he rushed to our father and threw his arms around him. Boots was the only one who moved. I was frozen in place. Pa looked as if he'd seen a ghost. And the lady just stared. Finally, she said, "You never told me you had kids, Manley. In fact, you never told me you was ever married."

Pa took a deep breath. "These ain't mine. I don't have a boy that size." He pointed with his chin to me.

"I'm Haidie, Pa," I said. "I dressed like this so's I could get work on the trail."

Pa stood staring at me a long time, before he put out his hand to me and started to cry. "I never thought I'd see you again." He picked up Boots and hugged him. "Bootsy, little Bootsy, you're all growed up," he said, the tears running down his face. Then he pulled me to him and hugged me, too.

I was glad to see Pa after all this time. But there was a lump in my throat the size of a buckeye, because I knew then that Pa hadn't planned on coming home. He'd deserted us, and maybe now he didn't want us. I wanted to cry, but I didn't. I'd already figured out that Pa might not be as rich as the Matchetts, but I thought he'd at least be respectable. Here he was, however, living in a place as small and shabby as a hired man's shack, wearing clothes as ragged as what me and Boots had on when we reached Denver. Maybe we shouldn't have shamed him by showing up the way we did. And then there was that woman. Who was she? That bothered me most of all. Had Pa forgotten he was married to Ma? He was as bad a sinner as Ambrose Tappan. I was glad to see him, but I was mad at him, too.

"Let's sit down. Do we have any coffee, Fanny?"

"We run out a week ago."

"We don't want anything, Pa," I said.

"The old maids already gave us hotcakes and bacon and eggs and—" Boots said, but stopped when I touched his shoulder. The woman named Fanny looked from Pa to us and back at Pa again, then folded her hands on top of her belly and said, "Explain yourself, Manley."

"I never knew it would come to this. I never knew you'd meet them." He took a deep breath. "These are my children, my son Boots and my daughter, Haidie."

"Daughter?"

Pa studied me. "You sure you ain't Cheet? It'd be like Cheet to pull a fool trick."

"I'm Haidie, Pa. I told you."

"Manley," Fanny said.

"Who's she?" Boots asked.

Pa cleared his throat and looked away as he stepped inside, and we followed him. The house was poor, but it was neat. Maybe that was Fanny's doing. Pa never was one to pick up for himself.

"This is my wife," Pa said, blushing and not looking at us.

"Your wife? What about Ma?" I knew how long it took to make a baby, and Ma was still alive when that baby got started.

"Did you bring her with you?" Pa asked.

"You got another wife?" Fanny asked. Her hands were on her hips, and she looked at him something fierce.

"Ma's dead," I told Pa.

"Well then, it's not bigamy," Fanny said.

I ignored her. "Ma died last year. November. You didn't

get my letter. It was still in the Georgetown post office waiting for you."

"November? We got married in October, with a preacher and a certificate. Are you telling me this ain't a proper marriage? I'd never have left the Progressive Club if you'd told me you had a wife somewhere," Fanny said.

"That's why I didn't," Pa said. He slumped onto a chair, looking miserable. He scuffed his boots around a little, then leaned back in the chair. "I didn't tell you 'cause I knew you wouldn't marry me, and I was in misery so deep after I got cheated out of my gold mine that I thought I ought to kill myself." He turned to me. "Fanny saved me."

"What?" Boots asked.

"Fanny worked at the Progressive Club as a . . . a . . ." Pa stammered.

"We've been to the Progressive Club," I said.

Now it was Fanny's turn to blush. She'd been a Red Feather Road girl all right.

"I came out here to get rich, and I was for about almost a minute. I was going to go back. But then I lost it all. I figured when I left that your ma wasn't long for this world. And I thought the two of you and Cheet would run the farm, that you wouldn't need me. After the way I bragged about finding gold, I was ashamed to go back."

"Cheet sold the farm cheap and kept the money and put us in an orphan home," Boots said.

"You could have come home, Pa," I said softly.

"No, your ma was so mad when I left, she said I wasn't to go back less'n I had a gold mine."

"She didn't mean it."

After a minute, he mumbled, "I know. But I couldn't go back all broke down like I am."

"You are not broke down. You are just down on your luck," Fanny told him.

"And a trusting fool," Pa said, shaking his head. Then he added, "I never figured I'd see you kids again."

"Are you glad, Pa?" Boots asked.

"Well, sure I am." But he didn't sound so sure. "Tell me about your ma."

Fanny went over to the stove and pretended she wasn't listening, but the room was so small that she'd have heard the conversation even if she'd had sealing wax in her ears.

I told Pa about how Ma had just worn out like an old dress. "For a long time, she expected you to come home. She sent me to the post office every week to ask for a letter. But after a while, she gave up."

"Your ma was sick when I left. I didn't expect she'd make it."

"Weren't you ever going to come home?" I asked.

"I thought so at first, but I gave it up. Maybe you'd remember me the way I was, not the way I turned out."

"You weren't so bad when we met. You owned a gold mine then," Fanny said from the stove.

"Well, I did, but as you know, I got cheated out of it."

"You really found a gold mine?" Boots asked.

Pa perked up. "I sure did. The Hangover in Georgetown. It started up real good, too." He grinned, the way I remembered, but then he hung his head.

"Did you lose it in a poker game?" I asked. Pa'd always

been pretty good at cards—it was a family calling. After all, he'd taught plenty to me and Cheet.

"No, I did not. I put it up as a stake, and I won five thousand dollars on it."

"Five thousand dollars!" Boots said. "I told you he was rich, Haidie."

Pa hung his head. "I didn't keep that money more than ten minutes. I didn't want to carry it around down there on Blake Street on account of the footpads. So when I saw a light on in a bank, I knocked on the door and asked to leave the money there, and the deed to the Hangover, too. It was for safekeeping."

"Did you get a receipt?" I asked.

"Well, sure I did." He paused. "But the next morning when I went to get the money and the deed, the banker said he'd never seen me in his life. I showed him the receipt, and he said it wasn't one of his, and that wasn't his signature, either. I could see I was in a bad way, so I told him he could keep the money if he'd just give me back the deed. But he claimed he'd won it off a fellow in a poker game. Then he smiled at me and said, 'Tough luck!' I went to the sheriff, but I didn't have any proof except for a receipt that wasn't any good." Pa paused. "Those are the stubborn facts."

"Was that banker Joel Thacker?" I asked.

Pa jerked up his head. "How did you know that?"

"We went looking for you in Georgetown. Folks there say he's done a purely poor job of running the mine."

"Serves him right," Fanny said.

"Isn't there anything you can do?" I asked. "Couldn't you

win the deed off him in a poker game? You were always a good cheater, Pa, just like Cheet."

"I don't even have a stake."

"Besides, your pa's down so low, he wouldn't even try," Fanny said.

Me and Boots stayed in that house, talking. We told Pa about the sisters, who turned out to be rich. I wondered if they would stake Pa to a game, but I let that idea go out of my mind as soon as I thought of it. They'd already taken in me and Boots. It wouldn't be right to ask them for money. And what if Pa lost it? I'd have to put on a dress and go work at the Progressive Club to pay them back. The idea made me smile. I'd grown but not enough for anybody at the Progressive Club to take a shine to me. Maybe Fanny'd go back to work there and I'd have to take care of the baby. That would be as bad as being locked up in the orphan home again.

"I'm fixing to dish up breakfast. You two's welcome to join us," Fanny said. She'd been frying salt pork and boiling porridge, but even Boots could see that there wasn't much, so we said no. I liked Fanny. She was nice to us, and she seemed good to Pa. It wasn't her fault Pa hadn't told her he already had a wife.

After a while, Pa said he had to go to work. He had a job that day at a stable doing what me and Boots had done in Central for Swindling Simpson.

As he put on his coat, Pa asked, "What are we going to do with you?"

Before I could answer, Fanny said, "They'll bunk with us. We haven't but the one bed, but you're welcome to the floor," she said. Then she asked Pa, "I'm thinking about supper. Is there any more of them out there?"

"Just Cheet, but he's not here," I answered.

Fanny nodded. "I told you with the baby coming, Manley, we'd need a bigger place. Now we'll need an even bigger one." It was real nice of her, not knowing until that morning that Pa had kin, to offer to put us up.

I said quickly, "The sisters want us to stay on for a while. We've got our own bed. We don't want to put you out." I didn't know if Miss Lizzie and Miss Arvilla would want us at all, now that we'd found Pa, but I could see he was embarrassed he didn't have something better to offer us. Besides, I had some thinking to do. I'd have to figure out how to get Pa's mine back. And how to forgive him.

He hugged us again, just the way he had every five minutes since we'd gotten there, and left for his job, and Fanny sat down in the chair and put her hands over her face. I thought she was going to cry, but she was just tired. "Your pa's in misery so low, he won't even try. I don't care if he's not rich, but I wish he'd pick himself up. He's got no pride anymore. He thought he was somebody when he owned a mine."

"We got to get it back for him," I said.

"You are a good child, Haidie, but there is no way to do that."

"We'll find a way."

"She's a liar," Boots said. "She's always been a liar, but she means well by it."

"Well, I appreciate the sentiment," Fanny told us. "Maybe just you two kids being here will perk him up. I surely hope so."

She looked down at her belly, and I said, "Maybe three kids."

* * *

"What are we going to do, Haidie?" Boots asked when we were halfway back to the Matchett house.

We were riding along Larimer Street just a couple of blocks from the Progressive Club. There were dance halls and gambling hells mixed in with outfitters and hardware stores and even a theater. I liked Denver. It was busy and noisy and exciting, and I hadn't seen a single orphan home. Maybe I could find a job to support me and Boots. Or if I went to work, I could give the money to Pa, and he could find a bigger house. "I'm thinking about it."

"You told Fanny we'd get Pa's mine back, but we're just kids. How are we going to do that? You surely did lie."

"Did not. I'll figure out something." I thought about that all the way back to the sisters' house, but I didn't have any idea. Boots was right. I was a liar.

We rode Outlaw into the stable, just as a man came out of the house and got into a carriage. Miss Arvilla stood at the door, her hand in the air.

"Come in, come in. Did you find your father?" she asked. Before we could answer, she called, "Lizzie, come down. The children have returned." Then she told Martha to bring us tea in the library.

"We found him," Boots said, as soon as the two women sat down. "We sure did."

"And?" Miss Lizzie asked.

"And he found a gold mine," Boots added.

"Oh, I do love happy endings," Miss Lizzie said.

"And we got a new ma, too," Boots finished. He looked at me. "Do we have to call her Ma?"

"Fanny. We'll just call her Fanny."

The sisters exchanged a glance.

"It's okay. Our ma's dead." I did not explain that Pa had married Fanny before Ma died.

Miss Arvilla was watching me. "But it did not go as you had hoped," she suggested.

"It did, and it didn't," I replied. Then I explained how Pa had lost the mine, and he was living in a shack, and now he was so discouraged he couldn't go on. "If we could just get that mine back for him. It doesn't even matter if it's no good. You see, Pa never succeeded at anything much in his life, and now he thinks he never will. But if he had that mine, he'd be somebody. That's the way I see it. We just have to get it back for him."

"Is it a major mine?" Miss Arvilla asked.

I shrugged. "All I know is it's not very well run. But people in Georgetown said the Hangover was a good strike when Pa found it."

"The Hangover?" Miss Arvilla said.

"Yes, ma'am, but I don't think Pa named it," I said, remembering I had been embarrassed to tell her the name earlier. "Have you heard of it?"

"Indeed I have." She turned to Miss Lizzie and said, "Mr. Thacker owns the Hangover."

"Joel Thacker's the man that stole it from Pa, stole the mine and five thousand dollars. Do you know him, too?"

"I'm afraid I do. That was Joel Thacker you saw getting

into the carriage when you rode up. He has asked me to marry him."

I took a deep breath. We sure were in the middle of it now. Miss Arvilla would warn him we wanted to trick him out of his mine, and then Pa would never get it back. She'd ask me and Boots to leave, too, and Pa would have to take us in. Things would be worse here than they ever were at the orphan home. We should have stayed there. "I'm sorry, Miss Arvilla. Me and Boots will leave now." I stood up.

"Where do you think you're going? Sit down," she said in a hard voice.

I slumped back into the chair. I'd forgotten what a sharp-tongued old maid she could be.

"Mr. Thacker is a pompous fool."

I didn't understand "pompous," but I knew what a fool was. I sat up a little straighter.

Miss Arvilla turned to her sister. "I've told you, Lizzie, that he is after Edwin's money. Why else would he declare himself after only a week? He said that in Denver the conventions of courtship do not apply. What foolishness. I could barely be civil in refusing him."

Miss Lizzie grinned. "So you have had a proposal of marriage and turned it down."

"More than one, if you will recall Mr. Stevens at home."

"Ah, yes. But he only pursued you because I had made it clear to him I was not available." Miss Lizzie took her sister's hand, and they both began to laugh. Then she turned to me. "Men are such fools. They think we cannot see it is our money they court, not ourselves, desirable though we may be."

"Now," Miss Arvilla said, leaning forward. "How do you

propose to recover the Hangover from Mr. Thacker? Shall we stake your father to a poker game?"

I grinned at the two old maids, and suddenly, I felt as happy as I'd been when I'd come up with the scheme to get me and Boots out of the orphan home.

"No, ma'am," I said. "Pa's too down in the dumps to play good poker. But you might stake Corny."

And then I explained to the sisters the plan I had come up with.

Chapter Nine

Mr. Edwin drove me to the Progressive Club in his buggy. He said Outlaw would be stole for sure if I left him tied up on Blake Street. Besides, if I was by myself, I would likely be set on by footpads, who would pound my face all to smash. We left Boots with the sisters. He was dog-tired after his day with Pa, and Mr. Edwin thought a boy that young might draw attention, although most gambling hells were happy to take a person's money no matter what his age.

The Progressive was busier at night than during the daytime, when we'd visited Emily. It was big and crowded and noisy with the sounds of men yelling and swearing and scraping their boots, women laughing, waiters shouting, the click of the roulette wheel.

"Corny's liable to be playing poker," I said, and we turned away from the roulette wheel and chuck-a-luck tables. We didn't see him, and I wondered if we were too early.

But we did see Emily, and I led Mr. Edwin to the table where she was sitting with another woman. They both smiled at Mr. Edwin, the way you smile at the man in the mercantile when you're hoping he'll give you a stick of licorice. Then Emily saw me and grinned. "Hey there, Haidie," she said.

"Hi, Emily. This is Mr. Edwin. He's a brother to the old maids."

Emily stood up and dipped her head at him, while the other woman said, "Some girls have all the luck," and slunk away.

"My sisters send their regards," Mr. Edwin said. "May we join you—unless you are otherwise occupied?"

Now, I thought the way he talked was real nice. Mr. Edwin was a banker, and he was rich, and I knew such men scoffed at dance-hall girls. But he was a gentleman, and he treated Miss Emily like a lady.

"Sure," she said. "And you don't have to buy me champagne. It's just cold tea anyway." She turned to me. "You find your pa yet?"

I nodded.

"Is he rich?"

"Not anymore. He got cheated out of his mine. We're going to get it back. That's why we're here. We're looking for a man named Cornelius Vander."

Emily thought that over. "Seems to me I heard of somebody like that, but that wasn't quite the name."

"He's real fancy. He wears a flowered vest and a top hat and—"

"Oh, him. That's Mr. Cornelius. Rodney Cornelius, I think it is. He comes in later in the evening—after the other poker players are drunk and get a little sloppy with their bets." She chuckled. "Now why don't the rest of them figure that out? He'll be here about midnight."

A waiter came over and asked, "Champagne?"

Emily shook her head. "They're just leaving." She said we'd better go before she got into trouble. So we stood up and started across the room. I turned to wave at Emily and saw that Mr. Edwin had left a coin on the table.

"We can sit in the buggy and wait, if you'd like. Or we can watch the action," Mr. Edwin said.

"Do you gamble?" I asked.

"Only with other people's money. I'm a banker."

Although it wasn't yet midnight, I said we ought to stay inside the Progressive, because we weren't likely to spot Corny if we were sitting in a buggy outside. So we wandered around the poker and faro and blackjack tables, watching the men gamble. I spotted a man using a holdout that was so obvious that I pointed it out to Mr. Edwin, who asked me how I knew about such things. "I come from a family of cheats," I said.

"Your pa cheat much?"

"He used to. As to now, I couldn't say. But my brother does. And Grandpap did, too. And I am myself awful good at it."

"So my sisters have taken in a tinhorn."

"Yes, sir," I said.

"And you and this Mr. Vander, or whatever his name is, think you are good enough to win a gold mine."

"Good enough to try."

"With my money."

"If we lose, I'll pay you back every cent, even if it takes the rest of my life. I don't want you to be out your money."

"That is of no consequence. I gather that without you, I might have been out a sister or two."

I'd been surprised that Mr. Edwin had agreed to help me and Boots. When Miss Arvilla told him about Joel Thacker, he said he'd had his suspicions. "I did not introduce him to you so that he could court you, Arvie. I was merely being polite when he stopped by the house to discuss a business deal. He seemed taken with you, and I believed you would do what you wanted without any advice from me. In fact, you are contrary enough to go against my advice, so I kept my silence. But I have investigated, and I can tell you that Mr. Thacker is a man of little principle and that, desirable as you may be, my dear sister, you are not the object of his affection so much as is our money."

"You did not have to waste your time in inquiry, Edwin. I have figured that out on my own. I only thought to amuse myself, but his proposal disgusted me, so obvious was it after less than a week of acquaintanceship. I would have denied him entrance to the house on his next visit, but now that Haidie has come up with a scheme to fleece him of the mine he stole from his father, I believe I'll keep him on my string a bit longer. Haidie's scheme lacks only one thing, and that is money. What do you say we advance it to him?"

"A capital idea, but I think it unlikely he would agree to play against a young boy."

"Oh, that is not the plan at all. Haidie is to go in search of his friend, a Mr. Vander, who is believed to be the greatest card cheat Haidie has ever seen." Then Miss Arvilla added, "Even more accomplished than he is himself."

"I'd like nothing better than to cheat a cheater. Oh, I have missed my sisters and their scheming ways."

* * *

So there we were in the Progressive Club, hoping to find Corny. I stood near a blackjack table, looking over a man's shoulder, but he jerked his head at me and said, "Get along, kid."

So I joined Mr. Edwin, who was standing at the bar, a glass of beer in his hand. He put the beer to his lips every now and then, but he didn't drink much. "Sheep dip," he muttered, when I glanced at the glass.

We stood there, watching the door, until long past midnight. "Maybe your friend is otherwise engaged tonight," Mr. Edwin said.

That could be. But it was also possible that whoever had questioned Corny's honesty in Omaha had followed him to Denver, and Corny had gone on to Central or Black Hawk or even Georgetown. "What say we give it up for tonight?" Mr. Edwin asked. I nodded, disappointed, because the plan had seemed like such a good one, but as we made ready to leave, I spotted Corny coming through the door, looking like a dude and brandishing that cane with the gold-plated cast-iron knob. "There he is," I told Mr. Edwin, pointing to Corny.

Mr. Edwin wasn't impressed. "That is the man to whom you would entrust your future?"

"The very same."

"He looks like a greenhorn."

"You'd have him look like a sharper?"

"Your point is taken."

We watched as Corny, head high, glanced this way and that. He stopped a moment at the roulette wheel, then went to the bar just down from us and put his foot up on the rail but shook his head when the bartender asked if he wanted champagne. "A glass of beer, sir," he replied. With his arm resting on the bar, he studied the poker players, lifting his glass every now and then the way Mr. Edwin had and taking only tiny sips.

"Why would anybody flash a diamond ring that size when he could be set upon by footpads?" Mr. Edwin whispered.

I decided he didn't know the first thing about gambling—or cheating. "Glass," I told him. "It reflects the cards he deals, just like a mirror."

"You are indeed an impressive young man, Haidie, learned in the way of evil doings. It's no wonder my sisters were captivated by you."

Corny stopped watching the poker players and returned to his beer, looking into the mirror behind the bar as he studied the room. At last, he saw me in the mirror, and a grin spread over his face. "Why, what do I behold? It is my young friend, Haidie, is it not?" He picked up his glass and crowded into the bar next to us. "I never saw a sight that pleased me so much. And this, I presume, is your father." He raised his glass. "Sir, I congratulate you on the fine young man you have sired. I never met a boy I admired as much as this young lad, and his brother promises to be every bit as accomplished."

"This isn't Pa. This is Mr. Edwin Matchett. He's a banker and the brother of two ladies who came overland with me and Boots."

"Then you have not located your father."

"We did."

"And did he find a gold mine?"

"He found it, and he lost it. That's why we came here looking for you. Jake and Teresa said you would be at the Progressive."

"Then I am glad to be of assistance. This young man," he said, turning to Mr. Edwin, "this young man helped save the lives of several who were threatened by ruffians. Young Master Haidie is a personage of courage. Now tell me, what is it you have in mind? I hope it involves fleecing, for I have always enjoyed getting the better of a scoundrel."

"It is much too complicated to discuss here," Mr. Edwin said. "Would you call tomorrow at my home, where Haidie, my sisters, and I will explain it to you?"

"It would be my pleasure. You bet." Corny tipped his hat, and I wondered if he still kept his gun there. I figured that was a sure bet.

* * *

Corny called at eight the next morning, and Martha escorted him into the dining room, where we were just finishing breakfast. He would not give up his hat, but placed it under his chair as he sat down, so I knew for sure that the gun was still hidden inside it.

"We had not expected you so early, Mr. Vander," Miss Lizzie said, after the introductions were complete. Without asking if Corny wanted to eat, she told Martha to have the cook fix a plate, and in a moment, Corny was digging into fried ham, eggs, hotcakes, and wheat bread, muttering as he ate that Miss Lizzie was too kind.

We waited until he had finished and we were all drinking coffee, which me and Boots had developed a taste for on the trail. "Now that I am refreshed, I should like the details of the little escapade you have so kindly invited me to join," Corny said.

"It is a simple one, Mr. Vander—or is it Mr. Cornelius?" Miss Arvilla asked.

"On that, we shall decide in a moment."

Miss Arvilla nodded. "As you wish. We would like you to engage a gentleman of our acquaintance in a poker game and win a gold mine from him, along with five thousand dollars." She corrected herself, "Six thousand dollars, the additional thousand being for your services. My sister, brother, and I will advance you the money for the game."

"And what if I lose?"

Miss Lizzie spoke up. "Haidie has assured us you will not. But if you do, then the loss will be ours. Of course, if you lose, there will be no money with which to pay you." Miss Lizzie grinned at her sister, then asked Corny, "Is that not a good incentive, sir?"

"Helping Master Haidie is incentive enough," Corny said. "But the one thousand dollars is, shall we say, the cream on top of the milk."

"Here is the plan, then," Miss Arvilla said, as she dismissed Martha and rose to pour Corny more coffee. "Haidie's father was cheated out of his gold mine and an additional five thousand dollars by an unscrupulous man who, it seems, is a business associate of my brother's. We will introduce you to him as a friend recently arrived from the East who wants to invest in Colorado mines. We shall ask him to take you under his wing and help you find the proper vehicles for your money. Then you will entice him to play poker and will win by whatever methods you choose to employ."

The plan was a simple one, but Corny frowned. "What makes you think he would agree to take me on?"

"Oh, he will, after he is assured you are Edwin's friend."

Miss Lizzie glanced at her sister, then said slyly, "You see, sir, the man is courting my sister and has already declared his intentions. He would do anything to win her."

"To win our money, that is," Miss Arvilla added scornfully. "So if for no other reason, he would take you as a client to please me."

"He is a man of good taste, even if the money is not considered," Corny said, bowing his head a little.

"I hope you are not so obvious when you play poker," Miss Arvilla chided him.

"I see you are not a woman who seeks flattery," Corny told her.

"Then we see eye to eye on that point at least," she replied.

So we agreed that Corny would pose as a wealthy man, Cornelius Vander, kin to one of the richest men in America, anxious to buy up gold properties, an investor whose knowledge of mining was as thin as gruel. Mr. Thacker would be so accommodating that he surely would not object when Corny suggested a poker game.

"It sounds as good as cheese," Corny said, "but I have one request. I should like to have Haidie with me. He will act as my ward and my factotum. It is always wise to have an accomplice."

I grinned at that. Now I could indeed be Corny's capper, and I'd be able to see Joel Thacker getting fleeced, too.

Miss Lizzie said that as I was to be a part of the scheme, she would buy me a set of gentleman's clothes—and one for Corny, too, because he was too flashy for an eastern investor. Only she didn't say "flashy." She said "grandiloquent."

"I acquiesce," Corny said, "but I insist on keeping my hat."

Well, I knew that.

* * *

Miss Arvilla gave Corny an envelope of money "for expenses," and her brother took us to a tailor shop where we were fitted with new clothes. Then Corny disappeared "to make arrangements," he said. All that took time, so it wasn't until two days later that we sat in the living room, Corny dressed in a black suit, white high-collared shirt, and wine-colored cravat, spats over his boots, and me in a suit that was a miniature version of Corny's—but without the spats—and as tight and uncomfortable as a hoop skirt. Boots had ridden Outlaw down to see Pa, but Mr. Edwin and his sisters were sitting with us. We had drunk about a thousand cups of tea and were ready to give up on Mr. Thacker, when we heard that raspy sound of the doorbell.

When Martha escorted our mark into the room, I stared, sizing him up as I tried to figure out what kind of man would steal a gold mine. Cheating at cards was one thing—after all, when you joined a game, you knew the chances of that—but outright theft was wrong.

Mr. Thacker didn't look like a thief, but then, I knew the best scammers looked just like somebody's brother. He was tall, burly, with dark brown hair and brown eyes as soft as those of that buffalo we killed. His nose was long, and his mouth wide, but it was his hands that interested me. You could tell by them that he surely had not labored in a mine. His fingers were tapered and soft, just like a gambler's hands. And that worried me a little, because hands like that could feel the slightest shaving or pinprick on a card. He might be a good poker player himself.

"This is our friend from the East, Mr. Cornelius Vander, and his ward, Haidie." Edwin glanced at me. We'd never talked about what name I should take. I hoped he didn't say "Richards," because Mr. Thacker might remember Pa's name and would suspect me right off.

"Vander, Haidie Vander," I said, before Mr. Edwin could continue.

"A pleasure," Corny said, standing up and shaking Mr. Thacker's hand.

"The pleasure is mine, sir," Mr. Thacker said in a voice as smooth as pudding. He studied Corny, but he didn't pay any attention to me, didn't even shake my hand, for that matter.

Then he went to Miss Arvilla and took her hand. "My dearest lady." He turned to Miss Lizzie. "Miss Elizabeth. I trust you are well."

"Never in a better state of mind," Miss Lizzie said.

At last, he shook Mr. Edwin's hand. "Edwin."

"Thacker."

When all that business was done, Mr. Thacker sat down. He looked for a place next to Miss Arvilla, but I was sitting there and didn't offer to get up. They all made small talk for a moment, until Mr. Edwin said, "I am trying to dissuade Mr. Vander from investing in mining. It is my belief that most mining properties on the market are borrascas—worthless, if you will—not bonanzas, and that it is folly for a man who is not an expert to put his money into mining. Do you not agree?"

"Hold on there, Edwin, I cannot say as I do agree. I myself have run across various investment opportunities that are as good as gold, so to speak." Mr. Thacker smiled at his little joke, although no one else did.

"There, you see, Edwin. By no means does everyone agree with you." Corny turned to Mr. Thacker. "I hope I may confide in you, sir, as a friend of Edwin's family, that I am here representing investors whose names I cannot reveal, but with whom you would undoubtedly be familiar. They have a great deal of money to spend. I myself am one of the investors, although a modest one."

"Cornelius Vander"—Miss Arvilla paused a moment to let the name sink in—"comes from a prominent eastern family and trusts Edwin, as they have been friends for many years."

"And I say you should keep your money in railroads and steamships and leave mining to those who understand it," Mr. Edwin said. He stood then and said, "Business calls. Thacker, disabuse Mr. Vander of the idea of buying gold mines, will you."

He left, and no one spoke, as Mr. Thacker seemed deep in thought. "Vander," he said at last. "An odd name, I'd say. Is it Dutch?"

"It is abbreviated. The original name was somewhat longer."

"Cornelius Vander," Mr. Thacker mused. Then he grinned. "I believe it must have been Vanderbilt."

Corny ducked his head. "As to that, you must keep it to yourself. I am indeed a member of that illustrious family, but ours is a poorer branch that has chosen a poorer name. It was changed due to a falling-out, but peace has been restored, and my more fortunate relatives have turned to me to handle their investments in the West. Can you imagine what would happen to the price of a mine if the owner were to discover the Vanderbilt family was interested in it? You must keep this intelligence to yourself."

"Of course," Mr. Thacker said.

"Edwin may be right in saying mining is a poor investment for us, but my instructions are to acquire such properties." He gave a woeful smile. "I suppose my relatives can afford to lose something, if Edwin's advice proves prescient."

Miss Arvilla excused herself and said she would see to tea, and Miss Lizzie followed her out of the room. As soon as the doors were slid shut, except for a small crack, Mr. Thacker said, "I hope I am not being too forward in saying that I am something of an expert in mining properties, having dealt in them for several years in California and now in Colorado, and would be pleased to offer my services."

Corny gave him a long look and drew back, almost as if he had been offended.

"I still hope to convince Edwin to aid me."

"Of course. Of course. But if he does not—great minds do not always agree, we are told—I would be happy to serve

in that capacity. I have references, the finest of them being
Edwin himself. If you should like to meet later, sir, I would
be happy to discuss opportunities with you—away from the
ladies, of course."

The two of them agreed to meet the next day at the
Criterion Saloon on Larimer Street, and just after they set
the time, Miss Arvilla entered the room carrying the tea tray.
Miss Lizzie was right behind her with a plate of little cakes.
It was almost as if they'd been listening behind the doors for
the two men to make their appointment, before joining us.

"Martha was indisposed, and I had to make the tea myself. I hope you will find it satisfactory," she said.

"Dear lady, anything made with your hands is more than
satisfactory," Mr. Thacker said smoothly.

Miss Arvilla didn't reply, but she sent her sister a look
of such scorn that had he seen it, Mr. Thacker would have
known immediately that his courtship with Miss Arvilla was
borrasca.

＊ ＊ ＊

"Your job," Corny told me the next afternoon as we rode to
the Criterion in Mr. Edwin's buggy, "is to watch to make
sure how Thacker cheats. I know his kind. Of course, most
men cheat a little. You bet. They consider themselves to
be fools if they do not. But they are clumsy. Still . . ." He
paused, thinking.

"Did you see his hands? They're a gambler's hands," I
said.

"You are an observant lad. I did indeed. It's possible that
he is a man of the pasteboards. If he swindled your father out

of his money, then he is unscrupulous and I believe would go
to any length to win at cards." Corny reached into his pocket
and took out two decks of cards. "If I tell you to go to the
bartender and ask for a fresh deck, you will return with one
of these."

"What if Mr. Thacker asks?"

"These will do."

Then Corny told me signals to use if I caught Mr. Thacker
cheating in various ways. "He will let me win at first, because he wants to be in my good graces. But I may lose, to
show him I am a novice. It is all part of the game. If I begin
to win big, however, he will become angry, and that's when
the cheating starts. If he puts up your father's mine, then he
will be desperate, and you must watch him closely."

We were late reaching the Criterion. Corny had dawdled
on purpose to put Mr. Thacker on edge, making him think
perhaps Corny had changed his mind. I wondered if Mr.
Thacker would do the same thing—leave us waiting to show
he had more important things to do—but he was standing
just inside the doors and held out his hand as soon as he
saw us. He and Corny shook hands. Once again, Mr. Thacker
paid no attention to me.

"We were detained. Edwin is not at all pleased that he
has not dissuaded me from investing in mining properties,
but he allowed as how you are as knowledgeable about them
as anyone, far more so than himself," Corny said. He looked
around the room. "It is not Delmonico's, is it? But then this
is the wild West. I wonder is the whiskey drinkable?"

"You might be surprised."

We went to the bar, where Mr. Thacker ordered two

whiskeys. When they arrived, he threw his down, but Corny sipped, then made a face. "You, sir, are a better man than I. My stomach cannot tolerate such swill. I believe I will switch to beer." When Mr. Thacker turned to the bartender to order the beer and another whiskey, Corny glanced around the room, his eyes flickering when he saw two men sitting at a table, and I knew he had lined up confederates.

"Shall we find a table where we can talk in private?" Mr. Thacker asked. Corny reached into his pocket to pay for the drinks, but Mr. Thacker told him, "You are my guest, sir. Do not insult me." He put a coin on the bar, then the three of us found a table in the back of the room, where the crowd was thinner.

As we sat down, I glanced about. The Criterion wasn't as fine as the Progressive. There were no mirrors on the walls or paintings of half-naked ladies. But it was crowded and noisy, and there were dance-hall girls just like Emily sitting at some of the tables, drinking champagne that, as Emily had told us, was really cold tea. Men were gambling at other tables. I saw one jump up and throw down his cards and stomp off, and wondered if he'd been beaten honestly or had been cheated. I'd have bet on the latter. As Cheet said once, only a fool loses, when he can win by cheating.

Mr. Thacker didn't throw back his whiskey this time, but only sipped it and leaned toward Corny. "Mr. Vander, your timing is exquisite. Just this morning, I obtained knowledge that one of the finest mines in the territory is available, and at a good price. This intelligence is confidential, so I must ask you not to reveal it to anyone, even to Edwin."

Corny frowned. "That is quite a coincidence, sir."

"Yes, you are prudent to be skeptical. There is so much flimflam in the mining world, I am afraid, and promoters would take advantage of a novice—a greenhorn, as they are called here. I am not suggesting you are such a personage, of course, but I would advise you to deal only with a man you can trust, a man who comes highly recommended." Mr. Thacker leaned back in his chair, giving Corny time to conclude he was just such a man.

"Your advice is taken," Corny said. "What is this prospect?"

Mr. Thacker looked around the room, then leaned close to Corny. "The Mighty Warrior, sir. It can be bought for half its value." He leaned back with a satisfied look on his face.

"The Mighty Warrior?"

"Surely you've heard of it, one of the finest prospects in Colorado. It is owned by a partnership that has found itself in great trouble because of the unscrupulous actions of one of its members. It seems he put up his stake in a poker game and lost it. He was the primary investor. The winner of the shares now wants to unload them. So controlling interest in the Warrior is available for a pittance."

"I should like to see the mine before committing myself."

"That is not possible. If it is known the shares are on the market, the price would skyrocket. But I can show you assays and engineering reports. And samples of the ore."

Corny frowned and tapped his forefingers together. "Well, I don't know. I will have to study on it. I had not expected to be presented with an investment so quickly. And I have a few ideas of my own that I want to pursue."

Mr. Thacker leaned forward until his chest was almost on the table. "My dear fellow, if you are to invest in mining, you must learn that agreements are finalized in the blink of an eye. To wait is to court folly. Faint heart never won fair lady, as the expression goes."

"That may be fine in courtship, but as for investments, prudence is the order of the day."

"Then I suggest you keep your money in steamships. Mining requires a man of decisiveness."

Corny appeared chastened. "I will admit I am at times too cautious. My cousins—my investors, that is—have warned me not to let opportunity slip through my fingers." He put his elbows on the table, his fingers together to form a steeple. Then he leaned back in his chair, balancing it on two legs, and looked around the room. "What game do they play there?" he asked, nodding at the table he had glanced at when we were at the bar.

"Poker, most likely."

"Ah, perhaps we might indulge ourselves in a game while I consider your proposition."

Mr. Thacker frowned. "A game of chance?"

"Perhaps."

"I would not recommend it here, sir. You would risk your purse. Cheats and scoundrels abound. But if you're so inclined, I might suggest a safer place."

"One where you play?"

"Oh no. I never play cards."

Corny sat forward quickly, the chair slamming onto the floor. "You don't gamble?"

"I never have and never will. I know my limitations. But I do not judge others who care to risk their capital. Feel free to pursue the diversion on your own."

Corny stared at him, and my mouth dropped open. I'd never considered that Mr. Thacker might not gamble with Corny. The plan that Corny had called as good as cheese now stunk like Limburger.

"I have offended you. It is a habit of mine to speak against gambling. I beg pardon," Mr. Thacker said.

Corny blinked a couple of times, then recovered. "A man after my own heart. It was a test, sir. I myself would not trust in a man who gambled."

Mr. Thacker looked pleased with himself, but I was horrified. We'd played our cards, and we'd lost. I pushed back my chair, trying to think how I'd tell Pa, but Corny reached under the table and put his hand on my knee.

"I would like to see the reports on the mine you mention, sir, but I must tell you that I have intelligence on another property that interests me far more. I did not mention it, because I did not know how far I could trust you. But I see now you are a man of honor."

Mr. Thacker dipped his head, as if he were accepting a compliment.

"The property is in a place called Georgetown. Do you know it?"

Corny was too obvious. He couldn't just outright ask about the Hangover, or Mr. Thacker would be suspicious. I cleared my throat to warn him, but he only tapped my knee again.

"I know the area well. In fact, I myself have investments there."

"Then I will tell you." Corny leaned forward and whispered, "The Blue Flag." He sat back, his face appearing as satisfied as a cat with a bird. I frowned, because I didn't have any idea what he was talking about.

Mr. Thacker frowned, too. "I don't know it."

"Splendid. That means it has not yet drawn attention." He lowered his voice even more. "The Emerald Isle, the major producer in the district, apexes on the Blue Flag claim." He grinned, and glanced at me, explaining, "It is all well and good to find an underground ore vein, but the fellow who owns the claim where the vein apexes, or emerges on the surface, has the right to follow it wherever it goes." He turned to our mark. "Is that not right, Mr. Thacker?"

"I see you are not totally ignorant of mining law."

Corny tried to look confident, but instead, he just looked like a stuffed shirt who knew only a thing or two about a subject.

"And how do you know about this, Mr. Vander?" Mr. Thacker asked. I wondered the same thing.

Corny tapped his head. "As you say, I am not totally without resources. I cannot give you the source of the information, as it was told to us in the strictest confidence. But I can assure you, the intelligence is not to be questioned. In fact, sir, I came here with the express desire of purchasing the Blue Flag." He lowered his voice to a whisper. "You see, we have had experts examine the mine—they have done it covertly—and the results would astonish you."

"Then you have played me for a fool, and you have wasted my time." Mr. Thacker started to get up.

"Not so quickly, sir." Corny tugged at Mr. Thacker's arm, and the man sat back down. "I will admit that I was not completely honest with you, but can you blame me? The name

Vanderbilt would invite all sorts of skulduggery. Although you come recommended by Edwin, I had to make sure of the man I was dealing with. It was only prudent. Forgive me, Mr. Thacker, but I thought it necessary to put you to the test, and you passed admirably, sir, admirably."

I did not have the slightest idea what Corny was talking about, but I figured we had nothing to lose, since we couldn't win back Pa's mine in a card game. So I leaned forward as if I were interested, and didn't say a word.

"I fail to see how this interests me," Mr. Thacker said.

"It should interest you a great deal. I would like you to acquire the mine for Mr. Vander . . . ah, my investors. I believe you can purchase the property for a much smaller sum than I can."

"Have you tried?" Mr. Thacker asked.

"Unfortunately, yes. The owner said he would not sell."

"Then I don't see how I—"

"Hush, man. Let me explain. The mine is in the Georgetown District. Its discoverer has an inflated idea of what the mines there can produce. Fool that he is, he does not realize he has the key to the entire district. That one mine can control everything. He is not a miner, you see, but a teamster who believes he knows more than he does. He would be suspicious of me. In fact, if he suspected who I represent, he would undoubtedly try to find other speculators to bid against me and drive up the price. But you are a local man and could deal efficaciously with him. You would acquire the Blue Flag, then sell it to us, at a suitable commission, of course."

"I see," Mr. Thacker said, nodding. He looked down at

the table as if he was thinking, but I could see that his eyes had a peculiar gleam in them.

"Is it not an ideal plan, profitable to you, to me, to my investors, and even to the owner of the Blue Flag?"

"All would benefit," Mr. Thacker said. "Who is the lucky man?"

"A country bumpkin of a personage by the name of Jacob Crowfoot."

My head jerked up at that, and it was all I could do not to grin at Corny. It had never occurred to me that Corny would come up with a backup plan, and do it so quickly. I wondered why he hadn't told me about it.

"Don't know him," Mr. Thacker said. "Where can I find him?"

"I believe he stays at the Denver House."

"I shall look for him there. Perhaps we can indeed do business together, Mr. Vander. I shall seek him out at once."

As Mr. Thacker stood up, Corny raised a hand. "Just one more thing, sir."

"Yes?" Mr. Thacker narrowed his eyes.

"You will forgive me if I do not completely trust someone I have known such a short time." When Mr. Thacker bristled, Corny added, "In fact, I do not trust anyone I have known a long time." He laughed as if he had said something funny. "I would insist on one thing, and that is you take my ward, Haidie, along with you. He is not a bright lad . . ." Corny paused, while I tried to look stupid. "And he was too often with the wild boys at home. I would like him to learn a little about how business is transacted. I am afraid he needs a lesson in ethics, too. He has had one or two little run-ins with the authorities, and I have brought him with me to straighten him out."

Now I tried to look like one of the toughs in the orphanage.

"I do not care to have such a lad looking over my shoulder, Mr. Vander."

"He'll be no trouble. He never says anything." Corny leaned forward, as if I wasn't there. "Just keep your hand on your purse."

"But sir—"

"That is my condition."

At last, Mr. Thacker nodded his head. "I believe we understand each other, Mr. Vander, and in short order, I hope the Blue Flag is yours. Come along, boy."

✳ ✳ ✳

This business of the Blue Flag was all news to me, of course. I glanced back at Corny as I followed Mr. Thacker through the crowd of gamblers, hoping he would mouth some word of instruction, but he only beamed and nodded and made a shoving motion with his hand, and I knew I was on my own.

Mr. Thacker all but forgot me as he rushed along the street. But after a time, he slowed, and said, "Now, boy, we must have an understanding."

"Yes, sir."

"Are you honest?"

I smirked. "Sure."

"What is your feeling about Mr. Vander?"

I looked away.

"Well."

"He's swole-headed."

"Is he honest?"

"Too honest for me. He's a skinflint, too. Makes me account to him for every penny I spend."

"And you would like a little cash of your own to fling about."

I shrugged.

"Then I suggest you keep your mouth shut as to what you see, and I will reward you handsomely."

"How much?"

"If all goes well, a hundred dollars. Have you ever seen a hundred dollars in your life?"

"How about two hundred?"

"Greedy, are you?"

"Not so greedy as you, sir."

Mr. Thacker laughed and clapped me on the shoulder. "I believe you might do business if you decide to leave your guardian. Now, the agreement is you are not to say a word to Mr. Vander about my dealings with Mr. Crowfoot. You will agree with me when I tell him how I acquired the property. Is that understood?"

"If you say so."

As we continued to the Denver House, I worried about what Jake would say when he saw me. He and Corny must have cooked up something, but Jake wouldn't have known that Corny would send me along with Mr. Thacker. What if he said something to me that queered the game? Jake wasn't as sneaky as Corny, and he might just blurt out, "Hello, Haidie."

We found the Denver House, and Mr. Thacker asked for Jacob Crowfoot. "Can't say as I know him, but you're welcome to look," a man said. We went inside the barn of a hotel, where the "rooms" were outlined by wagon covers hung from the ceiling. "Jacob Crowfoot, show yourself," Mr. Thacker called. A few men stuck their heads out from behind the panels of material, but none of them was Jake.

Then in a minute, Teresa came from the back of the room. I hadn't thought about Teresa. She would give me away in a second if she recognized me. I slipped behind Mr. Thacker and shook my head and put my finger to my mouth. She started to say something, but I butted in and said, "Ma'am, we're looking for a Mr. Jacob Crowfoot. Do you know him?"

Teresa gave me a long look. Either she was in on Corny's game, or she realized something was afoot, and she said, "He's at the Elephant Corral."

I put my hands together as if I were praying, and she nodded once. "Could you describe him, ma'am?" I asked.

Mr. Thacker turned to me and said, "I'll do the talking, boy. You shut your mouth."

Teresa ignored him. "Why yes, he's a big man, brown hair getting a little thin. And he has a big dog with him. Ugly dog. Be careful, that dog's a mean one."

Now I had another worry. What if Tige came running to meet me? I sure wished Corny had told me about his backup plan. "I could take you over there," Teresa said.

"No, ma'am, we'll find him," Mr. Thacker told her.

"How come you didn't want her to come along?" I asked, once we were back out on the street.

"Females get greedy. You offer them a hundred dollars, they'll want two." I was startled by that. Had Mr. Thacker figured out I was a girl? But then he added, "Girls and certain young men. Now I mean it, boy, when I tell you to keep your mouth shut."

We walked along to the Elephant Corral, Mr. Thacker humming a little, feeling full of beans, I guess, that he was going to make a big score from Corny. I spotted Jake right off. He was standing in the mud with his mules, Tige tied up to the wagon. I worried Tige would recognize me, but he was gnawing on a bone as big as he was. Mr. Thacker spotted Jake, and we approached him.

"I'm Haidie Vander," I said, emphasizing the last name.

Jake nodded, then held out his hand to Mr. Thacker. "And you'll be the boy's pa, Mr. Vander, I'd wager."

"Joel Thacker. The boy is an associate of mine. We've come looking for you, Mr. Crowfoot."

"For me?" Jake sounded puzzled—and a little stupid.

"Indeed we have. I've come with a little proposition for you."

"Well, I'm always interested in that," Jake said good-naturedly. "I'm interested in any kind of proposition, less'n it has to do with my gold mine." Then he gave such a dopey grin that Mr. Thacker couldn't help but believe Jake was the easiest mark in Denver.

Chapter Ten

I thought we'd go into a gambling hall like the Criterion, where Corny had met Mr. Thacker to talk about the Hang-over, but instead, Mr. Thacker led Jake, with me trailing along behind, up to Larimer Street and into a bank that wasn't as big as the Matchetts' library. We climbed a staircase along one wall and went into a little office on the second floor.

The office was as shabby as the orphan home where me and Boots had lived, with only a desk and two wooden chairs. There wasn't a rug on the floor or pictures on the wall, not even curtains on the windows, which were open and let in the noise from the street. A man cursed his mules, and Jake went to the window and waved. "Hey, looky up here where I am," he cried.

"Have a seat, sir," Mr. Thacker said, sitting down in one chair. Jake sat in the other, and I perched on the windowsill.

Jake crossed an ankle over a knee and looked around, disappointed. "This ain't so much," he muttered.

"Indeed not. I prefer to put my money into investments, not into appurtenances."

"What's a 'purtenance'?"

"Furnishings, sir, fancy chairs and pictures in gilt frames, a waste of money. It is enough that we have such fittings below, to satisfy patrons who are impressed with those fripperies. But you, sir, are a man of more substance. I believe you would prefer to deal with someone who does not waste money."

Jake looked even more confused, but he nodded. Then he glanced at me. "Who's that?"

"The son of a friend. His father, a man of the cloth, has passed on, and I have taken the boy under my wing, charged with teaching him the fundamentals of business. Pay him no mind."

I remembered Cheet then and wondered how many crooks thought nobody would suspect them if they pretended to be priests or priests' sons.

Jake nodded, apparently satisfied, and all but ignored me after that.

"Shall we get down to business?" Mr. Thacker asked.

"What business is that?"

"Why, mining, sir. Mining. As a banker, I am keenly interested in the mining business, as you yourself are."

"Oh, I am!" Jake told him. "I got the dandiest mine in the Georgetown District."

"That remains to be seen."

"It's the Blue Flag. I've had fellows offer me a million dollars for it."

"A million? Surely not a million." Mr. Thacker frowned.

"Well, close. A thousand anyways. One did. But I wouldn't sell, not to him, not to nobody."

"Everything has its price."

Jake shrugged.

"Just as a point of conversation, what is *your* price?" Mr. Thacker picked up a piece of ore sitting on his desk as a paperweight and began examining it. He looked a little bored, as if he didn't really care much about the mine.

"Why, there ain't any price. Georgetown's the richest district in the Colorado Territory, and I aim to have a good piece of it."

"And the Blue Flag is the key to the district?" A breeze came through the window and ruffled the papers on the desk, and Mr. Thacker set the piece of ore on top of them.

Jake shifted in his chair, glancing past me, out the window. He didn't answer.

"Sir?" Mr. Thacker said.

"I'll tell you a little story," Jake replied. "I never had money in my life. I grew up on a farm so poor we had to buy the rocks to haul away." He laughed at his joke, but Mr. Thacker didn't get it. Jake ducked his head and continued. "I worked myself 'most to death to get my team of mules, and they're a good team, not a brown mule in the whole lot. I got to be a good freighter, made enough money to get me a wife. I come out here and started hauling to the mining camps, and I seen how fellows get rich just from a hole in the ground. And I says to myself, 'Why, if they can do it, Jake Crowfoot, you can, too.' So I got me a pick, and every trip to Georgetown or Black Hawk or Central City, I spent a day or two looking for a gold mine. And I found one, a nice little piece of ground. I like it better than supper. It ain't very big, but it's right in the middle of the district. I done some work on it. It's a dandy."

"How does the ore assay?"

Jake looked canny. "I ain't telling." He frowned. "How'd you hear about the Blue Flag anyways?"

"I keep up on the mining districts."

Jake narrowed his eyes. "How come you want to talk to me?"

"A proposition, sir. You see, as a banker, I am always on the lookout for good investments, and I consider the Blue Flag to be . . . well, not a good one but a modest prospect. Of course, as you say, there has been little work done on it, and it takes capital to develop a mine. Do you have it, sir?"

Jake shrugged.

"I thought not. You would be well advised to sell your little mine while you can, while the district is still hot. So along that line, I am making you a most generous offer of two thousand dollars."

Jake stood up, indignant. "Two thousand dollars! You think I'm a blockhead? You think you can get me up here and steal my mine from me? Why, I should have brought my whip—" Jake stood and made for the door.

"Now hold on there, Mr. Crowfoot. That was just my opening bid. We can negotiate from there."

"No negotiating. I won't sell. My wife'd just spend the money. I aimed to have a gold mine, and now I do, and you ain't taking it from me. I want everybody to know that Jake Crowfoot is a man of property. Owning a mine makes me somebody."

"Then what do you propose?"

"I ain't proposing nothing."

Mr. Thacker rose and pointed to the chair, but Jake didn't

sit down. Instead, he stood behind the chair with his hand on its back. Mr. Thacker seated himself and began to roll the ore sample between his hands, thinking. "So what you want is a gold mine in the Georgetown District."

"Not just any mine," Jake said. "You can't play me for a fool."

"Why no, of course not, Mr. Crowfoot. I can see that." He bobbled his head a few times. "What if there were to be another mine in the district that is even better than the Blue Flag?"

"There's nothing better than the Flag," Jake told him.

"Of course, you don't know that, since you've had no significant production. You only *believe* it to be so. I have in mind one that is already a producer, one with a proven record."

Jake squinted. "What's that?" He sat down on the edge of the chair.

I leaned forward so far that I lost my balance. Now I understood Corny's game. He'd get Jake to trade the Blue Flag for the Hangover. I had to bite the inside of my mouth to keep from grinning. It was a good plan. I just wished I'd come up with it.

Mr. Thacker raised his chin a little and smiled. "The Senator."

I stopped biting my cheeks and gaped. The Senator! What in the world was the Senator? I was glad Mr. Thacker was staring at Jake instead of me, or he'd have known from my face that something was wrong. I felt as bad as I had when Mr. Thacker announced he didn't gamble.

But Jake played it right. He scoffed. "The Senator's played out. You can't pull that on me. You think I'm too dumb to know what's going on? You brought me up here to cheat me. I got better things to do with my time." Jake turned away from Mr. Thacker.

"Now hold on again, Mr. Crowfoot. There are other mines in Georgetown. I happen to be myself the owner of a fine mine there, the Hangover."

As he turned back to Mr. Thacker, Jake glanced at me with the tiniest flicker of his eyelids. "I hear it's got troubles."

"Nothing serious. Nothing a man of intelligence and hard work couldn't change. I believe you are that man."

Jake looked flattered. "Well, I have a way with mules. I guess men ain't much different."

"Quite right." Mr. Thacker smiled. "I would trade you a working mine for a prospect. You might ask why, and I would tell you that I have the capital to develop it. And I, sir, am a speculator. It is the gamble that stirs my blood." He paused. "A fair trade, then?"

"Not so fast. How do I know it ain't played out?"

Mr. Thacker removed some papers from his desk and laid them in front of Jake. "Just look at the shipping records, sir. I have here a producing mine, while you have only a hole in the ground." When Jake's head snapped up, Mr. Thacker added quickly, "Of course, it may be a valuable hole, but that has yet to be seen. I am trading you a sure thing for speculation."

While Jake tapped his forehead with his finger as if he was trying to sort out what Mr. Thacker had said, the banker turned to me. "Boy, go get us a bottle of whiskey." He reached into his pocket and held out a coin.

Jake jerked up his head. "Not so fast. I know about whiskey. He'll put something in it that'll make me stop thinking."

"Then the bottle will be for me."

I didn't want to leave. Jake was doing just fine on his own, but I didn't trust Mr. Thacker and thought he might try something when I was out of the room. Maybe Jake did, too, because he said, "The boy stays right here. I don't want him going out blabbing my business."

"As you wish," Mr. Thacker said. He glared at me. "Shall we execute the trade, Mr. Crowfoot?"

"Nah, you seem awful anxious. I expect you know something I don't. Besides, my wife won't like it. I want a gold mine, but she expects a diamond ring and a carriage lined with blue silk. She's the damndest woman." He shook his head.

Mr. Thacker laughed. "And an uncommon beauty, I am sure."

"She ain't common, that's for sure."

"I understand women, so I will make a most generous offer—the Hangover and one thousand dollars."

"No, I wouldn't do that."

"How much do you want?"

"Your mine and seven thousand dollars."

It was a good thing Mr. Thacker wasn't looking my way or he'd have seen me grin. That was five thousand dollars for Pa, a thousand for Corny, and a thousand for Jake.

"Why, that's highway robbery. I'll give you three."

"Seven or it's no go. My wife always said if she had seven thousand dollars, she'd be a rich woman." Jake gave that dopey grin again. "I sure would like to make her rich. She'd make it worth my while."

"I'll go five, and that is a great concession on my part."

Jake stood up. "Keep your mine then. Now that you've got me in the mood, maybe I'll find somebody that'll give me a better deal."

Mr. Thacker sighed. "It is against my better judgment, but I am a generous person. I would rather satisfy another man than reap the best profit." He reached into his desk and pulled out a document. "Have you your deed with you, sir?"

"I always carry it. Safest place I know." He patted his shirt. Corny must have drawn up a fake deed and given it to Jake. He'd sure been busy since he left the Matchetts' house.

"Then we can make the exchange. The boy will act as witness. Then I will get a bank draft."

"Cash," Jake told him.

"Cash?"

"Cash. I don't trust no drafts."

"But there are evil men out there who would entice you into a poker game and rob you of every penny. You could not only lose your purse but your life." He raised his chin a little. "I myself have killed two men who have tried to get the best of me."

"Cash," Jake said.

Mr. Thacker shrugged. "As you say."

The two of them signed a bunch of papers. Then Mr. Thacker handed me the pen and I dipped it into the inkwell and wrote carefully "Haidie Vander" where it said "witness."

"Now that business is taken care of, you will excuse me while I get your cash from the safe." He closed the door as he left the room, and Jake and I grinned at each other, and I threw my fist into the air. I wanted to shout "Huzza!" But neither of us said a word out loud because for all we knew, Mr. Thacker was listening at the door. We waited for a long time, both of us as nervous as chickens. Jake sat with his foot on his knee, slapping the other knee with his hand, while I tapped my foot on the floor. Every now and then we'd look at each other and grin. After a time, Jake studied the deed to the Hangover, then nodded, satisfied. "I'm not as dumb as he thinks," he mouthed. "I've signed contracts before."

Then I mouthed, "Aren't you afraid he's arranging for somebody to rob you?"

Jake shook his head. "Tige's tied up out there."

We kept on waiting until I began to wonder what Mr. Thacker was doing. Maybe he was onto us. He might even have gone to the sheriff. "Do you think—"

Jake cut me off, because we heard footsteps. Just as the door opened, Jake asked me, "Say, kid, do you know where I can buy a diamond ring?"

"Nah, I don't know anything about rings," I replied.

"There is a jeweler just up the street. You can trust him to sell you a diamond instead of glass. He is Mr. Manning on Holliday Street. You must use my name, and he will give you the best price," Mr. Thacker said as he came into the room. Then with a great flourish, he counted out the seven thousand dollars and handed the money to Jake, who counted it again. "You don't trust me?" Mr. Thacker asked.

"Trust you like the chicken trusts the fox," Jake replied, then grinned so widely that Mr. Thacker couldn't be offended. Mr. Thacker then handed him the deed to the Hangover.

Jake put it into his shirt. The two men shook hands, and Jake went out the door. I got up to follow him out, but Mr. Thacker said, "Where do you think you're going, boy?"

I swallowed a couple of times. All I wanted to do was get away from Mr. Thacker. He'd told us he'd killed two men, and I knew he'd threatened to kill Pa, too, when Pa'd tried to get back his mine and money. What would he do to me if he found out I was part of a plot to fleece him of the Hangover?

"I got to get back. Mr. Vander doesn't like to let me out of his sight for more than about a minute."

"He sent you with me. He won't expect you back."

"But you already got the mine."

"Yes." Mr. Thacker looked pleased with himself. Then he pointed to the chair and told me to sit down. "You and I have an understanding, boy."

"Yes, sir?"

"You forget about the hundred dollars I promised you?"

I'd rather leave than get the money. But that would make Mr. Thacker suspicious for sure. So I said, "Two hundred."

Mr. Thacker opened his desk drawer and took out five twenty-dollar gold pieces. "A hundred now. A hundred when the transaction with your guardian is complete."

"I didn't bargain on that."

"Do not play me for a fool. If I give you the full amount now, what is to keep you from telling the old boy about my transaction for the Blue Flag?" He mused, "That's the depositors' money I took. I'd be ruined if anything went wrong."

I shrugged. "What's there to tell? Mr. Vander will pay you back the seven thousand dollars."

"Oh, he will, will he? Perhaps you are not such a bright lad, after all. Do you think I will tell him I paid seven thousand? Oh, no." Mr. Thacker leaned back. "I paid *twenty*-seven thousand dollars for that mine, and threw in a property worth as much. He is a Vanderbilt, is he not? He is used to dealing in enormous sums and will be pleased the mine does not cost him even more."

I gaped. Mr. Thacker was a bigger cheat than me and Corny a hundred times over.

"I see I have impressed you," Mr. Thacker said, leaning back in his chair and putting his thumbs in his vest. "You will get your second hundred dollars after Mr. Vander has paid for the Blue Flag in full."

"If you're making so much, then maybe I ought to get five hundred," I said.

"Ah, such a greedy boy. We see eye to eye. Perhaps when this business is over, you could come to work for me. That is, if you want to leave that pompous fool Vander."

"Maybe, but I want my money first," I said.

"You will have to wait until morning, when we complete the transaction." He removed a cigar from a box on his desk, then with a cutter attached to his watch fob, he snipped off the end. He took his time lighting the cigar, then leaned back and blew smoke into the air. He glanced at the box, then at me, but instead of offering it to me, he shut the container. I was glad. I'd never smoked a cigar and didn't want to start now.

"Why not tonight?" I asked.

Mr. Thacker reached into his vest pocket and removed his

watch, opened it, then snapped it shut and returned it to the pocket. "The wait will be good for your guardian. It will put him in an anxious mood. You may tell him I will call upon him at ten in the morning. If everything goes as I expect, you can walk me to my conveyance after the conclusion of our transaction, and I will give you the second hundred dollars. Call on me later at the bank, and we will see about joining forces."

"You aren't going to meet him at the Criterion?" I didn't want Mr. Thacker going to the Matchett house. If he found out what we were up to and pulled a gun, he might hurt Miss Arvilla or Miss Lizzie. He'd realize sooner or later that he'd been taken, but I didn't want it to happen in front of the two ladies.

"I have other fish to fry there. I expect to impress a certain lady with my financial acumen."

"One of the old maids?" I asked.

"Watch your language, boy," Mr. Thacker warned. Then he added, "Women always appear younger to me when there is a fortune attached."

"Mr. Vander won't want you to go to the house. He'll be mighty mad if you don't meet him at a saloon. He told me he didn't like talking business with you in front of the ladies," I protested.

"Then you tell him that if he wants the Blue Flag, to be ready to finalize the transaction at the Matchett house at ten in the morning. And you will keep our little transaction a secret." He paused and looked me over. "I hope you are an accomplished liar."

"Oh yes, sir. I can lie like crazy."

✳ ✳ ✳

At last, Mr. Thacker let me go. I thought Jake might be waiting on the street, but there was no sign of him, which was just as well, because I had a feeling Mr. Thacker was watching me from the window. I strolled down Larimer Street as if I was in no hurry to get back to Corny, but the minute I turned the corner, I started to run. I stopped when I ran into Jake and Tige.

"I was getting worried about you," Jake said.

"He thinks me and him are going to be a team, that I'll be his capper." I shook my head. "But I made a hundred dollars out of him."

"And I made a thousand." Jake slipped me six thousand dollars and the deed, all wrapped in a bandana, and I slid the package into my shirt. "I kept my thousand." Jake grinned. "I'm going to spend it on a diamond for Teresa."

"You don't have to," I said, and reached under my lapel. I was so used to wearing Corny's "headlight" pinned to my coat that I'd put it there that morning. "This is for Teresa."

Jake looked it over and whistled. "Ain't that the finest thing! Teresa never had a friend as good as you. Wait till she sees it."

With all that money and the Hangover deed, I was afraid of being robbed, so Jake walked me to the Matchett house, then took off, just in case Mr. Thacker decided to call that night instead of in the morning.

I didn't even ring the bell, just rushed into the sisters' house and yelled for Corny. He was in the library with Miss

Arvilla and Miss Lizzie, and all of them hurried out into the hall.

"Well?" Miss Lizzie asked, while I was still catching my breath.

Miss Arvilla glanced around, then pointed to the library, and we went inside, shutting the door.

"I got the Hangover!" I said. I took a deep breath. "And six thousand dollars. Jake already kept his thousand."

"Splendid," Corny said, and Miss Arvilla clapped her hands.

"Oh, I wish I could see his face when you don't show up to claim the Blue Flag," Miss Lizzie said.

"You just might, ma'am, because Mr. Thacker is coming here at ten o'clock in the morning," I told her.

"What?" Miss Arvilla asked. "I thought he would meet Mr. Vander in one of the saloons."

"I tried to convince him to do that, but he said he was coming here." I leaned forward. "He wants to impress you."

"Then you must leave this instant, Mr. Vander. We want you to be long gone before Mr. Thacker arrives."

Corny thought that over. "No, ma'am," he said. "I do not trust what Thacker might do when he finds out he's been fleeced. It is said he is a dangerous man—"

"He's killed two men, and he tried to kill Pa," I interrupted. "And if he doesn't get his money back, his bank will go bust."

Corny nodded. "He is likely to blame you two ladies and your brother. I would not want to be responsible for what he might do."

"We have fought Indians, Mr. Vander. Surely one angry man, even one with a gun, is no threat."

"Perhaps you do not know the evil a man will do when he is up against it. No, dear ladies, we will have to play the game a little longer," Corny said. "Haidie, I require your assistance once more. This time, I shall lay out the entire plan. I did not before, because I wanted you to be surprised, to act as lively as a boy. This time, I will need your help as a man."

* * *

Later that night, I rode Outlaw down to Pa's house and pounded on the door. This time, Pa opened up, a man standing behind him. I grinned and said, "Why, this is just dandy."

* * *

Mr. Thacker's buggy pulled up as the clock in the Matchett house was striking the hour of ten. He didn't mind making Corny wait till morning to get the mine, but he was too anxious to get his money to be a minute late. My heart was beating in time to the clock, because so much could go wrong. We had to play Mr. Thacker finer than we had the day before or everything would be lost. If we made a single mistake, me or Corny could get killed or the sisters hurt, and we might even lose the Hangover if Mr. Thacker went to the sheriff.

We were gathered in the parlor, Miss Arvilla in the middle of the love seat so that Mr. Thacker couldn't sit next to her. I waited in front of the window, while Mr. Edwin stood in the doorway. Miss Arvilla had told him to go off to work, that the four of us could handle Mr. Thacker, but he'd said no. "Sister and I crossed by ourselves and understand danger," Miss Arvilla told him, but Mr. Edwin still refused to budge. Miss Lizzie had taken Boots out to the stable to keep him safe.

When Mr. Thacker rang the bell, Miss Arvilla held up her hand to stop Martha from answering the door right away. Martha waited until the second ring before she let Mr. Thacker into the house and ushered him into the parlor, leaving the doors open, as she'd been told to.

Mr. Thacker shook Mr. Edwin's hand, bowed to Miss Arvilla but did not kiss her hand, because her hands were folded tightly in her lap and she didn't offer him one. Nor did she move over so that he could sit beside her. He ignored me but said to Corny, "Well, sir, perhaps your boy has told you. The deed is done. You will be pleasantly surprised at how efficaciously I have worked for you." Mr. Thacker stuck out his chest, glancing at Miss Arvilla to see her reaction to his news.

"Yes, of course," Corny said. He did not stand to greet Mr. Thacker, but only reached for his coffee cup on the table next to him.

Mr. Thacker stopped grinning and glanced at me for the first time, but I only gave him a stupid look. "I have the title to the Blue Flag Mine, sir," he told Corny, his voice a little louder. He held out the deed.

"Ah, so you do. I am so sorry to have put you out. You bet. If I had known where to reach you, I would have sent the boy." Corny gave a sigh and put down his cup. "I am afraid my investors are no longer interested in the Blue Flag. They have changed their minds. They do that on occasion. They can be squally. It is very frustrating, I assure you. They now are interested in the Tenmile District. Perhaps you have something of interest there."

"But . . . I have the Blue Flag," Mr. Thacker repeated, thrusting the document into Corny's hands.

"And I have told you my investors have changed their minds. Would you have coffee?" Corny pointed to a silver coffee service on the table, and Miss Arvilla rose to pour.

Mr. Thacker ignored the coffee. "But sir, I have gone to great trouble and expense to acquire the Flag for you. It was my understanding you would purchase the mine and reward me for my efforts."

"So it was, but this is business. You understand that, of course. One does not always win in such negotiations. If you had presented it to me last evening, I would have completed the transaction, because the intelligence from my investors arrived by post only this morning."

I was glad Mr. Thacker didn't see me smirk at that. He would have to blame himself, because he'd decided to make Corny stew.

"But Mr. Vander." Mr. Thacker's face had begun to turn red, and his hands, which were the size of Bibles, had turned into fists.

Now Corny put the cup aside and stood up. "I am sorry, Mr. Thacker."

"You owe me, sir. I have put myself out for you."

Corny shrugged. "That is the way of business. It is merely an inconvenience."

Mr. Thacker turned to Mr. Edwin. "Inconvenience! Make him see that he is obligated to me. He must reimburse me the twenty-seven thousand dollars I spent for the mine."

Behind Mr. Thacker's back, I smiled at Miss Arvilla. I had told them all about the banker's plan to jack up the purchase price. Even now, with a losing hand, he was trying to increase the stakes.

"That is between the two of you," Mr. Edwin said.

"Am I to believe you spent such a sum without so much as a contract?" Corny asked. "I would hardly call that prudent."

"And in addition, I traded a valuable mine," Mr. Thacker said.

"Then you are in a poor way indeed. But as I say, we do not always win in business." Corny poured himself more coffee, tasted it, and said to Miss Arvilla, "My dear, the coffee has gone cold."

Miss Arvilla started to rise, but Corny waved her back to her seat. "It is of no consequence. I must see about packing my bags."

He stood and bowed to Mr. Thacker as if to dismiss him and started for the door, but Mr. Thacker grabbed him. "I will have satisfaction, sir."

Corny was startled and stepped back. I moved in front of the window and drew back the curtain, letting in the light, while Mr. Edwin took a step forward. "Thacker, be easy," he said.

"Easy!" Mr. Thacker thundered. "I am out a sizable sum and a valuable mine that I traded to acquire the Blue Flag. And you tell me to be easy! Why, I think this is your fault, Matchett. You introduced this fraud to me."

"And warned you to dissuade him from investing in mines," Mr. Edwin said.

"If I did not know better, I would think you were in this together."

"Mr. Thacker, how dare you! We don't give a continental what you think," Miss Arvilla said. Mr. Thacker took a step toward her, but at that moment, the bell rang, and Miss Arvilla called, "Martha."

We all froze, a little confused, while Martha came from deep inside the house to answer the door. "A tradesman, no doubt," Miss Arvilla said, raising her chin at Mr. Thacker, as if daring him to take a sock at it.

He might have, too, but it was Pa who'd rung the bell! He rushed into the room, a second man behind him. I gasped when I saw the gun in Pa's hand.

"What the—?" Mr. Edwin said, while Corny cringed. Mr. Thacker looked confused, glancing from Corny to Mr. Edwin to Pa. Only Miss Arvilla seemed calm. "Sir, what is the meaning of this?"

"I want my mine," Pa said. "It was stole from me, and I want it back."

"Who is this?" Mr. Edwin asked.

"I have no idea," Mr. Thacker said, his eyes shifting back and forth.

"I am Manley Richards, the owner of the Hangover. That banker stole it, and I intend to get it back right now," Pa repeated.

Corny picked up the deed to the Flag, which Mr. Thacker had set on a chair, and held it against his chest, as if to protect himself. "We do not deal with highwaymen."

"Mr. Richards," the man with Pa told him. "You must calm yourself. The sheriff will handle this."

"I tried. The sheriff didn't do nothing," Pa said.

The man with Pa held out his hands, palms up in a hopeless gesture, as he looked at us. "I tried to make him see reason, but he says this thing has boiled up inside him for a year. He is near broke, with a wife and three children and another ready to be born. When he heard a man yesterday talk about the Hangover, he made up his mind to take it back. We followed Mr. Thacker here. Mr. Richards is a violent man. I accompanied him to try to avoid bloodshed."

"Bloodshed?" Miss Arvilla said, her eyes wide. "Mr. Thacker, what have you brought into our home?"

Mr. Thacker held up his hands. "I know nothing about this. Nothing."

"Nothing, is it? You stole my mine and my money. I give it to you for safekeeping, and when I went for it, you said you never seen me," Pa said. "Well, I followed you here, so you seen me now. And I seen the deed. Give it over," Pa told Corny.

But Corny, stubborn at being told what to do, only held the deed closer to his chest as he inched toward the table. "I refuse to deal with ruffians. Besides, this is not the deed to the Hangover but to the Blue Flag."

"Don't you give me the cold shake," Pa said, pointing the gun at Corny and slowly advancing. Corny glanced at his hat with the gun hidden inside, but it was on the other side of the room.

All of a sudden, the man with Pa turned to Mr. Thacker. "I know in the sight of God what Mr. Richards says is true. Admit it, sir, and prevent bloodshed. I can sense you are the evil one in the room."

Mr. Thacker's eyes went wild.

"You cheated an honest man, and you must atone for it. Now, sir, on your knees. Beg forgiveness of this poor man and of the Lord."

"I did nothing. You can't blame me for taking advantage of a fool."

Pa didn't seem to be listening. Instead, his eyes were on the deed, and he ordered Corny to hand it to him.

"I will not," Corny said. "I will not condone robbery."

"You will," Pa said.

The man tried to grab Pa's arm, but Pa shook him off as he kept moving toward Corny. Suddenly he said, "You're my meat now," and fired the gun.

Corny said, "Ugh," and crumpled, grabbing at the table, his fingers grasping the cream pitcher. Then he fell to the floor, moved his feet and arms a little the way the buffalo had when we shot it, and was still. The man Pa'd brought with him went to Corny and put his ear on Corny's chest, then stood up and crossed himself. "Dead," he said.

We all stood there a moment, frozen. "You killed him," Mr. Thacker told Pa in a voice filled with horror. "And it wasn't even the deed to the Hangover he had."

The man with Pa grabbed the gun and pushed Pa into a chair. Then he turned to Mr. Thacker. "No, sir, you prodded him into it. He told me in the sacredness of the confessional what had happened. You are the one guilty of murder. You killed this man with your greed and your evil ways. I have known men like you. You set in motion the events that led to this poor man's death, and ruined another man's life. You are the one who is guilty."

"I'm . . . I'm . . . I did only what a normal man would have done when confronted with an opportunity." Mr. Thacker looked around the room. Miss Arvilla had her hands over her face, but now she removed them and stared at Mr. Thacker. Mr. Edwin slowly looked up from where a red stain was spreading over the Persian carpet. Even I had moved around to face Mr. Thacker. He could tell we were all against him.

"It appears this poor man only sought what was his. I believe what has been said, that you are a swindler and killer, Thacker, and when we tell my friend the sheriff what took place here, you will be arrested," Mr. Edwin said.

"But—" Mr. Thacker pointed at Pa. "He's the one who fired the shot."

Pa wouldn't look at him. He sat in a chair, his hands over his face, muttering, "I'll lick any man . . . I'll lick any man . . ."

Then Mr. Thacker looked down at Corny, lying on the floor.

"He's as cold as Greenland," Miss Arvilla said.

"Go to it! Go to it! Hurry, man," Mr. Edwin told Mr. Thacker, pointing to the door. "They hang men in Denver for this. You might pull this theft in California, but Denver will not stand for it. I will not have you ruin the reputation of my sisters with your senseless greed."

"But the body?" Mr. Thacker said.

"I will make arrangements," Mr. Edwin told him. "I am not without influence."

Mr. Thacker glanced at each one of us and, seeing the stubbornness on our faces, he picked up his hat. "I will be on the afternoon stage to California."

"We will wait until three o'clock to inform the sheriff of this unfortunate death. You have my word," the man who'd come with Pa said.

"Your word? And who are you?"

"As you can see"—he held out a large gold cross—"I am Mr. Richards's confessor."

* * *

To my horror, Mr. Thacker grabbed my ear just as he was leaving the room and yanked me out the door before anyone could stop him. "You come with me, boy," he said, pulling me down the walk to the buggy.

"Let go," I screeched, my hands grabbing at his wrist. But he would not, and I thought he'd pull my ear off.

He didn't release me until we reached the gate. "What do you have to say for yourself?" he demanded.

"Sir?"

"Your patron is dead, so I guess you'll want to go along with me. We could make a pair, you and me. In California with a boy like you, I could do all right."

I swallowed a couple of times. Corny was lying on the floor in a pool of red, and Mr. Thacker was planning how he could use me to trick somebody else out of money. I didn't know what to say.

"First off, I want my hundred dollars back," Mr. Thacker told me.

"What?"

"You heard me. I gave you five twenty-dollar gold pieces, and I want them. The deal is off. You didn't earn them."

"You killed a man, and you want my hundred dollars back?"

Mr. Thacker had let go of my ear and held the lapel of my coat now. He said in a shouting-bad voice, "I didn't kill anybody. You saw it. If the law comes looking for me, you'll tell them what you saw."

I had my out now. "I guess that man in there's right. You're the one responsible for Mr. Vander's death."

Mr. Thacker tightened his grip on my coat, while I tried to figure how to get loose of him. I'd just about decided to stomp on his foot, when Mr. Thacker suddenly let go of my coat and shoved me against the fence. Then he smacked me across the mouth. He reached for my throat.

"Haidie!"

I glanced up and saw Boots running toward me. He'd been in the stable, where Miss Lizzie was keeping him away from the house. *Oh no, Boots,* I thought. If he said something, he could ruin everything. "Go back," I called. "I'm all right."

I should have known that wouldn't stop him.

"Don't you never hurt Haidie," Boots yelled at Mr. Thacker. My brother picked up a stick and began beating Mr. Thacker, but Mr. Thacker just shoved it aside. Then he grabbed for me before I could dodge. Just as Mr. Thacker put his hand on my arm and started to wrench it behind my back, however, out of nowhere came a dog as big as a backhouse. He lunged at Mr. Thacker and grasped his leg between his teeth.

"Tige!" I yelled, shooting a glance into the trees across the street, where a man was hidden. Tige, looking uglier than a mud dobber, sank his teeth into Mr. Thacker's leg and shook him good before I could call him off. I was never so glad to see an ugly dog in my life.

The minute Mr. Thacker was loose, he made for the buggy and whipped up the horse. Then as he took off, he yelled at me, "Think you can give me the cold shake, do you? I'll come back someday, boy. You better keep a sharp watch. I'll fist you good."

Me and Miss Lizzie grabbed Boots and ran for the house. Then we locked the door, and rushed into the parlor, where I pulled down the shades. Everyone was just where I had left them.

"That man tried to hurt Haidie, but I whipped him with a stick," Boots said proudly.

"What a family!" Miss Arvilla said.

Suddenly Boots saw Corny lying on the floor and his face went white. "Did that man kill Corny?"

"No, of course not," Pa said, standing up. Then he reached for Corny's hand and pulled Corny to his feet.

Corny looked down at the red soaking into the carpet and sighed. "I have ruined your carpet with the dye, I fear. And I broke your cream pitcher, too."

"And I shot a hole in the floor," Pa added.

Miss Arvilla grinned. "It is nothing. Every time I look at the stain, I shall remember what fun we had. Oh, sister, I wish you could have been here. Mr. Richards's mine has been returned to him, and we have rid ourselves of a scoundrel." Then she glanced at the window. "You are sure he's gone, aren't you?"

"Oh yes, ma'am," I replied. "And Ben Bondurant will be

at the Wells Fargo to make sure he's on the stage for California. Ben says if Mr. Thacker doesn't get on that stage, he'll beat him to smash."

Mr. Edwin sighed. "I think we should all stay here until we are sure Thacker has departed. Do you think he will mend his ways?"

Corny snorted at that as he picked up the broken pieces of the cream pitcher and set them on the table, then set his napkin on the red stain to soak it up. "Perhaps for a day or two. But as nigh as I can come at it, I believe that once Joel Thacker reaches California, he will be restored to his malevolent ways." He went over to the man who'd come with Pa and introduced himself, saying, "Sir, I have not had the pleasure."

Until then, Boots hadn't paid any attention to the man, but now he looked him over and shouted, "Cheet!"

Cheet grinned and held out his arms. "Well, hello there, Boots. You grew some."

Instead of going to Cheet, Boots took a step toward me. "We ain't going to the orphan home again, even if they do pay you ten dollars to take us back."

"Cheet couldn't do that," I said. "We're with Pa now, so we aren't orphans anymore. Pa'll take us to Georgetown where his mine is. We've got the Hangover back, Boots."

"How come you're here?" Boots asked Cheet.

Cheet grinned at him. "Oh, I got to missing you, and I knew you'd gone west to look for Pa. So I came here, too. I didn't find him till yesterday."

"You mean you lost all the money you got for the farm," I said, crossing my arms.

"I swore off gambling."

I scoffed. "You did lose it, then."

Cheet cocked his head. "Well, it don't matter, because Pa's got a gold mine."

"No thanks to you, Cheet."

"Actually, the gold mine is mine," Mr. Edwin said. We all turned to stare at him. "I put up the money for this venture, so technically, the Hangover belongs to me." He put up his hands. "Oh, do not worry. We are all confederates in this crime. I have no intention of keeping the ownership to myself. Forty-nine percent will go to Manley Richards. With less than the majority ownership, Mr. Richards will not be tempted to gamble away the mine."

"I wouldn't never again—" Pa said, but Mr. Edwin stopped him.

"The balance is to be put into a trust for the benefit of Haidie and Boots," he continued. "I would hope these boys might go to college one day."

The sisters looked pleased, but Cheet blurted out. "Boys? There's only one boy here. Don't you know Haidie's a girl?"

"A girl!" Mr. Edwin's mouth dropped open, while Miss Arvilla put her hand to her chest and smiled.

Corny broke into a grin that split his face. He came toward me, his arm outstretched. I started to shake his hand, but instead, he took my hand and kissed it, then said, "You, young miss, are the smartest liar I ever saw."

Pa grinned, and I thought that was because of the compliment Corny had paid me, but he wasn't looking at me. Instead, he was staring out the window at the dust stirred up by Mr. Thacker's carriage. Then he pushed back the curtain and called, "Tough luck!"

* * *

And so, I was unfrocked, as Miss Arvilla put it. She said she had suspected ever since the trail, when she saw me with the Indian doll, that I wasn't a boy. Only a girl would look at a doll like that, she said.

Boots and Cheet moved with Pa and his wife and baby to Georgetown, where Boots went to school. Pa took over management of the mine and gave Cheet a job. But I stayed in Denver with the sisters. When I saw us all together, I forgave Pa for marrying Fanny, and Cheet for putting us in the orphan home. There wasn't any reason for me to keep on being angry. After all, what I had come West for was for us to be a family again.

I stayed with the sisters and attended their fancy academy. I'd seen for myself what happened to women who didn't have any schooling, and I didn't intend to wind up as a hoor at the Progressive Club, like Emily.

I'd known that once we reached Denver, I'd have to become a girl again, and now, with Mr. Thacker threatening to smash me, it was as good a time as any to put on a dress. I couldn't say I looked forward to it, but I found I didn't mind it as much as I'd thought.

Oh, I kept my boys' clothes, and I put them on whenever I wanted to ride Outlaw astride. Miss Lizzie frowned at that, but not Miss Arvilla. In fact, sometimes, when Mr. Edwin was away and Miss Lizzie was indisposed, Miss Arvilla borrowed a suit of her brother's, and the two of us made the rounds of the gambling halls. When she saw Emily there and remembered her story, Miss Arvilla offered her a job at the school.

I taught Miss Arvilla poker. She became a pretty good player. In fact, she almost measured up to me as a liar and a cheater. I told her that, and for some reason, she took it as a compliment.

Acknowledgments

Writing these acknowledgments is redundant, because these are the people who have helped me with so many of my books. They've become "my team." So once again I thank my longtime agent, Danielle Egan-Miller, and her staff. Danielle kept watch over the manuscript of *Tough Luck* and never gave up on it. My editor, Elisabeth Dyssegaard, cleaned up the manuscript, and, alas, knew exactly where to cut. Her assistant, Jamilah Lewis-Horton, handled the detail work and kept me on schedule. My family's always there when I'm stuck, especially my daughters. Dana helped come up with the title for *Tough Luck* (although I did like *The Road Less Graveled*), and Kendal prodded me when I doubted myself. Bob, Lloyd, and Forrest had my back. So did my sister Mary and my brother, Michael. And the Western History and Genealogy Department of the Denver Public Library was a great source when I was stumped with questions about the West. I'd thought when I finished *Where Coyotes Howl* that I had retired from writing novels. Thanks to all of you for keeping me going.